GORE VIDAL wrote his first novel, *Williwaw* (1946), at the age of nineteen while overseas in World War II. During four decades as a writer, Vidal has written novels, plays, short stories, and essays. He has also been a political activist. As a Dem___  ___upstate New York, he received the ___ ___century. From 1970 to 1972 he w___ ___rty. In California's 1982 Democrat___ ___ a half-million votes, and came in s___ ___

In 1948 Vidal wrote the ___ ___er *The City and the Pillar*. This was followed by *The Judgment of Paris* and the prophetic *Messiah*. In the fifties Vidal wrote plays for live television and films for Metro-Goldwyn-Mayer. One of the television plays became the successful Broadway play *Visit to a Small Planet* (1957). Directly for the theater he wrote the prize-winning hit *The Best Man* (1960). In 1964 Vidal returned to the novel with *Julian*, the story of the apostate Roman emperor. This novel has been published in many languages and editions. As Henry de Montherlant wrote: "*Julian* is the only book about a Roman emperor that I like to re-read. Vidal loves his protagonist; he knows the period thoroughly; and the book is a beautiful hymn to the twilight of paganism." During the last quarter-century Vidal has been telling the history of the United States as experienced by one family and its connections in what Gabriel García Márquez has called "Gore Vidal's magnificent series of historical novels or novelized histories." They are, in chronological order, *Burr, Lincoln, 1876, Empire, Hollywood*, and *Washington, D.C.*

During the same period, Vidal invented a series of satiric comedies – *Myra Breckinridge, Myron, Kalki, Duluth*. "Vidal's development . . . along that line from *Myra Breckinridge* to *Duluth* is crowned with success," wrote Italo Calvino in *La Repubblica* (Rome). "I consider Vidal to be a master of that new form which is taking shape in world literature and which we may call the hyper-novel or the novel elevated to the square or to the cube." To this list Vidal added the highly praised – and controversial – *Live from Golgotha* in 1992.

Vidal has also published several volumes of essays. When the National Book Critics Circle presented him with an award (1982), the citation read: "The American tradition of independent and curious learning is kept alive in the wit and great expressiveness of Gore Vidal's criticism." In 1993, he won the National Book Award for *United States: Essays 1952–1992*.

Vidal recently co-starred with Tim Robbins in the movie *Bob Roberts*.

BOOKS BY GORE VIDAL

NOVELS

Narratives of a Golden Age
Burr
Lincoln
1876
Empire
Hollywood
Washington, D.C.

Williwaw
In a Yellow Wood
The City and the Pillar
The Season of Comfort
A Search for the King
Dark Green, Bright Red
The Judgment of Paris
Messiah
Julian
Myra Breckinridge
Two Sisters
Myron
Kalki
Creation
Duluth
Live from Golgotha

SHORT STORIES

A Thirsty Evil

————

PLAYS

An Evening with
Richard Nixon
Weekend
Romulus
The Best Man
Visit to a Small Planet

————

ESSAYS

Rocking the Boat
Reflections upon a Sinking Ship
Homage to Daniel Shays
Matters of Fact and of Fiction
Pink Triangle and Yellow Star
Armageddon?
At Home
Screening History
A View from the Diners Club
United States: Essays 1952–1992

GORE VIDAL

Narratives of a Golden Age

HOLLYWOOD
A NOVEL OF AMERICA
IN THE 1920S

An *Abacus* Book

First published in the United States by Random House Inc 1990
First published in Great Britain by André Deutsch Ltd 1990
This edition published by Abacus 1994
Reprinted 1996

A CIP catalogue record for this book
is available from the British Library.

ISBN 0 349 10526 X

Typeset by M Rules
Printed and bound in Great Britain by
Clays Ltd, St Ives plc

UK companies, institutions and other organisations wishing
to make bulk purchases of this or any other book
published by Little, Brown should contact their local
bookshop or the special sales department at the address below.
Tel 0171 911 8000. Fax 0171 911 8100.

Abacus
A Division of
Little, Brown and Company (UK)
Brettenham House
Lancaster Place
London WC2E 7EN

Narratives of a Golden Age

Mary McCarthy once made a famous list of those things that "serious" fiction simply cannot deal with, starting, I believe, with a sunset and ending with a Cabinet meeting where actual politics are alluded to. Middle-class marriage is all that matters whether it be in sultry Toronto or vivid Baltimore. For the truly bored, there is literary theory whereby even Baltimore can be deconstructed, leaving the reader with the constituent elements of a novel, words strewn at random, ready to be rearranged or not, depending on the theory of the day.

I circle my subject, as you can see, because I have always thought that history (after pure invention – *Gulliver's Travels* or *Alice in Wonderland*) is the only form of narrative that has universal appeal; also, because of its often mythological origins, it tells us more about ourselves as, let us be seriously scientific, genetic arrangements than any mirror set in the roadway so that we can see just how we look as we cross the road to get, like the celebrated chicken in the story, onto the other side. The idea of placing history in fiction or fiction in history has been unfashionable, to say the least, since Tolstoi. We are assured that the result can be neither fiction nor history. Yet the record of the breakup of the author's own marriage the preceding summer is, most people would agree, the very stuff of solemn – no, *serious* fiction, the common experience. It is also, for many of us, as deeply boring as one's friend Brian, who wants to tell us just how and why he left Doris shortly after the exchange student Sonia signed on for his Barth Barthelme Burke and Hare course at East Anglia. In any case, even this sort of dim fiction is historical, too, because it describes something that actually took place, if only dully, in recent time. But then to place a novel within history is more the rule than not. The Second World War was history and tens of thousands of novels have been set within the details of that very real war. Literary theoreticians to one side, there are few texts without contexts.

In the case of American history, I had the curious fortune to be brought up in a political family at the capital of the country and I knew first-hand, or at interesting second- or third-hand (the republic is not much older than my lifetime plus that of my grandfather), what the politics had been that had resulted, say, in the Second World War or even, but this required turning myself into an historian, some of the reasons at the back of our separation from England. I always knew that sooner or later I was bound to use this material. But how?

In 1966 I decided to write a novel about growing up in Washington D.C. during the Depression, New Deal, Second War and the Korean misadventure. From early triumphant Franklin Roosevelt to a young senator not unlike my friend J. F. Kennedy; from the world empire of 1945–1950 to the National Security State of the early fifties. I used real characters like Roosevelt, though I never presumed to enter his mind: he is observed only by fictional characters whose lives are lived within the context of actual events. *Washington, D.C.* proved to be a popular novel, particularly on Capitol Hill. But one British reviewer, unable to believe the mild pre-Watergate corruptions that I note, called me "the American Suetonius," which I did not like since I was reporting, not inventing, the world of our rulers while an American reviewer thought that the book was closer to a glossy MGM film than to serious fiction. He knew, even then, that serious novels did not contain sunsets and Cabinet meetings while serious people certainly did not have butlers and chauffeurs nor did they know, much less quarrel with, presidents.

Part of the not-so-endearing folklore of my native land is that we have no class system; this means that any mention of it by a novelist will provoke deep, often quite irrational, anger. After all, our teachers are paid to teach that we are a true democracy (not a republic and certainly not an oligarchy) and our meritocracy is easy to break into if you will only take your academic studies seriously.

My attempt, fairly late in my career, to write an "autobiographical" novel raised more questions in my mind than ever it settled. I have never been my own subject, and history has always distracted me from my own education, sentimental or otherwise. I was also aware at school that our history, to the extent that I knew anything about it first hand, was not only ill-taught but seriously distorted.

Why not write "true" history and then, for added points of view, set imaginary characters in its midst? After all, this has been pretty much the main line of Western literature from Aeschylus to Dante to Shakespeare to Tolstoi as well as to hordes of other narrators from Scott to Flaubert.

When the decision was made by Bismarck to educate the lowest order so that it would be able to handle complex machinery and weapons, intellectuals knew that there was risk involved. If *they* could read, might they not get ideas? *Wrong* ideas? The argument about education went on for a generation or two and involved everyone from Mill to the Reverend Malthus. Meanwhile, *they* did learn to read. But what should they read? What actually went on inside the palace was out of bounds and there were to be no Cabinet meetings, ever; on the other hand, sunsets were nice, and so the good and the beautiful and the true became the Serious Novel as we know it – cautionary tales designed to keep the lowest order in its place as docile workers and enthusiastic consumers.

The great elimination of subjects to which Mary McCarthy adverted a generation ago has been underway for some time. The popular novel of the last century was, more or less, a sort of religious tract warning against intemperance, disobedience to authority, sexual irregularity and ending, often, with a marriage, an institution guaranteed to control the worker whose young children, hostages to fortune, would oblige him to do work that he did not want to do. No wonder modernism erupted with such force a century ago. Joyce, Mallarmé and Mann, each in his own way, chose not to observe the world from the point of view of a (contented?) victim of society. Modernism chose to illuminate the life of the interior whether it be of a man dreaming a new language for the night or of how a genius submits himself to the devil as spirochete.

I suspect that I was drawn to the idea of my own country as a subject by those schoolteachers who are paid to give us a comforting view of a society that, after eliminating the original population of the continent, lived more or less happily with slavery while imposing an often demented monotheism on one another as well as on the other breeds that came under its restless rule. Nevertheless, I believed that there *was* an American idea (if not "exceptionalism") worth preserving and so I set out to trace it from 1776 to its final interment in and around 1952 when the old republic was replaced by our current national security state, forever at war with, if no weak enemy is at hand, its own people.

Needless to say, I knew none of this in 1966 when I wrote *Washington, D.C.* I had begun at the end, as it were, and except where personal knowledge contradicted the official version I tended to believe what I had been taught and told about the country. The next book was the first chronologically, *Burr*; here I dealt with the years 1776 to 1836 and at its center I placed a family connection, the sardonic vice-president himself, Aaron Burr, "first gentleman of the United States" as he was often called and in his mad way he was a sort of Lord Chesterfield set loose in a world of pious hypocrites.

Burr's popularity with that small public which reads books voluntarily was the first sign that there does exist an intelligent public highly dissatisfied with the way history is taught in the schools. I had also created a family through whose eyes I was able to tell the story of the republic. Although I invented Burr's illegitimate son, Charles Schermerhorn Schuyler, he seems to me very real indeed. In *1876*, after a long life in Europe, he returns as a historian-journalist to cover the first centennial of the United States; this was the year that the winner of a presidential election was cheated of his victory by federal troops. Ironies abound, and Charlie is very much at home. He is also trying to marry off his widowed daughter, Emma, and succeeds at some cost. *Empire* introduces Emma's daughter Caroline Sanford and half-brother Blaise: brought up in France, they lust for distinction in the United States. Blaise's hero is William Randolph Hearst who has discovered that history is what you say it is in the popular press. This dubious argument is not without a certain charm for Blaise but it is Caroline who buys a moribund paper in Washington D.C. and goes in for yellow journalism.

I was told by knowing reviewers that no woman at this time could have done such a thing but, of course, less than a generation later, a family friend, Eleanor Patterson, did exactly that with great success (her unfortunate marriage to a Polish count gave Edith Wharton much of the plot of *The Age of Innocence*).

In *Hollywood* both Hearst and Caroline decide that the movies will be the next great thing, the source of dreams for the whole world. Caroline lets Blaise have her paper: then she produces and acts in films with rather more success than her friend Hearst who is constantly running for president. Meanwhile, the context of these imaginary people is the very real one of the First World War, the League of Nations, Woodrow Wilson, William Jennings Bryan, Warren Harding, the young embattled Franklin Roosevelt. It was odd for me, in *Hollywood*, to write about the youth of so many people that I had known in their old age.

Now I have rewritten *Washington, D.C.*, the summing-up novel, in order to bring together all the strands of the story. *Lincoln* is set somewhat apart, as only Caroline's father figures in it in a minor way; yet without our Civil War we have no history and so that story adds resonance to the comings and goings of the real and the imagined.

It is not for me to judge what the figure in this particular carpet is. Personally I prefer a flawed republic to the murderous empire that began in 1898 and is now, as I write, firmly established as a militarized economy and society with no end in view. But I am not a judge so much as an enthralled narrator of a family, at points somewhat like my own, and of a country whose curious mystique has always haunted me, so much so that I have decided to call this series of novels, not too ironically, *Narratives of a Golden Age, 1776–1952*. No, it was not all that golden for any of us at any time but we kept thinking that it might be until, thanks to Vietnam, we came to realize that, like everyone else, we are simply at sea in history and that somehow our republic had got mislaid along the way.

I leave to a writer, no doubt unborn, the sequel, *What Happened to the Empire, 1952 to* – date to come. More soon than late.

Gore Vidal, 1993

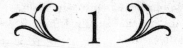

1

1

Slowly, William Randolph Hearst lowered his vast bear-like body into a handsome Biedermeier chair, all scrolls and lyres and marquetry. "Tell no one I'm in Washington," he commanded. Then, slowly, he blinked his pale blue eyes at Blaise Delacroix Sanford. Although Blaise was now forty-one and the publisher of the Washington *Tribune*, he was still awed by his former chief and mentor, gone gray in *his* fifty-fourth year, the most famous newspaper publisher in the world, owner of dozens of journals and magazines and, most curiously, the recent begetter of that worldwide sensation, a photo-play serial called *The Perils of Pauline*.

"I won't, of course." Blaise sat on the edge of his desk, flexing leg muscles. Unlike the Chief, Blaise was in excellent physical shape: he rode horseback every day, played squash in his own court, fought age.

"Millicent and I've been spending the winter at the Breakers. You know, Palm Beach." The Chief's face was Indian-brown from the sun. Just past Hearst's head, Blaise could see, through the window, a partial view of Fourteenth Street until, with a dry soft sigh, the Biedermeier chair crumpled in on itself like an accordion and Hearst and chair were suddenly as one with the thick Persian carpet, and the view of Fourteenth Street was now unobstructed.

Blaise leapt to his feet. "I'm sorry . . ."

But Hearst serenely ignored gravity's interruption of his thought. He remained where he was on the floor, holding in one hand a fragile wooden lyre that had been an armrest: the Orpheus of popular journalism, thought Blaise wildly, unnerved by the sight. "Anyway, what I sneaked into town for was to find out whether or not there's anything to this Zimmermann-telegram thing, and if there is, how are you going to play it? After all, you're the Washington publisher. I'm just New York."

"And everywhere else. Personally, I think it's a hoax. . . . Why don't you try another chair?"

Hearst put down his lyre. "You know, I bought a whole houseful of Biedermeier furniture when I was in Salzburg and I shipped it back to New York, where I never got around to uncrating it. Don't think I will now." As slowly as Hearst had sat so, majestically, he rose to his full height, at least two heads taller than Blaise. "Sorry I smashed that thing. Bill me for the damages."

"Forget it, Chief." In his nervousness, Blaise called Hearst the name that he was known by to all his employees but never to his equal, Blaise. As Hearst settled himself into a fortress-like leather armchair, Blaise picked up the so-called Zimmermann telegram. Blaise had received a copy from a reliable source at the White House and so, apparently, had Hearst. The telegram had been secretly transmitted from London to President Wilson on Saturday, February 24, 1917. It was now Monday and, later in the day, Woodrow Wilson would address a joint session of Congress on the subject of war or peace or continued neutrality or whatever with the Central Powers, specifically Germany, in their war against the Entente Cordiale, or France and England and Russia and, lately, Italy. If authentic, the telegram from the German foreign minister, Arthur Zimmermann, to the German ambassador in Mexico, a country for some time more or less at war with the United States, would end once and for all the neutrality of the United States. Blaise suspected that the telegram was the work of the British Foreign Office. The boldness of tone was the sort of thing that only a desperate country, losing a war, would concoct in order to frighten the United States into coming to its aid.

"My spies tell me that the telegram has been sitting around in London since last month, which means that that's where it was written, *if* it didn't start here first." Hearst withdrew his copy from a pocket; then he read in his high thin voice, "'We intend to begin on the first of February unrestricted submarine warfare.'" He looked up. "Well, that part's true, the Germans are really giving it to us, sinking just about every ship in sight between here and Europe. Dumb of them, you know. Most Americans don't want war. I don't want war. Did you know Bernstorff was Mrs. Wilson's lover?"

The Chief had a disconcerting habit of moving from subject to subject with no discernible connection; yet there was often some mysterious link that connected his staccato musings. Blaise had indeed heard the rumor that the German ambassador and the widow Mrs. Galt, as the second Mrs. Wilson had been styled a year earlier, had been lovers. But then Washington was not only Henry James's "city of conversation" but Hearst's city of fantastic gossip. "If they were lovers, I'm sure it was all over by the time she married the President."

"You never can tell unless you were in the room, as my mother keeps telling me. The money my mother has! And she's pro-English, too." Hearst began to read again. "'We shall endeavor in spite of this to keep the United States of America neutral. In the event of this not succeeding we make Mexico a proposal of alliance on the following basis: Make war together, make peace together, generous financial support and an understanding on our part that Mexico is to reconquer the lost territory in Texas, New Mexico and Arizona.'" Hearst looked up. "At least whoever wrote this isn't promising them my place in California."

"Who do you think wrote this, if not Zimmermann?"

Hearst looked grim. "Thomas W. Gregory, the attorney general. That's what I hear. He's pushing Wilson harder and harder to go to war now. Luckily, the rest of the Cabinet want Wilson to hold out because," Hearst squinted at the telegram, "this part here is what this war is all about. I mean, Zimmermann or Gregory or the English or whoever wrote it suggests that the president of Mexico approach the Japanese and get them into the war against us. Well, that's the big danger!"

Blaise moved off his desk and into his chair. Back of him hung a life-size painting of himself, his half-sister and co-publisher

Caroline, and their editor, Trimble. Blaise knew, everyone knew, that whenever Hearst was in need of a scare story for his newspapers, he would invoke the Yellow Peril. Although Blaise was neutral on the subject of Japanese expansion in China, others were not. On February 1 when Germany had delivered its ultimatum to the United States that all shipping from American ports to those of the Allied Powers would be fair game for German submarines, or U-boats as they were popularly known, the Cabinet had met, and though Gregory among others was eager for a declaration of war, the President, remembering that he had just been re-elected as "the man who kept us out of war," wanted only to sever relations between the two countries. He had been unexpectedly supported by his secretaries of war and Navy; each had made the case that the United States should allow Germany its head in Europe and then, at a future date, the entire white race would unite as one against the yellow hordes, led by Japan. Hearst had played this diversion for all that it was worth. Blaise had not.

Trimble entered the room, without knocking. He was an aging Southerner whose once red hair was now a disagreeable pink. "Mr. Hearst." Trimble bowed. Hearst inclined his head. Trimble said, "We've just got a report on what the President is going to say to Congress . . ."

"War?" Hearst sat up straight.

"No, sir. But he is going to ask for armed neutrality . . ."

"Preparedness. . . ." Hearst sighed. "Peace without victory. A world league of nations with Mr. Wilson in the chair. Self-determination for all."

"Well," said Trimble, "he doesn't say all that in this speech." Then Trimble withdrew.

Blaise repeated the week's Washington joke. "The President wants to declare war in confidence, so the Bryanites – the pacifists – in his party won't turn on him."

"Not to mention me. I'm still in politics, you know." Blaise knew; everyone knew. Hearst was preparing to run yet again for governor of New York or mayor of New York City or president in 1920. He still had a huge following, particularly among the so-called hyphenates, the German-Americans and the Irish-Americans, all enemies of England and her allies. "Did you see *The Perils of Pauline?*"

Blaise adjusted easily to the sudden shift of subject. The Chief's mind was a wondrous kaleidoscope, unshielded by any sort of consciousness. Like a child, whatever suddenly bubbled up in his brain, he said. There was no screening process except when he chose, as he often did, to be enigmatically silent. "Yes, I saw several of them. She's very handsome, Miss Pearl White, and always on the move."

"That's why we call them *moving* pictures." Hearst was tutorial. "She has to keep running away from danger or the audience will start to run out of the theater. You know, on this war thing, I'm for staying out just as you are for getting us in. But I'll say this – if the people really want a war, then I'll go along. After all, they're the ones who're going to have to fight it, not me. I'm going to ask for a national referendum, get a vote from everybody, you know? Do you want to fight for England and France against your own people, the Germans and the Irish?"

Blaise laughed. "I don't think they'll let you put the question like that."

Hearst grunted. "Well, you know what I mean. There's no real support out there. I know. I got eight newspapers from California to New York. But of course it's too late. This thing's gone too far. We'll get a war all right. Then England will cave in. Then the Germans will come over here, or try to. Have you thought about flags?"

"Flags?" This time the Chief's unconscious mind was ahead of Blaise.

Hearst pulled a copy of the New York *American* from his huge side pocket. On the front page there were red-white-and-blue flags as well as several stanzas from "The Star-Spangled Banner." "Looks nice, don't it?"

"Very patriotic."

"That's the idea. I'm getting tired of being called pro-German. Anyway I'm about to start a photo-play company, and I'd like you to come in with me."

Blaise adjusted to this new shift with, he thought, admirable coolness. "But I don't know anything about the movies."

"Nobody does. That's what's so wonderful. You know, while we're sitting here, all over the world illiterate Chinese and Hindus and . . . and Patagonians are watching my Pauline. You see, to watch a movie you don't need to know another language the way you have to when you read a paper because it's all there – up there, moving around. It's the only international thing there is. Anyway the point is that Mother, who's the rich one, won't lend me the money and I don't want to go to the banks."

At last Hearst had startled Blaise. It was true that Phoebe Apperson Hearst controlled the vast mining wealth of Hearst's late father, but Hearst's personal empire was more than enough to finance a photo-play company. Of course, Hearst lived more grandly than anyone in the United States on, it was said, five million dollars a year, much of which went for the acquisition of every spurious artwork for sale anywhere. "Well, let me think about it." Blaise was cautious.

"What about that sister of yours, Caroline?"

"Ask her."

"You don't want to sell me the *Tribune*, do you?"

"No."

Hearst rose. "That's what you always say. I've got my eye on the *Times* here. It's a lousy paper, but then so was this till Caroline bought it and fixed it up."

Blaise's sudden pang of envy was, he hoped, not visible to the other. Caroline had indeed bought and revived the moribund *Tribune*; then, and only then, had she allowed her half-brother to buy in. Now, jointly, amiably, they co-published.

Hearst stared down at Fourteenth Street. "Four," he said, "no, five movie theaters just on this one street. I've got my eye on a place up in Harlem, an old casino, where I can set up a studio." Idly, he kicked at the remains of the Biedermeier chair. "I have to stay in New York. Because of 1920. War or not, that's going to be the big political year. Whoever gets to be president then can . . ." Hearst tapped the Zimmermann telegram which lay on Blaise's desk. "I think it's a fake."

Blaise nodded. "So do I. It's too convenient. . . ."

Hearst shook Blaise's hand. "I'm heading back to Palm Beach

now. We'll get this war anyway, like it or not. Remember my proposal. I'm only starting up in Harlem because New York is my base. But the place to be from now on is Hollywood. You got that?"

"No," said Blaise. Like a circus trainer, he led the great bear to the door. "But I'm sure *you've* . . . got it."

2

The Duchess was late. As Jesse Smith waited for her in Madame Marcia's parlor, he studied or pretended to study Dr. Janes's *Vermifuge Almanac*, a thick volume filled with lurid charts of the heavens and strange drawings of even stranger creatures of which one, a monstrous crab, gave Jesse or Jess – "No final 'e,' please, boys, that's only for the ladies of the emporium" – heartache as well as heartburn, for in his recurrent nightmares there often figured a giant devouring crab of utter malignity; and Jess would wake up with a sob, according to Roxy, on the few times during their short marriage that they had spent an entire night together.

Quickly, Jess turned over several pages until he arrived at a neutral pair of scales, more soothing than the lobster with the sting in its tail or the menacing lion. It was not that he feared being eaten by crab, lobster, lion. Suffocation was the night terror, as heavy lion's paw covered nose and mouth.

Jess took a deep shaky breath. Madame Marcia's apartment smelled of boiled chicken and stale incense from a brass Benares dish filled with what looked like the burnt contents of a pipe but was actually the latest Indian Hindu sandalwood incense, to which Roxy had also been partial.

Madame Marcia's parlor was separated from the inner sanctum by a curtain made of strings of different-colored beads to give an *Arabian Nights* effect; but the beads were so dull that the effect was more like threaded penny candies. Nevertheless, half the great men and women of Washington, D.C., were said to have come here in order to glimpse the Future and so circumvent – or hasten – inexorable fate. A functioning sorceress, Madame comfortably advertised herself as "A president-maker and a president-ruler." Behind the cascade of beads, Jess could hear Madame humming to herself in a toneless voice that suggested the higher realms of spirit until one caught from time to time, the lyrics of a brand-new song made popular by the Ziegfeld Follies of 1916, and heard, for almost a year now, on every Victrola in the land. Jess gazed without much interest at a gaudy diploma on the wall that admonished one and all that, by these presents, one Marcia Champrey was a minister in good standing of the Spiritualist Church.

Madame Marcia had been Daugherty's inspiration. "I've never been to her. But they say she's just what the doctor ordered, and the Duchess needs a lot of doctoring." Like all politicians, Daugherty spoke code; and Jess, who had grown up in the actual shadow of his Ohio hometown Washington Court House's actual colonnaded courthouse, understood the code. Also there was nothing that he would not do for Harry M. Daugherty, who had befriended him when he was first starting out; done his legal work for nothing; introduced him to those Ohio politicians who always came to Daugherty for aid at election time – *their* elections, of course. Although Daugherty had been chairman of the State Republican Committee and was now forever a part of history because he had nominated William McKinley for governor in 1893, thus launching the sun, as it were, into the republic's sky, Daugherty himself had no political luck; had failed by seventy-seven votes to be nominated for governor; had now settled for being the hidden power behind whatever throne he could set up. Of course the highest throne of all was currently empty or, to be precise, occupied by one Woodrow Wilson, a Democrat, an unnatural state of affairs which would be corrected in 1920 by the election of a Republican president. But that was three years away, and there were certain arrangements that must first be made. Madame Marcia was one.

"Is she always so late?" Madame Marcia glided into the room, at an odd angle to the floor. She had once been a dancer, as she had told Jess on his previous visit, with the Frank Deshon Opera Company. "At sixteen," she would add, in case someone were to count the years that had passed since her name had appeared in very small letters on a very large poster whose date marked her as an artiste from the long-ago age of McKinley. Now the dancer was a spiritualist minister and a guide to the stars in the dark days of Woodrow Wilson when every day, for Republicans, was like today, February, with wet snow falling and a cold north wind.

"No. The Duchess is the soul of punctuality." Jess rose, as he always did, when a lady, any lady, entered a room, any room. "The weather . . ."

"The weather, oh, yes." Over the years, one by one, Madame Marcia's Brooklyn vowels had gradually closed until she sounded refined and deeply spiritual. She wore priestess black, and a string of pearls. Only the thick scarlet hair struck a discordant Frank Deshon dancer note. Jess had first met her with Daugherty, who swore by her, whatever that meant. Although Jess believed fervently in every sort of ghost and ghoul, he had no particular interest in any spirit world other than the one in his hall closet where, back of an old winter coat and a stack of galoshes, horror reigned. Only his driver George dared enter that closet; and return unscathed and sane.

"Mr. Micajah is keeping well?" Madame Marcia sat in a straight chair, and smiled, revealing pearl-like teeth rather more authentic in quality than the pearls she wore. Micajah was Daugherty's middle name. Real names were discouraged by the lady. "Otherwise I might be influenced when I consult the stars." Daugherty maintained that she had no idea, ever, whose horoscope she was casting: hence her high price. She was a legend in the capital and much consulted by some of the highest in the land, usually through intermediaries, as the faces of the highest would have been recognizable to Madame Marcia, thanks to photography and the newsreels.

"Yes. He's gone back to . . ." Jess stopped himself from saying Ohio. "Home. But his – uh, friend is here. The Duchess's husband."

"An interesting – even *significant* – horoscope." Madame Marcia had been given nothing more than the date and hour of birth of the Duchess's husband. Of course she had a Congressional Directory in her inner sanctum and she could, if she were so

9

minded, check the various birthdates with the one in hand, assuming that its owner was in the Congress. But, as Daugherty said, even if she knew *whose* horoscope it was, how could she predict his future without some help from the stars or whatever? The whole town knew that she had predicted the elevation to the vice presidency of the current incumbent, Thomas R. Marshall. Without supernatural aid, this was an impossibly long shot.

"I've never seen such a cold winter. Worse than New York ever was. . . ."

"Why did you come to Washington?"

"Fate," said Madame Marcia, as though speaking of an old and trusted friend. "I was associated with Gipsy Oliver at Coney Island. Mostly for amusement's sake. But" – Madame's voice became low and thrilling – "she had gifts as well as – worldliness. Dark gifts. Amongst them, that of prophecy. I was, I thought, happily married. With two beautiful children. My husband, Dr. Champrey, had an excellent practice, specializing in the lower lumbar region and, of course, the entire renal system. But the spirits spoke to Gipsy Oliver. *She* spoke to me. Beware of the turkey, she said one day. I thought she was joking. I laughed – more fool I! *What* turkey? I asked. I know turkeys, and don't much care to eat them – so dry, always, unless you have the knack of basting, which fate has denied me. Well, lo! and behold the next month, November it was, I was preparing a Thanksgiving dinner for my loved ones, when Dr. Champrey said, 'I'll go buy us a turkey.' I remember now a shiver come over me. A chill, like a ghost's hand upon me."

Jess shivered in the stuffy room. This was the real thing, all right. No doubt of that.

"I said, 'Horace, I'm not partial to turkey, as you know. Just a boiled chicken will do.'" She exhaled. Jess inhaled and smelled boiled chicken, old sandalwood. "'Why not splurge?' he said. Then he was gone. He never," Madame Marcia's bloodshot eyes glared at Jess "came back."

"Killed?" Jess had always known that he himself would one day die violently. Roxy said he was mad as a hatter. But Jess *knew;* and so he was never alone in an empty street or alleyway or, for that matter, bed, if he could help it. When George did not sleep with him, one of the clerks from his emporium would oblige. In Washington he always shared a room with Daugherty, next to the room of the invalid Mrs. Daugherty. Whatever town Jess was in, he cultivated policemen. He read every detective story he could get his hands on to find out how to survive the city jungle with its wild killings, human swarm, dark alleys.

"Who knows? The son-of-a-bitch," she added, suddenly soulful. "Anyway, I had had my call." She indicated the Spiritualist Church diploma. "I don't need *any* man, I'm happy to say, except when I feel we've known one another in an earlier life." She smiled at Jess, who blushed and took off his thick glasses so that her face might blur; he adored women but, what with one thing and another – like his weight problem and diabetes – what was the point? as Roxy had said in the third month of their marriage. Jess had wept. She was firm, yet loving. Roxy would never go for a turkey and not return. She just went for a divorce, and as Jess was worth even then a small fortune, more than one hundred thousand dollars, he could keep them both in high style. Today they were better friends than ever, each devoted to gossip; each able to remember almost to the week when a couple was married so that when the first baby was born they could – she without fingers, he with – work out the time of conception and whether or not it was blessed in the Lord's eyes. Each delighted secretly in the fact that the Duchess's son by her first husband was born six months after the wedding which was to end in divorce six years later. Roxy shared Jess's high pleasure in this sort of knowledge, proving that there were, Jess decided, blessings yet to be counted, particularly if Roxy should end up in Hollywood as a photo-play star, their common dream – for her.

The Duchess was in the room. "I let myself in." The voice was dry and nasal and whenever a word had an "r" in it the Duchess made that poor letter go through her thin dry lips, over and over again, as if she were French. But she was quintessentially a Midwesterner of German extraction, born Florence Kling. The head was large, the body small. The Duchess suffered from what Madame Marcia would call renal problems, and her ankles were often swollen while her sallow normal color was often dull gray with illness. She had only one kidney, which obliged her to drink quantities of water. Often bedded with a hot-water bottle on even the most stifling of summer days, she would try, sometimes in vain, to sweat. But today the small blue eyes were bright and there was even a suggestion of color in her cheeks due to the north wind, while the end of her somewhat thick nose was also rosy – moist, too. Like a trumpet, she blew her nose into a large handkerchief and said, "I hate incense. So foreign, so bad for the air."

"*Chacun à son goût.*" Madame Marcia was gracious. "Let me take your wraps." As the Duchess was divested, she turned to Jess. "We're invited to Mrs. Bingham's but . . ." The Duchess was about to name her husband; then saw the dark brown myopic eyes of Jess so unlike her own small gray far-sighted ones; remembered the rule of *omertà*. ". . . but I don't want to go alone. So you can take me, can't you?"

"Sure thing, Duchess."

"Now, Madame Marcia," the Duchess made the priestess sound like the patroness of a disorderly house, "I've been hearing so much the last couple of years about you and I'm really glad to meet up with you though I can't say I'm all that much a believer in all this." The Duchess's face set in what Jess was convinced she believed was a jovial expression but the long sheep-like upper lip and thin mouth produced an effect more alarming than not.

"Dear lady," Marcia sighed and blinked her eyes. "We are such stuff as dreams are made on. . . ."

"I don't like Shakespeare." Jess was always surprised by how much the Duchess knew and, usually, disliked. But then she had had a hard life which was probably not going to get any easier. She could hear storm warnings more clearly than anyone else he knew, like those animals that were able to anticipate earthquakes, much good it ever did them. "I saw the Frank Deshon Opera Company once." The Duchess did a complete reversal; she was also a perfect politician when she chose to be. "They played Cincinnati. I went with my . . . brother. That was way before your time, of course. . . ."

"Oh, my *dear* lady!" Madame March was properly hooked.

"Now what do I do? I feel like I'm at the dentist's." Madame Marcia took her client's arm and steered her into the back room. "It will be painless, I promise you."

"Now, don't you listen, Jess." The Duchess touched the beads.

"I never listen when I'm not supposed to."

"Says you! Those big ears of yours flap like nothing I ever saw outside the circus."

Jess resolved not to listen; and heard everything. "The subject," as the Duchess's husband was referred to, "was born November 2, 1865, at two P.M. in the Midwest of the United States. Jupiter." Then something, something. Then, "Sign of Sagittarius in the tenth house." Jess stared into the small coal fire set back in an iron grate. Washington was just like Ohio, nothing big city at all about these R Street brick houses. But then everyone liked to say that Washington was just a big village which happened to be full of big people of the sort Jess was naturally attracted to as they were to him.

Lately, Jess had started to keep a notebook in which he recorded the name of every important person he met in the course of a day. In Washington his fingers soon got tired, adding up the day's score. Even so, he was looking forward to Mrs. Bingham's reception. A wealthy widow, Mrs. Bingham conducted what Jess had first thought was a political "saloon" like a bar and grill until it was explained to him what a salon was. Mrs. Bingham was also the mother-in-law of the publisher of the Washington *Tribune*, a paper most friendly to Ohio Republicans, unlike the Washington *Post*, whose owner, John R. McLean, an Ohio Democrat, had died the previous summer, leaving his son Ned to do right by the Duchess and her husband. Ned and his wife Evalyn were now their close friends; and so, marvelously, was Jess, who had never dreamed that he would be taken up by a rich and glamorous couple of the highest society. Evalyn was especially magnificent, with the most diamonds of any one woman on earth, among them the Hope Diamond, a bluish chunk of old bottle to Jess's eye, worn on a long chain about her neck and as full of evil, it was said, as Jess's downstairs closet. But unlike Jess, Evalyn was unafraid.

"I feel extra-marital entanglements may cause grief." Madame Marcia's voice richly hummed through the beaded curtain. The Duchess's nasal response was pitched high. "That's somebody else's husband you got there. But that's all right. Go on."

"The stars . . ." Madame Marcia's voice dropped to a whisper and Jess sighed voluptuously as he thought of all the sin in the world, and so much of it of the flesh. The Duchess suffered because her husband was a ladies' man and there was nothing she could do but turn a blind eye, as she did to their neighbor Carrie Phillips, wife of James, who, like Jess, was a dealer in dry goods, as well as fancy and staple notions and infants' wear.

Carrie was handsome and golden and well-born – related to the Fulton of the steamboats, it was said. She was also part German, and that was cause for many a quarrel in the parlors of Washington Court House and of nearby Marion; worse, of many a quarrel between Carrie and her lover, who was obliged to placate both his pro-German and anti-German constituents. On this subject, Carrie could be fierce; otherwise, she made the great man happy, thought Jess, whistling softly to himself "My God, How the Money Rolls In!"

"That," the Duchess's voice rasped, "was all pretty interesting. I'll say that. Food for thought." As she strode into the sitting room, Jess thought of what her husband had once said about her: "She can't see a band without wanting to be the drum-major." She liked people to think she was her husband's dynamo, but Jess doubted this if only because *he* liked people to think that she was his spur. Daugherty thought they were more of a team, like a pair of old-time oxen pulling a cart, with her bellowing the most and with him pulling the most. But thanks to Jess's mother and to Roxy and to *her* mother, he knew more about women as people than anyone, and it was his view that the Duchess was a joyous slave to her apparently lazy, charming, lucky husband, who called the shots.

"Jess, you'll settle up?" The Duchess was now safely inside her various wrappings. Madame Marcia's smile was sweet and faraway.

"Okay, Duchess." Jess was aware that the "D" of Duchess had produced a sudden jet of saliva. Fortunately no one was drenched. He dried his lips with the back of his left sleeve; he would have to dry his thick moustache later, when unobserved.

"You'll pick me up at Wyoming Avenue. Five o'clock sharp. Wear something spiffy."

"Yes, ma'am."

The two ladies parted, amid powerful assurances of mutual high esteem and deep – on Madame's side compassion.

"What's the damage?" asked Jess, reaching for his wallet.

"The damage," Madame Marcia gazed ethereally out the window at the black afternoon sky, "has been done." Then she blinked her eyes, as if coming out of a dream. "Mr. Micajah's paid already. The lady's not very strong," she added, probing, Jess could tell. "She has a renal complaint."

That was on the nose. Impressed, Jess nodded. "She's been sickly quite a lot lately."

"Bright's disease, I should guess, not having done her horoscope. *He's* sickly, too."

"The picture of health." Again, she was on target. Jess was impressed for the first time. The subject's fluctuating health was one of the few secrets in public life; private, too. When he went off to Battle Creek, Michigan, the town thought that he was just getting away from the Duchess and politics, but he was actually trying to bring down blood pressure, moderate his heartbeat, dry out his system. Jess had gone with him once and was amazed at how pale the ruddy face became once he'd stopped drinking, and how frail he was for all his highly visible not to mention remarkably handsome robustness.

"I think you should tell Mr. Micajah – as he is paying – what I did not tell the lady." Madame Marcia drew the curtain against the February sky.

"Something bad?"

"These things are open to interpretation. If one were always right, I'd be living in a palace on Connecticut Avenue like Blaise Sanford. Of course, our occult gifts do not extend to ourselves. In that sense we're a bit like doctors, who never take care of themselves."

"Never take their own medicine either." Jess had seldom been free for long of doctors – asthma, diabetes.

"There, they are wise. Mr. Micajah made it clear to me that if I found in the stars what he thought I would that I should impart it to – the Duchess, which I have done. I have seldom seen so glorious a chart or one so brief. I can see why *he* is melancholy and

15

moody and wants all of life that he can seize before he rises to the heights. . . ." She stopped.

Jess's heart was beating faster. This was it. Clever Daugherty. Clairvoyant Madame? "Will he be president?"

Madame Marcia nodded solemnly; then she turned to gaze with bemusement at herself in a dust-streaked mirror.

"Yes. With those stars and that rampant lion, he cannot fail. I told her that. I told her everything, except . . ." For a moment she seemed to have lost her train of thought. What *was* she thinking of? The turkey that never was, or . . . ? She turned away from the mirror; crossed to a table where amongst numerous beautiful objects a small porcelain cup held a number of toothpicks; she selected one and most deliberately went to work on her lower teeth. "I did not tell her what I want you to tell Mr. Micajah. After glory in the House of Preferment, the sun and Mars are conjoined in the eighth house of the Zodiac. This is the House of Death. Sudden death."

"He'll die?"

"We all do that. No. I see something far more terrible than mere death." Madame Marcia discarded her toothpick like an empress letting go the sceptre. "President Harding – of course I know now exactly who he is – will be murdered."

3

From the beginning Caroline Sanford Sanford and Eleanor Roosevelt Roosevelt were friends. For one thing, there was the ridiculous redundancy of their names: each had married a cousin with the same family name; for another, each had gone to school in England with Mlle. Souvestre. As Caroline, now forty, was seven years older than Eleanor, they had not known each other at school. But each had been molded – even hewn – by the formidable Mademoiselle, a square-jawed spinster of extraordinary intellect and character and a freedom from all superstition, particularly the Christian one – which had alarmed Eleanor's Uncle

Theodore, the President. But as Theodore's favorite sister had survived the same school uncorrupted, he had decided that his tall gawky fatherless – and motherless – niece might "find herself" abroad in a way that she could not at home in Tivoli, New York, close to the Hudson River, less close to the edge of the great world – *her* world, because she could not have Hudson Valley friends to the house for fear that her alcoholic brother, stationed in his second-floor window, might open fire on them with a hunting rifle. Although he had, thus far, always missed, one could not rely forever on an alcoholic tremor to preserve life.

It had been an inspired notion to get Eleanor out of Tivoli, out of America. In fact, Caroline liked to take some credit for having helped persuade – or was it her half-brother Blaise? – the then Governor Roosevelt to let his niece go out into the world of free-thinkers. After two years, Eleanor had returned to America better educated than anyone of her class except, perhaps, Caroline herself, but then Caroline had been brought up in France, the country to which her American father had gone into eccentric exile after the Civil War.

At thirty-three, Eleanor could speak excellent French as well as some German and Italian. She had not succumbed to Mademoiselle's velvety atheism; rather, she had reacted to it with a renewed Protestant vigor and spoke often and unaffectedly of "ideals," a word seldom to be heard on the worldly Caroline's lips, but then Caroline was, with Blaise, the publisher of the Washington *Tribune,* a newspaper much influenced by William Randolph Hearst's "yellow" *sensational* journalism, while Eleanor was a noble matron, the mother of five young children, of which the oldest was at the Misses Eastman School with Caroline's daughter, Emma. Finally, Eleanor was very much the shy but purposeful consort of the assistant secretary of the Navy, Franklin Delano Roosevelt, a charming Hudson Valley gentleman farmer generally thought to be, in Senator Lodge's phrase, "well-meaning but light." Caroline was not so certain how well-meaning the ambitious Franklin was – she was impervious to his aggressive, even cruel charm – but she knew that whatever intellectual and moral force he might lack, Eleanor more than made up for. Each complemented the other. Each saw politics as a royal road to be travelled the full distance. Like Franklin's cousin and Eleanor's uncle, Theodore, Franklin had been elected to the New York state legislature; now he held the same office that Theodore had used in order to gain for the United States the Philippines and for himself the presidency.

"What is President Wilson's mood?" asked Caroline. "About Germany *now*?"

"He doesn't confide in his under-secretaries. But Franklin thinks war is upon us." She frowned. "I hope not, of course."

"Your Uncle Theodore Rex, as Henry Adams calls him, howls for war."

"Uncle Tee is – sometimes – too emphatic, even for us." Eleanor smiled her diffident large-toothed smile, and dipped her head, an odd gesture, as if to apologize for the too small chin, the too large upper teeth which kept her from full admission to that celebrated bevy of beauty, her mother and two aunts. But Caroline found her charming in appearance if a bit overpowering. She was as tall as most men. Fortunately, Franklin was even taller than she, both slender, long-limbed, full of nervous energy. Eleanor lived two blocks from Caroline's house, and each liked to walk, whenever there was time, in their common village, Georgetown, still mostly Negro but, here and there, eighteenth-century townhouses were being restored by the canny white rich. Caroline had taken two row houses and knocked them into one. The result was more than enough for a single lady whose fourteen-year-old daughter was away at school all day. On the other hand, the seven unwealthy Roosevelts were all crowded into 1773 N Street, a small red-brick house belonging to Eleanor's aunt.

Now Eleanor sat before the fire in Caroline's drawing room, an assembly of furs about her neck, studying the schedule for the day. She is like a general, thought Caroline, every contingency prepared for in advance. She had a full-time social secretary, as well as women to look after her children, and, of course, she herself presided over the political wife's necessity, the cardcase, with which, each morning of practically every week, she must make the rounds, stopping at the houses of congressional, diplomatic, judicial wives in order to leave a card as an act of homage. In turn, they would deposit their cards on her vestibule table. As a resident of the city for nearly twenty years, Caroline was a near-Aboriginal and so seldom planted cards anywhere unless it was on someone older than she or a friend new to the city.

"We have," said Eleanor, "twenty minutes before we must appear at Mrs. Bingham's."

"*You* must. I just do. . . ."

Eleanor's laugh was high, while her normally pale gray skin suddenly became pale pink. Although Eleanor blushed easily, Caroline suspected that this was not the result of shyness, as everyone thought, but the weapon of a marvelous social tactician for whom the blush was an evasionary tactic like that of the sea-squid which could spread a cloud of ink all round itself and thus vanish in order to chart a new course. "Naturally, I do it for Franklin. We must keep on the right side of Congress, and they all go to Mrs. Bingham's."

"Except this week. They've adjourned. I told her not to bother, but she has mortal longings. She hungers now for the diplomats who stay, and for the Administration, which never leaves town, the way they used to."

"They can't. Not now. Not with 'Preparedness.'" Eleanor frowned. "Do you think we'll go into the war?"

"That was my editorial. Yesterday. Yes, I do."

"I thought it was your brother's. He's been so . . . eager to have us go in."

"Well, now I'm eager, too." Caroline found herself staring at a bust of Napoleon, a gift from her original mentor in the newspaper business, William Randolph Hearst, whose gifts, like his life, tended toward the inappropriate but were no less revealing for that.

"The young men all are." Eleanor undid the button to her right glove; soon she would be shaking hands, graciously, like her uncle, but with far less noise. "I mean the ones in the Administration, like Franklin and Bill Phillips. I'm rather more – Don't tell anyone." She regarded Caroline anxiously, and Caroline found her charmingly innocent, since no one of sound mind would confide in a

19

newspaper publisher. But Caroline nodded sympathetically, as she always did whenever President Wilson pretended to confide in her; *he* was not innocent, of course, just self-absorbed and so, at times, tactically obtuse. "Well, personally, secretly, I rather like the way Mr. Bryan resigned as secretary of state."

"Peace at any price?"

"Almost. Yes. Aren't you?"

"Almost. No." Caroline was brisk. "It is too late, thanks to Herr Zimmermann's telegram. Even Mlle. Souvestre would favor war."

"Yes. That went too far. So discouraging. I suppose I'm getting used to the idea now. But when Mr. Bryan resigned as secretary, I thought him very brave. I'm not a pacifist, of course. I can't be. Franklin would be furious. He's getting to be just like Uncle Ted. War at any price. Now, thanks to Mr. Zimmermann . . ." Eleanor gazed forlornly at her schedule.

At first, both Caroline and the Anglophile Blaise thought the telegram was an invention of the British; as a result, humiliatingly, the *Tribune* was one of the last newspapers to record this shocking affront – and shock it certainly was – to the American people. Yet when the President requested congressional permission to arm American ships, the request had been filibustered to death on the Senate floor: and the Congress had then adjourned on March 3, leaving the nation's business unfinished.

On March 5, the President had taken his second oath of office in a simple ceremony at the White House to which neither Blaise nor Caroline had been invited. But then the President was vindictive not only in the large necessary things but in the small insignificant ones as well. To Caroline this was perfect proof of his greatness, since every major political figure that she had known was equally dedicated to disinterested revenge.

Jacques, the lesser half of a couple from Martinique, appeared in the doorway. "The car is here, madam."

Caroline rose while Eleanor perversely buttoned the glove that she had just unbuttoned. The process would now have to be repeated once they were in company. There was something compulsive about the younger woman's energy that Caroline found both touching and mysterious. But then the dread – and for

Caroline, if not for all the world, charming – Uncle Theodore had set inordinately high standards of activity, ranging from every sort of fidget in a room to mad dashes up and down the Amazon in order to slaughter any animal or bird that dared place itself in his path. Happily, the women of the family had never been taken in by him. From serene wife, Edith, to brilliant daughter, Alice, to the various Norn-like sisters, the ladies were never strenuous, unlike the menfolk, who never ceased to give unconvincing imitations of Theodore Roosevelt's strenuosity and superb manliness against every odd. Even distant cousin Franklin, who resembled the presidential Roosevelts not at all, had taken to tossing his head as if his thinning locks were a lion's mane and, of course, flashing large teeth in imitation of the one who had been what he – like all the others – wanted to be, the president. Yet Eleanor broke the sexual pattern. Serene and controlled in manner, she was over-active in deed. She climbed the rigging of ships; she paid more calls than she needed to; she over-organized her household; she was always in a desperate hurry, thought Caroline, hurrying to catch up with her at the motor car's door, where the Irish chauffeur stood, face anxious with sobriety.

"*Why*," asked Caroline, out of breath, "are you always in such a hurry?"

"Because," said Eleanor, "I think that I am always late."

"For what?"

"Oh . . ." She leapt into the back seat of the car. "Everything," she said. The toothy smile was sudden and very winning. "Life."

Caroline settled down beside her. "That takes care of itself soon enough. Us, too."

"Then one must hurry to do it all." Caroline wondered, not for the first time, if Eleanor disliked her husband. They were so well matched a political couple that only an underlying tension of some sort could explain Eleanor's perfectionism and irrational fear of being late – of being left behind?

Mrs. Benedict Tracy Bingham was Caroline's finest invention. At the century's turn when the youthful Caroline had taken over the moribund Washington *Tribune,* there was no place for the tone of the paper to go but down, down to as many common readers as possible – or out of business altogether. Caroline had imitated Hearst. Murders became her hallmark, particularly when the body – always female, always beauteous – was pulled from the canal. Caroline had a prejudice against the Potomac River which her editor, Mr. Trimble, honored whenever he could. Next to bodies floating in pieces along the canal that paralleled the river, robberies of the rich inhabitants of the city's west end were highly popular, and when Mrs. Bingham, wife of "the Milk King," as Caroline dubbed him, lost a few trinkets to a burglar who had found his way into her Connecticut Avenue house, Caroline had arbitrarily elevated Mrs. Bingham, a lady unknown to her, to First Ladyhood of Washington's society, enlarging the house to Windsor Castle and making all her jewels crown. Mrs. Bingham had been thrilled; had cultivated Caroline; had forced the Milk King to advertise in the *Tribune*.

In return, Caroline had helped Mrs. Bingham clamber along the heights of Washington society, an affair of mutually exclusive villages that tended to exclude the largest village of all, the government. Accustomed to the political salons of Paris, Caroline had encouraged Mrs. Bingham to specialize in members of the House of Representatives, a group no Washingtonian had ever wanted to cultivate. As Caroline had predicted, the statesmen were pathetically grateful for any attention, and so, *en masse* at Mrs. Bingham's, they proved a sufficient draw to fill her drawing room with an interesting assortment of other villagers. Now, widowed, blind, malevolent of tongue, Mrs. Bingham had arrived; had become an institution; had, somewhat to Caroline's bemusement, married her daughter, Frederika, to Blaise, and so the milklaced blood of the Binghams was now conjoined with the purple of the Sanfords and the Burrs in the form of a fat child. I have a lot to answer for, thought Caroline, as she and Eleanor entered the drawing room, where peacock feathers made Indian war-bonnets of a number of blameless Chinese jugs while Tiffany's largest lamps illuminated everyone's worst angle.

"It's Caroline." Mrs. Bingham's blind eyes turned in Caroline's direction. She looked older than she was, thanks to a regimen prepared for her by Dr. Kellogg himself. She lived on wheat that had been shredded; and so belched constantly from too much roughage of the sort necessary only to her late husband's cows, source of her wealth, glory. "And Mrs. Roosevelt. Franklin, that is." Mrs. Bingham did not even try to disguise her disappointment. But Eleanor, one of the right Roosevelts, was quite used to being taken, thanks to her husband, for one of the wrong ones.

Mrs. Bingham took Eleanor's hand. "Everyone speaks of your husband. So energetic. So handsome. Where is he?"

"He's been in Haiti and Santo Domingo, inspecting our Marines." Eleanor did not lie; but she did know how to avoid and evade the truth. Actually, when relations with Germany had been broken off, Franklin had been called back to Washington by the Secretary of the Navy. In the best Roosevelt tradition, he was now complaining to everyone about his long-suffering chief, Josephus Daniels, an amiable Southern newspaper editor, who hated war and alcohol and so had been entrusted with the American Navy.

"Well, he must be very busy these days. He's pro-German, you know." Mrs. Bingham when not spreading gossip of the most astonishing sort was given to occupying untenable positions, to the great annoyance of no one but her daughter, who was not, Caroline noted, present.

"Really?" Eleanor was not used to Mrs. Bingham.

"Yes. Really. Beethoven, Mozart, Goethe, Romain Rolland. Those are my idols."

"Rolland is French," murmured Caroline.

"Who said he wasn't? Not I." Eleanor had drifted off. Mrs. Bingham held Caroline's arm firmly. "We must talk. Not now, of course." The deep voice was conspiratorial. "But *he's* here. With *her* brother. And it's true. Seventy-five thousand dollars it cost to buy *her* off. Now the letters are in *his* hands."

Caroline bowed to the father of her child. Senator James Burden Day inclined his head while his wife, Kitty, smiled vaguely at her husband's mistress of sixteen years. Caroline was certain that Kitty did not know because, if she had, there would have been terrible scenes and threats of divorce in the American style so unlike that of Paris where, at least in these matters, things were better ordered. Of course, Caroline's husband had divorced her when he discovered the father's identity. Happily, there was no jealousy involved, only money. She was wealthy; he was not. In any case, her cousin had known that she was pregnant with someone else's child when he married her because he had needed money as much as she had needed a husband's good name, which was also hers, Sanford. In time, they parted. In time, he died. In time, Caroline went on, as there is nothing else ever to do with time.

While Mrs. Bingham told her of scandals too squalid even for the *Tribune* to publish, Caroline noted that her lover was growing stout, that the once thick bronze curls were now gray in front and fewer, and the blue eyes smaller in a lined face. Yet they still made love at least once a week: and, more important, there was always a good deal to talk about. But now she was forty, with a fleet of ships ablaze behind her. There was no going back in time, while what lay ahead was less than comforting if only because she did not know how to be old; and rather doubted that she'd ever develop the knack.

Everyone, even Blaise, urged her to marry again, as if one simply went to a party and selected a husband. But the few possibilities were always married, as her first lover had been and still very much was. Of the possibilities, she had allowed herself several short affairs, without great joy. Now she found that she was attracted to men half her age, which would have been acceptable in France but not here, where she could well be burned at the stake. Women were not allowed such vile license in the Puritan republic. Women were not allowed much of anything unless they were rich in their own right, her one glittering advantage, seldom taken advantage of.

Mrs. Bingham accepted the worship of two new congressional couples who, when they heard Caroline's name, saw, as it were, divinity. Aware that a newspaper proprietor was the source of all life to the politician, Caroline encouraged lit candles, murmured prayers, whispered confessions because, put simply, she liked power very much.

Suddenly she felt less sorry for herself, as Mrs. Bingham, punch cup in hand, told her with acrid breath that one of the he's of her story was standing across the room, a stout dim-looking man named Randolph Bolling, brother to the second Mrs. Woodrow Wilson. "Which," said Mrs. Bingham, delighted with the horror of it all, "is why *he is* with *him.*"

"*Who* is with *whom?*" Caroline had always had difficulty following Mrs. Bingham's higher gossip. Now, half in half out of her dotage, Mrs. Bingham no longer bothered to identify with a name those free-floating pronouns that bobbed in such confusion on the surface of her swift sombre narratives.

"He – *her* brother." Mrs. Bingham frowned with annoyance. She disliked the specific. "Randolph Bolling. Over there. With the sheep's head. Well, he brought *him.* The great speculator. Over there. The Jew. Quite handsome, to give the devil his due."

Caroline recognized Bernard Baruch, a very tall, very rich Wall Street speculator who affected a Southern accent so thick that it made Josephus Daniels sound like a Vermont Yankee. Baruch was a New Yorker of Southern origin. He had made a fortune by remembering to sell those stocks which he had bought *before* they cost less than he paid for them, a gift Caroline entirely lacked. She had sat next to Baruch once or twice at dinner and enjoyed his flow of gossip, in which every one of *his* pronouns was firmly attached to a famous name. Like so many newly rich men of no particular world – he was a Jew, she had gathered, only when it suited him – Baruch had been attracted to Washington, to politics, to the President. It was said that he had personally given fifty thousand dollars to Wilson for the election of 1912; it was also said that he used his White House connections to get tips on what stocks to buy. Caroline was hazy about all this. But not Mrs. Bingham, who was now in full swift torrent. "*Mrs. Peck,*" she said the name accusingly, much preferring *she.* "The President's old mistress – she's in California now – was threatening to sell the President's letters to the papers last fall before the election, and so Randolph Bolling got Mr. Baruch to go to her and buy the letters for seventy-five thousand dollars, and that's how the President could marry Edith Bolling Galt, who's getting fat, and the President could win the election, just barely. . . ."

A plain small woman with a large head marched toward Mrs.

Bingham, followed by a plump bespectacled man with a moist palm, as Caroline discovered when it closed all round her own hand. "Mrs. Harding!"

Mrs. Bingham produced her most ghastly smile for the wife of Ohio's junior senator, Warren Gamaliel Harding, who, after James Burden Day, was the handsomest man in the Senate. "This is an old friend." Mrs. Harding pushed her escort forward. "From Washington Court House, in Fayette County. Jesse Smith. Say hello to Mrs. Bingham. Say hello to Mrs. Sanford, Jesse." The hellos were duly said. Then, to make conversation, Jesse said to Caroline, "I'm a friend of Ned McLean. And Evalyn, too. His wife, you know. With the diamond."

"I'm not." Caroline was gracious. "A friend, that is. I wish," she was expansive in her insincerity, "that I was."

"I can fix it," said Jesse. "Any time."

"Jesse can fix anything." But Mrs. Harding sounded dubious.

"Where's the Senator?" Mrs. Bingham came to the only point that mattered: wives were to be tolerated, no more.

"He's gone to Palm Beach. With the McLeans. He hates the cold. So do I. But I've got so much to do here. You see, we went and bought this big house on Wyoming Avenue that's in two parts. We live in the one part and we rent out the other. Well, there's no end of bother with tenants, isn't there?"

Mrs. Bingham said, "I wouldn't know."

"You must come see us when we're settled in. You, too, Mrs. Sanford. I've been to your brother's lovely home."

"Almost as big as the McLeans'." Jesse made his contribution.

"My daughter finds it quite large enough these days." With her usual swift thrust, Mrs. Bingham reminded them that Mrs. Blaise Delacroix Sanford was none other than her own daughter Frederika – my protégée, thought Caroline, who was more glad than not to have got Blaise married to someone who could put up with his uneasy temper, so like their father's, though unlike that once larger-than-life now smaller-than-death monster, Blaise was not yet mad. Caroline quite admired her sister-in-law's strength of character, particularly the way she had, socially at least, dropped her mother once she had leapt to the top of their world. Neither

26

Blaise nor Frederika ever appeared at Mrs. Bingham's "at homes" to the Congress, nor was Mrs. Bingham invited to the Sanfords except for a private meal in the bosom of the family, the very last place that Mrs. Bingham ever wanted to be. Caroline herself was less strict than Frederika. Also, Mrs. Bingham was her invention; and never to be abandoned. She was good value, too, if one could separate her inventions from those shiny disreputable truths for which she had a magpie's eye.

Mrs. Harding was staring at Caroline. She had left her card upon first arrival in the city in early 1915; and that had been that. "You must come to us, Mrs. Sanford. We're simple folk, but I know you're a friend of Nick Longworth . . ."

"And here," said Caroline, saved by the appearance of a handsome creature all in blue, "is Mrs. Longworth."

"Caroline." The women embraced. "Mrs. Bingham." Alice Roosevelt Longworth's cold gray-blue eyes were aslant with controlled laughter. Mrs. Bingham had that effect on her. "Mrs. Harding!" Alice's eyes went suddenly wide; laughter was choked off at the source.

"I was just telling about your Nick and my Warren." The "Warren" came out in a staccato roar of "r's" which sounded to Caroline like "Wurr-rren."

"They play poker," Alice announced brightly. "In your apartment . . ."

"*House,* in two parts," began Mrs. Harding with a look of steel in *her* cold gray-blue eyes. Caroline was not certain which of the two would win if war came. Alice's wild sense of humor was a sword on which she might yet herself fall. While Mrs. Harding – what was her name? – Florence – would never give way. Ordinarily the two ladies would not have met but for the fact that Alice's husband was a congressman from Ohio, whose senator was Warren Harding: as a result, neither lady could ignore the other. But thus far Alice had collected the most points. "I must come see your apartment – I mean house. I don't go," she turned to Caroline, "because I'm not invited to the poker games. Only boys allowed. Even though I'm a very good poker player." She turned to Mrs. Harding. "Maybe you and I should have all-girl all-night poker games, Florence." Alice said the name with sufficient space all round it to leave room for a shroud.

"I'm Jesse Smith," said Jesse Smith, taking Alice's hand. "From Ohio, too."

"Lucky," said Alice, "you."

"I think you know my friends the McLeans. She plays poker, Evalyn does. Pretty good, too."

"Oh, God!" Alice had long since ceased to attend the Ohioans. "Cousin Eleanor! She's like a lighthouse, isn't she? So tall, so full of light. I must go tease her." Alice left them for the fireplace, where Eleanor stood, listening politely to Mr. Baruch. They were the only couple in the room in proper scale to each other. Like kindly giants, they stood before the flames and greeted Alice.

Mrs. Bingham knew all. "Her father will run again, in 1920. He'll be nominated, too. He's made his peace with the regular Republicans."

"My Warren thinks the world of Colonel Roosevelt." With a hunter's eye, Mrs. Harding studied Alice in the distance, the quarry that had got away so far. "The Colonel needs Ohio, if he's going to go anywhere at all, and my Warren can swing it for him."

"But surely Mr. Wilson will run again, and win again." As Caroline spoke, she wondered if she ought to try to have another child; or was she too old? Menopause had not yet begun; even so, the *Tribune*'s Society Lady never ceased to warn its readers against having a child so late in life and so long after the first. Of course, there was no husband, but nowadays a respectable widow could simply take a long trip around the world and return with an adopted child, and an elaborate story of a family retainer, in France, at Saint-Cloud-le-Duc, dead in childbirth. Last wish for baby: America. Adoption. *What else could I do?* Every four years, coincidental with the presidential election, she thought of having a baby or going back to France for good or entering, at last, upon a furious love affair. Also, any mention of Theodore Roosevelt had the effect of turning her inward. Although she quite liked the former President despite – or because of? – his noisy absurdity, the thought of his absolutely requited self-love made her affections turn not toward him but herself. He aroused the competitive

28

instinct in her. She could still start over. She had not lost her looks; she might still find . . . what?

"I think I shall go to California," she said, to the general astonishment of her companions and self. With that, she abandoned them for the father of her daughter, Burden Day, who had come to the Senate in 1915, the same year as Warren Harding. Before that he had been in the House of Representatives, where during his first – or was it second? – term he had deflowered her, for which she was in his debt. Otherwise, she might have been like Mlle. Souvestre, a vast untended garden, gone to seed.

"Jim," she murmured. He had just left the group around Alice and Kitty. *Kitty: The Unsuspecting Wife.* Caroline tended to think in headlines, capitals, italics, and bold *bold* Roman. She might no longer be much of a woman but she was truly a good and inky publisher. "Or should I call you Burden now?" With Jim's elevation to the Senate, Kitty had decreed he be known as Burden Day, which had a presidential sound, she thought, though to Caroline the name suggested a spinsterish old gentleman, at Newport, Rhode Island, in exuberant thrall to needlepoint.

"Call me anything. You look beautiful. What else?"

"I do have something else in mind. The beauty's only nature's trap. I want another child."

"By me?" Burden's smile was immaculate; but his voice had dropped to a whisper. Nearby, the Austrian ambassador spoke of peace to the secretary of the interior, who cared only for oil.

"By you. Of course. I'm hardly wanton yet."

"I suppose it could be arranged." He grinned; reminded her of the boy that he had been when they first met. "Funny," he added, and she smiled broadly, aware that when anyone said "funny" it was fairly certain that all mirth had fled. "Kitty said almost the same thing to me last year."

"And you obliged."

"I obliged. She never really got over Jim Junior's dying."

"Now?"

"Happy. Again. How's Emma?"

"Our daughter wants to go to college. She is very brainy, not like me."

"Not like me, either."

"Come see her. She likes you." Actually Emma was perfectly indifferent to her actual father, so much for the mystical inevitable tug of consanguinity. But then Emma was indifferent to most people; she was withdrawn, self-absorbed, neutral. She read books of physics as if they were novels. Surprisingly, the one person that she had liked was Caroline's husband of convenience, of course she had thought that John Sanford was her father. But as he was now dead, that was that. Caroline did find it unusual – even unfeminine – that Emma had never once noticed the physical resemblance between herself and her mother's old friend James Burden Day. But then Emma never looked at a mirror in order to see herself as opposed to hair or hat.

"She's made friends with the Roosevelt girl." At the fireplace, Alice was holding forth to cousin Eleanor, whose patient smile was beginning to resemble Medusa's petrifying rictus.

"Hard to imagine, a *Democratic* Roosevelt." Burden stared at the cousins, alike in appearance, unlike in character.

"What do you think of him?"

Burden shrugged. "He doesn't come my way. He's a bit too charming, I'd say. He's also too much the warrior. He can't wait to get us in."

"You can?"

"I'm a Bryan Democrat. Remember?" Burden stretched his arms, as if measuring them for a cross of gold. "The war's not popular where I come from. Maybe the Easterners should go and fight it and let us stay home . . ."

"And fight Mexico?"

"Well, at least we'd get some loot out of it. There's nothing for us in Europe except trouble." Mrs. Harding marched by, Jesse Smith two paces behind her. She greeted Burden; then affixed herself to the Russian ambassador, Bakhmeteff, whose wife was the aunt of Ned McLean, Caroline's friendly competitor at the *Post*.

"Now *he* has a problem. Warren Harding, that is." Burden took a glass of champagne from a passing waiter. It had been Caroline's idea for Mrs. Bingham to break with Washington tradition and serve champagne as well as the inevitable tea and heavy cake.

Official Washington was gratified except for such devoted teeto-talers as Josephus Daniels, who had gone so far as to ban wine from the officers' mess of the Navy. Currently, Mrs. Daniels was notorious for having presided over a tea where *onion sandwiches* had been served. She would never live that down was Mrs. Bingham's considered judgment. Even in Washington there were limits to vulgarity.

"Are there so many hyphenates in Ohio?" Caroline found the whole problem of German-Americans and Irish-Americans fasci-nating. The Administration found it alarming. If the United States went to war with Germany, how would a million or so German-speaking American citizens respond?

"No more than I've got, proportionately. But Harding's got one, a lady friend, who's a dragon, they say. She's threatened to expose him . . ."

"Expose him?"

"Both of them. She'll tell all if he votes for war with her native land."

"That is unusual. *Cherchez le pays.*"

"Senators are known by the women they keep." Burden grinned. "Actually, he's a nice fellow, if you don't count his speeches."

"That's what we say about all of you. Except Senator Lodge. We like his speeches. It's he that . . ." They were then joined by Mrs. Bingham, blind eyes agleam with excitement. "Mr. Tumulty's here. From the White House. You're being called back, Senator. All of you. All Congress."

"Called back for what?" Burden looked, again, his age; and Caroline decided not to have another child – by him.

"A special session. To receive a communication by the Executive on Grave Questions of Internal Policy. Those are Mr. Wilson's very words. I'm sure it's war at last. So exciting, isn't it?"

Caroline's heart began to pound – from excitement? Burden's face was suddenly ruddy. "I'm sure it isn't war just yet. When is the special session?"

"April sixteenth, Mr. Tumulty says."

Burden looked relieved. "That gives us a month. Plenty can hap-pen."

"Plenty is happening," said Caroline, the editor. "The President's busy arming those ships that you willful men in the Senate said he shouldn't." Although the celebrated American Constitution was a perfect mystery to Caroline, this did seem wrong. "How can he?" She turned to Burden.

"Oh, he can, if he wants to. He can call it 'military necessity,' the way Lincoln did."

"Lincoln! War!" Mrs. Bingham was ecstatic. "I wasn't born then, of course," she lied. "But I've always wanted to live through a war. I mean *a real one,* not like the Spanish nonsense."

"I suppose that's all that anyone ever wants to do." Caroline was not well-pleased. "Live through it."

4

James Burden Day walked up the steps to the north portico of the White House, where he was greeted by an usher who led him across the entrance hall to the small electric elevator. "Mrs. Wilson will be waiting for you in the upstairs hall. The President's in bed. The chill stays with him."

Burden was struck by the calm of the White House. There was no sign of emergency. A few politicians could be seen, showing friends the state apartments. Of course, the executive offices were in a separate wing to the west of the mansion, and although telephones never ceased to ring in the offices, there was, as yet, none of that tension which he remembered from the days of McKinley and the Spanish war, not to mention the tremendous bustle of the Roosevelt era when children and their ponies were to be seen indoors as well as out, and the President gave the impression of presiding simultaneously in every room with a maximum of joyous noise.

The Wilson White House was like the President himself: scholarly, remote, and somewhat lady-like. The President had been entirely devoted to his first wife. Now he was besotted by her successor. He was easily the most uxorious of the recent presidents; he also had the fewest friends. Ill-at-ease with men, Wilson preferred the company of women, particularly of his three daughters, gracious replicas of himself, ranging from the sad plainness of the spinster Margaret, who wanted to be a singer, to the dim beauty of Eleanor, married to the secretary of the Treasury, William G. McAdoo, to the equine-featured Jessie, married to one Francis B. Sayre.

The elevator stopped. The glass-panelled door opened. Burden found himself in the familiar upstairs corridor that ran the length of the building from west to east. In the old days, the President's offices had been at the east end and the living quarters at the west, with the oval sitting room as a sort of no-man's-land at dead center. But Theodore Roosevelt's family had been big; ambitious, too. He had added the executive wing to the mansion, while converting the entire second floor for himself and his family: successors, too, of course.

The wife of the most despised of his two despised successors stood opposite the elevator, waiting for Burden. Edith Bolling Galt Wilson was a large, full-breasted woman whose wide face contained small regular features, reflecting the Indian blood that she had inherited, she claimed, from Pocahontas. The smile was truly charming. "Senator Day! Now tell me the absolute truth. Did the usher refer to me as Mrs. Wilson or as the First Lady?"

"I think he said 'Mrs. Wilson.'"

"Oh, good! I hate 'First Lady' so! It sounds like something out of vaudeville, with Weber and Fields and me as Lillie Langtry."

Burden was aware that she was the focal point of a heavy jasmine scent that ebbed and flowed in her wake as she led him to the end of the hall where a desk with two telephones had been placed beneath a great fanlight window that looked out on the executive offices to the west and the State War and Navy Building to the north. At the desk sat Edith's social secretary, Edith Benham, an admiral's daughter who had replaced the magnificent Belle Hagner, a queen of the Aboriginal City, and secretary to the first Mrs. Wilson as well as to Mrs. Roosevelt and Mrs. Taft. It had been suggested that as Edith Bolling Galt had never been included in Mrs. Hagner's list of those who were invitable to the White House,

Miss Hagner herself was no longer to be found there with her lists, her files, her telephones at the desk below the fan window. Kitty had talked of nothing else for a week; and Burden had listened less than usual.

"I do hope Mrs. Day will come to tea April twelfth." This was Mrs. Benham's greeting.

Burden said that he hoped that she would, too. "Edith is a treasure," said Edith. "Of course, she's Navy. We're surrounded by Navy here. You know Admiral Grayson." A small trim handsome man in mufti had come out of the southwest suite. "Senator," he shook Burden's hand; another Southerner, Burden duly noticed, more amused than not that it had taken Virginia less than a half-century to reconquer the White House with Woodrow Wilson, who had, as a boy, actually gazed upon the sainted features of Robert E. Lee in the days of their common country's terrible ruin. Now the South had returned in triumph to its true home, city, nation; and the President was surrounded, as was proper, by Virginians. "He's doing very well, sir." Grayson spoke to Burden but looked at Edith. "Only don't tire him. He's strong as an ox but susceptible to strain. The digestive system . . ."

". . . is the first to record the disagreeable." Edith smiled, like a little girl, Burden noted; hence the President's famous nickname for her, "little girl," which had caused much mirth considering Edith's ship-like tonnage, inevitably decorated, festooned, bannered with orchids. "I was horrified when I first learned about Mr. Wilson's breakfast . . ."

"Two raw eggs in grape juice." Grayson was prompt. "It solved the dyspepsia as much as one can. Anyway, let him conduct the conversation." Grayson gave more instructions, to Burden's deep annoyance. He was perfectly capable of talking politics in his own way to what, after all, was just another politician, no matter how elevated and hedged round with state. Then Edith led him into the bedroom.

Woodrow Wilson was propped up by four pillows; he wore a plaid wool dressing gown; and his famous pince-nez. Beside the bed, on a chair, sat his brother-in-law Randolph. Between them, on the coverlet, there was a Ouija board, and each had a hand on top of the table-like contraption that moved as if of its own will over a wooden board on which had been drawn the alphabet, stopping, as the spirit dictated, at this or that letter, which Randolph duly noted on a pad of paper. Wilson held a finger to his lips as Burden and Edith sat beside the bed, a huge affair of carved dark wood that Edith had had moved from the so-called Lincoln bedroom at the other end of the corridor. Actually, the "Lincoln bedroom" had been Lincoln's office while the bed, known reverently as *his* bed, was never used by him. All that anyone could recall was that Mrs. Lincoln had bought it for a guest room. In any case, Burden regarded the bed as singularly hideous despite its provenance; but then he disliked anything to do with the Civil War era. Red plush, horsehair stuffing, gas-lamps were mingled with his own memories of growing up poor in the Reconstruction South before his family had moved west.

While the two men played with the Ouija board, Edith whispered to Burden. "The place was – is – so run-down. You must ride herd on everyone here twenty-four hours a day, which poor Mrs. Wilson, being sick, couldn't do, and Mrs. Taft was too grand to do. Now, of course, all the money goes to Preparedness and so we just scrimp along."

But they scrimped most pleasantly, thought Burden. A fire burned in the fireplace, while above the mantel a splendid American landscape afforded some relief from all those replicas of dim politicians and their wives that gave the White House rooms a sense of being mere stage-sets for an audience of glum, peering ghosts. The window opposite Burden framed a wintry view of the becolumned State War and Navy Building, where lights were already burning. On a table, beneath the window-sill, the President's Hammond typewriter was set. It was said that not only could he type as well as any professional but he alone wrote those high-minded mellifluous speeches that had so entranced the country, including Burden, who was generally immune to the oratory of others.

Both Edith and Burden watched the President intently. But then he was most watchable, Burden decided. Roosevelt was always in motion, and so always the center of attention. But there was nothing of particular interest in T.R.'s chubby face or the rather jerky movements of his stout little body. On the other hand, Wilson was lean, large-headed, and nearly handsome. The long face ended in a lantern jaw; the pale gray eyes were watchful; the thin gray hair cut short; the sallow skin deeply lined. Grayson kept him physically active, particularly on the golf-course, where Edith often joined him; reputedly, she was the better player. At sixty, the twenty-eighth president of the United States, re-elected to a second term five months earlier, looked quite capable (in Virginia's interest?) of being elected to an unprecedented third term in 1920. Such was the nightmare of the professional politician; and Burden himself was nothing if not professional, and like the rest of the tribe, he too saw himself abed in this house, if not with a Ouija board. Mildly dismayed, he gazed upon what might yet be the first three-term president.

Randolph announced the message from the spirit world. "Use mines to sink German submarines. Signed Horatio Nelson."

"I wonder how Nelson knows about mines. Or submarines." The President's voice was resonant, and only an ear as sharp as Burden's could detect Virginia beneath the correct professorial diction. If Wilson had not written more books than his nemesis Theodore Roosevelt, he had written weightier ones – solemn histories that were used as university texts, which made him something of an anomaly. The historian suddenly torn from his study in order to make history for others to write about. Most politicians disliked him for this suspected – true? – doubleness. But Burden found it intriguing. The President seemed always to be observing himself and others as if he knew that sooner or later, he would be teaching himself – others, too.

The fact that there had never been a president quite like Wilson made him all the more difficult to assess. For one thing, did the professional historian, who preferred the British parliamentary system to the American executive system, inhibit the president in his duties? Certainly Wilson had begun his reign with a dramatic parliamentary gesture. Instead of sending a message to be read to the Congress like his predecessors, he himself went up to the Capitol and read his own message, the first president to do so since John Quincy Adams. He had behaved like a prime minister in the Congress, except no one there could ask him a question in that constitutionally separated place. He also enjoyed conferring directly with members of the press; thus, he could mitigate if not circumvent their publishers. Finally, as he could not alter the checks and balances of the Constitution, he was obliged to maintain his power through his adroit mastery of the Democratic Party, a delicate task for one who belonged to its minority eastern wing made up of Tammany Hall and Hearst and worse, while the party's majority was Southern and Western and far too long enamored of William Jennings Bryan.

Burden knew that he had been summoned to the White House because, with his elevation to the Senate, he was now leader of the Bryanite wing of the party, which hated war, England, the rich, and, by and large, Woodrow Wilson, too. Wilson's re-election had been a very close thing indeed, thanks to his own party's suspicion that he wanted to join the Allies in the war against Germany. Only the inspired slogan "He kept us out of war" had, finally, rallied the faithful. Now war was at hand. What to do?

Wilson motioned for Randolph to remove the Ouija board; and himself. Edith also took the hint. At the door she said, "Don't tire yourself."

"That's hardly possible, little girl, in a sickbed." She was gone. Then Wilson noted the elaborate bed, rather like a Neapolitan hearse that Burden had once seen at the base of Vesuvius. "Though I'm not so sure about *this* bed." Wilson removed a sheaf of papers from his bedside table, and placed them on the coverlet.

"Have you seen Mr. Bryan?"

Burden shook his head. "I think he's in Florida."

"The Speaker?" Wilson stared at Burden out of the corner of his eye, a disquieting effect. But then they were embarked upon a disquieting subject. The speaker of the House, Champ Clark, was the *de facto* heir of Bryan. He had opposed Wilson at every turn and he had been, in 1916, a serious candidate for the presidential nomination. Had it not been for the maneuvering of such Wilsonian Bryanites as Burden, Champ Clark might now be enjoying a chill in the Lincoln bed.

"The Speaker's Southern. Southerners – Southwesterners – tend to peace at any price – in Europe, anyway."

"I know. I'm one, too. That's why I'm far too proud to fight." Wryly, Wilson quoted himself. This single phrase had enraged every war-lover in the land, particularly the war-besotted Theodore Roosevelt, who sounded no longer sane. Wilson picked up the papers. "I tell you, Mr. Day, I have done everything a man could possibly do to stay out of this terrible business. I'd hoped Germany would be sufficiently intelligent not to force my hand – to allow us to go on as we are, neutral but helpful . . ."

"To England and France."

The President was not tolerant of interruptions. He had taught others for too many years: ladies at Bryn Mawr and gentlemen at Princeton; and at neither place had the students been encouraged to interrupt the inspired – and inspiring – lecturer. "England and France. But also there is – was – cotton to the Central Powers, at the insistence of the anti-war ten-cent cotton senators . . ."

"Of which I am one."

"Of which you are one." Although Wilson smiled, his mind was plainly on the set of papers which he kept distractedly shaking as if to dislodge their message. Burden noted that two of them were tagged with red seals. "It is curious that if I am impelled to go to war, it will give pleasure to the Republicans, our enemies, and pain to much of our party."

Burden was still enough of a lawyer to seize upon a key word. "Impelled," he repeated. "Who impels you?"

"Events." Wilson gazed vaguely out the window, toward a row of lights where his clerk-like secretary of state, Robert Lansing, was, no doubt, busy doing clerkly things, so unlike his predecessor, the Great Commoner, who was incapable of clerkdom or indeed of anything less mundane than Jovian thunderings for peace.

"I know that many of you thought I was . . . uh, striking a bargain during the last election. That you would get out the vote because I had kept us out of war, despite so much provocation. Well . . ." He had either lost his train of thought or he was preparing to indulge himself in the presidential privilege of abruptly abandoning a potentially dangerous line of argument. "Someone asked me the other day – an old colleague from Princeton – what was the worst thing about being president." Wilson looked directly at Burden, the face solemn but the eyes bright behind the pince-nez. "Luckily, he didn't ask me what the best thing was. I might never have thought of an answer to that one. Anyway I could answer what was the worst. All day long people tell you things that you already know, and you must act as if you were hearing their news for the first time. Now Senator Gore tells me," there was plainly a bridge from repetitions of the obvious to Oklahoma's blind senator, whose opposition to the war had set in motion a series of parliamentary maneuvers designed to smoke out the President's intentions, "that I owe my re-election entirely to his efforts for me in California."

"But you do owe your majority to California."

Wilson had gone to bed on election night thinking that his Republican opponent, Charles Evans Hughes, had been elected; so, indeed, had "President" Hughes. The next day the Far Western returns came in and Wilson was narrowly re-elected. Burden knew that this might not have happened if that professional spellbinder Gore had not been persuaded to leave his sulky seclusion in Oklahoma City and go to California and take the stump for Wilson. Gore had done so on condition that he could guarantee that Wilson would continue to keep, as he had kept, the peace. On election night Gore had wired Tumulty the exact figure by which Wilson would carry California.

Now Wilson was faced with his own less than courageous record. At various times, he had managed to be both war and peace candidate. This sort of thing never troubled the public, whose memory was short; but senators were constitutionally endowed with long memories and, often, mysterious constituencies as well. Some were obliged to follow the prejudices of their pro-German constituents. Others saw themselves as architects of a new and perfect republic, and their leader was La Follette of Wisconsin, far more dangerous in his idealism than any of the Bryanites, who were bound to be swayed by popular opinion, a highly volatile substance produced, often at whim, by William Randolph Hearst in his eight newspapers, not to mention all the other publishers, to a man for war. Thus far, Hearst was still the voice of the Germans and the Irish; and his papers in the great Northern cities played shamelessly to that city mob which he still counted on to make *him* president in 1920.

"I expected to be a reformer president." Wilson sounded wistful. "There was so much to do right here at home, and we did do so much, so fast."

Burden agreed, without reserve. The sort of reforms that Roosevelt had always spoken of with such transcendent passion Wilson had actually accomplished with gentle reason, combined with the subtle twisting of congressional arms. But then, as he liked to say, anyone who could master the Princeton faculty *and* the alumni association would find a mere Congress easy to deal with. Was it Senator Lodge who had said, "But he never did master them. That's why politics was his only escape"?

"What position will they – will *you* take if I were to ask for war?" Wilson had collected himself.

"It will depend on what your reasons are. I always thought you missed your chance – if war is what you want – when the Germans sank the *Lusitania,* and so many American lives were lost. The public was ready for war that day."

"But," Wilson was cool, "I was not. It was too soon. We were – we are – not prepared."

"Two weeks ago," Burden was enjoying the game, "when you sent Ambassador Bernstorff home, the people were ready, again. Now comes the Zimmermann business. . . ." Although Burden was most sensitive to Wilson's aversion to advice of any kind, he knew that he had been invited to the President's sickbed to give him a reading of the Senate's mood. He took the plunge. "The time has come. The thing is here. You can't wait much longer. The press is doing its work. Gallant little Belgium. Raped nuns. Devoured children. The Hun is the devil. If there is to be war, prepared or unprepared, now is the time."

Wilson stared at the papers in his hand; and waited.

Burden proceeded. "Isn't that why you've called a special session? To ask us to declare war?"

"If I do, how many would oppose me? And on what ground?"

Wilson's usual Presbyterian moralizing and cloudy poetic images tended to evaporate when faced with a political problem. He was now very much the political manager, counting heads.

Burden named a dozen names, the leaders. "Actually, there is a clear but weak majority in each house that is against war, and nothing will stir them unless you have some new example of Hunnishness."

Wilson took off his pince-nez; rubbed the two indentations on either side of his nose – like red thumbprints. "I do believe that the Germans must be the stupidest people on earth. They provoke us. Sink our ships. Plot with Mexico against our territory. Then – now – they have done it." He held up the red-tagged papers. "Today three of our ships have been sunk. The *City of Memphis*. The *Illinois*. The *Vigilancia*."

Burden experienced a chill as the names were read off. "I have tried – I *believe* with absolute sincerity, but who can tell the human heart? least of all one's own – to stay out of this incredibly stupid and wasteful war, which has so suddenly made us, thanks to England's bankruptcy, the richest nation on earth. Once we are armed, there is no power that can stop us. But once we arm, will we ever disarm? You see my – predicament, or what was a predicament until the Kaiser shoved me this morning." The President's face looked as if it had just been roughly brought forth, with chisel and mallet, from a chunk of gray granite.

"Why," asked Burden, "have you taken so long when it's been plain to so many that your heart has always been with England and the Allies?"

Wilson stared at Burden as if he were not there. "I was three years old," he said at last, "when Lincoln was elected and the Civil War began. My father was a clergyman in Staunton – then, later, we moved to Augusta, Georgia. I was eight years old when the war ended and Mr. Lincoln was killed. In Augusta my father's church was a . . . was *used* as a hospital for our troops. I remember all that. I remember Jefferson Davis being led a captive through the town. I remember how he . . . My family suffered very little. But what we saw around us, the bitterness of the losers in the war and the brutality of the winners . . . well, none of this was lost on me. I am not,"

41

a wintry close-lipped smile divided for an instant the rude stone face, "an enthusiast of war like Colonel Roosevelt, whose mentality is that of a child of six and whose imagination must be nonexistent. You see, I can *imagine* what this war will do to us. I pray I'm wrong. But I am deathly afraid that once you lead this people – and I know them well – into war, they'll forget there ever was such a thing as tolerance. Because to fight to win, you must be brutal and ruthless, and that spirit of ruthless brutality will enter into the very fiber of our national life. You – Congress – will be infected by it, too, and the police, and the average citizen. The whole lot. Then we shall win. But *what* shall we win? How do we help the South . . . I mean the Central Powers to return from a war-time to a peace-time basis? How do we help ourselves? We shall have become what we are fighting. We shall be trying to reconstruct a peace-time civilization with war-time standards. That's not possible, and since everyone will be involved, there'll be no bystanders with sufficient power to make a just peace. That's what I had wanted us to be. Too proud to fight in the mud, but ready to stand by, ready to mediate, ready to . . ." The voice stopped.

There was a long silence. If the sun had not set, it had long since vanished behind cold dense clouds, and the room was dark except for the single lamp beside Wilson's bed and the fading coals in the fireplace. Although Burden was used to the President's eloquence, he was not entirely immune to its potency. Wilson had the gift of going straight to the altogether too palpitating heart of the business.

"I am calling Congress back two weeks earlier. On April second. I shall . . ." He put the dangerous documents on the table beside the bed. "How ironic it is!" He shook his head in wonder. "After all the work we've done to control big business, guess what will happen now? They will be more firmly in the saddle than ever before. Because who else can arm us? they'll say. Who else can administer the war?"

"Who else?" Burden had had much the same thought. If ever anyone benefited from an American war it was the trusts, the cartels, the Wall Street speculators. "We shall revert to the age of Grant."

Wilson nodded bleakly. "Then, if the war should be a long one, and we be weakened, there is the true enemy waiting for us in the West. The yellow races, led by Japan, ready to overwhelm us through sheer numbers. . . ."

Edith Wilson entered the room and switched on the lights, dispelling the apocalyptic mood. As Burden got to his feet, he noticed a number of Chinese works of art arranged on tables and in bookcases, no doubt an on-going reminder of Asia's dread hordes. "From my house," said Edith, aware of Burden's interest. "This is not the easiest place to make livable." She gave the President a sheet of paper. "From Colonel House. I've decoded it for you." Then she caught herself. "Oh, dear," she turned to Burden, "you're not supposed to know such things."

"That Colonel House writes in code to the President? I'd be surprised if he didn't. He's in Europe now, isn't he?"

Wilson nodded. Then he glanced at the letter; looked up at Burden. "Well, he thinks we should recognize the new Russian government. The Czar has abdicated. But Russia is still in the war, and so . . ." He stopped; and stared at Edith, plainly not seeing her, mind elsewhere.

"We need every ally now, I should think." Burden was diffident; he was also intrigued at the thought of a president's wife decoding high secret papers from the President's unofficial emissary to Europe, the rich and secretive Texas Colonel House.

"Yes. That's my view. Our ambassador is very enthusiastic about this revolution. So like our own, he tells me. He thinks we should lead the way, and recognize them."

"Henry Adams predicted all this twenty years ago." Burden suddenly recalled the joy with which Henry Adams had spoken of wars and revolutions and the certain fall of civilization.

"Is he still alive?" Wilson pressed a buzzer.

"Very much so. But he never goes out, never pays calls. Still lives across the street there." Burden pointed in the direction of Lafayette Park, as Wilson's Negro valet, Brooks, entered. Then Burden shook the President's hand. "You will get," he said, "whatever you want on April second."

"How many will vote no?"

43

"Ten at the most."

"You encourage me, Senator."

"You inspire me, Mr. President."

"That was my aim." Again the wintry smile. "Now I only wish I could inspire myself." With the help of Brooks the President got out of bed.

Edith showed Burden to the lift. "He does not sleep well," she said.

"Neither would I, at a time like this."

A maid came toward them, carrying a basket of pecans. "They just came, Miss Edith. The silver service brought them."

"Thank you, Susan. Take them in to Mr. Wilson." Edith opened the door to the elevator. "There are still things to laugh at," she said. "Susan's been with us twenty years, but we lived such a quiet life that she's still in shock, living here. She's made up her mind that the Secret Service are really the 'silver service,' and there's no correcting her." Edith started to say more; then said, "Good-by."

5

Armed with badge and documents, Blaise Sanford entered the Capitol on the Senate side. In addition to what looked like the whole of the Washington police force, troops were stationed at every entrance, as if invasion was imminent, or were *they* the invasion? Would there be martial law? he wondered.

Blaise himself had written a highly balanced either-or editorial for the morning's *Tribune,* to the distress of the editorial writers, who were openly disrespectful of anything either he or Caroline wrote. The *Tribune* was essentially Republican and pro-Allies, thanks to Blaise's influence, with occasional accommodations to the Democrats, thanks to Caroline's long-standing friendship with James Burden Day. When half-brother and half-sister disagreed on a policy, both positions were given equal space, to the consternation of those few Washingtonians who took editorials seriously.

A thin warm rain demonstrated spring's arrival. Illuminated

from below, the Capitol dome resembled a white gibbous moon against the black sky. There was a smell of narcissus and mud in the air, but the usual pervasive smell of horses was absent. The President's recent carriage drive to the Capitol to make his inaugural address was said to be the last such drive any president would ever make. The world was Henry Ford's at last. Blaise took refuge beneath the porte-cochere, where tonight neither cars nor carriages were permitted, thus insuring that everyone got equally, democratically, wet.

Fortunately, the Congress was inside. So no senatorial cabals could block Caesar's way. Now journalists, diplomats, wives and children were converging on the Capitol, where as each was admitted he was given a small American flag, the gift of an unknown but well-organized patriot.

In the main rotunda, Blaise was stopped by the editor of the *Atlantic Monthly,* Ellery Sedgwick. "I'm going in to see the President," he said. "He's in the Marble Room. Come on, let's say hello. Tumulty's made me a temporary member of the Secret Service. That was the only way I could get in."

Blaise looked at his watch; it was eight-thirty. The speech was scheduled for eight-thirty. But when it came to Congress, nothing was ever on time. The senators were still entering the chamber of the House of Representatives, where, for lack of chairs, many would be obliged to stand.

"I'm going to Henry Adams afterward. Are you? Informal supper. *He's* coming." Sedgwick indicated Henry Cabot Lodge, who was turned in their direction. White-haired, white-bearded, white-faced Senator Lodge gave them a jaunty wave; the bumblebee nostrils were dilated with excitement. As Theodore Roosevelt's man in the Senate, he was the head of the war party.

At the door to the Marble Room, a Secret Service man stood guard. When the two publishers tried to enter, he stopped them. "Mrs. Wilson's just gone to the gallery, and he's about ready. You better take your seat, Mr. Sanford."

As Blaise started to do as requested, he caught sight of the President. Wilson was standing at the ornate room's center. He was quite alone, back to the door, eyes downcast. In his left hand he held the cards on which his speech was written. Blaise thought the moment too intimate to watch but, like Sedgwick, he was rooted to the spot as, slowly, like a man in a dream, Wilson walked across the room to a great dusty mirror. Then Blaise saw the President's reflected face. Everything seemed to have fallen apart. The mouth was cretinously ajar and double chins flowed over the high hard collar. The eyes were round and staring while the muscles of the face were slack. Had this been Paris and the President a French boulevardier, Blaise could have named the drug that he had been taking – Opium. But this was the Capitol; and the President was a puritan. Abruptly, Wilson became aware of the image that Blaise could see in the mirror. With both hands, he pushed up his chin, smoothed out his cheeks, blinked his eyes; and the mouth set. In an instant, he was again the lean, dour, hard-faced Woodrow Wilson, whose cold clear eyes were now as watchful as any hunter's. Metamorphosis duly noted, Blaise slipped away not wanting the President to know that he had been observed.

In the crowded galleries, great ladies begged for seats while plenipotentiaries threatened war, to no avail. Fortunately, the managing editor of the *Tribune* was in Blaise's seat; and gave it up. Frederika was next to him, looking pale, youthful, subdued. Next to her was Blaise's fellow press-lord Ned McLean and his wife Evalyn, bedecked with diamonds, each unluckier than the other if the press – *their* press – was to be believed.

"Blaise, old boy!" Ned held out a hand, across Frederika. Blaise shook it. He didn't like being called "old boy" or indeed anything by Ned, an intolerable young fool, who then proceeded to offer him a silver flask.

"This could be very dry, you know." Ned's eyes popped comically. He was like a movie comedian, thought Blaise, declining the flask from which Evalyn took a long swig. "A ridiculous time to declare war," she said, drying her lips with a fret-work gloved hand on whose fingers diamonds glittered. "Eight-thirty. Imagine! Just when we're thinking about going in to dinner. Isn't that so, Frederika?"

"But we never really *think* about it. We just go in. Don't we, Blaise?"

Blaise nodded, eyes on the opposite gallery, where, somehow,

Caroline had got herself placed between two of the President's daughters. Mrs. Wilson was now taking her seat, with gracious smiles and waves to friends on the floor beneath.

"There's the widow Galt." Like so many Washington ladies, Evalyn enjoyed depicting the Wilsons as an amorous couple, given to never-ending venery. Blaise had been with Evalyn at the theater when the President had first appeared in public with the widow Galt she had worn what looked to be every orchid from the White House observatory. "What," Evalyn had asked, "do you think they'll do *after* the theater?"

Frederika had answered: "She will eat her orchids and go to bed."

Below them, the elegant Connecticut senator, Brandegee, bowed low to the press-lords. Brandegee had tried to interest Blaise in coming to the Senate from Rhode Island, where the seat was relatively inexpensive, certainly cheaper than the cost of maintaining Blaise's inherited house at Newport. "You'll like the Senate. Despite some bounders, it's the best club in the country." But Blaise had no interest in public office. Power was something else, of course, and a newspaper publisher had more power than most, or power's illusion, which was, perhaps, all that there ever is. The image of Wilson's collapsed face in the mirror was already inscribed on memory's plate as one of those startling never-to-be-erased images. If *that* was true power, Blaise was willing to forgo it. Wilson's face had revealed not so much anguish as pure terror.

From the chamber below, Burden waved to them. He was standing with a group of Democratic senators at the back. "Has anyone seen the speech?" Ned McLean assumed what he took to be the appropriate keen expression required of the publisher of the Washington *Post* on so awesome an occasion.

"No," said Blaise, who had tried his best – cost no object, as Hearst would say – to get a copy from the White House through a friend of the President's stenographer, Charles L. Gwen. But, apparently, the President had done his own typing on the night of March 31 and into the early morning of Sunday, April 1 – on April Fool's Day. Blaise was still unable to comprehend this occasion, this war.

Although Wilson had then met with the Cabinet, he chose not

to show them his speech. He did say that he was still undecided as to whether he should ask for a straight declaration of war or simply acknowledge that as a state of war already existed, Congress must now give him the means to fight it. Technicalities to one side, the Cabinet proved to be unanimously for war. Just below Blaise, the pacifist secretary of the Navy, Josephus Daniels, looking warlike, was taking his seat with the rest of the Cabinet, and the Supreme Court. The Vice President was now in his throne beside that of the Speaker of the House. Over their heads a round clock gave the time, eight-forty.

"He's late," said Frederika.

"Did you hear how, just now," Ned was leaning over the railing, "someone took a poke at Cabot Lodge? Look at that eye! All swollen up."

"Who did it?" Frederika was deeply interested in the more primitive forms of warfare.

"A pacifist," said Ned.

"What fun!" Evalyn removed a pair of diamond-studded opera glasses from her handbag, and trained them on Lodge. "Must've been a real haymaker. . . ."

The Speaker got to his feet, eyes on the door opposite his dais. "The President," said the Speaker; then he added, as the chamber became silent, "of the United States." The Supreme Court rose to their feet first, followed by everyone else on the floor and in the galleries. Then Woodrow Wilson, holding himself very straight, even rigid, entered the chamber. For a moment, he paused. In the stillness, rain tapping on the skylight was the only sound. Then, like thunder, the applause broke out. Quickly, Wilson walked down the aisle to the well of the House, not acknowledging any of the hands outstretched to him. He stepped up on the dais; turned and nodded to the Vice President and Speaker. Then they sat down, and the process of history began.

Wilson held his cards above the lectern; and spoke as if to them. But the voice was firm and the cadence, as always, uncommonly beautiful. Blaise found the voice neither American nor British, the first all nasality and the second all splutter. Wilson's voice was a happy balance between the two.

"Gentlemen of the Congress." A quick polite look up from the cards; then he addressed his text most intimately. "I have called the Congress into extraordinary session because there are serious, very serious choices of policy to be made, and made immediately. . . ." Wilson outlined briefly the problem. But as Wilson was a teacher of history as well as now a maker of it, he was obliged, in the great tradition of those who must engage in war, to address a Higher Principle than mere chagrin or hurt feelings or assaults on American persons and property. "The German submarine warfare against commerce is a warfare against mankind." Blaise suddenly felt weak: Americans would be fighting, really fighting in France, the country where he had been born and brought up. He was forty-two; he must now go to war, for two countries.

Everything seemed unreal, the dusky ill-lit chamber, the April rain on glass, the straining faces not to mention ears, many of them cupped as half-deaf statesmen tried to amplify for themselves the voice of the nation that had broken its long silence – last heard, when? Gettysburg? "Last best hope of earth"? Government of, by, and for the people. All these ultimate, perfect, unique concepts to describe mere politics. Nations were worldless embodiments; hence, the extraordinary opportunity for the eloquent man on the right rainy April evening to articulate the collective yet inchoate ambition of the tribe. Since such an opportunity might never come again, Blaise knew what was coming next; and it came.

"The challenge is to all mankind. Each nation must decide for itself how it will meet it." What then, Blaise wondered, almost laughing, would Paraguay do? or the Gold Coast? or Siam? Firmly, Wilson drove the first nail into Peace's pretty coffin: ". . . armed neutrality, it now appears, is impracticable." More nails. "There is one choice we cannot make, we are incapable of making: we will not choose the path of submission. . . ." There was a deep exhalation throughout the chamber, and then what sounded like a gun-shot. Bemused, the President looked up as the Chief Justice, a huge aged Southerner, held high above him his hands, which now he clapped like a battle signal, and the troops, if that is what we are, thought Blaise, himself included, shouted in unison. Ned

McLean gave a rebel yell; and took another drink from his flask. Evalyn's eyes were bright as diamonds. Across the chamber Caroline sat, very still, between Wilson's applauding daughters. There were going to be many more arguments at editorial meetings, thought Blaise.

Wilson's face was somewhat less sallow after this demonstration than before, and the voice was stronger as he drove in the last nail. "With a profound sense of the solemn and even tragical character of the step I am taking . . ." Tragical for whom? Blaise wondered. The dead, of course. But was Wilson saying that the nation was now embarked upon tragedy as a nation? Could so large a mass of disparate people ever share in anything so high and dreadful and intimate as tragedy? Tragedy was for individuals, or so Blaise had been imperfectly taught. Then he understood. Wilson meant himself: ". . . tragical character of the step *I am taking.*" This was grandeur, even lunacy. True, Wilson was, for this instant, the personification of a people; but then the instant would pass and other vain men, some seated even now in this chamber, would take his place.

"I advise that the Congress declare the recent course of the Imperial German Government to be in fact nothing less than war against the government and people of the United States. . . ." Wilson put the blame for war on Germany; then asked for war. Again, the cheering was led by the plainly drunk and weeping Chief Justice. Rebel yells sounded. Something was beginning to tear apart. Was it civilization? Blaise wondered, no enthusiast of that vague concept, but was its cloudy notion not better than men like baying hounds, howling wolves?

As if he had anticipated what wildness he was provoking about the camp-fire, Wilson moved swiftly to high, holy ground. "We are at the beginning of an age in which it will be insisted that the same standards of conduct and of responsibility for wrong done shall be observed among nations and their governments that are observed among the individual citizens of civilized states." Frederika, surprisingly, sardonically, murmured in Blaise's ear: "Does he know Mr. Hearst?"

Blaise almost laughed; she had at least broken the magic spell that the wizard was spinning amongst his war-drunk savages. "Or Colonel Roosevelt," Blaise whispered back, to the annoyance of the now elevated Evalyn. Ned was asleep. ". . . fight thus for the ultimate peace of the world and for the liberations of its peoples, the German peoples included; for the rights of nations great and small and the privilege of men everywhere to choose their way of life and of obedience. The world must be made safe for democracy." One person began to applaud, loudly.

The President had already started his next sentence when he stopped, as if only now aware of the significance of what he had said. The applause began to mount, as others joined in. What, Blaise wondered, wearily, is democracy? And how can it or anything else so undefinable ever be assured of safety? Human slavery was something so specific that one could indeed make the world a dangerous place for it to flourish; but democracy? Tammany? The caucus? Money? Had there ever been so many millionaires in this democratic Senate?

Blaise looked up at the clock. It was now nine-fifteen. The President had been speaking for almost half an hour. Magic had been unleashed in the chamber, and ancestral voices had begun their whisperings, and old battle songs sounded in the rain's tattoo: *for we'll rally round the flag, boys, we'll rally once again, shouting the battle cry of freedom.*

The warlock now spun his ultimate spell. "It is a fearful thing to lead this great peaceful people into war, into the most terrible and disastrous of all wars, civilization itself seeming to be in the balance. But the right is more precious than peace, and we shall fight for the things which we have always carried nearest our hearts. . . ." Oh yes, thought Blaise. Let us kill for peace! Frederika had broken the spell for him; yet he recognized its potency; saw it work upon the savages beneath who gave the wizard not only their belief but their fury as well, which, in turn, fueled the warlock's own. Thus, magic begets magic. ". . . with the pride of those who know that the day has come when America is privileged to spend her blood . . ." There it was, at last, the exercise's object, blood. They were sinking now into pre-history, around the blazing fire. Blood. Now for the sky-god's blessing upon the tribe. It came, in the last line. "God helping her, she can do no other." So there it was: Protestant Martin Luther at the end. Never had Blaise felt more Catholic.

Wilson looked up at the gallery. The eyes were wide and bright, and – was he now all alone to himself or was he as one with the hunters all round him? Blaise could not tell, for everyone was on his feet, including Blaise, and the drooping Ned, arms knotted loosely about Evalyn's neck.

Blaise leaned over to watch the President's progress down the aisle to the door. Lodge stepped forward – the face was definitely, satisfyingly swollen – to shake Wilson's hand; and murmur something that made the President smile. Just behind Lodge, the great La Follette sat, arms crossed to show that *he* was not applauding the witch-doctor, as he chewed, slowly, rhythmically, gum.

"Who would have thought," said Blaise to Frederika, as they pushed their way through the crowded corridor, "that only yesterday there was a majority for peace?"

"Do you think they really know what they're doing? I mean, it's such fun – for men, and I suppose there'll be money in it."

"A lot, I should think, for those who are . . ." Who are what? wondered Blaise. After all, he was son and grandson of the rich. Because he had not the urge to increase his wealth – as opposed to the circulation of the *Tribune* – did not mean that he was any different from Mr. Baruch, the New York speculator who had bought himself a high place in the Democratic Party as money-giver to the President himself, in order to benefit from the exchange. But Mr. Baruch was no more to be censured for his straightforward desire to make money than all the paid-up millionaire members of the Senate club who differed only in their approach to transitivity from the paid-for members.

Caroline intercepted them in the painted corridor, which smelled of damp wool and whisky. Ned McLean's had not been the only flask. "I promised Uncle Henry that I would report to him. He will feed us, he says."

Blaise said no; Frederika said yes; and so they all embarked in Caroline's Pierce-Arrow.

"How did you end up with the Wilsons?" Frederika often asked Blaise's questions for him.

"I am cultivating Mr. McAdoo because he means to be president, too, and I always like my moths better before they break out of the cocoon."

"How do you go about cultivating someone like Eleanor McAdoo?" Frederika had old Washington's sense of unreality when it came to the Federal theater that changed its program every four or eight years – sometimes sooner if a player happened to be, excitingly, assassinated.

"I begin by being inordinately kind to her very plain sister Margaret. This gains me points with everyone in the family."

"How sly you are." Frederika was equable. Blaise was constantly disappointed by the lack of friction between the sisters-in-law. He had hoped for more drama between the two Mistresses Sanford, particularly in so small a city. But each kept to her own set; and when the grand Frederika Sanford held court at Blaise's Connecticut Avenue palace, Caroline often appeared, most graciously, to smile upon old Washington, Frederika's world, and those Republican magnificoes who courted Blaise, who feted them. Caroline's court in Georgetown was smaller and more selective. Dinner was never for more than ten. Caroline's guests were notable for their conversation; this meant rather more foreigners than Americans and of the Americans more New Yorkers than Old Washington inhabitants.

The departure of the Roosevelts from the White House had restored the city to its traditional countrified dullness. Although the fat, bad-tempered President Taft was depicted as highly lovable and cheery, thanks to the journalists' inability to break with any cliché, he and his proud pompous wife had not provided much of a center to the Federal drama. The arrival of the Wilsons had been exciting; but then she became ill and he, remote at best, simply became his office. This meant that the eloquent President was most visible and successful in public, while the private bookish Woodrow Wilson was hidden away upstairs in the White House, nursing a sick wife; and adored by daughters.

Caroline's efforts to penetrate the Wilson White House had been half-hearted at best. As people, they had not interested her, but now, with this new development, everything was to be seen in a different, lurid light. History had begun to lurch forward or backward or wherever, and Wilson was astride the beast, as old John Hay used to say of poor McKinley. Suddenly, even Edith Wilson began to glow in the middle distance, while the war had created a definite nimbus about the equine head of Miss Margaret Wilson.

Henry Adams's ancient servant – as old as he? no, no one could ever be so old – showed them into the study, which had been for Caroline the center of her entire Washington life, a schoolroom and theater all in one, and presided over by the small, rosy, bald, snowbearded Henry Adams, grandson and great-grandson of two occupants of the White House across the street. He was the historian of the old republic and, with his brother Brooks, a prophet and a seer of the world empire-to-be, if it was to be.

The old man greeted them in front of his modestly spectacular fireplace carved from a block of Mexican green onyx shot with scarlet over whose mantel hung William Blake's drawing of the mad Nebuchadnezzar eating grass, a constant reminder to Adams of that ludicrousness which tends to shadow human grandeur. In the twenty years that Caroline had known Adams, neither the beautiful room with its small Adams-scale furniture nor its owner had much changed, only many of the occupants of the chairs were gone, either through death, like John and Clara Hay, joint builders of this double Romanesque palace in Lafayette Park, or through removal to Europe, like Lizzie Cameron, beloved by Adams, now in the high summer of her days, furiously courting young poets in the green spring of theirs. To fill his life and rooms, Adams had acquired a secretary, Aileen Tone, a gentlewoman as dedicated as he to twelfth-century music, visibly represented in one corner of the library by a Steinway piano, the equivalent of a wedding ring to Caroline, who was delighted that the old man should be so well looked after. As always, there were "nieces" in attendance. Caroline had been a niece in her day. Now she had settled for friendship, the essential passion of the Adams circle.

Adams embraced Caroline like a niece; and bowed to Blaise and Frederika. Like royalty, he was not much of one for shaking hands. "He has done it! I am amazed. Now tell me, what was he like?"

Adams sat in a special chair so angled that the firelight was behind him; even so, the eyes kept blinking like an owl's at noon. Caroline encouraged Blaise to describe what had happened at the Capitol; and Blaise, as always, was precise, even sensitive to detail. Caroline was particularly struck, as was Adams, by the scene before the mirror. "What could it mean?" Caroline affected innocence, the one quality Adams liked least.

"He's in too deep. That's what it means." Adams was delighted. "Anyway, it's done at last."

"You approve?" Caroline expected the usual Adams ingenious negative; instead she was surprised by the old man's enthusiasm.

"Yes! For once in my life I am with the majority – of the people we know, that is – and I don't dare say a single critical word. All my life, I've wanted some kind of Atlantic Community, and now – here it is! We are fighting side by side with England. It is too good to be true." He smiled the famous bright bitter smile. "I can now contemplate the total ruin of our old world with more philosophy than I ever thought possible."

"You see it all ending in ruin?" Blaise was still handsome, Caroline decided; a large concession, since, like Lizzie Cameron's, her taste was now beginning to run to youth in men.

"Well, things do run down. After all, haven't I predicted that from the beginning? – of time, it seems like now. And haven't I been right? The Russian Revolution – all mine. Well, Brooks can take some credit, too. Odd how proprietary one feels about one's prophecies . . ."

"Unless they are wrong," said Caroline.

Then Eleanor Roosevelt and her social secretary, a blond pretty girl, entered the room, bringing the cold with them. "It's Caroline's fault." Eleanor was apologetic. "I was going straight home from the Capitol, in such a state, when she said you might receive us, and who wants to be alone right now?"

"Where's your husband? No. Don't tell me. At the Navy Department, ordering Admiral Dewey to seize Ireland."

"We buried the Admiral two months ago." Caroline found Eleanor's secretary uncommonly charming; and wondered at Eleanor's courage in engaging someone so much more attractive than herself. Unless, of course, Eleanor was in love in the Souvestrian sense.

"Send the coffin to Ireland." Adams was exuberant as William passed around champagne. In the next room, a buffet had been set. Eleanor stared at it closely, even longingly. She liked her food, Caroline had noticed; yet she kept the worst table in Washington.

"Franklin is at the Navy Department, with Mr. Daniels. Everything's starting to happen. My head goes round. I *am* grateful, though, we have Mr. Wilson living across from you."

"Oh, child." Caroline recognized Adams's special ancestral voice, prophesying doom. "It makes no difference to the course of history who lives in that house. Never has. Energy – or its lack – determines events."

"Don't say that to my Franklin, please." Eleanor was unexpectedly firm. "You ought not to discourage any young person with ideals, who might accomplish something very fine." When Eleanor realized that she suddenly had the room's attention, the silvery skin turned to deepest rose – the Puritan rose, thought Caroline, fond of so much sweet humorless high-mindedness.

"I think maybe he's just the one I should say it to. Ah, the magnificoes have arrived. Like the Magi. My star, no doubt. Welcome, to my manger, or *manger â la fourchette.*" In the doorway stood the British ambassador, Sir Cecil Spring Rice, and Senator Henry Cabot Lodge, whose swollen, red cheek gave much delight to Adams, who enjoyed tormenting his one-time Harvard pupil. As Blaise and Frederika and Eleanor moved toward the buffet table, Caroline and the social secretary remained to greet the magnificoes.

Spring Rice was an old friend of old Washington. He had been posted to the embassy in youth; had penetrated the heart of the Adams circle, known as the Five of Hearts; had become Theodore Roosevelt's closest friend, and best man when the widower Roosevelt remarried. Now, old and ailing, he had returned in triumph as British ambassador to Washington. He wore a blond-steely beard like that of his king; he had eyes not unlike those of his President. He was, it was thought, most energetically, dying.

"You have prevailed." Spring Rice gave Adams an exuberant French sort of embrace.

"I always do, Springy. Who hit you, Cabot?"

"A pacifist. But you should –"

"See *him*. I know all the latest argot of your charming Scollay Square. Who would have thought Wilson would ever have had the courage?"

Spring Rice indicated Lodge. "There's his backbone. With some help from Theodore, our work is done. That is, just started." He took champagne from William and raised his glass. "Now it begins." Their end of the room drank solemnly.

"Our last hygiene session." Lodge smiled within his beard at the Ambassador, who explained.

"For the last two years, whenever I was about to burst, as Mr. Wilson delayed and delayed, Cabot would let me come to his office and denounce your government, until the fit had left me – hence, hygienic."

"Poor Springy," said Adams.

"Happy now," said Lodge.

"Will the Allies want American troops?" Caroline knew the answer that the readers of the *Tribune* did not know and that the President had avoided, except for the one reference to the "privilege" of spending America's blood.

"Surely we shall be the forge," said Lodge. "Providing arms. Food. Money. No more."

Spring Rice smiled at Caroline. "No more," he repeated, and then added with the eager indiscretion of the professional diplomat to the right audience, "but Mr. Wilson did say something odd to Mr. Tumulty on the drive back to the White House. . . ."

"You know *already* what he said?" Adams looked like a jovial gnome, blinking in the light.

"British intelligence never sleeps, unlike British governments. . . ."

"What did he say to Tumulty?" Lodge was suddenly alert. While it was understandable that his friend Roosevelt would not like the pacific professor who had taken his place as chief of state, Lodge's dislike had something queer to it, Caroline had always thought, as if a scholar from superior Harvard had been bested by one from inferior Princeton; in fact, Lodge's worst condemnation of any Wilson address was to say that although suitable, perhaps, for Princeton it was not up to Harvard's standards. Of course, Lodge had been the only intellectual in the higher politics until Wilson had, in two years' time, gone from Princeton to the governorship of New Jersey to the presidency. There had never been so high or so swift a rise for anyone not a general. Although it was natural for Lodge to be jealous, why to such an extent? Perhaps Alice Longworth had been right when, at the funeral of Mrs. Lodge, the previous year, she had said, "Cabot will turn merciless without sister Anne."

"As they drove through the cheering crowds, between the long rows of sombre troops at damp attention." Spring Rice smiled at Caroline, "See how I like to add color to my cold political dispatches."

"Like me." Caroline nodded. "But, perhaps, if I may be editorial, fewer adjectives, more verbs."

"More light," was Adams's contribution.

"What did he *say?*" Lodge was like an ancient terrier, sharp eye upon the hole to a rat's residence.

"The President said, 'Did you hear that applause . . .'"

"Vain schoolteacher! No. No. A vain *Maryland* preacher." Lodge had found his worst epithet.

"But he was right," said Caroline. "I was there. It sounded like thunder or –"

"The breaking of a dam?" Spring Rice provided a journalistic image.

"I have never actually listened to a dam while it was breaking." Caroline was demure.

"What . . . *what* did he say?" Lodge did a small terrier-like two-step.

"If you'll stop interrupting me, Cabot, I'll tell you. He said, 'My message was a message of death for our young men. How can they, in God's name, applaud that?'"

"Coward!" Lodge fired the word.

Caroline turned on Lodge and with none of her usual endless, or so she thought, evasive tact, fired in turn: "That comes ill from someone too old to fight."

"Caroline." Adams put his arm through hers. "Take me in to supper." But it was Adams who led the trembling Caroline; the old man was soothing: "It does no good to chide enthusiasts. They are like little automatic engines. They feed upon whatever energy is in the air, and today there is a great deal."

"Too much for me. I'm sorry." Adams patted her arm; then saw to his other guests.

The conversation was now general. The Allied leaders would soon be in Washington. Spring Rice's chief, the foreign secretary, Arthur Balfour, would be the first to arrive *before* the French, Caroline noted, accepting from – what was her name? Lucy something – cold duck *en gelée* from the table whose candlelit splendor was more Faubourg Saint-Germain than Adamsesque Quincy, Massachusetts. But then each year, until the war began, Henry Adams would settle himself at Paris, where he paid court to Lizzie Cameron, meditated on twelfth-century music, and denigrated his own highly acclaimed *Mont-Saint-Michel and Chartres*, so many decades in the making and now, ever since 1913, a published book that the public was not invited either to buy or to read by its prickly author. Yet Caroline could never have had an American life – or at least one in Washington – without the always wise, always benign Henry Adams, known to those not his "nieces" as sublimely caustic and harsh in truth's high service.

"You don't like Mr. Lodge?" Lucy's voice was low and faintly Southern. She was a popular extra woman who was to be seen at large rather than small dinner parties in the west end of Washington. Who was she? Caroline, who cared nothing for those genealogical matters that sustained the city's social life, had, in self-defense, learned the endless ramifications of who was related to whom and the famous question hence not asked when a name was brought to general attention: "So, then, who was *she*?" – establishing the wife's place in the scheme of things. "Saint-Simon without the king" was a piece that she had wanted to write for the *Tribune* until Blaise had said, with a brother's straightforward malice, "Without Saint-Simon, too."

Lucy's pale face gleamed in the lamp-light. "Camellia-petal skin," a phrase much used by the *Tribune*'s Society Lady. Dark blue eyes. Eleanor must dote on Lucy, a beautiful version of herself.

What would – indeed, would not – Mlle. Souvestre have said? "I've known Mr. Lodge too long to dislike him. He is one of the facts of life here. Naturally, I preferred his wife, Nannie. Sister Anne they called her, too."

"Mr. Roosevelt admires him . . ."

"They are best friends . . ."

"I meant *your* Mr. Roosevelt."

The eyes were very fine, Caroline decided. Mlle. Souvestre would have approved. Also Lucy – she was, somehow, a Carroll of Carrollton, which meant a Roman Catholic, which would also have pleased Mademoiselle, who, like most French atheists, respected the Church. Lucy *Mercer*. Caroline was relieved that she had remembered. After all, if she did not know her adopted city better than a native, she had no right to publish a family newspaper for largely political families. Lucy's father, Major Carroll Mercer, had founded the city's most fashionable country club, in the Maryland village of Chevy Chase, where membership was so highly restricted that Woodrow Wilson refused to play golf there while young Mr. Roosevelt did.

Aileen Tone had joined them. She was not at all dim, as companions were meant to be. "I keep trying to persuade Lucy to sing with us, with Mr. Adams and me, but she won't."

"Because you remember me in my youth. I am, now – in my old age – a baritone," said Lucy. "You remember my girlish alto."

"Perfect for Richard Coeur de Lion." Aileen turned to Caroline. "We are studying the old musical notations, trying to work out how twelfth-century music must have sounded. We're making progress, we think, with Richard's prison song."

"*Oh, Richard, oh, mon roi, tout le monde t'abandonne,*" Caroline croaked the French ballad, so beloved, for obvious reasons, by Marie-Antoinette.

"Eighteenth-century," said Aileen. "Lovely, of course. . . ."

"I have been struck once today." Senator Lodge was at Caroline's side. "But I struck back a powerful blow with my right fist. Now . . ."

"You will use your vigorous left one on me?" Caroline smiled sweetly.

"No. I respond only in kind. You denounce me. I denounce you."

"Oh, dear." Aileen sounded alarmed. "Mr. Adams won't like this."

"I was only going to match Caroline's observation that I am too old to fight with a compliment. She is too shrewd not to know why I called Wilson a coward. We should have gone to war at the time of the *Lusitania* but he was afraid that he would lose his hyphenates in the election. Because there is no Democratic Party without the Germans and the Irish."

"The Germans usually vote Republican," Caroline began.

"But if I'd favored a war against Germany then, they'd have *all* voted against him." Lodge was smooth. "And there are twelve million of them among us, including the German Jews, like Kuhn and Loeb and Warburg, who hate England and love the Kaiser, and now that our good Mr. Morgan is dead, there's no one to keep them in line. Fear of them made Wilson pretend to be neutral. But once he'd got their votes – those of the Irish, too – he now comes in for the last act, to claim a great victory, so that he can then be our first three-term president."

Caroline took pleasure in Lodge's statesman-like plausibility. For all she knew – indeed, for all *he* knew – he believed what he was saying. But mischief was upon her. "After the speech, I saw you shake his hand. What did you say to him?"

Lodge was superb. "I said – what else? – 'Mr. President, you have expressed in the loftiest manner the sentiments of the American people.'"

"'Sin boldly!'" Caroline had been reminded of the phrase by Wilson's unexpected casting of himself as Martin Luther.

Lodge looked startled; then recalled the context. "Trust a Catholic to know Martin Luther."

"I don't," said Lucy; and waved toward Eleanor.

"It is not only good Protestantism but it is good sense," said Caroline.

"What, then, is the sin here?" Lodge sounded as if he were conducting a catechism.

"Pride, Senator Lodge."

"What else, Mrs. Sanford?"

"What else is there? What else caused Lucifer to fall?"

"Lucifer was the son of morning. Wilson is a little schoolteacher and nothing more."

"He is the son of our morning, Cabot. And in full pride, too. And sinning boldly through this war, which you love and he – to his credit – does not."

"How do you know that he does not – or that I do?" Lodge's face was pale except for the red circle on his right cheek where pacifism's fist had struck. "He is guileful. Deceitful. Bold, too, at least as sinner. Yes, you may be right. But if he does not love, as you put it, this war, you will admit that he loves himself and his glory, and so perhaps he is not unlike . . ."

"I concede, Cabot. *You* are Lucifer!" Caroline was giddy with fury; sorrow, too.

"I?" Lodge stepped back, as if to avoid a second blow in one day. "Lucifer?"

"Curious," said Henry Adams, who had appeared as if by magic. "God has nothing intelligent to say anywhere in *Paradise Lost* while Lucifer's every word is ravishing, which makes him quite unlike our own dear Cabot."

"You see?" Lodge beamed at Caroline. "I'll let you assign to Mr. Wilson the grand sulphurous role. But remember, it is he – not I – who is fallen, falling . . ."

"But Lucifer took a number of other angels with him." Milton had begun to go round in Caroline's head.

"I promise you," said Henry Adams, "Cabot would have remained safely behind in Heaven, close to God's throne as angel-majority leader, singing hosannahs."

"That is because I am from Boston, where the Lowells speak only to Cabots and *I* alone may speak to God."

Caroline wondered whether or not anyone that she knew in America would now be killed in the war, which had claimed, the previous week, her favorite half-brother, aged fifty-four, the Prince Napoléon d'Agrigente. Plon had been at his regiment's headquarters in a paper mill near the river Somme. During the night, there had been a bombardment. The next day his body was identified only because of a dented gold cigarette-case on which his initials were intertwined with those of a lady as unknown to Caroline as she no doubt was to his grieving widow. Although Plon had not been much younger than Senator Lodge, he had insisted on rejoining a regiment to which he had once been, ornamentally, attached. As Caroline smiled warmly at Cabot Lodge, she most sincerely wished him at the very frozen center of hell.

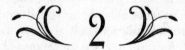

2

1

A smell of frying country sausage delighted Jess's nostrils as he let himself into the Harding half of 2314 Wyoming Avenue. The Duchess kept her husband well fed and as dry as she could, considering his passion for poker and bourbon and tobacco and the company of those insidious tempters, the politicians.

"That you, Jess?" The voice from upstairs was like a crow's.

"It's me, Duchess."

"You have your breakfast?"

"No, ma'am."

"Well, you're too late. Go and sit down."

Jess sat in the modern bay window that looked out on a desolate yard. The house, still on the raw side, was not quite finished, unlike the gracious Harding home in Marion with its numerous subtle decorative touches reminiscent not only of all the other opulent Marionite households but of Jess's mother's own residence in nearby Washington Court House, not to mention the long-planned but never completed nest for Roxy, who preferred apartment living, leaving Jess alone to face the horror of the downstairs closet. Jess felt tears come to his eyes as he thought of Roxy. The doctor had warned him that as a borderline diabetic case, with high blood pressure, he would be given to sudden floods of tears for reasons physical not sentimental. Harry Micajah Daugherty appeared from the study, unlighted cigar in his thick fist. "Jess, boy."

"Whaddaya know?" This was Jess's usual greeting to anyone he knew back home and, often, to those he didn't know but happened to see in the vicinity of the courthouse, original center to his world that was now extended not only to Columbus and the state house, but to imperial Washington and the Capitol.

"I know there's going to be a hot time in the old town tonight, for sure." Daugherty whistled tonelessly the song that had come to be associated with the Spanish-American War in general and with the hero of San Juan Hill, Theodore Roosevelt, in particular.

"They say T.R. hit town late last night."

Daugherty sat himself in a deep armchair whose antimacassar was slightly askew, like Daugherty's eyes. Jess could never make up his mind whether to look into the brown eye or the blue one. On aesthetic grounds, he preferred the crystalline quality of the blue. On matters of trust, however, he preferred the homely dog-like sincerity of the brown, despite its slight inadvertent twitch and vestigial cast. Otherwise, Harry M. Daugherty was a perfectly ordinary thick-set, fifty-seven-year-old politician with a small quantity of straight gray hair; no facial hair and, save for an occasional odd squint, no facial expression either. Daugherty now began to whistle three notes in ascending scale.

"How's the Missis?" asked Jess.

The notes were whistled now in a descending scale. Daugherty shook his head, unpursed his lips. "Not good, Jess boy. Not good. A martyr, that girl, to the arthritis." And as he did so often at the mention of his invalid wife, Lucie, he began to whistle, with a slight tremolo, "Love's Old Sweet Song." Even the tough Duchess was obliged to admit that theirs was a true love story, in marked contrast, Jess knew – delighted to know everything about his great friends – to the Harding marriage. But then the Duchess was five years older than the Senator. In fact, she was the same advanced age as Harry Daugherty; and plain women who were older than their husbands were accustomed, when dealing with sticks, to handling the short end, as they said in Fayette County.

Harry had been well pleased by Jess's organization of the Madame Marcia meeting. Until then, the Duchess had never really taken to the idea of Warren and herself in the White House. The

Senate suited her just fine. Warren, too, she said; and he would echo her. But what Warren said and what he thought were often two different things, according to Harry Daugherty, who knew Warren – or W.G., as he called him – best of all.

Twenty years earlier, when Daugherty had begun to realize that his own career would never go much higher than that of a party chairman, he had decided to conduct a high-powered career by proxy. When he had met the remarkably handsome Warren Gamaliel Harding early one morning in the front yard of Richwood's Globe Hotel, some fifteen miles from Marion, he had decided there and then that this handsome young state legislator and newspaper publisher was going to go all the way to the stars, or so Daugherty now told the story, and as he did, W.G. would half-smile that smile of his and stare off into space, eyes half-shut, head half-tilted. Jess had known both of them long enough to have heard the story become more and more elaborate, as W.G. had risen, in a zig-zag way, with a lot more zags than any of them had anticipated. After two terms in the state senate, W.G. had zigged into the lieutenant governorship of the state; served one term; went back to editing the profitable Marion *Star,* with considerable help from the Duchess, who was inexorable when it came to collecting monies due. Six years later, in 1910, W.G. zagged disastrously when he ran for governor and was defeated. But two years later Daugherty had reversed the Harding fortunes when he maneuvered the Republican magnates into letting Warren give the nomination speech for William Howard Taft at the party's convention. In a matter of hours, the handsome, sonorous, gray-haired, black-browed young politician was a national figure; and two years later, in 1914, he was elected to the United States Senate in the first election where senators were chosen not as the founders had intended, by state legislators, but by the people themselves. Now Daugherty was scheming to place his friend in the White House. What W.G. thought of all this, deep down, was a mystery to Jess. What the Duchess thought was often voiced: "I've seen the inside of the White House. There's no taste or refinement there, which is maybe the fault of the Wilsons. Anyway, how can a body stand having all those people around all the time? Why, you can't turn around you don't see somebody lurking back of a potted palm, his eye on you."

The Duchess was now in the room, busily straightening up, which meant throwing cigar stubs into the grate of the coal-fire. "Where are you two going to go meet Colonel Roosevelt?"

"Mrs. Longworth's house. Your favorite house, after the White House." Daugherty enjoyed teasing the Duchess. As she had no sense of humor, she could tolerate quite a bit of joshing at her own expense.

"I've still never set foot there. Nor she here. And. I." The Duchess spelled it out. "Am. The wife. Of the Senator. From Ohio. And Nick Longworth's just a representative of a lot of no-good Germans from Cincinnati. Which he wouldn't be today if my Warren hadn't helped him get back in after he got licked in '12, as well he should've been, the lecherous drunk."

"Well, he *is* in Congress. And Alice is still the President's daughter . . ."

"*Ex*-President. So stuck up. With her painted face. And cigarettes. And," the Duchess's thin mouth became a wide slit rather like that of a letter-box, "her cocaine."

Jess sat bolt upright. This was what he lived for. The real inside about everything. Whaddaya know? was now answered in spades, "How do you know that?"

"The dentist." The Duchess looked very pleased with herself. "I go to him. She goes to him. He prescribes it for her. He told me. She's had that bad jaw ever since a horse kicked her head in. Well, he gives her cocaine, and she asks for more and more and tells him she's a hopeless addict."

Harry sighed. "Speaking as a lawyer, Florence, if the guilty party admits guilt like that, she isn't really guilty. But just making fun, which is her style."

"There is nothing, Harry, that I don't know about dentists," was the Duchess's stern if somewhat tangential response.

United States Senator Warren Gamaliel Harding, Republican of Ohio, entered the room, carrying his frock coat over one arm. He wore bright red galluses and a stiff detachable collar, snowy white in contrast to his olive-tinted face, whose regular features were ever so slightly blurred, giving satisfaction to those who enjoyed believing the never entirely discredited legend that the Hardings were a Negro family that had only recently, in the last but one generation, passed over to white.

"Harry. Jess. Duchess." The deep voice rolled from the highly placed chest and abdomen. Although Harding had not yet passed the shadow-line between stout and fat, there was already an ominous sameness and lack of demarcation between stomach and chest, mitigated somewhat by the skillful hang of the trousers. "Have some breakfast, boys."

"Can't." The Duchess was firm. "Tillie's cleaned up."

Jess helped W.G. into his frock coat. Daugherty watched attentively – *his* creation. But Jess wondered, at times, if it might not be the other way round. Daugherty talked strategy morning, noon and night while W.G. just gazed off into the distance, smiling at whatever it was he saw there. He seldom committed himself to anything; seldom gave a political opinion, as opposed to learned soliloquies on what he found in his favorite reading, newspaper sports pages. Yet whenever Daugherty would discuss the election of 1920, their common grail, it was W.G. who appeared to direct the discussion, as he did now, seated in an old rocker, going through a sheaf of carbon copies of telegrams and letters while the Duchess headed toward the back part of the house to tyrannize the servant.

"Now then, here's the Colonel's first telegram. Last month. He's happy, as you might figure. Patriotism. Preparedness. And so on." Harding adjusted his spectacles. "I committed myself to one Roosevelt division, that he himself would raise. Volunteers. Volunteers."

Harding sighed. "I don't know what I can tell him. Now . . ." Harding's voice trailed off.

Daugherty was on his feet, slowly coming to an energetic boil, like a Ford Model T engine, thought Jess, who envied his brilliant friend not only his formidable brain but his energy, which he could crank up himself. "You've done all you could, W.G. You tacked your amendment – the *Harding* amendment – onto the preparedness bill, and it passed, and it's not your fault that Baker and Wilson refused to honor it, and ignored the will of Congress, due to partisan fever . . ."

"Don't," said Harding mildly, "make a speech. It's bad for the digestion this early in the morning. *My* dyspepsia's already starting to churn."

"So what are you going to tell the Colonel today?" Daugherty sank into an armchair.

"Three not one." Harding's smile was seraphic.

"Three what?"

"I'm going to see to it that when the next draft bill comes up, a provision will be made not for one but for *three* divisions of volunteers to be raised by the Colonel just like he did during the war with Spain, when he encouraged the brave to volunteer, to rally to the flag!" W.G. belched softly, punished for breaking his own rule against matutinal speechifying.

"They'll strike you down." Daugherty was flat. "Wilson won't give the Colonel a latrine to dig."

Harding put away his papers. "That will be between the President and the Colonel. I shall have done *my* duty by the Colonel, which is all that matters, isn't it, Harry?" Harding's gaze was benign.

Daugherty nodded. "Well, it's clever as hell, W.G., and that's the truth. You're just about the only link there is between that madman and the Regular Republicans, if he really wants to make up with us . . ."

"And he does just as much as we want to make up with him, to welcome him home, even if he did split our party in two and got the Democrats elected, which he now regrets most of all." Harding relit the dead cigar he held in his hand. "I think," he said at last, dreamily, exhaling blue-white smoke, "that I'm going to suggest to him that he be our standard-bearer next time around."

"Why?" Daugherty was suddenly alert, the brown eye blinking hard.

"Well, Hughes came a cropper, and Taft's forever out, so who else is there?" Harding smiled, generally, at Jess, as if he was a delegation of suffragettes.

"You know who else." Daugherty looked away.

But Harding never, at least in Jess's presence, responded to Daugherty's prodding. "If he gets his divisions and goes off to war, he'll come back a hero for a second time . . ."

"So he better not get his division."

"I reckon that's just what Mr. Wilson is saying to himself this morning. Anyway, like always, I want my friends to be happy."

"Colonel Roosevelt's your friend?" Daugherty chuckled.

"Oh, yes. Or he will be, after this morning."

To Jess's delight, he was allowed to accompany *his* great friends to the house of Mrs. Nicholas Longworth in M Street. The morning was damp, the sun pale, the press overexcited. A dozen journalists and photographers stood outside the narrow red-brick house. When they saw Senator Harding, they surrounded him, shouting questions. Jess was thrilled to think that he had just seen this much-sought-after man at home in his galluses while the press, eyes and voice to the people, must content themselves with a mere formal glimpse, a brief bloviation, Harding's favorite noun to describe speechifying, and a mystery.

"Now, boys. Relax. I'm just the proprietor of the Marion *Star*, a small-town publisher, not like you big Hearst fellows and your – Oh-oh! There's the *World*. I better keep my trap shut." W.G. chatted for some minutes, giving pleasure but no news. Then he entered the house, followed by Daugherty and Jess.

The downstairs hall was crowded with journalists of the progressive sort, as well as friends of the great man. Although Jess hated the progressives to a man, Harding knew exactly how to jolly them along. But Alice Longworth was not about to allow him any role in her house other than that of courtier, if not suppliant, to the warrior-king. "Senator!" She took his arm, and led him into the dining room. Jess looked at Daugherty – What to do? As if summoned, Daugherty marched right into the dining room and Jess did the same, very much aware that he was on history's stage, for at the head of the table sat Theodore Roosevelt with Senator Lodge on his right and a half-dozen other political grandees. Jess made himself invisible next to a break-front filled with unused wedding presents, his emporium owner's eye noted.

The appearance of Harding was electrical. Roosevelt leapt to his feet. Lodge languidly rose. Whatever they might have thought of Harding, and Jess was quite aware of the social disdain such people had for simple folk like W.G. and his Duchess, the presence of Ohio in that room, with all the state's wealth not to mention electoral votes, made even the fat small shrill Colonel reverent. "Mr. Harding!" Each pumped the other's hand. "You don't know what this means. I'll never forget your loyalty, Senator. Never. I don't mean to me." Roosevelt turned to the others, catching Lodge in a small yawn. But then Jess noticed that the Colonel had not seen the yawn because the eye that he had turned upon Lodge was plainly blind, damaged, it was said, in the White House by a medicine ball. "I mean to the whole country. Alone in the Senate, Mr. Harding saw the need for volunteers as well as conscripts."

"Alone?" murmured Lodge.

But Roosevelt was now moving about the dining room, voice raised high. In the hallway, Alice was conferring with her sad-eyed husband, Nick, a bald man with a full moustache, who came from one of Cincinnati's greatest families, and knew the McLeans better than anyone. But then old John McLean had begun his career in Ohio when he inherited the Cincinnati *Examiner;* later, he bought the Washington *Post.* Jess took considerable pride in his state: three recent presidents, Hayes, Garfield, McKinley; and then the Longworths, the McLeans – Harding?

Harding had finally been allowed to speak. "I just happened to be in the neighborhood," he said with a shy bob of his head – and he was shy, at least in the presence of those who could never forget his, or their, origins. "So I thought I'd pay my respects, Colonel, and tell you that no matter what kind of a draft bill we come up with next, there'll be a Harding amendment added – for three, maybe four, divisions of volunteers, and the sooner we let *you* raise them, Colonel, the sooner we've got this war won."

As Roosevelt seized Harding's hand in both of his, Jess noticed how gray the famous face was; gray, too, moustache and hair; while behind the dusty pince-nez, there were tears. At fifty-eight Theodore Roosevelt was a very old man. But then he had nearly died the previous year from a fever that he had caught big-game hunting in some South American jungle. "I swear to you, Senator,

I will be true to your trust, and let me tell you what I plan to tell the President today." The high voice suddenly lowered to a whisper. "*I will go to France with my troops, at their head, and I will not return. Because I know that three months in the field will see me to the end . . .*"

"I think, Theodore," said Lodge, "that if you could convince Mr. Wilson that you were never coming back, you'd get your division this afternoon."

"Root's already made that sour joke," said the Colonel, far too great a man to have a sense of humor.

Alice appeared in the doorway. "Mr. Tumulty's just rung from the White House. The Logothete will see you at noon."

"*President* Logothete," Nick corrected Alice. Jess wondered what a logothete was: something pretty awful, probably. The Colonel liked big fierce words.

"Good! Good!" The Colonel clapped his hands. Alice poured coffee from a great pot on the sideboard. "I shall come as a beggar. On my knees. Wailing . . ."

"Mr. Wilson will like that." Lodge was judicious, then W.G. nodded to Harry: time to go. But as the Ohioans stood up ready for departure, there was a disturbance from the reporters in the hall, as three more guests arrived. Jess recognized the Democrat James Burden Day, who had come to the Senate in 1915, the same year as Harding. With Day was a tall, willowy young couple, the man busy fending off reporters and the woman trying unsuccessfully either to put her large hat on or take it off.

"Senator Day!" The Colonel gave Burden a powerful hand-clasp.

"I'm your escort," said Burden. "To the White House, in case you've forgotten the way. The President thought you'd need a Democrat for protection."

"Democrats wherever I look!" Roosevelt kissed the woman's cheek. "Stop fussing with your hat, Eleanor. It's now too late to put it on *or* take it off."

"I think," the voice was high and fluting, "that I've driven a pin straight through my head."

This was the Colonel's niece, whom Jess had read about, and her husband, another Roosevelt, named Franklin. As Wilson's assistant secretary of the Navy, Franklin had been much cultivated by Daugherty, who was always interested in those departments of the government that let contracts.

"Well, Colonel." Franklin's smile was even wider than his cousin Theodore's; fortunately, his teeth were not reminiscent of a New England cemetery. "If ever we needed anybody here now it's you."

"Let's hope *your* President agrees. I've got a thousand names already." The Colonel gave his wallet pocket a tap. "Volunteers, ready to sign up the second I give the word."

"I'm sure you'll have no problem." The young Roosevelt was all easy charm and lightness and quickness of eye. He immediately shook hands with Lodge; then turned to Harding. "I hope we're still on for golf at Chevy Chase."

"Saturday." W.G. nodded. "Weather and the Duchess permitting. Now, Colonel . . ." Harding had turned toward Roosevelt, who had turned away from him, to his young cousin.

"What I'd give to be in your place, Franklin! And at your age, too."

"But you *were* in my place, in 1898, and you got us the Philippines. I'm afraid I won't have the same opportunity . . ."

"Probably not. That was rare luck, finding Admiral Dewey in time, and my poor Mr. Long always out of town . . ."

"While my poor Mr. Daniels is always in town, with the President." The young Roosevelt's smile was just a bit on the false side, thought the connoisseur Jess, even for a politician of the la-di-da patrician sort, who sounded more like an Englishman than an American.

"No. I don't mean the Navy Department. Once a war starts, *any-one* can handle that job."

Franklin's smile was fixed, while his small, close-set gray eyes stared down at his tubby cousin, who had now begun to walk about, arms flailing, just the way that Jess had enjoyed seeing him and his imitators do for so much of his life. "No. Your opportunity's more like mine *now*. To do battle! To enlist. As a private, if necessary. Then go where the action is. There is nothing more fitting for a man than to fight for his nation, with his bare hands, if necessary."

"But surely, Uncle Tee," the tall Mrs. Roosevelt was both diffident and firm, "anyone can shoot a gun, while very few people have Franklin's experience at the Navy Department for four years now . . ."

"Job for a clerk!" The Colonel smote the dining-room table a mighty blow. "The prizes go to the warrior, to the hero, not to the clerk safe at home behind the lines."

Although Franklin's smile was now in place, his cheeks were darkening with rising blood. But he spoke smoothly. "We must serve where we can do the best for our country, not ourselves."

This last was aimed at his famous cousin, who suddenly clicked his teeth fearsomely, three times; then shouted, "If you choose to imply –"

But Alice Longworth's voice was loudest of all. "Oh, good. A quarrel! Father, go for him. Remember your Japanese neck-hold . . ."

"I believe," began Senator Harding, moving toward the Colonel, Jess and Daugherty on either side of him.

"Try," said the elegant Senator Lodge, "what they call a right hook of the sort with which I recently floored a pacifist . . ."

"Try," said Alice, "this."

To Jess's astonishment, she was, for an instant, gone. Then the room burst into laughter. Alice had done a back-flip, landing with perfect balance on her feet, dress barely ruffled.

"Really, Alice." Cousin Eleanor was unamused. But Jess was ecstatic. He couldn't wait to tell the Duchess that her dentist was right and that the stuck-up Alice was indeed a dope fiend.

Jess was truly sorry to leave the M Street house, where, for this particular moment anyway, the whole country's attention was focussed; and yet, except for the privileged Jess, no one was aware of the low vice and high drama those brick walls contained, all lacquered over as they were with Rooseveltian world-glory. Jess had always wanted to be a detective. Now he knew that he had the makings of a great one like the fictional Nick Carter, based on the very real Mr. Pinkerton, whose glory still continued, even after death, in the agency that bore his name. Had it not been for dry goods and a fear of the dark, Jesse Smith might have made his mark in the world of detection. Now he satisfied himself with second-best, with his position on the inside of the top world, where he knew such things as who was a secret dope fiend and who was a secret presidential candidate. "Roosevelt's running" was Daugherty's gloomy comment as the three men got onto the half-empty electric trolley car, bound for the Capitol.

"That's why I'm in his corner." Harding was mild; he smiled at an old lady, who promptly looked out the window at Pennsylvania Avenue, vast and desolate in its April mud.

"If he gets to go to France, he's got the nomination." Daugherty chewed on an unlit cigar.

"He won't be going to France." Harding smoothed his thick eyebrows with a moistened thumb. The old woman was now watching him, with obscure horror.

"Then if Wilson won't let him go, he's really got the nomination in the bag."

"Harry, sometimes you go and look just too far ahead." Harding turned to Jess, who was holding a copy of the *Tribune*. "Give me the sports page, Jess."

"I wonder," said Harry, popping his eyes, the brown as well as the blue, at the demoralized old woman, "just what Burden Day was doing at the Longworths'."

"He's an escort, Harry. To get the Colonel from the frying pan to the fire." W.G. was deep into the sports page. "Well, here's the real story of why the captain of Army's football team didn't get to play Navy. Hazing, it says. He locked up one of the cadets in a locker and then went and forgot all about him. Damn fool thing to do."

"That's real absent-minded," said Jess, who admired Army's captain more than any of the other football gods, including Hobe Baker.

"I suppose they'll be graduating all the West Pointers and Annapolis boys a year early, for the war." Daugherty stared at the Post Office, which always looked to Jess like one of Carrie Phillips's beloved Rhine castles that had got itself mislaid on the Potomac.

"Remember that punt of his?" W.G. sighed. "Beautiful, it was. What I'd give to be able to do something like that, all those yards."

2

Burden Day had indeed been chosen by the President himself to get Colonel Roosevelt through the newspapermen at the north portico, not that anyone could control the Colonel, who had brought along someone called Julian J. Leary, as an extra buffer. In the motor car, Burden had found Roosevelt surprisingly small, even subdued, until they arrived under the porte-cochère to be greeted by a news-reel camera crew, a dozen overcoated journalists and photographers, and the Secret Service, whose numbers had doubled since the declaration of war. From all over the country there were scare stories: German-Americans were marching, meticulously armed, on Washington while German spies were everywhere, with dynamite, prepared to eliminate the city of Washington from the map.

There was a slight chill in the air, as Burden and Leary helped the Colonel from the car. Farther down the lawn, lilac was between bud and flower – always April, Kitty had said unexpectedly that morning, when presidents are killed, and wars declared, and the Republic imperilled. Was it something to do with the awakening of spring, with life's resurrection? Then why so much death at April and so little glory? – barring, of course, the Ned McLeans' annual Easter gala at their lordly estate, Friendship.

"Colonel!" A dozen voices said the name. Roosevelt came to swift vivid life and began to impersonate himself, left arm moving vigorously as right fist pounded, from time to time, into left palm. He seemed almost exactly like the Theodore Roosevelt who had dominated for twenty years the public imagination while reigning in this house for nearly eight of those years.

"Will Mr. Wilson run for a third term?" asked a journalist.

"You ask him. I won't. We're beyond politics now. All of us. This is war. We are not Democrats. We are not Republicans." Roosevelt could, like every politician, spin this sort of web effortlessly, but Burden watched rather than listened to him and saw how dull the eyes were while a second round face now circled, ominously, the first. It was against nature for T.R. to be old; but nature had been undone by time. Now a prematurely old man of fifty-eight was imitating himself with less and less plausibility, particularly as he tired. But Burden quite believed him when he said that he wanted to lead his own men into battle; and die upon the field. He also knew that, old or not, patriotic or not, Theodore Roosevelt had returned to the center of his party's stage and there was no one, including Wilson who could stop him from returning as sovereign to this house which he was now entering as temporary suppliant.

In the entrance hall, a dozen old retainers waited to greet the Colonel, who spoke warmly to each. He had what all good politicians had, the gift of intimacy with strangers, the ability to cut through all shyness and preliminaries and be himself, or something very like. All good politicians with the possible exception of the slender figure standing alone at the entrance to the Red Room, watching, as if at a theater, the performance of his rival, who had accused him not only of being a dread word-monger or logothete but a coward as well, the worst Rooseveltian epithet, since the Colonel had long since convinced the nation, if not himself, that as a man he was astonishingly brave, morally as well as physically.

Suddenly, Roosevelt looked up and saw the President; and each man, simultaneously, remembered to smile. Wilson's long discolored teeth were equine while Roosevelt's, though worn down by decades of grinding and clicking, were still hugely bovine.

"Mr. President!" Roosevelt crossed the entrance hall, Burden close behind him. Mr. Leary remained with the ushers and attendants. Simultaneously, Wilson's secretary, Joseph P. Tumulty, a classic Irish politician of the school of Jersey, appeared from the Red Room to join in the round of greetings. When Irish eyes are smiling, thought Burden, there's sure to be a knife. . . . The possibilities of alternative lyrics of a murderous nature were endless. But Wilson's clear eyes were Scots, and not smiling at all despite the baring of mottled teeth, while Roosevelt's face was like a carved coconut of the sort carried into battle by Polynesian warriors.

"Colonel Roosevelt, I'm so glad you could take time to see me." The courteous-killer Virginia note. "Come in. Come in. Please, Senator Day." Thus, Burden was invited to witness an historic confrontation. The men had not met since the election of 1912.

Before that, President Roosevelt had come once to Princeton, where college president Wilson had received him. Roosevelt, in turn, had acted as host to Professor Wilson at Oyster Bay, Long Island. Beyond that, the two men had existed for one another as, simply, enemies, mirroring one another as each challenged the other: Roosevelt for war at any time and in any place; Wilson for peace, or seeming to be for peace, under circumstances that had a tendency to shift rather more than the President's high-minded rhetoric could ever quite justify. Roosevelt was at least always in bellicose character; once Wilson had been obliged by events to go to war, he could now no longer depict his rival as an eccentric jingo when he himself was war-lord.

Wilson gestured for Roosevelt to sit before the fire, face to the window, an old trick that Roosevelt finessed by moving his chair so that the direct light was not in his face. Wilson sat opposite him, smiling politely; at the door Tumulty sat in a straight chair, pretending he was not present, while Burden sat comfortably in a sofa just out of range.

Roosevelt looked about him at the room. "We've moved a few things," said Wilson, vaguely. "I'm not sure what."

"Well, there was a president between the two of us – can't think of the name – and I wasn't asked here all that often in those days." Burden had never seen the Colonel try to please, if not an elder, a superior. He was startled at just how winning and boyish the Colonel could be when he wanted something. "No. I always think of this room as the room where I said, after I was elected in 1904, that I wouldn't run again in 1908."

"I wonder," said Wilson, "if you hadn't said that, if I'd be here at all."

"I don't know. But I do know that Mr. Taft would *never* have been here." Roosevelt was flat. "I can guarantee that. But I made a promise to the country, and I kept it."

"*Never* to run for re-election?" Wilson was like a kindly tutorial guide with a promising student.

"Exactly! Never to run for re-election." Roosevelt gave a dazzling smile. "*In 1908.*" With a crash, the door to 1920 was kicked open. Wilson for a third time versus Roosevelt for a second time in his own right, though, for all practical purposes, a third term, as he'd inherited most of the murdered McKinley's second term. "But all that's past, Mr. President. To say the least. I want us to win this war, and to lead the world, and I want to do my part, as my four sons, all of age, will do theirs."

"I know. Mr. Baker has spoken to your oldest, I think. Mr. Baker was much moved . . ."

"I want them to have their crowded hours of glorious life, as I've had mine, and will still have." Wisely, the Colonel did not leave the President an opening for a negative. "As a state paper, I regard your declaration, and its argument, as the equal of Washington and Lincoln. But it needs one thing yet to make it live, and that is for us, you and me, to inspire the nation to carry out your dream." When it came to flattery, Burden was amused to find that the Colonel could give as lustily as he took. Since Wilson was entirely human when it came to simple vanity, he visibly expanded under his predecessor's praise.

The dialogue went well, better than Burden had dreamed, considering what the two had said and thought of one another, all of which was now, the Colonel exuberantly declared, so much "dust in a windy street, if only we can make your message good."

Thus, Roosevelt welcomed Wilson to Roosevelt's war. Then the volunteer division was mentioned. Before Wilson could respond, the Colonel was on his feet, superbly impersonating himself. "I am willing to go forth to my fellow Americans and preach the sword of the Lord and of Gideon. I can raise armies of volunteers of the best – the flower – of the nation, as we did once before in my time, and before that, too, in Lincoln's day . . ."

"But in Lincoln's day, there were too few volunteers." Wilson's voice was suddenly urgent and, again, Burden heard not the elegant neutrality of the Princeton professor's voice but that Southern cadence of – what other word if not freedom but rebellion? "That is the problem before us. We must conscript the young men. Draft them. Find a new word for draft, if necessary, but no matter what the word, there is so little time to do so much in." The President interrupted himself. "I know that you think I should have led us into this war a year ago, but if I had, only you – worth ten divisions – would have followed me."

"All that is past." The Colonel sank into his chair. "You are president. I am not. The burden's yours. God help you. I will go, for what it's worth. Clemenceau has asked me to come to France, just as a symbol of our will to fight. . . ."

Burden was fascinated to watch so skilled a politician as Roosevelt make so fundamental a mistake. For a French premier to request the aid of an ex-president was to insure a presidential veto.

"All Europe finds you fascinating, Colonel. As do we." Virginia was replaced by Princeton. "But we must not discourage those men we draft by setting up a special corps of volunteer soldiers." Before Roosevelt could interrupt, Wilson was quick to add, "Not that uses cannot be made of the volunteer spirit and of – of the sword of Gideon. I am also wary of allowing ourselves to become too much enamored of one side or the other, in which I follow General Washington, perhaps, more than yourself, which is why," and now Wilson began to weave his own artful magic, "I want peace without victory for all sides, if humanly possible, since victory for one is defeat for the other, and should that happen the cannons will sound once more, and there will be more blood in the next generation. So I have presented us not as an ally of the Allies nor indeed as an enemy of the *people* of the Central Powers, but as an 'associated power,' to see peace made, justice done, and – ah, life enhanced." Adroitly, Wilson led Roosevelt away from the specifics of his visit; and spun for him one of his verbal webs, so plausible, so beautiful and so, very often, misleading. Wilson had once confessed to Burden that whenever he was faced with an office-seeker, the surest way to get him off the subject was "to control the conversation yourself and take the high moral ground. Often he will be ashamed to mention his interested errand." Of course, Roosevelt knew the trick, too; he also knew when to allow a certain smoke to obscure conflicting interests. He shifted the conversation from his own particularity to the generality.

"As you and I close ranks, so the whole country must." The Colonel turned his head toward the window and the white April light. "I suggest to you now, privately, what I shall soon be writing about in the Kansas City *Star*. They now want me to be a regular newspaper writer, every week, and if there were the time . . ." A slight pause made it clear that if the Colonel did not get his military command he would be regularly heard from in the press, as the not-so-loyal opposition.

If Wilson had grasped the implicit warning, he chose to ignore it. Chin held high, righteousness itself embodied as a Presbyterian elder, Wilson nodded encouragingly; and let the other talk. So far, on points, they were even by Burden's calculation. "I refer now to the German-language press, which has been, from the beginning, disloyal to this country. I would, as a military necessity, shut all those papers down."

Wilson blinked his surprise. "Isn't this – arbitrary? Surely, they are guaranteed the same freedoms –"

"This is war, Mr. President. Lincoln suspended *habeas corpus*, shut down newspapers, and we'll have to do the same. . ."

"I hope not. After all, we shall have a military censorship that will apply to everyone. This should keep the Germans on a tight lead."

"They are also centers of treason – or potential treason anyway. Why run a risk? We must – you *must*, sir, tighten everyone's lead in the name of victory. Many would-be traitors – German sympathizers – pretend to be peace-lovers, to be – what's their phrase? – 'conscientious objectors.' Well, I would treat them conscientiously! I would deny them the vote. If they are of military age and refuse to fight for their country, then they must forgo their citizenship."

Wilson was taking all this remarkably well, thought Burden. He continued to nod politely, judiciously – most judiciously when he observed mildly, "I suppose the Supreme Court could find some way to disenfranchise them."

"Supreme Court!" Roosevelt's fist struck his own knee so hard that he winced, and the pince-nez fell loose on its cord and dangled on his shirt-front. "You are the commander-in-chief. And this is war. So you, *you*, are president, court and congress all combined. Do what needs doing, do it fast. The world's almost ours at last!" Roosevelt was on his feet. "We have all the gold now. All the money power. England and France, Germany and Russia, they will never recover from this blood-letting. Their empires are as dead and gone as Nineveh and Tyre. Oh, what a glorious time you'll have of it!"

"Shall we trade places?" Wilson's smile was genuine.

"Yes! This minute!" Roosevelt roared with laughter. "Why, if I had enough Rough Riders I'd come in here like a Mexican bandit and take over . . ."

"I'd help you," Wilson sighed. "You are more suited for this than I."

"I think so, too." Roosevelt was blunt. "But history has ruled otherwise. If these states are still under a lucky star, as we were when I was here, you shall be – glorious, Mr. Wilson, and I'll retract all my partisan statements."

"Logothete, too?"

"I thought you'd fancy that one. Secretly, of course."

Wilson laughed for the first time. "I don't like it. But I'd never deny it. I am a man of words. Like you." He thrust.

Roosevelt did not blink, and his response was mild. "But there is also action . . ."

"Ah, Colonel, words are the greatest action of all, words are what bind us to Heaven – and to hell. At the end, as well as in the beginning, there is only the word."

Roosevelt stood now in front of the fireplace, legs wide apart, hands behind his back, just as he had stood so many times in that same spot when he had been the president. "Then, perhaps," he said, smiling, "if that's the case, I should select my words with more care."

"In this matter, Colonel, you are the judge, not I."

Burden had a curious sense of time having doubled. This was 1917; yet, simultaneously, this was also 1907; and there were two presidents in one Red Room.

Then the Colonel broke the spell. He crossed to Tumulty, who rose, respectfully. "Now here's the sort of fighting Irishman I like." He slapped Tumulty on the back. "By Jove, Tumulty, you are a man after my own heart! Of course, you have six children. . . ." Burden knew then, for absolute certain, that Roosevelt would be a candidate in 1920. Why else memorize the exact number of the egregious Tumulty's brood? "But I'll tell you what. You get me over to France, and I'll put you on my staff, and Mrs. Tumulty won't have a thing to worry about." Roosevelt turned to Burden. "Senator, you're still a strapping lad. You come, too."

"Shall I pack my toga?"

"No. Turn it in. Plenty of senators in this country. In fact, far too many."

"We are in perfect agreement on that." Wilson stood up. "I suppose you'll want me to volunteer, too."

"It would set a fine example." Roosevelt chuckled.

"I could go as a chaplain, I suppose."

"Don't underestimate yourself, Mr. Wilson. I would put you in charge of the great guns. You're a born artilleryman, as Mr. Taft and I discovered in 1912. Anyway, you have your place already. The first place. You are my commander-in-chief. I've come here to get my orders." Roosevelt gave a fairly smart salute, which the President gravely returned. Then in a general storm of farewells and good feeling, the Colonel was gone, leaving Burden with the President and Tumulty. From the entrance hall, Rooseveltian "bullies" could be heard. Wilson looked, quizzically, at Burden. "Well, that was an experience," he said. "He's like a great big boy."

"Who can charm the little birds out of the trees," said Tumulty.

"What about the big birds?" Burden could not guess what Wilson would do.

But the President was still bemused. "I always found him charming, personally. But there is now a sort of sweetness about him that was not there before. Four sons, he has," Wilson's voice lowered, "and he wants them all to go to war, with him. . . . I'm glad I have daughters." Wilson's mood lightened. "Anyway, he's hard to resist. I can see what it is the people love about him." Wilson sounded to Burden, wistful. As a public man, Wilson aroused admiration – and hatred – but no affection.

"But what will you do?" Burden was direct. "Does he get his division of volunteers?"

"Senator Harding wants him to have *three* divisions," said Tumulty.

Wilson spread wide his arms and stretched his back. "If it were up to me, why not? But I leave the military to the military. At the moment, they fear that special volunteers – like these – will wreck our whole system of drafting men. Also, he's no general."

Wilson's hand rested now on a large bronze head of Abraham Lincoln. "Thank God for Lincoln! You know, when I taught history, I taught Lincoln. And I was struck how, when the war came, he made every mistake it was possible to make. Well, thanks to his bad example, we won't make the same mistakes *now*."

"One of his mistakes," Burden was now trying to draw Wilson out, "was the appointment of opposition politicians as generals."

"Yes," said Wilson, turning to Tumulty. "See if the coast is clear. I don't want any photographs of me with the Colonel."

Tumulty and Burden left the Red Room. The Colonel could be seen through the open door, talking to journalists. Tumulty turned back into the Red Room. "He's got the Pathé news-reel cameras photographing him, and won't be budged."

Wilson then appeared in the doorway, and with a comic timing worthy of a Mack Sennett movie, he tiptoed across the hall to the elevator, with mock-terrified glances over his shoulder, as if pursued by a ghost in a graveyard.

And that was that. The Colonel would not get his division. But there was an excellent chance that he might get another four-year lease on the White House. In a curious way, with or without military glory, Theodore Roosevelt could no longer lose. After a decade's absence, luck was now with him again, which meant, at his age, to the end.

3

Kitty sat on a boulder overlooking Rock Creek, her eye on the baby, as it tottered ever closer to a clump of shiny poison ivy at the foot of an English walnut tree whose green fruit glowed in the summer sun. "Why not," said Kitty, "put the parlor here, over the creek, and our bedroom over there?"

"The road's too near." Burden had taken off his jacket and

unbuttoned his shirt, and felt free of all things worldly except Kitty, who had become surprisingly pretty as she aged; she was no longer the somewhat hard-faced young woman that he had felt obliged to marry because her father was the master of the Democratic Party of their state. If nothing else, Caroline had taught him never to disguise his motives from himself. In early days, Caroline had shocked him. Now he shocked her whenever he chose to reveal just how the affairs of the republic were conducted. Admittedly, the shock to her system was not moral: rather, she appeared to resent the lack of form to American life, so unlike France, where everyone knew what to expect, including the exact nature of the almost always predictable unexpected.

On the other hand, Kitty was a natural politician, true heiress to her father, the legendary judge, not only as a political tactician but now as possessor of her late father's fortune soon to be transformed from abstract stocks and bonds into wood, brick, stone.

Burden himself had never been able to acquire money. Somehow or other the munificent seventy-five hundred dollars a year salary of a United States senator was hardly enough for them to live on, even though their large house in American City was always profitably rented. When it came time to go home to vote or to campaign, they would check into the Henry Clay Hotel across from the state capitol, and pretend that they had been living in town all year, just folks, with only the odd trip to Washington.

The first installment of Kitty's inheritance had gone to buy one and a half acres of Rock Creek Park, mostly wooded hills whose undergrowth was as green and thick as any jungle. In fact, the park was almost too much of a jungle for Burden's taste, as he seized his daughter's pinafore just as she was about to bury her face in a cluster of poison ivy which could, within hours, cover its victim with oozing itching blisters, torment for an adult, hell for a child.

"Diana!" Kitty's voice sounded too late. "What is it about poison ivy? Jim Junior had a dowsing rod for the stuff."

Burden settled himself on a fallen log opposite Kitty, Diana on his knee. Birds silently circled overhead, their singing-mating season past. Now they were solicitous parents and providers, as well as flight instructors to the young – and mourners for those who fell to earth.

"The architect says that *this* should be the parlor, facing south." Burden tried and failed to imagine a room where they were sitting. Jungle or not, he preferred the open. Unlike most boys brought up on a farm, he did not prefer the indoors, as long, of course, as he did not have to do chores. "She'll grow up here," he added, looking down at Diana, a grave as yet speechless child, who sighed.

Kitty took a crust of bread from her handbag. Then, bread in hand, she extended her arm. The miracle, as Burden always thought of it, occurred in a matter of seconds. A large thrush made several close passes in order to get a good look at Kitty before he settled on her wrist. Then he took the bread in his beak, shook it free of encumbering crumbs, and rose to a branch of the nearest tree, where he ate the crust and watched Kitty.

"How do you do it?"

"I've always done it." Kitty's relationship with the animal world was intimate, collusive, extra-human. All creatures came to her without fear; and she was there. As a girl, she had befriended a full-grown wolf, dying of hunger during a hard winter. The wolf had followed her about like a dog; then, according to the Judge, while she was at school, the wolf had attacked the hired man and the hired man had shot the beast in self-defense. To which Kitty had replied with a terminal coldness, "No, Father. You just had him killed." Father and daughter never spoke of the subject again but father and son-in-law did discuss the matter years later, and the Judge had said, with puzzled awe, "How did she know – how *could* she know that I killed the brute when there was no one there to see me?" It was decided then that Kitty was psychic, at least with animals and birds. She seemed less interested in people as opposed to voters. She knew as much of Burden's alliances and arrangements as he did; yet he was certain that she knew nothing of Caroline. He also suspected that if she did know, she would be indifferent. Odd, he thought, not to know your own wife as well as – a thrush did. When Jim Junior had died at six, it was Burden who had wept. Kitty had simply busied herself with the funeral arrangements; then she had quarrelled with her Negro cook over the refreshments for the wake, a bit of Romanism popular in their Protestant state. That was the end of their son.

Although a cool west breeze was rustling the branches of the taller trees, Burden was still uncomfortably hot. But then everyone said that this was the hottest summer in memory, the first war-time summer. "High ceilings." Kitty looked up at the tallest tree, an oak.

"The highest." Burden was knowledgeable. "A Norman facade. Gray stonework. A terrace. A pond. A porch to the side . . ."

"Let's hope the war won't interfere."

"Building goes on. Even if food doesn't." Burden moved from log to ground; and the inevitable grass stains on his trousers. "The President's fit to be tied over Section 23."

"You can't blame him." The animal psychic was now the political psychic, having skipped any sort of rapport with those human beings between the two poles of her life.

"They're trying to do to him what they did to Lincoln when they set up that joint congressional committee to oversee the war."

"Same thing." Kitty nodded. "And all tucked inside the food bill, which is sly. But you won't let it go through?"

"No. But there'll be a real fight. Can't you just hear the talk? Oh, the talk!" More than ever, the Senate encouraged personal oddity. Originally intended as a house of lords for the American patriciate or its assigns, the members of the upper house were selected by the various state legislators that were themselves paid for by the moneyed class. But since 1913, senators were now popularly elected. As a result, a new breed of lordly tribunes of the people had appeared in the sleepy chamber; and they delighted in tormenting the gentlemanly old guard of the patriciate. Also, since any senator who had got the floor to speak could speak as long as he was conscious, a great new age of filibuster had dawned, and a leather-lunged senator might, in the last hours before adjournment, talk to death a piece of legislation or threaten to do so in exchange for favors.

Even so, Burden was delighted to belong to so powerful a club, in which he had found his place as chief conciliator of his party's chief, the schoolmaster president, whose control over the Senate's

Democratic majority was fragile at best. This meant constant work for Burden, who must placate – when not outright bribe – the Bryanites, the isolationists, the pro-Germanites and all the rest, who chose to reign in committee rather than serve their president.

"I wonder who she'll marry." Kitty gazed fondly at Diana, almost as if she were a plump raccoon arrived at the kitchen door for a handout.

"Isn't that tempting fate?" Burden felt a swift chill; and shuddered. He had once speculated on Jim Junior's future and promptly lost him to diphtheria.

"No. She'll marry in this house, or from this house." Kitty had a sort of second sight. "I suppose she'll be happy, too."

"Yes." Burden was noncommittal. Kitty was fond of him; he of her; no more.

"Did your father like your mother?" This was sudden.

"That was so long ago. I don't recall." Burden had grown up on a farm in Alabama, surrounded by veterans of the lost war like his father. Burden had always been amazed at how Mark Twain had managed to make so idyllic that harsh crude muddy – always mud – world of mosquitoes and chiggers and wet-heat and poisonous snakes the color of the mud. Of course, Twain had been writing of an earlier generation before the war, but even so Burden had been aware all his childhood that this was not the way life was meant to be. There had been a very great fall, which his father, unlike so many veterans, was eager to explain and describe, the pale blue eyes fierce and crazy, as they must have been that day at Chickamauga when the bullet felled but did not kill him and he was taken prisoner. Later, among the ruins, Obadiah Day had begun his life all over in the delta mud. Of his children – seven, eight? Burden did not know the count – all but two had died of bloody flux, as the cholera was known. Burden did recall how much of his childhood seemed to have been spent in the local cemetery, watching small boxes being hidden under red dirt. He also recalled hours spent listening to his father speak of how They had ruined the South, corrupted the Negroes, foreclosed on the land of the best true stock of the country. *They* were a shifting entity composed of all Yankees and bankers and railroad men and, sometimes, of plain aliens, of whom Catholics and Jews were the worst. Curiously, the Negroes, no matter how out-of-hand, were never held directly responsible for their behavior. If a nigger went bad it was They who'd gone and turned him.

In time, the defeated Confederates turned to politics, the only weapon that they could use against Them. The political picnic and the under-canvas rally became the true church of those who had been dispossessed in their own land, and Obadiah was among those who had helped form the Party of the People in order to redress the people's wrongs, and the party flourished everywhere in the South, and Obadiah himself was elected to a series of small state offices. Then came the day when he heard the fourteen-year-old Burden speak at a rally, and joyously he had welcomed his son to the great struggle, much as the Baptist had received the Messiah on Jordan's shining bank. So, at Alabama's edge, James Burden Day had come into his kingdom to do his father's work and rout Them in the people's name.

Clearer to Burden now than the crowd itself – and every crowd to Burden was like a lover met and lost or, more likely, ravished and won – was the image of his father, still surprisingly young in appearance, despite white hair, still brilliant of that bright blue eye not covered by a patch, still lean enough to be able to wear the butternut-gray patched Confederate uniform that he had come home in, with the bullet that struck him at Chickamauga on a string about his neck after he had insisted that it be gouged from his thigh by a friendly doctor so that, should he die, no part of Them would be eternally mixed with his bones. Together, father and son had fought in the ranks of the People's Party until Burden had gone west to a new state to practice law; and though he never ceased to be, he swore to his father and murmured to himself, a true Populist, he had been obliged to start an entirely new life in a brand-new dry dusty state as opposed to his old wet, muddy one. Obliged to use a family connection to get an appointment at Washington in the Comptroller's Office, he had disappointed his father. But they were reconciled when Burden had promised the old man that he would never give up the struggle and that when the time was right he would go back to his new state and lead their party. When the time was right, he did go back and marry Kitty, and with *her* father's help, he was elected to Congress not as a Populist but as a Bryanite Democrat. Father no longer spoke to son. Yet Obadiah and a second wife continued to live in Alabama; and though Burden had sent him a message after his election to the Senate – where, after all, did he not continue to fight Them? – he got no answer from the old man, who was still, at heart, the furious boy struck down a half-century earlier at Chickamauga – two minutes before noon, he had noted the time before he lost consciousness. To live without such a father's pride was, to Burden, unendurable; particularly when he himself had never lost their common faith in the people, their people. What was a party label? What was – anything?

"Will it be you?" Kitty rose. She took Diana from him. The child was falling asleep in the warm sun. The sweet heavy odor of honeysuckle was everywhere, as was the vine itself, a yellow-green tapestry clinging to the laurel.

"Me? What?"

"If Mr. Wilson does not run for a third time, which no one has."

Kitty never ceased to calculate, despite the distractions of a child, house, the wild beasts of the field and – the what? – of the air. "It's far too soon to even guess. The war will be short. That's one thing – in his favor. He'll be a victorious war president. And not too old. So if he wants it, he'll probably have it."

"It does no harm," said Kitty, removing the drowsy Diana's thumb from her mouth, "to place ourselves in position in case something goes wrong. If it does, our only competition will be Mr. McAdoo."

"That's a lot of competition." Burden frowned, as he always did, when he thought of the enormous advantage that the President's son-in-law *and* secretary of the Treasury had over everyone else in the party. McAdoo had already so positioned himself to inherit the Wilson legacy that it would be impossible to contest him unless the whispers of corruption that always surrounded the vast gray granite Treasury Building proved true.

"Then there's the Colonel."

"Surely, he must die sometime." Kitty was sweetly relentless.

"At sixty-one? With the nomination already his? If ever there was a life-restorer, it's that. Almost as good as a Federal pension to insure longevity. There are," said Burden, as always bemused by the fact, "seventy-three widows of the War of 1812 currently collecting pensions from the government."

"Young girls who married old boys."

"Now they are old girls made immortal by a pension." Their Negro driver, Albert, joined them. He was a native Washingtonian, and a consummate snob. For years when Burden was in the House of Representatives, Albert would refer to his employer, behind his back, as "the Senator." Burden's eventual election to the Senate was, Kitty maintained, more thrilling for Albert than either of them. "I always felt we were common," Albert would say, "when we were in the House with all that tobacco-chewing white trash from nowhere." Albert's mother had been called Victoria, after the queen; and she had called him Albert, after the consort. "Very psychological," Kitty would say, looking wise. "He's very much a mother's boy."

Albert reminded Burden that he had agreed to go out on the river with the Assistant Secretary of the Navy. So Burden collected Diana while Kitty collected laurel to decorate the Mintwood parlor; and then they descended the hill to the road, and the waiting car.

The *Sylph* looked its name – swift slender craft of a type unknown to Burden, but then he was the perfect landsman and could not tell one boat from another. But he was grateful for the day's outing, anything to escape Washington's airless heat.

The Assistant Secretary was all in white and most nautical-looking, as was Cary Grayson, the President's physician, and Grayson's young wife, Altrude, Edith Wilson's closest friend. Obviously, the Assistant Secretary of the Navy had discovered that the most direct route to the President was through the Graysons, and as Franklin Roosevelt's luck would have it, Grayson was Regular Navy. He was also a very small man; and the gracious Altrude, very much in the Edith style, loomed over him. There was another couple whom Burden did not know – "fashionables," as he thought of the eastern gentry whom he had met, from time to time, in Sanford-land. Finally, in the new uniform of a woman sailor, yeoman third class, the charming Lucy Mercer, Eleanor's social secretary. Lucy's escort was a young man from the British embassy.

Once they were under way, Burden relieved himself of jacket and tie and enjoyed the cool, somewhat rank breeze off the Potomac River as they headed downstream toward Mount Vernon and the Chesapeake. For a moment, the frantic war-time city seemed remote; war, too, except for a pair of destroyers, if that's what they were, anchored off the Navy Yard.

As Burden accepted a mint julep from a steward, Franklin smiled contentedly. "If only Josephus Daniels could see us now."

"Surely his prohibition of alcohol does not extend to guests of the Navy."

"To everyone, including the President." But Burden noticed that Franklin drank only lemonade, while the others were now all forward, waiting for the ship to draw abreast Mount Vernon, which the *Sylph* would duly salute, as antique Navy custom required.

Franklin made agreeable small talk. He had far more charm than his presidential cousin, at least for Burden, who was something of a connoisseur in these matters since everyone in Washington wanted to charm senators, particularly those, like Burden, of the majority party. Ordinarily, Burden and the Navy had no links. Burden's committees were Agriculture first last and always, with Foreign Affairs for amusement, and Banking for grave necessity, since that committee, a twin to the House Ways and Means Committee, was the fountain of all expenditure; hence, government patronage. But as Burden was only in his first term, he carried no great weight other than the power that accrued to him as the link between the Bryanite senators and the President, a position recently relinquished by the blind Senator from Oklahoma, who could abide neither President nor war. But the true link between Burden and the young Roosevelts was Caroline and, to a lesser extent, Blaise. The Roosevelts tended to move in high fashionable circles, keeping their distance from such low showy fashionables as the Ned McLeans.

"Where's Mrs. Roosevelt?" The mint julep was uncommonly

pleasant; and the sun, filtered by a heavy white haze, was, for the first time in days, bearable.

"She's gone up to Canada, with the chicks. I'm supposed to join her in August. Only . . ." Franklin stared at the Virginia shore.

"Only what?" But Burden knew. Franklin was planning to run for the Senate from New York in the fall election.

"Do *you* think I should run?"

"I don't know that much about the state. But if I were you, I wouldn't quit this job first. Just take a leave of absence."

Franklin laughed without much joy. "I will. If I can get away with it. I think old Josephus would like to see me well and truly gone."

"But the President –"

" – has been most understanding. Everyone tells me I've a safe berth here if I lose, only . . ." Again the pause; the word "only" seemed to provide a barrier for Franklin, who, while appearing to have no secrets, managed to evade all intimacy with considerable grace.

"Only you'd rather not lose."

"Exactly."

"Do you have Tammany's support?"

"No. They've got their candidate. So I shall be reform, I suppose. Another Uncle Tee in Democratic clothing." He swallowed some lemonade; and grimaced. "I've a sore throat. Too much talking. I argue and argue and nobody listens. You see, I've worked out a way to bottle the German submarines. But the British can't be budged. And our admirals are so slow, so slow. The solution, Burden, is this."

Burden never much liked being called by his first name, particularly by someone who was not only a decade his junior but so far beneath him in the national hierarchy. Yet it was a part of this Roosevelt's considerable charm to lift, spontaneously, others to a level of intimacy with himself, a member of that sovereign patriciate that still held a number of seats in a Senate which had been entirely theirs until democracy had so rudely sprung the chamber's door and let Burden, among others, in.

"It's so clear. We seal off the North Sea with a mine barrage from Scotland to Norway so that no submarine could ever get through, which would seal them up tight in their own ports. Well, it took me weeks to get to the President, who's now given the go-ahead. But the British are still dragging their feet even when I said we'd do the same for the Dover Straits, which would protect *their* home waters. But they are sound asleep." He scowled, as he drank more lemonade. Burden noticed that Franklin's face was now glistening with sweat despite the cool breeze. The handsome head with its thin chiselled nose looked fragile; the small eyes were not only too close together but due to the face's asymmetry one was higher than the other.

Suddenly, they were athwart the pillared mansion of the first president. Franklin sprang to his feet, as did Burden, who remained at self-conscious attention while a bugler "aft" played taps.

When the fashionable couple joined Franklin in the stern, Burden made his way forward to where the English diplomat and Yeoman Third Class Lucy Mercer were seated. Both rose in defer-ence to senatorial rank.

Burden sat between them. A steward plied them with Josephus Daniels's lemonade. Like everyone else in the small Washington world, Burden found Lucy uncommonly attractive, and mysteri-ous. Why hadn't she married? Of course, she was a member of Maryland's Catholic gentry and there were not so many Catholic bachelors available in the capital. On the other hand, a short trip to Baltimore and she would be surrounded by her own kind. Yet she had chosen to live in Washington and work for Eleanor Roosevelt and fill in at dinner parties until she had joined the Navy. "Now you are a fighting woman," said Burden.

"It was Mr. Roosevelt's idea." She smiled, and looked away.

"Your military service," said the Englishman, "is *distinctly* selec-tive."

Burden had more than once claimed credit for the sublime euphemism "selective service." The word "conscription" was taboo, reminding everyone of the Civil War's bloody riots. But since Wilson could no more rely on volunteers than Lincoln, a new phrase was devised. A few years earlier when it looked as if the bor-

der troubles with Mexico might turn into a full-scale war, Wilson
had issued a ringing call for volunteers: and hardly anyone had rallied to the colors. This time he was taking no chances.
Conscription was to be swift and absolute and under another
name. On June 5, ten million men between twenty-one and thirty
had been registered under the National Defense Act for "selective
service" in the armed services, which sounded rather better than,
say, cannon fodder in France.

Privately, Burden hated the whole enterprise. The wounded of
the Civil War had been all round him in his youth, and the general
poverty of the delta during that time was directly due to the loss of
manpower and money in the war. Publicly, Burden supported the
war; yet he could never rationalize to himself the brutal manner in
which the United States had violated its own sacred Monroe
Doctrine in order to fight a war in Europe, something the original
republic had guaranteed to all the world that it would never do.
However, as a practical politician, he had been able to rationalize
the necessity of making the world safe not for democracy – a
quixotic enterprise, since the United States had yet to experiment
with so dangerous a form of government, as those militant women
who wanted to vote never ceased to remind their sexual masters –
but to enrich the nation. This had already begun, as the
Englishman, Mr. Nigel Law, reminded him. "Your speech in committee, sir, was much applauded in London."

"It was just plain old common horse sense." British accents
tended to cause Burden to assume the folksy, down-home style of
a vaudeville rube comedian. He chewed an imaginary piece of
straw. "Can't let our best buddy go broke."

"What speech was that?" Lucy's blue eyes shifted from the blue-
green Virginia shore to Burden's imaginary straw.

"About the loan to England. Last month the President was told
that without quick help from us, England could no longer support
the pound. Fact, in twenty-four hours, they would have had to go
off the gold standard, so I said to my fellow statesmen, who don't
much care for foreigners in general and the English in particular,
if the pound goes, the dollar's going to go, too, so we better prop
them up, which we did, and which we're still doing, thanks to Mr.

McAdoo and his Liberty Loans, which are gathering up every spare dollar in the country." The rhetoric of the Liberty Loan campaign – all Hunnish ghoulishness – had got on Burden's nerves. Even a Republican hack like Harding had complained about it, to no avail.

"To your everlasting credit, Senator." Mr. Law was slightly overdoing it, for England, of course.

Burden smiled. "Actually, it is to *your* everlasting debit. Anyway, we've got everybody's money now, which is most satisfying." He turned to Lucy. "Mr. Roosevelt's sick. You ought to get him to a doctor."

For the first time, she looked at Burden with interest. "You could tell?"

"From the way he's sweating."

"He says it's just a sore throat. Yes, I'll get him to a doctor when we're ashore."

"Will the Lever bill pass the Senate?" The diplomat did not believe that sore throats and fevers should be allowed to thwart diplomacy.

Burden nodded. "But we'll cut it up a bit first." The President had wanted to control the price and distribution of food; and he had chosen that successful mining engineer Herbert Hoover to be its director. But in a recalcitrant mood the Senate had made it a provision of the bill that a joint congressional committee on the war be set up, to monitor the President. The historian-president was quick to rally his troops in the Senate; and it was Burden who was now in the throes of eliminating Section 23 from the Lever bill.

"Your president has the most extraordinary powers, doesn't he?" Mr. Law looked somewhat wistful.

"Only in war-time."

"Then, if I were an ambitious president, I'd keep the country forever at war."

"It couldn't be done." Burden was flat. "Our people don't like war. Why should they? We've got all the space we need right here. All we want is open doors everywhere so we can go and do business. Any president who tried to get us into an unpopular war would soon be an ex-president. Look how hard it was for Wilson to get us into this one." Burden realized that he had said too much.

Mr. Law looked at him as if he expected him to continue. But Burden was not about to place on Wilson responsibility for a war that he had done rather more than not to stay out of. "If Germany had not been so stupid and provocative, we might still be at peace and the pound sterling . . ."

"Fallen into the dust," said Mr. Law.

"Your family's from Washington, aren't they?" Lucy diverted the conversation.

Burden nodded. "Part of them. The part that stayed on in the District while my branch went west. I lived for a time with relatives here, when we lost our farm in the panic." Comfortably, they sank into genealogy, which meant Burden's connection with the ubiquitous Apgar clan. Lucy, too, was connected to them by marriage, as was Caroline, as was everyone that was worthy from Albany to New York City to Washington, D.C. Burden stared into Lucy's beautiful eyes and felt a sudden pang, a need to be loved yet again by a girl, not necessarily one who was Catholic, complicated and, probably, virginal. But he must start again, soon. In three years, he would be fifty and at the end of anything remotely like youth. There was Caroline still, but that was known country. Also, with time, she had shown her true nature, which was that not of a wife or lover but of sister and friend. He valued her, but she was not what he now furiously craved, skin, flesh.

Franklin joined them, pale in the heat but supremely jaunty. "The Lock Tavern Club," he announced. "For a late lunch on the pier. With a sunset." As the large hand rested idly on Lucy's shoulder, Burden realized that the two were in love, and he was not.

4

Blaise was also at sea; alone, too, if not in the least furious. Frederika had proved to be the best of all possible wives. She was present when needed and otherwise engaged when not. She was also uncommonly shrewd about people and Blaise was not. From Connecticut Avenue, they presided over the grand life of the capital, their paths intersecting with that of the other Mrs. Sanford, Caroline, who generally chose to emulate the Henry Adams circle, now reduced to Adams himself and a handful of what he called "nieces."

"At least there is air to breathe." Blaise turned and saw Mrs. Wilson, in a fresh nautical sort of gown, looking much refreshed. The presidential party had gone aboard the *Mayflower* just before noon, when all the air had been burned away by a bronze disk of a sun. The President had been unusually subdued. Mrs. Wilson had been flushed and somewhat breathless, while a number of her relatives cooled themselves vigorously with palmetto fans and murmured to one another in their soft Southern accents. The *Mayflower* was headed toward Chesapeake Bay and, thanks to wartime censorship, no one in Washington suspected that the President, defeated by the heat, had temporarily abandoned the capital.

"Do sit, Mr. Sanford." Graciously, Edith indicated one of two chairs side by side on the stern. She took the other. "As far as I can tell this is about the only pleasure they allow the President, though I'd say this comes more under medical necessity than anything else. Not," she was quick to add, "that he isn't made of the purest iron. I do enjoy your sister."

"And she you." Blaise was equally quick at Washingtonese.

"We don't see enough of her or of you and Mrs. Sanford. She's in Newport?"

Blaise nodded. "I stay on to memorialize the government, and the war."

Edith chuckled, a pleasant low sound. "I must say, on the one hand, there is nothing worse for a president than to have Congress in session all summer, making trouble, but then when you think of this terrible heat and some of those terrible men and their wives, I rejoice that they are stuck here with us."

"Poor Cabot Lodge wanted so much to go to the North Shore, to be near Henry Adams at Beverly Farms . . ."

"Poor Cabot Lodge," Edith took up the refrain as if they were part-singing. Then she started a new verse. "Beverly Farms," and stopped. "Isn't that the house Mr. Adams built . . . ?"

"With Mrs. Adams back in the seventies. After she died, he never went back, until now."

"Of course it wasn't murder, was it?" Edith looked suddenly eager, like a child about to be told a favorite story.

But Blaise could not satisfy her. "She killed herself, as far as anyone knows. She drank that stuff you develop photographs with. He's never referred to her since, as far as I know. But then my sister is his great friend. He just tolerates me."

"He doesn't even know me." But Edith did not seem distressed. Astride the world, it is possible to overlook any and every slight. From the beginning Blaise had been amused at how wholeheartedly Edith had taken to her royal estate, sprouting ever more orchids as well as ever more gracious, kindly, regal airs.

"Washington is not a city but a dozen villages," observed Edith, as everyone who lived there sooner or later observed more than once. "And there are no connections between most of them."

"Except for Pennsylvania Avenue, which connects all the villages to the White House."

"That's what I always thought. But it really isn't true. We're very isolated, you know."

"The war . . ."

"Doesn't help. But I think of the presidents as sort of ceremonial prisoners. And *my* village, the Galts and the Bollings and all the rest, hardly ever notice who's in the White House. I must thank you, by the way, for your treatment of us, of the President. We don't get to read much about us that's pleasant nowadays."

"Perhaps," Blaise remembered to smile, "censorship has something to do with it."

"Mr. Creel is aboard. You told me you'd like to meet him. See? I never forget." The smile was, as always, girlish and beguiling. Blaise thanked her. George Creel had suddenly appeared on the national scene in the wake of a storm of legislation, mostly inspired by the President, to establish control over every aspect of American life. Censorship of the press came under Mr. Creel, who had, in April, been designated chairman of the Committee of Public

Information. Mr. Creel was a young journalist from the West. As a publisher, Blaise was extremely wary of how the various newly legislated powers of censorship might be used. In the first thrill of war and Hun-hatred, an Espionage Act had been passed, which made it possible to put in jail for twenty years, and to fine ten thousand dollars anyone who conveyed "false reports or false statements with intent to interfere with the operation or success of the military or naval forces of the United States or to promote the success of its enemies. . . . Or attempt to cause insubordination, disloyalty, mutiny or refusal of duty, in the military or naval forces of the United States, or . . . willfully obstructing recruiting or enlistment service."

When this splendid annulment of the First Amendment became law the previous month, on June 15, Blaise had received direct word from William Randolph Hearst in New York that the law was specifically directed against the two of them. "Do something," was the Chief's injunction to his former disciple.

Edith rose, as George Creel, a youthful forty-year-old, appeared, straw hat set on the back of his head. In the presence of the sovereign lady, the hat was removed. Edith made the introductions, then said, "I must help the President with Colonel House's latest reports. Oh, what a tangled web we weave . . ." she intoned, mysteriously, and vanished into the salon.

"Whose web?" asked Blaise, indicating for the younger man to sit. Blaise offered Creel a cigar, which he took.

"Colonel House. I suppose Mrs. Wilson thinks he's been given too much of a free hand in Europe." Creel put the straw hat back on. As this was news to Blaise, he affected boredom. "I've always thought he was just a message-bearer, a sort of courtier."

"She would agree with you about the courtier." Like so many energetic young men new to public life, George Creel could hold nothing back that might demonstrate in the most astounding way his own involvement in public affairs. "She thinks he says yes too often to the President."

"Doesn't everyone?"

"I try not to. Of course, I've only been in this job three months . . ."

"What *is* this job?"

Creel looked surprised. "Information. We try to give the good news about our side, and the bad news about the Huns. In a way, it's like advertising, though the President doesn't care for the word."

Blaise nodded. Creel was now coming into focus. Blaise had expected a bumptious Midwestern journalist; instead, he was faced with a bumptious advertising man, a thinker in slogans, a perfect man for Hearst if not Blaise. "Who decided to abandon press conferences altogether?"

Creel looked away. "Well," he said – lying? – "I saw no point to them in war-time. I mean, yes, our troops are now in France and, yes, they'll fight when they're ready, but what's the point in *not* answering that question every time you meet the press? After all, he can't talk about the military situation, and he won't talk partisan politics, so why see the press at all? Except someone like you, sir, in a private way."

"You have the power to shut down a newspaper or arrest an editor who might simply disapprove of the way the war's being run . . ."

"That," said Creel cautiously, "is the purpose of the law that Congress passed and the President must execute."

"Could this mean the suspension of free speech?"

"In cases where national security so requires, yes. But I'm not the Czar." Creel laughed without much joy. "I must work with the secretaries of State, War and Navy. Well, Mr. Lansing has already said that he doesn't trust me because I'm a Socialist! So after one meeting with him, I gave up on the State Department. Now I work only with War and Navy. You know, I've already talked to your sister, Mrs. Sanford."

"I didn't know."

"Senator Day arranged it. I told her that it would be a great thing if she were to serve *ex officio* on my committee."

"And do what?" Blaise was not surprised that Caroline had told him nothing, since that was her way, but he was surprised that the country's official censor and propagandist should be interested in her.

"I think the ladies can make all the difference. Look at the Liberty Loans. Mr. McAdoo's going to get his two billion dollars, thanks to the way he's been using movie people like Mary Pickford and Charlie Chaplin to sell the bonds, and important ladies all around the country to organize the sales, showing that women – at least those women – really believe in our democracy."

"Which the suffragettes don't?"

"I'll say!" Creel blew a huge smoke ring at the Maryland shore. "They undermine the picture I want to paint of us as the first democracy in the world, fighting for other democracies everywhere."

"But it's not easy for us to claim to be a democracy if women can't vote." Blaise was serenely hypocritical. He liked neither votes for women nor democracy.

"So," Creel beamed, "thank God for Mary Pickford! I've asked Mrs. Sanford to go west. To Hollywood. To influence the motion-picture business. I work pretty well with Pathé News. Fact, with all the news-reel companies. But most of those companies are in the East. Problem is, I've got no one out there where just about all the photo-plays are being made. So Mrs. Sanford said that she might go out and see what she could do for the cause."

The ancient competitiveness between half-brother and half-sister now reasserted itself. "What can she do when she doesn't know any of the movie people?"

"But they all know her. They know the *Trib*. That's what matters. Besides, she did meet Mary Pickford the same time I did in New York at that Liberty Bond rally where the stars raised a million dollars in – what was it? – an hour."

"So she will organize bond rallies . . ."

"No, sir. She will persuade – as my representative – Hollywood to make pro-American, pro-Allies photo-plays . . ."

"Which means anti-German . . ."

"Yes!" Creel's eyes shone. "The audience for the movies is the largest there is for anything in the world. So if we can influence what Hollywood produces, we can control world opinion. Hollywood is the key to just about everything."

*

The lunch with the President was something of an anticlimax after Creel's revelations. A half-dozen of Edith's relatives, all named Bolling, and several naval aides took their seats in no especial order, while the President presided at one end of the table and Edith at the other. "You sit here," she had said to Blaise.

The President now seemed in better health and spirits than Blaise had seen him for some time. "I think *any* place is better to be than Washington," Wilson observed, then the sudden surprisingly attractive smile. "The only real pleasure for me is knowing that Congress will be in session straight through the summer." He looked at Blaise. "And without, thanks to Senator Day, Section 23 to harass me with."

"We'll have wine," Edith said in a low voice to the steward.

"But no one is to tell Mr. Daniels." Wilson's hearing was acute. "Actually, Mr. Daniels is turning into quite a sea-dog." Wilson's long nose twitched, a premonitory sign of amusement. "Not long ago he was seated one evening aboard a battleship, talking to the admiral, when the officer of the day came to make his report to his superior. The officer stood at attention and said the usual – 'I wish to report, sir, that all is secure.' So the admiral turned to his superior, the Secretary of the Navy, Mr. Daniels, who simply stared at him until, finally, he realized that he was supposed to say something. So Mr. Daniels gave a great smile and said, 'Well, I declare!'" Wilson mimicked perfectly Daniels's deep Southern accent. "'That's just fine! I'm mighty glad to hear it. Mighty glad.'" The laughter was genuine. Blaise, who had been several times to the theater with the President, was quite aware of the great man's incongruous skill as a vaudevillian, mimic and not inexpert tap-dancer. One evening, while courting Edith, he had been seen tap-dancing across Pennsylvania Avenue, singing "Oh, You Beautiful Doll."

The great big beautiful doll herself helped herself to lobster, and said, "You know, as a boy, Mr. Wilson always wanted to go to Annapolis. He has a real affinity for the sea, which I don't. When we were in rough water last year, off Long Island, I was so ill that I took down a bottle of brandy from the cupboard just as the boat hit a wave and I fell to the floor – or deck, as we're supposed to call it. Mr. Grayson found me, on my back, green of face, a brandy bottle clutched to my bosom."

"A rare sight," said Blaise, who had taken a liking to both Wilsons, to his own surprise as he was a Republican who would have preferred Elihu Root as president, over-qualified for the post as that brilliant man was. But Wilson was agreeably intelligent; and his first term had been remarkably successful. Now, like the world, he was on an uncharted sea.

"Is it true that Senator Lodge has said that Mr. Wilson is the second-worst president, after Buchanan?"

"He's never said it to me." Blaise was tactful. Lodge's intemperate tongue had caused Henry Adams, at his own table, to shout, "Cabot, I will not allow treason to be spoken in my house."

"If he did," Edith was bland, "I shall begin to study the Administration of Mr. Buchanan, who must have had all sorts of virtues if Senator Lodge really hates him all that much."

Blaise noted, yet again, that the President never mentioned politics at meal-time; also noted that a naval physician, an aide to Grayson, never took his eyes off Wilson, whose chronic dyspepsia had once threatened to make him an invalid.

At Edith's end of the table, with a brother to her left and Blaise to her right, she could indulge herself while the President told Pat-and-Mike Irishman stories, to the delight of George Creel.

"It's sad about Colonel Roosevelt, who should be friendly, since he and Mr. Wilson have so much in common . . ."

"Including the job."

". . . *and* a war. Though this one is going to be far more terrible than that little one with Spain ever was. But they always seem to misunderstand each other."

"They are rivals. That's all," said Blaise. Then he fished. "The Colonel's pretty certain to be the Republican candidate in '20 against Mr. Wilson, I suppose."

"Do you *really* think Mr. Wilson will run again?" Edith's small dark eyes were suddenly mischievous. Did she know? Blaise wondered. Did Wilson know, for that matter.

"Why not? He'll have won the war."

"But General Pershing will get the credit, and the people always elect generals, if they get a chance. But never admirals. I wonder why."

"They might make an exception for Josephus Daniels."

Edith laughed. Blaise let her off his inquisitorial hook. Certainly, the President looked fit enough for a third term, and vain enough too. For all Wilson's charm and good manners, he was still an odd combination of college professor unused to being contradicted in a world that he took to be his classroom and of Presbyterian pastor unable to question that divine truth which inspired him at all times.

After lunch, the President decided that he would like to take a walk, and the captain docked at a small island in Chesapeake Bay, with the exotic name Tangier. Blaise and Creel each escorted a Bolling lady ashore.

The town itself proved to be two parallel streets with freshly painted wooden houses like so many white building blocks set side by side. At the back of each there was a garden and at the front rather grimly, a family cemetery.

There was no one in sight as the Wilsons led the way down the first street, their Secret Service man nervously looking to left and right: were they walking into an ambush? Even Blaise began to feel edgy, while Creel came right out with it. "There's something wrong here. The paint's fresh on that house there – someone's still painting it, but there's nobody in sight."

"Spies?" Blaise could not resist.

"Or worse." Creel was grim.

One of the Bolling ladies said, "Well, this *is* a fishing village. So I expect everyone's out fishing."

"Wives, too?" Creel started as a cat – brown – crossed his path.

"The cats have stayed." Blaise looked at the President, who stood, puzzled, in the middle of the street.

"No cars, no buggies," Creel began.

"Not allowed," said the ship's captain, who had joined them. "That's the charm of the place. Though where everybody is is a mystery to me."

Blaise moved to the head of the presidential procession, joining Mr. Starling of the Secret Service.

"There's somebody at last," said Edith behind them. "On the curb there, the old man with the child."

In the shadow of a willow tree, an elderly man was seated, holding a small boy on his lap. "Good afternoon, sir," said Edith.

"Lovely day," said the President, and, hand in hand, they moved across the street toward the old man.

With genial suspicion, Starling said, "Hi, Grandpa."

"Say, mister," the old man was equally suspicious and by no means genial, "who's that man over there with his woman?"

"Why, that's Mr. Wilson. The President of the United States."

"This ain't a plot like last time?"

"Last time? A plot . . . ?"

"That's really him, the President?"

"You're squeezing me," wailed the child. At which the old man dropped the boy in the dust and stood up. "We thought you was the Germans, coming to take Tangier the way the English did back in 1812. Come out!" he yelled. And the street began to fill with the good people of Tangier.

"Tangerines, I guess we have to call them," said Creel, journalistically stirred by so much human interest.

Blaise suddenly remembered Creel's name from long ago. "You worked for the Chief, at the *Journal* in New York."

"That's right. I wondered if you'd remember me. Then I turned honest and went on to Kansas and from there to the *Rocky Mountain News*. But I am, forever, school of Hearst."

"So am I," said Blaise. "It leaves a mark."

Then they gathered about the President, who saw fit to address not only his island constituents but the yachting party as well. "Tangier is the logical place from which to invest Baltimore by sea. So the British fleet arrived here a hundred and five years ago, and took the island. But the local parson, one Joshua Thomas, told them that they would fail to take Baltimore because the Lord of hosts was not with them, and, as it turned out, he was not with them then, and I promise you," the conversational voice of Woodrow Wilson had now become the magical voice of the great seducer of the imagination, the evoker of the higher spirit, the very essence of the virtuous republic that he had been chosen to

106

personify, "that the Lord of hosts is not with the Germans now, and never will be as long as we are true to that great covenant we made with the spirit of all mankind when we made ourselves independent of the old world with its intrigues and inequalities, and all of us as one, *e pluribus unum,* embraced a freedom for all that was truly something new under the sun."

It was like a tap, thought Blaise, which these orators could turn on and off at will. Did they, he wondered, actually listen to themselves? Or were they simply conduits for a kind of mass energy to which they were attached in some mysterious popular way, able to articulate instinctively the emotions of the mute and the many? "That," said Woodrow Wilson, turning off the tap, "is enough sermon for any Sunday afternoon in Tangier."

The President was enthusiastically cheered.

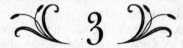

3

1

Caroline lay tied to the railroad track, the hot sun in her face while in her ears the ominous sound of an approaching steam engine. A high male voice called out, "Look frightened."

"I am frightened."

"Don't talk. Look more to the left."

"But, Chief, she's got too much shadow on her face. You can't see the eyes."

"Look straight ahead." The slow-moving steam engine was now within a yard of her. She could see it out of the corner of her right eye. The engineer stared down at her, hand on – what? – the brake she prayed. A stone pressed into her back, just below the left shoulder blade. She wanted to scream.

"Scream!" shouted William Randolph Hearst; and Caroline obliged. As she filled the air with terrified exhalation, a man on horseback rode up to the railroad engine and leapt into the engine room, where he pulled a cord, releasing a quantity of ill-smelling steam from the engine's smoke-stack. As the train ground to a halt, he ran toward Caroline and knelt beside her.

"Cut!" said the Chief. "Stay right where you are, Mrs. Sanford."

"I have no choice," said Caroline. The sweaty young man – a cowboy belonging to Hearst's ranch – smiled down at her reassuringly. "It won't take a minute, ma'am," he said. "He's got to change the camera so he can get a real close look at me untying you."

"Why doesn't he just show a card on the screen, with the information that two weeks after Lady Belinda's eleventh-hour rescue she was home again in London, pouring tea. I think I can do that rather well."

Hearst was now standing over her, his vast bulk mercifully blocking the sun. "That was swell. Really," he said. "Joe's rolling up the camera now. It won't take a minute. I never knew you were such a pro."

"Neither," said Caroline, "did I."

"Actually, there's nothing easier than movies," said Millicent Hearst, whom Caroline had known since she was the younger partner of a vaudeville sister act. "Either you look nice on the screen or you don't. If you do, they'll love you. If you don't you can act your butt off and nothing's going to happen."

"You're certainly very effective on the screen." Caroline spoke brightly, still flat on her back, with the dusty cowboy to one side of her while, to the other, Mr. and Mrs. Hearst gazed down on her, observing the social amenities with a flow of good talk.

"Actually if Millicent weren't so old, I could make a star out of her." Hearst was his usual kindly, tactless self.

"I'm not all that much older than Mary Pickford." Millicent's voice had never ceased to be Hell's Kitchen New York Irish. "But it's a mug's game, acting, and the hours they keep here in the movies you wouldn't believe."

"But I do. In fact, one of those hours has passed," said Caroline, "since I was tied up."

"We're ready," said Joe Hubbell, the cameraman, just out of Caroline's range.

"All right. Let's get started." The Hearsts withdrew. The cowboy and Caroline waited, patiently, to be told what to do. As they did, Caroline admired, yet again, Hearst's instinct, which had now drawn him to the most exciting of all the games that their country had yet devised. As he had invented "yellow journalism," which obliged reality to mirror not itself but Hearst's version of it, now he had plunged into movie-making, both amateur like this film and professional like the Hearst-produced *The Perils of Pauline,* the most successful serial of 1913. Now in summer residence at San Simeon, a quarter-million-acre ranch to the north of Hollywood, the Chief was amusing himself with a feature-length film in which he had gallantly starred his houseguest, Caroline, who was several years older than Millicent, and by no means as conventionally pretty. Once Caroline had accepted George Creel's assignment to be the Administration's emissary to the moving-picture business, she had started her embassy by paying a call on her old friend Hearst, who disapproved of the war in general and Wilson in particular. Nevertheless, he was most lavishly a host not to mention meticulously a director.

An hour later, Caroline, no longer Lady Belinda, was freed from her track by the cowboy, whom she was directed to kiss full on the lips. He had blushed furiously, and she had been intrigued to find how soft a young man's lips could be, not that she had had much experience with young men or, for that matter, old, she also noted that he smelled, powerfully, of sweating horse.

Caroline and her maid, Héloise, shared a tent close to the wooden house of the Hearsts atop Camp Hill. Since there were always a dozen houseguests as well as an army of servants, gardeners, ranchhands, the hill was now a city of temporary tents, surrounding the elaborate wooden house, which was taken down in winter and put up in summer.

"And here, right here," said Hearst, "I'm going to build a castle, just like the one you and Blaise have at Saint-Cloud-le-Duc."

They were seated in the Chief's principal sitting room, with its rough-hewn beams and unfinished pine walls on which were hung perhaps the largest collection of false old masters that any American millionaire had ever accumulated. But then it was always said of Hearst that after thirty years of the wholesale buying of art, he could always tell a good fake from a bad one; and of the world's forgeries, he chose, invariably, the ones with the most accurate brushwork. "He has," the art merchant Duveen was supposed to have said, "an excellent cocked-eye."

While Caroline drank sherry, Hearst stood over a round table on which was placed what looked to be a wedding cake covered with velvet. Like a matador, he removed the covering to reveal the model of a castle with two towers, all meticulously detailed in plaster. "This is it," he said. "What I'm going to build up here."

"It is," Caroline was guarded, "like nothing else."

"Nothing else in California, anyway. Can't wait to get started." Hearst's major-domo of twenty years, George Thompson, was now as round as an owl and as rosy as a piglet; for more than twenty years he had appeared at the same hour with Coca-Cola in a silver-embossed mug for the Chief; and now sherry for Caroline. "Good evening, Mrs. Sanford." She smiled upon him. After all, it was George who encouraged the Chief to traffic with fashionables like herself in addition to the Chief's own preference, politicians and theater folk, while the friendly Millicent tended to keep her distance from her husband's friends. She preferred New York to California; motherhood to glamour; respectability to Hearstian fame; and Roman Catholic strictness to Protestant easiness. She was said to be quite aware that she had been superseded in the Chief's affections by a showgirl, who was either twenty years old or seventeen; if the latter, she was the same age that Millicent had been when she and her sister had danced their way off the stage of the Herald Square Theater, where they had been two of the many maidens in *The Girl from Paris,* and into Hearst's great heart. Now history was repeating itself with Miss Marion Davies, the daughter of a Brooklyn politician named Bernard Douras. Blaise had approved the *Tribune* story of the romance, which Caroline had read with delight and promptly spiked as a Matter of Taste, all important for the *Tribune* as the war-time President's favorite Washington newspaper now that Ned McLean's *Post* was known as "the court circular." Actually, the vaudeville-loving President would probably have enjoyed very much the highly suggestive but never absolutely libellous story of the young showgirl for whom the fifty-year-old Hearst had, if not forsaken his wife, abandoned her to the rigors of respectable domesticity while he squired, without cigarettes, alcohol or bad language, his chorus girl through the only slightly subdued night life of wartime New York. Miss Davies had left her convent – always a convent, Blaise had decreed – when a mere girl to join the chorus of *Chu Chin Chow, Oh, Boy!* and now her apotheosis in the *Ziegfeld Follies of 1917.* There were whispers at San Simeon that when the Missis left, the Miss would arrive. But Hearst was silent on all personal matters; and Millicent seemed unperturbed.

"So George Creel wants you to organize the movie business." Hearst sat in a throne opposite Caroline while George lit the kerosene lamps. The electricity at San Simeon was home-made and unreliable. "Stories about Huns raping Belgian nuns?"

"Surely your papers have told us all that we want to hear on that subject." Caroline was smooth, relaxed by sherry. "I thought, perhaps, Huns raped by Belgian nuns, to encourage women to resist the beast."

"I always said," Hearst did not even smile, "that *you* were the newspaperman, not Blaise."

"Well, I did buy the *Tribune,* and I made it popular by copying faithfully your *Journal.*"

"No. You've got a better paper. Better town, too. Particularly now. I'm thinking. . . . You know, Creel worked for me on the *Journal.* Ambitious. Movies." Hearst stared at a Mantegna whose wooden frame sported wormholes only down one side; thanks to Hearst's usual haste, there had been no time for the forger to drill holes in the rest of the frame. "I think movies are the answer."

"To what?"

"The world." Hearst's glaring eagle eyes were fixed on Caroline and the hair that had been blond when they first met was now gray. "I always thought it was going to be the press. So simple to print. So simple to transmit with telegraph. But there's the language problem. By the time Jamie Bennett's stolen all our stories for his Paris *Herald,* the news is old hat. The beauty of the movies is they don't talk. Just a few cards in different languages to tell you what the plot is, what they're saying. Everyone in China watches my *Perils of Pauline,* but they can't read any of my papers there."

"You're going in?"

Hearst nodded. "I do this for fun, what we did today. Though if it looks okay, I'll distribute it. I've got my own company. You don't mind?"

"I'd be thrilled, of course." Of all professions that Caroline had ever daydreamed of for herself that of actress had not been one. As a girl, she had been taken by her father back-stage to see Sarah Bernhardt; and the sweat, the dirt, the terror had impressed itself upon her in a way that the splendor of what the public saw from the front of the stage had not. As for movie-acting, Millicent, an old showgirl, had grasped it all. Either the camera favored you or it did not. At forty, Caroline assumed that she would look just that; after all, there were, officially at least, no leading ladies of forty. She herself was interested only in the business end of the movies; she had also been commissioned to investigate the propaganda possibilities of this unexpected popular novelty. It had not been until such movie favorites as Charlie Chaplin and Douglas Fairbanks had taken to the market-place and sold Liberty Bonds to millions of their fans that the government had realized how potent were the inventors of Hollywood; and Creel had agreed.

But Hearst, as usual, was idiosyncratic. "Distribution companies, theater chains, those are what matter. The rest is a bit like the theater, a gamble. Except you almost can't lose money on a film unless somebody like the director – what's his name – the two girls, the initials?"

"D. W. Griffith." Caroline knew all the names from her own paper.

"Decides he wants to make the biggest movie in the world by spending the most money, building things like all of Babylon. I hear he's broke. And Triangle wants to sell out. I've made a bid. But Zukor and Lasky have got more cash than I do – in hand, that is. This business is like a cornucopia, like Alaska in '49. A million dollars just for Mary Pickford. Incredible. Only danger is these Griffith types. Stage-door johnnies who start to think big once you give them a camera to play with. Though," the thin lips widened into a smile, "it is the best fun there is, making a movie. Sort of like a printer's block, the way you can keep rearranging all the pieces. But without a paper's deadline. You can keep at it until you get all the pieces in the right order. They call that part – just like we do – editing. Then it just doesn't lie there dead on the page, it moves."

"Let's sell our papers and go to Southern California." Caroline was always easily fired by Hearst.

"If I were younger I would. But," Hearst frowned, "there's New York."

"That's right. Didn't we endorse you for mayor, this fall?"

Hearst's face was blank. "The *Tribune*, on orders from Wilson I expect, has told me to tend to my papers, and support the incumbent, the hopeless John Purroy Mitchel."

Caroline was all mock wide-eyed innocence. "That must be our new editorial writer . . ."

"*That* was my old friend Blaise. You must've missed the issue. Anyway, I've got Murphy. I've got Tammany. So if I win . . ."

"You'll be the Democratic candidate for president in 1920."

"And the president in 1921, when I take the oath of office. It's about time, don't you think?"

Caroline had never understood Hearst's ambition other than to suspect that there was, simply, nothing more to it than sheer energy. "I have never known an election when there were so many candidates so early, and so – so unashamed."

"Nothing to be ashamed of." He rinsed his teeth noisily in Coca-Cola. "The people don't like third terms. They also don't like Wilson. Roosevelt's a wreck and a spoiler and the people are tired of him. McAdoo . . ." He paused.

"James Burden Day?" Loyally, Caroline said the name, which did not interest Hearst. "Champ Clark?" The Speaker of the House was the leading Bryanite; and already at work. "And those are just the Democrats."

"The Republicans will nominate Roosevelt, who's done for, or Leonard Wood, who I can do in any day of the week. He's a general," Hearst added with disdain.

"So is Pershing, and when we win . . ."

"There won't be a general on any ballot. Remember what I say. This war's too big. The ordinary man hates officers, West Pointers particularly. Every man who's gone through training will want to get back at the men who gave him such a hard time."

"Why wasn't this true in the other wars?"

"Well, it was true in my little war against Spain. I don't count Roosevelt, who was already a politician when he rode up that hill with my best reporters covering him. The true war candidate – back then – should've been Dewey. Dewey of Manila. Dewey the conquering hero. So what happened? Nothing."

"He was stupid."

"That's usually no drawback. Anyway, *this* time something called selective service is going to crowd the military out. These boys aren't volunteers for this war. They're being taken captive to go fight alongside people they hate, like the English, or against their own people."

"Your Irish and German supporters?"

"You bet. Or if they're just ordinary buckwheat Americans they won't know where they are once they're in Europe, or why they're supposed to be mad at something called the Kaiser. That means when they get back, if they get back, they're going to blame Wilson and their officers for the whole mess. You know, you ought to put some flags on your front page. There's this new color process. Good red. Pretty good blue. Looks nice and cheery. Patriotic. People like it."

Caroline had always regarded Hearst as a mindless genius; or an idiot savant; or something simply not calculable by the ordinary criteria of intelligence. Yet there was no getting round the preciseness and practicality of his instincts, including his occasional odd forays into socialism. Recently he had convinced Tammany Hall of the necessity of municipal ownership of public utilities. If such a thing were to come to pass and if Hearst were to become president, the entire Senate, at his inauguration, would converge upon him and strike him down, like Caesar, in the name of those sacred trusts that had paid for their togas.

Twenty sat down to dinner in a long timbered room hung with Aubusson tapestries. On the table huge crystal girandoles alternated with bottles of tomato ketchup and Worcestershire sauce. Caroline sat on the Chief's right in deference to her high place as a fellow publisher. Seated on Caroline's right, at her request, was Timothy X. Farrell, the successful director of ten – or was it twenty – photoplays in the last two years. Farrell had come to see Hearst on secret business, which Caroline had quickly discovered involved a screen career for Marion Davies and a new production company for Hearst, who had also just acquired, he told Caroline, casually, the Pathé Company from its war-beleaguered French owners.

Farrell was thin and dark and nearer thirty than forty; spoke with a Boston Irish brogue; had been to Holy Cross when he had got the call to make movies at Flushing, New York. He had moved on to Santa Monica, California, where he had worked as a carpenter and general handyman for Thomas Ince. Now he was a successful director, noted for his use of light. Caroline was in a new world of jargon, not unlike – but then again not very like – journalism. Farrell was touchingly eager to make films celebrating the United States, freedom, democracy, while attacking, of course, the bestial Hun, monarchy and the latest horror, Bolshevism, now emerging from the ruins of czarist Russia and connected closely, Creel maintained, with various American labor unions, particularly those that sought to reduce the work day from twelve to eight hours.

"What we need is a story," said Farrell. "You can't just start shooting away, like the Chief. He's old-fashioned. He thinks *Perils of Pauline is* the latest in the movies. But it isn't. That serial's four years old. Four years is like a century in the movies. Everything's different now. The audience won't pay their dollars – or even nickels – to see just anything that moves on a sheet. But they'll pay as much as two dollars for a real story, and a real spectacle. Griffith changed everything."

"You, too," Caroline remembered to flatter. A film director was no different from a senator.

"Well, I got lucky last year. *Missy Drugget* had the biggest gross of any film for the year, in the States." Farrell frowned. "That's another problem with this war. Our overseas distributors – crooks all of them to begin with, but now there's a war they can really cheat us, and they do. Goldstein was going to do something about it. But now I guess he's going to jail."

"Who's Goldstein, and why jail?"

"*Spirit of '76.* Remember? About the American Revolution? Came out just before April, before we were in the war. Well, your friends in Washington thought," there seemed to be no sarcasm in Farrell's naturally urgent voice, "that any mention of our own revolution was an insult to our ally, England. You know it might confuse our simple folks to be told how we once had this war with England so that we could be a free country. Anyway, under one of the new laws, the government went and indicted Bob Goldstein,

116

the producer, and they say he's going to get ten years in prison."

"Just for making a movie about how we became a free country?"

Farrell seemed without irony, but his voice was hard. "Free to put anyone – everyone – in jail. Yes."

"Why hasn't the press taken this up?"

"Ask Mr. Hearst. Ask yourself." The eyes were arctic blue with black lashes and brows.

"What is the exact charge against Goldstein?"

"I don't know. But it's all covered by the . . . what's its name? Espionage Act, which didn't even exist when we made the picture."

"Your picture, too?"

Farrell flushed. "Yes. Me, too. I did the lighting and camera work as a favor. But they don't go after the small fry. Now, I'm working with Triangle. They're the group that Mr. Ince did *Civilization* with. He's a friend of Mr. Hearst, which is how I happen to be here, I guess."

"Will Mr. Ince be arrested, too?" Caroline remembered that Ince's *Civilization* had been a pacifist film. Since Hearst not only had been against the war but was considered pro-German, Caroline suspected a connection between the anti-war films of some of the best movie-makers and Hearst himself. In fact, Hearst had been so anti-Allies that the British and French governments had denied his newspapers the use of their international cables. In a fit of over-excitement, Canada had banned all of Hearst's newspapers and should a Canadian be caught reading so much as the Katzenjammer Kids comic pages, he could be imprisoned for five years.

"I doubt it. He has connections. He knows the President. But I'll bet he wishes he'd stuck to 'westerns.'"

After dinner, Hearst led them into a tent that served as a theater; and here he showed them a western of his own making, *Romance of the Rancho.* The hero was Hearst, looking rather bulkier than his giant horse; the heroine was Millicent, who sat next to Caroline during the performance, complaining bitterly about her appearance. "I look like a Pekingese. It's awful, seeing yourself like this."

"I wouldn't know," said Caroline, who was attracted to the idea of film not as an art or as light or as whatever one wanted to call so collective and vulgar a storytelling form but as a means of preserving time, netting the ephemeral and the fugitive – there it is! now, it's past, gone forever. Millicent, *now*, was seated beside her, face illuminated by the flickering light upon the screen while, on the screen, one saw Millicent *then*, weeks ago – whenever, unchanging and unchangeable forever.

As applause for *Romance of the Rancho* ended, Hearst stood up and gave a mock bow, and said, "I wrote the title cards, too. Couldn't be easier. Just like picture captions." He looked at Caroline. "Now we'll see something that's still in the works. A super western epic." The lights went out. A beam of light from the projector was aimed at the screen, which suddenly filled with a picture of Hearst's train-of-all-work coming to a halt. Caroline recognized the sweaty cowboy with whom she had worked that day. Obviously he was much used in Hearst's home movies. She was struck at how startlingly handsome his somewhat – in life – square, crude face became on the screen. She noted, too, that his eyebrows grew together in a straight line, like those of an archaic Minoan athlete.

There was a murmur in the tent as a slender woman got off the train. She was received by the cowboy, hat in hand. A porter then gave him her suitcase. The camera was now very close on the woman's face: a widow's peak and a cleft chin emphasized the symmetry of her face, high cheekbones made flattering shadows below large eyes. Slowly, the woman smiled. There was a sigh from the audience.

"Jesus Christ," murmured Millicent, now all Hell's Kitchen Irish, "ain't you the looker!"

"I don't believe it." And Caroline did not. A title card said, "Welcome to Dodge City, Lady Belinda."

Then the cowboy and Lady Belinda walked toward a waiting buggy; and Caroline stared at herself, mesmerized. But this was no longer herself. This was herself of two weeks ago; hence, two weeks younger than she now was. Yet here she was, aged forty, forever, and she scrutinized the screen for lines and found them only at the edge of the eyes – mascara could hide the worst, she thought automatically. Then as she smiled what she always took to be her most transparently insincere smile of greeting, usually produced in honor of a foreign dignitary or the president of the moment, she noted that Lady Belinda – she regarded the woman on the screen as an entirely third person – looked ravishing and ravished, and the only lines discernible in the bright sunlight were two delicate brackets at the corners of her mouth. For twenty minutes the incomplete film ran.

When the lights came on, Caroline was given a standing ovation, led by Hearst. "We've got a brand-new star," he said, sounding exactly like a Hearst story from the entertainment page of the *Journal,* where a different chorus girl, at least a half-dozen times a year, went on stage in the place of a stricken star, and always triumphed and became the Toast of the Town.

Arthur Brisbane, Hearst's principal editor, shook Caroline's hand gravely. "Even without blue eyes, you hold the screen." Brisbane was notorious for his theory that all great men and presumably women, too, were blue-eyed.

"Perhaps my eyes will fade to blue in the sun." Caroline gave him her ravishing smile; and felt like someone possessed. She was two people. One who existed up there on the screen, a figure from the past but now and forever immutable, while the other stood in the center of a stuffy tent, rapidly aging with each finite heartbeat entirely in the present tense, as she accepted congratulations.

"It's a pity you aren't younger," said the merciless Millicent. "You could really do something in pictures."

"Lucky that I don't want to, and so I can enjoy my middle age."

The cameraman, Joe Hubbell, came up to her. "It was really my idea, sticking the film together like this. So you could see it."

Hearst nodded. "We've Joe to thank. I never look through the camera lens and I don't see rushes. So when Joe kept telling me that Mrs. Sanford is really something, I thought he was just being nice to the guests."

"He was," said Caroline. "He is." She was thoroughly bemused and alarmed, like one of those savages who believe that a photograph can steal away the soul.

After most of the guests had retired to their tents, Caroline and a chosen few went back to Hearst's wooden house, where George poured Coca-Cola, and Caroline talked to Farrell about the uses of film for propaganda purposes. "I don't think you – or Mr. Creel – will have to do much arm-twisting. Everybody in Hollywood does the same thing anyway, particularly now we're in the war, and you can go to jail if you criticize England or France or . . ."

"Our government. In order to make the world safe for democracy," Caroline parodied herself as an editorial writer, "we must extinguish freedom at home."

"That's about it." Farrell gave her a sharp look. "Personally, I don't see much choice between the Hun and the Espionage Act."

"You are Irish, and hate England, and wish we had stayed out." Caroline was direct.

"Yes. But since I don't want to join Bob Goldstein in the clink, I shall make patriotic films about gallant Tommies, and ever-cheerful doughboys or hayseeds or whatever we'll call our boys."

Caroline stared at Hearst across the room. He was in deep conversation with a number of editors from various Hearst newspapers; or rather the editors, led by Brisbane, were deeply conversing while their Chief listened enigmatically. For the first time in her life, Caroline was conscious of true danger. Something was shifting in this, to her, free and easy-going – too easy-going in some ways – republic. Although she and Blaise had contributed to the war spirit – the *Tribune* was the first for going to war on the Allied side – she had not thought through the consequences of what she had helped set in motion. She had learned from Hearst that truth was only one criterion by which a story could be judged, but at the same time she had taken it for granted that when her *Tribune* had played up the real or fictitious atrocities of the Germans, Hearst's many newspapers had been dispensing equally pro-German sentiments. Each was a creator of "facts" for the purpose of selling newspapers; each, also, had the odd bee in bonnet that could only be satisfied by an appearance in print. But now Hearst's bee was stilled. The great democracy had decreed that one could only have a single view of a most complex war; otherwise, the prison was there to receive those who chose not to conform to the government's line, which, in turn, reflected a spasm of national hysteria that she and the other publishers had so opportunistically created, with more than usual assistance from home-grown political demagogues and foreign-paid propagandists. Now the Administration had invited Caroline herself to bully the movie business into creating ever more simplistic rationales of what she had come, privately, despite her French bias, to think of as the pointless war. Nevertheless, she was astonished that someone had actually gone to prison for making a film. Where was the much-worshipped Constitution in all of this? Or was it never anything more than a document to be used by the country's rulers when it suited them and otherwise ignored? "Will your friend Mr. Goldstein go to the Supreme Court?"

"I don't think he has the money. Anyway, it's war-time so there's no freedom of speech, not that there ever has been much."

"You are too severe." Caroline rallied to what was, after all, her native land. "One can – or could – say – or write – almost anything."

"You remember that picture with Nazimova? *War Brides?* In 1916?"

"That was an exception." In 1916 a modernized version of *Lysistrata* had so enraged the pro-war lobby that it had been withdrawn.

"That was peace-time."

"Well, no one went to jail." Caroline's response was weak. How oddly, how gradually, things had gone wrong.

"It'll be interesting if they get Mr. Hearst."

"They've tried before. Remember when Colonel Roosevelt held him responsible for President McKinley's murder?"

"That was just peace-time politics. But now they can lock him up if he doesn't praise England and hit the Germans . . ."

"And the Irish?" Caroline had got Farrell's range. "For not coming to England's aid?"

"Well . . ." Farrell accepted Coca-Cola from George. "Your friend Mr. Creel's moving fast. I've been invited to join the moving-picture division of his committee, to work with the Army Signal Corps, to glorify our warriors."

"But they haven't done anything yet. Of course, when they do . . ."

"We'll be ready. You're very beautiful, you know." As no one had said such a thing to Caroline since she was nine years old, she had taken it for granted that whatever beauty she might ever have had was, literally, unremarkable and so unremarked.

"I think that you think," she was precise in her ecstasy, "that my picture projected a dozen times life-size on a bedsheet is beautiful, which is not the same thing as me."

"No. It's you, all right. I'm sorry. I have no manners." He laughed, then coughed. "My father kept a bar in Boston. In the South End."

"Your manners are very agreeable. It's your taste I question. But without zeal, as the French say. At my age, I can endure quite a few compliments without losing my head."

Caroline allowed Mr. Farrell to escort her to her tent, where, in the moonlight, to the howls of appreciative coyotes, a man not her lover kissed her. She noted that his lips were far less soft and alluring than those of the Minoan cowboy.

"Women are not destined to have everything," she observed to Héloise, who helped her undress. "Or, perhaps, anything." But this sounded too neat; as well as wrong. "I mean, anything that we really want."

2

For Jess Smith, Christmas meant the main street of Washington Court House, with the electrified Christmas tree in the front yard of the county courthouse and enough snow and ice to keep the town's doctors busy setting bones and pouring plaster-of-paris. Also, it made him feel glad to see the business his emporium was doing. For some reason, the war was stimulating people to buy up everything in sight; and as he stood near the main entrance, just across from the cashier with her high black money-register, he inhaled the fragrant odor of Christmas holiday money, a heady combination of damp wool and rubber galoshes. Automatically, he greeted half the customers with his usual "Whaddaya know?"

Jess greeted Roxy with the same phrase as she came down the stairs from her mother's flat. Roxy had doubted the propriety of living in her former husband's store, but Jess would not hear of her moving out. "You're my best friend," he'd say. "After Harry Daugherty," she'd say.

Roxy gave his plump cheek a sisterly kiss and together they went out into the cold evening. Roxy still dreamed of going to Hollywood and becoming a movie star. But until she got around to making the trip, she saw every photo-play that came to town. Currently, at the Strand, Geraldine Farrar was playing in *Joan the Woman*. Roxy loved historical movies in general and the over-weight Farrar, an opera singer, of all things, in particular. As there were no gangster movies available, Jess had agreed to go with Roxy after a simple supper at the Blue Owl Grill. With luck, there might be a good serial with the feature, which was already a year old and only re-released because of the war.

"It's about Joan of Arc," Roxy explained as they crept down the icy street, half-blinded by the lights of automobiles, come to town for last-minute shopping.

"I don't recollect the name." But Jess knew every name in town; and he greeted passersby cheerily.

"You should have some interests outside politics." Roxy nearly fell, which Jess took to be fate's swift punishment for suggesting that his life was anything but idyllic, barring a tendency to put on too much weight. Jess propped Roxy against the wall; then, arms carefully locked, the couple entered the Blue Owl Grill, where the owner said "Whaddaya know?" first, an old joke with the old-timers; and Jess was shown to his table at the back of what was, despite all the recent patriotic fuss against all things German, an old-fashioned German beer hall with solid German food and known, until recently, as the Heidelberg. The owners were a Swiss German couple, fierce in their neutrality.

"Bratwurst and sauerkraut." Jess always ordered the same supper. "Sausage and *liberty cabbage*," said the immense German waitress, without a smile.

"Can you imagine?" said a woman's voice. "Changing the names just because they're German." It was Carrie Phillips, alone at the next table. Even though she was Jess's age, she looked more than ever like a Viking goddess, with dark gold curls framing a face unaided by cosmetics.

"I sometimes think people are crazy," Carrie added, to Jess's unease. All in all, it was not a wise time to speak up in public for the Germans, or indeed for anything German. Wagner could not be played in many cities, which suited Jess fine, but earlier that week Congress had declared war on Austria, and Jess prayed that this did not mean the end of the Strauss waltz, the only dance that he could do happily and with some grace. Jess had not been prepared for so much ill-feeling. Neither had W.G., the love of whose life was sitting at the table next to Jess and Roxy.

"Where's Jim?" asked Roxy.

The seated Carrie put on her coat, with Jess's help. "He's gone to get the car. We're going back to Marion tonight."

"On these icy roads? My!" said Roxy. Relations between Jess and his emporium and Jim Phillips and his Marion emporium had always been surprisingly good, since in the age of the motor car the distance between the two towns had shrunk to practically nothing, making them competitors. But Jess was not ambitious, while what ambition Jim had was more than compensated for by the branch of Uhler-Phillips that he had opened in New York City, right on Broadway itself. After the Hardings, the Phillipses were the first family of Marion, maybe even of Fayette County. All the more irony that, unknown to the Duchess and to Jim, W.G. and Carrie Phillips had been deeply in love for a dozen years. At first Daugherty had been distressed; then he had realized that when there could be no real scandal in the sense that the lovers would ever want to be married or that there might be a child, he had accepted the situation, as did those who suspected, who were few, as opposed to those who *knew,* who were many, at least in Marion.

The affair had begun in the wake of the Duchess's kidney operation, which had coincided with the equally ailing Jim Phillips's removal to the sanatorium at Battle Creek, Michigan. During the summer when W.G. would take to the Chautauqua circuit, speaking in a different town six days a week, Carrie would come join him in the homely anonymity of a variety of small-town hotels.

Jess thought the whole thing truly romantic. Certainly they were the best-looking couple in Ohio; on the other hand, they were not all that well matched. She was a bit nose-in-the-air, like Alice Longworth. She loved Europe; worse, she prided herself on her German heritage; worst, she would not stop talking about it. "Just think," she said, "Jim and I were booked this summer on the *Bremen*. I'd hoped to stay over in Germany for maybe a year, working on my German. Then this war . . ." She frowned. Several heads at nearby tables turned. Jess blushed; and pretended that he was a soldier at the Front.

"Well, it won't take long." Roxy was cheerful. Jess had finally persuaded her to cut off the Mary Pickford curls; as a result, the short not quite natural red hair made her look younger than her thirty-five years. More *gamine,* as she would say. Roxy had also spent a year in Europe and could be almost as high-toned as Carrie. "Now that our boys are all over there," Roxy was unexpectedly patriotic. The heads returned to feeding.

"I don't think," said Carrie, coldly, deliberately, elegantly, which for her meant the affectation of a slight German accent, "that our boys will have an easy time with the greatest army on earth. We . . . they," she took her time in changing the pronoun, "are winning in France, and now with the Russians just about out of the war, Ludendorff will drive the Allies into the sea."

"Us, too." Roxy's tone was hard.

Jess put his napkin over his face; he had just been wounded in action. He shivered, as he always did, at the thought of guns, bullets, death.

"We're not allies." Carrie was suddenly girlish and sweet and ominous. "Didn't you see what Mr. Wilson said? We're for the war to end, and that's all. We're not taking sides one way or the other. Peace without victory. No," Carrie smiled at her own reflection in the back of a heavy spoon on which was engraved in Gothic letters *Heidelberg,* a memento of the pre-Blue Owl world, "the only possible way for us to beat the Germans is with a general like Johann Josef Pfoersching."

"Who?" Jess dropped the napkin and speared a dumpling from Roxy's plate.

"John J. Pershing is what he changed his name to." Carrie was triumphant: America's commanding general was a member of the race of supermen, not to mention women. The patrons of their corner of the Blue Owl were now all talking at once.

"Well, I never," said Roxy, thoughtfully, forgetting her year in Europe and lapsing into Ohioese.

"I don't think many folks know this." Jess was uneasy. If Pershing should be a double agent, taking his orders from the Kaiser . . . What a plot it would make, he thought excitedly; now he was a spy-master as, earlier, he had been an amateur detective, alert to clues and able to spot a murderer in a crowded room simply by the way he moved.

"I'm glad that W.G. finally tried to talk some sense to the Senate for a change, about all that Liberty Bond hysteria. I was disgusted by it, and I told him so, too. The way they went on about German crimes, and the Huns, and quite forgetting all the crimes those French darkies are committing, and the English . . ."

"Against the Irish, anyway," said Roxy without thinking. Then they were joined by sallow, small, lean Jim Phillips. "The car's outside, Carrie." Jim greeted Jess fraternally as a fellow Elk, smiled at Roxy, helped Carrie to her feet. "We got us a nasty drive ahead, what with the snow's starting up again."

Carrie towered over her husband in the same way that the Queen of England did over hers; and she stood as ramrod-straight. "You tell our friends in Washington how I . . ." She changed whatever it was she meant to say. "How we miss them."

"You do that," said Jim.

Merry Christmases were exchanged. Roxy looked at Jess, who looked at Roxy. "She does go on," said Roxy.

"I wish she wouldn't." Jess drank beer from a pewter mug. "I really wish she wouldn't."

"Sir." Jess looked up at a stout young man with the lower half of a moustache; the rest had not grown in or was not there to grow in. "If I may interrupt you in your meal, sir." The man withdrew a wallet from his inside pocket; and opened it halfway so that only Jess could see that it contained a badge. The voice whispered, "Silas W. Mahoney, United States Secret Service."

"Sit down." Jess could barely speak. Terror and excitement caused him, literally, to lose his breath. For an instant he actually ceased to breathe. This was as high as you could go in the world of detectives: the government's own secret investigators, forever at work, capturing criminals and protecting presidents – freedom, too.

"What've you done, Jess?" Roxy was more querulous than alarmed. Mr. Mahoney slid into a chair between them. Fortunately the grill room was now so crowded that the comings and goings at Jess's table went unnoticed.

"It's about Mrs. Phillips," said the Secret Service man, removing a small notebook and a pencil from his jacket. "As you know, this is war-time." Mr. Mahoney expected the news to have more effect than it did. But Jess was still breathing hard, and Roxy was unimpressed by the law in general and by Mr. Mahoney in particular, who said, very slowly, "Mrs. Phillips is a woman of some influence here in Ohio, and in Washington, too."

"The branch store is not in Washington," said Roxy with a swift coolness that Jess admired and envied, "it's on Broadway, in New York City. Uhler-Phillips is an influence only in dry goods, Mr. Mahoney."

"I didn't get your name." Mr. Mahoney poised his pencil over the notebook.

"This is my wife," Jess began.

"I'm his ex-wife, Roxy Stinson . . ."

"Smith," Jess added; he was beginning to enjoy the situation. Mr. Mahoney made a notation. "Now just why are you investigating Mrs. Phillips?"

"We have reason to believe that she is a German agent. That she provides the Wilhelmstrasse with secret information."

Roxy burst forth with a great laugh, of the sort known in Fayette County as a horse-laugh. "Well, I reckon she could tell the Germans what the markdown will be on blankets after the Christmas sales are over, and I think she's very good on lingerie. Uhler-Phillips has the best selection in this part of Ohio –"

"Roxy!" Jess was stunned. He prided himself on Smith's wide range of exciting hand-stitched silk undies.

"I don't think you understand the danger that a woman of her thinking poses to a great nation in time of war." Mr. Mahoney tried to sound reasonable but, plainly, Roxy was rattling him.

"I don't think," said Jess, finally in control of an excitable self, "that she'd have any information from around here that the Wilhelmstrasse would want to know about."

"Mr. Smith, when it comes to intelligence, the smallest detail can be of significance."

"You're right there!" This was the real thing all right. Mr. Mahoney could have stepped off the page of a Nick Carter story.

"Look, Mr. Mahoney," Roxy was now waving to the waiter for the check, "Mrs. Phillips is a vulture for German culture, and that's it. She works for the Red Cross, like every patriotic little lady in these parts, and there's nothing for her to spy on anywhere around here."

"But what about Washington?"

"What about Washington?" Roxy looked blankly at the Secret Service man. "I don't think she's been there in years. Has she, Jess?"

Jess shook his head. "No occasion to. She doesn't even go to New York except to sail for –"

Roxy kicked him under the table. Fortunately, Mr. Mahoney could not write and listen. He had missed the dangerous verb. "But then, I guess, Washington comes to her, when Senator Harding is back home in Marion."

An alarm sounded in Jess's head. Fortunately, he was able to subdue his nerves by pretending that he was a counter-agent, a master detective, who knew far more than this insignificant cog in the vast Pinkertonian machine. He was guileful. "The Senator and Mrs. Harding are close friends of Mr. and Mrs. Phillips. Fact, they went to Europe together a few years ago . . ."

"To visit Germany, wasn't it?"

"No. It wasn't." Jess was suave, like Raymond Griffith, his favorite film star, elegant, unflappable, and seldom out of a tuxedo. "France and Italy mostly, looking for works of art." W.G. had come home with two marble statues of naked women, while the Duchess had bought a fully clothed lady called Prudence the Puritan.

"I see," said Mr. Mahoney, who, Jess had noticed, could not both think and speak either, which eased Jess's task. "They often make trips together . . ."

"They did. But that was in younger days. Now the Senator is busy in Washington or out on Chautauqua, and Mr. Phillips's health is not so good, and she's so busy with the Red Cross . . ."

"Why do you think she said what she said about General Pershing?"

This was a surprise, to which Roxy rose. "So you were listening in –"

"That's my job, Miss Stinson . . . Mrs. Smith."

"I think she thought it a good joke that our commanding general against the Germans is a German. I think it's pretty funny, too." Roxy was on her feet. "We don't want to miss the feature," she murmured. Jess helped her into her coat.

"I'd like to know," Mr. Mahoney doggedly began.

Roxy cut him short. "If you want to know whether or not General Pershing is a German spy, I suggest you go to France and ask him. Anyway," she added with true Roxy zest, "a well-set-up young man like you ought to be in France, anyway, fighting for his country, instead of bothering Ohio ladies."

That took care of Mr. Mahoney, Jess could see. But if there was to be a real investigation of Carrie, then the affair with W.G. would come to light; and if that happened, all was lost. Even as Jess complimented Roxy on her cool handling of the detective, he was wondering just what he dared tell Daugherty over the telephone, which might very well be tapped into by the government. Suddenly the whole country had become very exciting and dangerous, and Jess was both thrilled and terrified as his dreams of spies and detectives and ghosts in the broom closet were now all starting to come true.

3

Burden Day congratulated the President on his recent birthday. Wilson's thin face looked more bleak than ever. "Thank you, Senator. Sixty-one is a riotous age. You have it to look forward to. Meanwhile, tell Senator Reed of Missouri that I really do celebrate my birthday on December twenty-eighth and not, as he thinks, on December twenty-fifth." Burden sat on a sofa beside the fire while the President sat in a straight chair opposite. Comment was no longer made on why it was that the President chose to conduct his business from a small upstairs study rather than from the presidential office in the new west wing. Doubtless he liked the proximity of Lincoln's ghost or, more likely, Edith's ample presence.

Although the Senate was in a brief recess for the Christmas holidays, few of the Westerners had gone home. Burden and Kitty had sent for relatives; and like a kaleidoscope, the Senate continued to turn, rearranging its component pieces in ever new combinations. Last week's ally was this week's enemy. Only the politicians' code of a favor for a favor gave any shape to the very odd club that had made for itself so powerful a place in the scheme of things that even the President, with all his war-time powers, was often at the mercy of the savage-tongued Jim Reed – a member of his own party – not to mention the more or less crazed Henry Cabot Lodge of the opposition.

On this, the last day of 1917, the President had asked Burden to come see him in the late afternoon and together they would go over some of the points that the President would make to the new Congress on the progress of the war and, most important, on the peace that would follow. Burden had long since discovered that Wilson did not crave advice; consequently, he tended to nod his head and hum agreement, grateful for the room's fire. Half of the White House had been shut off to conserve heat; or so Tumulty had piously informed the press. Certainly the downstairs hall had been somewhat colder than the portico outside.

As the beautiful voice droned on, Burden did his best to keep awake. If Wilson did not want advice, Burden did not want to be read to. Finally, the President put down the pages, typed by himself, Burden noticed, recognizing the characteristic blue of Wilson's typewriter ribbon. "You get my thrust. I have a group working on the details. A sort of inquiry, you might say, on what to do after. Because there is – was – no point to our joining in this war if at the end we cannot find some way to stop these wasteful bloody enterprises."

"You agree with Mr. Taft, which should impress the Regular Republicans." Burden decided to advise. "If I may say so, I think it a bit too soon to speak as if we had already won the war when the Germans have been smashing the British to pieces, and we haven't done much of anything yet – in the field, that is."

To Burden's surprise, Wilson took this well. "I agree," he said. "I don't plan to make a speech tomorrow, but I'm trying to sort out what should be our position when it comes time to . . ." He stopped.

Burden finished, in his own way, the master of eloquence's thought. ". . . to justify a war so unpopular with so many people, particularly those in my part of the country, who are your main supporters."

A dull red spot formed atop each presidential cheekbone. "I was under the impression that the war is now more popular with the average American than it ever was with me. And in spite of all the bad news from France."

"Will there be a coal shortage?" Burden had been persuaded to ask this question by several senators from the mining states. "And will you – take action?"

Wilson looked glum. On the day after Christmas, the President had seized the railroads, and placed them under McAdoo.

"Will you nationalize coal, too?" The object of Burden's visit, if not of Wilson's invitation.

"There are . . . imperatives, yes. New York City is close to a real shortage; and tonight the temperature is below zero up there. We've made them cut down on electricity . . ."

"'No lights on Broadway.'" The theaters had been furious in their response; the President adamant in his.

"It will be worse than that." Wilson stood up. In the firelight he seemed like a scarecrow, ill-defined and not physically coherent. He shuffled to his desk and opened a drawer, which Burden by now knew was known as The Drawer, where the red-tagged important messages were piled. Wilson removed several documents. "Russia is now out of the war. The Bolsheviks have accepted Germany's terms, not that they ever had any choice. I'd hoped we could keep the new Russian government as an ally, but now their whole country is falling apart." Wilson glanced at one of the messages. "From our consul at Harbin. He says Irkutsk – which is in Siberia, I think – is in flames. The Bolsheviks have killed a number of their own people, as well as various French and English officials."

"Do you think this is true?"

"I don't *think,* Senator. I read what I am told is an account of what happens when extremists seize a country the size of Russia, the size," Wilson sat again in his straight chair, "of the United States. I believe we have done everything possible to keep a line of communication open to those people. I have no choice. If Russia leaves the war, that will free an entire German army to reinforce the Western Front. Then what?" Wilson sighed. "We have had such bad news." The President took off his pince-nez; rubbed the two small red marks on either side of his nose that matched, in miniature, the now fading ones on his cheeks. "There is England, too. We're being drawn into their net. I have never seen anything like their 'propaganda,' as George Creel likes to call it. How can we convince the world that we are truly disinterested – asking for no territory, nothing – when England makes us look like a partner in imperialism rather than what we are, a republic that wants only peace . . ."

Wilson could do this sort of thing by the hour, and although Burden admired the President's genuine high-mindedness, he himself tended to the literal, the objective, the useful. As if sensing Burden's distraction, Wilson replaced one red-tagged document with another. "This came yesterday. It's from Brest Litovsk, an appeal from the Bolshevik Trotsky. He's an American, I gather – at one time anyway. Now he's in charge of the Russian delegation. He rejects, thank God, the substance of the German agreement, but then he requests that the Allies make peace, which certainly pleases me, but then he adds this intolerable rubbish." Wilson read from Trotsky's statement: "'If the Allied governments in blind obstinacy, which characterizes the falling and perishing classes . . .'"

"Us?"

Wilson nodded. "'. . . again refuse to participate in the negotiations, then the working class will be confronted with the iron necessity of tearing the power out of the hands of those who cannot or will not give peace to the nation.'" Wilson put down the paper. "There is great mischief here. Should these Bolsheviks prevail, what effect might they have on our own people, on all our home-grown Communists and radicals and labor agitators?"

Burden was not impressed by Wilson's alarm, if it was true alarm and not simply political play-acting. "Since we never imitated Russia when they had a highly colorful czar, I doubt if Mr. Trotsky of New York City, or wherever he is from, will have much effect either. But I thought," Burden shifted to the real politics of the matter, "that Mr. Root had made a deal with the provisional government last summer."

Elihu Root, the most brilliant as well as the most conservative of American statesmen, had been sent by the President to Petrograd to keep the Russians in the war. As counterweight, Wilson had sent with him two colleagues, of whom one was a genuine American Socialist. At the same time, to complicate matters, a World Socialist Congress was meeting in Stockholm. After much public agonizing, Wilson had refused to issue passports to the American delegates, citing their "almost treasonable utterances." Deeper and deeper, thought Burden; but then he knew that as he himself was entirely of his place and time and class and so both isolationist and populist, the President was now as one with the, to Burden, un-American Eastern ruling class, always more prone than not to foreign adventures in collegial tandem with regimes that Burden would have only politely tolerated.

"I'm not sure 'deal' is the word to use." Wilson's nose twitched fastidiously. "In May their government agreed to continue the war with Germany while we extended to them over three hundred million dollars' worth of credit at a very low rate of interest."

"They were bought."

"They were bought." Wilson was equally flat. "But, as Mr. Frick said of Colonel Roosevelt, they did not stay bought." He waved the red-tagged paper like a flag. "That was May when they loved us. Now it is December and . . . they do not. They encourage the worst elements of our labor movement. Read this . . . No. I just read Mr. Trotsky to you. He proposes that our workers overthrow us." Wilson got up and replaced the documents in The Drawer. "By next year, according to all projections, our labor unions will have increased their membership by four and a half million."

"Good news for the Democratic Party."

"Let's hope not for Mr. Trotsky. He's trying to make capital – surely the wrong word – out of Thomas Mooney, who is innocent, he tells us, of the San Francisco bombings . . ."

"I've always thought he was." Someone, in July of 1916, had interrupted a Preparedness Day parade with bombs. Nine people had died, and the labor radical Mooney had been arrested, found guilty of murder and condemned to death.

"I was not at the trial." Wilson was legalistic. "But our ambassador in Russia wants me to commute the sentence, which I don't think I can do, as the whole matter is under the governor of California. Colonel House thinks I should intervene, or *seem* to. So I'm setting up a mediation committee, and should they find new evidence, as such commissions tend to do, I shall ask the governor, most respectfully, to refrain from his auto-da-fé until there is a new trial, and so on, and so forth. They blackmail us!" Wilson rubbed his forehead. He looked ill. One of Burden's friends, a doctor, had assured him that Wilson was prematurely arteriosclerotic, with a long and secret history of strokes. Like all doctors, sworn to secrecy, this one could not bear to remain silent on a matter so exciting. But then he was not the President's physician, who was, suspiciously, in constant attendance. Also, it was well known that Grayson allowed his patient no more than three or four hours of office-work a day, broken by numerous automobile and horse-back rides and golf. In frantic war-time Washington, the White House was the most tranquil place to be. Yet no one could say that this president was not entirely master of the nation's politics and, probably, of its war-time allies as well. Burden had never known a mind so capable of swiftly relating one fact to another in order to achieve as large a view as possible of what was necessary to itself. But Wilson's necessity might not be that of Leon Trotsky, of Lloyd George in England, of Clemenceau in France, while even to many senators in his own party, the President's world-view was eccentric. There were still quite a few old-fashioned populists in the Congress who believed implicitly Trotsky's charge that the United States had gone to war to protect J. P. Morgan's loans to the Allies. Burden himself, on demagogic days, inclined to that bright simple view.

As always, the President, once done with moralizing about man's estate, descended to practical politics. It had been Burden's experience that the great Wilson, in the unlikely event that any of the President's many selves should ever be raised to that prime category, was the party manager. No congressional district was alien to him. On his desk he kept what looked like a large sentimental family picture album. Inside were the highly unsentimental photographs of every member of the House of Representatives and Senate. During the early days of the Administration, he had studied each face; and committed it to memory. Burden was almost alone in knowing that in the next year's election Wilson was planning to purge those Democrats, mostly Southern and Western, who had ever defied him. Burden had warned him against this sort of reprisal but Wilson was grim. He would weed *his* garden, and that was that.

At the moment the President was not looking to future elections; rather, he was still shaken by the recent election of the Hearst Tammany candidate for mayor of New York City, a Brooklyn County judge named John F. Hylan. When Hearst saw that his own candidacy would divide the Democratic Party, he and the Tammany boss, Murphy, had selected Hylan to defeat the incumbent, John Purroy Mitchel. The election had been unusually bitter. Colonel Roosevelt had campaigned for Mitchel, denouncing his ancient enemy Hearst as "one of the most efficient allies of Germany on this side of the water." Hearst was the Hun within the gate, more dangerous than the one without. "Hearst, Hylan and the Hohenzollerns should have been a winning slogan for Mitchel," said Roosevelt. Then Hearst's candidate had won by 147,000 votes. So much for the Roosevelt magic.

"I don't understand that city. I never have." Wilson shook his head.

"I do," said Burden, "it's anti-war, anti-English, anti-French. What I don't understand is Hearst. Why, with all he's got, does he bother?"

"To come here, my friend. He thinks he'll be nominated in 1920; and elected. That's the arrangement he made with Murphy." Wilson was now very much the nuts-and-bolts politician. "Hearst stays out of the mayoral race, pays for Hylan, supports him with his papers, and a grateful Tammany delivers the New York delegation in the summer of 1920, an eternity away."

"But if we all survive this eternity, it will be you, Mr. President, not Hearst."

Wilson smiled. "If I have done that well with the war and then the peace, I might think myself worthy . . ."

"You are modest. You'll be elected by acclamation."

"No, Senator. Never that. I am not a popular sort of man, like Roosevelt. Nothing is ever easy for me. Nothing. Nothing at all."

Burden nodded a sorrowful assent to this astonishing falsity. In exactly two years, Wilson had been elected both governor of New Jersey and president. No American politician had ever had such a rapid, lucky rise. But then no one knew how Wilson himself saw those elections, or how he saw himself in relation to the field, much less to history. Vain about his intellectual achievements, he was oddly modest about his political prowess. It might, Burden thought somewhat enviously, be the other way around. The schoolteacher Wilson was very much, as Lodge liked to remind anyone who would listen, run-of-the-mill, but as political manager and eloquent if sometimes monotonous enunciator of man's better nature, Wilson was unique.

"Do you know Hearst?"

Burden nodded. "I saw a good deal of him when he was here in Congress."

"Amazing to think of him in so humble a job."

"He was a bit amazed, too. I had to show him how to introduce a bill."

"I wonder," said Wilson, not listening, "if he could be charged with treason."

Burden unfolded his legs; and his two feet struck the floor simultaneously. "For what?"

"For aiding the German cause in war-time. Of course, I'm not a constitutional lawyer and I've never properly studied the Espionage Act, but it seems that we might charge him, somehow, with aiding and abetting the infamous Paul Bolo Pasha, a proven German spy. After all, Hearst used to entertain him in New York." During the election, much had been made of Hearst's connection with the unsavory Bolo, who had later been given money by Bernstorff in order to subvert the French, who had promptly imprisoned him. Put on the defensive, Hearst had said that he had met Bolo only once; then he printed even more colored flags on the *Journal*'s front page.

"Well, Mr. President, I'd be very careful with Hearst. He's capable of anything."

"So," said the kindly old Presbyterian minister in the chair opposite, "am I."

"Yes," said Burden; and left it at that.

"Do you remember that dreadful photo-play serial – *Patria* – that Hearst made two years ago?"

Burden nodded. Whenever news was dull, Hearst would invoke the Yellow Peril. But in *Patria* he had outdone himself. He had combined the Yellow Peril with Mexican outlaws, each bent on the destruction of the United States. The Japanese government had complained bitterly. "I used to see it at Keith's," said Wilson. "Ridiculous, I thought. But I had to write him a letter, asking him to desist. Moving pictures have such a – powerful effect on public opinion. They can actually alter circumstances." Wilson laughed. "I have just made a paraphrase of Burke, which suits us all: 'Expediency is the wisdom of circumstances.'"

Burden nodded his appreciation; then he made his own gloss: "Wisdom is to find it expedient to do nothing at all."

Edith entered on Burden's diminuendo. "The clan is gathering. Do stay, Senator."

"No. No. It's late. I have my own clan gathering and then . . ."

"New Year's Eve at the McLeans'."

"Exactly." Burden bade the President a happy New Year; he had received not only the information that he wanted on the possible seizure of the coal mines but a dozen other messages of the sort that politicians exchange without the use of sometimes compromising and always ambiguous spoken words.

Edith led Burden onto the cold dimly lit landing. The only comforting light came from the open door to the upstairs oval sitting room, where the voices of her family were slightly louder than those of his. "I have the book." Edith crossed to her secretary's desk beneath the fanlight at hall's end. Burden had entirely forgotten what book he had asked for. She returned with a thin volume. *Philip Dru, Administrator* was the title. Burden remembered: a novel by Colonel House, published six years before. Now that House was the President's alter ego in Europe, Burden was curious to know more about this courtly wealthy Texan, who wanted only to serve as the President's loyal eyes and ears if not always tongue, for, according to Edith, "He is something of a yes-man. A few weeks ago I showed him Mr. Wilson's address to Congress, the one where he took over the railroads – and the Colonel didn't like it one bit. And he told me why. And I was really impressed. So I told him to tell the President the next day. Naturally, I warned Woodrow, and he was upset because he thinks the world of Colonel House. Well, the next day, Woodrow says he's sorry Colonel House doesn't like the message about the railroads, and the Colonel got all nervous and said, 'Well, I've reread it since and I now agree with every word of it.'"

That, thought Burden, was the only way to handle the President; and he admired Colonel House all the more. Burden took his leave with the book, which, he had been told, dealt with the first dictator of the United States, a most enlightened and benevolent man who, having solved all domestic problems, solves those of the world as well by setting himself up as the chief of a world concert of nations.

4

The fact that the McLean estate, Friendship, had once been a monastery never ceased to delight Blaise, as he and Frederika descended from what she called "our land yacht," a huge enclosed sedan, driven by a Russian refugee, who spoke French and claimed to have been captain of the Czar's personal guard. "All in all, *not* a good reference," Frederika had said.

Friendship was an extraordinary place to have within the limits of the District of Columbia, and Blaise quite envied the Ned McLeans their eighty acres of ponds and streams and parks; he did not envy them the somewhat common old-fashioned house with the low ceilings favored by the glum heat-conservers of the previous century. But now, after the icy night air, the warmth of the house was an agreeable shock. The Friendship conservatories had produced a thousand rare plants; and the rooms smelled of wood smoke and gardenias. Once outer coverings had been surrendered, they were warmly received by the butler. In the long run, Blaise decided that the only people one ever really got to know in life were servants and bartenders and maîtres d'hôtel. He had had more conversations with the headwaiter at the Cosmos Club than with his mother-in-law, who now stood, blindly, in the doorway to the main drawing room.

"It's Mother," murmured Frederika in much the same tone of voice that a fourteenth-century woman might have warned her family of plague.

Simultaneously, the butler announced, "Mr. and Mrs. Blaise Delacroix Sanford," and mother and daughter embraced, while Evalyn approached, wearing on a chain that huge ominous lump the Hope Diamond, and the glittering Star of the East in her hair. Evalyn greeted the rival publisher with a somewhat frothing champagne kiss. "Isn't it wonderful!" she exclaimed.

"*You!* As always." Blaise wondered what "it" was.

"Yes!" Evalyn embraced Frederika, who had fought Mrs. Bingham to a standstill.

"Can you tell?" Evalyn looked at Blaise conspiratorially, but turned her body toward Frederika. "I'm pregnant."

"That is wonderful." Frederika had a way of drawing out her syllables that made the listener feel as if he alone of all the world's population had attracted not only her interest but delighted wonder.

"Vinson needs a little brother, I said to Ned."

"What," asked Frederika, "did Vinson say?"

"He is only six."

"I," said Mrs. Bingham, eager to dispense terror, "would get rid of that diamond first if I were you."

"Oh, it's all right now. I had a priest exorcise it. In Latin, too." Evalyn pointed to a fantastic six-foot-high arrangement of purple orchids. "Alice went up to that thing and in her loudest voice said, 'Good evening, Mrs. Wilson.'"

There were two hundred for dinner; then dancing until 1917 was safely done for. Blaise got Alice Longworth at dinner, as he often did at her request as well as his. Alice was aging well; and Blaise wondered what his life would have been like had they married, a thought that had occurred, briefly, to each of them but at different times. She was certainly the best of company, but then Frederika was far from dull. On the other hand, Alice was, forever, *the* President's daughter. Washington and Jefferson and Lincoln were simply pale precursors set in place by history, like so many John the Baptists, to prepare the world for the wonder of Theodore Roosevelt, soon to be president again, or so Alice – and Blaise – thought. Since anything that did not relate to the messianic mission was trivial, she was probably better off with the passive, amiable, hard-drinking Nick Longworth, a wealthy Ohio congressman, who was seated across the table next to an overdressed, plain woman who was, Alice said, Mrs. Warren Gamaliel Harding, "*our* Senator's wife." Alice made the "our" sound like an embarrassing possession, a dog that has just squatted at the center of a rare rug. "Nick has them to the house for poker. I am wonderfully tactful and very, very kind. It is said that she has one kidney, out of a possible two."

"Usually, you'd only mention that if we'd just been served kidneys."

Alice poked her fork into the mess on her plate. "Terrapin.

See? I am very, very tactful nowadays because we need everybody, Father and I. Of course she could have only one terrapin, located in the third chin."

"I think she can hear you." Mrs. Harding's ice-blue eyes were fixed without fondness on Alice while Nick, ever the courtier, murmured in her ear.

The dinner was grand, as all McLean occasions were. Thus far, Ned was not yet drunk; and Evalyn was in her element. It was said that she was even richer than Ned, from Western gold mines. Blaise found her a relief from the other hard-panners, as the Western new rich were called. Unlike the other ladies, she revelled in her low birth and vast income; bought more diamonds than anyone since Marie Antoinette and, in general, created euphoria all about her. Who else would have lit up their palace so splendidly when the lights were dimmed throughout the country and Broadway's Great White Way switched off?

"Where's Caroline?"

"At the other table, I think." Blaise had caught a glimpse of his sister in deep conversation with Ned McLean's aunt, wife to what had been the czarist Russian ambassador, now ambassador no more. Blaise hoped that Caroline would remember that she was a publisher and collect news.

"Is it true she's acted in a photo-play?" Alice looked, suddenly, more jealous than sardonic.

"It was just a joke, made by Mr. Hearst."

"Hearst!" That changed the subject for good. "Father still thinks he's the most dangerous man in the country, *and* a German spy."

"I can't see what he could spy on, outside the Ziegfeld Follies."

Alice moved yet again; this time for scandal's jugular. "Have you met *her*?"

Blaise nodded. It seemed that everyone was interested in the Chief's "secret" love, Marion Davies. "She's very young, very blond. She stammers, and she calls him 'Pops.'"

Alice roared; then began to stammer "Pops" over and over again until the removal of the terrapin allowed Blaise to address his other dinner partner.

After dinner, more guests arrived, and an orchestra played in the ballroom. As Blaise watched the dancers, he was aware that someone had sat down beside him in the next chair. It was the British ambassador, Cecil Spring Rice, looking old and tired.

"Dear Blaise. It is hard to believe that there's a war going on."

"Half a world away is . . . half a world away. The whole thing still seems unreal to me, and I'm really French, you know." Blaise assumed that he had made so untrue a confession in order to console the Englishman for the blood-letting. Certainly the sons of the British ruling class were being used to manure the fields of France; and for what harvest?

"This is to be my last New Year's in Washington. So I came here to see the show for one last time."

Blaise knew that there had been problems between Spring Rice and the Lords Reading and Northcliffe, recently sent over by the British government to represent the politicians; also, Spring Rice's long friendship with Roosevelt and Lodge did not recommend him to the Wilsons. "When do you go?"

Spring Rice shrugged. "When they tell me to. I assume sometime in April when I shall be sixty and get my pension. How it's changed since I was young. . . ." He was in an elegiac mood. "I came here first as a very young secretary. We thought this a minor capital then. Buenos Aires was more desirable, more worldly. Now . . . look."

Blaise looked at the Hope Diamond as it swung back and forth like the pendulum to some highly sinister clock.

"The thing has now come round to us." Blaise agreed. "But I'm not so sure that we'll know what to do with – all the world."

"You'll think of something, I'm sure. Anyway, you are not Germany." Spring Rice frowned. "But then Germany is not Germany anymore either. I used to think one could generalize, in a vague way, about a nation, a people, a tribe. But one cannot. The Germany of my youth was the most civilized country in the world, and my German colleagues the most intelligent and professional. Then . . ."

"The Huns?"

"There are Huns in every country, I am convinced. The military – the Huns – took over my Germany."

"Why didn't your Huns take over your empire?"

"We're far too lazy for that sort of thing. Sloth has always saved England from itself."

"Will it save us?" Blaise had noted, with some amazement, the ease with which the Administration had been able to whip up so much hatred in the American people. Although there was nothing that Blaise did not know about the manipulation of public opinion, even he had been startled by the efficiency and speed with which the likes of George Creel had managed to demonize all things German. If this could be done so rapidly with a people whose relatives compromised a sizable minority of the American people, it could be done again and again by any administration, and for any purpose.

"You are not a slothful nor a lazy people." Spring Rice was precise. "You are also more susceptible than we to – storms of emotion."

"Just what I was thinking. My sister has been in Hollywood, where they are now making photo-plays about bestial Huns, and millions of people go see those moving pictures, and believe what they see."

"As," Spring Rice smiled, "they believe my dispatches and your editorials."

"But we have *some* shame, don't we?"

The Ambassador nodded. "We do. But I am never sure about those who govern us. The President did me the courtesy of explaining what it is he does."

"Tell me. I've never known."

"Apparently, he is a barometer in human form. He registers precisely the popular mood. Then, when it is no longer – variable? – he acts in accordance with that mood."

"Which you and I and the photo-plays have created for him."

"We make some of the weather. But not all. Actually, he seems to me much more like a swimmer, trying to avoid one wave from crashing over him while trying to find another one, which he can ride to shore."

"You preferred Roosevelt. I know." Blaise quickly apologized for the gaffe. "I'm sorry. I shouldn't have said that."

"I heard nothing but the music, dear Blaise, and saw nothing but my beloved wife over there, teaching a senator the fox-trot."

"What you have done – *do* for England!"

"Only my all. You know," Spring Rice was, for an instant, serious, "the President – and Colonel House, his Buckingham – believes that there should be a post-war league – a covenant – of all countries, to keep the peace."

"So do I. So does Taft, who gave him the idea."

"So, I suppose, do I. But then I'm a barometer, too, an old infirm foreign barometer, admittedly, but I can usually predict the weather in these parts – at least the storms, when I – the barometer – start falling. These people, your people, will never join such an organization."

Blaise was surprised. After all, it was the received opinion of those who led the state and molded public opinion that such an organization was highly desirable. If they could so easily make the people hate all things German, they could certainly make them love a bureaucratic means of forever keeping peace. "I see no obstacle. Republicans are even more in favor of a league than Democrats."

"It won't work like that. Americans are too used to going alone in the world. You're also at the start of your own empire, and no rising empire ever wants to commit itself to peace when there are still so many profitable wars to fight."

"You astonish me."

Caroline and a lean, dark blue-eyed man approached them. Although introductions were made, Blaise did not hear the man's name. Plainly, he was not from Washington. Caroline was splendid, all in gold; and looked a decade younger than she had before the trip to California, where, on Creel's instructions, she had excited the motion-picture business to even greater, if possible, propaganda efforts. Spring Rice was led away by Ned McLean, whose sobriety was now drawing to a close, along with the year.

"I've heard so much about you." The accent was Boston Irish. This was the sort of thing one met in California, thought Blaise, censoriously. He wondered if Caroline was having an affair with him.

"Well, I've heard nothing about you." Blaise radiated what he hoped was charm. "But that's Caroline's fault."

"Your fault," said Caroline. "We don't see each other outside the office."

"We don't see each other *in* the office either." Blaise was genial. "There is an editor who keeps us apart. What are you doing here?"

"Visiting Caroline." Yes, this was her lover. Women, Blaise noted, not for the first time, had no taste in men. Of course, the Irishman was younger than she, and, happily, their French upbringing had released them from that powerful American taboo, the monster older woman who, like a vampire, drains – dissipates – the rare essence of innocent young manhood. French women, in bed as well as in the market, valued *les primeurs*. "Timothy has never been to Washington before. So I wanted to show him a typical party."

"It's just like DeMille," said Timothy.

"DeMille who?" asked Blaise.

At that moment, all the lights in the ballroom went out. Then one end of the room was lit up with a thousand red, white and blue lights that spelled out "Good Luck to the Allies in 1918." There was cheering. The orchestra played "Auld Lang Syne." There was loud singing. Blaise kissed Caroline's cheek, and shook Timothy's hand. Caroline then kissed Timothy on the lips. "I am," she said to Blaise, through all the noise of paper-crackers and band music, "going to make a movie in 1918."

Then the lights came on again and the dancing started up. Blaise turned to Caroline, who was definitely having an affair with Timothy. "I'm getting deaf," he said. "I thought you said you were going to make a movie in 1918."

"I did, Blaise. I am." Caroline and Timothy joined the dancers. Frederika appeared for Blaise to embrace. "His name," said Frederika, omitting the Happy New Year, "is Timothy X. Farrell. He directs – or is it conducts? – photo-plays."

"I had hoped he was a chauffeur," said Blaise, in a good mood. "Anyway, whatever Hearst does, she does. Perhaps she found him in the chorus of the Follies."

"Good for her, I say. She was bored." Frederika took a glass of champagne from a waiter.

"She isn't bored now." Then Blaise and Frederika began the new year with a waltz.

145

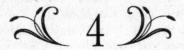

4

1

For Caroline, love had always meant – if anything – separation. In the golden days of her affair with Burden she was allowed to see him only on Sundays in Washington; with rare excursions elsewhere, to exotic river cities like St. Louis, and to the wonderful blankness of hotel rooms. She had not needed Burden – or anyone – every day. She had had a full life, beginning with her seven years' war against Blaise for her share of the Sanford inheritance. Although Blaise had won the war in the sense that she had received her capital when she was twenty-seven and not, as their father's will required, twenty-one, she had scored the greater victory by acquiring a moribund Washington newspaper and making a success of it, largely because Blaise had always wanted to be a publisher, like his friend and sometime employer Hearst. But it was Caroline not Blaise who had re-created the Washington *Tribune*. Finally, at a peace conference in exotic St. Louis, she had allowed him to buy into the paper while she kept control.

But control of what? she wondered, as she carefully crossed the icy sidewalk in front of Henry Adams's Romanesque villa across from the Byzantine-classical St. John's Church, whose gilded cupola mocked the demure primness of Lafayette Park. Whatever urge that she might have had for political power had been entirely extinguished by her years in Washington. Seen close to, the rulers of the country were no different from the ruled, or if they were, she could not tell the difference. Money mattered, and nothing

146

else. For anyone who had been brought up in a nation whose most famous play was called *The Miser,* this was more agreeable than not, particularly if one had enough of what mattered. The problem now was what to do with what remained of her life. Tim, as she now somewhat self-consciously called Farrell, had entered her orderly life like a sudden high wind at a Newport picnic, and everything was in a state of disorder.

In Los Angeles, their days were spent in the surprisingly small barn-like buildings where photo-plays were created at a very rapid rate; and their nights at early "supper," as it was called in California, with the world-famous men and women who were the stars, each tinier than the other; only their large heads in proportion to their small bodies demonstrated some obscure Darwinian principle that when evolution required movie stars those best adapted to the screen – large heads atop small neat bodies would be ready to make the journey to Southern California "because there's sun all year round," the town proclaimed. Actually, there was fog almost every morning and a thousand other places would have been more suitable except for one crucial detail – the Mexican border was only a hundred miles away. Since all the moving-picture makers in California were using equipment developed by that protean genius Edison, and since none acknowledged his patents, the village was filled with hard-eyed detectives, waiting to catch a glimpse of something called the Latham Loop, which, if found in use, could lead to gunfire and endless lawsuits.

Caroline had enjoyed the frontier life. She had also enjoyed her first affair in many years. Although Irish and often drunk, Tim was, to use the popular new verb, enthused by sex, and Caroline felt herself grow younger by the day. She also never ceased to ache in every joint, because, as Héloise wisely and proudly said, "you are at last using *all* your muscles." Caroline felt like a wrestler in training as she and Tim tried to make as little noise as possible in the Garden Court Apartments, from which – except for them – all movie people had been excluded by the Iowan management. Tim explained to Caroline that most of Hollywood's residents were peaceful retired Middle Western farm folk who were stunned to find their village suddenly overwhelmed by beauty and vice, by Jews and process-servers.

Tim had gone back to California right after the New Year. In due course, Caroline would join him, but for now she remained in Washington. Hearst had already proposed that she buy into his new venture, Cosmopolitan Pictures, currently making movies in his own New York studio at Second Avenue and 127th Street. But Caroline was wary of Hearst. For one thing, he could absorb her too easily; for another, she and Blaise had been startled to learn that Hearst was negotiating to buy the Washington *Times* in order to do for it what she had done for the *Tribune*. Blaise had agreed with her that they should keep Hearst out of Washington even if it meant buying the *Times* themselves, and merging it with the *Tribune*. Finally, if Caroline was to fulfill her war-time task, Southern California was the place to be. Also, that was where Tim was. Seize the day, as Burden had liked to joke when their bodies were new to one another.

Henry Adams had always been of movie-star size but now, with age, he was almost no longer present in the room. The large bald bearded head seemed unattached as it floated close to the floor in the study that always smelled of lilies and roses no matter what the season. It was here, thought Caroline, as they embraced, her Washington life had begun; now was it here that it would end? Was she fated to end her days at the other end of the United States, wearing puttees and riding breeches, shouting orders through a megaphone at tiny actors, once the Santa Monica fog had finally burned away?

"I'm early."

"I'm late. Far too late." Adams helped her to a chair beside the fire. All in gray, Aileen Tone greeted her softly. It was Caroline's impression that Adams was kept like some rare fragile Fabergé egg in a carefully arranged, all-cushioned and heated, nest: would the egg then hatch? Yes, if death was the final hatching.

"Theodore, Rex that was, is in the town. But why do I tell you when you are the town."

"The voice has been heard, it's true. Is he coming to lunch?"

"Here? Oh, no. I have standards, not high, I confess, except in the case of nieces, but certain big fish can never make it up the river to me. *She* comes, though. My eldest niece, Edith, and daughter Alice."

"I like her – or '*she*.'" It was taken by some as a sign of Roosevelt's fragile health that his wife Edith had come to Washington with him in the wake of the President's Fourteen Points (four more than God's, was the current joke) that had been submitted to the Congress. The principal point involved a league of all the nations that would, at the first sign of stress between any of its members, soothe and adjudicate and make war unthinkable.

Theodore Roosevelt had rushed to town to address the National Press Club. He had denounced the War Department that had refused his services and, indirectly, the President. He had been scornful, as usual, of Wilson's "peace without victory"; and declared, "Let us dictate peace by the hammering guns and not chat about peace to the accompaniment of the clicking of typewriters." At the time, Caroline had duly noted the first verb. But Blaise had vetoed a *Tribune* essay on the necessity or non-necessity of a dictator in time of war, something that such a pacific figure as Harding of Ohio thought desirable. In American life there had been no Bonapartes or sun kings – only the ambiguous Lincoln. If nothing else, because of their French birth, Caroline and Blaise had been inoculated against that virus. But Henry Adams's brother Brooks had apparently succumbed. "He cries like an infant for a dictator," said Adams, a faint smile perceptible within the beard. "Then he howls, like Cabot, whenever Wilson does anything dictatorial. There is no pleasing my brother."

"Or you?"

"Oh, I delight, humbly, in the crash of all that I have ever held dear. But I've always been boringly in advance of everyone. Poor Brooks considers the world to be going to the devil with the greatest rapidity, and I console him, as best I can, in my merry way, by telling him that the world went there ten years ago."

"*That* is consolation." Caroline found it hard to believe that Uncle Henry, as he was known to her without quotation marks, would be eighty in a few weeks.

Adams picked up a slender volume. "You know George Santayana?"

Caroline nodded. Half-Spanish, half-Boston, he had taught philosophy at Harvard alongside, when not at odds with, Henry James's brother William. He had written a number of works on the reason of life or the life of reason. Caroline had never read him; but she remembered vividly the dark shining eyes at their one Boston meeting.

"He's just written some very elegant propaganda. No doubt inspired by the great Theodore. Aileen, do read the marked page." As she took the book from Adams, he turned his still-bright gaze upon Caroline. "I am now blind."

"No," Caroline began.

"Yes." Adams was matter-of-fact. "Three months ago, the light went out. Do read, Aileen."

Miss Tone obliged. "'In their tentative many-sided way the Germans have been groping for four hundred years towards a restoration of their primitive heathenism.'"

Adams interrupted. "Now that makes sense. Remember, the Teutonic tribes were the last to be Christianized, and they still resent the experience. That's why, ever since, they have been at war, in one way or another, with Christendom."

"You make them sound most sympathetic." Caroline had been painlessly separated from Christianity by Mlle. Souvestre; and had no longings.

"You are a Bolshevik, I suppose. That's the latest thing. It's also the future thing. Brooks is right. We have lived to see the end of a republican form of government, which is, after all, merely an intermediate stage between monarchy and anarchy, between the Czar and the Bolsheviks."

"Everyone says you've become a Roman Catholic," announced Alice Longworth, as she entered the room with her stepmother, Edith – "long-suffering Edith" was the Homeric tag Caroline mentally attached to the older woman, who had coped marvelously well with five boys of whom the most tiresome was her husband, while relations with Alice were always edgy.

Adams greeted the ladies warmly. "I've heard the rumor, too.

My conversion is a German war-aim, and will fail like everything else they put their hand to. 'Subjectivity in thought,' as Santayana describes them, 'and willfulness in morals.'"

"Is that *you*, Uncle Henry?" Alice had not heard the "them."

"No. The Germans. I think poor Springy started the rumor about me, to liven our spirits."

"I do miss him," said Alice.

Edith took the throne by the fire where, in earlier days, Clara Hay had always sat; now Clara was dead and of the original Five of Hearts only Adams remained. "Theodore thinks Mr. Wilson had him sent home, out of spite."

"Theodore *would* think that." Adams was mild. "I'm sorry he couldn't come. Politics?"

"What else?" Edith sighed. "He sits in poor Alice's dining room like a pasha, and they all come to him. He's with the New York delegation now. He wears himself out. And his stomach is upset."

"Wait till he dines tonight with cousin Eleanor and the wrong Roosevelt." Alice's gray-blue eyes glittered in the winter light from Lafayette Park. "Eleanor has become the Lucrezia Borgia of Washington – none survives her table."

To Caroline's surprise, they were joined by no one. "I want you three all to myself," said Adams. "I'm tired of men, and allergic to politicians, and grow rabid at the sight of a uniform."

"All my brothers are overseas. Father is jealous."

"Yes." Adams's voice was, for an instant, ominous. But then he lightened the mood. "You'll doubtless be calling on your successor across the road." He put his arm through Edith's and led them into the dining room, where his usual late breakfast or early lunch was set up.

"Oh, you can imagine that." Edith was amused. "I suspect I'm the last person she'd want to see, coming in the door like the Ghost of Christmas Past."

"They say," said Alice, who always said what they were saying, "that her brothers are stealing everything that's not nailed down."

"Now, Alice." Edith's voice was both weary and warning.

"Mother insists that if you were not actually in the room during the crime it could not have happened." But Alice dropped the subject. Edith was the only person who seemed to intimidate her; certainly, her father did not. Once criticized for Alice's escapades, the then President had famously said, "I can regulate my daughter or I can preside over the United States. But I cannot do both."

As Adams and Edith exchanged news – illness, funerals, wills – Alice murmured to Caroline, "Franklin thinks Eleanor doesn't know, and I think she does."

Caroline's response was swift. "She wouldn't say if she knew."

Alice was surprised. "Why not?"

"I would have to tell you all about our mutual schoolteacher . . ."

"The atheist Mlle. Souvestre. I know. I think I *really* know." Alice's malice had the same sort of joyous generalized spontaneity as did her father's hypocrisy.

Caroline let the bait slip by. "Eleanor will notice nothing until there is something to notice, and it is my guess, as a fellow Catholic, *de la famille,* that Lucy Mercer will not go to bed with Franklin until she is safely married."

Alice was deeply interested by so European, so papist a viewpoint. "You mean married to Franklin?"

"Preferably. But marriage to anyone makes adultery a possibility, even a necessity. Don't you think?"

Alice, for the first time in Caroline's long experience of her, blushed. Plainly, a lucky hit. But if Alice had found a lover she had been superbly discreet. "At last I understand vice. We Americans are so much simpler. If it itches, scratch it. But no fuss, no divorces, no marriages – I mean, just for *that.* I saw them together, out driving, Franklin and Lucy, coming from Chevy Chase. I told Franklin I'd seen them, and that he'd almost wrecked the car staring at her, and he said, cool as could be, 'Beautiful, isn't she?' I have them to the house, when Eleanor's out of town." Alice frowned. "But they could never marry each other. She's Catholic. He isn't."

"Worse. She's Catholic. He's political. He can't have a career and be divorced." Caroline had always felt that Eleanor's position was impregnable, thanks to Franklin's astonishing ambition – astonishing because, amiable and charming as he was, he seemed curiously lacking in any real political sense, as he had recently demonstrated when he ran for senator from New York, only to be sunk without a trace by the Hearst-Tammany money machine. Luckily, he still had his job at the Navy Department; still had the magical name.

Henry Adams and Edith Roosevelt were bemoaning the loss of Springy.

"He was best man at our wedding in London. I don't think Theodore has ever had so wise a friend."

"Nor I so civilized a one." Adams mournfully ate cornbread, a dish that Caroline delighted in only at his table. "Springy's great unsung contribution was his manipulation of the Jewish bankers in New York – and their press. Almost to a man, they were for the Kaiser . . ."

"The editor of the New York *Times* did hold out." Caroline had been much involved in the newspaper intrigues of 1914. Kuhn, Loeb & Company had threatened to take over the pro-Allies *Times,* while other pressures were brought to bear on the press by Jacob Schiff and the American brother of the German Warburgs. Wilson had steered a delicate course. A number of pro-German Jewish bankers had given money to his campaign, assuming that he would "keep us out of war" against their beloved Germany. Wilson had mollified them by appointing Warburg to the Federal Reserve Board and the country's leading Zionist, Louis Brandeis, to the Supreme Court. Caroline had been present at the White House when Wilson suddenly quoted Scripture to Spring Rice: "'He that keepeth Israel shall neither shun her nor sleep.'"

"Springy can also take credit for Mr. Balfour's note of last November, when he undid all the zealous work of Christendom by restoring Holy Zion to the Jews. I believe Mr. Schiff now plans to rebuild the Temple, out of his own pocket."

"But surely you must be a Zionist, Uncle Henry." Like everyone in Washington, Alice knew that the very thought of the Jews made Adams apoplectic. "They will then all be in one place which you won't ever have to visit."

But Adams saw fit to respond, sweetly. "But I *do* want to visit. And now that the British have taken Jerusalem away from the Turks, I wish to gaze reverently upon our holy of holies, the petrified heart of Christendom."

"I think, Henry," said Edith Roosevelt in the tone that she used to quiet her husband, "that you are becoming blasphemous . . ."

". . . at breakfast, too," Alice added.

Aileen Tone changed the subject. Caroline thought of love and age. Lately, she found that she had become like every other woman of her acquaintance and age, totally self-absorbed. Only that morning, Emma had said, "You must stop staring at yourself in mirrors."

Caroline had rallied sufficiently to say, "How else can I see myself, except in a mirror?"

"You are intolerable," said Emma, now in her second year at Bryn Mawr, and interested in mathematics. But that was Emma's problem. Caroline had now become Caroline's problem. Of course, there was a way to see oneself other than in a mirror and that was on the screen. Caroline, Caroline decided, looking down at the pale blind ancient Henry Adams, was not herself, was mad. At the door to the study, she suddenly kissed Adams on the cheek.

"Try not to forget us," the old man said. Thus the fifth and final Heart bade Caroline farewell.

2

A recent bombardment had shattered a grove of trees, stripping them of leaves, branches. In the diffuse light, they looked like a company of dead men stripped of flesh. Between the trees, there were trenches, demarked by barbed wire. On the ground, the dead, American dead. Some looked as if they were asleep. Some stared in horror at the end. Some were unidentifiable as to species.

The Red Cross nurse moved slowly through the woods. From time to time, she would stop at a figure on the ground; stare hard at the face. She wore a dark cloak, creased and soiled; and a man's muddy boots. Finally, at the edge of the grove, she knelt beside a body. She reached out a hand as if to touch the forehead of the staring face. Then stopped; froze.

"Cut!" Tim's megaphoned voice was authoritative. "That was lovely, Emma."

Caroline – known to the studio and "in art" as Emma Traxler – stood up and stepped off the set and into the bright Santa Monica sun. The gray diffuse light of Belleau Wood in France was the work of a gauze net over a platform where skeletal trees and living dead men and lifeless dummies had been carefully arranged by Timothy X. Farrell and his art director.

"Set up the close shot." Tim turned to Caroline. "We have a visitor. Mr. Ince himself."

An agreeable man not yet forty, Thomas H. Ince was a legend, as he might have put it, in his own time. With Griffith and Mack Sennett, he was Triangle Films. In name, Ince wrote, directed, produced. In practice he supervised most of the studio's productions, now working overtime to supply America's hunger for the movies. Here, at Santa Monica, he had built a self-contained village-studio, created solely for the making of photo-plays indoors and out. But Inceville, as it was called more seriously than not by everyone including its creator, was already too small and a new studio village was being constructed some miles to the south at Culver City.

Caroline's first discovery had been that there was no Hollywood in the sense of a movie capital, only villages set in orange groves and onion fields with dusty roads to connect them. As the studio closest to the sea, Inceville was the pleasantest of all the thirty or forty studios.

Triangle's principal rival and soon-to-be owner, Famous Players-Lasky, occupied a small barn-like structure near the corner of Sunset and Vine Street; and it was here, in a blaze of klieg lights (named for the brothers Kliegl: "Who kicked the 'l' out of the Kliegls?" old-timers liked to proclaim) that famous plays were photographed with famous players, the first of whom had been Sarah Bernhardt, who played both Queen Elizabeth and *La Dame aux Camélias*. According to Caroline's French brother Plon, when Bernhardt saw her portly self on screen, she had fainted with horror. "But then," Plon had added, "we all did. Out of respect."

Currently, the world's greatest photo-play star was under contract to Famous Players. At twenty-five, Mary Pickford was still playing pubescent long-haired girls, for which she had been given a million dollars for two years of her time by the Messrs. Zukor and Lasky. She had already made *The Little American,* to the delight of George Creel, and now she was in something called *M'liss.* Patriotism was abroad in the land, and Caroline was now doing more than her part in a seven-reel photo-play that would, Mr. Ince assured her, "make a fortune. I know. I can tell. But don't ask me how."

Beneath an umbrella, Ince and Caroline were served tea, while the six-man orchestra, which was used on the set to inspire the actors, now played light dance music. In the first of Caroline's many weeping scenes, she had discovered, as so many amateurs do, that it is difficult to weep on cue. Tim had suggested that she think of someone close to her dead. She thought of her daughter, Emma; not a tear came. She thought of Plon, who was dead; and scowled, with anger, that she should have lost him in so stupid a war. The orchestra was asked to help inspire tears. The conductor, a violinist, said "I have just the thing. Mary and Doug and Mr. Chaplin all cry like babies when I play. . . ." With that, the orchestra, standing in a hospital set where the wounded and the dying were being ministered to by Caroline, played "Danny Boy," and Caroline laughed. Finally, a stick of camphor was given to Héloise, who held it close to Caroline's face, so that the pungent fumes would make tears while the orchestra softly played "There's a Long, Long Trail a-Winding." The result had been deeply satisfying for Caroline; and authentic, too, according to the delighted Tim.

"The question is . . ." But Caroline was then obliged to shut her mouth as the make-up man repainted her face, starting with the lips. Caroline no longer looked at herself in mirrors. If she wanted to see herself she could watch the rushes. But after staring at herself on the screen for half an hour on the first day, she had had enough. She allowed herself to be painted by others; moved here and there at Tim's orders; and dressed as the wardrobe mistress decreed. Luxuriously, she had given herself up. Let them invent her.

"The question is, how long can we keep you a secret? But then, you tell me. You're a publisher, Mrs. Sanford. You know more about that than we do."

"Not really." The mouth had been finished; now the lines about her eyes were being painted over. "It's bound to come out, and I don't mind at all if . . . well, if I'm not too shameful."

Ince stared at her appreciatively, as if she were a work of art that he had got on loan from a museum. Caroline had seen the same look many times on Hearst's face. "No chance of that. And believe me I'd tell you if there was any danger for you, because it's all on my head, too. No, you're a novelty, and that always works. We've got a raft of Russian royalty out here, all trying to get work with us. Even the socialites are showing interest. Just had a message from Mrs. Lydig Hoyt that she might do a photo-play or two, as war-work."

"Your cup," said Caroline, who knew the New York lady, "run-neth over."

"But where she's just a society name, good for some ballyhooly in the press, you have this face." He looked suddenly sad. "Wasted, if you'll forgive me, all these years when we could have used you. Oh, how we could have used you! Like Marguerite Clark . . ."

"Not Mary Pickford?" Now that Caroline had entered a world of perfect fantasy, she was subject to all sorts of irrational likes and dislikes that she would never have entertained in the real world. Mary Pickford, almost young enough to be her daughter, was the chief rival to be overthrown, while the Gish sisters' wistful charm enraged her.

"Not Mary. There's only one of her, and considering what she costs, there may not even be one of *her* much longer. No. You're something that really hasn't happened before – a woman of forty who looks younger, of course –"

"Who looks her age."

"Whatever. But looks extraordinarily beautiful on screen. We've had a lot of famous actresses who were around the bend, like they say, starting with Bernhardt. But you're not an actress. You're unknown – to the public, anyway – and you're playing your age . . ."

"And here is my son."

A tall dark man of thirty with a small nose and round blue eyes, suitable for shutting in death scenes, saluted them. He wore a torn French uniform. The plot: An American, he had enlisted in the French army. Lost in action at Belleau Wood, his mother, a society butterfly, became an heroic nurse, a second Florence Nightingale; and her search through the battlefields for her lost son was like the stations of the cross, Tim maintained, or Dante's descent into hell. Caroline grew nobler and nobler as the death and destruction all about her grew worse and worse. Caroline was also working herself into an hallucinatory mood: she really was home in France, searching for Plon. From that point of view, the transference of actual self to fictional character was working perfectly, and Tim was awed by the ease with which she became, as they called it, the character.

"Hi, Emma. Mr. Ince. You keeping track of how much film we're using up today?"

"No, I'm just a tourist!"

"Well, don't forget that western you told me about. Did you know," he turned to Caroline, eyes even rounder than usual, "Mr. Ince discovered William S. Hart?" Then Tim pulled Caroline's "son" onto the set and covered him with mud.

"I must've made a hundred westerns," said Ince. "They're fun. Always the same plot. No problems."

"Unlike *Civilization*?" One of the reasons that Caroline was acting as vicereine for Creel in Hollywood was to make sure that nothing like *Civilization* was ever made again. Although it was regarded as Ince's two-and-a-half-hour masterpiece, the pacifist theme popular in 1916 was now, in 1918, treasonable even blasphemous, as the subtitle indicated, *He Who Returned*. The plot concerned the return of Christ as a German submarine engineer, who preaches peace with the usual result. But Ince had cleverly covered himself. Since Wilson was then running for president as the peace candidate, Ince added an epilogue to the film, showing Wilson himself thanking Ince for having made so powerful a contribution to peace and, as it turned out, his own re-election. A man of no particular beliefs, political or otherwise, Ince was now concentrating on films like Caroline's *Huns from Hell*. Meanwhile, his partner, D. W. Griffith, had gone to London to make pro-Allies films; and it was rumored that once the war was over he would make his future photo-plays in the East. The failure of Griffith's expensively ambitious *Intolerance* had so wrecked Triangle that Famous Players had then bought two sides of the Triangle, Ince and Sennett, as well as the debonair screenlover Douglas Fairbanks and the bucolic William S. Hart.

"This is the last Triangle film. So we want to go all out. Open at the Strand in New York. Charge a dollar-fifty a ticket."

As he talked, Caroline thought not of movies but of France. She had made no effort to go back even though there were so many things that she could be doing there, if somewhat less heroic than what she was now playing. Mrs. Wharton – the ancient friend of Henry James – had organized the seamstresses of Paris, and was making clothes for the troops. Saint-Cloud-le-Duc had been taken over by the French government as a hospital, to Blaise's alarm but her secret delight. She could see herself, gently smiling, moving from bed to bed amongst the familiar *boiserie* while . . .

Caroline stopped the image in her mind. She was beginning to think like a movie, always a bad sign. But then she had been think-ing for years like a newspaper – in headlines, sub-heads, bold roman, italics and, of course, pictures artfully arranged upon the page, bigger and bigger pictures as reproductions luckily improved at the same rate that people were able to read less and less text. Once a year the book critic of the *Tribune* would write a despairing piece on literature's approaching end while the drama critic would deplore the effect on the theater of the public's pas-sion for moviegoing. As yet, there was no critic for the moving pictures. But that would come, Caroline decided, as she bade Mr. Ince farewell. They would meet again that evening, socially. There was a Mrs. Ince and children. There was an elaborate social life already established in what was known as the "movie colony," set down like a pillar of fire in the midst of bewildered Iowans.

Tim led her onto the set of a ruined church. There was a section of nave, containing the high altar on which a crucified Christ loomed, amidst the wreckage. Behind the altar a round window contained a few fragments of stained glass. Above the roofless set was the same gray gauze that had filtered the light of Belleau Wood.

"Most authentic," Caroline commended the art director, a newly arrived Russian who spoke no English but, somehow, between bits of French and sign language was able to create anything that Tim required. The make-up man kept fiddling with Caroline's face like a painter with an unfinished canvas. He added white greasepaint to the white layer already in place. We look like dead people, she thought. Yet, on the screen, a transformation took place: the ghoulish white faces in life came alive, while the imagination of the audiences made lips red, cheeks rosy. But not the young old, she thought, grimly, trusting to Tim's instinct that a middle-aged woman could be "ravishing" on screen.

Tim and the cameraman whispered to one another. Two technicians presided over a pair of blazing klieg lights that made the crucifix glow eerily in the dimness. A third light was in place to illuminate Caroline's face. She noted, professionally, that the light was sufficiently high on its arc to erase her lines. Daylight was the worst for an aging woman. Only when the sun was low – rising or setting – could one look at all like oneself and not haggard. Because of the cruelty of natural light, the original film stars had been extremely young, like Pickford and the Gish sisters. But now, thanks to new cameras and controlled lighting, all this was changing, but then everything kept changing in the movie business, unlike life.

Caroline began the task of convincing herself that she would look absolutely "ravishing" in front of the altar, with the highest arc light full in her face. As always, even the thought of light, and her eyes began reflexively to tear. She suffered from "klieg eyes": somehow, dust or light rays caused an inflammation of the eyes that could lead to temporary blindness. The make-up man, quick to see the tears, mopped them up. Should her eyes get worse, ice would be applied to tortured lids.

Tim and Pierre, a French actor who was playing a German officer mutely in broken English, joined Caroline at the altar. As befitted a professional movie actor, Pierre was small, with the obligatory large head, which had been so shaved that the painted white scalp looked like an enamelled Mont Blanc. He wore a monocle.

"Now," said Tim, "this is where you find out that your son has been taken prisoner. Pierre, you are pleased with the situation. You sit, there – at your table below the altar. You're writing dispatches. While she is pleading with you, you keep on reading and writing. Don't look up. Then when she begs you to tell her what prison he's in – we'll follow the script. By the way, do you both know it?" Both claimed knowledge of the script. Caroline always learned her part while driving in to the studio. There had been a time when actors simply made up their lines as they went along, telling one another jokes or dirty stories that had nothing to do with the scene. But they had not counted on the ingenuity of the first audience that had been brought up on movies: many had become skilled lip-readers, who appreciated every nuance of the acting and were horrified whenever an actor betrayed them with nonsense or, worse, obscenity.

"Then you look up, Pierre. You see she's beautiful. You stand up. You come round the table. To your right. You try to take her. She resists. You chase her to the altar. She seizes the crucifix – don't worry, it's very light wood – and she clubs you with it. You fall backwards. We end with a close shot of it, of Nurse Madeleine holding the crucifix. Horrified . . ."

"Transfixed." Caroline delighted in this sort of thing.

"Anything you can think of. Okay. Go to it."

They took their places. At first the camera would be on Pierre. Then Caroline would move so that she was at the center of the picture and at the very edge of the traditional nine-foot distance between the acting space and the camera. In the original photoplays, the camera did not move. But now cameras could be put on automobiles or trolleys and the actors were less constrained.

"Okay!" Tim's voice was authoritative.

"Quiet on the set!" said the assistant. The six-man orchestra was in place back of the camera. The conductor said, "What will it be, Miss Traxler?"

Die Meistersinger." Caroline had already worked out the sort of music she would need to inspire her to heroism.

"German," an unidentified voice sounded.

"Shut up," said Tim. Then the command that started filming, "Interlock."

"My son . . . they say you would know. Where, Colonel von Hartmann, *where* is he? Now."

"Name?"

They went through the standing-sitting part of the scene. Then Caroline made her move into the bright discomfort of the klieg light that conferred, along with burning eyes, glory. Fortunately, glory was not mixed this time with unscripted tears. She delighted in the power of the great light, even as it began to melt the white greasepaint on her face, even as Wagner began to melt her brain.

"You Americans will never learn to fight. Never. Germany will triumph over your mongrel race." Caroline wanted to smile – the French-accented English was ludicrous coming from what looked to be a Hun straight from hell.

"We will – all of us – do our duty, as my son did his," Caroline declaimed into the camera.

"Go on," said Tim.

"I don't have any more words."

"Make them up. Both of you, after he gets up from the desk."

"Henry Adams," Caroline began in her best society-hostess voice, "felt that you Germans were essentially heathen, and your wars are always against Christianity."

"Is interesting," said Pierre, leering up at her. "It maybe *expliquer* why they like to break down the churches. I have only one lung, madame. Otherwise I fight for la France."

The Hun colonel rose from his table; placed his monocle securely in his eye; smiled a slow lascivious smile. "You is very beautiful, madame."

"That is what all you Huns say."

Pierre rose to his full Napoleonic height, an inch shorter than Caroline. "In my script it say now I rape you, madame."

"In my script, too. Rest assured that I will resist like a tigress. I am incredibly brave."

"Is because you never have real man before." Pierre was now in front of her, a foot closer than she to the camera in order to appear taller. He had made more than a hundred photo-plays in Europe.

"Who is Henry Adams?" he murmured gutturally.

"A beloved friend, who died this spring."

Pierre sprang at her; she pushed him away. "Old?"

"Over eighty." She shrank from him. "He was the wisest man I ever knew." Caroline bared her teeth – a tigerish effect, she prayed. *The Meistersinger* was driving her to heights never before attained by mere woman.

"Very good on German character." A Hunnish leer made Pierre's face positively alarming. He reached for her neck. She backed away, toward the altar, terror mixed with resolve in her face. "You should read his last book, *The Education of Henry Adams.*"

With a lunge, Pierre tore her dress at the neck, exposing her collarbone. "My English is not so good enough," he hissed.

At the altar, they were back into the script. "No. Never!" Caroline shouted.

"If you want to see your son alive, you must."

"How *can* you?"

Pierre thrust her back onto the altar; his eyes glittered; he was ready to rape.

"Oh!" was what the script required and "Oh!" was what Caroline said as she turned, saw the crucifix, picked it up and then, holding it worshipfully high, as if in prayer, counted to three and slammed the crucifix down on Pierre's shaved pate. He staggered backward; crumpled to the floor, unconscious or dead – the script did not specify since Caroline would soon be escaping through the horrors of Belleau Wood, where she would meet the American Marines who had, single-handedly, defeated the entire German army, or so the Creel-inspired title cards would instruct the audience.

Tim was ecstatic. "You were wonderful – both of you." He included Pierre, who was now on his feet, rubbing his head. Caroline smiled gallantly at Tim through the dead white mud of her makeup, which was now streaming down her face and into sensitive eyes. The make-up man was upon her with a sponge.

"You didn't mind our chat while I was being raped?"

"I'm afraid I was so excited watching, I didn't listen. You didn't keep to the script?"

"Script ran out," said Pierre gallantly. "We talk books."

"Doesn't matter." Tim had picked up the crucifix. "You were both moving too fast for anybody to read your lips. Anyway, it *looked* great." He held up the crucifix.

"That always has an effect on you Irish," Caroline observed.

"Well, we *are* Catholic."

"No, you're not. I'm Catholic, darling Tim. You're Irish. It's not the same."

"One more shot." Tim was concentrating only on the film. Caroline moaned, as the white make-up was again brushed onto her face.

"Am I to be raped again?"

"No. That was perfect. I want a close shot of you. At the altar. When you turn, pick up the crucifix, turn back to camera. I'll be very close on you then."

"Never say no to a close shot." Caroline repeated movie wisdom through clenched teeth, as bluish lip rouge was applied.

"Then," Tim turned to Pierre, "we get your reaction. When you see the cross, you are, suddenly, horrified at your own evil. You look from cross to the face of the woman you were about to rape . . ."

"Good. I like."

"Will all *that* be on the card?" But Tim ignored Caroline and returned to his place beside the camera. In due course, the word "interlock" was said, and Caroline did become if not another person another self, as she stood at the altar and did what was required of her.

Meanwhile, in real life, the German army was everywhere triumphantly on the move, even as they were demonstrating otherwise in Santa Monica, trying to obscure for millions of people all around the world that at the time this particular photo-play was being filmed in July of 1918, German armies had occupied more of Europe than anyone had ever held before, including Napoleon Bonaparte. The Germans were fifty miles west of Paris. They were the masters of northern Italy, the Balkans, Poland, the Baltic states, the Ukraine; and they had encircled Holy Russia's Holy City, Kiev. More than ever, it was necessary for the Allies to pretend that they were winning. So, if not in the field, on film American Marines kept on destroying the Huns and a simple American mother, armed only with her virtue and her haunting photogenic face, with the odd crucifix to hand, was able to save herself from the carnal lusts of the bestial Hun. This was more potent than newspapers, thought Caroline, as she watched Pierre in his "reaction shot," eyes wide with horror, hands raised to ward off the terrible blow. As always, Hearst was right. But what to do with so novel a means of – what? George Creel would say propaganda. But that was too simple and eventually the audience would learn all the tricks. Even now, at the beginning of movies, the public's passion to know everything about the stars would eventually inspire skeptical curiosity about the what and the why of so powerful a means of entertainment. In a sense, the Allies could actually lose Europe with the average American, three thousand miles away, persuaded that all was well, and the Hun stopped in his tracks by Caroline Sanford, known in art, as the French would say, as Emma Traxler, the newest, least-known photo-player in Hollywood.

As Mrs. Sanford, Caroline was known and courted by the already startlingly inbred world of movie people. Although Hollywood was simply one of a series of small villages strung out along the Pacific from Culver City to Santa Monica, the name had come to signify "movies," and those who worked in the movies were referred to by the bewildered natives as "movies," implying people who moved restlessly about, at great speed, shattering all ten of God's commandments.

Actually, Caroline had found the famous photo-players somewhat on the dull – not to mention overworked – side. They lived in comfortable Spanish-style houses along Franklin Boulevard or at the beach or in the high canyons that fissured the wild Hollywood Hills. Since it was an article of faith that the American public could not fall in love with a screen star who was married in real life, many a father of five, like Francis X. Bushman, was obliged to pretend to be a virtuous bachelor, living alone, waiting, wistfully, for Miss Right to leap from the darkened audience onto the bright screen to share with him the glamour of his life. Meanwhile, Mrs.

GORE VIDAL

Bushman and the children were hidden away from the public's gaze.

Mrs. Smythe received Caroline and Tim in what was known to the fan magazines as her sumptuous drawing room, atop a hill with a view of miles and miles of orchards, and the brown Pacific in the far distance. Mrs. Smythe was small and nervous, and swathed in magenta silk. The voice was more Liverpool than intended Mayfair; but she knew a lot of the world. She had moved to Southern California for her health. Mr. Smythe was president of a firm that made soap. While he gallantly stayed in war-time England, Pamela Smythe had "come out" alone. In no time at all she had established herself as an important hostess, thanks to her alleged wealth and allegedly titled friends. The movie people loved titles, largely, in Caroline's view, because they were obliged to impersonate so many grand people in photo-plays. Now, with the fall of the Czar, White Russians were everywhere. All were titled and balalaikas were played at the drop of a blini and Mary Pickford invariably wept as she listened to yet another lament for the far-off river Don, and serfs aplay.

Dinner parties began at six-thirty because the stars must be in bed by ten unless it was a Saturday night, in which case there might be dancing at the Biltmore Hotel in Los Angeles, and heavy drinking and gambling at one of the few late-night places, or receptions at gracious homes like this one.

"Caroline!" Mrs. Smythe had fallen into the new world's habit of first names. Caroline responded with a "Pamela" that sounded like three names quite worthy of her sister-in-law's slow delivery. Tim was given a radiant smile. "All old pals tonight." Montana was now mingled with Liverpool-Mayfair.

"A round-up at the old corral." Caroline completed the sentiment, as a heavily painted woman approached Caroline, arms outstretched.

"Allow me to present," said Mrs. Smythe, somewhat alarmed at the tableau-in-the-making, "the Countess of Inverness."

"Millicent."

"Caroline." Caroline embraced her old friend. They had been in the same class at Mlle. Souvestre's. Millicent was the niece of an

American president whom neither Caroline nor anyone else could remember as he had been one of the worthy nonentities between Lincoln and Theodore Rex. After school Millicent and her mother had stayed on in London, and Caroline had been presented at court by Millicent's mother. Caroline had then moved on to New York while Millicent married the Earl of Inverness, a local blockhead, who had made her life miserable, as everyone had warned.

"You know each other." Mrs. Smythe was sad. But then the arrival of Douglas Fairbanks shifted the room's attention dramatically, leaving Millicent to weep on Caroline's shoulder. "He is simply vile," she moaned.

"I think him rather attractive." Caroline gazed without shame at the small man with the not-so-large head who had captured the hearts of half the women on earth.

"I don't mean that actor. I mean my husband."

"Is he here?"

"If he were, would I be?" This was said with such dramatic emphasis that a bowl of orchids was nearly overturned. Plainly, Millicent was finding solace in that same drink which, when awash inside her husband, made life vile. Apparently, the Earl, like Jamie Bennett, publisher of the Paris *Herald,* and Ned McLean, publisher of the Washington *Post,* was not only given to long drinking bouts but would, if the occasion was sufficiently public and preferably grand, publicly relieve himself. Jamie had done so many years earlier in a vase at the house of his fiancée, whose brother had then horsewhipped him out of New York and across the Atlantic to Paris for good. Ned favored fireplaces, joyously putting out flames, while the Earl augmented punch bowls: "At the *American* embassy in front of Mr. Page, *our* ambassador. Everyone saw."

"What did you do?"

"I slugged him." Millicent held up a powerful hand, whose rings were set with numerous irregularly shaped stones.

"You must have done great damage."

"I tapped the claret, as they say over there." Millicent looked grimly happy. "We shall divorce once the war is over. That's why I'm here. To get as far away as possible from my life. You know the feeling."

"I've never not known the feeling. That's why *I'm* here."

Although Caroline would have liked to mingle with the famous small people, Millicent pulled her down on a sofa. Japanese servants offered them wine. The tea party was a thing of the past in this part of the West, except among the English, who, like so many Saint Teresas scrubbing floors, worked in the movies while living as if still at home in Surbiton. On the other hand, the six-thirty dinner party was a local novelty that Caroline endured only because she, too, must be up at dawn to face the early sun, which flattered her, while hiding from the noon until the sun was again aslant.

"I'm going back to Washington to live."

"You'll liven us up."

"I'll certainly liven up Alice. What airs she puts on." Millicent had once been the only presidential relic in town; and she had not ceded her high place graciously to Alice Longworth. But Millicent's marriage to an earl somewhat redressed the balance. Caroline saw endless trouble ahead, and news for her Society Lady. "They haven't forgotten me, have they?" At less than fifty, Millicent had skillfully managed to erase her good looks with whisky, which she now poured into a glass from a silver flask attached to a chain about her neck. Yes, thought Caroline, she'll be a joy at the McLeans' if not the Wilsons'. The age of Millicent, Countess of Inverness, would occasion riot and merriment from the Gold Coast of Connecticut Avenue to the moral grandeur of Thomas Circle. "Quentin's dead. Did you know?" Millicent drank her whisky. "A friend wired me from London. Such a nice boy. He was killed in an airplane, fighting an air duel, they said, with the Germans. How strange – an *air* duel!"

Caroline realized then that she had been too long out of the real world. She did not even look at the local newspapers except for the *Kine Weekly,* which gave news only of the movie business. She was up too early; kept too busy; asleep too soon. It was like life in a sanatorium; the only news from outside was business telegrams from Blaise. Now she must write to the Colonel and Edith Roosevelt and – what? to Alice?

One of the little people actually came to Caroline just as Millicent turned to say hello to a White Russian who had swum across the Black Sea, or some other large body of water, to freedom.

Caroline looked down into the bright, glassy, red eyes of Douglas Fairbanks, who promptly noted the state of her eyes. "Klieg eyes," he said. "What are *you* doing, making a photo-play?"

"It's like being a Mason, isn't it? These eyes." Caroline uncontrollably wept; tears triggered by his reminder. Quickly, gracefully, as if he were on the screen, he removed not a sword from its scabbard but an atomizer from his pocket and sprayed her eyes, having first noted that she was not wearing eye make-up. The effect was cooling. He produced a silk handkerchief. "Take it. Keep it."

"You are kind." Caroline mopped her eyes. "It does help," she said; and it did. "I'm doing an appeal for Mr. Ince. For France. In French. I was brought up there, you see." She got, she thought, wildly off the subject; but only into more confusion.

"Why French? The cards are always translated."

"But it won't be *me*, will it? Talking to my . . . sort of . . . native land." Why should a movie star so reduce her to confusion?

"I guess not. Remember the other night, at Mr. DeMille's, I said I'd written a book, which I wanted you to read. Well, I brought it." Fairbanks presented her with a thin volume entitled *Assuming Responsibilities*.

Caroline smiled her delight. "How," she said, as it was expected of her, "do you find the time?"

Fairbanks told her. He had astonishing charm off-screen, unlike so many of the little people, who were like dolls until properly lit and told to move about in that nine-foot-square area where the photo-play had its cramped limited life in the present, a mere prelude to the screen's blazing immortality.

". . . Theodore Roosevelt is my idol," he ended.

"Well, you are both strenuous. I can see that."

The smile flashed like so many light bulbs on a theater marquee. Contrary to dark rumor, the hundreds of teeth were brightly real. "That was a wonderful idea of yours at the Washington *Trib*, to have photo-plays reviewed by the regular drama critic."

Caroline continued to marvel how men and women who were known, literally, to the whole world still managed to keep track of every obscure newspaper reference to themselves in the national press. Who knew what marvelous reviews Douglas Fairbanks was receiving in Shanghai and Lisbon and Caracas? *He* probably did as he counted his vast revenues, yet his eye was also fixed coldly on the drama editor of the *Tribune* because "after that wonderful review of *The Americano* two years ago, he stopped reviewing movies."

Caroline remembered none of this. "I suppose," she improvised, "that *The Americano* was so important a . . . a breakthrough as a photo-play that he treated it as he would a real play or . . . or *The American* by Henry James."

"Pardon?"

Caroline plunged on: never look back. "But I agree. He – or someone else – should realize that a photo-play is every bit as serious a work of art as a Belasco play . . ."

"I'll say!" The handsome jaw set, as she had seen it set a dozen times on the screen. "We're making something absolutely new in history, and we're making it for everybody, and everybody everywhere sees us. You don't know what a weapon this is."

"Oh, yes, I do. I'm here from George Creel, remember. To get you to help the Allied cause."

Fairbanks nodded vigorously, gracefully. Caroline wondered why he did not appeal to her sexually. Was it because everyone everywhere had seen him nod his head like that? and smile? and make love? A half billion people times two represented quite a lot of horns for the actual lover of a movie player to wear. "Of course *you* do. I forgot. No, I came from the theater . . ."

"*A Gentleman from Mississippi!*" Caroline suddenly recalled a handsome young actor on the Broadway stage. He had been quick-moving and, yes, graceful. But now she understood why he had kept moving so restlessly about the stage; he had been shorter than the leading lady.

Fairbanks was delighted. "That show ran two years. You must've been a kid. That was – what? 1910. Anyway, I was like all the stage actors then – a lot now, too – I thought this was just an easy way to pick up a few bucks. But then there was Griffith, and Chaplin and . . ."

"Pickford." Caroline could not resist. Fairbanks was supposed to be separated from his wife and having an affair with "America's sweetheart." Thus far, the starry-eyed American public had not been taken into Hollywood's confidence. War-time censorship had also made it easy for Hollywood to control its own press; and control was necessary. Although most people had accepted the fact that Mary Pickford was a twenty-five-year-old woman who still played very young girls, if "Our Mary" had been suspected of having an affair with a thirty-five-year-old married man and father, her – and his – movies would have been boycotted and every church in the land would call for God's wrath to strike California's Sodom, and turn to tiny bleak salt pillars all the dolls.

Fairbanks took Pickford's name in easy stride. "You've just named the members of our company. We're starting our own studio, with our own distribution. Why should Zukor and you, Tom," he included the newly arrived Mr. and Mrs. Thomas Ince in the conversation, "make all the money? Now we'll keep it all, and only do photo-plays that we really like."

Mrs. Ince smiled, vaguely, at Caroline. The wives, if they were not in the business, spent a lot of time smiling vaguely at one another, and discussing domestic problems and the superiority of Japanese over Filipino servants. From the beginning, Caroline had felt very much at home in this self-contained colony: Washington's obsession with politics quite equalled Hollywood's obsession with its own glamorous product. As a newspaper publisher, Caroline was in the happy position of being equally useful to both sets of colonists.

"As soon as Griffith gets back from London, we start organizing."

Ince smiled sadly. "Well, there's nobody like him. I'll say that. He's the best director there is. But don't let him wreck you the way he wrecked Triangle, spending all that money. . . ."

Caroline enjoyed shop-talk, particularly now that she herself was at work in the same shop.

Later, enveloped in the icy darkness of a cold compress over her eyes, she said to Tim, as they lay in bed together, "What shall I do when everyone finds out that I'm Emma Traxler?"

"Everyone won't. Outside of the few people you actually know, the world will only be interested in what's on the screen, which is Emma, not Caroline. Anyway, do you care?"

"I suppose not. If I did I wouldn't be doing this, would I?"

"I don't know! Anyway, Emma Traxler's going to be a real honest to God star."

"I'm jealous of her already. She'll have the fun and the glory, and I'll just be Mrs. Sanford, the Washington matron."

"I wouldn't fuss." Tim yawned. She removed her compress. They made love. He slept. She tried to sleep but she could not stop thinking of that crucifix, and what sort of wood it was made of that it should be so very light.

3

Burden sat on the terrace in front of the Chevy Chase Club and watched the Sunday golfers setting out or returning from the course, which in the silvery October light looked like the background of a Gainsborough, all dim green hollows and muted green leaves amid leaves already turned earth-brown. The sky was hazy; the day warm. Earlier, he had played nine holes of golf with William G. McAdoo, at Mac's invitation. Whatever the Secretary of the Treasury had in mind, he had not managed to express it while they were enjoying the – mephitic air? For a month, the Spanish-influenza epidemic had spread throughout the western world. Kitty had been struck hard. Luckily, Diana was in good health and Burden himself stayed clear of crowds, and practiced not breathing, an impossible prophylactic against the killer plague. The Senate had been badly hit. It was indeed like a medieval plague, transmitted from person to person, but precisely why some were susceptible and others not was no more understood than why at this particular time in history the plague should occur. The Judgment of God was suspected by some; the German high command by others. Many believed that German scientists had poisoned the reservoirs of the western world. The fact that the influenza had surfaced most virulently in Germany was put down either to carelessness or, again, to God's inscrutable judgment. Alarmists declared that many millions would die before the plague had run its course. Even greater alarmists suggested that the plague would end when the last of the human race had expired, burned first by fever, then drowned in pneumonia's tidal wave. All this, and a world war – and in an election year.

As they were about to leave the ninth hole, a club steward had hurried up to McAdoo: the White House. Most urgent. In silence the two men had walked back to the clubhouse. McAdoo had gone inside, while Burden enjoyed the peopled solitude of the terrace, and pondered why and for what end McAdoo had been sounding him out. The why was easy. McAdoo wanted very much to be the Democratic candidate in 1920. Did he have in mind a McAdoo-Day ticket? Certainly it would be not only well balanced but probably a winner. Burden had the support of Bryan and Champ Clark and the other Southerners and Westerners who still formed the largest single bloc in the Democratic Party, while McAdoo had the Eastern city bosses, the Wall Street bankers; he had also been a highly successful secretary of the Treasury and member of the War Conference Board that currently governed the United States. The fact that he was the President's son-in-law both hurt and helped equally, and so could be factored out of the final equation. But what of the President himself? He had only two more years in which to make the world safe for democracy.

Thus far, Germany had not been defeated – rather the contrary, and the newly arrived Americans were not yet the overpowering fresh force in the field that George Creel's obedient press proclaimed them. Even so, the fact that there were now in France a million troops from across the Atlantic had turned, psychologically, the tide, and that wise prophet Henry Adams had been proved correct when he had said as early as 1914 that Germany was far too small and insignificant a power to be the world's conqueror. In the end, in all honesty, Woodrow Wilson could be able to claim victory. Thanks to him, America's timing had been impeccable. The late entry into the war meant few casualties, while the high-minded appeals to the people of the world over the heads of their selfishly partisan leaders had been, Burden thought but did not say, uncannily like those of the Bolshevik Trotsky. Finally, "peace without victory" was utopian; hence, impossible; hence, acceptable to all. The odds were that if Wilson wanted a third term as president, he could get it. But might he not, like the American dictator in Colonel House's novel, want to lead the whole world? If he were to establish himself as Lord Protector of Democracy somewhere in Europe, then why not McAdoo-Day in 1920? Or the other way around.

McAdoo sat down beside Burden in one of the large white enamelled wooden chairs that characterized the club's comfortable spaciousness. A Negro waiter brought them whisky. "To ward off the flu," said McAdoo. He was tall, loose-knit, with a bat's pointed ears and pursed mouth; at times, he looked like an unfinished sketch of his father-in-law. "Can the executive branch trust the legislative with secrets?"

Burden was light. "No. Never."

"But I will. Remember, this is secret."

"I am mute."

"The President just got back from New York with Colonel House. . . . At that point each man drank. The subject of the assistant president, the *éminence grise,* the Texas Machiavelli, was too enormous for either to embark on. "The President was just given a message from the German chancellor. Germany is ready to accept the Fourteen Points. And stop the war – now."

Burden took this in easy stride. But then the war had never been quite real to him. Now its end was equally unreal. "What about the Allies?"

McAdoo sighed; stared at clouds. "They have made so many secret arrangements."

"As Trotsky told the world . . ." In a fit of mischief, the Bolshevik government had revealed all of the Allies' various secret treaties, so often deplored by the moralizing President, who had himself entered into something very like a secret agreement with Japan over that busy nation's seizure of Shantung in China. Wilson had been embarrassed but unshaken. For him, the Fourteen Points were the only basis for America's entry into the war and that was that. Now Germany had come to him for peace and not to the Allies, who were certain to be bent on revenge and recompense.

"Then we have our war-lovers." McAdoo looked weary. "They want unconditional surrender."

"You don't get that until you've won an unconditional victory. We haven't won much of anything, and the German army's still intact, still in France."

"The War Department estimates that for us to take Berlin would mean a million American lives."

"I think even Cabot would find that high, or Colonel Roosevelt." Although the great jingo affected euphoric pride in the wounding of one son and the death of another, those close to him said that he was quite stricken by the finality of real war so unlike the familiar noise of his own ceaseless theatrical trumpet to arms.

"They want an armistice now."

"What does the President say?"

"He plans to take it up with us, the War Conference Board, tomorrow. This won't be easy."

"The Allies?"

McAdoo nodded. "Then there are the war-mad here at home – and overseas."

Burden understood the war-mad at home: vast fortunes were being made legally and illegally out of the military. Burden had recently joined the Senate Naval Committee, where he had got himself a sub-committee on procurement. Every day he was solicited and lobbied. Bribes were offered both openly and subtly. He had succumbed to neither, but other senators had been weaker than he – or was it stronger? Since the morality of Washington was always relative to need, one man's Gethsemane might be another's Coney Island.

"You will have your problems with the Army." Burden offered a secret for a secret. "General Pershing will oppose any armistice. He wants to fight another year, and ride in triumph through Berlin."

"Pershing?" McAdoo turned to get a full look at Burden. With the sun back of his head, he looked more than ever like a giant bat. "He wouldn't dare."

"I don't know *what* he'll dare, but I have it on the best authority that he'll come out publicly against any sort of negotiated peace."

McAdoo shook his head. "Generals," he murmured.

"They are stupider than most people," Burden agreed.

"Thanks for the warning." McAdoo was grateful. "But for now the problem will be the Allies. They want their ton of flesh. But we have all the trumps."

"We have all the money." It had taken Burden some time to grow accustomed to the phrases "debtor nation" and "creditor nation" and why it made any difference who was what. Great Britain had been the world's foremost lender of capital until it ran out of money in 1914. When J. P. Morgan – later backed by McAdoo's Treasury – paid for Britain's overdraft, the United States became the principal creditor nation. Yet New York, outside Fifth Avenue, was as shabby as ever while it was said that even after four years of war London still shone imperially.

"We have all the money." Burden looked at his watch. He did not want to be late two Sundays in a row. "Anyway, they'll fall in line if the President says just three words."

"Which three?" McAdoo smiled. "'I love you'?"

"No. 'A separate peace.' We went to war not to help the Allies but to get the Germans to accept the Fourteen Points. Germany has now done so. Like it or not, the war's over. And we've won it."

McAdoo nodded. "True. But the British and the French will have to agree at some point. Colonel House tells me, in confidence, that the British and French leaders dislike the President even more than he mistrusts them." McAdoo shook his head. "Imagine Pershing wanting to drag out the war so that he can look like a hero."

"So that *he* can be president."

McAdoo gave Burden a sharp look: yes, this was the object of their Sunday game of golf. "If the people found out that just because he wanted to march down the Wilhelmstrasse one million Americans would die, he'd be hated."

"They voted for Grant. He killed more than a million."

"A different war. A different time. A better cause. Should I resign?"

Burden had expected the question; and had prepared an

answer. "No. You've made a huge success of the Liberty Bonds. You're at the center of a government that's won a war. Stay there."

"I am kept on a tight leash."

"Better that than roaming about baying at the moon for two years, trying to collect delegates." Burden was blunt.

McAdoo affected not to hear the part about the delegates. He was tangential. "You know the best way to get to the President? Mention someone he hates. Tell him something he doesn't know about an enemy. Make it up, if you have to. He warms up immediately. Then you can do anything you want with him."

Burden rose. "Thanks for the game."

They shook hands. McAdoo said that he must wait for a White House car to pick him up. Out of deference to "gasless Sunday," each had come to the club in a horse and buggy. As Burden crossed the high-ceilinged main hall of the club, he wondered what had gone wrong between father and son-in-law. He also thought, with envy, of the vast amount of Wall Street money that McAdoo could call upon if he should make the race for president. Since Burden could deliver as many votes as McAdoo could deliver dollars, the combination was irresistible; only the order was wrong. Why not Day-McAdoo? The Secretary of the Treasury was better known to the whole country than the Senate's deputy majority leader, but where the voters were, there Burden was entrenched, a second Bryan without the first Bryan's primitivism; also without, to be honest, his magic.

Halfway across the hall, Burden found himself face to face with a white-faced Franklin Roosevelt, who had been weeping. Caught off-guard, Roosevelt managed a smile, then quickly covered his face with a handkerchief and blew his nose.

"You look," said Burden, "awful."

The face that emerged from behind the handkerchief was now its usual jaunty rather vacuous self. But the color was pasty; the close-set eyes glassy. "I've just got out of the hospital."

"Flu?"

"Pneumonia. I got it in Europe. I was there two months. I've never been so sick."

For all Franklin's Rooseveltian affectation of vigor, he was a sickly creature, as Burden remembered from the *Sylph*. Then the next association in his mind was abruptly anticipated. Lucy Mercer joined them; she was in civilian clothes. "Senator," she smiled. She was dreamily beautiful. What was the gossip about them? He had heard something; and forgotten it.

"There's been a peace offer." Franklin moved to deflect the subject – from what? Illness? Lucy?

"McAdoo just told me."

"Is he here?"

Burden nodded and said good-by. From Chevy Chase to Connecticut Avenue would be more than half an hour by horse and buggy. He should have asked McAdoo to drop him off in the White House car.

Although Burden was late, she was serene. "Gasless Sunday is ghastly Sunday," she drawled, "until now." They were in her upstairs sitting room, panelled in rosewood. Tea had been set up in front of the fireplace. On Sunday afternoons, only her personal maid was on duty to let him in and to see that the coast was clear of other servants. Later, she would lead him down the back stairs to a side entrance. The master's bedroom was at the opposite end of the marble palace, while the master himself was at the opposite end of the country. "He should be back tomorrow."

As she was so much younger than Burden, he had always taken her for granted, a part of the city's large chorus of decorative girls. Now she poured tea for him on Sundays. Thanks to Caroline, Sunday was now associated in his mind not only with pleasure but with freedom from himself. What Sunday could mean to a woman was beyond him. After all, if they were reasonably adept at traffic management, they had six other days in the week as well.

"Why should Franklin Roosevelt be crying at the Chevy Chase Club, with Lucy Mercer?" This was very much a Sunday question.

"Because," she handed him tea and a plate of Hyler's macaroons, "that was probably their last meeting. Unless," she was thoughtful, "it was the first meeting under the new dispensation. Eleanor has found them out."

"At last." Even Kitty had been concerned at Eleanor's slowness to discover what everyone in their small Washington knew. "How?"

"He came back from Europe with double pneumonia, which is twice as bad as plain pneumonia, which is good enough for the rest of us. Anyway, Eleanor got him to the hospital. Then she came home, and straightened up the empty house, the children were all away. Then she went through his suits from Europe to send them to the cleaners, and there were the love letters from Lucy. It was just like one of those simple-minded plays. I must tell Caroline when she gets back." Frederika's laugh was low and conspiratorial, as if there were only the two of them in all the world.

"Who told you? Alice?"

"Among others. Now comes the part where there is a difference of opinion. All are agreed that Eleanor, nobly – 'so noble,'" Frederika imitated Alice imitating Eleanor, "said that Franklin could have his divorce, but Lucy would have to take their five children. This was brilliant. After all, Lucy has been her secretary and she knows that those five children are like ten. Lucy agreed not to see Franklin again. And now a sad peace reigns."

"But they met today . . ."

"At the Chevy Chase Club, where Senator Day and Mr. McAdoo and everyone would see them, see how wretched they were, and we would discuss them, just like this. I think they want us to know that she, as a Catholic virgin, confronted by a Protestant wife and mother, has decided not to go on without marriage, which is out of the question. So the man weeps helplessly, and she enters a nunnery."

Burden brooded comfortably on the adultery of others. Then he said, "There's something wrong with this story."

"What?" Frederika brushed blond hair away from her eyes.

"I know nothing about women . . ."

"You should've waited for *me* to say that. In anger, of course my darling." Frederika was droll; and seldom too expected. "What's wrong with the story?"

"It's too much a woman's viewpoint. I mean, what about the man's?"

"Is that so different?"

Burden nodded. "It's always different, and when the man's a politician – and here I know everything – it's really different. First,

Franklin could never, under any circumstances, marry a Catholic. Second, Franklin, a divorced man with five children, could never, ever – like double pneumonia – marry a Catholic and expect to win so much as a race for sheriff of Dutchess County."

"So – what happened?"

"Eleanor threatened. He backed down. That's obvious. It's the terms that are curious. I mean, he's always known that he could never marry Lucy. But does Lucy – did Lucy – know that?"

"I see." Frederika was quick. "He could've led her on. Yes. I see that. Then Eleanor forced the issue. And he . . . he is deceitful."

"That's what adultery is all about."

"I meant," said Frederika evenly, "*doubly* deceitful, which you'll admit is once, at least, too much."

"Caroline thinks that he is triply deceitful. But I'm not so sure."

"Why triply?"

"She thinks that Eleanor is in love with Lucy and that Franklin broke it up for everyone's sake, meaning his own."

"If true, he's a master politician." They went to bed. In the act, he thought of Caroline not as she was now but as she had been that first time, which was indeed, to his amazement, truly her first time. In due course, he had become the father of her daughter, who was then attributed to her husband and cousin, John Apgar Sanford, whom she had promptly married. At least *that* secret had been well kept. Blaise knew it; but to Burden's surprise, Frederika did not, and Frederika had been, from time to time over the years, close friend to Caroline. All in all, Burden was grateful to Blaise for not telling his wife, now Burden's mistress in place of Blaise's half-sister, presently living openly in California with one Timothy X. Farrell, whose latest movie, *Huns from Hell,* had opened to splendid reviews at the Capitol Theater in Washington and at the Strand in New York. It was the war film to end all war films and had opened, luckily, just as the war to end all wars was about to end.

4

Jess and the Duchess sat in the last row of the orchestra of the Capitol so that she could see the screen without her pince-nez and he could barely see it at all. But what the Duchess wanted you to do you did. Although the figures on the screen were not as vivid as the myopic Jess might have liked, what he could see was very clearly a marvelous movie. The bravery of the American mother had brought tears to his eyes, and even the usually stony Duchess was obliged to hold her smelling salts in one hand and a handkerchief in the other. The organ played mournful music, suitable for the horrors of war. The night attacks. The bursting shells. Poison gas. Men writhing on the barbed wire. The hospital with the mutilated. For the first time, Jess understood something of war. Most photo-plays about the war had been slap-dash propaganda. No one had ever really looked dead or wounded in them, and the sets had looked like sets. But this was the real thing; and it was said that much of it had been filmed in France with an actual American mother, searching for her real-life son at Belleau Wood. Everyone had commented on the mother's beauty – like a Madonna, the papers said, a Mater Dolorosa, the high-toned ones had added. Now the organ music became ominous. The mother was in a ruined church. Jess hated anyone who would deliberately destroy a church, as these Huns had done. Worse, before the high altar, sat a bald German officer, with a monocle. How a monocle was held in place had always intrigued Jess, whose round eyes could not have held anything at all while his small nose could barely support a pince-nez. The Prussian officer was desecrating the church by using it as his office. Now the music intimated that something even more terrible was about to happen. Jess's hands were moist. Out of the corner of his eye, he noted that the Duchess had moved forward in her seat, the great thin mouth set as if she were the grieving woman on the screen.

The Madonna pleaded for the life of her son, begged to know where he was being held prisoner. Then – this couldn't be really happening, Jess assured himself, heart racing – the Hun smiled evilly; got to his feet; lunged at the devoted mother, who shrank back. There was a single sound from the audience, part gasp, part moan, when they realized that the Hun was about to rape the Madonna *in a church*. She fought him off; he stalked her, she fled to the altar; he followed. Jess had stopped breathing. Then she raised high the crucifix.

The audience, as one, moaned with terror and awe. The face of the Hun was a study in fear and horror as he saw the crucifix slowly descending upon him. The face of the mother was transfixed with a power higher than this earth's; she was transcendent now, at one with God. The crucifix connected smartly with the shaved head of the Hun, who fell backward down the steps of the altar, to a powerful crescendo from the organ. The Duchess gave a single dry sob into her handkerchief. Jess exhaled, tremulously, and hoped he was not having a heart attack. The picture ended with mother and son united by the American Marines on the Marne River, and as the organ played softly "The Marseillaise," the house lights came on and people dared not look at one another for fear that their tears would be visible as they walked, nobly, like the mother, up the aisle, to face the dull daylight of a Washington afternoon.

The Duchess blew her nose loudly in Fourteenth Street, and said, "I know that woman."

"Who? The mother?"

The Duchess nodded and studied the card in front of the theater. "Emma Traxler. That's her name."

"That's not an Ohio name."

"Chicago, maybe. Of course, it could be made up, like Mary Pickford." The Duchess hailed a taxi. "The Capitol. Senate side."

"Well, I think it's one of the best movies I've ever seen," said Jess, still shaken, "about the war, anyway. I felt like I was there, in the trenches, with all that noise."

The Duchess marched round to the door to the Senate cloakroom, which was behind the vice president's throne. As she and Jess were about to go in – the Capitol guards all knew and liked the Duchess despite or because of her bullying ways – the Senator came out of the bathroom opposite, arm in arm with Senator Borah, a tall, burly, lion-headed man from Idaho who was considered radical. It was typical of W.G. that he would go out of his way to befriend someone like Borah, who had furiously opposed the war-time draft, the Espionage Act, and Liberty Bonds. The first because you did not destroy Prussia by prussianizing the United States; the second because the First Amendment guaranteed free speech; the third because bonds pushed up prices, creating inflation. As a businessman, Jess entirely approved of number three, and so, secretly, did W.G. Although it was not politically wise to take such stands in a country mad for war, Borah was fearless while W.G. was careful. Mrs. Borah and the Duchess were on good terms; but then they were neighbors in Wyoming Avenue.

W.G.'s smile was huge when he saw his wife and just as huge when he greeted Jess. "Duchess, why aren't you off at your sewing circle?"

"War's over, they say. How do, Mr. Borah?"

"Mrs. Harding." Borah also smiled at Jess, not recalling him. Jess was used to this: the smile of recognition was recognition enough. Borah's head was like an apple whose two sections started with the part down the middle of his hair and ended with the cleft in his rounded chin. "You see the President's answer to the Kaiser?"

"I've been at the movies." The Duchess sounded as if she had, somehow, just won the war at the Capitol Theater. "The matinee was crowded, which goes to show that the war's about over."

Borah nodded. "Wilson's told the Kaiser that he'll have to abdicate before we talk business. First sign of gumption in a long time."

"I'm going to speak," said W.G. "This is all pretty historic."

Jess was allowed to accompany the Hardings into the holy of holies, the Senate cloakroom, a long narrow room, reminiscent of what indeed it was, a men's club, with a row of tall lockers along one wall, leather chairs, tables, sofas along the other. Two doors at either end gave entrance to the Senate floor.

Like everywhere else, the Senate was sparsely attended these days: those not ill with flu avoided public places. A dozen senators were in the cloakroom; some were writing at the tables; some chatted conspiratorially; a number paid court to the senator from

Pennsylvania, the Republican boss Boies Penrose, a man so enormously fat that once wedged into the largest armchair in the cloakroom, it took at least two pageboys to pull him out of his chair. Old and failing as he was, Jess knew, Penrose would decide, as he always did, who would be the Republican nominee in 1920. When he saw Harding, he waved absently; then he continued his conference with a pair of Western senators. Borah went onto the floor.

Harding and the Duchess sat side by side on a black leather sofa, and while the Senator studied his notes, the Duchess talked to Jess. "What Daugherty would give to be here," she observed.

"Maybe he'll get here one of these days," said Jess, who would have given an arm and a leg to be a member of this extraordinary club just as long, of course, as he never had to get up and make a speech. Even more than the dark and guns and the infamous downstairs broom closet, public speaking terrified him. Much of the awe in which he held W.G. was at the ease with which he could stand up before a crowd and talk and talk without the slightest hesitation or any sign of nerves. Of course it helped to be as handsome as W.G.; and as likeable.

"No. Daugherty lost for good two years ago. If you can't beat Myron Herrick in a Republican primary, you're never going to get elected in Ohio."

The senator from New Mexico came off the floor. He was a genuine cowboy with huge moustaches. He had been one of T.R.'s Rough Riders in the Spanish-American War, and he was a regular at the Harding-Longworth poker evenings. "Howdy, Duchess. Jess." Albert B. Fall never failed to remember Jess's name.

"I thought you'd gone home to repair some fences." The Duchess had no real interest in politics but she doted on elections. Like a baseball fan, she knew everyone's score. Fall was up for re-election in November.

"I'm on my way." Fall looked curiously at Harding, who was checking his notes. With his glasses on and thick white hair ruffled, W.G. looked more than ever like the editor-publisher of the Marion *Star* whom Jess had first met as a boy. "You speaking?"

"A bit of bloviation to swell the senatorial choir, Brother Fall."

Harding looked up; and smiled. "I shall call for brotherly love, as we accept once more in the concert of nations the good people of Germany no longer duped by their bad leaders now fallen from their thrones."

"That will please Carrie Phillips." The Duchess did not so much speak as hiss. Jess felt his face grow hot; palms start to sweat. W.G. stopped smiling. Senator Fall, who had no idea who Carrie Phillips was, merely said, "I just made pretty much the same speech. By the way, I'm getting Colonel Roosevelt to campaign for me."

"Bully," said Harding, in a bad imitation of the Colonel, "for you."

"He's high on *you*, W.G."

"He told Daugherty last May that if he was the candidate in 1920, he'd like having Warren on his ticket. That was when he was speaking in Columbus," added the Duchess, as if erasing with the odd detail her tactless mention of Carrie Phillips.

"He'll need Ohio, and that's you, W.G."

Harding took off his glasses and pocketed his notes. "The Colonel once said to me, 'I think I understand most things pretty well, except Ohio politics.'"

"Simple," said Fall. "Cincinnati is one place and Columbus is another. Lot of folks get confused." Then Fall joined Penrose and whispered something in the fat man's ear.

"Where is Daugherty?" asked the Duchess.

"Cincinnati. Or maybe Columbus." W.G. was relaxed. "I haven't heard. But then I've been on the circuit."

With the President's blessing, Chautauqua was more than ever popular, and those politicians who earned the major part of their income from speaking in the tents were encouraged to speak as much as they liked on condition that they, subtly or not, support the war effort. Harding's set speech for years had been the career of Alexander Hamilton, the result of once having read, while taking the cure at Battle Creek, a novel based on Hamilton's life. Jess had heard the speech a dozen times and could hear it a dozen more. Harding never altered a word or any of the six gestures that he always used, in the same sequence, as prescribed by the elocution book. But the coda of the unalterable speech was changeable.

Harding could always join his hero, Hamilton, with whatever contemporary issue he chose – in this case the winning of the war to end all war in democracy's name.

"Daugherty's a brilliant man." W.G. combed his hair, without a mirror, something the thin-haired Jess could never have done. "But he's got so many political hatreds now that I worry about him. He takes things too hard."

"He's a good friend." The Duchess had been made an ally very early in Daugherty's campaign to make W.G. president, a most unlikely enterprise, if Theodore Roosevelt was going to run, which he was. But vice president wasn't so bad, as even Daugherty tended to agree when he and Jess discussed, endlessly, the subject.

"I wish," said W.G., standing up, and straightening his jacket while the Duchess brushed dandruff from his shoulders, "that he wouldn't keep mixing up my politeness with folks as agreement or weakness. Somehow or other he's got the notion that I'm politically sort of below par. You know, easily 'strung.'"

"You're too nice to people. You trust everybody." The Duchess echoed Daugherty.

"Trust everybody, and you don't have to trust anybody. Anyway, you get more flies with honey than vinegar." Harding pulled in his stomach, held high his head. There was no handsomer man in public life, thought Jess. Then the Senator pushed open the swinging doors and walked onto the Senate floor and into the day's history.

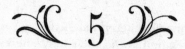

5

1

As the crucifix was raised high, Caroline shut her eyes. To date, she had watched *Huns from Hell* a dozen times, and each time she had found something new to dislike despite the fact that she had been compared favorably to Duse, the actress of muted effects. To herself, she seemed more school of Bernhardt, all artifice and embarrassing broadness of gesture.

The moment safely passed, she opened her eyes, and glanced at the President; who was absolutely concentrated on the screen while next to him, Mrs. Wilson gasped inadvertently as the crucifix, yet again, made its fateful rendezvous with poor Pierre's skull. For all eternity, or until the celluloid turned to dust or whatever celluloid was scheduled to become, Caroline would be raising and lowering that crucifix and Pierre would be falling backwards, backwards, backwards. Could *this* be hell, repetition?

At the end, a new title card had been added, to acknowledge the string of inexorable American victories from the Marne to the Argonne, as the Hun was driven back toward his lair across the Rhine. The guests in the East Room applauded the victories, undisturbed that the Allies, who had contributed so much, were not mentioned. "We'll have different cards in the different countries," Ince had said. "That way everybody gets to win the war except the Huns." To which Tim had responded, "There's quite a German audience, too. Why not let *them* win in the German market?"

There was more applause as the picture ended with a long shot of Caroline, gallantly walking into the future, wind from a machine in her hair, eyes aglow with a bad case of kliegitis, and everywhere desolation, broken only at the end by a cloud's passing and – look! the sun. It had taken two days to get this cloud effect from the pier at Santa Monica.

The lights in the East Room were switched on. The red-eyed guests of the President got to their feet. The President shook Caroline's hand. "You should be very proud of having produced this."

"I'm afraid it comes a little late for the war effort." Caroline, as always, marvelled that after two hours of watching her on the screen people could then turn to her in real life and make no connection at all between the giant shadow-image and the real-life miniature. She had given herself credit as producer because Triangle had run out of money halfway through and to shut down would have been fatal to Tim's career, or so she liked to think and he to say.

Huns from Hell had been astonishingly successful; and there was great curiosity about Emma Traxler. There were also numerous photo-play offers for her services, all sent in care of Mr. Ince, who thought that she should take her new career seriously. But Caroline understood luck, if nothing else. There were certain accidents in life that did not recur. This was one. Of course, she could be an old actress, but that was rather worse than being an old private lady who was not obliged, ever, to look into a mirror.

Edith Wilson took Caroline's arm, and led her from the East Room across the hall to the Green Room. "A few people are staying for coffee. Do join us."

"Of course, but . . ."

"Mr. Farrell, too." Mrs. Wilson was tactful. "I hadn't realized how – well, powerful, a photo-play can be. In a way, it's more exciting than the theater."

"Quicker, certainly."

"We should have had music. I told Woodrow to get the Marine-band pianist. But, poor man, he's dead – just like that. The flu. And where do you find someone good on such short notice?" The

188

Green Room was now beginning to fill up. From the War Council, there was the Californian Herbert Hoover, who was thought to be a genius of organization, or so Caroline read in the *Tribune*. Caroline had found him agreeably shy at dinner. They had talked of China, where he had been an engineer at the time of the Boxer Rebellion. They had not discussed food rationing, a subject which his chubby face, somewhat incongruously, personified.

George Creel and Tim came in together. Creel was delighted. "We'll show this all over Europe," he said to Caroline. "Show them just what they owe us."

Caroline was startled by the crudeness. "Surely they know better than we do what they owe us, if anything."

"You should take a look at their press! You'd think we hadn't been in the war at all. That's why a movie like this is so important. They'll pretend they won all by themselves and then they'll try to find reasons not to accept the German peace offer." The room was dividing into swarms. The largest flocked about the President and Colonel House, who was due to return to Europe, where he would have to convince the Allies that the Fourteen Points were America's immutable terms for peace.

"I don't think they'll want to go on fighting without us." Creel smiled. "Remember last summer? France was done for. England broke. Well, *we'll* arrange the peace whether the Allies like it or not. What will you do next, Mr. Farrell?"

Tim smiled his altar-boy smile. "Now the war's over – and won – I think I'd like to do something on Eugene V. Debs."

Creel was taken aback. "Debs? But he's on his way to prison." The leader of the Socialist Party had never much interested Caroline, but now that she was obliged to see some of the world some of the time through the eyes of her lover, she had become interested in Debs, who had received a million votes for president in 1912. Then, with violent rhetoric, Debs had opposed the war as well as capitalism. He was also given to praising if not, perhaps, reading Marx and Lenin, and he did not view the Bolshevik revolution as inimitable. Briskly, the United States government had charged Debs with violating, through the exercise of free speech, the Espionage Act of 1917. As briskly, a court had sentenced him to ten years in prison. Currently, he was free on appeal. But everyone knew that the Supreme Court would unanimously find him guilty, invoking Justice Oliver Wendell Holmes's celebrated condition of when speech was free and when it was not. Speech was absolutely free, he had ruled, except when there was "a clear and present danger."

If nothing else, Tim had confronted Caroline head-on with the realities of this, more than ever, strange country whose harsh contradictions she had tended to take for granted. Although she was not as sentimental as he about such abstractions as justice, her Cartesian education made her wary of illogical propositions. Either one could speak freely of political matters or not; if not, do not claim that there is freedom of speech when its exercise means ten years in prison. The "clear and present danger" proposition was, to Caroline, itself a clear and present danger to freedom itself. She had argued as much to Blaise, who had said that she had misunderstood the nature of a republic whose contradictions were, in some mystical way, its strength.

Meanwhile, Creel's swift energetic crude mind had now taken up the idea of a film about Debs; and found it good. "You know, it's inspired, Mr. Farrell. You're quite right. You've shown us the Huns from Hell. Well, we've taken care of them. So what's next? The Bolsheviks, communism, socialism, labor agitators, the enemy within our own country. That's where the real danger is now. Show Debs and Trotsky, working together to enslave every American, something not even the Huns thought of doing because we're both Christian nations with the same capitalistic systems. But the Bolsheviks have got a new religion that could just take off in this country. Look at the railroad strikes, the coal strikes – you can't tell me someone somewhere isn't manipulating our workers in order to destroy our freedoms . . ."

"Of which," Caroline was sententious, "freedom of speech is the most important."

"Absolutely . . ."

"Even when danger is clear and present . . ."

"Exactly!" Creel was beside himself with a new crusade. Caroline gave Tim a reproachful look. Tim shrugged. It was inevitable that the Creels would find a new enemy to take the place of the Huns. As Tim described the searing indictment of Debs that Creel would want him to make and that he would not, Edith Wilson drew Caroline into the President's orbit. "You know, that marvellous actress looks quite a bit like you. Naturally, she's older." That was the closest people ever came to working out the identity of Emma Traxler. At first, Caroline had been mystified to discover that no one realized that she was Emma. But Tim had explained it to her: "It's because people don't really look at other people if they know them." Tim's life work was to see precisely what he saw. "But a stranger who doesn't know Caroline Sanford will see you on a street and realize that you are Emma Traxler." This had happened more than once in New York and Washington. But so clearly was she identified with herself among those who knew her that she simply could not be anyone else. Also, Emma's hair was different, and her luminous Madonna face was the result of careful lighting which real life – light – cruelly refused to supply.

"Emma Traxler is Swiss, from Unterwalden in Schweiz. A very old family. I knew her in Paris when she was on the stage." Caroline loved inventing Emma. But then so did the press, who had changed her provenance to Alsace-Lorraine, that lovely divided borderland which had reputedly given the world so much, not least the creator of the Universal movie studio, Carl Laemmle, from neighboring Württemberg.

Colonel House took Caroline's hand in both of his. Edith withdrew. Like a kindly gray rat, House whispered compliments into Caroline's ear, particularly for the *Tribune*'s editorial policies. Behind him, the President held court.

"The Allies will be difficult, won't they?" Caroline had never been able to determine the nature of House's influence over Wilson.

Plainly, the little man was an adroit flatterer in the lay-it-on-thick Texas style; plainly, he was disinterested in the sense that he did not want money or public office, which impressed everyone but Caroline, who knew that to exert power in the world was the most exquisite of all interests; plainly, he was intelligent. The mystery, if mystery there was, had more to do with Wilson's singularly remote personality than any design, no matter how interested and interesting, of the Texas Colonel. Wilson had no men friends because he believed, as only a university professor could, that he had no equals; certainly this was the impression that he had made on the leaders of his own party, men who took themselves quite as seriously as he took himself. For someone so isolated by his own forbidding rhetoric and by the Constitution's war-time powers, a Colonel House was a necessary link to the world outside himself.

". . . I sail on the fourth of December. I expect, before I go, we'll be hearing good news from Germany."

"What about from France and England?"

"We have most of the cards, Mrs. Sanford. Fact, maybe all of the cards, for now. The real problem is afterwards, making peace."

"I've met some of your young men. They are formidable."

"The Inquiry?"

Caroline nodded. A year earlier House had set up a board of young scholars whose task it was to make plans for the new world that would emerge from the peace conference. Historians were put to work studying Europe's boundaries, language groupings, religions; also, they were allowed to study the secret treaties that the Allies had made with one another and with interested countries like Italy, which had been promised a large chunk of the Austro-Hungarian Empire in return for a collusive neutrality followed by war. The Bolsheviks had published the lot, embarrassing the President, who pretended that he had not known of the treaties. Since the Fourteen Points meant redrawing Europe's map, the unenviable task of the Inquiry group was to conform Wilson's generous "peace without victory" – a phrase invented by one of the Inquiry men, a *New Republic* editor, Walter Lippmann – and the secret treaties, which represented total victory for the Allies and not much peace.

The soft whisper was eminently soothing. ". . . the Kaiser will abdicate, and there will be a republic, and an armistice, and then the peace conference, where, I hope I'm not bragging too much, we'll go in, those boys of mine, certainly, the best prepared of the lot. We're ready for anything, including, if we have to, the partition of Schleswig-Holstein, along racial lines."

"How amazed the French will be! They think us totally ignorant . . . of European politics," she added, quite aware of France's
jealous contempt for everything American.

"The British Foreign Office has a sort of French mentality, too."
The gray rat's eyes gleamed with good humor. In the background
the President, eyes half-shut, seemed to be giving a sermon.

"Who will negotiate for us?" Caroline expected no answer but
often the way that a question was not answered was revelatory.

"I suppose we'll continue as we are."

"With you in Paris – or wherever . . ."

"And the President here, telling me what to do."

"No Lansing?" The President's dislike of his secretary of state
was common knowledge.

"Well, maybe, not too much Lansing." House chuckled.
"Anyway, it shouldn't take very long. We're ready for once."

"The President stays here?"

House nodded. "This work isn't for the chief of state. After all,
he's the British king and prime minister all rolled into one. He's
too huge for our sort of a conference. He should come over,
briefly, show the flag – they think he's God, you know. Then vanish into the empyrean, just like God."

On the way back to Georgetown, Tim was both exultant and
impressed. "If the South End of Boston could see me now."

"They were mostly South Enders there." Caroline was melancholy, and did not know why. "They just got out long before you
did." The chauffeur came to a stop in Wisconsin Avenue, as a long
line of dull black hearses slowly crossed the street en route to – or
from – the morgue. "I wonder if everyone will die?" Caroline took
her gauze mask from her handbag and slipped it in place over her
nose and mouth. Most people were masked when out of doors or
in a public place.

"That would solve a lot of problems." Tim was light-hearted. He
did not wear a mask.

"They say more people have already died of flu than died in the
war. Frederika's got it, my sister-in-law."

"Serious?"

"Yes."

An authentic Emma was waiting for them in the drawing room. She was large and fair and very like Burden. Obstinately, she had missed beauty wide. Caroline longed to do something with her but Emma was not to be altered by anyone. She was happy as a mathematician, a field forever shut to her mother. Now, because all the schools had shut down, Emma had come home. Caroline was glad that their relationship was sufficiently polite that no questions would be asked when Tim stayed over. Emma took everything in stride. Whether this was a sign of intelligence or of perfect indifference, Caroline could not fathom. But then she, too, had reserves of indifference ever ready to be called upon. "Five thousand people died yesterday, that they know of," was Emma's cheery greeting. She was curled up on a sofa beside a fire now fallen to coals and ash.

"In the country?" Caroline removed her mask.

"Here. In the District. Hello, Mr. Farrell."

"Hi, Emma." Tim was still euphoric from his White House success. "Did you see Creel's face when I said I wanted to do a movie about Debs?"

"I saw it. Luckily, he misunderstood you."

"Democracy should begin at home." Tim made himself at home; poured whisky neat into a glass. "The Chicago race riots last summer . . ."

"Aunt Frederika's worse," Emma cut in.

"Oh, God." Caroline sat beside the fire. Perhaps it *was* the end of the world after all. The plague would come to every house until everyone was dead. "Uncle Blaise?"

"He's with her. He's all right. He thinks he's already had it, a mild case."

"How seriously are you Catholic?" Tim turned, seriously, to Caroline.

"Not at all, ever. It's *this* life I fear, not the next, which isn't there."

"Lucky you to think that." He changed the subject. "I think the President recognized you. I caught him staring at you after the crucifix . . ."

"We're old acquaintances." Quickly, Caroline broke in: Emma

194

did not know of the mythical Emma. Fortunately, Emma did not go to movies. "What are you reading?"

Emma held up the book in her lap. "Uncle Henry's last book. About his education. I went to see Miss Tone today. She's still in the house. It's all very sad."

"Sadder for us than for him. He died in his sleep." She looked at Tim, as if this were, somehow, significant.

"He was smiling, Miss Tone said, when they came to wake him up."

"So much history – gone." Caroline wondered if now she would begin to speak in movie title cards, with numerous dashes and exclamation marks.

"The whole Negro question is really interesting, and no one's done it." Tim was not about to mourn Henry Adams.

"Why interesting?" For someone so deeply flawed with the politeness of class, Emma was curt.

"Look at the fix they're in. Twelve million of them live here in a country that's fighting to make the world safe for democracy, and most of them can't vote or have the same rights as white people."

"Maybe they don't want them." Emma was not of an imaginative or, indeed, generous nature, thought Caroline, who was not generous either but sufficiently imaginative to be able to understand what others felt. Perhaps it was this odd gift that had made it possible for her to become so easily the mythical Emma Traxler, who could become Madeleine, a mother at the Front.

"If they didn't want the same rights, why do you think hundreds of people were killed or hurt last summer in Chicago?" Tim was looking at Emma with interest.

"Perhaps," said Emma, "the white people thought that the Negroes wanted something which they shouldn't have, and so they attacked them first, the way they do in the South when they lynch one."

"Ingenious." Caroline applauded. Much of Washington's charm for her had been its Africanness both in climate and population. Racial equality had not meant much of anything to her or, she thought, to most Negroes, who ignored the white world as the white world ignored them, or so it seemed to her, each race living

195

in separate if contiguous universes in two separate but simultaneous Washingtons.

"No. They want the same rights. Particularly now they've been in the Army, fighting for democracy . . ."

"Such a meaningless word." Although Caroline's teeth were set on edge by all political rhetoric, the reverent intoning of the national nonsense-word "democracy" most irritated her. The much-admired Harvard professor George Santayana, now retired and withdrawn to Europe, had noted the curiously American faculty for absolute belief in the absolutely untrue as well as the curiously American inability to detect a contradiction because, as he had written, an "incapacity for education, when united with great inner vitality, is one root of idealism." That was it – American idealism, the most unbearable aspect of these people. For the first time in years, Caroline wanted to escape, go back to France, or on to Timbuctoo, anywhere that these canting folk were not.

Tim did not cant; but he came perilously close in his espousal of the rights of man – liberty, equality, fraternity. But where he believed or believed that he believed in these things, the French regarded them as mere incantations to ward off unpleasant disturbances like revolution. "Of course, democracy doesn't mean anything for them. There was this sign they were carrying in Chicago – a wonderful picture, crowded street, howling whites, blacks huddled together, police with guns, sticks – and this sign that says – like a title card, you know? – 'Bring Democracy to America Before You Carry It to Europe.'"

Emma looked at Tim curiously. "Are you a Red?" she asked.

"No. Catholic." Tim smiled at Caroline. "A believing one."

"Tim has a feeling for the masses only because he makes photoplays for them." Caroline's voice had set itself in the gracious-hostess register.

"So does Griffith, and *The Birth of a Nation* did more to revive the Ku Klux Klan than anything in years."

"Mr. Griffith," said Caroline, rising to the occasion, "makes movies for the white masses who are willing to pay as much as three dollars to see a very long photo-play."

"My history teacher was at Princeton when Mr. Wilson was president there." Emma was now stirring up the coals with a poker. She was too red in the face for Caroline's taste. Fever? Flu? Death? "He said that whenever a Negro applied for admission to Princeton, Mr. Wilson would write a personal letter saying that he was happy that the colored man had qualified but he felt it only his duty to warn him that as many of the students were from the South, he'd have a hard time of it if he came."

"They didn't come." Tim finished his whisky.

"They didn't come." Emma put down the poker and stared into the revived fire.

"I'm going to France," said Caroline, rising; then she heard herself, a fraction of an instant later. "Why did I say that? When all I meant was I'm going to bed."

"You mean," said Emma, "you'll do both. You *should* go. Uncle Blaise says he's going. He'll be at the Peace Conference."

"'Peace without victory.'" Tim remained in his chair. Caroline looked forward to a bed to herself. Lust came in cycles; departed the same way. Besides, she refused to brood morbidly on flu's silent sudden death in the act of love. Was it possible that Frederika, the serene, the competent, the droll, would die?

From the bedroom, Caroline rang Blaise. He sounded tired. "She's the same. The crisis hasn't come, whatever that is. These damned doctors are hopeless."

"Is she conscious?"

"She drifts back and forth. She makes no sense. What happened at the White House?"

"The Fourteen Points have won the war, and Colonel House sails to France in four days, to make eternal peace."

"Is he the official negotiator?"

"So he implies. Helped by all those bright young men at that boardinghouse in Nineteenth Street . . ."

"All Jews and Socialists."

"I'm going to Paris, as soon as it's possible." Caroline stemmed the familiar tirade.

"Should both publishers be there?"

"Mr. Trimble would be relieved to have us both out of town permanently."

"We'll see." Blaise sounded exhausted. "*I'll* have to see."

"Of course," said Caroline; and said good night. Before she turned out the light, she stared a long time at the painting of her mother, Emma the First. The lady's resemblance to the Empress Eugénie had not gone unremarked by the painter. Although the dark eyes stared at Caroline, there was no message, only a painted simulacrum of a woman that she had never known, yet Caroline had twice bestowed her mother's name upon her own inventions as if there were some unfinished business in the past to be completed if not now later.

2

Burden sat in his office, signing letters, while Miss Harcourt, old and gray and silent, perched on a straight chair beside his desk. She wore a man's shirt, tie and jacket; only a reluctant skirt was concession to the prejudices of her unhappy time and place. Miss Harcourt lived with her mother in northeast Washington; she had worked, superbly, grayly, silently, for Burden ever since he had first come to Congress as the old century turned to the new, now almost one fifth done.

The letters were appeals to various leaders about the country to support the Democratic Party in the coming election. Since Burden himself was not up for re-election, he could appear personally disinterested in requesting aid for the party. But the list, of course, carefully compiled over a decade, represented his own potential backers when and if the time should come for him to seize the crown. He was maintaining connections.

The last letter signed, he sat back in his high leather swivel chair; and felt somewhat light-headed. The afternoon sun cast a beam of light on the bust of Cicero opposite his desk. On either side of the white marble fireplace glass-doored bookcases contained law-books as well as statute books of the United States of America. Over the mantel hung an engraving of Lee surrendering at Appomattox, which did not displease his constituents, most of whom, though Westerners now, descended from Confederate soldiers. On the mantel was the bullet that had struck his father at Chickamauga – a skewed bit of black metal set on a marble stand. When the old man died, he had, with some bitterness, left his son the bullet as a reminder of who he was and what war was, a reminder of the people, the people, the people. Lately, words had a tendency to repeat themselves oddly in his head: maddeningly, unwanted series of echoes would start and then, mysteriously, stop.

The best thing to do was talk through the echoes. As "the people" tolled in his head, he spoke to Miss Harcourt. "Is Congressman Momberger in his office?"

"No. He too has been stricken. The Spanish flu. Late last night, Mrs. Momberger said."

"We must adjourn. Remind me to talk to Senator Martin today." "The people" stopped, leaving him with a headache.

"I called the Sanford house," said Miss Harcourt, who either knew everything and thought nothing of it or knew nothing and thought not at all. "*She* is past the crisis, they think."

"Oh, good. I must – tell Kitty to pay her a call when she's better." At first, he was positive that Frederika would die. Fate did that sort of thing to one. But she had clung to life or life had clung to her; and when he saw Blaise at the nearly empty Cosmos Club, Blaise had said that she'd be all right.

The telephone rang. Miss Harcourt answered it, then turned to Burden. "Mr. Tumulty wants to know if you could see the President this afternoon."

"Five o'clock." While Miss Harcourt so instructed the President's secretary, Burden got up and went to the tall window with its view of Capitol Hill. But he looked not through the glass at the familiar view but at his unfamiliar pale, old face reflected in the glass. He must take more exercise, like horseback riding. He thought of Caroline, as he always did when he thought of all those Sundays that he had ridden along the canal beside the Potomac, ending the morning at her house. Since they were not married, the affair had been allowed to come to a pleasant, natural end. Neither was jealous of the other. Gradually, they had come to meet less and less in secret and more and more in public. Finally, after the hardfought election of 1916 when Burden had spent weeks touring the country, without a word spoken on either side, the affair had stopped.

"Tell Kitty I'll be home for dinner."

Miss Harcourt inclined her head. Like most of the Senate secretaries, she was at permanent odds with the Senator's wife. After all, the secretaries spent more time with the senators than the wives did; and the wives were jealous of all those hours, days, years from which they were excluded.

The President and Admiral Grayson were putting on the south lawn of the White House, just back of the executive offices. A Secret Service man greeted Burden by name.

Burden crossed to the improvised putting-green. As he did, Wilson said to Grayson: "That's enough fresh air, Admiral."

"Never enough, sir." Grayson took the President's putting-iron. "I've got neuritis in my shoulder, so the doctor prescribes golf. True agony." Burden had never seen Wilson so relaxed, even boyish, despite aches and pains. "Let's look at the sheep," he said.

The south lawn of the White House was a miniature park that Edith Wilson had turned over to a flock of Shropshire Downs sheep, whose wool had sold for a good deal of money around the country as an encouragement to American women to knit for peace – without victory.

"How close is it, Mr. President?"

"An armistice? Maybe a week, two weeks. There's no trouble on the German side or our side . . ." Wilson left the thought unfinished. Halfway down the lawn, a bench had been so situated that passersby could not see it through the iron fence while the Secret Service man could see both passersby and bench. Burden had often daydreamed about the presidency; yet the actual reality of it never ceased to bemuse him, a combination of banality and grandeur, of dullness and true terror at the thought of so much energy concentrated in one man, in one place, time.

"They say I never consult the Senate. But I always consult you, don't I?"

"*Sometimes* you consult me." Wilson's dislike of the Senate was warmly reciprocated. Each senator was to himself a microcosm of the government and, combined with his fellows, sovereign, a state of affairs that the true sovereign, Wilson, was not about to acknowledge.

"I haven't discussed this with the Cabinet." Wilson gave Burden a statement, typed neatly on his own blue-ribboned typewriter. "But I want to get your view first. Tumulty approves. So does Colonel House. But they're not politicians – like us," Wilson added graciously. As Burden read the text, Wilson hummed a song from the last vaudeville program at Keith's before the flu closed it down. As the cheerful song droned in his ear, Burden experienced nightmare. The master political manager of their time and country had committed, at least to paper, a major political catastrophe.

Burden carefully folded the text twice, as if he could twice dispense with it. Wilson had stopped humming. "You disapprove?"

"Yes." There was no point in the usual evasive demur, suitable for the greatest autocrat in the world, as Wilson himself had referred to his constitutional war-time self. "You are making a direct appeal to the people to give you – you, personally, it sounds like – a Democratic majority in Congress so that you can single-handedly – I'm anticipating Lodge and Roosevelt – make the peace."

Wilson was sweet reason. "I also have reminded the electorate of all those domestic reforms which we – the Democratic Party – have made and which would be unmade if the Republicans were to win."

Burden gazed bleakly at the grazing sheep. What to do?

Wilson was surprisingly placating. "Vance McCormick and Homer Cummings and the whole National Committee, or so they tell me, want this statement now."

"Mr. President, without any sort of statement from you, we will organize the Senate with anywhere from a five- to ten-vote majority and, maybe, fifteen to twenty in the House. But if you interfere and tell the country that the Republicans can't make the sort of peace you can, that's a red flag to a bull –"

"Lincoln, McKinley, even Colonel Roosevelt made similar appeals."

"I haven't read their calls to arms lately, but a mild comment to the effect that you don't change horses in midstream is very different from warning, lecturing . . ." He had used the fatal verb. Wilson the lecturer stiffened. But Burden plowed on, ". . . the people by telling them that if they don't vote the way you want them to the Europeans will think that you've been repudiated. You are too personal, if I may say so."

The two familiar red smudges appeared at the top of each high cheekbone. "The office does have its personal side, Senator."

"All the more reason to depersonalize it as much as possible. Don't make yourself the issue –"

"I am the issue. If we lose the Senate, Lodge will be majority leader. He'll also be chairman of Foreign Relations. When I bring home a treaty, he can delay it, just the way he used to delay – and finally kill, I'm told – his friend John Hay. So you see why I must do everything possible to keep our majority in Congress."

Burden nodded. "I agree. And the best way of keeping our majority is to tear that thing up. Then speak humbly to the people, from whom your power comes, because you know that in their essential rightness they will, as always, or at least as in 1912 and 1916, do the right thing. You know the spiel."

Wilson stared at the sheep, who were, even to Burden's rural eye, remarkably uninteresting. Then the President sighed, and stood up. "They say one American in every four has or will have the flu."

Burden also rose. "They think, around the world, twenty million will die."

Together they walked slowly back to the executive offices, where the Secret Service man kept watch. "I wonder if I should wear a mask when I talk to Congress next."

"Or plugs in your ears."

"How they talk! How they talk. Anyway, so far, they haven't given me flu." Each man touched the same oak tree for luck. "How did my last speech go down?"

"Those who hate women's suffrage were not moved. But women are bound to get the vote in a year or two."

"I've always been against letting them vote. But then I thought to myself women cannot be stupider than men."

"We are as one on that."

"Also, I noted that in those areas where women are allowed to vote they tend to support me. I find this a sign of the highest wisdom."

"Well, Mr. President, it *was* Eve who ate the apple of knowledge."

Wilson laughed. "What a peculiar story that is, between us, of course."

The next morning Burden awakened with a high fever, aching muscles, and an uncontrollable cough. The doctor declared him a victim of flu. With that, he entered a nightmare realm where at times Kitty was ministering angel and at others demon-in-residence. One of his nightmares was that the President had released the text of what Burden had read; and nothing was altered. Later, the nightmares involved Roosevelt and Lodge campaigning across the land, denouncing Wilson. But bells also rang. There was an armistice that was celebrated prematurely; then there was an armistice that meant war's end. All this swirled about in Burden's fever-dreams, where, time and again, he was visited by his father in his corporal's uniform, young and fierce, and on his father's lips, over and over and over again, the words "the people."

Burden returned to life: and decided that he preferred death or whatever realm it was that he had occupied when the dreaming stopped and there was nothing. He opened his eyes and saw Kitty, reading a newspaper beside his bed. "What time is it?" he asked.

"Oh – hurray!" Kitty threw the newspaper into the air; she was entirely out of character. But then everything was not as it should be. For one thing, he had been transferred from his own vigorous body to an old man's wasted frame. The sunlight hurt his ancient eyes. He shut them. "The fever's all gone, the doctor said. But it takes time to get your strength back. Are you hungry?"

"Thirsty."

Kitty gave him a glass of water. With a great effort he sat up and drank, with difficulty because his lips were blistered from fever. Then he fell back on the pillow. "I've been sick," he said stupidly.

"Very sick," Kitty agreed. She smiled at him, but her face was haggard and the blue eyes dull and there was more gray than usual in her once-blond hair. "But now you're all right. Ever since late last night when you . . . you were all right again."

Burden held up one of his hands; a strange hand that he'd never seen before, gray skeletal fingers except for the large knuckles, which were red.

"You've lost weight." Kitty picked up the newspaper from the floor. "I'm your nurse now. We had two for the whole time, day and night."

"How long – was the whole time?"

"Two weeks."

"My God." Two weeks out of time, flesh, life. Death is nothing at all was the message.

"It's November twelfth now, and Germany has signed an armistice. See?" She held up the newspaper. A headline declared peace. The President would address Congress at noon; and give the terms. "There was such disappointment last week when everybody felt the war was really over because the Kaiser had abdicated and someone said the armistice was agreed to but then it wasn't. This time it's real. Everyone," she added, "has written or called." Kitty indicated piles of letters and telegrams and calling-cards on the secretary beside the window. "The President rang me twice, to see how you were."

Burden wanted to ask about Frederika; but with his old man's body he now had an old man's caution. "The election . . .?"

The election had been held on November 5. "Well, you were right." Kitty frowned, once more in her proper character as total politician. "The Senate has gone Republican by one vote and the House by forty-six."

In his astonishment, Burden forgot his great age. "It's not possible! What happened?"

"First, the President's idiotic appeal, as you called it – to his face, I hope. Then T.R. and the Republicans had a glorious time, accusing Mr. Wilson of trying to be world dictator, and that lost us the Germans and the Irish voters, and the women that could vote –"

"Why the women?"

"Because of all the Southern Democrats in the Senate who had voted against giving them the vote . . ."

"I told them. I told them."

"And then there were all the wheat farmers who felt we had paid more attention to supporting cotton, which is you . . ."

"Who was defeated?"

Kitty repeated the entire list by heart. But then she knew every senator not only as a man but as a senator, knew how he voted and why he voted as he did. As Burden listened to the names, he felt the usual combination of joy and dismay. Dismay for the friends ousted from the club; joy at his own survival. What Wilson had managed to do was create for himself, at a moment of military victory, the same sort of hostile Congress that Lincoln had been faced with during the last weeks of his life; and that his heir was to be impeached by.

"A disaster." Burden's lips were like sandpaper. He motioned for more water; she held the glass to his lips.

"Yes," she said. "And he has himself to thank for it. Of course, the National Committee wanted him to make a strong statement, but why remind everyone of why they don't like you? They say he's secretly pleased so many of the Southerners were defeated."

"Without them, Bryan's party is no party. Without Bryan, Wilson's nobody. I don't think he understands."

"There's been talk of you out in California. Two papers put you first on the list for 1920."

Burden sighed: would he ever again be strong enough to walk across the room, much less run for President?

Kitty then read to him from the various messages. She kept those that had political significance in a special box. She started with governors; then party leaders. He was building support, he decided. With Wilson handicapped by a Republican Congress, anything could happen in two years.

"McAdoo?" he asked.

"Very nice. Positive, I think." Burden and Kitty never needed to spell out anything of a political nature. They completed each other's sentences. The McAdoo letter was very positive, and it meant McAdoo-Day. How to reverse the order? Kitty read on.

There was a letter from Blaise. "Poor Frederika," she said suddenly and without malice. She did not know. He was certain of that. Unlike Franklin Roosevelt, he did not keep love letters in his pockets. Unlike Lucy Mercer, Frederika would not dream of writing one. Poor Frederika. But she was supposed to have recovered. Now he saw her dead; and his heart raced.

"All of her hair fell out, such lovely hair it was. No one knows if it will ever grow back."

Burden breathed more easily. "She recovered . . ."

"Like you. She was lucky." Then Kitty gave him the latest list of the dead, the dying, the ill. "What a winter this has been! But they say the epidemic is stopping now, nobody knows why."

Burden allowed oblivion to recall him. He slept and dreamed that he was, with many frantic gestures of his arms, airborne above a field where people had gathered to hear him speak not fly but fly he now did to their amazement and his joy.

3

Frederika looked ethereal, thought Blaise, who had never before known that word to come to him of its own. She wore an evening gown that was mostly black with some silver, and on her head a splendid bejewelled turban. They met in the study, where the Maltese butler – Washington's population was becoming exotic, thanks to the war-time increase of population – poured them sherry. Tonight would be Frederika's first social outing since death's reminder that there would one day be an invitation that could not be politely declined.

"I feel that the turban's transparent," said Frederika. "And everyone will be able to see the bald egg in all its wispy glory."

"No one will suspect." Blaise was soothing. "Tell them you've decided to be like – what's her name? The President's wife who always wore a turban."

"Dolley Madison. The doctor's just looked at Enid. She's all right. No cause for alarm, he says."

206

Blaise wondered if he would ever learn to accept his daughter's common name, bestowed at the christening because his ferocious mother-in-law had insisted that the child be named for her; and there was no denying Mrs. Bingham.

The butler said that the car was ready. They were to dine with Secretary Lansing, a man in every way the antithesis of the President, who seldom consulted him. Where the President was all intuition and the higher goals, the Secretary of State was the complete lawyer – dry, logical, often but not always predictable. For instance, to Blaise's surprise, Lansing deeply hated the Germans, and he could be very boring indeed on the subject of autocracy versus democracy, as if either nation was really the one or the other. But Lansing had been convinced that the Germans were bent on world conquest and that had the United States not gone to war, the Kaiser would have occupied the White House. Blaise actually enjoyed Lansing's company because the Secretary was a bore very much after his own heart. Also, Lansing could be surprisingly shrewd, which meant he saw things Blaise's way. Lansing was particularly interesting on that Yellow Peril with which Hearst periodically frightened the American people. Essentially, the Secretary was a lawyer whose speciality was international law and boundary disputes, and he wanted very much, as did Blaise, a *détente* between the United States and Japan, whose expansionism into China offended Wilson's sense of morality. When the Japanese representative, Viscount Ishii, had come to Washington to find out what the United States intended to do in eastern Asia, Wilson had spoken vaguely of Open Doors and China's integrity, while Lansing had tried to regularize relations between the two expanding empires. Lansing saw the need for good relations with Japan as well as China because of the markets that American industry would require after the war. He was also willing to accept Japan's presence not only in Shantung but in Manchuria and Mongolia as well. The resulting agreement was a masterpiece of evasion, which could not be entirely published, out of deference to Japanese public opinion.

Mrs. Robert Lansing received them at the door to the drawing room. Blaise had known her slightly when she was Eleanor Foster, the daughter of Harrison's secretary of state, whose house the Lansings now occupied. "You're practically hereditary now," Blaise had observed when Lansing was unexpectedly promoted after Bryan's departure.

Frederika was told how well she looked, and the turban was admired. Among the guests, there were the William Phillipses from the State Department and the inevitable Jusserands, representing French glory and civilization. Lansing himself was courteous and precise and, as always, a trifle long of wind, to which Blaise responded with a sense of bliss. He had always been attracted to bores, and when, in youth, Henry James came to call on his father, he had sat enraptured as those long sentences wrapped round and round him like skeins of comforting wool. Lansing's sentences were shorter but there were a great many of them. "The McAdoos were coming. Now they aren't coming."

"Most royal," Blaise observed. "Very French," he added for no reason except that Jusserand was holding a group of ladies in thrall to his exquisitely accented English.

"More British. More Hanoverian."

Blaise looked into the Secretary's handsome gray face with its near-invisible gray, clipped moustache. "Trouble between sovereign and . . . Prince of Wales?"

"I think," said Lansing, discreet too late – deliberately? – "that Mac's going to resign now that the war's over. They disagree too much, in a friendly way. But . . ." The sentence was strategically abandoned.

"What will he do between now and 1920?"

"I'm told that at such times politicians have a tendency to travel a great deal, and make speeches." Lansing had now done Blaise a favor. And Blaise would respond in due course. McAdoo's resignation meant that Wilson would be the candidate and, if he was, there was no presidential future for the Prince of Wales.

After dinner, the ladies went back to the drawing room. Port went round the table, cigars were passed. Blaise sat between Lansing and Jusserand. The Spanish flu had dominated the dinner-party conversation. The after-dinner talk was of the coming Peace Conference. Lansing was guarded, Jusserand diplomatic,

Blaise inquisitive. "Will Colonel House represent the United States at the Peace Conference?"

"Well, he's already there." Lansing pushed his port glass back and forth. "With his Inquiry Group. I'm told that M. Clemenceau is eager to begin." Lansing looked at Jusserand, whose white-bearded face gave him the look of a benign Zeus.

"There is so much work to do." Jusserand was vague.

"Our Paris correspondent tells me that M. Clemenceau has said that as it will not be possible for President Wilson to meet with the European premiers on an equal footing, he expects the secretary of state, Mr. Lansing, or some delegate with high rank, to lead the American delegation." Blaise enjoyed telling people what they already knew but did not care to comment on.

With a smile, William Phillips observed, "A Texas colonel does not rank very high outside of Texas."

"He does," said Blaise, "if the President turns him into a special high ambassador."

Lansing nodded. "The Colonel got the premiers to accept the Fourteen Points – anyone who can do that can probably negotiate. Besides, the President has the constitutional power to delegate to anyone he pleases. More interesting will be the delegation that goes with the negotiator . . ."

"Republican senators, if he's wise," said a Republican senator the sharp-tongued Brandegee from Connecticut.

"I suggested my predecessor Mr. Root." Lansing was cool. "But the President thinks him too old and, perhaps, too conserva-tive . . ."

"Only for M. Clemenceau." Blaise winked at Jusserand, who murmured to Blaise in French, "Happily, I am deaf in my right ear."

Suddenly, Mrs. Lansing was at the door, motioning for Lansing to come with her. He excused himself. Jusserand and Blaise con-tinued to speak to one another in French. Jusserand had been a part of Blaise's life for so long that he thought of him as a perma-nent fixture, not to mention a reminder of his own French origins.

"We enjoyed – that is, my wife and I – your sister Caroline's photo-play. It was amazing how very like the Front it is. All the details were right, and that actress with the crucifix was superb, absolutely superb."

Blaise alone knew that the actress was Caroline, and she had sworn him to secrecy. Thus far, no one that they knew had identified Emma Traxler, while the national press had not caught the scent. In time, of course, they would. Meanwhile, of their Washington acquaintances, only Caroline's half-brother had immediately identified the soulful mute giantess on the screen. "She says the movie is playing in Paris now. They like it, apparently . . ."

"Too close to life, I should think, for great popularity. You know, they are mad not to send us Root." Jusserand lowered his voice. "He has authority. He is respected. He's old but . . ."

"He's younger than M. Clemenceau, who is – what?"

"Seventy-seven. I agree, privately, of course, with Mr. Lansing that we should get the peace treaty settled, a difficult matter all by itself, and *then*, separately, later, go on to the creation of some sort of world league – a popular idea here, thanks to Mr. Wilson and Mr. Taft, but not taken very seriously in our wicked old Europe. What news of your place at Saint-Cloud?"

"Still a hospital. I'm trying to go over next month. . . ." Blaise felt in sudden need of relief: a congenitally weak bladder had, with age, grown weaker. He excused himself.

Blaise opened the door to the downstairs bathroom to behold Woodrow Wilson, comb in hand, standing at the mirror. "Mr. President," Blaise began.

Wilson quieted him with a gesture. "I'm not here," he whispered, and put away his comb. At the bathroom door, he paused. "Could you step by the library for a moment?"

When Blaise entered the library, he found Lansing seated by the fire; and Wilson standing in front of it. A portrait of Secretary of State Foster glowered down upon them.

"Come in." The President turned to Lansing. "Forgive me. But Mr. Sanford saw me, and I wanted to make sure he'd say nothing . . ."

"As a publisher?"

"As a gentleman." Wilson smiled an attractive smile. "Come, sit

210

down. The *Tribune* has supported us nobly, most of the time, at least."

"One can never entirely please an administration."

"Politicians demand quite a lot of pleasure," Wilson observed genially. He seemed both perturbed and delighted. "That's why I let Tumulty read the press for me. I see what he thinks I should – pleasurably – see."

Blaise was appalled; and smiled his own attractive smile. In a country like the United States it was dangerous for a president not to study the press if only to determine what superstitions were abroad and what potential panics beginning. Plainly, Wilson was much insulated from the world by wife, doctor, secretary. "I hope he gives you T.R.'s column from the Kansas City *Star*."

"I see those." Wilson smiled. "But then I must always listen to him and Taft. They are my predecessors, my ancestral voices . . ."

". . . prophesying war," Blaise completed the quotation.

"Exactly, Mr. Sanford. Mr. Lansing, do you mind if we put the problem to someone as knowledgeable as our mutual friend here?"

Although Lansing looked as if he minded very much, he nodded. "By all means, Mr. President."

"I have decided to go to Paris next month. Mr. Lansing would rather I not go. That is," Wilson anticipated Lansing's demur, "he sees nothing wrong with my making an appearance but he believes that I should not take part in the Peace Conference on the ground that I am on a higher plane – constitutionally, that is – than the premiers. They are chiefs of government, I am chief of state. Now, Mr. Sanford, you know the French far better than I. You know the issues as well as anyone. Should I take part or not?"

Blaise was not prepared for so weighty an after-dinner dialogue. He saw, as did the President, the dramatic possibilities of the legendary leader from across the seas whose never-ending supplies of men, weapons, food had more than any specific battle caused Germany to stop the war and replace the Kaiser with a republic. "If you could do it quickly, I'd say go."

"Why quickly?" asked Lansing.

"Because they will do their best to involve the President in details, in the secret treaties, in old quarrels like Alsace-Lorraine. He should not be wasted on such things. Let him go. Sweep public opinion behind the Fourteen Points. Get them accepted once and for all and then go home, leaving the conference in *your* hands." Without warning or preparation, Blaise thought that he had done very nicely. The President appeared pleased. Lansing was less somber than he had been when Blaise had walked into the room. Perhaps there was – perhaps this was – a middle course.

"I see what you mean." Wilson rocked back and forth from toe to heel as he often did while making a speech. "Certainly I can't be away too long for political – even constitutional – reasons."

"No president has ever left the United States to attend a conference of any kind." Lansing was dry. "The president should be like the pope, mysterious, separate, an awesome personage to whom others come."

"What does Colonel House think?" Deliberately Blaise asked the wrong question, which was, of course, the right one.

Wilson frowned; and stopped rocking. "I assume he will go on as before. He hasn't said he would not. Until now, he has spoken for me. When I'm there he knows that I will speak for myself. Naturally, when it comes to detail, he and his scholars will make sure that I know what I'm talking about. Also, Mr. Lansing and his staff will be with me, too. The point, I think," and Wilson was now entirely off the subject, without answering Blaise, "will be Article Ten, the league, the covenant of nations. Otherwise, the whole enterprise is meaningless. We didn't go into the war to annex coal mines or gain seaports. We went in to stop the intolerable business of military force being used to gain ends that might be achieved peacefully by a league of all interested parties. I think I can put the general case better than the Allied leaders, who don't truly accept the Fourteen Points – articles – but go along because the peoples of their countries are with me – for now. That's why speed is so important. Things change."

"To make the peace, yes," said Lansing. "But to tie it in with the establishment of a league might be too much for one conference."

"But *not* to tie it in is to admit that we are just another belligerent out for loot, like the French and the British and the Italians."

"What is wrong with that?" asked Blaise.

The President's face was now as rigid as unpolished granite: the Presbyterian elder was in the room. "*Everything* is wrong with that. We are not like other people. We must not be like other people. We will not, in this, *be* like other people."

"But we are only people, Mr. President." Blaise spoke gently, fearful of God's wrath.

"That is why we must at least try to be better than we are. Don't you see how little time I have? Lodge controls the Senate, and chairs the Foreign Relations Committee. Roosevelt," each syllable of the name was spoken like an ancient prophet's curse, "has already said that no one need listen to me at the Peace Conference because I was rejected by my own people two weeks ago. He also said," a smile hardened rather than softened the stone face, "that America's contribution to the victory was only two percent – he means the dead – of the Allied total, so England may ask for anything, having suffered more! Well, that will come back to haunt him in the next election." Abruptly, Wilson stopped. He had broken his own moratorium – no politics until peace.

"Perhaps," said Blaise, "you should ask your two predecessors to come to France with you. Then there would be a totally united front at home."

"I should not mind Mr. Taft. But . . ." Wilson shook his head.

Blaise rose. "I've intruded on great affairs too long."

"You'll say nothing?" Wilson extended his hand.

"Of course not. But when will *you* say something?"

"When I address Congress next week. Then Mr. Lansing and I will take to the high seas."

Blaise left the two men to what he suspected was a most edgy conversation. It was lucky for Wilson that Lansing was essentially a lawyer who would do whatever his chief wanted him to do. Also, being human, Lansing was no doubt delighted that he might be given a chance to supplant Colonel House in Paris. Yet Blaise shuddered at the notion of this particular president, all stiff brittle backbone, accompanied by two warring sets of advisers, face to face with old Europe's most unscrupulous political street-fighters. Clemenceau and Lloyd George would devour this simple

Christian. Blaise joined the ladies; and soothed Mrs. Lansing. "I will keep silent."

"You are kind," she said. "It's a worry, isn't it?"

Blaise assumed that she was referring to the President's decision, and he agreed that it was indeed a worry. Later, as he was putting on his mask to go outside – a ludicrous business, since he was more apt to catch the flu at a crowded dinner party than in the frosty November air – he realized that she could not have known the President's errand. What, then, was her worry?

Frederika – maskless as befitted one to whom the plague had done its worst – partly answered. "Mrs. Lansing thinks the President is losing his grip."

They drove through the empty streets of northwest Washington. "He seems very much in control." Blaise would not tell Frederika of the encounter. "On top of the world."

"She thinks otherwise. He's forgetful. Bad-tempered . . ."

"Wouldn't you be after losing control of Congress?"

"She thinks, which means that Lansing thinks, he's got arteriosclerosis."

"Everyone past sixty has that, more or less." Blaise was now middle-aged. Forty-two had seemed very old to him in the year that the century shifted from nineteenth to twentieth. Now that he had reached so great an age, he found it no different from twenty-two. He still maintained what Caroline referred to as his stable-boy physique, with its thick, slightly bowed legs. Recently he had become interested in sexual adventures of the sort that he had enjoyed in youth; plainly, a final flowering before – arteriosclerosis. He found it amusing that at practically the same age, Caroline was also having a similar revival with her photo-play director, a physical type Blaise found repugnant, somewhat to his surprise since in the past they had often been attracted to the same types.

4

Caroline waited at the back of the sound-stage while Tim set up the scene. The interior of a railroad warehouse had been re-created, faithfully, Caroline assumed, as she had never been inside of one. Presumably, such a warehouse resembled more than not the soundstage itself in what had once been the Harlem River Park Casino, converted by Hearst into a movie studio. Here he made Cosmopolitan Pictures, which were then released by Paramount, a distribution company owned by Famous Players-Lasky. To Caroline's surprise, Hearst had refused to move his company to Hollywood, because, he said, of Marion Davies's stage career. Actually, the Chief was, yet again, like some obsessed figure of legend, proposing to run either for governor of New York in 1920, or for the presidency if Wilson faltered. He dared not leave his Riverside Drive base in easily the largest apartment in the world, whose endless succession of rooms were crowded with works of art, some genuine.

Caroline had started her own production company, Traxler Productions, and despite Blaise's cheerful derision she had made three in six months, and each was making money. But then, unless one spent too much, it had not been possible to lose money on any movie until the flu epidemic. Before the epidemic, the entire country had taken to movie-going and those producers who were able – and willing – to deal with the movie magnates could become wealthy.

But the great wealth was not so much in the actual making of movies as in their distribution. Adolph Zukor, a Hungarian Jew, had become one of the first movie-makers when he persuaded famous players like Bernhardt to appear in not-so-famous photoplays. In the last seven years not only had Zukor's company absorbed a dozen other movie companies but he was now in the process of buying, through Paramount, hundreds of motion-picture theaters across the country. Wall Street was also interested in movie houses, if only as real estate, and First National was their vehicle and Zukor's principal rival. Currently, Zukor was the largest player of them all and both Caroline and Hearst wooed him, as he wooed them. Publicity was all-important to Hollywood and Hearst could be counted on to praise relentlessly his own films in his own newspapers. For Hearst's millions of readers, Marion Davies was queen of Hollywood even though she lived in New York and made her money-losing photo-plays at 127th Street.

Although Tim could make movies anywhere, Caroline did her best to keep him at work on the East Coast. She had taken to counting on her fingers the number of years that she had left as a woman still able to compete in the Lists of Love, as the English writer Elinor Glyn might put it, and though Caroline used both hands when she counted, she wondered if she was not being unduly optimistic ever to go beyond the fingers of a single hand, which meant five years with Tim, and then – no more fingers, love, whatever. She was exactly opposite to what she had been with Burden. Then she had relied on absence to maintain their interest in one another. Now it was presence that she wanted daily, nightly, until the last finger had been counted. What, she suddenly wondered, did the thumb mean? Should it be counted as a half-year, an aberrant year? She looked down at her hands and saw two white-knuckled fists.

"All right. José, you're scared. The union man's a Red and you know it but he doesn't know you know. You pretend to go along with him. But you're really scared, only you're trying not to look scared." The star, a former dancer from the Follies, was of regulation dwarf proportions, with a handsome Latin face at the front of a huge head that looked larger than it was because of masses of black curls. The union organizer was of normal size and proportions, which meant that he would photograph sinister on the screen. He had a somewhat ascetic face, which Caroline had thought all wrong, but Tim assured her that it was always interesting to cast against type. The photo-play had been written by one of the best Hollywood writers, a woman as most of them, curiously, were. In fact, the most successful photo-play writer of all was Frances Marion, who was being paid two thousand dollars a week by Hearst to do for Marion Davies what she had once done for Mary Pickford. Tim's lady writer was less expensive but somewhat temperamental. She and Tim were always arguing over "the theme," which mystified Caroline, since the story was a very simple one, inspired by George Creel, who now wanted the Bolsheviks to replace as quickly as possible the Huns as the on-going enemy of Americanism.

Currently, a dozen anti-Red photo-plays were in production. To Caroline's surprise, Tim had been eager to make one. They had then acquired the rights to a magazine story about the infiltration of a railroad union by American Communists, directed from Moscow. One worker, José, at first refuses to go along with the Red bosses of the union until he is persuaded by the daughter of the director of the railroad to become a double agent. There was, thought Caroline, rather too much plot. In the end, the workers see the light, which is not red but red-white-and-blue, and the strike is called off, but it is too late to save José, who, stabbed mortally in the back by the leading Red, played by a Georgian prince, walks along the tracks toward the director's daughter, who, unaware that he has been mortally wounded, waits for him with arms outstretched.

Caroline had thought that, perhaps, there were far too many scenes involving railroad tracks. But then, thanks to a life of privilege, she herself had never had a meeting much less a love scene of any kind, anywhere near a railroad. But Tim assured her that the effect would be overwhelming.

As José reaches the girl, he throws his arms wide – the crucifixion yet again – and drops dead. Then, from nowhere, happy workers appear and lift high his body and carry him back down the tracks, away from the girl, the camera, life.

Caroline deeply hated the entire project but George Creel was delighted. Despite Tim's preference for the down-trodden, he seemed quite pleased to be a tool of capitalism.

"Interlock!" Tim shouted, and the scene began. Caroline slipped out of the sound-stage and into a corridor that led to the office of the president of Traxler Productions, herself. Everything was suitably shabby, as befitted a onetime Harlem casino gone to slow ruin. But within the casino's shell Hearst had built a number of modern studios while not improving as the bankers liked to say, the property.

217

Caroline's secretary presided in the small outer office, answering the telephone, which rang constantly. Everyone wanted to act or write or do anything that would bring him into the magical world of giant images and somewhat diminished salaries: movie grosses for 1918 were a fraction of what they had been the previous year, and if the influenza epidemic kept the theaters empty much longer, 1919 would be a disaster for everyone except the bankers and their real estate. European production was also becoming competitive and Hollywood was in danger of losing its world market. Fortunately, Caroline, who had devoted years to making an unlikely success of the Washington *Tribune,* was used to drudgery and the deferral of pleasure. Also, this particular "business" was actually more pleasurable in its drudgery than the *Tribune* was in its glory, because at the paper she had been quite alone in her private life while now private life and work had combined in a way that she had never thought possible. She counted her blessings on one finger.

The secretary gave her a list of telephone messages; and a long cablegram from Blaise in Paris. He had been to Saint-Cloud-le-Duc. The wing that had been used as a hospital was now empty; in need of repair. Wilson was the messiah. Colonel House was not. That was cryptic, she thought. Blaise had been invited by the President to be an observer at the conference and, presumably, he was busy observing but not reporting to their readers.

In December, Blaise had sailed with the President and Mrs. Wilson on the *George Washington.* There were over a thousand Americans in the presidential entourage, and Blaise had reported that Wilson was in high spirits. No senators of either party had been chosen for the official delegation, a fatal move, Burden told her, but then since his near-death from flu, everything smacked of mortality. Except for old Henry White, there was no elder statesman in the delegation, only Wilsonian spear-carriers, and Lansing, who was on hand to act as the President's deputy, dedicated to eliminating Colonel House. George Creel was also present in order to make propaganda. But for once Creel was not needed.

On December 14, Wilson arrived in Paris as Europe's savior. From the news-reels, Caroline could see that the French crowds were unlike anything that anyone had ever witnessed before, even

218

those aged members of the Jockey who liked to claim that from a mother's arms they had seen Bonaparte ride in triumph through the streets, kings chained to his golden car. Actually it was the mothers, held in other arms, who remembered the imperial glory. Plon's mother-in-law recalled vividly the day at Fontainebleau when Napoleon stood on the outside staircase and said farewell to the Guard. Caroline could visualize that moment perfectly on film.

Photo-play scripts were piled high on Caroline's desk. They read like a combination of plays and feature journalism. But the most engaging thing about the form was that there was no way to tell a good one from a bad one. What seemed the worst writing on the page often came startlingly alive on the screen; and the reverse. There were two photo-plays about Napoleon by writers who had not bothered to read anything about him. Idly, Caroline wondered if she herself might be able to construct a story about the Emperor, relying not so much on expensive battles as on drawing-room skirmishes to save production costs: tears in the boudoir, history in bed. The secretary rang. "Mr. Hearst," she said, with quiet reverence: *their* Napoleon. Caroline picked up the receiver. Before she could speak the thin, high voice commenced. "This is the Chief."

"This," said Caroline, "is the squaw."

There was a pause. "I'm sorry," said Hearst at last, "I guess it's a habit."

"Mine, too."

Impervious to irony, Hearst was a slave to jokes, particularly very old ones. "I'm at the Beaux Arts. You want to have breakfast with us? I've got news."

Caroline was delighted, she said, to have a second breakfast; news, too.

The morning was cold and cloudy and the streets empty. The troops had not come home, and the flu still kept people indoors. Caroline had become fatalistic and no longer wore a mask.

The Beaux Arts in Sixth Avenue catered to New York's High Bohemia. Actors and actresses favored its high rooms, tall mullioned windows, Italian plaster-work. Here Marion Davies lived in quiet splendor at Hearst's expense. A Japanese butler showed

Caroline into the living room, where Hearst was standing beneath a portrait of himself that looked more like Hearst than he did. All natural pink and gold, Marion sprang like a cat from a sofa and threw her arms about Caroline and kissed her, wine upon her breath. The Chief did not like to drink himself and did his best to discourage others. Marion was not easily discouraged. "My movie . . ." The first "m" gave no trouble, the second did. But she went on, stammering breathlessly. ". . . doesn't start for another week. So Pops and I are having a real holiday here in town . . ."

"I'd rather be in Palm Beach." Hearst held up an early edition of the *American*. Even across the room, Caroline could read the headline "TR DEAD."

"Is this a joke?" Hearst was known for practical jokes, involving fake headlines and stories calculated to terrify guests, not much different in tone, Caroline had observed, from his actual papers.

"No. He died at Oyster Bay last night. I think we're first."

"I hope we're not last." Caroline prayed that Mr. Trimble had been on the job early that morning. Since Roosevelt's recent stay in Roosevelt Hospital, Caroline had ordered the obituary to be brought up to date; yet no one had really expected all that energy to be snuffed out on the eve of a political restoration. "What was the cause?"

"Some sort of blood clot. Last night. While he was asleep. I wouldn't mind going like that."

"Pops!" Marion helped herself to more breakfast wine, which turned out to be hock. In response to the news, Caroline drank a glass straight down. "You're much too young." Marion gazed fondly at the huge bear that Hearst had turned into, so unlike the slender, gaudily turned-out young man that Caroline had first met, twenty years earlier.

"This changes everything," said Caroline, trying to recall just what would be changed.

"Well, the Republicans don't have a candidate, that's for sure. TR had the whole thing sewed up. Months ago. He and Taft had buried the hatchet. That took care of the regulars. Then he was going to run with Beveridge to keep the progressives happy. He would've won, too."

"Against Wilson?"

"Yes. But not against me." This was said so matter-of-factly that Caroline almost did not take it in.

"You?" Caroline stared dumbly not at Hearst but at the headline.

"Pops has all sorts of letters to and from that awful man, who took money from the oil people like Hannah . . . what was her name?"

"Mark Hanna was *his* name." Hearst's smile was more than usually thin. "I was going to really get him this time around, the way he got me over McKinley, claiming it was me and the *American* – or the *Journal* then – that inspired the killer when there are those who think that *he* may have had a hand in killing McKinley."

"Roosevelt?" Caroline's head was spinning.

"That's the story. Roosevelt and Rockefeller were in on it, to keep McKinley from going after the Standard Oil monopoly, which is why Roosevelt never did go after Rockefeller until I forced him to, and then he did nothing much but make noise."

Like so many inventors of the news, Hearst himself was capable of believing anything. When Caroline first became a publisher, she was struck by the number of otherwise sane people who would suddenly produce a carefully documented "proof" that President Garfield's murderer, say, had been in the employ of the Jesuits or the Zionists. When the "proofs" were disproved, other documents appeared; and the plot widened. Now Hearst appeared to believe that Roosevelt had been involved in McKinley's assassination. "Will you include this in the obituary?" Caroline was light.

"No." Hearst led the way into the adjoining dining room. "But one day I'll do something with it."

"Poor Pops." Marion took her place opposite Hearst. Caroline sat to Hearst's right. As an elaborate breakfast was served by the Japanese butler, Caroline told of Blaise's cablegram. But Hearst was indifferent to the Peace Conference and to Wilson, whom he disliked largely because he was a dreary schoolteacher who had got the prize that he ought to have had. But Hearst was eloquent on the subject of his latest enemy, the Irish governor of New York, one Al Smith, whose combination with Tammany had denied Hearst the mayoralty in 1917. "Now the Governor's complaining because

I've been made the official greeter of the troops when they come back . . ."

"Wonderful spot for Pops," said Marion, looking wistfully at her empty wineglass. "Right in the center of all those news-reel cameras when the ships come in and the boys march off and there's the Mayor, who appointed Pops and just made Pop – that's my real old man – a city magistrate up to the Bronx." This flood was stopped by the filling of her glass.

"Roosevelt was their choice to take my place next week when the *Mauritania* comes in. Well, he won't be there, and I will. Mother won't," he added.

"Mother won't what?"

"Be there. My mother."

"She's got flu." Marion sounded satisfied.

"I didn't know she was here."

"She came for the holidays to be with the boys. I warned her. This place is sickly, I said. Anyway, she's mending now. She'll go back to California. She's given away twenty-one million dollars in charity . . ."

"Less than you've spent on newspapers and," Caroline looked at Marion and said, quickly, "art."

"I'm not in that league. But I'm losing money. Are you?"

Caroline was used to the Chief's candor with her. He treated her not as a lady or even as another man, he treated her as an equal, flattered her by his open envy of what she had done with the *Tribune*. "No. We're profitable. It's been a good year for the *Tribune* and . . ."

"I didn't mean the papers. You can't lose money with a war on. No. I meant with your photo-plays."

"Well, we're suffering like everybody else. But we're in the black."

"Red is what Pops is in," said the immediate cause of his losses, eating a truffled egg in aspic. "He pays too much for Mr. Urban and everybody –"

"I want the best. It's like a paper –"

"We had a scene where I meet my beloved in an English country house and I'm playing – I forget who. It's all a blur. I've been in

222

five movies in the last year, playing five different people, with five hundred different costumes. Anyway, Pops comes on the set and I'm standing in front of this fireplace, crying my heart out with – oh, I remember now! Ramon Novarro, who isn't my suitor but he's blackmailing me because of something. And Pops says, 'That fireplace isn't right for the period.' So Mr. Urban, the most expensive designer in the world, who tells Mr. Ziegfeld where to head in, says, 'It is, and the grays set off the blacks.' Don't you love it? Anyway, guess who wins? So while they all have to go looking through Pops's warehouses filled with junk because he knows he owns the right fireplace but can't remember where he put it, the picture stops but everyone goes on being paid."

"It's things like that . . ." Hearst began vaguely; and ended, mind elsewhere. "We should make an anti-Red film . . ."

"I am making one." Caroline never understood Hearst's use of the first person plural, sometimes collegial, other times imperial, editorial.

"So's Zukor. He bought the rights to that play . . . you know."

Caroline did know, and she, too, had wanted to buy it, *Paid in Full*, by Eugene Walter. "Tim's competing with it, he says."

"We can't have too many movies like that. When there's no epidemic, there's nothing like Reds for getting to everybody."

"There's a Marion Davies fan club in Moscow." Marion Davies was touchingly awed by herself.

"There's one probably everywhere in the world. And we thought newspapers were something. Funny how the Jews got in on this before we did."

Like everyone else involved in photo-plays, Caroline had given the subject considerable thought. "Don't you think it's because they're the same sort of people as the audience used to be? Just arrived immigrants who could only afford movies at the nickelodeon?"

"Then why not the Irish or the Italian immigrants?" Hearst shook his head. "Fashion," he answered.

"What does that mean?"

"Zukor and Loew own half the theaters in the country and Famous Players and Paramount, and they've just swallowed up

Triangle and most of the other little companies except you and me. Well, they didn't go to Yale like we did."

"Like you did. I am only a woman . . ."

"Let him have it, Caroline." Marion was tipsy; she was also, or so she had told Caroline, a secret suffragette.

"They were immigrants, and they were in the fur business, and Zukor made a small fortune guessing what the fashion for next year would be. Red fox," Hearst ended, cryptically.

"He was partial to red fox?" Caroline quizzed the oracle.

"He made a killing in June, figuring women would all be wearing red fox in October. Then he bought up the nickelodeons. Then he figured that you could make money with movies that run as long as plays, which everyone said was impossible, proving what had been good for the masses was now good for the classes. And it worked. Unbelievable. Here they are mostly Jewish furriers, who can hardly speak English, mostly from Hungary, of all places, and *they've* got the movies. Lucky, they're good Americans, I'll say that. They serve us well. Only where are *we* in all this?"

"Surely, D. W. Griffith –" Caroline began.

"He's Jewish, too. But denies it. Because he's a Southerner, and wants to be mistaken for a gentleman, God help him. Besides, he was an actor." Hearst employed the most horrible epithet of their class.

"*I'm* an actor." Marion glared over her wineglass.

"No," Hearst said mildly, "you're a star."

"All in all," said Caroline, suddenly a hard, cold business woman, "there's a lot of money in movies."

The Chief nodded. "Yes. Mine."

They were joined by Edgar Hatrick, the eager young man who was in charge of Hearst's movie enterprises. Since they were obviously about to discuss their business, Caroline excused herself and walked through chilly streets to the Plaza, a comfortable modern hotel that had replaced, in 1907, an earlier Plaza Hotel.

In the drawing room of Caroline's suite, the ten newspapers that she studied every day from all around the country were neatly stacked, and as she went through them, one by one, to see how different stories were covered, she found herself daydreaming about movies. They were insidious. They were like waking dreams that then, in sleep, usurped proper dreams. There was power here but she was not sure what it was. There was crude propaganda of the sort that she had made at Creel's insistence. But newspapers could do that sort of thing, too. There was more to this new fad than anyone had grasped, and she could understand why Hearst, too, was bemused by the whole thing. A moving picture was, to begin with, a picture of something that had really happened. She had really clubbed a French actor with a wooden crucifix on a certain day and at a certain time and now there existed, presumably forever, a record of that stirring event. But Caroline Sanford was not the person millions of people had watched in that ruined French church. They had watched the fictitious Emma Traxler impersonate Madeleine Giroux, a Franco-American mother, as she picked up a crucifix that looked to be metal but was not and struck a French actor impersonating a German officer in a ruined French church that was actually a stage-set in Santa Monica. The audience knew, of course, that the story was made up as they knew that stage plays were imitations of life, but the fact that an entire story could so surround them as a moving picture did and so, literally, inhabit their dreams, both waking and sleeping, made for another reality parallel to the one they lived in. For two hours in actual time Caroline was three different people as a light shone through a moving strip of film. Reality could now be entirely invented and history revised. Suddenly, she knew what God must have felt when he gazed upon chaos, with nothing but himself upon his mind.

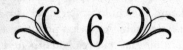

6

1

Blaise shook his stepbrother's hand. Since the death of Plon, André was now Prince d'Agrigente. Ten years older than Blaise, he looked as if he could have been Blaise's father. The hair was white. The face was white; only the black eyes seemed alive in all that arctic bleakness. Like Plon, he had married money; unlike Plon he had maintained good relations with his wife, whom he saw several times a year. She lived at Aix-les-Bains in a family house. He stayed in Paris, with his mistress and her two children, neither his, he would say with a bitter pride, as he had been impotent for twenty years.

Blaise gazed with more curiosity than fondness at the stepbrother whom he had hardly known. André stayed close to Paris and Blaise stayed close to the *Tribune*. "You're thin," said Blaise, as they entered the bar of the Crillon. For all practical purposes, the entire hotel had been taken over by the American delegation.

"You're not," said André, looking about curiously. "I've never seen so many Americans all at once."

"Come to America."

"Why bother? They come to us. Do you like them?"

"I am one."

"I don't think so."

"I do." Blaise found them a table near the bar. The room barked and growled with English. Most of the men were relatively young, and there were not many ladies on view, since the President had

226

insisted on absolute seriousness for the thousand or so American men who had come to Paris to arrange eternal peace for all mankind. Everyone took himself very seriously, the President most of all.

André ordered whisky; like the rest of his generation, he was very much in the English style. Blaise drank Pernod. "Is this president of yours as stupid as he appears?" André was above politics but not above Saint-Simon. The characters, not the politics, of important personages amused him.

"How stupid does he appear to you?" Blaise was surprised to discover he was deeply annoyed when Europeans criticized anything American; something he himself never ceased to do.

"Those speeches!" André's eyes rolled upward. "He is so . . . so Protestant."

"Well, that is the nature of his mission."

"A messiah? Well, I can see that. Everyone can see that when he drives through the crowds, and the crowds go mad with stupidity, too. I watched him make his entrance here. The saint from across the water. I suppose now he'll go home where he belongs."

"No. He stays until the middle of February. Then he goes home, to adjourn Congress. Then he says he'll come back."

Lansing had appeared in the door to the bar. There was an immediate hush. Then two men rose from a table and joined him, and the three departed. "Is that a great man?"

"No. Just the Secretary of State, one of the peace commissioners." When Wilson had appointed the American commission he had taken no one's advice. Arbitrarily, the President had chosen Lansing, House, a general from the Supreme War Council and, as token Republican, that ancient enchanter-diplomat Henry White, a man of no political weight save his friendship with Theodore Roosevelt, now storming Valhalla or wherever it is that strenuous heroes go.

After the President's triumphant entrance into Paris, even Blaise was optimistic that the treaty would soon be drafted. Technically this was the Preliminary Peace Conference which would agree upon the terms to which the Germans, when they eventually joined the conference proper, must submit. But despite worldly laurels, the President did not immediately have his way. Since the conference was not yet ready to begin, Wilson was encouraged by Prime Minister Lloyd George to show himself to a grateful England and by Prime Minister Orlando to a grateful Italy. Thus, two weeks had been agreeably wasted. The crowds were head-turning; and the head that was turned, as the premiers had shrewdly intended, was that of Wilson. He returned to his Paris quarters, the Palais Murat, tired but exalted.

During this time, Blaise had worked with Colonel House, whose staff occupied much of the third floor of the Crillon, under the supervision of his son-in-law, Gordon Auchincloss, a cousin of the ubiquitous Apgars. Blaise acted as an unofficial liaison with the French press, which tended to mordancy on the subject of their savior, taking their cue from Clemenceau, whose view of those who would change man's nature was sardonic when not sulphurous. The conservative André echoed the radical Clemenceau in this dark view of the human race. "It is pointless to ask us not to do everything possible to smash Germany to pieces. Look what they have done to us this time. Look what they did in 1870 . . ."

"Look what *we* did to them under Napoleon . . ."

"They kill more people these days, and the survivors remember longer. My dear Blaise, the Germans will come back one day if we don't split them up into little countries the way they were before Bismarck."

Blaise knew all the arguments; all the answers. That was the problem with politics, whether domestic or international. As the great questions were always posed in the same way, they invited answers that were equally predictable and unchanging. How anything was resolved remained to Blaise a mystery. He assumed that this particular conference would be "won" by the most patient faction. Sooner or later, Wilson would tire. Yet Blaise was also convinced that the President was most certainly an agent of history, occupying the right place at the right time, and when all force was so gathered in someone with a plan, the Clemenceaus and Lloyd Georges and Orlandos would be powerless. Even Blaise had been impressed by the size of the crowds in the three countries that had lost millions of men during the last four years while even more millions had died of flu.

George Creel joined them, as if he had been invited. André gazed at him with the amused curiosity of someone at a circus, eager to be delighted by strangeness. "How is room 315?" Creel liked to pretend that he and Blaise were in warring camps, which, in a sense, they were. Colonel House and Lansing were at permanent odds, a situation reflected in the staff of each. Although Creel was the master propagandist, Colonel House and his son-in-law were formidable manipulators of the press, as Blaise could appreciate rather better than anyone else. Because Colonel House was apparently so self-effacing, his was the only face that anyone of importance wished to confront. He who had been Wilson's eyes and ears was now thought to be the great man's brain. In due course, Wilson would grasp all this, and unless Blaise had entirely misunderstood human vanity, the President would free himself of the whispering Texas charmer. Lansing was too unimaginative to make trouble between Wilson and House, while Creel could do so only indirectly. On the *George Washington,* it had been Blaise's impression that Wilson was not well pleased by either man. Each had told him, in his own way, that he ought not to commit the prestige of the presidency to what, after all, would be no more than a sort of cut-throat poker game, where gamblers cheated and knives glinted. But Wilson was filled with missionary zeal, worsened by the crowds that proved to him that he was the divine instrument of all the hopes of every single sweaty component of those gray-pink-brown hordes which, like vast stains, flooded ancient squares and swirled headlong down wide modern streets. The smell of the Paris crowd had been enough to drive Blaise back to his room at the Crillon on the third floor, where Colonel House reigned in well-publicized secrecy. "Three-fifteen wants to get started as soon as possible. What about the second floor?"

"Lansing is having his problems with Clemenceau." Creel was direct. Then turned to André. "I assume you aren't his nephew, or a member of the Cabinet?"

"No. I am idle. I have always been idle. But I like nothing more than watching the ants run about after their hill has been kicked over." Blaise was delighted that his old-world connection made not the slightest effort to accommodate the new world.

"That's one way of looking at it." Creel was indifferent to malice. "Clemenceau would like to wait until things have settled down before the haggling starts. Lansing wants to start now, but leave the League of Nations until after the treaty is signed."

Blaise nodded. "Since the President is more interested in the League than in the treaty, Lansing shouldn't be surprised at the influence of the third floor." House always supported the President, to his face. Lansing dared argue, up to a point.

"Certainly," said Creel, vibrant in his own malice. "The Colonel is well supported by his family. They outnumber the delegation."

"A loving family man is everywhere admired." But Blaise had been surprised by the Colonel's unexpected recklessness when it came to his private arrangements. Save for Edith, Wilson had brought none of his own family, including his son-in-law Francis Sayre, who had worked for the Inquiry. Wilson had also discouraged everyone except the highest officials from bringing wives. Yet House had brought his sister as well as his daughter and her husband, Gordon Auchincloss, who had, in turn, brought along his law partner and *his* wife. Currently, House was trying to assign Auchincloss to the President as a secretary during the conference, and Mrs. Wilson was taking a darker and darker view of the less and less gray eminence of House. Wilson himself was sphinx-like, pursuing his own high destiny in his own eloquent way. There were storm warnings everywhere.

"Clemenceau used to live in America." Creel waved to a departing group from the Inquiry. Tonight would be an easy night for everyone. The next day the conference would begin at ten-thirty, January 18, the forty-eighth anniversary of Bismarck's declaration of the Second Reich in the fallen capital of France. With grim pleasure, Clemenceau had picked the date. "He was married to a New York girl, and then divorced."

"That," said André, eyes glittering, "explains his love for America."

"The divorce," asked Blaise, "or the marriage?"

"The experience."

"Did you see your . . . uh, sister's photo-play?" Creel knew there was some relationship between André and Caroline.

"My half-sister. No. I've never seen a photo-play, actually. I play bridge. One can't do both. But I have read about *Les Boches de l'Enfer,* and I see that someone has taken our grandmother's name, Emma Traxler. Is it Caroline?"

"No," said Blaise, not certain whether or not Creel was in on the game.

"No," said Creel, smiling to show that he did know. "She only produces movies."

"It sounds," said André, "like a magician, *producing* something from a hat."

"It is." Blaise took out his watch. The mistress of his youth had invited him for ten o'clock, the new fashionable hour in war-time Paris, a city still luxurious despite ration books and shortages. Creel saw the watch; and got to his feet.

"I have a late dinner or an early supper," said Blaise. "You'll be there tomorrow, for the opening?"

Creel nodded. "I'll watch until I'm thrown out."

"I'll do the same, I suppose."

House had told Blaise that it could be arranged for him to attend. But if a place had not been arranged for Lansing's Creel, Blaise was not about to provoke wrath by letting it be known that one had been arranged for House's Sanford. Actually, the preliminaries were open to a variety of privileged observers, while the actual conference was closed and secret – if seventy-two delegates from twenty-six nations could be relied on not to tell the world more than it wanted to know on the subject of new boundaries. The entire map of central Europe was being redrawn and, theoretically, Wilson held the blue pencil that would create new countries like Czechoslovakia while dismembering, if not erasing, ancient empires like that of Austria.

"I hope Colonel House is recovered." Creel said farewell to André.

"Oh, the flu came and went, like the President." When Wilson had come to the Crillon to visit House, he had passed Lansing's office but he had not stopped to greet that great officer of state. There had been scandal.

"But the gallbladder is still full of stones." Creel was gone.

"I don't understand Americans." André did not sound deprived.

"I wouldn't bother. You don't need to understand – us."

"Yes. You are one. Is Caroline?"

"Most of all. She has gone native."

"Our mother did, too. And brought us home your father, and you, too, of course."

"Yes. She is the link, Emma de Traxler Schuyler d'Agrigente Sanford. But no blood of mine."

"*Tant pis*," said André, reverting to their first language. Blaise wondered why Emma's descendants were all so proud of a woman who, Caroline had discovered, had deliberately allowed Blaise's mother to die giving birth to him so that she could then marry his father and the Sanford money. Of course, they all enjoyed their left-handed descent from Aaron Burr through Emma's father, who had been one of the many natural sons of that brilliant vice president who was now known only for the killing of Alexander Hamilton. In youth, Blaise had been excited and somewhat horrified to have two murderers, by marriage, in the family. But the arbitrariness of so many recent deaths from war and plague had quite erased murder's glamour in a flood of statistics that could only be grasped when one realized that Plon, say, was no longer there to talk to, ever again.

Blaise had been an adolescent when he first became the lover of Anne de Bieville, whose son, older than he, had then become his closest friend. Blaise had maintained the affair even at Yale, careful never to let on to his loud, loutish, virginal classmates that while they got drunk and babbled of girls, he was practically a family man.

The affair had ended quietly, thanks to the width of the Atlantic Ocean as much as to that of passing time. Blaise now looked into her face for the first time in a dozen years and found her the same but old. She was at least sixty-five. Since she had allowed her figure thoroughly to go, she was dressed like an odalisque in a sort of robe that did not try to reveal where her waist had been or even such details as the precise whereabouts of the breasts as they responded, as did all flesh, to inexorable gravity.

Anne met him in the foyer outside her drawing room, where twenty people were cheerily gathered. The house was shabbier than he remembered. The complaisant husband was long since dead, as was his friend, her son, swept away in the war. "We won't talk about him." Anne was firm. She held Blaise at arm's length so that her pale, far-sighted eyes might get a good look at him. "You've kept *your* figure."

"Yours . . ."

"Say nothing, my love. I am retired. But you're still like – what did Caroline always call you? – a furious pony. My style – once. Now I no longer ride."

"Outside the battle?"

"Outside the *war*. We can't talk now. But come tomorrow, or any day at five. I want to know so much. I saw Caroline in that film. She photographs so well."

"You're one of the few who recognized her. She's thrilled to be both famous and unknown."

"Emma Traxler is a magic name in Paris this season. Tell me about Frederika. No, don't. Save that. The Jusserands are here. My fault. You obviously see them every day in Washington. But they want to see you. There are also old friends from our old life. I almost got M. Clemenceau. But he is saving himself for tomorrow."

For the first time in years, Blaise felt entirely at home: but then, for the first time in years, he was in a room filled with people he had known all his life and for whom nothing ever changed. Their ranks could be – indeed had been – decimated by war but they still continued to be what they had always been and everyone was in correct relation to everyone else. There was no one present, no matter how vigorous and young and even rebellious, who could not "place" everyone else and himself in a web of family and history. In Blaise's chosen land, only Boston was like this; but he was not a Bostonian. He was French because he had spent the first twenty years of his life in Paris and at Saint-Cloud-le-Duc, and no one had forgotten him.

Blaise plunged into the warm bath; swam gracefully but swiftly through the Jusserands and those concerned with the Peace Conference, which now seemed a minor distraction. Here was the world, as they called it; of family, as they called it, of which he was forever, like it or not, a member.

"You know my mother." The young man looked literally familiar. Generation after generation, family resemblances could be, like butterflies, identified by inherited markings, not to mention traits of character.

"I am the right age." Blaise did not even mind being taken for middle-aged when he was, moment by moment, becoming younger and more like his – what had Anne called him? – furious blond pony self. Blaise identified the young man, correctly, as a Polignac. He was then presented to a dark, rather plump young woman, whom he did not immediately place though the name was a famous one, Charlotte, born Duchess of Valentinois as she wore no wedding ring. Blaise was amused at the ease with which he could re-enter the abandoned world of youth. Charlotte was the illegitimate daughter of an actress – with Negro blood, some said; Arab, said others – and the bachelor Prince Louis of Monaco, whose absence of issue had so alarmed *his* father, the reigning Prince of Monaco, that the girl had recently been legitimized and recognized as heiress to that convenient principality by the sea. Pierre de Polignac was at the Foreign Office. "Though I won't be in attendance tomorrow. I am seriously outranked. But I hear that you will be present."

"How?" Blaise was surprised. There had been nothing in the press.

"We have a list at the Quai d'Orsay that no one is supposed to see so of course I saw it."

"Very sensible. I shall watch the opening, anyway."

"We've all enjoyed," said the actress's daughter, "your sister in *Les Boches de l'Enfer*."

"Everyone recognizes her here, and no one at home." Blaise was delighted.

"Actually, *Figaro* gave away the secret," said de Polignac. "We get no credit. How long to go to America!"

Blaise spoke easily, without thinking, a principal pleasure in this society where, if one wanted to think, one could enjoy the most exhausting dialogue in the Henry Adams style; otherwise, conversation engulfed one warmly and the on-going narratives of each person in the *world* continued to unfold with sufficient surprises and odd turnings to keep boredom at bay.

Etienne de Beaumont was a spirited master of what Blaise liked to think of as the salon narrative. He was an elegant vivacious contemporary of Blaise, and they had known one another as boys. "Who would have thought you'd become an American!"

"Who would have thought that I was ever anything else?"

"I would." There was a mild excitement in the salon as the Queen of Naples made her entrance. She had lost her kingdom years before and now her brother-in-law, the Austrian emperor, was about to lose his empire to Woodrow Wilson's blue pencil. But the Queen was still as serenely beautiful as legend maintained, living a quiet life at Neuilly, undaunted by poverty. The ladies curtseyed low, as she passed. The men bowed.

"I was influenced by your relative, the Beaumont who went with Tocqueville to America, and wrote the book . . ."

"*That* Beaumont was a passionate monarchist like me, though I lack the passion. Anyway, Pierre de Polignac, who needs employment, is going to marry the Grimaldi girl, and become the prince consort of Monaco. After all, he has failed in literature. What else is there?"

"The Foreign Office?"

"He is only a decoration there."

"In Monaco?"

"A better-paid decoration. We have missed you. Are you going to open up Saint-Cloud?"

"It's not me but my house everyone misses."

"We are honest people. Oh, my God, the newlyweds." A middle-aged couple were moving purposefully in their direction, accompanied by a sturdy rather thick young woman of great vivacity and plainness.

Blaise recognized the man, who was a few years his senior; but neither woman was familiar. Apparently, it was the older of the two who had just been married to Louis de Talleyrand-Périgord, Duke of Montmorency.

"May I congratulate you?" Blaise shook hands formally with the groom, who seemed pleased to be remembered by their world's American now returned in triumph; the new duchess appeared energetic, if plain, while the plump young woman was alive with vivacity. To Blaise's amazement, she was American.

"I've met you a hundred times, Mr. Sanford, but you wouldn't remember. I'm a friend of Elsie de Wolfe." Names, mostly sapphic, were set off like fireworks.

Etienne was enjoying himself. "How," he asked the Duchess, "is your charming son?"

"Very well, thank you." But she was after bigger game; she turned to Blaise. "I've seen your beautiful residence at Saint-Cloud so many times *from the outside* . . ."

"You must see the inside . . ."

"Come back to us!" the lady exclaimed. "Our old world needs new blood. Of course, you are so busy with your newspaper. You know, my husband, the Duke, subscribes. Of course, all the papers come at once. So we have stacks of New York *Timeses* everywhere in our home."

Etienne's smile was of Cheshire-cat proportions.

The young American woman came to the rescue. "Cecilia," she boomed, her voice very deep. "It's not the New York *Times* he publishes."

"I know, Elsa, I know." The new duchess smiled upon Blaise. "I must go and pay my respects to the Queen of Naples. She must be so depressed by that boring republic in Germany and her poor father, the Kaiser, a prisoner in Belgium!"

The three swept through the room to where the Queen stood, back to a gilded mirror, Anne beside her. "Cecilia's marvelous. She gets *everything* wrong! A work of art." Etienne looked as if he had somehow invented the duchess. "You don't remember her?"

Blaise shook his head.

"She was not so much received in the old days when she was Madame Blumenthal born Ullmann . . ."

"Very rich. I remember." It was beginning to come back. "She wanted to have a salon . . ."

"And a name. Now she has both. She also has a grown son by M.

Blumenthal, and one of the conditions of her marriage to our friend Louis was that he pass on his title to her son, which he agreed to do in exchange for some of the Ullmann-Blumenthal millions."

"How nice to know nothing changes here."

"Well, some things change." Etienne frowned. "He would never have married her in our youth, no matter how hard up he was."

"The Dreyfus case?"

"That was only a passing symptom. The world changes, I'm afraid. Anyway, our poor Louis, now our rich Louis, is known as the Duke of Montmorenthal."

Although Blaise felt comfortably at home here, he was more stimulated by the anarchy of social relationships in America, where nearly everyone was a new arrival and blatantly self-invented. "I am more surprised by the fat girl," said Blaise. "*She* wouldn't have been here when we were young."

Etienne shrugged. "There have always been court jesters. This one is very energetic. She accompanies singers at the piano, professionally. Her name is Maxwell, Elsa Maxwell, and I should say she will be permanently unmarried. Is the family known in America?"

Blaise pleaded ignorance. Then he bowed low to the Queen of Naples; kissed Anne ceremoniously on both cheeks. "If you would like to be presented to Edith Bolling Wilson, queen of the United States, I can do it."

"I should like nothing more."

Blaise brooded upon physical attraction as the taxi drove him from the Faubourg Saint-Germain across the Seine to the nearly invisible rue de l'Arcade, which was just that, a covered sidestreet where, at number 11, the Hôtel Marigny occupied a narrow building two rooms and a staircase wide and five stories high.

In youth, Blaise had been totally absorbed by Anne; then one day he was not. He had changed his tastes; he now preferred girls to women. Happily, she had always understood that she was simply a gate through which he would pass en route to his own maturity – whatever that might entail. He had liked her, but in time she would have become the mother that he had lost at birth, and though he was sometimes curious about this personage her absence had caused him no distress. He wanted no surrogate.

Blaise walked the few yards from square to hotel. The night was intensely cold, and his breath was a dark gray cloud in the light from a single street lamp.

The heat was tropical inside the Marigny. A smell of boiled turnips, dust, incense. To the right of a fragile staircase, the manager's office – a room not much larger than a Crillon closet. Here, in the doorway, stood Albert, a pale man in his mid-thirties, with elaborate manners.

"The American gentleman." He showed Blaise into the office which contained a day-bed covered with Turkish material, a desk and a chair. "I'm afraid we're short of furniture. I only took over last year, and if it hadn't been for friends, I wouldn't have even these few sticks. I've seen you before, of course."

Blaise nodded, sat on the edge of the day-bed, refused a glass of sherry. "Our mutual friend has told me your . . ." Albert gestured gracefully. At sixteen, he had come from Brittany to Paris, where he had been employed as footman in one great household after another, of which the most notorious had been that of Prince Constantin Radziwill, of whom a jingle had been composed: "It is most incivil to mention ladies to Constantin Radziwill."

Over the years, Albert had fallen so deeply in love with the aristocracy that he had made himself an expert on genealogy, and he had come to know everyone's connections better often than they did themselves. Like Saint-Simon, he was fascinated – obsessed – by precedence. In the Faubourg, old ladies swore by him, and he was often consulted before a dinner to determine who should go in to dinner before whom and sit where. Once, Albert had been given the most dangerous of all challenges: if a lady were to invite to dinner the first duchess of France, d'Uzès, an ancient creation of the Bourbon kings, and the Princess Murat, a creation of the Bonaparte emperors, which would take precedence? Albert had answered severely, "No *lady* would ever invite the two together."

Albert spoke politely of the weather, of the United States; guardedly of certain figures in the great world. Blaise responded easily. Then Albert motioned for Blaise to follow him up echoing stairs to the first landing. Here, Albert opened a door so that Blaise could look into the room without being seen by its occupants. Three young soldiers in uniform were seated on a day-bed, drinking red wine while a butcher-boy, complete with bloody apron, sat reading a Socialist newspaper. Blaise studied the four; then murmured to Albert, "The blond soldier."

Albert then showed Blaise into a bedroom with a four-poster bed, heavy-duty velvet curtains at the window, a torn silk curtain in one corner, half-hiding bidet and washstand. Blaise's pulse was now beating erratically. He looked at himself in the mirror to see if he was turning – unhealthily? – red in the face. But the face that looked back at him was as usual except that, thanks to the dust with which the glass was streaked, he looked twenty years younger than he last remembered, and almost as young as the face that now looked over his shoulder.

Blaise turned, and shook hands gravely. The boy – he was no more than twenty – muttered a greeting. Like Albert, he was from Brittany. "I was mustered out last month." The Breton accent appealed to Blaise. "But I didn't go home. I should've. But I was having too good a time. I drink too much."

"Calvados."

"Anything," said the boy glumly. "I lived with this woman for two weeks. She took all my money. So I'm here."

"Like the other soldiers in the room."

The boy nodded. Blaise gestured for him to take off his clothes. He did, slowly; the fair skin flushed with embarrassment. He was plainly not used to the business. "The guy who's dressed up like a butcher," he said, letting his shirt drop to the floor, "he's really an upholsterer, but the crazy man who owns this place . . ."

"Albert?"

"No. This old man. He's very sick, very pale. He bought the hotel for Albert. Anyway, he likes talking about blood, things like that. So Albert, if he can't find a real butcher, gets a guy to dress up like one and tell the old man all about cutting up animals. The old man likes blood. He's really crazy." The drawers fell to the floor, and the boy stood in front of Blaise. The legs were like Blaise's, stableboy legs, and the golden hairs gleamed in the lamplight.

239

"What have I got to do?" The bluntness was so mingled with fear and embarrassment that Blaise's response was equally mingled; he felt both lustful and paternal. "Well," said Blaise, "you won't have to talk about blood."

"Good." For the first time the boy smiled, a hesitant smile. "I've seen enough of that."

Blaise was now undressed. The boy looked at him, and appeared relieved that Blaise was not a monster. "You're like a pony," said Blaise, running his hand across the smooth skin of the soldier's hairless chest.

"I smell like one," said the boy sadly. "But it's not me. I mean, I'm clean. But the uniform's the only one I've got. I've had to sleep in it for weeks."

In recent years, Blaise had indulged so little in masculine pleasures that he had almost forgotten just how splendid it was to be with a body that was the same as his but entirely different, and young. More than anything, the other's youth acted as trigger to both lust and memory, and Blaise was, suddenly, *briefly*, as one with his original self. The lack of complication was also a perfect joy. Women meant involvement even when, with prostitutes, responsibility was cancelled by cash: the habit of a relationship that was intended to lead to children was ever-present. But nothing of that sort obtained in a four-poster with a sweating boy. This was mindless pleasure; and freedom. Best of all, like all ordinary males unless otherwise trained by women or by an over-conscientious Albert, they did not kiss. That was only for man-father with woman-mother, after snake, apple spoiled Eden.

When they were again dressed, Blaise paid the soldier twice what was expected, and the boy gave him a shy smile revealing a crooked front tooth. "That was all right," he said, with a degree of surprise.

"You could do it for pleasure?"

"Well, maybe, if there was no woman . . ." They both laughed; and left the room.

Albert was gravely pleased that they were pleased. Blaise tried to remember the name of the society novelist who had paid for the establishment. He had been told the name, most recently by

Etienne de Beaumont. The man was a Jew, a semi-invalid, and, like Albert, obsessed with genealogy, with bloodlines as well as actual blood. Whoever he was, he had appeared on the scene after Blaise's day in Paris. Nevertheless, Blaise was deeply grateful to him for having made it possible to encounter, so unexpectedly, his own youth in a wintry arcade.

2

At the entrance to the Quai d'Orsay, Blaise was obliged to show various badges and documents. Fortunately, the gray misty morning had yet to produce rain; but the cold was penetrating and typical of a Paris winter. Then, through a crowd of journalists, the *Tribune*'s correspondent hurried to greet his publisher. He was English, brought up in France. He knew everyone and everything, or so he said and doubtless believed. "The President is ready. He's about to present to the world his Valentine." Mr. Campbell thought like a journalist.

Blaise observed how apt this was – February 14, 1919. After four weeks of intense and mostly secret labor, Wilson had completed his covenant of the League of Nations with small help and much hindrance from the conference, reduced, for practical purposes, to a council of ten, chaired by Clemenceau, with much work from Colonel House at the Crillon, where the Commission on the League of Nations met across the river from the Quai d'Orsay.

House's gallstones had ceased to trouble him, and he was able to obtain for the President the grail that he had been pursuing. He had also seen to it that the other nations, no matter how reluctant, would accept their handiwork. The previous evening, at seven o'clock, the twenty-six articles of the covenant had been accepted by the conference. Now the President would present his finished masterpiece to the conference in the great Hall of the Clock; and then hurry home to report to Congress. Blaise was to travel with the presidential party aboard the *George Washington,* due to leave that night from Brest.

"I've already cabled the text to Mr. Trimble. I got it last night at midnight, through a friend on the commission . . ."

"Gordon Auchincloss?" The House contingent relentlessly worked the press at Lansing's expense and, it was beginning to be noted, the President's as well.

"Just a friend." Mr. Campbell was cheerfully mysterious. Blaise was obliged to join the military section in the anteroom to the crowded hall, whose open doors provided a partial view of the horseshoe table at which sat the delegates of the victorious nations and their would-be clients.

The French were masters of this sort of theater, thought Blaise, as Mr. Campbell placed him in a gilded chair next to an unidentified marshal of France. Blaise had been told that his fellow publisher Lord Northcliffe was also present, but there was no sign of him in the anteroom. Would Northcliffe, thanks to the British prime minister, get a better seat than the publisher of Washington's most powerful newspaper, which meant the world's? Blaise indulged himself in imperial daydreams, thus identifying himself with the United States, whose president had brought peace to Europe in the present and was now about to impose a universal peace upon the future.

The red-carpeted hall was not large, sixty by forty feet, the reporter-Blaise guessed, all gilded and painted. At a horseshoe table, covered with acid-green baize, the delegates sat beneath the huge eponymous clock held in the arms of a rococo plaster maiden. By special dispensation, at the horseshoe's open end Mrs. Wilson reigned in gorgeous purple, Admiral Grayson standing next to her. At the head of the table, Clemenceau presided, Wilson beside him.

During the last four weeks Blaise had had one long meaningless talk with Lloyd George, or rather he had listened to the histrionic Welshman whose glowing insincerity was so commingled with animal charm that Blaise had quite liked him.

Blaise had found the Italian premier, Orlando, sad; doubtless because he had made so many secret treaties as a price for Italy's presence among the Allies that he now realized that he was not going to get as much of the shattered Austrian empire as his people expected.

Of the lot, Clemenceau most delighted Blaise. They spoke of people long dead, friends of Blaise's father. Clemenceau spoke of the American Civil War, during which he had been a correspondent for a French newspaper. He still remembered, he said, the look of the fallen Confederate capital, Richmond, shortly after the victorious Lincoln had left the city. He also remembered the fallen French capital, Paris, where Bismarck had imposed a German peace. Clemenceau had questioned Blaise closely about Wilson; and Blaise found him less suspicious than he had anticipated. Plainly, Clemenceau had started by thinking the President a knave like Lloyd George; now he seemed to think him merely a fool.

At the head of the table, Clemenceau wore a black skullcap and pearl-gray gloves of gauze to hide his eczema. The face looked to be a mask of yellow parchment – out of which stared, as journalists enjoyed noting, the eyes of a tiger. It was said that he had accepted Wilson's covenant as a *quid* whose *quo* would be ruinous reparations to be paid the Allies by Germany. The fact that a bankrupt Germany might turn Bolshevik, as Russia had done, did not concern him.

The President glanced at the clock. Then he picked up a sheaf of papers, and stood up. Wilson was more gray than usual, but when he spoke, the voice was as nearly jubilant as that priestly voice could ever be. Wilson had managed through luck or cunning or a combination of both to make the United States the first nation in the world as a result of a war that had cost his nation fifty thousand lives while Germany, Russia and France had each lost close to two million men apiece and England a million; a generation was forever gone from Europe, and summer as well as spring had gone out of the year.

Wilson's delivery was muted. He read what was, Blaise realized halfway through, nothing less than a declaration of interdependence of all the countries of the world. What Jefferson had done for thirteen British colonies, his successor was doing for the whole earth. Blaise looked about him with some awe at the rapt attention of Japan and China, of the colonial empires that included Africa, of the antipodean rulers, all present beneath a gold clock, as their teacher explained to them how peace could be kept like time. When he had got through the text, he put it down. Then Wilson spoke simply but movingly of the covenant. "A living thing is born, and we must see to it that the clothes we put upon it do not hamper it." This homely echo of Jefferson worked surprisingly well. "I think I can say of this document that it is at one and the same time a practical and humane document. There is a pulse of sympathy in it. There is a compulsion of conscience throughout it. It is practical, and yet it is intended to purify, to rectify, to elevate. . . ." Even Clemenceau appeared to be moved, while Lloyd George's blue eyes glistened as if aswim with happy tears.

When the President had finished, he sat down. There was no applause. The summing up had been improvised from a few notes, something that awed most of the statesmen and journalists in Paris. Even Clemenceau read carefully from a text, fearful that if he improvised he might betray himself. But Wilson's years as teacher of history proved peculiarly useful to him now as maker of history. In a sense, he was lecturing as if he himself was already a documented figure in the past. But then Blaise had an odd feeling that everything he was now witnessing had happened long ago. The great gilded clock above Wilson's head had already measured so much past time that now whatever it marked was, by its own circular process, enriched and done for.

The translator took over and read, rapidly, the covenant; and did his best with the President's improvisation. After a swift, silent, unanimous ballot, Clemenceau adjourned the conference.

Blaise was carried forward by a surge of excited journalists to the head of the horseshoe, where George Creel was arranging a photograph of the principals.

Wilson looked singularly miserable; and Blaise heard him say to Creel, "Don't let them use their flashes. They hurt my eyes."

But Creel could no longer control the situation. The principals stood in a row, the President slightly apart and averted from the cameras. The lights provided a terrible lightning glare. Wilson winced and blinked his eyes. "We will all look," he said to Lloyd George, "as though we were laid out in a morgue."

3

There were two boat trains to Brest that evening. The first contained Wilson's staff and outriders, among them Blaise, and the second was for the presidential party. The troops that lined the railroad siding presented arms as the first train departed, twenty minutes before that of the President. Blaise shared a compartment with the Roosevelts and Eleanor's youthful uncle by marriage, David Gray. Eleanor had come over to visit hospitals and be useful, while Franklin had just come from Brussels and Coblenz and the Rhineland, where he had collected a great many souvenirs, including a spiked German helmet that he kept beside him on the seat.

Dutifully, the Roosevelts waved at the crowd, who knew them not. *Noblesse* – or *politique* – *oblige,* thought Blaise: After all, Eleanor was the late President's niece. Now she quizzed Blaise about Wilson's speech. She was unusually pale, which, considering her normal lack of color, made her seem as white and insubstantial as a cloud, admittedly a large swollen cloud. She had been ill with pleurisy. "So we shall have a league of nations," Blaise concluded.

"I hope so," she said.

Although Franklin had been talking to David Gray, he had also been listening at the same time. He interrupted himself with, "Public opinion's with the President now. But let's hope he can get this through the Senate fast. Before the Republicans whip up the opposition . . ."

"Mother says . . . Mrs. James, that is, Mrs. Roosevelt," Eleanor giggled nervously, "that all of her set think Mr. Wilson is a Bolshevik, and she has stopped seeing the Whitelaw Reids because of that. Mother is very loyal."

"I wish all the Democratic senators were." Franklin frowned. "So many of them are paid for by the Germans or in so deep with the Irish that they forget that if it weren't for Wilson they wouldn't have been elected in the first place."

This was exaggerated, thought Blaise. The President's opposition within his party was the party's true core: the big-city bosses with their obedient immigrant masses and the populist Bryanites like Burden Day. As the party of the bankers and great merchants, the Republicans had always been the internationalists, and they looked to the world outside America for trade and profit, it was no accident that to the extent that the League was any one person's idea, credit must be given to the former Republican president Taft or to Elihu Root or even to the bellicose Theodore Rex, who had, when it suited him, come out for some such organization.

Eleanor was anxious about the American soldiers in Paris. "The stories one hears!" There was now a trace of color in her cheeks. "If their mothers only knew of the dangers."

"Just as well they don't." Franklin exchanged a rapid conspiratorial look with Blaise – the masculine lodge must now close its shutters.

"I am told," said David Gray sadly, "our officers are the worst. While the private soldiers ask for directions to Napoleon's Tomb, the officers ask for Maxim's."

"Exactly what I've heard!" The vein in Eleanor's temple throbbed. "Poor Franklin," as Alice Longworth would say, "he has Eleanor, so noble." Although Blaise quite liked Eleanor, he could not imagine being married to so much energy and high-mindedness.

"Well, they'll soon be home," she said. "Anyway, I hope it's not true, is it?" she was suddenly tentative, "that the French provide their troops with . . . with houses of assignation?" Eleanor was pale pink now, the most headway that the blood could make through that thick alabaster-gray skin.

Franklin nodded gravely. "Horrifying," he intoned, "but true. I was in Newton Baker's office when General March told him what the French had done, and Baker said, 'Don't tell the President or he'll stop the war.'"

"Good grounds," said Eleanor, grimly, and ignored the laughter of the three men.

4

Blaise lay on a deck chair beside David R. Francis, American ambassador to Russia; each was heavily swathed in woolen army blankets like cocoons from which each would, presently, emerge as a stately moth. The February sea had been too much for most of the passengers of the *George Washington* – except Blaise, who enjoyed the ship's shuddering encounters with gray-black waves, like boulders thrown up from the deep.

Ambassador Francis was also equal to the sea's turmoil. But he was less equal, he confessed, to the Bolsheviks. "At the beginning, we really did think they were an improvement." A spray of salt water caused him to wince; he dried his face with the corner of a blanket.

"I know." Blaise did not remind the Ambassador of his embarrassing comparison of Lenin with Washington and the Czar with George III.

"But how did it all come apart?"

"The French. The English. Clemenceau." Francis shook his head. "They want Russia destroyed, Russia in any form. I'm convinced it's not just Bolshevism."

"No more German Empire, no more Austro-Hungarian Empire, no more Russian Empire . . . one sees their point. England rules the waves, and France the continent."

Francis nodded. "But except for Austria, the empires are still where they were. Only the emperors are gone."

"There will be trouble?"

"There is trouble. Our boys are fighting right now in northern Russia, with the Allies, against the Bolsheviks."

"How many American troops?"

"Over five thousand." Francis stared unhappily at the pewter-dull western sky. Then a wave broke over the starboard bow, and the rubber of the sailors' mackintoshes shone like seals. "Thanks to the War Department, instead of reporting to me in Petrograd, they went straight onto Archangel and reported to the British commander. Now they're icebound, and the railroad to Murmansk is out, and then when the thaw starts, how do we get them out of there?"

"We fight our way out, according to young Mr. Churchill. He claims there are a half-million anti-Red troops, eager to overthrow the Communist government, if only we'd just stay and help them."

"It would be nice," said Francis, sourly, "if *he* were to lead them. I met with him and the President just before we left. He was full of . . ." The ambassador, a former governor of Missouri, controlled himself.

"What did the President say?"

"He listened, mostly. Finally, he told Churchill how we are irreversibly – his word – committed to getting our troops out when the weather lets up. Privately, Lloyd George thinks Churchill's one precious fool and that if we – the Allies – were to get into a full-scale war with the Bolsheviks so as to divide up Russia between us – Clemenceau's dream – the English people would all go Communist during the war."

Blaise was grimly amused. "At least Lloyd George understands the nature of tyranny in his own country."

Francis did not hear – or did not choose to acknowledge – this heresy: the winners were all democracies; thus insuring safety for themselves and everyone else from despots and levellers. "Anyway, we'll be out of Archangel by summer."

"But what about Siberia? I'm told that we have eighty-five hundred troops there."

Francis grinned. "Another War Department error. We told the Japanese that we'd send in seven thousand. So the War Department went and added another thousand, which gave the Japanese an opportunity to break the agreement, and send in tens of thousands of troops to keep *us* from annexing Siberia."

"Are we?"

"Going to annex? I don't see how. We're too far away and the Japanese are too close, and Admiral Kolchak is still fighting the Bolsheviks, and if he wins, Russia splits in two. It's a terrible mess for everybody."

Blaise presented himself at the door to Wilson's cabin just as the number of bells that meant three o'clock at sea were struck. Admiral Grayson ushered Blaise into a sizeable office with a large mahogany desk on which were placed two telephones connected, Blaise wondered, to what?

The President was dressed as if he were about to go golfing. The sea air had brought color to his face; the pince-nez shone in the light from the overhead lamp. "Mr. Sanford. How good of you to come." It was part of Wilson's charm to act as if each of his visitors had made an extraordinary personal sacrifice to call upon him, no doubt a necessary charm when dealing with wealthy Princeton alumni or difficult parents.

Blaise took the indicated chair at Wilson's right. Through the porthole opposite, he could see Marine guards patrolling; could hear their boots strike, rhythmically, the deck. Wilson noticed Blaise's glance.

"Mrs. Wilson can't bear the sound or the thought of those boys marching back and forth all day. But I find it soothing." The ship suddenly pitched; a telephone began to slide along the desk. The President steadied it.

"Is that your line to the Vice President?"

"The Vice President?" Wilson looked puzzled; then he laughed. "Yes, the Vice President. Well, we do have a wireless link to the War Department and they connect with the White House. So I suppose the Vice President is somewhere – out there – on the other end. Anyway, thanks to the wireless, I'm as much in touch with public affairs here as I was in Paris or even Washington." Wilson sounded defensive. Many of his own supporters were appalled that a president should leave the country for even a day, much less two months.

"You'll come back, then?"

"May I speak off the record?"

"By all means, Mr. President." Over the years, Wilson had come to trust Blaise if only because the *Tribune* was generally favorable to his Administration while the *Post* was unreliable, and the *Times*, now manipulated by Hearst through Brisbane, hostile. Also, Blaise had never betrayed a confidence on those rare occasions when he had been in receipt of one.

"I don't see how I can abandon the Peace Conference. Colonel House is superb, but he's not well. The French . . ." Even off the record, Wilson could not trust himself. "Clemenceau . . ." he began: and let it go at that. "So much can be undone if I'm not there."

"But you have your covenant . . ."

"Right here," said Wilson and opened his coat so that Blaise could see the famous document folded in his pocket.

"Over my heart. Though Edith maintains it's my spleen. But I shall not be splenetic, no matter how keen the fight in the Senate."

"Why should there be any fight at all?"

"*They* will have it. So I must have it." The underslung jaw set.

"But they . . . the Republicans . . . invented the idea, if anyone can be said to have thought of it first."

"And they would rather kill it than see us get the credit for this astonishing charter. Oh, there'll be a fight all right. But then I've never found that one could get anything worthwhile without a struggle." Thus spoke the Scottish clansman on the eve of a border war.

"Surely all western civilization is built on compromise." Blaise expected to get a rise from the President; and did.

Wilson looked at him sharply, even inquisitorially. "You've been talking to Colonel House."

Blaise nodded. "I was quoting his exact words."

". . . when he quoted Burke to me. Yes. We disagreed. My wife calls me the most obstinate man in America." The smile was faint and hardly proud. "But I know what I am up against. Lodge will do anything to destroy the League or, indeed, anything else that I propose."

"If there were a vote now in this particular Senate, you'd win."

"A two-thirds vote? Which is what I need for a treaty?"

Blaise nodded. Burden had explained it all; even with the new Republican majority, made not so secure by the independent Senator La Follette's unreliable support, there were enough Republicans and loyal Democrats to give the President his treaty. Blaise then gave the President Burden's detailed anatomy of the chamber and how the votes would go. To his surprise, Wilson had done no research at all into the Senate's mood. Burden's estimate of how this one and that one might vote appeared strange to him.

"Well, everything you tell me is comforting, in theory," he said at last. "But one can never underestimate Lodge's ingenuity. You know, all during the conference, he was seeing to it that the press and the delegates were constantly reminded that I do not have the support of the American people, that I have lost the Congress, that I represent no one but myself. You can't think what an effect this makes, and how difficult it is to dispel their doubts, particularly when dealing with those who want me – us – to fail."

Wilson sat back in his chair, face suddenly white and strained. "I put all this on the head of one man alone, Theodore Roosevelt." The name on Wilson's lips was a curse. "Sick in the hospital, about to die, he was plotting with Lodge and Root to destroy this mission. All three wanted the League long before I'd ever appeared on the scene. But out of Roosevelt's private rage and malice and, yes, malignant evil, he could not bear that anyone else might ever get credit for benefitting the world. He was without the slightest human compassion. He cared only for himself and his ludicrous career. Frankly, I regard his death as a true blessing and I pray that no such monster ever again appears upon the scene, preaching mindless war."

Blaise was shocked at the intensity of Wilson's hatred; but hardly surprised. In life, Roosevelt had indeed done everything possible to destroy Wilson, and now, in death, thanks to Lodge, the mischief continued. But Blaise also was certain that the President, trailing glory, would prevail as he had in Paris against far more worldly opponents than mere gentlemen from Idaho and Missouri and even Massachusetts.

The telephone rang. "Little girl," Wilson murmured, suddenly transformed from Old Testament prophet to uxorious mate. "Yes. Of course we'll go to the show tonight. Yes." Wilson hung up. "They were afraid that I was displeased with last night's program."

A sailor, dressed as a prostitute, had done a somewhat lascivious dance, and then chucked the President under the chin. The sailors had roared; the presidential courtiers had gasped; and the President himself had turned to stone. "They were a bit high-spirited . . ." Blaise began.

"I was . . ." Wilson stopped and frowned. "Well, not pleased, no.

251

For the sake of the office such things ought not to happen. But, personally, I'm relieved that people find me not entirely forbidding. In my life I've had very little to do with individuals, except to teach them, by no means a . . . friendly activity, or discharge the office of an executive, hardly an endearing activity."

Wilson sat back in his chair, and sighed. "You know, I could've done well in vaudeville." Suddenly, he let his face go loose and Blaise was reminded of the scene at the Capitol before the declaration of war. Slowly, Wilson shook his head. The face, totally slack, was cretinous and comical. The body drooped, complementing the face. "I'm Dopey Dan," he sang, "and I'm married to Midnight Mary." With that, he did an expert scarecrow sort of dance across the deck, whistling all the while. When he finished, he bowed.

Blaise applauded loudly. "Do that when you address the Congress, Mr. President, and you'll sweep the nation."

"Do that, and they'll put me away." Wilson laughed. "Or send me out on the Keith circuit with Midnight Mary, by no means the worst of fates." Blaise was more than ever confident that the President could easily handle Congress, not to mention the ghost of Theodore Roosevelt.

7

1

The Senate cloakroom was now divided by an invisible wall across its narrow middle. On one side the Republicans exchanged whispers with their leader Lodge, and on the other the Democrats brooded under the benign if not particularly able leadership of Gilbert M. Hitchcock, Claude Swanson and Burden himself, by no means, in his view, the ablest managers to see the treaty through the Senate.

Outside the cloakroom the sergeant-at-arms had thoughtfully assembled a number of army cots and blankets in case the senators filibustered today as they had the previous day, March 2, when La Follette of Wisconsin took the lead in exploiting the right of any senator to speak as long as he liked. Ostensibly, the bill to be talked to death concerned the leasing of public coal and oil reserves by suspect private interests. But as the Sixty-fifth Congress was obliged to expire March 4 and as a seven-billion-dollar Victory Bond bill had not yet passed, La Follette and his liberal friends were threatening, in effect, to leave the government without funds until the Sixty-sixth Congress assembled in December.

Since Wilson had no intention of calling Congress back between March and December, there was considerable urgency on the part of the Democratic minority to see that the appropriate bills were safely passed and the Congress sent home. If Congress were to come back in an emergency session, Lodge and his allies would then be able, in leisurely fashion, to dismember Wilson's covenant while the President was still in Paris at work on the final peace treaty.

In full health Burden enjoyed this sort of maneuvering, but nowadays he was in half-health at best. In the flu's aftermath, he was permanently, mortally tired, with an alarming tendency to fall into a sudden sound sleep no matter where he was. Kitty had begged him to stay away from the Capitol. But the President had begged him to stay at his post. So now he sat with Hitchcock at the Democratic end of the cloakroom, his feet resting on an army cot.

Thus far, everything that Burden and Hitchcock had tried to arrange kept coming undone. La Follette and his friends had given up their filibuster at six-forty on the morning of March 2, at the request of the Republican caucus, which did not want the party blamed for the failure of the Victory Bond issue to pass. There had been a trade-off. La Follette took seriously the stealing of the people's wealth. Lodge took seriously the destruction of Wilson's treaty. As party leader, Lodge had promised to aid La Follette later if he would end the filibuster now. La Follette obliged; the bond issue had been passed. But the financing of the government through a general-deficiency bill of $840 million was still pending. The Senate had then adjourned until ten in the morning, March 3, which meant that there would be only twenty-six hours in which to appropriate money to pay the federal government's debts. If the money was not forthcoming, Lodge would get his wish and Congress would be obliged to come back in the spring.

Burden looked at his watch. It was now eleven thirty-five. In twelve hours, at noon, March 4, the President would come to the Capitol to sign whatever bills Congress had prepared for him.

"Marshall's ready to recognize us." Hitchcock stared through the cigar smoke at Lodge, who was holding court from a black leather sofa. Surrounded by Republican senators, he looked most grandly the philosopher-king. "But they don't quit. When one finishes he signals to another one to spell him, and the Vice President can't do a thing."

From back of the swinging doors to the chamber, Burden could hear the slightly hoarse voice of – Francis of Maryland? Yes: the phrase "King Woodrow" was being repeated over and over again, to the gallery's delight. All Washington had converged on the Capitol to enjoy the fun. Frederika and Caroline were sitting together in the gallery, and Burden felt not unlike a superior rooster gazing upward at his very own hens, side by side, and easily the two most distinguished ladies in the gallery now that Evalyn McLean had dropped off to sleep in the diplomatic section. "At ten to midnight I'll make my try. I've told Marshall that when he recognizes me, I'll ask for a vote."

"Let's hope there's still a quorum. They could make a run for the depot."

"We'll send the sergeant-at-arms after them."

"We're not the majority." Hitchcock was sour.

La Follette entered the cloakroom. He seemed not at all tired after Saturday's filibuster. A large-headed, stocky man, most able in debate and fierce in his representation of the people against the interests. Burden had always assumed that like most instinctive populists, La Follette had pacifist leanings and so would support the League. But in this he was more Roosevelt-progressive than true people's man. Finally, he was more La Follette, the histrionic lonely warrior, than anything else. Lodge had cleverly used La Follette's genuine objection to the leasing bill in order to postpone altogether the vote on the appropriation bill. La Follette had obliged. Now Burden wondered what price he had demanded for his co-operation.

"Will we hear your magnificent voice this evening, Senator?" Hitchcock was orotund.

La Follette shrugged; and mumbled, "I've got a lozenge in my mouth."

"We'll hear you then," said Hitchcock.

"Will you speak *all night*?" asked Burden.

"If sufficiently inspired by my theme." La Follette went onto the floor. Burden noticed that Lodge had been watching La Follette closely – anxiously? No one knew what their common strategy was, other than to keep the Senate from coming to a vote before adjournment.

Burden went to the swinging doors and looked into the chamber.

Electric light emphasized more than daylight the prevailing greens. The effect was rather like looking into an aquarium where senators, like large fish, floated and the pages, like so many minnows, followed first one then another. The weary Vice President was in the chair, a study in bad temper.

A Democrat now took the floor, Martin of Virginia. The former majority leader warned his colleagues of the financial panic that would ensue if the finance bill was not passed before adjournment. He was eloquent. The Republican Lenroot of Wisconsin rose to ask if the bill was not passed, would the President call the Congress back *before* he had returned from France?

Martin was emphatic. "In two conversations, in the plainest possible English, he said that he had made up his mind, and it was final, that no extra session of Congress will be called under any circumstances until his return from France."

Burden caught the Vice President's eye. Marshall nodded. As agreed, Burden would be recognized just before midnight; and he would call for a vote. Burden went on to the floor and sat for a moment at his desk. Frederika smiled down at him; her hair had started to grow back, not blond but white beneath her temporary wig. Caroline gave him a sisterly smile.

Back of Caroline, Alice Longworth sat with her cousin Eleanor and Senator Borah. Alice, as usual, was doing all the talking, and Eleanor looked pained. Eleanor was as much for Wilson as her cousin was against him. Burden wondered how the friendship or, specifically, relationship was going to survive so much political passion. Senator Harding suddenly sat in the desk next to Burden. The handsome face was flushed; he enjoyed his drink. "I can't for the life of me see the point of all this." He shook his head mournfully. "It'd be so easy to just sit down and work out what's possible and what isn't with the treaty, and compromise."

"I don't think it's that easy, Mr. Harding. The President gave his word to the Allies that this was what we'd been fighting the war about, this treaty, this League of Nations, and so they gave in to him, which is why he can't go and change it now." Burden glanced at his watch: five minutes to go. The Vice President was also looking at his watch. Lenroot was speaking.

"Well, I'm not convinced it's the best thing in the world the way it is, and I still don't know why we fought that stupid war. This is between you and I." Harding smiled. "Naturally, in public I'm for democracy for everybody everywhere every minute of the day. But I think a lot of this Bolshevism that's going on in Europe and starting up here at home, too, is Mr. Wilson's doing."

Burden was suddenly aware of Lodge's presence in the chamber. The gallery applauded as Lenroot yielded the floor to Lodge, who addressed the Senate, document in hand. This was not according to Burden's plan.

Lodge's splendid Boston voice was high with tension. "Mr. President, I desire to take only a moment of the time of the Senate. I wish to offer the resolution which I hold in my hand, a very brief one." Then he read from the paper. "That it is the sense of the Senate that while it is their sincere desire that the nations of the world should unite to promote peace and general disarmament, the constitution of the League of Nations in the form now proposed by the Peace Conference should *not* be accepted by the United States . . ." There was a gasp from the Wilsonians in the galleries; and applause from the rest.

Burden was on his feet waving to the chair for recognition. Lodge persevered, as Marshall gavelled for order. ". . . immediately be directed to utmost expedition of the urgent business of negotiating peace terms with Germany . . ."

Burden had caught Marshall's attention, too late.

". . . and that the proposal for a League of Nations to insure the permanent peace of the world should be *then* taken up for careful consideration."

Burden was certain that there were not enough senators present to pass this or any other measure with the hope of surviving a later full vote; also, many of the senators present had been defeated in November while those who had been elected in their place had not yet been sworn in. As Lodge knew that his motion would carry no weight until the convening of the Sixty-sixth Congress, what was his motive? Lodge said, "I ask *unanimous* consent for the present consideration of this resolution."

Burden recognized a parliamentary trap when he saw one.

There was no possibility of unanimous consent now or ever. Burden turned to Harding, but Harding had vanished. Burden started down the aisle, ready to object to the propriety of the measure. But Claude Swanson of Virginia had got the Vice President's attention. Swanson said, "I object to the introduction of the resolution." Swanson had taken the bait.

Lodge remained standing during this, the venerable white head inclined to one side, like a listening bird; then he nodded his head judiciously as if some important point that had been too difficult for him to grasp had been at last cleared up. Swanson sat down.

With as much an appearance of humility as that bearded Roman head could permit, Lodge bowed gracefully to Swanson. "Objection being made, of course, I recognize the objection. I merely wish to add, by way of explanation, the following." Burden felt a chill: the trap had sprung. With relish, Lodge recited the names of those Republican senators who would have voted for his resolution if they were present and a vote had taken place. Lodge read off the names of thirty-seven senators, more than the one-third needed to defeat the League of Nations. As the gallery began to understand what was happening, applause broke out; then boos. The Vice President called for order.

Lodge left the floor, and the La Follette filibuster began again, with Sherman of Illinois first to speak. They would speak straight through the night until adjournment at noon. There would be no finance bill. There would be an extra session while Wilson was out of the country. There would be no League of Nations if Lodge could hold on to his thirty-seven senators, which Burden doubted. Even Lodge himself favored a league. The problem was as simple as it was insoluble. Wilson's league, as approved in Paris by the Allies, would not be accepted, while Lodge's league was so deliberately vague that even the most extreme isolationist might be able to support it at the proper time.

In the cloakroom, Lodge now held gracious court. As Burden went to his locker, where he kept whisky and soda water, he found Brandegee doing the same thing. "That was *my* idea," he said winningly. "The Round Robin."

"The what?" Burden was feeling not only tired but stupid.

"The thirty-seven signatures." Brandegee helped himself to his own dark restorative while Burden drank directly from the bottle and promptly felt less tired but no less stupid. "Do tell the President. I don't want Cabot hogging all the credit."

"Credit? For putting the covenant at risk?" Burden sounded more righteous than he intended. Actually, he quite liked this deeply conservative and even more deeply cynical political games-man who explained to him how, Sunday morning, he had found some accumulated mail at his house, including a letter from a stranger who implored the Senate Republicans to pass some sort of resolution declaring the League as presented unacceptable; otherwise, Wilson would go back to Paris and say that the Senate and the nation were behind him. "After I read the letter, I went straight to Massachusetts Avenue and explained it all to Cabot, and told him I could get more than a third of the Senate, enough to defeat the treaty, to sign and then he could present it at the last minute of March third for a vote . . ."

"He could never have got a vote." La Follette had entered the cloakroom from the hall, where, presumably, he had been in the washroom, emptying himself for the coming filibuster. He and his friends would speak all night and all the next morning until the adjournment of the session at noon.

"We knew we couldn't get a vote. We also knew that one of you would make the mistake of objecting, which Brother Swanson did, and then Cabot would meekly accept the objection and say that, naturally, as the full Senate wasn't here he quite understood, but that if they *were* present, the following senators had said that they'd vote to reject Brother Woodrow's League as it stands, and that's how we got the Round Robin into the record and now we'll be able to mail it all over the country to our many friends and fellow patriots."

"Beautiful work," said Burden without irony.

"I thought you'd appreciate it. I revere Brother Cabot, but I don't want him to be entirely credited for *my* last-minute rescue of this republic from the hands of a would-be world tyrant and his decadent allies in old Europe, so unlike our sunny land, where ne'er a shadow falls."

"Unless it's shot down by . . . Brother Frank Brandegee." Brandegee bowed low; then he joined Lodge and the rejoicing Republicans at the far end of the smoky cloakroom.

Hitchcock and Swanson were in a deep glum conversation with the Vice President. "I'm sorry," Burden said, "but before I could call for a vote, Lodge had the floor."

"Doesn't matter." Hitchcock rubbed his face. "They would've got that damned thing in the record one way or another."

"If I hadn't objected," Swanson began, but the Vice President stopped him. "You did. You had to. I'm going home. I'm turning the chair over to fellows who know there's going to be no vote tonight or tomorrow morning."

"What do we say to the President?" asked Hitchcock.

"You say, 'Good morning,'" said the silver-haired, silver-moustached Vice President, who, like most of his predecessors, felt that the accident of fate that had made him forever second was a cruel one. There goes Vice President Marshall, someone had recently said, with nothing on his mind except the President's health.

Burden agreed to spend the night captaining the Democratic minority from a cot in the hall. If anything happened, he would be wakened instantly. But nothing happened; and he awoke with a start to find a fresh-faced page staring down at him. "It's morning, Senator," said the boy. Burden inclined his head gravely, as if he had been meditating not sleeping. Why, he wondered, did everyone hate to be caught asleep?

In the great washroom with its high marble urinals and outsized basins, he shaved himself, as other weary senators came and went. Cold water on the face was the preferred restorative. The filibuster was still underway. La Follette had spoken for many hours on many subjects. As Burden stepped in the corridor, he could hear the hoarse rasping voice from the chamber. He hurried on to the President's room.

The Capitol was crowded with journalists, diplomats, citizens, all eager to enjoy the great filibuster, and Woodrow Wilson's discomfiture.

The President sat beneath a crystal chandelier at a desk on which last-minute bills would be placed, ready for his signature.

"Senator Day." The smile was warm. Wilson was not about to give any Republican the joy of seeing him distressed. Hitchcock was beside him. Admiral Grayson was behind him. Burden wondered, yet again, at the political wisdom of being always seen with one's doctor.

"I'm afraid we couldn't get the government paid for this time around."

"Well, I'm sure Mr. Glass," he nodded to the small imp-like replacement to Mr. McAdoo, "will be able to borrow enough between now and December to pay the light bill at the White House."

"I can also change stones into loaves and fishes." The Virginia drawl was acid.

Wilson got to his feet and motioned for Burden to join him at a distance from the others. "Tell me," he said in a low voice, "did Lodge make any reference to the League involving us with – what does he call it – 'international socialism and anarchy'?"

"Not last night, no. He's very vague. He has to be, since he favors the League, which he opposes."

"Solomonic. There is now pressure on me to commit the United States to a war on Bolshevism . . ."

"Russia?"

"In particular, but international socialism in general. I'm speaking tonight in New York. I'm going to say that according to my reading of the Virginia Bill of Rights, our *old* testament, any people is entitled to any kind of government it damn pleases, whether we like it or not. After all, I don't think the current King George really approves of us. Was the bill returning the railroads to their owners passed?"

"No. Mr. La Follette was too busy giving us his view of a future and better world. Or so I was told. I slept on a cot." Burden looked down at the President, who was half a head shorter than he. "When will you be back from Paris?"

"June. No," Wilson anticipated the question, "I won't call a special session before I get back even if none of us gets paid his salary."

"It will be hard."

Wilson winced; hand to his jaw. "My tooth. Always when you're about to take a trip, a tooth goes wrong. Let's hope the naval dentists . . ." Wilson stopped. The Vice President, Lodge and Hitchcock entered the room, each the picture of weary self-importance.

"Mr. President, the Sixty-fifth Congress adjourned at eleven thirty-five," said Marshall, adding roguishly, "not *sine die* but *sine Deo*."

"That depends, sir, upon which God it is that you serve." Lodge was amiably sanctimonious; he also never took his eyes off the President, his quarry.

But Wilson ignored Lodge. He picked up his pen, expectantly. "Is there any legislation awaiting the approval of the executive?" he asked formally.

Lodge said that there was none. Marshall said, "There is the prohibition amendment, Mr. President. But it's not ready. There's a stipulation that if the states don't ratify it in seven years, the damned thing is dead. We'll deliver it to your ship, where you can drink a toast to the prohibition of all alcohol in the United States."

"I will drink the toast only outside our territorial limits." Then Wilson motioned for a youthful watchful man to come forward. He presented him to Burden. "I think you should get to know my new attorney general, Mr. Palmer, and prepare him for his confirmation into this church *sine Deo*."

Burden shook hands with Palmer. "I'll escort you through the Senate maze."

Slowly Wilson crossed to the door. Then he turned. "Gentlemen," he said, "we shall see each other in December. I bid you good day." Lodge stared at Wilson's back as it receded down the corridor. Great mischief was brewing for Wilson. What, Burden wondered, if anything, for the state?

2

At thirty-five Cissy Patterson, the sometime – still? no one quite knew – Countess Gizycki was as handsome and as original as she had been at nineteen when her parents had bought her a Polish title and sent her forth from their palace in Dupont Circle to three wretched years of married life. Today Cissy's hair was redder than it had been when she was a girl, while maturity had given her a distinctly voluptuous look, somewhat undone by wit. Caroline regarded her, if not quite as a daughter, as a younger sister because, "Oh, how I envy you *everything*!"

Cissy looked about Caroline's office in the *Tribune* building with a view of F Street's streetcars, traffic jams, movie houses. Currently, an Emma Traxler production was playing to capacity audiences at the Capitol while Emma Traxler herself was on view at the nearby Mercury in "a very special vehicle," as Thomas Ince had called what looked to be suspiciously like a hearse for whatever ambition she might have had as a photo-play star. She had played a society adulteress at the turn of the century, which she herself had been in life. But in the photo-play, unlike life, she had fallen out of society, and threw herself from a window of the Waldorf-Astoria. The plot had been stolen from Mrs. Wharton, who had complained to Blaise, who had told Emma, who had warned Thomas Ince, who had said, "Let her sue." Emma Traxler's very mature beauty had been acknowledged by all, but the story was not good and Emma herself – Caroline, that is – was somewhat shaken that she had not noticed the story's shortcomings earlier. But then Tim had been in California during the shooting in New York.

"You must buy yourself a paper. You have the right ink in your blood." Caroline was brisk. "Your grandfather, father, brother, cousin all put out newspapers. So why don't you? There's nothing to it."

"I know there isn't, but what is there to buy? Hearst's got the *Herald* in the morning and the *Times* in the evening. You and Blaise have the *Tribune,* and don't want to sell, do you?"

"No."

"I wonder," said Cissy, "what happens to the *Post* if Ned finally drinks himself to death?"

"Evalyn publishes. Why not start something new?" Caroline held up the copy of the New York *Daily News* that Cissy had brought her. Cissy's older brother, Joseph, had started it in June, with some help from his cousin Robert McCormick, now running the family newspaper in Chicago. The *News* was half the size of an ordinary newspaper: tabloid-size, it was called, and Hearst had laughed at the notion. "No one wants a paper that you can't get a lot of pictures onto a page." But for once the Chief's cunning in journalistic matters had deserted him. Joe Patterson's tabloid was an instant success, and just as Caroline's brother had been made jealous by Caroline's not-so-instant success with the *Tribune*, now Cissy was jealous of Joe's astonishing coup, the first in the third generation. Until now, the family giant had been their grandfather Joseph Medill, whose Chicago *Tribune* had gone to his son-in-law, her father, and now to his grandson, her cousin, Robert R. McCormick. "The boys have got Chicago and New York. Well, why can't I have Washington?"

"Do you have the money to start a tabloid here?"

"In competition with you and Hearst? No. That Polish son-of-a-bitch is costing me a fortune."

"Kill him."

"Try and find him." Cissy glared at the painting of Caroline and Blaise and Mr. Trimble, their editor. "At least I got Felicia away from him." The battle between father and mother had rivetted the attention of the popular press for years. Mother had finally won but the cost had been high. Cissy now lived in lonely state in her father's Dupont Circle home; and dreamed of newspapers.

The secretary announced the approach of Blaise. Caroline nodded; he could come in. From the beginning, they had agreed that neither would ever surprise the other in his or her office.

Cissy was delighted to see Blaise. Cissy's reputation had been so damaged by her marital trials that she had then set out, perversely, to damage it all the more in the eyes of Washington's Aborigines. She was moderately promiscuous and she drank "like a man," as the saying went, and she sometimes fell, again like a man, upon others of her sex. Although she was too grand a Washington fixture ever to be shunned, the mention of her name caused a mournful Greek chorus of gossip, mostly invented, and all of it as pleasurable for Caroline to listen to as it was a matter of indifference to the restless, energetic Cissy. "I think I shall write a novel. I'll call it *Glass Houses*."

"Who will you throw stones at?"

"Alice Longworth. Who else? And my Polish beast. I begged the Reverend Woodrow to partition Poland until nothing was left."

"I suppose he laughed at your delicious wit." Blaise enjoyed Cissy, who had, thought Caroline, rather a soft feeling for Blaise.

"He was unimpressed. You've seen Joe's paper?" Cissy held up the *Daily News*.

Blaise nodded. "I've just won a bet with Hearst. On the circulation. He said the public would never buy a tabloid."

"They're certainly buying this one. I do nothing but envy others. This is a sign of bad character, I know." Cissy looked pleased with herself. "Captain Patterson, he calls himself." She added, with some malice: "It's like the Civil War, isn't it? And my cousin Bob wants to be called Colonel McCormick."

"Well, I'm just Mister Sanford."

"Monsieur is more like it." Cissy was on her feet. "There's a newspaper in Baltimore –"

"Don't," said Caroline. "Blaise bought it and sold it years ago."

"There is a curse on that paper," Blaise agreed. "No one reads it, and it always burns down."

"How lucky I am to have such experienced friends. Tell Millicent I'll ring her," she added, and left.

"Millicent?" Blaise turned to Caroline.

"Smith. Inverness. She's coming back to Washington to live. She's staying with me till she finds a place." Caroline stared down the street at the theater marquee, where she could just make out the "xler" of her other name. "Tim is buying a house in Los Angeles."

"To be close to the Mexican border?"

"I don't think the Justice Department would dare arrest him."

"I would," said Blaise, staring thoughtfully at the *Daily News,* which he held in one hand and the *Tribune* in the other.

"I suppose," said Caroline, "it will get worse. George Creel thinks it will. He says Palmer is running for president . . ."

"Why not? Everyone else is." Of the two of them, Blaise was the most susceptible to the anti-Red propaganda that was now sweeping the country, Hun now exchanged for Bolshevik as the new Satan.

That spring Tim had been caught in the middle when his strikebreakers movie was released and, to Caroline's horror, it not only favored the strikers, organized labor and the eight-hour week but made fun of the Bolshevik menace. The movie had been immediately withdrawn while Tim had been indicted under the Espionage Act, a singularly capacious bit of legislation which could be used to suppress almost anyone that the zealous Attorney General chose to punish. Caroline had used influence. Since the courts were busy, the case might be allowed to become moot if the Attorney General proved less than zealous. It was Caroline's impression that Palmer did not want to offend the *Tribune;* on the other hand, the *Tribune* dared not offend Palmer, whose house in R Street had been dynamited two months earlier, making him, almost, a martyr to capitalism while his neighbors, the Franklin Roosevelts, enjoyed miles of newsprint. The gallant Franklin had rung for the police while Eleanor, soon joined by her delighted cousin Alice, gave solace to the Palmer family, who had been sleeping in the back. No one knew who had done the deed but Communists were suspected. The actual perpetrator had blown himself up, leaving behind, most mysteriously, two left legs. The *Tribune* had revelled in the anatomical details, and a great nation shuddered at the thought of all its public men being, one by one, blown up in the night. Radicals were everywhere arrested while the Labor Department was now taking advantage of the war-time Sedition Act, which gave the secretary of labor the power to deport those foreign-born citizens whose looks and speech he found disturbing.

"Why did Tim do it?" Tactfully, Blaise had not asked her before; even so, she had still not thought of an answer.

"Well, he is . . . radical, I suppose."

"Boston? Irish? Catholic?"

"They can turn. *He* turned. I think it started when they sent that producer to jail for doing an anti-war film. But I don't know. I've never really talked about it."

"Do you think he's a Red?"

"I doubt it. He's too independent to be anything. He wants," Caroline took the plunge, "me to move to California." She looked at Blaise, who seemed genuinely startled . . . pleased?

"You won't."

"I might. I think I may have had enough of this," she indicated, vaguely, the portrait of the three publishers of the *Tribune,* "for a while. I like the movies . . ."

"And the climate. People always say that."

"Actually I *don't* like the climate. It's rather moldy. But the movies are still so . . . fluid, and you can get a grip on them still."

"You'd better work fast. The Jews have taken it all over."

"That's the challenge. Anyway, Hearst is there, or will be soon, he says, once 1920's out of the way . . ."

"And he moves to the White House . . ."

"San Simeon is more like it. He's richer than ever now Phoebe's dead . . . a lot madder, too."

Mr. Trimble was announced. Caroline could not believe that this frail old man who could not stand up straight had ever been the handsome red-haired young man of 1900. Was she as changed for him?

"The meeting's over," said Trimble, settling slowly into his customary chair beside Caroline's desk. The electric fan was directly upon him, stirring the heavy air. "I've had the first call, from a senator who was there, who will be nameless." Trimble still delighted in privileged information, not to mention those stories that the *Tribune* had been able to run before anyone else. "The President lost control, it would seem. The whole Foreign Relations Committee was on hand – Lodge, Knox, Borah." Which, Caroline wondered, had rung Trimble? – who liked Lodge more than either Sanford did.

"How – lost control?" Blaise sat on top of Caroline's desk, which he knew annoyed her.

"They gave him a hard time on Shantung. Why had he made a deal with the Japanese? which he then said he himself wasn't very pleased with either, which sounded weak. Then Borah started cross-examining him about all the secret treaties the Allies had made, and Wilson couldn't remember when he had first known about them and then when Borah asked him if he had known about them when he issued the Fourteen Points, he said no, which was madness – or a breakdown – since the Bolsheviks had already published them and *everyone* knew. The senators were kind of amazed."

"That is what they came there to be," said Caroline, suddenly sympathetic to Wilson.

"How did it end?" asked Blaise.

"They all had lunch after three and a half hours of grilling." Trimble removed a sheet of paper from his pocket. "He was right embarrassed when he was told that Lansing had said that the Japanese would've joined the League even without the Shantung agreement."

"You've written the editorial?" Trimble nodded. Caroline took the paper from his hand. She read quickly and gave it to Blaise, who began to rewrite as he read.

Trimble sighed. "I think the League pointless – for us, anyway."

Caroline experienced a small surge of anger. "Because you Americans want to have the freedom to annex the Mexican oil fields . . ."

"It's *we* Americans, *chérie.*" Blaise was mild. "We also want Siberia, but if we can't get it we don't want the Japanese to have it, so we'll all join the League and debate."

"Might be too late. We're both in Siberia," said Trimble, "and they've got more troops than we have. So when Russia falls apart . . ."

"Here." Blaise gave the page to Caroline, who read and agreed: the League was the hope of the world. Without the League, there would be another war with Germany within thirty years because of the Carthaginian peace being imposed by the Allies, who not only had broken the terms of the Wilsonian armistice but now meant to bankrupt Germany with reparations. Caroline and Blaise were always in agreement about savage old Europe's propensity to play king-of-the-castle games. But where Europe had a murderous tendency to sink into barbarism, the United States had not yet achieved a civilization from which to fall. Caroline prayed that the prim schoolteacher would be able to hold in line what was still, essentially, a peasant nation, ignorant, superstitious and inordinately proud of its easy pre-eminence.

Trimble took the revised editorial, and limped from the room. "I think they need a different system of government here," said Blaise, getting off the desk.

"So does Wilson. He still wants a parliamentary form of government – after he's gone, of course. What news from Saint-Cloud?"

"The hospital's moved out. It'll be ready for us by spring."

"I'll spend Easter there. You, too?"

"I probably will." Blaise smiled. "But you won't."

"Why not?"

"You'll be in Hollywood, with your man."

"Imbecile."

Millicent Smith, Countess Inverness, looked like a galleon with pale pink and yellow crepe-de-chine sails, filled now with hot August air. Two French windows opened onto the small garden at the back of Caroline's Georgetown house. Here every known form of ivy rioted, and no flower ever grew because of the dense shade of a huge magnolia tree. Amidst the ivy, armies of rats were dedicated, like Europeans, to war. "Caroline! I have messages for you. Somewhere. Héloise went to the doctor. Are we dining in? I've forgotten."

"Yes. Just us." Caroline poured herself a glass of wine. Millicent drank neat gin in great quantities and showed no ill effect. "Did you find a house?"

Millicent described what she had seen, and complained of prices as did everyone else, including most of the country's workers, who were on strike, inspired, according to the Attorney General, by Moscow. Millicent had had lunch with Alice Longworth, her White House rival. "She's in a very bad mood." Millicent's own mood lightened considerably at the thought. "Nick is never home. She complained of his drinking . . ."

"Then she's lucky he's out of the house." Caroline wondered if she would *stay* in Hollywood.

"But who is he with when he's not home? That's the question.

Naturally, I pretended not to know the rumors, and naturally she said nothing about them. She's so political, isn't she?"

"We all are. This is Washington."

"Now. But not in my day. When we were in the White House, it was considered bad form to talk about politics in mixed company. Like money, you know. But I suppose *he* changed all that."

"Colonel Roosevelt?"

Millicent nodded. "Bully," she said; and laughed. "Douglas Fairbanks does that all the time. I think he thinks he is Teddy Roosevelt. He's awfully attractive, you know."

"All the women in the world agree on that." Caroline had found it difficult to take seriously any of the great lovers of the screen. Aside from their doll-like proportions, she could never relate in any personal way to a face that everyone knew and that the owner himself could never forget that they knew in the unlikely event that he had ever tried. Although political faces were often as familiar as those of actors, the owners were, essentially, still-lifes, unlike the actor, whose face in life and in motion was always more interesting than a photograph forever fixed on the front page of a newspaper.

"I never go to photo-plays," said Millicent, "I simply like the rawness of the life out there in the West. The excess. The formality. So like London in the season."

Caroline could never, easily, follow Millicent's train of thought and so did not try. "Anyway, Mr. Fairbanks is involved with Miss Pickford."

"He gave me a rose." Millicent smiled secretly into her gin.

"That," said Caroline, with supreme fairness, "is something."

"You must act with him." Millicent knew Caroline's secret. In fact, by now most of her friends did. But thanks to her position as a publisher, the press had amiably left her alone: dog don't eat dog, in Mr. Trimble's phrase.

"I'm too old for him," said Caroline precisely. "While he is too old to be my son."

"Is it too late for *me* to act?"

"Yes." Caroline was cruel.

The nonfictitious Emma appeared, face ruddy from the heat.

"We've made it. In time for dinner, if that's all right."

"Of course." Caroline kissed her daughter's cheek. "Who's we?"

"Didn't I tell you? Giles." And Giles entered the room. An assistant professor of history at Bryn Mawr, Giles Decker was ten years older than Emma. He was blond and stout and eunuchoid, a type that had never not appealed to her daughter, who was put off by attractive men, none of whom, in turn, had ever presented her with a rose. Introductions were made. Millicent pulled herself together most regally; and smiled in a kindly way at the young. The kindly smile turned rapturous when Professor Decker said that he had written his dissertation on Millicent's uncle. "His foreign policy mainly."

"Did he have one?" asked Caroline. The uncle had been president in the lazy days before empire had seized the sleepy republic by the nape of the neck.

"Don't be rude!" Millicent sounded like Alice Roosevelt when anyone suggested that *her* father was not of god-like marble but human clay. "We had quantities of foreign policy. There was Nicaragua. Always. *Festering*, my uncle would say. And China, we opened up China, didn't we, Professor Decker?"

"Actually, Lady Inverness, no, the President didn't really. Actually, he . . ."

"See?" Millicent poured herself more gin and this time added angostura bitters. Like a pink dawn, thought Caroline, who realized that she would not have time for a bath before the early dinner, dictated by the absence of her regular cook, whose replacement feared going home in the dark.

"So nice to see that some of the young remember our heritage. But even the immigrants are interested in us, a few of them, anyway. When I suggested to Mr. Zukor that Uncle's life would make a marvelous photo-play for Mr. Fairbanks, Mr. Zukor was *very* interested."

"I am sure he would be now that Mr. Fairbanks has started his own studio with Mr. Zukor's golden goose, Mary Pickford. Mr. Zukor would do anything to get back his stars. As he says, the inmates are running the asylum."

All three said, "What?" and Caroline explained that when Fairbanks, Pickford and Chaplin, with D. W. Griffith, had founded their own production company, United Artists, Zukor had made his famous, by no means in-jest remark. After all, Zukor's Famous Players-Lasky was the supreme studio, thanks to its ownership of hundreds of movie houses where he could show, if he chose, only his own pictures, a policy known bleakly as block-booking. First National, Fox and Loew's were lesser competition, while United Artists, with help from McAdoo, who had got to know the stars through his Liberty Bond appeals, was now so profitable that Caroline had opened negotiations to use it for the release of Traxler Productions photo-plays.

"Giles was very upset about Mr. Farrell's movie, *The Strike-Breakers.*"

"What – or who – is a strike-breaker?" asked Millicent; but no one answered her.

"Why upset?" Caroline gave Giles her special three-quarter Madonna smile which had an astonishing effect, a knowledgeable publicist had told her, on adolescent boys from thirteen to sixteen and sapphic women of any age, two groups unnaturally dedicated to movie-going.

Giles, as it proved, was neither adolescent nor sapphic. "I saw it in New York before it was withdrawn and I was very disturbed by the Communist message, which surprised me, knowing that you were the producer . . ."

"And Mr. Farrell a Catholic," added Emma.

"One doesn't see *them* in London, thank God." Millicent made her contribution. "The Duke of Norfolk, yes. But even he has to mind his p's and q's, not like here where they don't even make good maids like they used to because they are always, if you'll forgive me," she smiled compassionately at the young, "pregnant."

"Well, Mr. Farrell is not pregnant." Caroline was demure. "I thought the film was simply against violence. In this case, on the part of the management."

"But *that* is a Communist theme, Mrs. Sanford. One must be wary when dealing with them. I know."

"How?" Caroline's tone was more blunt than she intended.

"Giles is very active with the National Civic Federation, and he writes for their review . . ."

"You must know their editor, Ralph Easley?" Giles now held a pipe in one hand but did not light it. Ralph Easley was a professional publicist who had been pursuing Communists all over the United States. He had caused a furor with an article called "If Bolshevism Came to America." Apparently, everyone would have to get up before dawn to take an icy shower and then, their cars taken away from them, trudge to work, where they would break rocks for a dozen hours. Easley had found Communists everywhere in American life, particularly in the press, the churches and the schools. He had attacked the *Tribune* for its editorial on the necessity of bringing American troops home from Russia. Needless to say, the conservative American labor movement admired him and wished him well in rooting out those Communists hidden in their ranks. Hearst also loved him. Caroline thought him a joke in bad taste, while Blaise thought that there might be something to his charges.

Caroline said that she had not had the pleasure of meeting Easley but she was aware of his busy-ness.

"We take him very seriously, Mrs. Sanford. I'm on the academic committee for freedom from anarchy, which works closely with Mr. Easley . . ."

"Giles has written an exposé of all the history departments, showing how they are controlled by Marxists."

"I thought," said Caroline, gazing upon her daughter's ruddy features with mild dislike, "that your discipline is mathematics."

"Emma is also a concerned citizen . . ."

"This concerned citizen," said the Countess of Inverness, "is about to change for dinner."

"So, I think, will I." Caroline would have her bath after all. She rose. "You two come as you are. It's only us – and at eight."

But Caroline was denied her bath. Just as Héloise was helping her out of her dress, Emma knocked on the door. "Come in, darling." Caroline was already feeling guilty about the sudden spasm of disaffection that she had felt for her only child. The late-afternoon light through the thick dark magnolia leaves was an intense deep hot gold.

Emma stretched out on a chaise-longue. Emma sat beneath a

painting of Saint-Cloud-le-Duc. Caroline thought of her, fondly, as a little girl, playing in the grounds of the chateau as Caroline herself had once played in the last years of the old century that seemed, in this age of telephones and automobiles and heavier-than-air craft, a millennium ago.

"Giles is very worried about you, Mother."

"Tell him not to be. I still have my . . . my wiles."

"He thinks you've been taken in by Tim, who is a member of the Communist Party."

"I wasn't aware there was a Communist Party in this country. After all, a condition of our freedom is that it be exercised only in support of the majority, as Mr. Debs has discovered."

Emma was humorless. "There's a *secret* party, just the way the anarchists are secret."

"*You* know their secrets?"

"Giles does, and so does Ralph Easley. They mean to overthrow the government. Look at what they did to Mr. Palmer."

"He lost a few front windows. They – whoever they were – lost their lives."

"You sound sympathetic."

"Really? I thought I sounded factual, and indifferent."

"Giles thinks – and so does Mr. Easley – that you should take a more active, a more unequivocal stand against Bolshevism."

Caroline wondered if her daughter had, somehow, been bewitched. "I have never known you to show the slightest interest in politics, and now you lecture me on the Red Menace."

Emma frowned and the stubborn jaw, so like her father's, jutted out. "I'm not. I mean, in the usual nonsense. But I'm serious about this, Mother. We could lose everything, our whole country, our freedom if they win . . ."

"Who are they?"

"Trotsky, Lenin, the Hungarians, the Germans. They're everywhere. Three thousand strikes this year in the United States alone. Why? Ask Lenin. He knows. He has this special committee. In Chicago. Direct wireless to Moscow. Who do you think ordered the strike in Seattle? Trotsky. We have his directives in a code, which we broke. We . . ." Emma was speaking more and more rapidly and less and less coherently. She kept interrupting herself, as a new subject exploded in her brain. But since she tended to begin in the middle of a statement, the subject was often unclear. "Naval warfare. Submarines. Under the treaty. The Red fleet now largest. Off Catalina Island. In June. Basic investment of a quarter-million dollars. La Follette, of course. Always La Follette. Connection between Moscow . . . the Third International was convened March this year. For every country. Everywhere. Workers unite! La Follette knows all about it. So does Borah. That's why Tim's film with your backing . . . last year ninety Communist films were made by Jews on orders from Trotsky, a Zionist. Everyone knows. Condition of the New York *Times* to support England in 1917. Homeland for communism in Palestine. Hearst only one who'll speak up. You *must* . . ." Emma was temporarily out of breath.

"Must? I must what?"

"Giles – and Mr. Easley – think you should write – or be interviewed – or something – on communism in Hollywood, and how you were tricked by Tim into making that Red propaganda film –"

Caroline slapped the arm of her chaise-longue so hard that she hurt her hand. "Are you absolutely mad? You know nothing of politics or movies or anything else except mathematics. I was hardly tricked . . ." Like her daughter, Caroline had veered off into what might prove to be a cul-de-sac. Tim had indeed tricked her about the film, and their relationship was seriously frayed. In the autumn she would go to California and see what could be done to put together the pieces. Otherwise, she might simply weigh anchor and sail splendidly off into high middle age, without human moorings of any kind.

"Well, if you made the film deliberately, then Mr. Easley's right and you did know what you were doing, because you're basically a foreigner, and should be deported under the Immigration Act of 1918 and also under the Espionage Act . . ."

"Shut up!" Caroline had never addressed herself quite so directly to her daughter. "You need help, plainly. One of those behaviorists or whatever they call them. I am not a foreigner. I've always had a foreign . . . I mean, an American passport . . ."

"Your mother was foreign. I know. She killed Uncle Blaise's mother . . ."

Caroline was on her feet, shouting at Emma in French.

Only Emma's superior smile at this proof of her mother's foreignness stopped Caroline cold. "You are very . . . trying, Emma. I put it down to the bad influence of Mr. Decker."

"No, Mother. It's been a long time coming. Waking up, really, to the way we're losing our country to you foreigners."

"Perhaps you should find yourself a different young man." Caroline was her silky self again.

"I don't think that I could, really. You see, we were married this morning. In Maryland."

Caroline had a hard time catching her next breath but, once caught, she was at perfect ease. "Then you are a fool," she said.

"I know," Emma sighed almost, for her, theatrically. "But then it's not my fault, is it? That I'm illegitimate."

"No," said Caroline, standing up. "It is not your fault. Now – *go away.*"

3

The President was at his typewriter, as Grayson showed Burden into the upstairs study. "I'll be just a moment." Wilson continued to type at a near-professional rate. Burden was always impressed by such skills. Like most of the Senate, Burden relied on aides to assemble his own speeches. When he did write a speech for himself, it was in near-illegible longhand. But the President could not only create his own eloquence, he could type it neatly with hardly an error. On the other hand, Wilson could not bloviate, as the windbag Harding put it: speak impromptu with incoherent passion. Burden himself had a definite gift along these demagogic lines. But he saved it for the stump. In the Senate he prided himself on sharp brevity.

Wilson pulled the sheet from the typewriter, let it drop onto his desk; rose and shook Burden's hand. The President's face was more than usually pale – from the August heat? The Sixty-sixth Congress due to convene December 19, 1919, had been called to Washington in May. The President had returned from France in July. Now the entire government was obliged to endure the equatorial heat. The President, Burden noted, had developed a twitch at the corner of his left eye; and, all in all, seemed on edge. At Wilson's gesture, Burden settled in his usual sofa at an angle to the desk. Neither liked being face to face to anyone.

To Burden's surprise, Wilson did not mention the League, which Lodge was slowly killing with amendments in the Senate. "What would you do about labor, if you were me?"

"You mean the strikes?"

"I mean the whole arrangement between the managers and the workers."

"When in doubt, do nothing. Are you in doubt, Mr. President?"

"Yes and no. I think we proved during the war that we could run the railroads as well as the owners. Well, now . . ."

"You think we – the government – should take them over?"

Wilson nodded. "It would be one way of bringing into line both managers and labor leaders."

Blaise shrugged. "I don't see much difference between the government running something and the owners running it. It will just make life more difficult for us if a railroad union strikes against the government."

"Or less difficult. Most countries keep control of vital necessities like water, electricity, transport. We don't. We allow anyone to gouge the customer, to exploit the worker."

Burden smiled. "With all your other problems, Mr. President, do you want to be called a Socialist?"

"Why not? I've been called everything else. It's because I'm terrified of Bolshevism that I think we might steal some of their thunder in order to keep them from stealing our country altogether. Have you seen my son-in-law, Mr. McAdoo?"

Burden shook his head. "I suppose he's in New York, practicing law."

Wilson sat back in his chair and allowed his head slowly to turn from left to right and then from right to left. Apparently a form of exercise. "There is pressure on me to make up my mind about next year. I've said that I don't want a third term, and my son-in-law certainly would like at least a first term." The smile was dour. "It would be useful for him if I were to rule myself out now. Then he'd have a year to get ready."

"Yes." Burden gave nothing away. He wondered if Wilson knew about the conversation at the Chevy Chase Club.

"I wish I could oblige you – him, that is – but I don't know. Until the League is safe, my work here is undone. When do you think the Senate will vote?"

"Lodge drags it out. He feels each day makes it harder and harder for us to support the League, and he's right. Why not accept his reservations, and get the thing over right now?"

"Never." Wilson's voice was unagitated. "As you probably know, this morning the Foreign Relations Committee adopted fifty amendments that would keep the United States from ever serving on nearly all those international committees that would instrument the League. Lodge also got a nine-to-eight vote reversing the Peace Conference's stand on Shantung."

As Burden spoke, the tremor in Wilson's eyelid became so pronounced that the President took off his pince-nez and, pretending to dry his brow with a handkerchief, brought pressure to bear on the wayward nerve. "So Tumulty told me."

"Did he also report that Knox and Borah and Johnson and some of the other irreconcilables, as they call themselves, plan to stump the country, particularly the West, propagandizing against the League?"

Silently, Wilson folded the handkerchief in four. "So we must all, now, go to Caesar."

"To our masters." Burden smiled, as he always did, when he contemplated the fiction that the American people in any way controlled their own fate. The Constitution had largely excluded them while custom had, paradoxically, by enlarging the franchise limited any meaningful participation in government by the governed. Naturally, the emotions of the people had to be taken into account, but those emotions could be easily manipulated by demagogues and press. If the irreconcilables were to play skillfully to

America's hatred of the foreign, then Wilson must play to their own high self-esteem in a world where they were now, so it was believed, not only the greatest power but the most shiningly innocent. It was so easy, given time. Without a thought in his head, Burden could rouse an audience to accept the League and a Pax Americana; then, as easily, he could excite them with the spectre of liberties lost to a British-dominated League, to be rejected out of hand in obedience to George Washington's sacred warning against foreign entanglements. This was all that there was to politics in the great democracy. Once Professor Wilson had grasped this, he had opted for a parliamentary system. But President Wilson now grasped the sceptre and the orb without question; and played the game.

"I go, too," he said replacing his pince-nez. "Mrs. Wilson and Grayson want me to take a rest, but I have no choice."

"You're taking to the stump?"

Wilson nodded. "I shall be trailing the senators from one end of the West to the other." Wilson named the cities that he intended to speak in, and Burden quickly grasped that this intensive tour of the nation was the beginning of Wilson's campaign for a third term, something no president had ever attempted.

Burden gave some advice on the cities to be visited. Wilson made notes. When they discussed Senate strategy, Wilson picked up the sheet of paper that he had been typing on. "This is anonymous." He smiled at Burden. "I want you to know about it, and Hitchcock, too. But no one else. Secretly, I am willing to compromise on the treaty."

Burden was astonished and delighted. The mad President who would not yield because he was doing the Lord's work was, once again, the master politician, capable of any adjustment to get his way. "I have listed four areas of interpretation of the treaty on which you – the Democratic leadership – will agree to compromise in order to get the League approved. But Lodge must never know that this comes from me. If he knew, he would want four times four in the way of adjustments. But these, I think, cover any differences and should be acceptable to all but the professional clowns."

Burden took the paper. "I am relieved," he said. "I think we'll have no trouble, now we can maneuver."

"But sooner or later the Senate – Lodge's friends, that is – will have to take their medicine." Wilson kept oscillating between rigid truculence and supple negotiation. Was this, Burden wondered, for effect? In many ways the mild scholarly man of 1912 was noticeably changed. He was more than ever irritable and thin-skinned while his once-formidable ability to concentrate on a subject was gone. Finally, in addition to Wilson's congenital arteriosclerosis, the President had been extremely ill in Paris, Burden had been told. Officially, he had had the flu, unofficially there were rumors that he had had a stroke. Simultaneously, there had been a falling-out with Colonel House, which explained the disarray on the American side when the final peace treaty had been hammered out in a spirit quite at odds with the lofty "peace without victory" that Wilson had proclaimed when he led the United States to war.

There would be no third term, Burden decided, as the President began to read from an inventory. "You know that I am *personally* held responsible for the contents of the house in the Place des Etats-Unis, just as I was responsible for the Villa Murat, which is only fitting. Our government should not pay for the glasses that Mrs. Wilson and I break, though she herself broke none and I only one. Yet they have written *ten*, which is, you'll agree, intolerable." Wilson stared up at Burden. He brought the same gravity to the broken glass as he had to the League of Nations.

"It would seem so, Mr. President. But why don't you turn all this over to Mr. Tumulty?"

"If only I could. But he wasn't there. I alone know for certain about that broken glass. It was in the bathroom, the first Sunday morning after we got back to Paris and settled in the new place. The other nine glasses, if broken, were broken by someone else. I do not rule out the French themselves. After all, every single one of them assigned to our household was a spy. I even heard two of them whispering together in English." He stared intently at the book in front of him. "And now this! The broken frame to the Fragonard copy, not even an original but a very common sort of copy, that was hanging in Mrs. Wilson's boudoir . . ."

Edith was suddenly in the room, serene and commanding. "Woodrow," she murmured. She closed the inventory book. "That's my work. How did you get it?"

"I saw it on Miss Benson's desk, and of course I must check each item, including Fiume, to which Italy . . ."

Burden caught the look of fear in Mrs. Wilson's eyes; more a fear of Burden being witness to . . . what? Wilson was not mad, as he had demonstrated with his masterful four points of compromise, but he was obsessed in some incalculable way. To him, the inventory was of equal moral weight with the League, and the two seemed to be blurring in his mind. Grayson was also in the room. Did they listen at the keyhole? Wife and doctor were resolutely cheerful and helpful.

"Time for a drive," said Grayson.

"It's gotten cooler."

"Equatorial days," said Edith. "My poor mother is near extinction in the Powhatan Hotel and she has six fans all going at once *and* a cake of ice in the middle of her sitting room."

Wilson, perfectly sane and normal, walked Burden to the door. "Many thanks for the . . . information. As for the other . . ." He held up a finger.

Burden nodded. "Only Hitchcock is to know."

They shook hands. Unusually, Edith did not walk him to the elevator. She and Grayson stayed with the President while Hoover, the chief usher, escorted Burden. Over the years, Burden had cultivated this dignitary. Often one could learn more from five minutes' idle chat with the chief usher or a Secret Service man than with any of the principals. "I see where you're going on a long trip."

"The President, Senator. I'm staying put. I wish he would, too."

"He seems fully recovered," Burden fished.

"Oh, he's fit as a fiddle except for this heat, and tiredness. We're all pretty strung-out after Paris, and now the Senate. If you'll excuse me, sir."

"I'm one of the good guys." At the elevator door, Burden was inspired to ask, "Who did break the frame of the Fragonard copy?"

There was the briefest look of alarm on Hoover's face. Then he was the soul of blandness. "The President is very conscientious, isn't he? Like it was his own property, that dirty palace."

Burden's own palace was clean at last and furnished, too. In the afternoon light the two-story mansarded gray stone house shone against the blue-greens of Rock Creek Park. They had decided to inaugurate the house with a casual tea, a popular thing to do in August if you lived on a wooded hill above the cool and cooling swift Rock Creek.

A half-dozen Negro waiters had been hired for this occasion. Kitty was already dressed in a long yellow-green gown while Diana was not yet undressed. She would be allowed to watch the arrivals from the great window on the first landing with its view of the driveway, now presided over by a special policeman both known to the guests and knowing. Burden always called him Sergeant, like the sergeant-at-arms of the Senate, who knew every senator and his ways.

Burden showered; then put on a white suit of the sort affected by Southern statesmen as well as by the late Mark Twain, whose white hair, moustaches, suit were all perfectly coordinated as he made an occasion for applause his strategic entrances at the top of the stairs that descended into New Willards' Peacock Alley.

Burden crossed to the side porch, his favorite spot in the house, and the coolest. Through the thick surrounding woods he could hear the shallow creek as it swirled over its rocky course. A bird – a cardinal, all scarlet – perched on a chair opposite him, waiting to be fed by Kitty. But she was too busy and Burden lacked intimacy with the wild. Fondly, Burden gazed over his two acres of woods, and wondered why anyone needed more of anything. He had started poor; he was now secure, thanks to Kitty's inheritance and the voters' indulgence. But the first was being spent and the second was, to say the least, volatile. Particularly now when a number of things were very much out of joint in the United States.

The war had been fraudulent. It had never been of the slightest concern to the United States whether or not Germany commanded Europe; indeed, most Americans believed, as a matter of course, that the entire point to their country was that it provided a safe refuge for those Europeans who could no longer endure the old continent's confusions and cruelties. Wilson, for reasons obscure, had maneuvered the republic onto the world stage. If there was a design to history, then Wilson had been obliged to conform to the inevitable. If there was no design, only chance, then Wilson had – through vanity? – made a bad choice. To the extent that the American people thought of foreign affairs at all, they inclined to tribal loyalties that, over the generations, vanished. Recent German immigrants had favored the Kaiser; recent Irish immigrants wished England ill. But neither tribe was eager to return, in any guise, to the ancient continent so thoroughly abandoned. Only the crudest, most unremitting propaganda could stir up so essentially placid a polity. As it turned out, the propaganda had been inspired and the Germans had been thoroughly demonized. But now with so much hatred still in the air, the professional politician knew, instinctively, that he himself might fall a victim to those emotions that had been called up from the deep. To make matters worse, a financial crisis had begun and the people at large were restive and in a mood to punish *them,* whoever *they* happened to be. He would soon have to decide how he would present himself for re-election in 1920.

At first the war had been deeply unpopular in the state; then, overnight, everyone had succumbed joyously to every anti-German, anti-Red, anti-Negro demagogue. The Ku Klux Klan was now reviving, this time in the cities rather than in the countryside, an ominous development. Would the voters punish Wilson – and Burden – for the war? Or would they accept the notion that, thanks to the pro-warriors, the United States was now pre-eminent in the world? – something hard to believe when you had to walk ten yards on a cold night to the privy. Not for the first time Burden wished that Bryan had been of even average intelligence, because he alone had had the ability to give voice to the confused majority. Burden and his mad father had parted company over Bryan. For the veteran of Chickamauga, all one needed to do was to organize the people so that there would be a representative government and a more perfect union for all. But Burden knew that this could never happen. One look around the Senate cloak-room was enough to demonstrate to even the most zealous populist that he had no chance to unseat the likes of Penrose. They – the true gilded They – owned it all, including himself. Was it not that clever Wall Street lawyer, McAdoo, who wanted to, in effect, hire Burden to be on his ticket as an enticement to the unrepresented?

Borah sat opposite him. "Daydreaming?"

Burden gave a start. He was apologetic. "I'm sorry, Senator. The heat . . ."

"And the flu." Borah was understanding. "It clings. I came a little early." A waiter brought them iced tea. Kitty was in the next room with Mrs. Borah, an attentive dragon, ready to scare off over-enthusiastic ladies. "Wilson's going to take a trip."

Burden nodded.

"Well, it should do him good. Get to see the country after all that time in Europe. See the folks. Johnson's going to cover California. I'm starting out in the Twin Cities."

"One hundred percent against the League?"

Borah nodded. "I'm also eager to get our boys out of Siberia."

"So is the President."

"But he put them there in the first place."

"I thought you were a T.R. man."

"I am. But I'm also for getting us out of places where we don't belong."

"Roosevelt thought we belonged everywhere, toting the white man's burden."

"I'm older now, wiser. I like to think there's probably enough for us to do right here at home. Once we start having colonies around the world we're their prisoner. I thought Wilson had more sense. But his head's been turned by all those kings and chancellors and bankers."

Burden was never sure how to handle Borah. They were personal friends with similar constituencies. But Burden had gone along with his party and Wilson, while Borah had remained in concert with what he took to be the majority of Americans. If the people were to feel betrayed by Wilsonian internationalism . . . Burden experienced a mild chill: he could be defeated. On the other hand, if the economy improved and the propaganda for the

284

League made rosy the prospect, Borah would have a difficult time. "I think the League is popular, to the extent people know about it."

"It won't be when I finish explaining how we'd lose control over our own armed forces, and how if England ordered us to send a hundred thousand troops, say, to Constantinople, we'd have to go, like it or not."

"I don't think it will work quite like that."

"It won't," said Borah, thin mouth no more than a straight horizontal line, "work at all. It's the banks that are doing this to us. New York's bad enough to have to live with. But London, too? No, thank you. We fought that war of independence once. Don't need a second round. Siberia!" Borah shook his head, with wonder.

"Would you let Japan have it?"

"Why not? They're next door. Anyway, whoever owns that icebox will still have to do business with us."

"What about this hemisphere?"

"Well, Mexico's our own back yard. So when they go grabbing our land and killing our people, I'm perfectly willing to go beat them up. I'm not a pacifist. Mexico matters to us. So we fight. Germany doesn't."

"What about Haiti, the Dominican Republic, Nicaragua, Panama, Honduras, Cuba?"

"What about them?"

"Each of those supposedly sovereign states is currently occupied by American Marines, answerable only to the President. We behave to them the way the Austro-Hungarian Empire behaved to Serbia and Montenegro and Slovenia . . ."

"Don't make my head ache. I don't want to think about those old bad places. Wilson really wants to be the first president of the world, doesn't he?"

Burden shrugged, somewhat disloyally. "He's never *said* anything about it. And after this last round in Paris, I don't think he wants to have anything to do with Europeans ever again. He hates the French, thinks Lloyd George a crook, the Italians vultures . . ."

"Well, I'm relieved that he has grasped the essentials. You know, I wasn't all that impressed with him at the White House. Fact, I was pretty shaken. Does he lie a lot, do you think?"

Burden laughed. "You mean more than you and me?"

"I never lie," the lion of Idaho lied; his devotion to himself was more religious than secular. To himself he was, simply, God, and he saw that he was good. Despite – or because of – this certitude, Borah was the most popular man in politics and not about to share his godhood with mere mortals. "No. What struck me was the feeble way Wilson lied to us about the secret treaties. He certainly heard about them when we heard about them, if not before, but then he says –"

"He's edgy these days. He's easily flustered. He was sick in Paris . . ."

"Encephalitis." Like God, Borah was nothing if not well-informed.

"I hadn't heard that. But he's still pretty weak, and shouldn't go to the country now, not in this heat."

"I suppose he'll be your candidate, won't he?" That was why Borah had arrived early, Burden decided. Even God needed an occasional political tip.

"Yes," Burden lied. "He is, barring accidents."

"You'll be his running mate?"

"He hasn't got that far. But he means to sweep the country for the League." As Burden improvised, he was somewhat disappointed to discover that his spur-of-the-moment lie, calculated to confuse the enemy, was the plain truth. Of course Wilson was preparing for re-election as the first three-term president. Of course he would need someone like Burden to balance the ticket. Would, Burden wondered, lightning strike? If it did, could he also, as insurance, run for the Senate as well? State law was ambiguous while political opinion was severe. Whoever ran for two offices would probably lose both, and, of course, Wilson would be ill-pleased at so public a lack of faith.

"You'll be a big help to him." Borah nodded in god-like acknowledgment of one of his own minor works.

"You'd be a big help – to whom?" With Roosevelt's unexpected death on the eve of his political rebirth, the Republican Party was a leaderless group of feudal lords like Penrose and Platt, with no hero – as opposed to a deity like Borah, who was too large for the presidential office, while Lodge was too old and odd and shrunken.

"I don't think I'd look right as vice president." Borah did not smile. "As for president, I'll have to wait till everyone catches up with me and realizes what a mistake this war was." At the doorway, Kitty gestured for the statesmen to join the party.

Kitty had managed to collect a bit of everything for their house-warming. The Senate was on hand in collegial force. The Lansings and the Phillipses represented the State Department. The Longworths and the Mombergers stood in for that vast herd, the House of Representatives. The ever-present lobbyists of the war years were no longer to be seen, smiling and waiting to present their petitions. Of old Washington, there were the usual Apgars, paying court to the ancient Mrs. Marshall Field of Chicago, who had recently, mysteriously, settled her court at the capital.

Blaise and Frederika stood in front of the carved stone fireplace filled with pots of flowers, something Burden had first noted years before in Caroline's house and, gradually, brought Kitty round to. Frederika was now wearing her own somewhat thin gray-blond hair. She looked younger than she had before the flu. "I'm trying to convince Blaise to be cool, like this, in the country."

"If Connecticut Avenue isn't country, what is?" Blaise was brusque.

"Virginia is." Frederika was prompt. "The Potomac Heights. We already own a hundred acres just past Chain Bridge. I want to build where you can hear the sound of water, cool water, like here . . ."

"Water? All I can hear is iced tea," said Blaise, reaching for a champagne glass, another of Caroline's importations that Kitty, temperance like most of their constituents, had long resisted.

"We can hear the creek when there isn't company. Where's Caroline?"

"Gone west. To be a cowboy." Blaise was mildly drunk.

"Movie star." Frederika was wistful. "I envy her. All that energy. Emma's married, you know."

Burden was startled that Caroline had said nothing. "When?" he asked, meaning to whom.

"A professor at Bryn Mawr," said Blaise, getting the order

287

straight. "Just now. She brought him home to Caroline's, and they quarrelled. They are now honeymooning with us in Connecticut Avenue."

"He is critical of Caroline's movie director," said Frederika.

The arrival of Henry Cabot Lodge obliged Burden to break away and greet the great man, who had grown frail in recent years. Without his wife, he seemed only half a person, and that half all senator. "There aren't many people left to talk to," he observed to Burden, with perfect if unconscious rudeness.

"There's history." Burden spoke with exaggerated deference.

"History," said Lodge, "does not respond. I love the park," he added, looking about the airy room. "We wanted to live here but didn't. And if you don't, early on, you won't. Colonel Roosevelt and I used to ride across your property, coming up from the ford."

"I remember."

Kitty brought the Attorney General over to Lodge, who graciously received him. A. Mitchell Palmer had been in a state of euphoria ever since his house had been blown up. The enemy was everywhere, and he had been singled out to save the democracy from Bolshevism. With practiced charm, Lodge strung him all the rope that was needed, while Burden continued his rounds, greeting the guests and making an appearance of making conversation.

"Jess Smith, Senator," said a voice he never could place. "I'm here with Mrs. Harding. The Senator's laid up." Jess Smith was owlish and slack of jaw. Mrs. Harding was slack of nothing; sharp cornflower-blue eyes glittered behind a pince-nez. "Really nice home, Mr. Day. Really nice. Which proves you've always got to build it yourself if you want something nice."

"I thought Wyoming Avenue was pretty grand." Burden's politician's memory seldom deserted him. He had been to their house once, and remembered everything, including her maiden name, Kling, and the fact that she had been divorced from a first husband before she married Harding, some years her junior, and that she had had a son by the first husband, and that her well-to-do father had disapproved strenuously of Harding on the ground that he was supposed to be several parts Negro. One could not know too much, was Burden's theory; or, more precisely, one could not forget too much.

"You must see us when Warren's back from Chautauqua. How he loves the circuit. The crowds – the hotels, the boardinghouses – and the hundred-dollar fee for each appearance, which is pretty important now that everything costs so much. You don't do Chautauqua, do you?" Mrs. Harding made it seem like a kind of religious observance, not lightly unobserved.

Burden said that he seldom had the time, much less Harding's gift of oratory. Mrs. Harding was not listening; she was staring at the Longworths, who were at the door to the dining room, where Cissy Patterson Gizycki stood, red hair set off by classic jade green. Alice looked grim for all her toothy smile. Cissy looked seductive, and Nick Longworth looked seduced, and drunk. "The Countess sure is a sketch," observed Florence Harding.

"She's no duchess, that's for sure," said the amiable Jess.

"She's always been popular here." Burden sounded to himself like one of his prim old-guard Apgar cousins instead of his usual rough Western tribune-of-all-the-people self. But then he had been in politics in Washington for more than twenty years; he had known, as girls, Cissy and Caroline and, for that matter, Alice the Great.

"It's a good thing the folks back home don't know what goes on here." Mrs. Harding fixed him with a hard stare just as his natural daughter, Emma, entered the room.

"I'm sure Washington's no different than Marion, Ohio, when it comes to – secrets," said Burden, scoring a bull's-eye.

Mrs. Harding turned a mottled red. Jess cleared his throat of non-present phlegm. "Marion is so correct it's dead," Jess said. "Now Columbus is something different, I'll say."

Burden, as host not to mention collegial senator, had gone too far. Warren Harding was known to indulge himself carnally, and it was not for Burden to betray the secrets of a lodge whose members were known by the women they kept. He changed the subject. "We asked your friends the McLeans –"

"She don't go out yet. At least not much since Vinson died. They thought the world of that boy. Always had guards with him so he wouldn't be kidnapped, and then this car runs bang into him. She's like a madwoman on the subject and of course she knows and I know that it's those diamonds of hers – that Hope one, in particular – but she won't part with them and now Vinson's dead."

"Tragical," moaned Jess.

Burden found Emma at the buffet table in the dining room. "Where's your husband?"

"You know?"

Burden gave her a senatorial kiss on the cheek. "Yes. Congratulations. Why such a hurry?"

"I had to. Marry, that is. We quarrel. Mother and I. We really tore it this time." Burden looked down into his own blue eyes, as she looked up into *her* own eyes, without recognition. This was simply her mother's old friend, not her father, demi-creator.

"These things pass." He was soothing. "Is he here, your husband?"

"No. He had a meeting. With a committee. Against Bolshevism. So many are in the history departments. One of the reasons. Particularly Henry Adams."

"Henry Adams?" Burden had not entirely followed her rapid delivery, and put it down to the noise in the room.

"Harvard's the worst, you see. But Hollywood's Red, too. Mother's a dupe, or worse. I hope not. If you draw it now, and you will. *We* will! Must . . ."

"Draw *what*, Emma?" Burden wondered if his own mother's hereditary deafness had finally claimed him.

"*The line!* We must draw the line." As she continued to speak rapidly, eyes narrowed as if observing her own thoughts rush by like the fastest of trains, Burden saw deliverance approaching him.

"The very man you should be talking to . . ."

But Emma was now out of control. "Laughed after the Winter Palace, 1917. Our opportunity. Kerensky told us. Did we listen? No! China. The final apple to fall from the bough . . ."

Burden seized the Attorney General by the arm, and drew him close, for protection.

"Emma Sanford . . . I haven't yet learned her married name, it's so new," Burden said to the Attorney General. "You know her mother, Caroline Sanford . . ."

"Oh, yes. This is a pleasure."

"Emma, this is Mr. Palmer. Mr. A. Mitchell Palmer."

"At last!" Emma was ecstatic. "I'm from Bryn Mawr. A letter. All of us. The June-second bombing. Trotsky – who else? Your anti-radical division. Superb. Wrote Mr. J. Edgar Hoover, the right person. In spite of –"

"Yes. It was pretty noisy, I'll say that. The explosion, I mean." But A. Mitchell Palmer had no idea what Burden had unleashed upon him. Emma has finally found her tongue, Burden thought, as he moved away, greeting guests; unfortunately, her mind now moved too rapidly for her tongue to express so many urgencies.

Burden completed his tour of the party where he had started, on the porch. A fragment of a waxing moon decorated the black-purple sky and the last of the season's fireflies glided lazily on the west wind. From the grape arbor, two figures entwined, approached, unaware that he was watching. Tactfully, he stepped behind a column as Cissy Patterson, lipstick smeared, stepped onto the porch, followed now by the slightly dishevelled drunken Nick Longworth. They went inside. Burden was not surprised. Nick was a compulsive womanizer, made uninhibited by the drink, while Cissy was restless, to say the least. Then, as fate, or herself, would have it, Alice Longworth stepped onto the porch from the far door. She could not have avoided the sight of her husband and Cissy together.

"What a cool night, after such a hot day." Alice sat in a chair with her back to the party.

"I've always loved the park," said Burden, with rather more feeling than so neutral an observation deserved.

"I can't think of *anything* I love." Alice was grim. When she did not smile the Rooseveltian toothy smile, the thin lips made a pursed sombre line, while in the half-light her gray eyes were dull. "This is no place to live."

"In our line of work, we must."

"*Your* line. Nick's line. I have no line."

"Go away."

"Where? I always thought I'd live somewhere else when father was gone. But now that he's really gone, there is no place. I shall be a fixture, like one of those awful Apgars."

"My cousins."

"Poor you!" Alice leapt like a cat to her feet; self-pity quickly sloughed off. Kitty came out on the porch.

"Mr. Lansing wants to talk to you, Burden . . ."

"I shall listen in," said Alice, "and report every word to Cabot. You know, when Wilson came back to the White House, I stood in the crowd on the sidewalk and I put a murrain on him, a very serious murrain . . ."

Burden was now at the door.

"What is a murrain?" asked Kitty.

"A hex. A curse. I am a witch, you know."

"Can you see the future?" asked Burden.

"Of course," said Alice. "But I never look. I don't dare. Would you, if you could?"

"No," said Burden; and crossed to the corner where Lansing and Hitchcock were waiting for him in the present that enveloped them all like the night with its half-moon and idle fireflies.

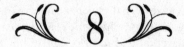

8

1

The President was standing in his open car. Edith sat beside him, clutching flowers. The President held his hat in his left hand, and waved with his right. The smile looked genuine; fatigue, too. Then the car with its Secret Service outriders pulled into a street lined with working-class people. As the President waved, they crossed their arms over their chests and looked away. Suddenly, one man held up a sign: "Release Political Prisoners." The President's hand dropped to his side. The smile vanished. Edith stared up at her husband, with a fixed awful smile, as the car, like a hearse, made its way through the sombre crowd.

The lights came on in the screening room. "Where was that?" asked Caroline, appropriately shaken.

"Seattle." Tim waved to the projectionist. "That's all. Thanks." Together they left the screening room and walked down the musty-smelling hall to the offices that Famous Players-Lasky had rented Traxler Productions, overlooking the corner of Vine and Selma. Soon they would have to decide whether or not they would buy or build a studio, or continue to rent.

"You can't use that." Caroline was firm.

"If I knew how, I would. But there's no story to go with it." Tim stared down at the row of pepper trees that bordered Vine Street. The Lasky studio, as everyone called it, occupied two city blocks. On Vine Street was the studio, a two-storied gray frame building while just back of it, on Argyle Street, was the fenced-in back lot, filled with technicians' sheds, New York streets, French villages, English mansions – every sort of setting that a photo-play might require.

Caroline studied a stack of photographs of herself. In the nick of time, for her at least, a cameraman had discovered that if black maline silk was placed over the camera lens years would be subtracted from those photographed, thus adding years to the acting lives of elderly players, of which Emma Traxler was one. Lines vanished or were reduced to mere platonic essences. At her worst, Emma simply looked faded but spiritual, and that was what the plot of *The Dangerous Years* called for: a widow with a fortune falls in love with her son's best friend at college, who wears knickerbockers to emphasize his youth. Although the actor was only a decade younger than Caroline, the new lens kept him a boy and Caroline a gamine in her late thirties. At the end, Caroline would commit suicide, something she very much looked forward to. Usually, she was to be seen at picture's end striding into the future during a long shot on a desolate moor, which was almost always the Burbank Golf Course after the mist-machine had disguised all the holes. Then a final close shot of her luminous face, transfigured, as Mr. Wurlitzer's organ played Tchaikovsky's Fourth Symphony, and the women in the audience wept. Somehow, mysteriously and without design, Caroline Sanford had become Emma Traxler if not for good then for the amount of time that she chose to spend in Hollywood with Tim, and that looked to be most of the year.

Tim had recovered from the fiasco of *The Strike-Breakers* through the simple expedient of rewriting the title cards to favor the railroad management and denounce the strikers. The result had been cheered in the popular press as a victory for capitalism; and no one had gone to see the movie. So, in the end, as Caroline observed, political integrity had been maintained.

"You've got to admit that that footage would make a swell ending to a story about the Wobblies. You know, the workers ignoring the President who had put so many of their leaders in jail."

"Why pick on poor Mr. Wilson?"

"Because he picked on poor Mr. Debs."

Caroline had made it a rule to ignore Tim's curious political line. "Philosophy" was too large a word to describe what seemed to her a perverse impulse to take the side of the unpopular and the weak. Since Americans only worshipped the strong and the bullying, she had at least convinced him that it was bad for his career to become too identified with the hated poor; yet, surprisingly, when she had suggested they make a film about Russia's October Revolution, he had not been interested. Plainly, he was more radical priest than revolutionary. She herself knew too much about politics to believe in anything other than the prevailing fact of force in human affairs. Henry Adams had been a thorough teacher.

When the secretary announced that Grace Kingsley of the Los Angeles *Times* had materialized, Tim left the office by a back door. Miss Kingsley's section on entertainment in the *Times* was read by everyone in Hollywood, and much reprinted elsewhere. The world could not get enough news about the movies, and Miss Kingsley was the principal conduit between the studios and public. A maiden lady, she was startlingly unprurient. She was not interested in love affairs or scandals, only photo-plays planned or in production or in release.

"Dear Miss Traxler." Miss Kingsley withdrew a long glove from a mottled hand and Caroline, though preferring the glove, shook the hand warmly. "It's so nice having you here close to home. My heart sinks when I have to go over to Burbank or that ultima Thule, Universal City. I feel like a pioneer, so much cactus, so many onions, and the Cahuenga Pass terrifies me."

Miss Kingsley made herself comfortable in a chintz-covered chair. "I've just come from Mr. Griffith. Thanks to Mr. Lasky, he's got financing again and he'll be able to finish *Scarlet Days*, certain to be a monument, I predict, to the western, which, if memory serves, he's never made before, at feature length. He also tells me – this is between us, of course, as I won't write it yet – that he's going back to the East when he finishes his contract with Artcraft here. But *then* another little bird has told me that he's just signed a three-picture deal with First National, and that will keep him here, I should think, for at least another halcyon year."

"Is his studio for sale?" Caroline revered Mr. Griffith, as did everyone; but she was far more interested in the studio that he had created at the juncture of Hollywood and Sunset boulevards: two sound-stages, a house whose owner had been moved out, and a laboratory where it was possible not only to experiment with·special effects but to create an entire movie from the printing of the negative to the editing to the making of copies for the distributors.

In Griffith's case, the entire process seldom took more than a month. Once he had decided on a story, he would get his artist in residence to draw each scene, which he then gave to the art director, who would call in the studio's carpenters, plasterers and painters, and the sets would be built. Meanwhile, Griffith would be rehearsing his actors; for years, he himself had been a stock-company actor, constantly on tour, and he had learned, firsthand, what thrilled the mass public. Then, in a great burst of energy, sometimes in as little as eighteen days, he would film the photo-play in an atmosphere very like a war, according to Tim, who had been involved as a cameraman in two of Griffith's early films. Although Griffith himself was relentlessly polite, he also enjoyed creating unease and tension all about him. Tim had learned what he could from him; and quickly moved on.

"I suspect . . . I cannot be positive . . . that he *will* sell once he's finished up his commitments here and removed himself to Mamaroneck in the East, Heaven only knows why."

"We would like to increase our production, as you know. Mr. Lasky has been very gracious, but we're crowded here. Mr. Farrell has found a place on Poverty Row . . ."

Miss Kingsley shook her head and sighed. "No. No. Not for Traxler Productions. You are a hallmark of quality. Down the road there they make a movie in a week. *Vulgar* movies."

Caroline gazed out the window at Poverty Row, which was just visible on nearby Gower Street. The cheap studios resembled a row of barns or garages haphazardly assembled in what was still a large orange grove.

"We could build, I suppose."

"Do! Like Charlie Chaplin. Now there's a charming studio. How I enjoy going there! So English, with tea being served all the time, and of course it's where I like to think home is, *this* area, the true Hollywood and not the Valley or Culver City, in spite of dear Mr. Ince."

Chaplin's studio was on the east side of La Brea, below Santa Monica Boulevard, while two blocks west of La Brea, his fellow United Artist, Douglas Fairbanks, had built *his* studio. Here he would eventually be joined by Mary Pickford if she, a good Catholic, could ever get divorced from her alcoholic husband, a source of constant interest to the entire world if not to Caroline, who wanted nothing more than an inexpensive sound-stage of her own.

"You are," Miss Kinglsey had opened her notebook, "contemplating a film about the Bolshevik terror in Russia."

"How did you know that?" Caroline was always surprised at how much the vague Miss Kingsley knew about everything that had to do with "home," the true Hollywood.

"One of my little birds. Now, you know that those Warner Brothers people spent fifty thousand dollars to buy Ambassador Gerard's book about Germany and the war, so there's now a serious trend, which I can detect, of doing real-life historical stories of a modern nature. Would you be working from a tome on the subject?"

Caroline was so thrilled to hear the word "tome" used in conversation that she said, without thinking, "Ah, yes. Yes! The tome will be *Ten Days That Shook the World,* if we can get the rights, of course."

Miss Kingsley's notebook nearly fell from her hand. "But that is a *pro*-Bolshevik tome, I am told."

"Oh, not the way we plan to do it."

"You will change the message the way you did in *The Strike-Breakers?*" Miss Kingsley was far from being the fool she seemed, and Caroline already regretted having spoken without a thought in her head.

"On that order, yes. Mr. Farrell is eager to alert all Americans to the dangers of communism, which is everywhere on the march. . . ."

Miss Kingsley hummed happily to herself and wrote and wrote

as Caroline improvised and improvised. Then Emma Traxler was questioned about *her* plans as an actress. Emma Traxler had made five films since *Huns from Hell,* and though each had made money none had equalled her startling debut. Even so, Caroline was amazed that she was something of a cult whom producers wanted to use. The previous year, Fairbanks had asked her to play Queen Berengaria to his Richard the Lion-hearted; and she had said yes, eagerly. But so far, there were no plans to make the film. "Everyone thinks I'm too contemporary for costume pictures," he had apologized when they last met in the Dining Room of the Stars at the Hollywood Hotel, where, surprisingly, a few stars occasionally dined.

"I have plans – hopes, I should say – to play Mary Stuart before I'm too old." Caroline enjoyed using the one word that Hollywood did not acknowledge.

"Dear, dear, dear," murmured Miss Kingsley, as if Caroline had confessed to some incurable disease. "No, no, no," she then added. "Never *old.* Will Mr. Farrell direct you?"

"I don't think that's his sort of thing. I'd like to use that young German director, Mr. Lubitsch."

"I saw his *Madame Du Barry.*" Miss Kingsley looked stern. "It was very *continental,* if you know what I mean."

"But then so was Mary Stuart, and so," Caroline practiced a husky laugh like Bernhardt, "am I."

"You seem thoroughly American, Miss Traxler." After Miss Kingsley had bestowed her highest accolade, they discussed Caroline's current film, now in its second week of shooting. She was free today because the company was doing a garden-party scene to which her character had not been invited. Graciously, Miss Kingsley declined an invitation to visit the set.

Caroline then walked her to the main door of the studio, where, as always, a small crowd of innocent fans waited to see the stars come and go, not knowing what the less innocent fans knew, that the stars tended to enter from the Argyle Lot, a block away. Mr. Lasky himself greeted Miss Kingsley at the door, where a studio policeman stood guard. Lasky was a small plump cheerful gnome of a man. Of the Jewish producers, he was the only one to be born in the United States. Where his partner, Zukor, was imperious and harsh, Lasky was easy and charming, and it was only a matter of time, everyone agreed, before Lasky would be devoured by the great predator. Caroline studied the various movie magnates with all the fascinated zeal of an anthropologist.

"I've got Maurice Maeterlinck and Edward Knoblock and Somerset Maugham and Elinor Glyn." This was Lasky's greeting to Miss Kingsley, who responded with, "Hooray! When do they come?"

"January. I'm getting them all. You want one, Miss Traxler?"

"Yes. Bernard Shaw."

Lasky frowned. "He won't come. I guess he's holding out. But when he sees how we've gone and got every famous writer there is, he'll hightail it out here pretty fast, let me tell you."

Caroline left Mr. Lasky and Miss Kingsley together, and made her way through the building to the back lot, where the New York City row of brownstones always reminded her how much she would like to appear in Mrs. Wharton's *The House of Mirth*.

A film was being shot in the street. Two gunmen came out of a shop, firing at the camera. Caroline ducked behind the street, where a metal frame held up the facades, which were so realistic that one could not tell they were not real. Thanks to San Francisco's 1915 Exposition, Hollywood had acquired a number of first-rate Italian plasterers, brought over to build fake Renaissance exhibit halls. At one point, Griffith had hired the lot of them to build Babylon for *Intolerance*, a set still to be seen, slightly peeling – all trumpeting elephants and fertility goddesses – at the confluence of Hollywood and Sunset boulevards.

Caroline's set was just beyond the New York street, a mansion with a lawn, surrounded by tall Eastern trees, which meant that the art department had transformed, most artfully, pepper trees into oaks.

Twenty ladies and gentlemen in fashionable attire drank tea while butlers circled them with trays of sandwiches. The director sat to the right of his cameraman, a homburg pulled over his brow. Directors prided themselves on the originality of their costumes. The star director at Lasky, Cecil B. DeMille, dressed as if for polo.

Others, usually from the theater, wore striped trousers and blazers suitable for a New York men's club. Emma's Oleg Olmstead was dressed for tennis except for a homburg to protect his head from the omnipresent sun. He waved to Caroline, who waved back and watched the scene, in which her film lover was made much of by the ingenue, a creature of a blondness undreamed of anywhere except Hollywood, where the perfecting – even the brutal re-creation – of nature was on a par with the best Italian plastering.

The scene would be observed by the stricken Emma Traxler in her luxurious bedroom overlooking the lawn – she had taken to her bed with what a script said was a cough but Emma decreed was a fever: the cameraman had enough trouble lighting her without having to deal with a face contorted by coughing. Once Emma's character realized that youth *always* calls to youth she, despite her wealth and high social position, would promptly take her own life, with a never-identified but swift-acting poison that caused her face, ever so gently, to relax into a final gentle smile.

When the scene ended, the extras were let go, and Mary Hulbert joined Caroline. Together the two women left the studio. "You don't know what this means to me, being able to work at anything, really." Mary had once been a pretty and vivacious woman whom life had so harassed that she was now distinctly wan and faded. A first husband, Mr. Hulbert, died; a second, Mr. Peck, had been divorced. A grown son was now living in New York City on what money she could give him.

A dozen years earlier, Mary had lived in a charming villa in Bermuda with her mother, and it was here that she had entertained the president of Princeton, Woodrow Wilson, when he used to take vacations on the island without his first wife. Caroline was certain that they had been lovers. Others thought not: after all, Wilson simply liked the company of women, particularly those who could recite poetry and talk, imaginatively, of him. For more than a decade, the two had exchanged letters, and the letters had figured in the last election. The *Tribune* had been offered copies. But Caroline had said no, on the ground that although they were affectionate they could hardly be called love letters. During that time, Caroline had met Mary and found her appealing. The letters

300

themselves were a mystery in the sense that Caroline had no idea whether or not Mary herself was behind their sale. In any case, they did not affect the election and one of the President's wealthy admirers, Bernard Baruch, was supposed to have bought them all up.

The previous year, Mary had presented herself at Caroline's hotel in Los Angeles, and they fell upon one another as long-lost friends, largely because Caroline delighted in the mystery of a relationship that had never been a secret to anyone, including the first Mrs. Wilson, who, complaisantly, would invite Mary to the White House to entertain the President, unlike the second Mrs. Wilson, who was quite pleased that Mary had chosen to pursue her destiny in California as – variously and unsuccessfully – a rancher, a writer, an interior decorator and an actress. Caroline had got her acting work. She had also commissioned Mary to write a photo-play about Mary Queen of Scots.

Caroline enjoyed the luxury of driving herself in a black, open Graham-Paige – no more chauffeurs. As they drove through the Argyle gate, the fans shouted, "Emma! Emma!" and Emma smiled her haunting Madonna smile; and thought grimly of her dentist's threat to remove a left incisor, which would, a dozen actresses had blithely told her, cause the flesh beside the nostril to fall in, which meant an asymmetrical face for the screen unless the other incisor was also removed, in which case one might have a whole new and quite unwanted face.

There was little traffic in what was still, for Caroline, a village. She turned left on Vine into Hollywood Boulevard, a most subur-ban sort of street, with large houses set far back from the sidewalk. Above and parallel to Hollywood Boulevard was rustic Franklin Avenue, where many of the stars lived among wooded hills that were still wild: owls and coyotes and mockingbirds made clam-orous the nights.

At Cahuenga and Hollywood there was a small cluster of shops, including the inevitable United Drug Company store, a bank, and a hardware shop. Behind the low shop fronts, on a ridge, was the de Longpre mansion, a twin-turretted Victorian house much admired by the locals. Caroline had been offered it by the owner, a painter, but she had said that she was far too shy to live in so conspicuous a house. As she was in her role as Emma Traxler, this was undoubtedly true. Other castles, usually the work of Chicago dentists or lawyers, had been equally unsuitable. She was now comfortably installed on the top floor of the Garden Court Apartments on Hollywood Boulevard just east of La Brea, from the Spanish word for "tar," a reminder of the famous La Brea tar pits where earlier residents of the planet could still be observed, embedded in life-enhancing oil.

Caroline parked on the Highland Avenue side of the Hollywood Hotel and thought, as she so often did, that Hollywood with its thirty thousand people had all the charms of village life and none of the drawbacks. Despite the constant attention of the world's press, it was possible to vanish into one's own house in the hills and be a part of dull wilderness, or one could step triumphantly onto the world's stage at the Hollywood or Alexandria Hotels. Fortunately, in the late afternoon, the world's stage, as represented by the hotel's south verandah, was not crowded and the solitary waiter brought them tea.

The automobiles that drove along Hollywood Boulevard usually slowed down to see who was going in or coming out or taking tea on the verandah. On good days, Caroline quite enjoyed being recognized. Today was good, were it not for the left incisor, which was now never far from her thoughts as she brooded on the nightmarish depression beside her nostril which could well sicken audiences as they gazed in horror at the terrible asymmetry of a once-perfect face. I am not really vain, she thought, eating a cucumber sandwich. I am simply mad, like everyone else here.

"What must it be like," asked Mary, "to be two people?"

"Isn't everyone? At least two, I'd say."

"Not so publicly, anyway. There you are one person on the screen, a woman of mystery . . ."

"A secret without a sphinx?" Brightly Caroline contributed to her legend.

"And then you're *the* Mrs. Sanford, everyone knows."

"Only everyone in the District of Columbia, which is a long way away. I really love it here."

"I can see you do." Mary lit a cigarette. The hand, Caroline noted, was unsteady. "If I didn't have so much trouble . . ." She stopped.

"Mary Stuart will solve that." Caroline had already given her an advance for the photo-play.

"You've been very good." Mary suddenly laughed, and Caroline had a glimpse of what charm she must have had in better times. "I've been very good, too. I haven't written a book."

"Perhaps," said Caroline Sanford, shoving the haunting Emma Traxler to one side, "you should. The *Tribune* would serialize."

"I will. One day. But I can't now. I must wait till he's . . . off the scene."

"But no one will care by then."

"Oh, but he's permanently historic, don't you think?" A slender handsome young man with astonishingly even features greeted Caroline, who said, "How would you like to be Bothwell to my Mary Queen of Scots?"

"I hate horses," he said, simply. "Have you seen Mr. Griffith?"

Caroline said she had not.

"He's probably hiding out inside. We're having our premiere at last, Clune's Auditorium."

"I can never remember the title."

"*Busted Posies.*" The young man laughed. "I play a Chink." He went inside.

"He would be a wonderful Bothwell," said Mary.

"Indeed he would, if I were twenty years younger." Caroline, who had never much minded the process of aging, now hated it on the ground that as she was doing it so well, why did she have to do it at all? A red electrical car passed by. A woman waved at Emma Traxler, who waved back. "Have you met Mrs. Wilson?"

Mary shook her head. "I am told she's jealous. I can't think why. After all, *she* married him."

"Would you . . . have married him?"

Mary's laugh was most attractive. "Oh, yes. But he never really asked me. I thought he would. In fact, I still have the lace I bought for the dress I expected to be married in."

Caroline looked at her with new interest. Photo-play plots were

303

seldom so unexpected. "Then you must have had very good reason to think that he would want to marry you."

"I did. After all, I was the choice of his first wife. She knew she was dying for quite a long time, and she liked to have me at the White House to . . . distract him. I did, or tried to. When I wasn't there, he wrote me every Sunday for years and years."

"The famous love letters?"

"Infamous, I'd say, and hardly love letters. More loving than love, and anyway more political than anything else. I think that's why he got so nervous when Mr. McAdoo said that I was showing the letters to people. He was always very candid about other politicians, and that was an election year."

Caroline was now certain that the President and Mary Peck Hulbert had had an affair. The brilliant openness of their friendship was a proof. Of course, the President was a very odd man indeed, like an intricate piece of machinery carefully coiled in upon itself. Yet he was more than susceptible to physical passion; hence, the unseemly swiftness of the second marriage over the strong objections of his advisers, particularly Colonel House and McAdoo. "How did McAdoo know you were showing the letters to people?"

Mary put a lump of sugar in her tea and then, heroically, removed it. "He didn't. Because I wasn't showing them. There was some sort of White House plot. Everyone was worried that if the President married Mrs. Galt, he might lose the election. Poor Ellen had been dead only a year. And then there was me. The fall and winter after Ellen died, he begged me to come stay in the White House. But I couldn't. My son had lost a great deal of money, and I was trying to get work as an interior decorator in Boston, not the best of cities for that sort of thing. . . ."

Caroline murmured no, and wondered at the diversity of Mary's interests. In her poverty, she had tried every profession except the obvious, marriage. "Why didn't you just move into the White House and marry him?"

"I should have." The response was quick. "But I was worried about my son, and money, and I was writing articles for the *Ladies' Home Journal*. They said they had lost some of my articles, which I knew was untrue, so I got – oh, this is terrible! – but I got the President to write the editor, who promptly found the articles, and printed them."

Caroline had now decided that Mary Peck Hulbert was a fool of astonishing dimension. To worry a president in time of war with something so trivial suggested true megalomania; to worry in such a way a grief-stricken man in love with her was monstrous. Caroline gazed upon Mary with absolute delight. "Tell me more. Of Mr. McAdoo, that is."

"Well, it appears – I don't know for certain – that he told the President that someone had written him anonymously, from California, saying that I was showing people his letters, so this – plus the fact that he had given me the seventy-five hundred dollars – would make it look like . . ."

Fled from the tea-table was luminous Madonna-like Emma Traxler; seated now in her place like an avenging angel was Caroline Sanford, yellow journalist. "He had made you a loan?"

"Oh, yes. You see, we were so broke. So I came to the White House in – well, it was just after the *Lusitania* was sunk, I remember – and I asked him to take over two mortgages for me for seventy-five hundred dollars, which he did, though he didn't tell me that he was about to marry Edith. But I suppose I must've *known*, I mean one can always tell that sort of thing, don't you think?"

"Yes. Yes. Yes. Always."

"I must go."

"Oh, no. No!"

"You've been so good to me, Caroline. . . ."

The two women were on their feet. "Let me drive you . . ."

"No. I'm only twenty minutes by electric car."

"Will you go hear him speak?" The President was due to speak the next night at the Shriners Auditorium.

"I can't," said Mary. "But I'm to have lunch with him and Edith the next day. Sunday. I'm dreading it, really."

"Shall I come with you?" Caroline reminded herself of a shark she had seen off Catalina Island as, like a torpedo, it struck and nearly wrecked a small boat.

"Would you?" Mary's response was so charming and so sponta-neous that Caroline almost missed the other's calculation. "I know you know them so well . . ."

"Not that well. But the *Tribune* supports him, and so they are both amiable."

"Meet me in the lobby of the Alexandria Hotel at twelve-thirty. I'll warn them." Mary then hurried to the corner of Highland and Hollywood, where a red car waited. Caroline waved brightly at her, as the electrical car glided east. Three men walked up the steps to the verandah. She recognized one of them. He bowed low; she bowed even lower. "Mr. Griffith." She spoke the name rever-ently.

"Madame Traxler." He had a stagey melodramatic voice and looked, suitably, like an American bald eagle. "You should be on a stage, working. I see you standing in a window. It's dawn. There are sheer white curtains behind you, billowing in a wind . . ."

"From outside or inside?" Caroline could not resist.

The great man laughed. "You know so much! Half the directors keep the wind indoors. I must talk to you soon. After the open-ing . . ."

"Mr. Barthelmess is waiting for you inside."

"Madame." A lower bow, and then he went inside; as he passed, she could smell whisky on his breath.

At the Garden Court, Héloise lived what she took to be a rugged western life in a Hollywood renaissance apartment. Tim's flat adjoined Caroline's and the management had made no fuss when a door between the two had been unlocked. But the Garden Court had only just opened, and Emma Traxler was the first star to take up residence. Héloise condescended to cook occasionally for the two of them; and then it was early to separate beds. Caroline found making movies very much like being in school again. One was up at dawn; one spent the day learning lines and trying to please oth-ers; and then one went to sleep, as they said hereabouts, with the chickens.

Caroline lay on a sofa, a pile of photo-plays on the floor beside her. At an escritoire, Tim made notes for the next day's work. In the small kitchen Héloise rattled pans.

This was domesticity, Caroline decided comfortably; also, simplicity. She had never lived in a flat before; she had never lived without many servants; she was truly free at last, all thanks to California and a new invention that had brought together some of the most extraordinary people in the world.

"Shall I die with my eyes open or shut?"

"Shut." Tim went on writing.

"Open, I think. I've been practicing. All you have to do is let them go slowly out of focus."

"You'll blink."

"I won't. I'm having lunch with your new star, Mr. Wilson."

This got Tim's attention. He put down his notebook. "When?"

"Sunday. The day after the speech."

"I'm photographing inside the Shriners."

"Why?"

"I don't know. I mean, I can always use that footage of him in Seattle in any labor story. *Anti*-labor, of course."

"Of course. But why photograph him at the Shriners?"

"Something might happen."

"You think they'll shoot him?"

"Wouldn't that be wonderful?" Tim's blue eyes were ablaze with pleasure. "But I've never had that kind of luck."

"Thank heaven. I quite like Mr. Wilson."

"No one has ever taken scenes from real life – you know, a president on a swing around the circle and then intercut it with a made-up story."

Caroline saw the possibilities; and the dangers. "What, then, is the made-up story?"

"Oh, something political. Maybe to do with the League of Nations even, but it's also got to be a personal story."

Caroline thought of Mary Hulbert, a story so wonderfully inconsequential yet odd that fiction could not properly account for it while lovers of the real world would reject it. She tried to visualize the President's letter to the editor of the *Ladies' Home Journal*. Then she looked at Tim and beheld the red flag behind him or, worse, the cross. "The possibilities for trouble are endless, my darling," she said, shifting to Emma Traxler, warm and understanding yet, gently, chiding. "A. Mitchell Palmer is longing to put you in jail for treason and only the *Tribune* has stopped him."

"Keep on stopping him." Tim was blithe.

"Why bother with politics?"

Tim looked inspired. "Because I have to."

"Are you a Communist?"

"I might be. One day. Why not?"

Caroline sighed. "You will ruin yourself."

"I thought it was a free country."

"Did you? Then don't *think*, my darling, ever again. Because your mind is not your most . . . formidable asset. It is your heart that does you – and me – so much credit. I am talking exactly like a title card so that you won't."

"What have I created?" Tim was delighted with Emma Traxler, less pleased with Caroline Sanford. "I'm sure you never talked like that before I met you."

"No one," said Caroline, "talks like that outside photo-plays. The only freedom that an American has is to conform, as you've discovered." Caroline did not in the least mind the disparity between the country's shining image of itself and the crude reality. She was entirely on the side of the rulers, ridiculous and unpleasant as so many of them were. She felt a certain generalized pity for the people at large, but there was nothing she could do for them except report murders in the press, and commit suicide on the screen – with her eyes wide open, she decided; and though smelling salts be broken under her nose, she would not blink, she vowed. "Leave politics alone."

"The Warners are doing all right with that ambassador's book . . ."

"That's leftover anti-Hun material." A mockingbird started its song outside the window, and Caroline got up and looked out over Hollywood. In the distance, the huge remains of the Babylon set beautifully, insistently, filled the eastern sky with prancing plaster elephants. Hollywood, she decided, could be anywhere – except on earth and in time.

The Alexandria Hotel was very much in the United States and in present time. The lobby was crowded with Secret Service men, state troopers, police, political delegations, all waiting for a signal from on high that the President would receive them. The intermediary was the President's Secret Service man, Mr. Starling, who sat at a gilded desk near the elevators. He had a list of names in front of him, a telephone, and the abstracted look of someone who had chosen invisibility. As it was, only those who had business with the President were presented to Starling by a tense assistant manager.

To Caroline's surprise, Mary was late. As she came across the famous million-dollar rug that covered the floor of the lobby, Caroline noted that she had a slight limp.

"I missed the red car. They only run on the hour where I live." Mary started toward the main desk but Caroline led her to Mr. Starling, who rose when he saw her. "Nice to see you again, Mrs. Sanford."

"Mr. Starling." Caroline smiled a Sanford smile. "This is Mrs. Hulbert. We're expected for lunch."

Starling frowned at the list on his desk. "I thought it was Mrs. Peck."

"I am Mrs. Peck, too." Mary was suddenly the First Lady of the Land. Starling gave her a long curious look: then he led them to an elevator. "This goes directly to their floor. The policeman will take you on in." Starling went to his telephone, and the ladies ascended.

"Mr. Griffith lives here." Caroline made conversation. "Or used to. Actors like hotels better than houses."

"Poor things." Mary was compassionate.

A policeman met them at the door to the elevator and escorted them into the drawing room of a large suite, where Edith Wilson stood. At close to six feet tall, she could appear quite menacing in the fullness of her flesh. She greeted Caroline warmly. Then, with perfect courtesy, she extended her arm to its full length and took Mary's hand in hers. "I am so happy to meet you, Mrs. Peck."

"And I you, Mrs. Wilson. You know, I've gone back to my old name, Hulbert."

"I *am* sorry," was the ambiguous response. Brooks, the Negro

309

valet, opened the door to the bedroom, and the President entered, smartly turned out in a blue blazer and white trousers. He looked somewhat sunburned, and yet not at all healthy. The eyes behind the pince-nez were dull. But the smile was genuine. "Mary," he said, and he shook her hand for a long moment. "You don't change," he added.

At the far end of the room, Brooks helped a hotel waiter prepare a lunch table for five. The President gestured for the ladies to sit. "Mrs. Sanford, I still remember how we watched your photoplay with you, and never guessed that it was you we were watching."

"I guessed, Woodrow." Edith was serenely knowing.

"You *suspected*," he corrected her. "But neither of us was certain. Now you act in everything!"

"It just *seems* like everything."

"How do you weep so easily?" asked Edith. "I mean, never having acted before."

"But we've all of us been acting all the time all our lives . . ."

"I have," agreed the President. "But I thought I was unique."

"You were a born actor," said Mary, fondly. "I'll never forget the King Lear you did on the beach at Bermuda, just for Mark Twain and me."

Very good, thought Caroline, glancing at Edith, whose smile looked as if it had been carved in the firm butter of her round full face.

"I wasn't there last night at the Shriners." Caroline decided on an intervention. "But the *Times* is delighted, and Mr. Farrell, you remember, my director, said it was thrilling."

Wilson nodded vaguely, eyes on Mary, who was lighting a cigarette. Edith continued to smile. "But aren't you speaking too often? I mean for your . . ." Caroline substituted the word "voice" for "health."

"Of course he is." Edith was firm. "But once he's made up his mind . . ."

"I must match the opposition. Hiram Johnson is all over the state, attacking the League. The worst is the . . . the . . ." Wilson paused; and frowned. Edith's smile was impenetrable. Caroline suspected aphasia, something she herself suffered from when

310

tired: the needed word, no matter how simple, was suddenly not there.

". . . the acoustics," said Mary, accurately, to Edith's great displeasure. "Those sounding-boards are never in the right place."

"But San Diego was even worse," said Wilson, pleased to be on course again. "They have something new called a voice-phone. You must remain absolutely still and speak into it and somehow it connects with loudspeakers – like radio, I suppose. I've never had such a difficult time. I like to move about, you know, but there I was, under sentence of death, if I moved."

"It was terrible for Woodrow. But thirty thousand people heard him as if he was talking into each one's ear."

"No. No." Wilson frowned. "That's not true. Just opposite me there was a section that could hear absolutely nothing, nothing." The face was red. He shook his head and coughed. "Asthma," he murmured into his handkerchief. "Imagine! Now."

Suddenly, Admiral Grayson was in the room. He greeted Mary and Caroline, and took the President's pulse and smiled and said, "Lunch is ready. This was to have been our Sunday of rest."

Caroline thought that this was directed at Mary, but as the President led them to the table, he described their misadventures that morning. "I wanted to see an old friend of my wife's – my late wife's – who lives here but has no telephone. So, first thing, we went down the back way, and escaped the press and the crowds, and drove to her house only to find she wasn't there. Then the Secret Service discovered that she had gone to the train station to get a look at me, so off we rush to the station, and there she is . . ."

"You can imagine," said Edith, "the sight of the two of us tearing about Los Angeles, with the Secret Service either too far behind or ahead . . ."

"Like Mack Sennett," said Wilson. "Do you know him?" He turned to Caroline, who radiated an Emma Traxler silent affirmation.

"Tell him I can't get enough of Ben Turpin. He reminds me of the Senate . . ."

"He reminds me of you, this morning, so undignified." Edith was placid. "Anyway, there was Ellen's old friend on the train in the station, so we did have an intimate talk, surrounded by a thousand curious voters. Then I hurried back here to arrange for lunch, and Woodrow followed me."

Caroline could see why Edith was less than pleased to divide the Biblical day of rest between a lady-friend of the first wife's and her husband's former mistress. Mary didn't add to Edith's joy when she said to Wilson, "Do you remember this dress?"

It helped even less when Wilson nodded and said, "You wore it in May of 1915, at the White House."

Edith raised her menu. "What," asked Edith in a voice of muted thunder, "is – or are – abalone?"

Fortunately, the President's passion for movies now surpassed that of his ancient passion for Mary, so Caroline gained innumerable points in Edith's eyes by telling as many Hollywood stories as she could think of. The President was particularly interested in what his son-in-law, McAdoo, had accomplished with United Artists.

During lunch, Tumulty would look in from the next room, and say, "Converts, sir," and Wilson would be obliged to go into the next room and shake hands with visiting delegations. Mary and Edith would then discuss the merits and demerits of California, a state that they had, finally, rejected for retirement as being too far away. Edith did not specify from what.

Finally, converts and lunch done with, they sat in the sitting room of the suite, and Mary described how persons unknown but suspected had ransacked her house and stolen letters from Wilson. "Which darling Caroline was offered and rejected, which is why I invited her here."

"Who offered them to you?" Edith turned to Caroline but her eyes never left the President's weary face.

"A journalist that we know. He wouldn't say how he'd got them. Journalists never do. I turned them down, of course."

"To think, poor Mary, you've had to go through all this for me." Wilson sighed.

"Well," said Edith, with an attempt at lightness, "where there's so much smoke there must be *some* fire."

"But surely *you* were not von Bernstorff's mistress." Mary's sudden savage riposte made it quite clear why Wilson had once delighted in her company. Before Edith had married Wilson, she had indeed known – how well? – the notorious German ambassador.

Edith handled the assault with a liquid Southern charm that involved a simulated Negroid chuckle of delight followed by, "I declare, the stories that they invent about us are a lot more interesting than the movies."

Fortunately, Wilson had not noticed – or taken in – this exchange. "I've considered resigning," he suddenly said; and put his finger to his lips, as a not entirely mock warning that all this was secret.

"But you look so well." Mary was interested now in her own problems, and Caroline could see that a letter from the President to, perhaps, her landlord might be required.

"Not on grounds of health. On the League of Nations. If I have difficulties with the Senate, and I pray after this tour I won't but if I do, I shall propose that we all resign, the Vice President and I *and* the senators opposed, and that we then hold a national election to determine whether or not the League be accepted."

Caroline could not believe that the President was serious; but when she saw Edith's Buddha-like bobbing of the head, she realized that Wilson had entered a new and dangerous phase. "The governors are willing, we hear," said Edith. "They are the ones who must call the election, state by state."

"Then you'll have that parliamentary government you've always wanted." Mary allowed herself to be distracted, for the moment, by history.

Wilson smiled. "I hadn't thought of that. But I suppose that is what we'd be doing, going to the country, as the English say, and on a great issue rather than the usual politics. It would be such a pleasure to concentrate those bungalow-minds in the Senate on something that matters." Then Mary returned with gentle persistence to the financial problems of her son; and of the high cost of living in Los Angeles. Edith smiled and glowered at the same time.

Caroline was embarrassed by the monotony of Mary's self absorption. On the other hand, the President gazed at her raptly,

313

as if she were still enchanting and he enchanted. Then Grayson entered. It was the end of the audience.

Edith rose. "You were so good to come see us," she said to Mary, who had just begun to describe the possibility of going into partnership with the interior decorator Elsie de Wolfe, as a Los Angeles associate.

Edith left the room, to get Mary's coat. Caroline moved – no, glided – to the window, to put as much distance as she could between the star-crossed couple. She tried not to listen, as she gazed toward Culver City set amongst so many aggressive onion fields whose flatness was abruptly broken by the colonnaded Southern-mansion-style studio of Thomas H. Ince, her first producer, whose callers were received not by the usual studio policeman but by a gracious Negro butler in full livery.

"What can I do?" Wilson's voice was low but not low enough for Caroline's sharp ears.

"You could help my son. In New York. Here. I've written his name and address."

"But what about you?"

"Such a pretty coat," said Edith; and Caroline turned to face the curious triangle. Farewells were made. But Wilson insisted on accompanying the ladies to the elevator. Edith remained behind, in all her bland immensity.

As the policeman held the lift door open, Mary suddenly recited, "'With all my will, but much against my heart, we two now part.'" There were tears in Wilson's eyes as the two women entered the elevator; and the doors shut. In silence, Caroline and Mary rode down to the lobby. Next to the cashier's grille, Mary paused. "Do they know you here, dear?"

"I suppose so," said Emma Traxler known to all.

"Could you help me cash just the tiniest check? I've been so busy working on your picture, and now, of course, it's Sunday. . . ."

Emma Traxler obliged a reluctant cashier to cash the check. At least, the President had been spared the indignity of endorsing Mary Hulbert's check.

2

The Vice President of the United States stared into Cicero's blank marble eyes while Burden sat back in his leather swivel chair, feet on his desk. "That," said Marshall, finally, "is about as good a likeness of old Bryan as I've ever seen."

Burden nodded gravely. It was an on-going source of joy to him that no one had ever recognized the life-size bust as being of Cicero. One and all thought it Bryan, Burden's political progenitor.

After one of the hottest summers in memory, autumn had been hot, too; and now, in October, the leaves had not turned but simply burned and fallen and the Capitol looked chalky and bare on its brown hill.

Marshall sat beside the fire and lit a cigar that had cost rather more than the "good five-cent cigar" which he had once so memorably said the country needed. "You been to the other end lately?"

Thus they referred to the White House at the opposite end of Pennsylvania Avenue.

Burden shook his head. "Tumulty won't even let me speak to *Mrs.* Wilson."

"It's been bad," said Marshall. "Now it's worse. The President's dying."

"Who told you?" Burden's amazement was not so much at the startling news as at the fact that anyone had been able to learn anything about what was going on behind the padlocked White House gates.

"I can't say. Tumulty says he'll get word to me. But doesn't. Grayson is a doctor, and they don't talk – except when they do. Mrs. Wilson is presidentess. . . . And all they do is feed us the official line about how there was the nervous breakdown, whatever that is, on the train, and so they had to come whipping back to Washington. It sounds like he had some sort of stroke, which is why he can't appear in public. Now this morning they found him flat on the bathroom floor. It seems he's paralyzed and his kidneys don't work, and the sons-of-bitches refuse to tell the country or me, the vice president, anything at all. What news I get is through the grape vine."

Although Burden personally liked Wilson, the matter was now beyond personality. It was not a man that was sick, but a political system that was paralyzed. "Have you talked to Lansing?"

"Not today. He's been running the Cabinet in an *ad hoc* way, and they all go on looking after their departments like they do anyway, but dear God, we've got a steel strike on our hands and a coal strike – and winter coming on – and there's martial law in Omaha, thanks to that nigger-lynching, and there's Lodge –"

"There's Lodge. If I were you, I'd collect Lansing and go to the White House and ask to see the President and if they say no, invoke the Constitution and remove him from office until such time as he is able to exercise his duties." Burden's line was hard; and precise. The American government could not function without an executive despite the pretensions of peacock-like senators.

"I just don't dare." Marshall looked forlorn. "Lansing mentioned the subject to Mrs. Wilson and she about bit his head off."

Burden thought how different things would be if he, and not Marshall, had been vice president. "How long can they string everybody along?"

"Who's to stop them? Do you realize," Marshall's cigar had gone out, "that he could die, and Grayson and Tumulty and the lady could go right on pretending he was just fine?"

"He still has to sign bills. Hitchcock has got four of them right now, on his desk, including prohibition, and if he doesn't sign or veto them, they'll be the law in ten days."

"Christ, Burden. You know and I know that any one of our secretaries can sign our names just as good as we can."

The two men lapsed into silence. The first American regency had begun and there was nothing to be done about it as long as the President's wife and doctor said that he was competent. Meanwhile, the League, for which Wilson had given if not his life his health and probably sanity, could still be salvaged. Lodge had agreed to the principle of two leagues. One in the eastern hemisphere and one in the western, where the Monroe Doctrine roamed. In concert, the two would be stronger and less dangerous than one. Finally, as much as Lodge hated Wilson and all his works – the anti-League forces that he led proudly called themselves the Battalion of Death – Lodge was also an internationalist New England senator and he saw the folly of letting go so potential an instrument as a world league to be led by the United States; hence, his invention of an Augustus of the west and one of the east. But now there was no president to deal with, and his lawful successor sat helplessly staring into Burden's fireplace, a dollar cigar between his teeth.

It was not until November 17 that Burden and Hitchcock were summoned to the White House. Hitchcock had been once before and he warned Burden not to show surprise at what he saw.

"What about what I hear?"

Hitchcock did not answer, as the White House gates were unpadlocked, and their long Packard drew up to the north portico. The day was cold and dry and there were, everywhere, dirty drifts of old snow, left over from the recent coastal blizzard which always coincided so neatly with coal miners' strikes. Currently, nearly four hundred thousand miners had refused to go back to work and their leader, John L. Lewis, publicly doubted if General Wood's men could dig enough coal with their bayonets to warm the nation.

Mrs. Wilson and Admiral Grayson were waiting for them in the upstairs hall. Each wore an incongruous smile; each looked as if he had not slept for a week. Otherwise, the usually busy corridor was like a hospital's terminal ward. No secretary sat at Miss Benson's desk, on which, Burden noted, Mrs. Wilson's handbag and knitting rested. Plainly, she spent a good deal of time at the desk, guarding the door. "We have wonderful news, gentlemen," said Mrs. Wilson. "He's in a wheelchair, and this afternoon we're going outside for the first time."

"The recovery has been astonishing, really astonishing," said Admiral Grayson.

"From what?" Burden was not feeling in the least like a courtier. Hitchcock gave him a hard look but the conspirators were prepared for the questions.

"First, exhaustion from the tour. Then what we feared might be

317

uremia. Then a prostate condition which has come and, with medication, gone."

"We wanted no operation, Woodrow and I, though some doctors did. Thank God, we didn't. Now he's on the mend." With a bright laugh, Mrs. Wilson led them into the bedroom.

The President was carefully arranged in a wheelchair in front of a window whose light put him in silhouette so that it was difficult to make out the features of the right side of his face, while the left was turned to the window. He wore a shawl from which he extended his right hand and, firmly, shook hands with each senator.

The President was completely unrecognizable. For one thing, he wore a long white beard that looked like a vaudevillian's prop. The normally lean face was now cadaverous; and the speech slightly slurred. The rumor was true, after all. Wilson's left side was paralyzed. Whatever his other problems, he had had a severe stroke. "I am not the picture of rude health," he said, with half a smile. The left side of the mouth, though turned away, could be seen to fall as the right went up. "But compared to what I was a few weeks ago, I am a boy again." He gestured with his right hand at Grayson, who, reluctantly, withdrew. To Burden's surprise, Edith sat nearby, taking notes on their conversation. What were the regents up to?

"We have had quite a few royal visitors." The President was deliberately chatty. "The Prince of Wales wanted to know which room his grandfather had slept in, that was back in Buchanan's time. I told him how his grandfather had escaped one night, through a window, to go to a party. He wanted to know which window." Wilson raised his right hand, almost airily, then let it fall into his lap. "Then the King and Queen of the Belgians returned our visit to them. I wore a sweater, thinking it less compromising than a dressing gown. The Queen told the press that a sweater was worn, which came out as 'torn,' depicting me as some sort of derelict, and a hundred good ladies have sent my wife balls of wool to repair me." The head swivelled toward the senators. "I want the revised preamble to the treaty deleted. If it isn't, I'll pocket-veto the treaty, reservations and all."

"Then, sir, am I to instruct the senators of our party to vote against the treaty if the preamble stays?"

Wilson nodded. "Don't you see if I refuse to veto but don't accept the treaty with reservations – just put it in a drawer – Lodge can't say that I killed my own League?"

"But isn't that what you're doing?" Logic, no matter how exquisite, that rested upon a false hypothesis tended to annoy Burden.

"No." The voice of the history teacher was flat and cold. "It will be clear to the country when the Democratic senators vote against the treaty that the treaty no longer is what it was. Then when the Senate goes into recess, the public and the press will have the time to convince at least two-thirds of the senators that Lodge's game is simply partisan malice and not a reflection of those crowds I saw in the West, day after day, until . . ." The voice stopped.

"Surely," said Burden, "some treaty is better than no treaty at this point . . ."

"The President must take his medicine," said Mrs. Wilson. She was on her feet. The senators rose. Wilson extended his right hand to each man; again, the grasp was startlingly strong.

"Perhaps," said Hitchcock, always tactless in Burden's eyes, "the time has come to hold out the olive branch."

"Let Lodge do that." The white-bearded old man looked to be carved from ice.

In the hallway, Mrs. Wilson turned to Hitchcock. "I think you're right, Senator. I would accept any reservations to get this awful thing settled, so that he can get well again. But he said, 'Little girl,'" her obsidian-dark, narrow Indian eyes were bright with tears, "'don't you desert me. I couldn't bear that. I have no moral right to accept any change in a paper that I have signed without giving all the other signers, even the Germans, the right to do the same thing. It's not that *I* will not accept: it is the nation's honor that is at stake.'"

Hitchcock was visibly moved. Burden was, he hoped, invisibly enraged. "What does Colonel House advise?"

"I don't know. We've not seen him." This confirmed the rumor that House had been excluded from the President's councils. "I'm told he is in Washington. But our door is shut now, I'm afraid."

"Even to Lord Grey?" The British foreign secretary had arrived the previous month to assure everyone that His Majesty's Government would not strenuously object to Lodge's various reservations as long as there was, at the end, a world League of Nations. But the President would not see him because, according to Alice Longworth, whose gossip was always lurid but no less accurate for that, one of the British embassy aides had made an unforgivable joke about Mrs. Wilson (Question: "What did Mrs. Galt do when the President proposed to her?" Answer: "She fell out of bed"), and though Mrs. Wilson had demanded the aide's dismissal, Lord Grey had said no, and now his lordship was being punished and the door was shut to him as well as to Colonel House.

"The Prince of Wales brought up the subject! Imagine involving a boy in such a matter! We only saw him because his parents had been so nice to us when we arrived in the middle of their Christmas holidays. Anyway, we owe nothing to Lord Grey, quite the contrary." A bell rang from the bedroom.

"Don't go," she said, and hurried into the sickroom.

"Let's talk to the Vice President." Burden was hard.

"I did. He won't make a move. You know how they keep in touch with him?" Hitchcock was now whispering. "Tumulty tells this friend of his on the Baltimore *Sun* what's going on here and he tells Marshall."

"Then maybe we'll have to go to law to get these people out." Burden was amazed at his own anger and perfect lack of compassion. Either the nation was serious or it was not. Either there was a functioning president or there was a dangerous absence that could not be filled by a loyal wife and a naval doctor.

"But he's not disabled. He vetoed the Volstead Act. He's out of bed . . ."

The loyal wife returned. "The President says that Democrats are to vote against the treaty but instead of saying that they are *defeating* it, they are only *nullifying* it."

On that note, the Minority Leader of the Senate and his deputy departed. Burden saw nothing but disaster ahead; and a Republican president the next year.

3

Jess and the Duchess sat with the McLeans in the Senate gallery. Once again all Washington had assembled to see the Battalion of Death crush the President and the League of Nations. Below them, W.G. waved to the Duchess as senators streamed onto the floor. In fact, the entire Senate would be present to hear Lodge present his committee's report. Then, after a discussion, the League would be put to a vote. W.G. had already been asked by Lodge to open the debate for the Republican side in support of the revised League which then the Democrats would, confusingly, vote to nullify.

"Warren's very nervous," said the Duchess to Evalyn McLean. "He's been practicing for days in front of the mirror."

"I thought he just made it up as he goes along." Evalyn was now very like her old self; on the other hand, Ned was sober, a sign of some new development in his character, or liver.

Jess looked about the crowded gallery. The self-styled Colonel of the Battalion of Death, Alice Longworth, was accompanied by Ruth Hanna McCormick, daughter to Mark Hanna, wife to Medill McCormick, recently elected senator from Illinois, young and aggressive and ambitious, and brother to Robert McCormick of the Chicago *Tribune*. Medill was going to be president one day, everyone said, including Alice, who doted on his wife, a lady as fiercely partisan as she. The two women held court at the end of the row. A number of senators clustered about Alice, who was like that woman who knitted beside the guillotine in one of Jess's favorite movies. Whenever she dropped a stitch, she said kill, kill, kill.

Jess had actually heard Mrs. Longworth call Senator Lodge "Senator Wobbly" because he had been intent on establishing some sort of non-Wilsonian league. Meanwhile, whenever any senator dared suggest that the magnificent Theodore Roosevelt had ever so much as dreamed of a league, she would send him a stern note from the gallery. Alice had been chosen by Heaven and herself to be the keeper of the Roosevelt flame as well as the promoter of the Roosevelt heir, General Leonard Wood, the progressive Republican candidate who had so recently delighted the country by breaking up strikes with troops in an all-out war against what he called "radicalism," to which Jess could only say "amen." But Daugherty thought General Wood would fizzle out. When he did, the party would turn to W.G. Thus far, W.G. had been noncommittal.

There was a stir in the chamber as the Vice President sauntered through the swinging doors and climbed the steps to the high throne, and muttered something to the parliamentarian who was never far from his side. Then Thomas R. Marshall brought down his gavel hard. The Senate was in session, and even Alice Longworth was stilled.

Senator Lodge, more than ever like a bumblebee gone white from too much – presidential pollen? – delivered the Foreign Relations Committee report on the treaty, with fourteen reservations, one for each of Wilson's famous Fourteen Points. Then Senator Harding rose to endorse the committee's hard work.

Jess thought W.G., as always, magnificent. He used all six of his famous gestures in the most natural way. The voice had enormous power. The arguments, whether good or not, thrilled Jess and the gallery. Even Alice Longworth rose and cheered him when he proclaimed, "It is my deliberate conviction that the League of Nations Covenant as negotiated at Paris either creates a super-government of the nations which enter it or it will prove the colossal disappointment of the ages. I cannot believe this republic ought to sanction it in either case."

As the hours passed, Jess grew wearier and wearier, but the Duchess would not budge until the thing was over. At shortly before eleven in the evening the mellifluous Senator Underwood, a rival to Hitchcock for the minority leadership, proposed an unconditional resolution to ratification.

The Vice President then asked for a vote; and the President's league was briskly defeated at the request of the President, who would not accept any of Lodge's handiwork. Then Lodge, master now in his own house, asked for a vote on Wilson's own treaty, *without* reservations. Since all the Republicans save one voted against the League, the war between Lodge and Wilson was over; and Lodge was the victor.

As the gallery cheered, the Duchess rose and applauded the

Senate as if she had just watched the curtain fall on a particularly satisfying play. Then she and Jess pushed their way through the mob to the rotunda, where Harding was waiting for them.

"We've just had an invitation," he said.

"You go. I'm going home." The Duchess was firm. "My ankles are killing me."

"Well, I guess I did wrong by accepting Alice Longworth's invitation to go over to their house for a late-night supper."

Jess knew that Mrs. Longworth's refusal to invite Mrs. Harding to her house on any non-poker occasion deeply rankled. The Duchess's first reaction was shock. "Why now?" she asked.

Harding pretended to misunderstand. "Because we've all missed our supper. And since she's the colonel of our battalion, she wants to feed her troops."

"Well, if it makes her happy," was the Duchess's dour comment. As they started across the rotunda, Senator Lodge, at the head of what looked to be a parade of admirers, stopped to shake Harding's hand. "That was a superb speech, Senator."

"I hope it didn't do any harm." W.G. was his usual genial modest self.

"No. Only good."

Jess was breathing hard now: too much history.

"I have never been through anything like this before," said Lodge; then frowned. "No. The fight to annex the Philippines was almost as bad." He turned to Senator Wadsworth. "I remember right after that vote I met your father-in-law, John Hay, on this very spot, and how pleased he was, we all were." Lodge then swept past them.

The Duchess, possibly eager to annoy Mrs. Longworth, insisted that Jess come, too.

By the time the Hardings arrived at M Street, the small house was crowded. There were the irreconcilables: Senators Borah, Reed, Brandegee, Moses; and the reservationists, Freylinghuysen and the Wadsworths; and the reservationist Democrat, the blind Senator Gore, and his wife.

"Well, that speech was a humdinger!" Folksily, Alice greeted W.G. "You must be very, very proud, Mrs. Harding."

"Oh, I've heard Warren do better."

"But never in a better cause." Jess stared with wonder at all the stuffed animal heads on the walls – game shot by Theodore Roosevelt. Alice, who never remembered Jess nor tried to, saw him staring up at the huge head of a mightily antlered moose. "I'm putting Wilson's head right next to Father's bull moose."

Nick Longworth had not been at the Senate. He had dined at home with his French brother-in-law. Now he greeted the guests with the announcement "The cook's gone home."

"We've got a great many eggs," said Alice.

"*I'll* cook them." The Duchess marched off to the kitchen, leaving the Colonel of Death's Battalion to savor her victory in the drawing room, her chosen battlefield, among her chosen troops.

Brandegee toasted Alice, who said, "We'll do this again in March, when the final vote comes due – like a foreclosure or whatever they call it, on a mortgage, on Mr. Wilson."

Although Jess was not quite sure why the whole process had to be repeated, it was now clear that the President had lost his League and W.G. had got the country's attention in a big way. He couldn't wait for the next day's newspapers. Meanwhile, W.G. sat between Nick and Borah on a sofa, and seemed unusually content.

In August, the all-powerful Penrose had asked Harding if he'd like to be president, and W.G. had said, characteristically, that as he couldn't run for two offices at once, he preferred to keep the one he had: he'd file for the Senate. This had only excited the fat man all the more. Ohio was the key to the election, and Harding was Ohio's favorite son. After Wilson's imperial approach to war and peace, the country needed a rest, a return to the noble good quiet McKinley sort of man. Later that month, during a hot night on the verandah of the house in Marion, W.G. had discussed the matter with Daugherty and Jess. After the Duchess had taken her ailing kidney to bed, W.G. had given all the reasons why he could not be nominated, starting with everyone's favorite, General Leonard Wood. Daugherty had dismissed the great paladin with the single word "Epaulets."

"What does that mean?" asked Jess.

W.G. answered him. "Harry figures that no man who was a general in the war is going to get the vote of any man who wasn't a general." W.G. chuckled. "Could be. But Wood's got all the rich Easterners behind him, and they can usually go out and buy you the job."

"Not this time." Daugherty was positive. "He's got no following. Nobody likes him. Everybody likes you."

"Well, a lot of people here in Marion and over in Washington Court House think the world of me, but I have a feeling there are a lot of places out in Nevada where nobody gives a damn." W.G. chewed tobacco comfortably; then spit over the railing in a perfect arc.

Jess envied him this necessary skill in dealing with the plain folks. For years, Jess had tried to chew tobacco but his natural tendency to salivate too much had ruined more than one shirt, including several not his own.

"Then there's Governor Lowden." Harding dried his lips with the back of his hand. "He's got Illinois, and he's rich."

"Too rich. His wife's a Pullman. Not even the Republican Party is going to vote for anybody with railroad money."

"There was Lincoln," observed W.G. mildly.

"He was just a hired hand, a railroad lawyer. Lowden married the boss's daughter. So that leaves you."

"You know, Harry, even in my daydreams, I've never seen myself as another Lincoln." W.G. was droll.

Daugherty laughed. "I'll tell you a secret. Nobody else has either. But I'll tell you another secret. This country doesn't want another Lincoln, ever again. Why, he killed half a million men, and started up all this darky problem. No, sir, we praise Lincoln but we won't elect anybody like that ever again. Same goes for Wilson. Folks want a quiet time now, to make some money."

There was a long silence broken only by the sound of W.G.'s rocking chair. Then an owl hooted in a nearby tree, and Jess shuddered; owls terrified him with their fixed staring eyes and sharp murderous beaks that could slit your throat.

"I suppose," said Harding at last, "we should start moving around and getting the idea talked about. Outside Ohio, there's no way I'm going to be anybody's first choice, but if I'm everybody's *second* choice, I'll make it." Jess was awed by W.G.'s simple clarity. Even Daugherty, who preferred to do the talking, was struck. He turned in his chair to face Harding, who was now stretching his shirt-sleeved arms. "But the only problem is, what do you do when you're there, and there's no war?"

"Well, you throw out the first baseball of the season."

"That's seemly," Harding nodded, "and enjoyable. But what else in a quiet time?"

"Pray that it *is* a quiet time. Life's full of surprises. Look at Wilson. He never expected to be a war president or, maybe, a president of the world. So now the man's a wreck. But every so often history just goes to sleep. Let's hope we hit one of those long snoozes."

"And let the folks make money." Jess added his two bits.

"If I didn't know everybody in public life, I'd say I wasn't big enough for the job, wasn't worthy." Harding stood up. "But I do know everybody, so – why not?"

"Good night, Mr. President," said Daugherty, as Harding opened the screen-door to the house. Harding looked back and smiled; then he shook his handsome head and let the screen-door slam shut behind him.

Now Warren Gamaliel Harding listened respectfully to Senator Borah talk about Senator Borah while Senator Gore, a young-looking man with white hair, ate scrambled eggs with a fork that he held in his right hand while his left forefinger made sure that the eggs were securely on the fork. But how, Jess wondered, fascinated, could he tell so accurately just where his mouth was if he couldn't see the fork? Of all the Democratic senators, Wilson hated Gore the most. While of the President, Gore had said, "He finds it disturbing if you look above the third button on his waistcoat."

W.G. regarded the dark-eyed Mrs. Gore as the most attractive of the senatorial wives, but then she was supposed to be part-Indian. Jess amused himself, thinking of the two together, one part-Indian and the other part-Negro. It was a good thing that the public was never let in on half the secrets Jess Smith had found out, starting back in Washington Court House and ending, for now, right here at the heart of the United States Senate.

Alice Longworth proposed a toast. "Down with Wilson." Everyone drank except Senator Gore, who continued his delicate balancing act. Of course he had been blind since the age of ten and he had had a lot of practice.

4

In the large picture-window of Pamela Smythe's "palatial home" above Franklin Avenue stood the greatest of living writers, Elinor Glyn, back to the setting sun. Reverently, Mrs. Smythe presented Caroline to the author of *Three Weeks,* and Caroline nearly curt-seyed to the robust woman, swathed, like a sofa, in a purple velvet cloak that somewhat muted the turbulent masses of a glorious red wig that had been parted down the middle of an ursine head out of which peered the intelligent features of a green-eyed Irish girl, somewhat long in the tooth.

"Emma Traxler!" The voice was deep and convincingly upper-class, unlike that of Mrs. Smythe, whose diphthongs occasionally suggested sea-caressed Liverpool.

Caroline's hand was engulfed in bear-paws, as bright small intel-ligent eyes stared down into hers. Task as a hostess accomplished, Mrs. Smythe welcomed other guests, who always arrived as the sun set, dined in the first hour of darkness and then, after an hour of charades, hurried home to bed in order to be able to present rested features to the benignly slanted early-morning sun.

"Miss Glyn. What a . . . pleasure. For me." Caroline had selected the exact polite word. But then, from the human point of view, Hollywood was absolute pleasure. Real Russian grand dukes were to be seen alongside self-invented Russian grand dukes, and the con-men were usually more convincing than the Romanovs, thus explaining, Caroline had duly noted, the revolution. In any case, jammed together in a relatively small place, some of the most exotic creatures in the world could be found, panning furiously for movie-gold.

"Mrs. Kingsley tells me you have never been more superb! And according to *Kine Weekly, Flower of the Night* will gross three million domestically, and with your fans in poor little England alone . . . *ma foi!*"

Caroline mumbled modestly. Out of the corner of her eye she saw Tim talking to a pretty girl whose famous three-not-two names she could never remember. She did know, as the world knew, that the girl was being groomed by Famous Players-Lasky to replace Mary Pickford, who, that day, had been married to her longtime lover and current partner in United Artists, Douglas Fairbanks, who had recently built an already-fabled – that is, publicized – love-nest for the two of them on one of the wilder Beverly Hills.

"I would so much like to *create* for you." Miss Glyn was now all business. "You are that rare thing, a woman *d'un certain âge* . . . you speak French, of course?"

"Oh, as little as possible."

But Elinor Glyn was now in full high-priestess flow. "A woman of a certain age," she translated, helpfully, "but with allure. What I call, for want of a richer, more specific – for obvious reasons – word, 'it'!"

"It?"

"It."

"It." Caroline offered Miss Glyn her Madonna smile instead of a contract at Traxler Productions. "I would have thought that only women of childbearing age could have 'it.'"

"It is not a reference to menstrual flow." Miss Glyn was sharp and, to Caroline's delight, earthy. "But to that innate seductive power that some women are born with – like you, Miss Traxler – and that other women must acquire the hard way like me . . ."

"Surely not too hard," Caroline murmured.

Miss Glyn was not used to listening. "Nay," she said, as if the word were in everyday use and not a blossom plucked from the pages of a vivid fiction, "even a woman of my essential substance, willful, commanding, yes, in appearance and, perhaps, oh, the tiniest bit in real life, can still, when the moon shimmers in the sky and there is a scent of orange blossom upon the air, cause a dashing young Romeo to fall to his knees in an ecstasy of desire . . ."

"The position, I hope, is only temporary . . ."

"Romeo must *start* on his knees. The rest depends on – Kismet."

"And *it.*"

"He would not have been on his knees in the first place without *it.*" Miss Glyn was patient. "Now I hear Mrs. Hulbert's Mary Queen of Scots photo-play is a real revulsh."

"Let us say," Emma Traxler was now her legendary compassionate generous self, "that there are problems."

"I am a descendant of Mary Queen of Scots." Miss Glyn played the bold English card, which never failed to impress Americans, particularly the ones who worked in movies. On the other hand, the real thing was often viewed with suspicion like the young Austrian archduke who had just entered the room. Chinless, in the best Habsburg tradition, Leopold was thought to be inauthentic by half the hostesses of the Hollywood Hills.

"How they must fear you at Windsor, those German usurpers."

"They are Stuart, too, though less than I. Frankly, I would like to have, as they say out here, a 'crack' at Mary. Of course, I'm under contract to Famous Players, but you could always lend yourself to them . . ."

"Or they you to us."

"Alas, not now. Anon, perhaps. You see, they are capitalizing mercilessly upon my name, particularly Mr. DeMille, who is truly salacious, don't you think?"

"He goes as far . . ."

"One ought not, ever, to be too obvious in appealing to the fiercer emotions. Certainly the man, the hero, the actor must always be smiling and yet, of course, not leering like the village idiot. He should smile with good cheer, and should he through – what shall I call it? – not *it* – *youthful heedlessness* make a mistake he does not do so deliberately."

"As in life."

"Yes," said Miss Glyn, not listening, her eyes on the beautiful figure of Mabel Normand, one of the few truly amusing as well as erotic stars in the movies. A Boston girl, Normand was considerably sharper than the usual bovine American star. She was known to play jazz on the set, while her addiction to cocaine had given, as Tim had observed, a new meaning to the phrase "powder-room."

Someone was now at the piano, playing New Orleans jazz, and Mabel Normand, all in silver, kept the beat with her whole body; and electrified the room.

"I'm writing a series of little books, *The Elinor Glyn System of Writing*. In due course, I shall deal with photo-play writing, but first I must master this extraordinary medium, which Mr. Lasky won't give me time to do as he is so busy having me pose with Mr. DeMille and whatever tart they happen to be promoting. How I long to do *Three Weeks* again, properly! To bring true sensuality to the screen with the kind of accuracy Mr. DeMille is incapable of, particularly when it comes to showing our aristocracy as they really are."

"I know Lord Curzon." Caroline delivered the knockout blow.

"How?" Miss Glyn was astonished. It was well known that Miss Glyn had had an eight-year affair with the onetime viceroy of India, and that he had then married a Mrs. Alfred Duggan, leaving Miss Glyn to read the news of his remarriage in the *Times*.

"London, I think. I can never remember where I meet people, do you?"

"In the case of so great a personage . . ."

"But that's even worse. For me, anyway. If one has heard a great deal of the . . . the personage *before* one meets him, then it is all a muddle between what one has heard of him and what he is actually like. Anyway, everyone knows the Leiters . . ."

Miss Glyn sighed her relief. "The American Wife," she intoned, as if it were a movie title card. "Yes, of course. So tragic her death. Is it true what they say of Mrs. Hulbert and your president?"

"What do they say?" The enchantingly unworldly Emma now took over from the tough-as-nails Caroline. "And who are they?"

"Rumors. Purloined letters. A passionate affair that almost brought to ruins the Ship of State upon the rocks of mad and unbridled desire in Bermuda."

Caroline listened in awe as Elinor Glyn dictated to her a page of romantic conjecture. When she had finished, the lovers alone on Bermuda's pink coral strand, it was Emma not Caroline who said, shyly, "I do hope you're right. I hope they were able to seize some happiness. They say she was very attractive then."

"No trace of *it* now," was authority's verdict.

At dinner Caroline sat next to the most attractive of the men, William Desmond Taylor, an English director of her own age. Across the table, Tim was flanked by Mabel Normand and the three-named young girl who had appeared in Taylor's recent movie *Jenny, Be Good* Although the press had predicted that she would never take the place of Mary Pickford, she and the movie were praised. "Did you go to the wedding?" Caroline asked the question of the day.

Taylor shook his head. "To my surprise I wasn't asked, even though Mary and I have known each other forever. I used to direct her, not very well, I'm afraid . . ."

"Perhaps that's why you weren't invited."

Taylor laughed. "If that were to be a law out here, none of us would go anywhere. No. Astrology determined the day and the hour and probably the guest list, too."

"Astrology?"

Taylor nodded. The Negro butler said, pointedly, "You better tuck into that guinea hen while it's hot."

"Thank you." Taylor was as polite to butlers as to stars: the perfect extra man, he'd been called. "Well, at Doug's request, Mary got her divorce from Owen Moore some place in Nevada, on a good day . . ."

"Isn't she Catholic?"

"Only when it suits her. Then Doug's astrologist told him that he could begin a new – a *fabulous* new life – thirteen days after the Ides of March, which is today, March twenty-eighth, 1920."

"Do you believe in astrology?"

"Only when it suits me." They laughed.

Caroline congratulated him on being elected president of the new Screen Directors Guild and he said, politely, that without Tim's help he would have lost. As they spoke of their common business, she noticed that he was attractive to her, something that men, by and large, were not any longer. Tim had become less lover than younger brother in a relationship that had always been based upon a mutual fascination with the telling of stories through enlarged moving pictures. She was addicted now to this shadowy fictional life; and he was in love with it. She had noticed that the few times, lately, that he had found her physically attractive was after a long day in the cutting room, looking at Emma Traxler, whose haunting autumnal beauty aroused him in a way that the forty-four-year-old Caroline Sanford did not in life.

Caroline was pleasantly amazed at the tranquillity – or was it numbness? – with which she had accepted what seemed to be the end of the affair. It was rather as if she were watching a photo-play, starring Emma Traxler, whose genius as an actress was never, never to surprise an audience. They wanted her noble and mag-nanimous and brave, and she gave them exactly what they wanted with, as Marion Davies would say, bells on. What Caroline Sanford wanted was something of a puzzle. Naturally, she wanted to watch the movie to the end; and perhaps gasp once or twice into a damp handkerchief in the dark as, on the screen, Emma strode off, res-olutely, through machine-made mist, across the moors, which meant from the first hole to the second hole of the Burbank Golf Club. But after the lights came on, what next? Golf?

"I play golf at least once a week," Taylor was saying, his words matching her thoughts, rather the way dreams, at their end, adjust so neatly to the real world's noises. "Do you play?"

"Not for years. I must take it up again. I have a membership – or Tim does – at Burbank." Tim was plainly smitten with Taylor's *Jenny, Be Good* girl. Caroline wondered how many times he had been unfaithful – a word that made no sense if one lacked all reli-gious faith. She herself had said no to quite a number of young men whose interest in her, she suspected, had more to do with her power to project their images onto a screen than her own faded allure. Perhaps she should try someone her own age, she thought, looking at William Desmond Taylor, who gave every impression of being, in his bright English way, the man – as well as director – for her.

"I thought your death scene wonderful," he said in a low voice, as if there was already some subtle intimacy between them. "Your eyes, in the close shot – and the way the light fades from them, to darkness . . ."

Caroline and Emma simultaneously knew ecstasy. This was what being "understood" meant. "Tim and I quarrelled for days over that scene. To die with eyes open or shut. So we did it both ways. My way won, I'm happy to say. How vain," Caroline remembered in time to laugh, "one becomes."

"Hardly vanity. It's a business. The things you do well you should be grateful for. Looks, too. I was an actor for years before I started directing. You must build on what's there. . . ." Happily, they talked shop.

After dinner, Caroline and Taylor sat in Mrs. Smythe's Tudor drawing room, and she confided to him her difficulties with Mary Queen of Scots. He knew, he said, an excellent writer. He himself would love to direct her in so distinguished a film – if, of course, Tim was not interested. She said, quite accurately, that Tim had never been much interested in historical studies of a romantic nature. Taylor's handsome graying head nodded thoughtfully over the pre-Prohibition brandy that the butler had brought him. "We could make it at Doug's studio. Doug *and* Mary's studio." He smiled; the eyes were boyish, a quality Caroline did not highly esteem in men but in Taylor's case it was understandable as he had made a number of highly successful movies about such bucolic American figures as Huckleberry Finn and Tom Sawyer and other lads from the nation's not so distant Arcadian past. "We could release through United Artists," he said, staring at her mouth.

Caroline felt herself flushing. "I have," she whispered, erotically, she hoped, "a four-picture contract through Traxler Productions with Lasky, and any loan-out arrangement of Emma Traxler must be agreed to by Mr. Zukor." Honeyed words, she knew.

"Tom Ince's Associated Producers Incorporated could, through Mr. Zukor, arrange a loan-out against a fifth Lasky picture and then, with me, we could set up a separate unit at Pickford-Fairbanks with distribution through United Artists at fifteen percent less than Mr. Zukor charges for a Paramount release." Was ever woman in such manner wooed? thought Caroline, besotted. If only Elinor Glyn could hear the real language of courtship, Hollywood-style.

Mabel Normand jittered over to them, toes turned inward, hands outward, her trademark. "Deal me a card? I'm strung out.

333

Hi, Miss Traxler." Mabel spoke rapidly in a manner that Caroline was quite used to. Cocaine-users were edgy and in constant need of the sudden rush of energy to the brain which – Caroline had experimented – lasted no more than a quarter of an hour. Morphine was more benign and dreamy, and preferred by Washington's ladies while opium was the stuff of dreams in Paris. Caroline could easily have got used to opium; her half-brother André was a two-pipes-a-day man. But at this hazardous stage of her life she preferred her senses unclouded.

She noticed that Taylor was displeased by Mabel Normand's request. "No cards for you, my darling." He opened his cigarette case, and she removed a gold-tipped black cigarette. Was that how it was done? Caroline wondered. Mabel frowned, and hurried away. Caroline was aware that Taylor was watching her intently.

"Yes," said Caroline. "I understand."

"You don't understand how tough it is to get her off the stuff. Mabel!" he called after the star, who was now at the entrance hall.

"What?" She turned at the door.

". . . Be good." She was gone. "'Mabel, be good' is a private joke, and not much of one, I suppose." He looked suddenly attractively haggard. In the popular movies that Mabel had made with Chaplin as her co-director, her name had often been in the title: *Mabel's Busy Day, Mabel's Married Life, Mabel's New Job.* Now *Mabel's Cocaine Habit* was becoming a problem.

"There are cures, aren't there?"

"For some people. Not for others. Like drink."

"I must get to bed at the usual early hour." Caroline was on her feet. Most elegantly, Taylor kissed her hand.

"No!" a voice tolled. "For the full romantic effect, you must kiss the *palm* of her hand." Elinor Glyn loomed over them.

"Perhaps, Miss Glyn, the full romantic effect is inappropriate." Caroline glittered from the sheer force of Emma's habit.

"It is always appropriate in the best society."

"Oh, what worlds you have seen, Miss Glyn, beyond my wildest daydreams."

"I'll ring you," said William Desmond Taylor.

Caroline was mildly disturbed that Tim was not in the least

jealous. They sat in her sitting room with its view of Griffith's Babylon by moonlight. "I wouldn't," said Tim, "let Miss Glyn near Mary Queen of Scots."

"Of course not." Caroline looked at the three photo-play scripts that she had already acquired on the subject. The worst, predictably, had been Mrs. Hulbert's, but then Mary had only used the script as an excuse for long conversations with Caroline about herself, with the odd request for a small loan. The collapse of President Wilson had disturbed her far less than one of her son's recent financial misadventures. It had been with relief that Emma Traxler had, gently, cast her off. But not before Caroline had acquired sufficient material for a movie about a woman of enormous charm and perfect self-absorption who throws away every possibility in life because she has never noticed that anyone else exists.

Caroline turned on the gas-fire. The night was damp and cold. "I'm getting arthritic," she heard herself say. "I must go to your Bimini Baths. Where are they again?"

"Third and Vermont." Tim wore only underwear, the thin body looked discouragingly boyish. Taylor was as elegantly thin but hardly boyish. "It's built over an artesian spring. You know, he dopes."

"Who what?" Caroline pretended not to understand, as she poured tea from a Thermos bottle prepared by Héloise, who had taken to Hollywood's hours like the proverbial chicken.

"Bill Taylor. Mabel Normand says he was the one who got her on cocaine."

"Surely she was born with a . . . sniffer, or whatever they call it, in her nose, like a silver spoon."

"Are you thinking about him for *Mary*?"

"Yes. After all, he's had so much success in period. Like *Huckleberry Finn*," she added for her own amusement. "We could do *Mary Queen of Scots* on the Mississippi on a raft."

"I've got a rough cut of the Wilson footage."

"I must talk to Blaise." Mention of Wilson reminded her of neglected duties, of her displaced if not lost self, Caroline Sanford. Of the Washington *Tribune*. Of the coming election.

"Are you interested?" Tim was drinking quite a lot of whisky, she noticed.

"No. Not really. The paper is well run without me. But we must take some sort of position. Blaise is bound to be far too Republican. I'll be –"

"I meant in the Wilson footage."

"Oh, that." She sounded more vague than she intended.

"You're not. I'm off to bed."

"No." Emma Traxler made a weary reappearance on the scene. "I'm sorry. I've had a hard day. The Griffith studios aren't available after all."

Tim stopped at the connecting door to his suite. "Work's always hard if you're not used to it."

"What an unusual observation to make to me," said Caroline Sanford, the first self-made woman newspaper publisher in the world. "I am supposed to be an inspiration to every suffragette in the land."

"Your face . . . ?"

"My newspaper."

"Good night." He was gone. Habit, thought Caroline, counted for more than love. Could she do without the habit of Tim? As she stared at the dark row of prancing elephants in the gray moonlight, the musical horn of a foreign-made car sounded below her in Sunset Boulevard, like a motif in a romantic *opéra-bouffe*. But what was Emma Traxler but a figure from Offenbach? Now in danger of turning into one from Strauss, the Marschallin. She had better turn back into her true self, if there was such a thing left. As if to remind herself of that true self, she picked up the latest stack of pages from her daughter, an excited testimonial to Caroline's perfect failure as a mother.

Apparently, Tim's new picture would be picketed by anti-Communists, while Emma Traxler was on a list of suspect Americans. Emma Sanford wrote page after page about the wonders of living in a free country while exulting, simultaneously, in all the publications that her group had managed to shut down as well as teachers fired, politicians defeated, labor organizers imprisoned. The child was mad. Was the country, too?

Caroline had no real sense of the new United States or, indeed, of the old. She had known the most rarefied of American society, the Hearts of Henry Adams; and she had delighted in the District of Columbia and, most lately, in the exciting unreality – even sur-reality – of Hollywood; but what, finally, did she know of the actual Americans, starting with her daughter and son-in-law? Were there many others like them out there, with lurid dreams of absolute conformity to some rustic ideal? True, the sometime peasant nation had finally encountered civilized old Europe at last, and Europe had offered it war and revolution and Bolshevism. No wonder the real and would-be peasants were distressed. But what was the *true* origin of their mindless panic? What were Americans afraid of? She wished Henry Adams were alive to explain it all. But then in lieu of his comforting presence and wisdom, she tore up her daughter's letter, and threw the pieces into a wastebasket. She felt nothing at all about her own child. But then Mlle. Souvestre had always said that when a woman's daughter is no longer a child but fully grown and married, the two women, even though one be demi-creatrix of the other, are wise to part.

Caroline finished her tea and went into the bedroom so seldom visited now by Tim. Plainly the time had come to renew herself; this time with William Desmond Taylor. After all, the clock never ceased to tick even when she was not aware of it. Somehow or other, most of the day was now quite gone.

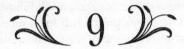

9

1

Jess enjoyed the bright April sun rather more than he did the New York *Times* editorial that he was reading. "Harding is eliminated. Even if his name is presented to the convention . . ." Jess felt the saliva beginning to drool down his chin; he wiped it off with the *Times* and hoped he hadn't smudged his face. At the far end of the front porch, the candidate himself was seated, talking to the folks who wandered by. All in all, the last two primaries had been discouraging. Harding had carried Ohio as a native son, but even so, General Wood with all of his unfair millions of dollars had acquired – bought was more like it – nine of the state's forty-eight delegates, and, unkindest blow of all, Daugherty himself had failed to be elected a delegate.

A week later, at Daugherty's insistence, Harding had entered the Indiana primary. Wood, Johnson and Lowden had all run ahead of W.G., who managed to win only two of fifty-six counties. Jess knew the reason. There was, simply, no money for Harding. The rich bankers and Roosevelt men were financing Wood, and Mrs. Lowden was financing Governor Lowden. Jess and his co-chairman Daugherty had raised barely a hundred thousand dollars against all those millions, and that was why the New York *Times* could now write magisterially, ". . . everyone will know that he is an impossible candidate." Although W.G. had been deeply distressed by Indiana and spoke, in public, of his own impossibility as a candidate, in private, he was surprisingly serene. "This will all come my way, barring divine intervention," he had told Daugherty and Jess, while the Duchess, reinforced by more astrological bulletins from Madame Marcia, agreed.

Harding's strategy was to be himself. He had particularly ingratiated himself with Lowden by promising not to go after any of his delegates, and the grateful Lowden had reciprocated. Harding had done some simple adding and subtracting and come to the conclusion that if no candidate could be nominated on the first ballot, everyone's number two would win on the hundredth, or however many ballots were needed. So he would see to it that he was everyone's second favorite. Daugherty had accepted the strategy, and the two men had quietly crisscrossed the country, ingratiating themselves to everyone and disturbing no one.

"Jess." Jess put down the *Times* and there, to his horror, was Carrie Phillips. She was elegantly got up, he noted, with the eye of a fellow dry-goods dealer and arbiter of fashion.

"Carrie Phillips," Jess whispered so that W.G., whose back was to them at the far end of the porch, would not hear or, God forbid, the Duchess, who was inside busy telephoning, her principal activity these days.

"I thought you weren't coming round here now." Jess's rocking chair was at the porch's edge, and he was able to lean over so that their heads were practically touching.

"Oh? I was just out for a stroll, that's all. It's a free country."

Jess knew that a "final" exchange of letters had passed between Carrie and W.G. For one thing, Jim now knew everything. For another, though the press had as yet shown no special interest in Harding's campaign, there was always the danger that an ambitious reporter might do some snooping before the convention and what with everyone in Marion knowing everyone else's business, W.G.'s image of a good family man might easily be altered to . . . to the Satyr of the Chautauqua, thought Jess wildly.

"I just wanted to sneak by and say hello. That's all. See? I'm on tiptoe." So, on tiptoe, Carrie approached W.G., who was now alone in his rocker at the other end of the porch, reading not the *Times* editorial but the sports page. When he saw Carrie, he beamed. But

339

she put her finger to her lips and whispered something that caused him to lean forward, head lowered, hand clutching the porch rail. Now *their* heads were together; and Jess felt ill. What would Daugherty say? What would the Duchess do?

The Duchess said nothing at all, which was most ominous. Instead, she appeared in the doorway to the house and, for a long moment, glared at the adulterous couple. W.G., as if he had eyes in the back of his head, which indeed he may well have had when it came to his wife, sat back in his chair but did not turn around or otherwise acknowledge the appearance of the Duchess on the scene.

Carrie continued to talk in a low voice to W.G., ignoring the Duchess, as well as the feather-duster that suddenly came hurtling her way. Then the Duchess, now very red in the face, stepped back inside to collect a metal waste-basket, which she aimed with astonishing accuracy at Carrie, who leapt quickly to one side, while continuing her conversation with W.G., who was now looking back over his shoulder at the Duchess.

As Florence Kling Harding went back inside for more ammunition, Jess looked around to see who was watching this spectacle: several old citizens of Marion, used to such displays, and an unfamiliar well-dressed man, who stared in horror at this domestic scene. Jess prayed that he was not a newspaperman.

The Duchess returned, holding in her arms a four-legged piano stool whose swivel-seat was of considerable weight. With the strength, as it were, of ten, the Duchess hurled the homely piece of household furniture at Carrie. En route, the stool narrowly missed the handsome head of Ohio's famous and, literally, favorite son, and only by a ballet leap to the right did the golden adulteress avoid concussion. Overcome by *force majeure*, Carrie graciously blew a kiss at Harding, and sauntered down Mount Vernon Avenue, enjoying the spring sunshine. The triumphant Duchess withdrew. She had said not one word; nor had she any reason to when her actions were so eloquent.

With some dignity, Harding had got to his feet, and said, to his wife's back: "Florence, this is not becoming, not seemly at all."

Later that day Daugherty arrived in Marion, and Jess reported everything, as they sat in the bar of the newly restored Old Heidelberg, where whisky in teacups was available to regular customers in contravention of the Eighteenth Amendment that prevented the American citizen, whose fundamental charter assured him life, liberty and the pursuit of happiness, from drinking alcohol. Jess, who was not a constitutional scholar, did wonder, from time to time, how the U.S. could be, as everyone knew, the freest country on earth when there was a government busy prohibiting whatever it thought people shouldn't have. In Europe, it was said, the decadent old races were laughing at their recent saviors. Fortunately, every town had its Old Heidelberg, and Jess sipped at Scotch whisky from Canada, while Daugherty said, "We've got to get her – and *him* – out of town until after the convention. No!" The brown eye blinked fiercely while the blue eye was tranquil. "Until *after* the election."

"Him? W.G.?"

"No. No. Jim Phillips. He knows everything, and it beats me why Carrie keeps coming around like this unless . . ."

"They want to be paid off?"

Daugherty nodded. "Of course this'd come at a time when we've spent just about everything."

"What about Ned McLean?"

But Daugherty's active mind had moved on to other subjects. "Jake Hamon's worth a million to us down in Oklahoma. But his price is a third of the Navy oil lands, and I don't see how we can promise that."

Jess had been immensely impressed by the large loud Oklahoma oil man with his showy mistress and extravagant ways. But Jess had seen no reason to trust him; neither did Daugherty. "W.G.'s counting on a deadlock." Daugherty was thoughtful. "If Wood and Lowden get stuck they'll stay stuck and there's no compromise except W.G."

"Johnson?"

"Never. He's a red rag to the conservatives. But W.G. figures that maybe a quarter, maybe more, of the delegates will remember him from four years ago when he made that great speech to the convention. Or even from eight years ago when he nominated

Taft, and since he's stayed in touch with a lot of them, they'll . . . I wish I was as sure of this as he is."

Jess was puzzled. "I thought you was the one supposed to be charging him up?"

"That's the way he wants it to look. He's going to be all maidenly and blushy and modest with a lot of 'I'm not worthy,' while I'm the keen, hard-driving manager who seems to be prodding him, like a bullock home at sundown. 'Course he's the ideal middle-of-the-road candidate, which he thinks is what the country wants, and if that's so . . ."

"You think he'll make it?"

Daugherty shrugged. "How? All the money's with Wood and Lowden, and the Republican Party's the money party. Jess, you remember Nan Britton, don't you?"

Jess nodded. All Marion knew how, even as a very young girl, Dr. Britton's daughter Nan had developed a crush on the handsome editor of the Marion *Star*. She had never made any secret of the fact that she used to cut out pictures of W.G. from the newspapers for her scrap-book; and she would even moon about the Mount Vernon house, to W.G.'s embarrassment and the Duchess's rage. After Dr. Britton's death, Nan had moved to New York City; and Jess assumed that by now she was married and settled down.

"She's up in Chicago. She's got a job as a secretary, and she's living with her sister Elizabeth."

"Nice-looking girls, both of them. I suppose they're all married and . . . and grown up," Jess added, vaguely. He felt the saliva begin to form in his mouth. He took out his handkerchief, ready to mop rather than spray, a habit that maddened Daugherty.

"Elizabeth is married." Daugherty withdrew a slip of paper from his pocket. "To a man called Willits. He plays the fiddle or something for the Chicago Opera Company. Nan's living with them. Here's their address."

"Why?"

Daugherty finished his tea and stared, moodily, at the travelling salesman across the smoky tavern. "W.G. has been carrying on with Nan for . . . I don't know how long. I found out some time in 1917 when he got her a job as a secretary in New York and used to sneak up there to see her in these different hotels, where in one of them . . ." Daugherty stopped. "Well, that's neither here nor there."

"Carrie *and* Nan?" Jess, unable to be active with his own beloved Roxy, was filled with envy. On the other hand, with the Duchess for a wife, a man deserved some solace elsewhere. "Is she making trouble?" Jess understood blackmail well enough.

"No. Not yet anyway. She's in love with him . . ."

"Is he in love with her?"

"What a question!" Daugherty looked at Jess with such disgust that, reflexively, Jess dried his lower lip just to make certain that he himself was not disgusting. "How do I know? What do I care? We're politicians, for God's sake. We love the people, the ones who vote, anyway. All I know is W.G.'s still sweet on her. He writes her letters."

"Letters." An alarm bell went off in Jess's head.

"Yes. Letters."

"Like President Wilson did to Mrs. Peck?"

"These are a bit homier, Jess." Daugherty was sardonic. "W.G. swears there's nothing compromising, but hell, any letter to a girl half your age, telling about hotel rooms and times and places, is going to look real bad."

"You want me to buy the letters?"

Daugherty shook his head. "No. She won't sell them. I've tried. I think she thinks someday the Duchess will die or disappear and she'll marry W.G. But that's not the problem." Daugherty gave Jess an envelope which, from its size and heft, contained currency. "I want you to go to Chicago, and give her this money."

"So then she *is* blackmailing him."

"No. Child support. For their daughter, born last October."

Jess stared at Daugherty, as though he'd just made a complicated joke that Jess was too dense to comprehend. Should he ask for the punch line again? "Does . . . does W.G. admit that it's his?"

Daugherty nodded. "He helps out all he can."

"But the convention's in Chicago." Jess was getting panicky.

"Convenient, isn't it?"

*

On Sunday, June 6, 1920, Jess found himself for what was now the third time in the small parlor of the Willitses' four-room apartment – 6103 Woodlawn Avenue at the corner of Chicago's Sixty-first Street. He had memorized the address.

Nan was alone and weeping. "I waited and waited at the Englewood Station, but he never got off." Even now, with her red eyes and nose, she was an attractive woman. There was no sign of the baby, who was being boarded with a nurse nearby.

"Well, that's why I'm here. W.G. was very upset. But the Duchess was with him every minute and there was no way he could get off at Englewood. But he sent me on to tell you he'd try tomorrow about this time, which is Sunday, so your sister –"

"Oh. I can get them to go to church or something." Nan dried her eyes. Then she picked up a bamboo-framed photograph of herself holding a baby. "There's Elizabeth Ann," she said, "taken on the day she turned six months. He won't see her, you know."

"Well . . ." was the best that Jess could do.

"She is the spitting image of him, isn't she? I just pray he'll go over and see her or maybe I'll take her out in the park like I usually do and he can sort of stroll by in a casual way and say hello. What's happening at the convention?"

"It don't start till Tuesday and they won't be voting till Friday. Nobody's locked it up yet. I suspect the thing will be decided in smoke-filled rooms." Jess, like most of the country, quite fancied the phrase, attributed widely by the press to Daugherty, who had given an interview to the effect that if the convention was deadlocked early, the Senate magnates would then decide, in a smoke-filled room, who was to get the nomination.

As of today, the *Literary Digest* poll showed Harding seeded sixth place in the hearts of his fellow Republicans, while according to the number of pledged delegates at the convention, Harding was fourth, with Wood, Lowden and Johnson each far ahead of him. It was a very long shot on which Jess had made only very small bets. Daugherty was busy but pessimistic. W.G. was oddly relaxed, as if he knew something others did not, while the Duchess was convinced that the stars had already made their choice. The previous week, Madame Marcia had been emphatic, and the Duchess kept repeating: "Trine aspect to the moon in the sign of Aries."

"I've been reading how he's stopped smoking and drinking entirely."

"Well, that's the Duchess. She doesn't want any photographs of him with a cigar or, worse, a cigarette, which is what lounge-lizards smoke, so he just chews tobacco when no one's looking. Chewing don't show in a picture." But Nan wasn't listening. She was at a tall sideboard, where, among the dishes, there were stacks of newspaper cuttings of W.G.. "I think he's put on a little too much weight here. But *here,* in the *Delineator,* he looks wonderful. That was taken when he was on Chautauqua, and I was staying down the road at a hotel where . . ."

"Dearie?" The voice was low, and entirely familiar to both of them. Jess jumped to his feet while Nan ran to open the door. There stood Senator Harding, who, when he saw Jess, stepped quickly into the room before Nan could embrace him. "I happened to be in the neighborhood," said W.G. in a voice so matter-of-fact that Jess, if he had not known better, might have thought that an Ohio senator was simply paying a proper visit to a constituent's daughter, currently domiciled out-of-state. "So I thought I'd drop in and see you and Elizabeth. At Judge Scofield's specific request, back in Marion."

"Elizabeth's gone out. For the day."

"Well, then I'd better be –"

"No. No. Do sit down. She'll be back any minute. I mean, she . . ."

Jess was overwhelmed. Not even Roxy had ever done so much acting on his behalf as Nan and W.G. himself were doing. As Jess crossed to the door, W.G. said, "I think they're all over at the Congress Hotel, at our headquarters. In the Florentine Room. Same room," he turned politely to Nan, "as Theodore Roosevelt used back in 1912."

Jess said good-by to the lovers, who ignored him.

The Florentine Room was a marvel of dark carved wood and gold-embossed leather and heavy metal chandeliers. Portraits of Harding hung on every wall, while refectory tables were covered with literature, buttons, straw hats. A dozen volunteers supervised the display, while Daugherty and the Duchess stood to one side of the main door, as if to protect themselves from a sudden horde of fans.

"Where's Warren?" was the Duchess's first question.

"I think he's in your suite at the La Salle. I've been over to the Coliseum." Jess had indeed visited the hall where the convention would take place, and he was much impressed by the latest acoustical sounding-boards at the back. "I also saw the suite you took in the Auditorium Hotel." He turned to Daugherty, anything to avoid the Duchess's hard blue stare. "Everything's set up there. What about here?"

"We've got forty rooms here," said the Duchess, "that's seven hundred and fifty dollars a day for ten days. Daugherty's spending money like it was water . . ."

"What else is it for now? We spend, and we elect . . ."

They were joined by George Christian, a hometown boy whom Harding had taken for a secretary. He was a dark intense capable young man of an old Marion family. "Well, we've got our people in every hotel where there's a delegation. All information on every delegate is kept up to date here at headquarters. We've got five hundred full-time organizers, and by next Friday we expect to have close to two thousand. We're just being real low-key, and cheery, and we sure hope you'll remember the Senator if there's a problem . . ."

At this moment the sound of male voices singing in unison drifted in from the lobby.

"My God," said the Duchess, "what's that?"

"You're tone-deaf, Duchess," said Daugherty. "That's the Republican Glee Club of Columbus. Every day this time they're going to sing their hearts out here on the mezzanine, all seventy-five of them. Now they're greeting . . ." Daugherty listened a moment and they all heard the mournfully sung phrase "Wabash far away." ". . . the Indiana delegation. Then, in the evenings, they're going around to all the hotels, where they'll serenade all the other candidates, building up good will."

"Trine of the moon," muttered the Duchess to herself. Then she said, aloud, "They say the price for Southern delegates is now five thousand dollars a head."

"That's for the ones on sale," Daugherty confirmed. "The committed come higher."

The chairman of the Republican National Committee entered the Florentine Room, followed by various members of the press. Will Hays was very young and, to Jess's critical eye, very ugly, with ears that stuck out, a pointed nose, no chin, and a somewhat mouse-like squeaking voice with a strong Indiana accent. He was supposedly neutral but everyone knew that he inclined to himself as the dark horse: he was a pet of the Senate cabal. "Somebody said the Senator was here." When Hays saw the Duchess, he gave her a rodentine smile and shook her hand. "Mrs. Harding, you tell the Senator anything we can do we'll do. The Credentials Committee is here in the hotel, in the annex, and if there's any hitch, we're rarin' to go."

"I'll tell him, Mr. Hays."

"How're the Southerners?" asked Daugherty.

Hays rolled his eyes most comically; and retreated. Jess stared at the poster of Warren Gamaliel Harding on the wall opposite him and wondered what would happen if the world knew that the noble-headed Roman senator was at present in bed with Nan Britton on the other side of Chicago.

2

The week was, for Jess Smith, one of perfect confusion. He was sent on numerous errands, often with envelopes of money for Southern delegates. W.G. held forth in the Florentine Room; he seldom smiled. Daugherty commanded his two thousand troops with great precision but to what end no one could say. Wood and Lowden were still the principal candidates and Harding was just one of a dozen horses, ranging from shadowy to Stygian darkness. Worst of all, a decision had to be made by Friday night whether or not he would file for re-election to the Senate. If he did not file before midnight, he would be unavailable for re-election. If he did file, he would, in effect, be declaring that he did not expect to be nominated for president. All week he had wanted to file for the Senate, while the Duchess was still under Madame Marcia's spell. Now, Friday, the day of the ballotting, *she* was urging him to file for the Senate while *he* was suddenly enigmatic.

Jess sat for a time in the gallery, with a palmetto fan which not only did not cool him when he used it but made him all the hotter for the energy he was expending. Everyone was in shirt sleeves. Below him, the state delegations were talking to one another so loudly that no one could hear the speakers who appeared, one by one, on the flying bridge, as it was called. Here they were requested by a large sign to stand inside a white circle so that the curved sounding-board behind them, in conjunction with a complicated bit of telephone equipment, could make any speaker audible to the thirteen thousand people in the auditorium. But no sound system could compete with the chatter of the delegates as they clustered about their state banners.

Suddenly there was a hush in the auditorium as the convention's chairman, Henry Cabot Lodge, old and waxen-looking, appeared on the flying bridge. He stood a moment looking out over the sweltering hall. At five o'clock in the afternoon, it must have been over a hundred degrees inside, thought Jess. But Lodge looked cool, and the voice was cool. "We shall begin," said Lodge, "to ballot the states."

There was a general sigh of relief and some applause. Jess got out his pad of paper and pencil. One by one, in alphabetical order, the states were named, and each state's spokesman answered with the state's vote. There were ten candidates. Some were native sons like Nicholas Murray Butler of New York and the governor of Massachusetts, Calvin Coolidge, filling in until the state's delegation could make a deal with the winner; others, like Herbert Hoover, were supported by disinterested enthusiasts. In fact, Hoover would have been the whole country's choice if the people could express a preference. As it was, the irrelevant galleries were filled with Hoover enthusiasts while the relevant floor was not.

It was clear that neither Wood nor Lowden was about to yield.

Wood ended the ballot with 287½ votes, Lowden with 211½. Johnson had 133½ votes and Harding 65½, 3½ votes fewer than New York's Professor Butler. When the vote was complete, Jess hurried from the auditorium to the Harding suite in the Auditorium Hotel. Daugherty himself let him in. Harding was stretched out on a sofa, a bottle of whisky and two glasses near to hand. He looked exhausted. Since he had not shaved that day, he looked pale as a ghost. George Christian was on the telephone. The Duchess was nowhere in sight.

"I guess I'd better file for the Senate." Harding spoke to himself as much as anyone.

Daugherty said, "You've got till midnight. Let's pray nobody finds out, because this thing isn't going to break our way today or maybe even tomorrow."

Harding poured himself a shot of whisky. The hand, Jess noticed, was steady. Christian put down the phone. "Well, the senators are going into action. They've united to stop Wood."

"How?" Daugherty had picked up a second telephone.

"They're putting the pressure on the favorite sons to go for Lowden."

"You can't have more'n *one* vice president." Daugherty was sour. Then he spoke into the telephone; and his voice was low and warm. "Might I, please, speak to Senator Penrose: this is Harry Daugherty in Chicago." The answer was a brisk negative. "Thank you very much, anyway," said Daugherty and put down the receiver.

"Penrose is home, dying," said Christian.

"Well, while he's busy dying, he's got a special line to the Pennsylvania delegation. And he's been using it. One word from him . . ." An aide put his head inside the door. "Senator Fall would like to speak to Senator Harding."

Harding leapt to his feet, straightened his clothes and combed his hair all in one rapid move.

"Tell him to come in."

Jess admired Fall very much. For one thing he looked like a real cowboy with his piercing eyes and full moustaches. He was also one of W.G.'s best friends in the Senate.

The two men shook hands warmly. Then Harding led Fall to the far end of the room, where they could not be overheard by anyone except Jess, and even Jess had a problem eavesdropping because both Daugherty and Christian were loudly working the telephones, giving orders, offering deals.

Fall was doing his best to cheer up W.G. "Borah and Johnson are threatening to bolt the party if either Wood or Lowden is nominated."

"Why?" W.G. looked uncharacteristically confused.

"They're concerned about all the money those two have been spending. Borah's particularly upset at the way Lowden's people bought up those Missouri delegates. He's saying the presidency shouldn't be bought."

"A bit late in the day for that," said W.G., an edge of sarcasm in his voice.

"Well, you know what they're like."

"I know this is good for us." W.G. smiled. But then the telephone rang. Christian answered it. The second ballot was completed. Lowden had picked up forty-eight votes and Wood only two. Harding had lost four and a half votes.

"Well, our fellow senators have done all that they could do, for now." Fall was not displeased. "Only New York could've started a stampede when Butler pulled out, and it didn't."

"I suppose," said W.G. suddenly, very much like his usual calm self, "we'll be here all night."

But before the end of the fourth ballot Jess watched with fascination as the senatorial cabal went into action on the stage of the auditorium. A dozen of the most powerful men in the country were holding, very much in the open, a crucial meeting. Wood's lead had refused to collapse, despite all their efforts, yet Lowden's votes showed no signs of serious erosion. Lodge stood on the flying bridge, as the fourth ballot was being tallied. Then he announced the outcome. Wood was within 177 votes of being nominated. There was cheering as the figures were read aloud. The senators, the true masters, or so they believed, of the convention, Senate, nation, had finally come to a conclusion. The solemn Senator Smoot walked up to the bridge and said, in a loud voice, "I move that the convention do now adjourn until tomorrow morning at ten o'clock." There was a startled silence. Then before there could be any vocal response from the delegates, Lodge said, "Those in favor of the motion to adjourn will signify it by saying 'aye.'"

There were a few ayes to be heard.

"Those opposed, 'no.'" Lodge looked more than ever as if he had been recently embalmed.

The nos nearly swept the chairman off the bridge. But Lodge, grasping the lectern hard, picked up his gavel and said, with a small smile, "The ayes have it and the convention is adjourned until tomorrow morning at ten o'clock."

That, thought Jess, with a shiver, was power at its most brutal. Also, Daugherty's prophecy was about to be fulfilled. Tonight the senators would select the next president, and no doubt the hotel rooms where they met would be filled with smoke. But would W.G. emerge from the smoke? Jess had been deeply disappointed by Harding's lack of appeal thus far. No one was passionately for him, unlike the supporters of Wood and Lowden and Johnson. On the other hand, no one was passionately against him. That had been Harding's strategy from the beginning. If the chieftains cancelled one another out, only he would be left, ready to pick up the crown.

Jess entered the Blackstone Hotel, where the major delegations were staying. Will Hays's suite was now the hub of the senatorial junta. As Jess crossed the crowded lobby to the elevators, he was stopped by a distinguished-looking man with a stack of pamphlets in one hand. "I can tell, sir, that you are a delegate . . ."

Jess was too flattered to say no. "Whaddaya know?" he asked reflexively.

"What do I know?" The man smiled. "I know that one of the candidates for president is a Negro, and I know that only disaster can befall a white country that elects a Negro . . ."

Jess realized that this must be Harding's nemesis, William Estabrook Chancellor, a professor at Wooster College in Ohio. Whenever Harding was a candidate for any office, Chancellor would appear, at his own expense, with his pamphlets and genealogies, and though he had done no great harm in the past,

Jess could see how he could make a terrible difference in a close race. Jess refused the pamphlet, and hurried to the elevators.

In the headquarters of the Ohio delegation, Jess found W.G. himself. There had been a considerable transformation since the Coliseum. Harding was now handsomely dressed, newly shaved and exuding confidence. There were fifty or so men and women in the drummers' room – a long narrow room with a long narrow table where, ordinarily, salesmen showed their wares. Harding sat comfortably on the table in front of a large poster of himself. "Now I know there's a temptation to go along with what you think might be the winner, General Wood, and I know there are a couple of fellows pledged to me who're trying to persuade you to switch tomorrow on the first ballot and throw the nomination to General Wood. But he's not going to be nominated, ever. It's as simple as that, and neither is Governor Lowden. We're still very much in business, and we're still the state that the Republicans have to win to win the election. . . ."

Jess looked about the room to see what effect W.G. was having on the great man of the delegation, old Myron Herrick: he was nodding in agreement. As Governor Herrick was the central fact of Ohio politics, W.G. was still holding on to his native state, despite signs of rebellion.

At the far end of the room, Jess spotted Daugherty. He was sitting, back to Harding, and writing in a notebook. Jess made his way to Daugherty as invisibly as he knew how. "Whaddaya know?" Jess whispered.

"We'll know in an hour. They're all meeting up in Will Hays's suite."

"Did W.G. file for the Senate?"

Daugherty nodded, and put his finger to his lips. "But we're going to make it. Here. Tonight."

"How?"

3

Blaise asked Lodge the same question. They were seated in a corner of the suite that Will Hays shared with the publisher of *Harvey's Weekly*, George Harvey, a onetime friend and now dedicated enemy of Woodrow Wilson. Earlier, Blaise had dined with Lodge and Brandegee and Curtis of Kansas in suite 404, where "the thing" would be sorted out. A dozen senators were now in more or less permanent session while their host, Will Hays, was in and out of the sitting room, conferring on the telephone in his bedroom, meeting with mysterious strangers in Harvey's bedroom, giving reports to the senators.

Lodge looked most regal as he sat at the room's center, a painting of Niagara Falls behind him. Whisky on a sideboard was occasionally attended to by the Conscript Fathers, who had, most of them, voted for its prohibition to every American.

"The 'how' is the easy part." Lodge was tutorial. "When we give the word, the favorite sons will withdraw, and the delegates will vote for our choice. The 'how' is deliciously simple. It's the 'who' that's giving us trouble."

Hays came in from the bedroom. "I got through to Penrose."

"Is he dead?" asked Harvey, who was showing signs of too much whisky and too little sleep.

"Not so's you'd notice." Hays was agreeable. "Anyway he's gone and dropped Wood."

The senators were delighted. Brandegee drank a toast to Penrose. "Apparently old Penrose asked Wood for three places in the Cabinet and Wood said never, and Penrose hung up on him."

Wadsworth of New York said, "That just rules out Wood, but it doesn't help Lowden and Johnson . . ."

"Johnson is not possible," said Smoot.

Brandegee sighed. "He says he'll bolt the party. Do you think we could hold him to that?" The others laughed. Then Brandegee said, "So what about Massachusetts's favorite son?" He looked at Lodge.

"I was seventy a month ago." Lodge looked grim. Blaise wondered what it must be like to have wanted something all one's life and then, simply, thanks to the calendar, watch it slip away.

Brandegee smiled. "I was thinking of your *other* favorite son, Governor Coolidge."

Although like most thoughtful Americans Blaise preferred the nonpolitician Herbert Hoover – Franklin Roosevelt was on record as saying that Hoover would make a superb president for either party – Coolidge was an intriguing figure, much admired by everyone for having told the police of Boston that they had no right to strike against the public safety.

Smoot shook his head. "He's got no following, and he looks like nobody at all, which is exactly what he is."

"I don't think," said Lodge thoughtfully, "we should nominate a man who lives in a two-family house."

Harvey said, "I'm for Will Hays, of course . . ."

"So am I," said Will Hays, "but I can't be nominated – just now, anyway."

Smoot sat down on the arm of an overstuffed sofa. "I think Harding's our best bet."

But there was no great enthusiasm for Harding. Brandegee observed that he *looked* like a president, but was that enough? Lodge remarked that in Washington Harding lived in a two-family house and so must be denied the manorial splendor of the White House.

Blaise remained until midnight, listening to the great men discuss the various nominees. By one o'clock in the morning, he realized not only that they had no common plan, but that despite Lodge's airy assurance the delegates would do as they were told, the convention was out of anyone's control and if Wood and Lowden both remained in the race, there would be no way of breaking the deadlock until fatigue caused the delegates to turn to Johnson or to Harding.

At two o'clock, Blaise, unnoticed, left the suite, as did Senator Smoot. "Who's it going to be?" asked Blaise.

"Well, it's going to be the one with the fewest enemies. So that rules out Johnson." The elevator door opened. Inside was a reporter from the New York *Telegram*, a man Blaise knew by sight and Senator Smoot by name. When asked the inevitable question,

Smoot said, in a low voice, "We've all decided on Harding. He's the man."

"Can I print that?"

Smoot smiled. "But no attribution. Yet. Tomorrow we're going to let Lowden run for a few ballots, then, in the afternoon, we'll nominate Harding."

The reporter ran from the elevator across the lobby to a pay telephone. Blaise looked at Smoot with wonder. "But there was no agreement to back Harding, or anyone else."

"Well, Mr. Sanford, in politics you don't always say what you mean. Fact, the smart politician seems to go along with events. My band of brothers up there were eliminating not designating, and though they don't come right out and say 'Harding's our man,' that's what they were doing when they shook their heads over Johnson and Coolidge."

Blaise suddenly remembered that he, too, was a newspaper publisher. "The New York *Telegram's* going to put that story on page one."

"That's why I told the lad what I did. Then the AP will pick it up and by noon every delegate will be reading how we picked Harding for them."

"Do you think it'll work?" Blaise was impressed by Smoot's confident mastery of politics at its most arcane.

"Yes, I do."

The two men parted and Blaise went to the telephone and rang Trimble in Washington, with a somewhat more plausible-sounding story in which he predicted, one way or another, a victory for the Senate's reigning oligarchy.

Harding, accompanied only by Jess, entered Hiram Johnson's suite, where W.G. was warmly greeted by Johnson and a dozen men, unknown to Jess except for the advertising man Albert Lasker, who had so famously changed the inedible Puffed Berries to the popular Puffed Wheat by simply changing its name; he had also invented the phrase "schoolgirl complexion," a state of being that could only be maintained by a constant use of Palmolive soap.

Hair neatly parted in the middle, Johnson looked as stalwart and stern as ever. "Can I have a word with you?" Harding was very much master of the situation; and Jess wondered why. Johnson led Harding into the bedroom, with Jess beside him. Jess carefully shut the door, expecting W.G. to tell him to wait outside. But W.G. had not even noticed him.

"It's been decided at last," said W.G., with his most charming smile.

"Who's decided what?"

"Our fellow senators. Wood's out of the picture. Lowden can't make it, as we'll see on the first four or five ballots tomorrow – today, that is. Anyway, I want you on my ticket."

Johnson's scowl was horrendous. "*You* . . . ?"

"Ohio and California, that's hard to beat."

"You . . . for *president?*"

"Hiram, I know I'm not in the big leagues like you. Never have been. That's why I need you. You're one of the finest and most popular men in public life . . ."

"Not popular enough for Lodge and Brandegee and Wadsworth . . ."

"Well, you know how they are. You scare the fellas a lot of the time. Anyway, please don't go and close the door on me. Just wait a bit and sort of mull it over. All right, now?" Harding shook Johnson's hand while embracing the smaller man's shoulders with his left arm. Then Harding, followed by Jess, left the room, leaving Hiram Johnson in what was plain to Jess a perfect rage.

4

Blaise had breakfast at the Blackstone with Alice Longworth and the noticeably hung-over Harvey. To Blaise's amazement Harvey said, "We decided on Harding. It was really the only thing we could do."

"Harding!" Alice was appalled. "But he's so . . . so . . ."

"Second-rate." Harvey agreed. "But he has the fewest enemies.

He's also what the delegates want now that Wood and Lowden have cancelled each other out."

"*When* was this decided?" asked Blaise. "I was there till one, and nothing had been decided."

"It was around two-thirty, I guess. We even asked Harding to come over to the suite so we could tell him. Then we asked him if there was anything in his private life that might disqualify him, and he said no . . ."

"Other than Negro blood," said Alice.

Harvey laughed. "Somebody brought that up to Penrose on the phone and Penrose said, 'Considering the trouble we've been having with the Negro vote that could be a big help.' "

While Alice delivered herself of a number of home truths about W.G. and the Duchess, Blaise was confident that Harvey was lying. He had lied about Wilson in the past; and now he was lying again in order to make himself seem integral to the process of king-making. Blaise was confident that no choice had been made and he very much doubted that Harding had been sent for and questioned like a candidate for a bank teller's job. For reasons of Harvey's own, he wanted to make himself central to Daugherty's now-famous predictions of four months earlier – that around eleven minutes after two in the morning, fifteen or twenty weary men would turn to Harding.

"Why not Knox?" asked Alice plaintively.

But Harvey was called away to the telephone. He returned, looking most owlish and wise.

"The first ballot's being taken. Lowden's having his run. Wood's slipping, Harding's picking up the odd vote here and there. Johnson's falling."

"Was Senator Borah in 404?" asked Alice.

"Uh . . . no, no, he wasn't, but we kept him informed, and he . . . he has acquiesced . . ."

"Acquiescence isn't really his style, is it?" Alice was sharp. Blaise wondered if she believed Harvey. "Anyway, why don't my old boys just jump on the bandwagon now and put Harding over on the next ballot? Why drag it out?"

"Logistics." Harvey was plausible. "There was no time to get to all the delegations before the convention started. But the word's being spread now."

"Surely Cabot doesn't want Harding." Alice was ill-pleased by democracy's vagaries.

"Cabot only wants to destroy Woodrow Wilson and the League of Nations." For once, Harvey was precise. "He doesn't care who is nominated as long as he doesn't live in a two-family house. Back home, that is."

"Cabot's standards are so high," said Alice, unable to eat her egg.

Blaise wondered why no one had considered her husband as a potential candidate. After all, Nicholas Longworth was now a floor leader of the House of Representatives, which made him a very important man. But no one ever thought of charming easy bibulous Nick for anything at all.

5

If the senatorial cabal had pre-ordained the convention, the delegates themselves had not been instructed. Blaise found the first five ballots to be reminiscent of Friday. Wood and Lowden see-sawed. Johnson slipped and Harding rose imperceptibly.

Blaise made his way through the equatorial heat to the stage, carrying his coat over one arm, trying not to breathe the fetid air. At the stage, he found Brandegee looking rather ill. "What's going on?" was Blaise's less than brilliant question.

Brandegee shook his head. "Nothing's going on. That's what's going on."

"I thought you senators made up your mind last night to go for Harding."

"Who told you that?"

"My newspaper."

"George Harvey's more like it. He's the ultimate horse's ass. We made no decision except we'd all like to see Hays nominated, and I have so instructed the Connecticut delegation, to support Will Hays on the next ballot."

"If Connecticut goes for Hays . . ."

"Connecticut won't."

"But you're the senator."

"But I'm not the state. The delegates want Harding. They told me to go to hell. The thing is a complete mess."

"So much for the senatorial cabal."

"So much for the newspapers that invented us," said Brandegee. "Our only hope now is a recess. Then we get Lowden to pull out, and Hays will win."

Blaise wanted to ask why, of all people, Hays? But at such a moment it was pointless to ask. Why anybody?

Lodge announced a recess. There were a few cheers; many boos. The president-makers now had three hours to make Will Hays president. Meanwhile the rumor was being spread that Harding not Hays was the choice of the Senate. To what end so much cleverness? Blaise wondered. Was it to make Harding's nomination possible or impossible?

As the delegates began to file from the hall, Blaise saw Daugherty fiercely remonstrating with Lodge on the flying bridge. "You cannot defeat this man this way," Blaise heard Daugherty shout to the icy Lodge, who murmured something about "party unity" and turned away.

Jess joined Daugherty in a room at the back of the stage where W.G. was already secretly installed. Daugherty was sweating; and nervous. Harding was entirely at ease. "Where's the Duchess sitting?" he asked.

"To the left of the flying bridge," said Jess.

"The next ballot should do it." Harding combed his hair in a mirror, and Jess wondered if he would make an appearance before the convention when he was nominated. It would certainly be dramatic, but then perhaps it wasn't allowed. Jess couldn't remember what the procedure was from earlier conventions.

There was a rap at the door. Jess opened it a crack. It was Toby Hert of Kentucky, Lowden's floor manager. Behind him was Governor Lowden himself.

"Come in!" Jess sprayed himself.

Harding and Lowden shook hands most warmly. "I expect," said the Governor, "you know why I'm here."

"You were always my own personal choice." W.G. was gracious in victory.

Toby was to the point. "We've released all our delegates, and most of them are going to you. But a lot of votes out there are being bought up for Hays."

"How much?" asked the practical Daugherty.

"Anywhere from one to ten thousand dollars."

Daugherty whistled.

"It's too late for Hays," said Lowden. "You're the next in line, and no one will ever be able to say a group of senators forced you on the delegates . . ."

"Oh, they'll *say* it." Harding smiled. "But we know it isn't so. My friends in the Senate actually tried to stop me. But I shall forgive them, as they know not what they do."

"You can say that again," said the exhausted Daugherty.

Blaise sat back of Mrs. Harding as the ninth ballot was called at four-fifty. Hays showed no strength at all. So much for the bosses in the smoke-filled room. There was no significant change from the previous ballot until Kentucky stood up and gave Kentucky's votes not to Lowden but to Harding. This was the signal that Lowden was no longer in the race. A great shout went up.

Dourly, Lodge pounded his gavel. The Duchess removed her hat and put it on her knees. In her right hand she held two long hat pins, as if ready to fight to the death for the stars' choice for president. Then Daugherty was in the seat next to her. "He'll be nominated on the next ballot. Pennsylvania's come our way." The Duchess made a convulsive gesture and plunged the needles into Daugherty's leg, or so it looked to Blaise, and must have felt to Daugherty, who turned very pale but rallied. "W.G.'s in the back right now. With Lowden. After he's nominated, we're taking him over to the La Salle. We've already hired a bigger suite with its own elevator."

The Duchess nodded, too overcome for words.

*

360

Jess sat with Nan Britton high up in the galleries. Together they shared a brown paper bag of peanuts. The heat was stifling, but neither cared as the tenth ballot began. Apparently, W.G. had seen Nan three times in the past week, and there was even a plan to meet her the next day in the park, where she'd be perambulating the child. Jess wondered what Daugherty would say if he knew, wondered if he should tell Daugherty or not. So far, W.G. had taken the elevated train all by himself to Sixty-first Street three times, unrecognized. Nan said that he had said he was "crazy to do it," but he couldn't help himself. Love.

The great moment came when Pennsylvania was called, and the chairman of its delegation, aware of his historic mission, gravely intoned, "Pennsylvania casts sixty-one votes for Warren G. Harding." An exhausted cheer from delegates and onlookers acknowledged Harding's victory.

Lodge announced that the vote was unanimous for *Lowden;* and was roared down. Then he got the name right, but the boos continued. Wisconsin would not support anyone but its own La Follette, while Wood still had more than a hundred votes.

With a sneer, Lodge brought down his gavel hard; and in his hoarse patrician voice shouted, "Warren G. Harding is unanimously nominated by this convention as the Republican candidate for president of the United States!"

"I can't believe it," said Nan.

"I can," said Jess. "Daugherty and me, we always knew we'd pull it off one day and now we have."

6

The Democratic nominees for president and vice president sat in Tumulty's office overlooking the south lawn of the White House. Burden kept them company while Tumulty was organizing the president. The presidential nominee, Governor James Cox of Ohio, was a small, thin-haired, apple-faced man; he wore a three-button suit with all three buttons neatly in their holes; he seemed both self-important and awed. The vice presidential nominee was the thirty-eight-year-old Franklin D. Roosevelt; though incapable of awe for anyone except, perhaps, a fellow Roosevelt, he was very nervous. "Will we see *her,* do you think?" he asked Burden at one point.

"Who knows?" Burden was less than helpful. If ever a political party had selected a pair of exquisitely balanced losers, it was the supercilious Roosevelt, whose imitation of T.R. was rather less convincing than that of most vaudevillians, and the worthy but lifeless Cox, who had only won the nomination after forty-four ballots during which the two leading contenders, Bolshevism's foe A. Mitchell Palmer and William G. McAdoo, had destroyed each other. Burden had done what he could for McAdoo, but the party's natural leader had been undercut by his father-in-law, the President, who had let the word seep out that he himself would like a third term to fight for the League. As Wilson was currently incapable of conducting the office of president, it seemed most unlikely that such an invalid would be granted another four years. In any case, even had Wilson been in excellent health, the country, if not his party, would have rejected him.

When Harding's tongue had slipped during a recent speech, transforming "a return to normality" to "normalcy," the nation, as one, heaved a great sigh of relief – no more great men for them! – and Harding's odd word was greeted with absolute satisfaction as a summing-up of the national mood.

Burden gazed at Roosevelt with only mild dislike. If ever a politician had been born with a set of loaded dice, it was this tall, elegant creature in his white trousers, dark jacket and white shoes, more suitable for a vigorous game of croquet than a race for the vice presidency. Happily, he would soon be defeated and no more heard of on the national scene, as there was now every sign that the Republicans, once back in power, might occupy the White House for as long as they had the first time, from Lincoln to Cleveland.

In a sense, Burden was glad that McAdoo and he had not been nominated. Though they were stronger figures than the two edgy men sitting opposite him in Tumulty's sun-flooded office, the country was in a mood for normalcy and sleep and money-making.

Burden's own race for the Senate was proving more difficult than usual, and Kitty was already in American City, directing the campaign. On a trip east to raise money in New York, he had found Franklin doing the same thing; at Roosevelt's request, he had agreed to help him and Cox through a difficult meeting with the President, whose endorsement could do them almost as little good as his enmity, because, in the end, Wilson was the only campaign issue. Was the country for or against the League? for or against larger-than-life presidents? for or against a leading role in a world as mysterious as the Kingdom of Heaven to the simple majority?

"I've not been forgiven for Christmas." Roosevelt lit a cigarette. Cox stared glumly at the south lawn of the house that he would never live in. "Poor Lord Grey was at a loose end. The President wouldn't see him because of – you know, that joke one of the embassy boys made about Mrs. Wilson. So Eleanor and I asked him to join us, and Mrs. Wilson's been raising hell ever since."

"I wonder why he fired Lansing?" Cox turned away from the window. "I mean, what was the real reason? It couldn't have been because he was holding Cabinet meetings while the President was sick."

"*She* never liked Lansing." Franklin had, to Burden's view, an exaggerated view of the role of women in the public lives of their husbands, even a woman who was generally considered to be the acting president in what had been for over a year a kind of regency.

"It was a number of things," said Burden. "First, the President never liked him. Second, Lansing did talk to the Vice President about the possibility of removing the President from office . . ."

"Lansing was in on that?" Cox was intrigued.

Burden was happy to know something that the titular head of his party – until the first Tuesday in November – did not. "Yes. So was Marshall. So was I. So, I'm afraid, was Cabot Lodge. That's when we sent Senators Hitchcock and Fall over here to see how the President really was." Wilson had put on a splendid show. As the senators were departing, Fall had said, unctuously, "We're praying for you, Mr. President"; and Wilson had responded with his vaudevillian timing, "Which way?"

"Finally," said Burden, "when Lansing's aide, that ass Bill Bullitt, testified to us that Lansing thought the League was useless, the President decided it was time for Lansing to walk the plank, and so he did."

"Some months later," added Franklin.

"The President's stroke intervened . . ."

"And the regency began." Franklin put out his unsmoked cigarette.

"I don't think there *is* a regency." Burden startled both men. "I've been here a number of times, and I quite like Mrs. Wilson, and no matter what you hear, I don't think she and Grayson are running the country."

"So who is?" asked Cox.

"Tell no one," said Burden; then he whispered dramatically, "Nobody."

"You mean it's as if," Cox frowned, "there was *no* president at all?"

"That's just the way it is, and I don't think the Republicans will ever bring up the subject, because there's a good chance that the folks may like the idea and decide to abolish the office and save us all a lot of money."

"Heaven," said Franklin, "forbid."

The thick and untidy Tumulty appeared. "He's on his way. He'll meet you on the south portico. Have you seen this?" He held up a pamphlet with the headline "A Negro President?" Under the headline was a blurred photograph of Harding, looking duskier than life.

"Of course," said Cox. "Terrible stuff. I've said not to use it."

"Do you think it's true?" asked Franklin.

"Who knows?" Burden was indifferent. "Anyway, every time Harding runs for office, the same madman appears with all his so-called proofs."

"This could give us all the South, Southwest, and a lot of Ohio *and* California, which we desperately need. . . . Tumulty looked mournful.

"We've got the South," said Cox.

"Nothing is certain in this business," said Franklin, riffling the pages of the pamphlet.

"Anyway, forget about it. The President's said no." Tumulty sighed. "I think it would elect the two of you, but what do I know? And anyway, you're going to win, but even so . . ."

"What does that mean, the President said no?" The small, cold, close-set eyes of Roosevelt stared at Tumulty, their sudden full level attention emphasizing the unpleasing asymmetry of the oval face.

"It means, Mr. Roosevelt, that if anyone tries to send one of these through the post office, the postmaster will confiscate it."

"By what authority?" Franklin was now very much on edge.

"Under the President's war-time powers, which have still not been rescinded. Specifically the Espionage Act of 1917."

"We must," said Burden, with a friendly smile at Franklin, "do something about all those dictatorial powers we gave to Caesar . . ."

"*After* Mr. Cox's administration." Franklin laughed; blew his nose; said, "Why does the Potomac affect my sinuses worse than the Hudson?"

"Home's best, I suppose." Burden beamed.

Tumulty was at the window. "Here he comes. Let's go outside."

On the south portico, Woodrow Wilson was arranged in an odd-looking wheelchair. Despite the warmth of the day, a shawl covered his paralyzed left side. Except for a Secret Service man, he was alone. Plainly, Mrs. Wilson did not wish to appear as either regent or interpreter. The President's neck was wasted, face haggard, mouth's left side fallen. Cox murmured to Roosevelt, "I didn't know he was still so sick."

As they stepped into the portico, Wilson extended his hand. "Thank you for coming. I'm very glad you came."

"Mr. President." Cox appeared overwhelmed by the extent of the ruin before his eyes. "I have always admired the fight you made for the League."

Burden thought this singularly infelicitous. Had it not been for the fatal fight, Wilson not Cox would be the nominee and in rude health, as the English put it. Wilson's blind zealotry had wrecked the League, the party and himself. When it came to practical politics, Burden's level of human compassion was never high.

"The fight can still be won," said Wilson, passing on the suicide weapon, like a Japanese warrior surrendering to the next generation, a sword suitable only for disembowelling oneself. Burden noted that although Franklin floated about, as it were, exuding euphoria, he only made amiable noises, saying nothing about the League or anything else. Perhaps he was more intelligent than Burden suspected.

"You will enjoy the White House," said Wilson. Without the left side of the mouth and tongue to help form words, the voice was indistinct; also, after he spoke, there was a tendency for the mouth to remain open. "We have done so much of the time, though now, of course . . ."

Cox was plainly not up to the requirements of so essential and painful a scene. "Mr. President," he orated, "we are going to be a million percent with you and your Administration, and that means the League of Nations!"

Again, the President murmured, "I am grateful. I am very grateful." Franklin flashed the hereditary Roosevelt teeth like talismans, and set off a string of meaningless happy syllables; then Cox and he shook hands with the President and Tumulty led them back to the executive offices. Burden would have followed had Wilson not grasped him firmly by the wrist. "Stay," he said.

Once the candidates were out of sight, Edith came onto the portico. She greeted Burden warmly if wearily; then she and Burden sat on either side of the wheelchair. "We had trouble finding the right sort of chair until I remembered those wonderful ones at Atlantic City, you know? Where the boys push you up and down the boardwalk. So we bought one. Only five dollars." Edith looked pleased with herself.

"I can walk now," said Wilson.

"You can stand up and walk with help," amended Edith.

"I can't raise my left leg yet. But that will come soon. Too late." Wilson struck the arm of his chair. "I should've fought for it. But there was Mac . . ." The voice trailed off.

Burden thanked whatever deity presided over the fortunes of politicians that Edith and Grayson and everyone else close to the President had managed, with the greatest difficulty, to keep him from running for a third term. He seemed as completely unaware of the extent of his unpopularity as he was of the extent of his physical debility. He had even sent the new secretary of state, Bainbridge Colby, to the Democratic convention in San Francisco to drum up support for a third term. Burden, as a delegate from his own state, had done his best to explain the political situation to Colby. But the President had given his instructions, and Colby was obliged to obey his master.

McAdoo had led on the first ballot. One word from Wilson and his son-in-law would have been the candidate and probable winner. When Postmaster General Burleson had wired the President urging him to support McAdoo, Wilson had turned into King Lear upon the heath. He threatened to fire Burleson; then he ordered Colby to present his name. In the end, not even Colby dared to present Wilson's name to the convention.

"Mac is an excellent executive but he has not the power of execution."

"You mean," said Edith, who had heard this line many times before, "the power of *reflection*."

"Surely, that is what I said." Wilson turned to Burden. "I shall practice law when we leave here. In Washington, with Mr. Colby."

Burden wished the new law partners well, as Edith looked at him oddly, not certain how he would use this information. "Of course, I'll write history. Or try to. I'm a bit out of practice. He's not at all like T.R., is he?"

Wilson's attention to any one subject was no longer great, and the transitions were apt to be both abrupt and cryptic. Edith translated, "Mr. Franklin Roosevelt, Woodrow means. I," she added, "would not like to be poor *Mrs.* Roosevelt."

"Surely all . . . *that* is over."

The previous winter Lucy Mercer had married one Wintie Rutherfurd.

"But the way he treats her. Don't think we haven't heard all about the night that she left him at a very lively party and then went home and found she'd forgotten her key, and so she had to sit up in the freezing vestibule until he got home at dawn."

"I think I'd have rung for the servants," said Burden, who had also heard many versions of the same story.

Wilson pushed himself up straight with his good arm. "You were kind to come," he said.

Burden shook his hand. "I'm glad you're doing so well."

"It is remarkable, isn't it?" Was this ironic?

Edith was bland. "And how hard he works – we both work."

The prematurely ancient face looked up at Burden; the dull gray eyes glittered like a wolf's in the bright sun; the long teeth, too, were distinctly lupine, while the voice was suddenly a low growl. "It is a terrible thing to be helpless." Yes, thought Burden, the wolf knew that he was in death's trap, yet still he wanted to kill.

An usher escorted Burden up the stairs to the main floor of the White House, which resembled a deserted hotel off-season. Rugs had been taken up in the Green, Blue, Red rooms. Only the East Room was in use, as a movie theater. Each day, the Wilsons and the Graysons sat in lonely splendor, staring at flickering images on a bedsheet hung from a crystal chandelier.

Burden shuddered, inadvertently; and then made his way to Rock Creek, where an amiable widow was waiting for him in his own shut-for-the-season house. As his car turned off Connecticut Avenue and into Rock Creek Park, he realized why Wilson had forbade the use of the so-called evidence of Harding's Negro ancestry. Wilson wanted Cox and Roosevelt to lose: the wolf's last kill.

ℭ 10 ℌ

1

On the fifty-fifth birthday of Warren Gamaliel Harding, November 2, 1920, the American electorate made him president. Although less than half of those who could vote actually voted, Jess could tell from the figures on the blackboard in George Christian's living room that W.G. was winning by close to two to one. Also, both Senate and House of Representatives were securely Republican, and the age of Woodrow Wilson was now as remote as that of Cleveland.

Jess was one of a half-dozen trusted volunteers who had sat in the house that Christian had rented next to the Hardings' and spoke by telephone to various agents around the country to get a sense of who would be coming back to the new Congress and who would not. A number of famous senators had been defeated; and new names had taken their places.

The telephone rang. Jess answered. It was that amiable war hero Charlie Forbes, calling from Seattle. "Tell the *President*," said Charlie, sounding hardly drunk at all, "that he has swept the whole Northwest."

"Whaddaya know?" said Jess; the word "president" was beginning to register.

"Tell him happy birthday, and we'll see him in Washington."

That, decided Jess, would be his last call. He put down the phone. From the next room he could hear W.G.'s laugh, followed by the Duchess's familiar "Now, Warren!"

In the dining room of the rented house, the President-elect sat at the head of the dinner table, the remains of a birthday cake in front of him. Daugherty and Christian sat on either side of him while the Duchess and W.G.'s father, old Dr. Harding, studied the returns at the other end of the table.

"That was Charlie Forbes just now," Jess said to W.G.'s end of the table. "Clean sweep in the Northwest."

"Good old Charlie." In his moment of triumph, W.G. was aglow with a generalized human warmth, while Daugherty was at ease for the first time in more than a year. The energetic Christian was busy with the various newspapermen who came to the house, requesting bits of "color," as they called it. So far, the only color was that W.G. had stuck his napkin into the top of his trousers and left it there.

It was the Duchess who asked, "Why such a low turnout?"

"The ladies – God bless them." Daugherty's blue eye was misty not with sentiment but fatigue. "This is their first presidential election and most of them never got around to registering to vote."

"George." The Duchess turned to Christian. "I left two bottles of champagne by the front door of *our* house. You take them over to the newspaper boys. Of course, those bottles never came from us, as we observe the laws of the land."

"The President," said Daugherty, "technically speaking, has not yet sworn to uphold those laws, so he can, as a former senator and not yet president, commit a felony in good faith."

"But nothing unseemly," said W.G., chewing on the end of a dead cigar. Jess wondered what on earth it must be like to find yourself president during dinner, just like that. Of course, it hadn't been all that fast. For more than a year, Daugherty and Harding had been at work in state after state, gathering support. Now here it all was.

"Oh, and George," the Duchess was not yet finished, "don't give *anything* to the news-reel people. I've told them once we're in the White House, they won't be let in, not after those pictures of me and Warren they took last week when we weren't looking."

"Now, now, Duchess." W.G. was placating.

"I've also kept a book," said Florence Kling Harding, eyes bright as blue searchlights. "Everybody who's ever snubbed us in

Washington's been listed *with* the snub. Well, *they're* not setting foot in our White House, ever, let me tell you."

"Poor Alice Longworth," Daugherty observed.

"I think we'll make an exception for her." W.G. grinned.

"She's the worst, why, she –"

"Dearie, Nick's a leader of the House. So we're going to *have* to let them in the door."

"Well, only when it's absolutely official."

Christian appeared in the doorway. "Associated Press wants to know, did you say, when you were nominated in Chicago, that 'we drew to a pair of deuces, and filled'?"

"Certainly not," said the Duchess.

Harding sighed. "Would I ever say anything so unbecoming of what was – until now – the greatest moment of my life? No. I never said it. Governor Lowden was with me. He can testify I asked him to pray for me."

Christian disappeared. "Not that it'll do any good," W.G. observed, sadly. "Once they knot one of those phrases of theirs about your neck you have to wear it forever."

Daugherty laughed. "Like Hiram Johnson's who's supposed to've said when you offered him the vice-presidential nomination, 'You would put *your* heartbeat between me and the White House?'"

"So puffed-up," said the Duchess. "I'm glad we got Calvin Coolidge instead. *He* stays out of the way. I wish I could say the same for her."

Jess was perched on a chair between Harding and Daugherty. Outside there were cheers and, from time to time, passing automobiles would sound their horns. All Marion was up for the night to celebrate.

Hands linked behind his head, Harding summed up: "It's like this Senate group – what did that New York *Times* man call them? The 'Senate Soviet.' They were supposed to've got together in Will Hays's smoke-filled suite . . ."

"That part's mine," said Daugherty, "looking into my crystal ball last spring."

"Then they decided – for every sort of sinister reason – that I was going to be the candidate the next morning." Harding frowned for the first time since glory had draped him like a Smith's Emporium Genuine Gold Thread and Chinese Dragon Silk Dressing Gown Deluxe. W.G. discarded his well-chewed stub and deliberately lit a proper Havana cigar. Despite warning hums from the Duchess, Harding puffed deeply and contentedly and said, almost dreamily, "Yet the next day, on the first four ballots, the thirteen senators who were supposed to've agreed the night before that I'd be their candidate all voted *against* me."

To Jess's surprise, Daugherty nodded agreement. Usually, Daugherty liked to take credit for what was supposed to have happened in Will Hays's suite at eleven minutes after two of that famous Saturday morning. Actually, Daugherty had not known of the meeting until morning, by which time other forces were at work. "That's why," said Daugherty, "when Lodge called for a recess, I thought I'd have a stroke."

"That was because you didn't know Lowden and I were having a con-fab on what to do." W.G. gazed benignly at a group of wide-eyed young relatives gathered about the Duchess. "Even up to the ninth ballot, my senatorial colleagues were still hoping to nominate Hays. But by then Lowden and I were in accord. On the ninth ballot, ten of my supposed senatorial managers voted against me while the three who switched to me had been in the cards all along, as the press would say."

"But does that mean," Jess could not contain himself, "that the senators had *nothing* to do with getting you the nomination?"

W.G. nodded. "When the number-one and number-two candidates cancel each other out, number three is usually chosen. Well, I was number three. Simple as that. They couldn't stop me once Governor Lowden and I had got together. The fact that some of them were still trying to get it for Hays between the eighth and ninth ballot shows how little they know about these things. Fact, most folks would've been pretty scandalized if the senators *had* managed to stop me."

"As it is," said Daugherty, "once we were in, that four-flusher Harvey and some of the others started talking about the smoke-filled room, pretending that they were the bosses. But they weren't. You did it. You were the convention's choice."

W.G. rubbed his eyes. "And that's pretty much the way we planned it. Of course, for a while there I was afraid . . ." When the President-elect did not complete his thought, Jess wondered if it might have something to do with the galleries, with all those people who truly wanted Herbert Hoover, who wasn't even, in the party's eyes, a candidate. Yet they kept yelling, "Hoover, Hoover!"

Christian entered, smiling. "Governor Cox has conceded."

"Don't you believe it!" said the Duchess. "That Jimmy Cox is treacherous as can be. George, you check –" But everyone else in the room was now too busy cheering and applauding as a crowd of journalists and photographers surrounded the President-elect.

Daugherty drew Jess to one side and gave him an envelope. "She's on the seven-A.M. from Chicago. She'll go straight to the Marion Hotel. Meet her by eight."

"Is she . . . alone?"

"Say your prayers, Jess. Just as I say mine. I'm going to bed. We done it."

"We done it," Jess repeated. Then he wondered what on earth they were going to do with Nan Britton for the next four years.

Jess found Nan in the coffee shop of the Marion Hotel. Except for a tired woman behind the counter, there was no one in sight. Nan was reading the Chicago *Tribune*, which she must have brought with her: yesterday's headline predicted a Republican victory. Jess had a copy of the Marion *Star*, with the great news: *Harding Sweeps the Nation.* Jess said, without thinking, "Whaddaya know?"

Nan said, "I know it's wonderful! I was so worn out I actually slept in that Pullman car and it wasn't until I was getting up at six-thirty that I asked the porter who won and he said, 'Harding's the man, miss.'"

"You want your usual waffles with jam, Jess?" The old woman behind the counter regarded them without curiosity.

"With a side order of chipped beef." That had been W.G.'s breakfast election day. While breakfast was being assembled, Jess gave Daugherty's note to Nan, who read it, and nodded and put it in her handbag. She was certainly pretty, Jess decided, but for a president who could have his choice of Mary Miles Minter or Gloria Swanson or, maybe, why not, Mary Pickford, newly married though she was, Nan was a bit on the plain and unglamorous side. As if to emphasize the fact, back of their booth stacks of *Photoplay* magazine featured the marriage and home life of Mary Pickford.

"I guess you'll be staying in Chicago." Jess fished, not subtly.

Nan nodded, a sad expression on her face. "My sister's willing to adopt Elizabeth Ann if . . ." Nan sighed.

"I'm sure they'll fix it real fine because, 'My God, How the Money Rolls In!'" He hummed a line from that popular song and started in on his waffles. Nan picked at toast.

"What's happened to Carrie Phillips?" she asked, with an unsuccessful attempt at casualness.

"Well, she and Jim lit out this summer for Japan and points east to find some new silk specialities for the store and they're still travelling last anybody's heard." It was said that Albert Lasker, on orders from Will Hays, had given the Phillipses fifty thousand dollars to get lost until after the election. Jess suspected that the sum was probably less. Carrie loved to travel, while Jim was too important a man to be involved in something so crude as a payoff.

"Look." Nan removed a large glossy photograph of W.G. from her handbag. "I'm going to ask him to sign it for me."

"You do that," said Jess. After all, this was now Daugherty's business, not to mention that of the Secret Service. He had done his job as courier.

"I suppose they'll go on straight to Washington." Nan was wistful.

"No. Texas. The McLeans are joining them, with their own private car and two or three senators and Doc Sawyer, who's going to be surgeon general now so's he can come to Washington and look after the Duchess's kidney."

"Doc Sawyer? A general?" Nan laughed, and it was a comical thought: the local doctor was a small insignificant wisp of a man whom no one ever noticed except the Duchess, who had given him the run of her remaining kidney. He had saved her life a dozen times.

"Then they plan to go on to Panama. You know how W.G. likes to travel."

"Do I know? Why, even out on Chautauqua, no sooner would we

hit one town than he was already phoning on ahead to the next. 'Can't you ever stay still?' I'd say, and he'd say, 'Dearie, I'm a travellin' man.' He'll love being president, don't you think?"

"Who wouldn't?" said Jess, thinking how much he and Daugherty were going to enjoy the Harding Administration. But as for W.G., Jess was not so certain. He wouldn't be able to just slip away from the Duchess, say, and take the train to New York and meet Nan or Theda Bara at the Biltmore. The July trip on the Chicago elevated to see Nan was probably the last public train that he would ever set foot on again. From now on, he was national property, guarded by the Secret Service and watched by the press, who lad a lot more and better eyes than even the Duchess. Jess suddenly felt sorry for W.G. "He'll be able to go anywhere he likes," he told Nan, "with his own railroad car and his own yacht."

"But I'll never be with him, will I?"

"No, honey, you never will be. In public, anyway."

Will Hays, still master of the Republican National Committee, entered the coffee shop. He looked, even this early, like a fresh wide-eyed mouse asearch for cheese. "Good morning," he said to Jess, instantly recognizing the face if not the name of a part of the presidential entourage.

"Whaddaya know?" Jess greeted Hays, who then sat at the counter, and ordered coffee, and read several newspapers all at once. Everyone said that he would be in the Cabinet. According to Daugherty, even Jess could have an important job somewhere high in the government, but Jess thought he preferred the freedom of anonymity. There was a lot of business to be done during the next four years, and he had never liked the idea of going to an office on any regular basis.

2

Through the steam, small figures could be observed like midget ghosts. Blaise blinked his eyes to accustom them to the heat and the mist; thus blurring his vision all the more. Then he found his host. With only a towel wrapped about his head, this small muscular man was talking to another small less muscular man, with no towel. Although Blaise was hardly tall, he towered over Douglas Fairbanks and Charlie Chaplin, who were discussing their joint enterprise, United Artists.

"Mr. Sanford. Blaise." Fairbanks greeted him as formally as a naked man could. With his right hand he shook Blaise's hand; with his left he covered his genitals in *a pro forma* gesture of modesty, which he then quickly forgot. Blaise and Chaplin shook hands gravely and Blaise could not help but note, again, how much smaller than real life, in every way, these larger-than-life world fantasies were. He also noted that Chaplin was not, as everyone seemed to think, Jewish.

"You do yourself very well," said Blaise. As a part of the Santa Monica Boulevard studios, Fairbanks had built himself a private gymnasium as well as a Turkish bath, with professional trainers and masseurs on constant duty. Now that Fairbanks had come into his supreme own as an athletic star with *The Mark of Zorro,* he worked constantly on his body. In fact, over the entrance to the gymnasium hung a sign, *Basilica Linea Abdominalis* to remind the star and his friends that the waistline was, for Fairbanks at least, center not only of his body but his world. As a result, Fairbanks's hips were easily the narrowest that Blaise had ever seen on a man close to forty.

Suddenly, as the Puck-like Chaplin proceeded to do a small dance, depicting an adulterer caught by an angry husband in a hot shower, they were joined by Fairbanks's trainer, tall and out of place among the small stars, and a handsome Army flier who had been an all-American football player at West Point. The fact that the West Pointer had three testicles of equal size delighted the stars and in no way embarrassed the Army officer, whose body looked like a sculpture meant always to be seen in the nude and in the round and in every detail perfect save for the genital joke. As a result of the heat and the curious company, Blaise's susceptibility to his own sex was abruptly switched off. Also, the ultimate anti-aphrodisiac, Fairbanks wanted to talk politics to the publisher of the Washington *Tribune.*

"I was asked to join Al Jolson's group, when they came out for Harding. But I'm the original T.R. man, and even though Harding was finally their choice – the Republican choice – I just couldn't. I suppose I should've. Mary was tempted, too. But then we were really rooting for Mac, and of course he didn't get nominated. So we sat it out."

"Just as well, I'd say." Blaise had not voted because as a resident of the District of Columbia, he could not. But now that he was established at Laurel House on the Virginia side of the Potomac, he would no doubt register as Frederika had done with unexpected rapture in finding herself, at last, Woman Enfranchised. She had then forgotten to vote.

"I know," said Fairbanks, "how people object to movie actors talking politics. But why shouldn't we speak out? We're citizens, too. We pay a lot of tax."

"It's very simple, Dougie." Chaplin's voice was curiously light, and very English. "We don't talk in the movies, and they love us. But if we start chattering in public, they might hate us."

"You," said Fairbanks thoughtfully, "never stop talking."

"That's only in private with you. With those I love. Anyway, I speak only to instruct and delight my friends. But for the world, Charlie is forever silent." With that, he did his curious shuffle-walk out of the steam-room, and even without the famous large shoes, the effect was weirdly comic.

After the hot dry room, cold plunge, massages, they were draped in towels and arranged upon wooden chaise-longues, while a waiter served tomato sandwiches and Château d'Yquem, which Blaise loathed and their host, a natural teetotaller, did not drink. Blaise contented himself with soda water.

Fairbanks discussed football with the Army officer and Chaplin discussed Caroline with Blaise. "She's about to work with an old friend of mine, William Desmond Taylor, a real gentleman, of what used to be called the old school. So unlike the new school. I myself am self-educated." In imitation of a rabbit, Chaplin nibbled one corner of a tomato sandwich.

"Like me." Blaise was agreeable. "I quit Yale . . ."

"For us of the new school of gentlemen, Yale is just another lock to be picked. Of course, I'm from the London streets, poor but never, ever proud. Now, Taylor's a real gent. Irish, I think. Protestant, of course. He enlisted in the war, aged forty-one or so, while Doug and I, young and the stuff of which cannon fodder is made, were exempted *if* we sold Liberty Bonds."

"You financed the war."

"The thing is this." Chaplin suddenly looked at Blaise, who found it highly disconcerting to be looked at by a face that he himself had looked at for so many hours over the last seven years. Without the toothbrush moustache, Chaplin did not even look like Charlie Chaplin; yet there was something about the eyes that held Blaise's attention in much the same way that the eyes of the face on the screen did. The little man was all energy and force, and perfect coldness. "Poor Taylor's got himself into a terrible position with two stars and one lady, or so the last-named would depict herself. I wonder if beautiful Emma – your Caroline – knows what she's getting into."

"I had the impression that he was simply going to direct her in *Mary Queen of Scots* ."

"He's one of the best directors we have, which is saying nothing at all since anyone can direct and just about everyone does. But he's better than most."

"Better than Timothy X. Farrell?" If Chaplin knew so much, Blaise saw no reason to hold back what he himself knew, which was obviously less than any of Caroline's Hollywood coevals.

"Different. I like Farrell. But he's going to be in trouble if he keeps on making political movies. This country is far, far too dedicated to freedom to allow freedom of speech." Chaplin's rabbity smile was sudden and entirely engaging. "I'm joking, of course," he said.

"Of course."

Fairbanks was now walking on his hands, towel fallen to the floor. "Doug is very vain, you know. All those muscles. You've heard of Mary Miles Minter? My favorite name after Pola Negri."

Blaise nodded. "She's supposed to be the new Mary Pickford."

"So the great furrier Zukor decreed. But her nose is too large for our screen, and her talent too small. Worse, she has a mother, the lady I referred to. The mother was once an actress called Charlotte something. She put baby Mary on the stage, and baby Mary, who is still only nineteen and gloriously nubile, in due course found her way here. Guided by Charlotte, she attained stardom in a trice, and a huge salary of which thirty percent goes to her mother."

Blaise wondered why he was being told all this; and why Chaplin should care. "Thirty percent is high."

"Very high. Now when little Mary Double M was about fifteen, already a star, she had an affair with a friend of mine, a director, by whom she got pregnant. Charlotte warned the director that if he ever saw the child again she would have him jailed for tampering with a minor, who was also a hot screen property. Then Triple M underwent an abortion. Now Mary Miles Minter is in love with my friend Taylor, as is her mother, Charlotte. So you see, what Emma Traxler, born in war-torn Alsace-Lorraine of noble yet haughty stock –"

"I think it was Unterwalden . . ."

"No matter. She wears, at all times, an invisible coronet to which even the vilest Jacobin doffs his Phrygian hat. Although the Three M's are presently locked in their room in a palace on New Hampshire Boulevard – rather the way one does with a cat in heat – the child sometimes escapes to see Taylor. Meanwhile, Charlotte, in constant, *scorching* heat, throws jewels through his window, emitting heart-rending howls of unslaked lust."

"Who," asked Blaise, aware of the menace in this lightly rendered saga, "is the second star?"

"Mabel Normand." With a look of mild distaste, Chaplin watched Fairbanks do a back-flip. "He's going to break that thick neck of his one day or have a heart attack or both." He turned back to Blaise. "We all love Mabel. I most of all. I've acted with her, directed her, and *she's* directed *me*. She's superb in comedy. In everything. But she's falling on hard times. Goldwyn just fired her and she's gone back to Mack Sennett, a step down in this business. She's also in love, or thinks she is, with William Desmond Taylor. How he directs all the traffic in that bungalow of his, I dread to think. Now Emma Traxler, the Transylvanian princess, has been added to the . . . story."

"My sister is a superb manager of traffic," said Blaise truthfully.

"I would hate for anything to happen . . ."

"To Taylor?"

"No. Men can take care of themselves. To Mabel Normand. What brings you here, Mr. Sanford?" The transition was swift.

"I had heard that my old friend Hearst was trying to buy the Los Angeles *Herald*. So I thought I'd put in a bid, to keep things lively."

"I keep telling Doug we should use all this money we make to buy the press. All of it. Then there'd be no more of those sordid scandals about us. None of it, let me assure you, Mr. Sanford, remotely true. Every star, male as well as female, goes to his marriage bed a virgin, and it is because of this prolonged chastity that our performances . . ." With a crash, Fairbanks fell to the floor.

"How satisfying!" Chaplin clapped his hands. "Poor Doug," he called, "did you hurt yourself? Was something small but essential to United Artists broken?" A swift glance at Blaise, and Blaise was hot with embarrassment: Chaplin had read his mind in the steamroom.

"My son." Chaplin was now an old-world gypsy crone, swirling about the collapsed Fairbanks. "It is the gypsy blood! I know. I know. The Tokay. On the steppes. The balalaika. Then the hot gypsy blood like quicksilver in your veins." Chaplin snapped his fingers like castanets, and danced over Fairbanks. "You cannot deceive a loving gypsy mother. *I* know for whom you wait, hanging upon a mere tenterhook. It is the glorious young Englishwoman who has set atingle all your senses. Oh, my poor son! Born for the priesthood! A catamite at Mount Athos for lo! these many years. Now lost to God by a pair of saucy blue eyes!"

The aged crone suddenly became a haughty English girl. "I cannot, don't you know? leave my father the Duke of Quimsberry, now aboard his magnificent yacht moored not a stone's throw from this moonlit gypsy camp in the Vienna Woods." Chaplin became a Russian Cossack dancer. He leapt in the air. "Dance, little fool! Dance!" he roared. "My gypsy blood is aflame. You madden me! So if it's a fuck you want, it's a fuck you'll get, Lady Sybilla." Then, as Lady Sybilla, he cried, "I thought you were a gentleman! True, gypsy blood runs through you yet –" A gasp. "Runs through both of us now. Oh, may this night never end. But hark! What is that, coming toward us, through the Vienna Woods? Oh God! It is the yacht of my father the Duke." With that, Chaplin, before their eyes, turned into a very large, steam-powered yacht, making its way slowly through the Vienna Woods, just missing the odd tree in its stately progress.

"Charlie," said Fairbanks, "has found his voice."

Although Caroline had insisted that Blaise stay with her, he had moved into the brand-new Ambassador Hotel, midway between Hollywood and Los Angeles, where the *Herald* was located. The hotel itself was very large and modern and somewhat reminiscent of an armed camp, with private guards and public policemen everywhere. Currently, Los Angeles was in the midst of what the press called a crime wave, partly the work of transients who had come to this new El Dorado only to find the best gold already panned, and partly the work of local criminals at war with one another over the various drug territories, none particularly lucrative since a card – or gramme – of cocaine cost two dollars. Morphine was expensive but less popular. In any case, when it came to serious crime, the police stayed aloof; either paid off or frightened off. But transients were dealt with brutally.

The Coconut Grove of the Ambassador resembled its name. Here, later in the evening, among false palm trees, popular singers would sing and a full orchestra would play, over and over again, "Look for the Silver Lining," while those movie stars who did not have to work the next day would dance. Caroline had warned Blaise gravely that Saturday night at the Grove was the one place where Blaise and Frederika must be seen if they wanted to be accepted as forever young and fashionable.

Frederika sat comfortably beside a palm tree, while Blaise drank gin and coconut milk from a hairy coconut shell, all beneath the gelid gaze of plainclothes police and uniformed hotel guards. The Grove was half filled with serious diners; the orchestra played soothing dance music; a few couples danced.

"I see what she sees." Frederika looked about her with a tourist's fascination. "I only wish I'd seen more movies so that I'd know who everyone was."

"It's all a bit like – like Mardi Gras, isn't it?" Blaise was not used to tropical or near-tropical societies. A day with the ownership of the *Herald* resembled what he'd always imagined it would be like to do business in Tahiti.

"That's what makes it so – different. Caroline showed me her *Mary Queen of Scots* sets. Very authentic-looking, except for a tomato in the kitchen. I reminded her that North Europeans weren't partial to tomatoes then. She was apologetic."

Blaise was intrigued not by the anachronism but by the kitchen. "What would the Queen be doing in a kitchen?"

"Well, darling, it is Scotland. I suppose she cooks haggis for Bothwell."

On the arm of her latest director and lover, William Desmond Taylor, Caroline made a slow, majestic entrance. At the door, photographers were allowed pictures; then they tactfully vanished.

"You've never looked more radiant." Blaise needled Caroline.

"I know," she said, giving her sister-in-law a kiss. "It is an inner light, actually. Either one has *it*, as Elinor Glyn would say, or one has not."

Blaise found Taylor charming; very much the British gentleman as represented on the Broadway stage. He was tall, slender, and about Caroline's age. Blaise wondered who on earth he really was. Caroline had told him so many of the original names and origins of the stars that he was suspicious of everyone, particularly Emma Traxler, the tragic fire-opal of Alsace-Lorraine, whose lady-mother had been drowned by Huns in her own moat. The spirit of Hearst now informed the Hollywood studios, and the result was beyond anything that the old yellow journalist ever dreamed of.

"When do you start shooting?" Blaise enjoyed using Hollywood jargon.

"April Fool's Day," said Taylor, smiling at Caroline. "We've got the right script at last. From Edward Knoblock."

Blaise nodded; apparently, he was supposed to know the name.

"He wrote *Kismet,* that play which ran for years," said Caroline. "He's from New York but lives in London. He was one of the writers Mr. Lasky imported, along with Maeterlinck and Maugham and Elinor Glyn and all the others. He's staying with William, and working on the script."

Could this, Blaise wondered, be his sister, Caroline? The friend of Henry Adams and Henry James, now praising the author of *Kismet*? Or, perhaps, more to the practical point, was this simply Caroline's *Doppelgänger,* Emma, an aging actress trying to survive in a fast, furious, unsentimental world? Frederika was positive that Caroline's face had been tightened by surgery. Blaise thought not; on the other hand, she did look disturbingly perfect in a style that was not altogether human.

Taylor asked Frederika to dance, and half-brother and half-sister were able to talk. "The *Herald,*" Caroline began.

"Too expensive . . ."

"I'm told Hearst has already got it . . ."

"Through Barham? Probably. It was too late . . ."

"My fault. I should've made a move last year, but . . ."

They spoke in their own rapid private language; no ellipsis ever needed filling. Then he asked, "What's happened to Tim?"

"Nothing. He's still living at the Garden Court. Since you're obviously curious, we've locked the door between our rooms."

"I see."

"Why should you?" Caroline watched Taylor and Frederika waltz decorously at the center of the dance floor. "Anyway, it's all very friendly. We still work together, in a business way. He's found someone younger."

"And you've found someone older. He *seems* all right." Blaise was still brooding upon the saga of Taylor and the two stars and the one mother. "He must be very popular."

"Too much so." Caroline was now her old candid self. "He is trying to get Mabel Normand to stop taking cocaine, and he is trying to keep Mary Miles Minter from killing herself for love."

"Of him?"

"So it would seem."

"Where do you fit in?"

"A woman of a certain age, warm, compassionate – wise, too, as only such a woman can be. One who has known heartbreak . . ."

"Is this you or Emma Traxler?"

Caroline laughed. "A bit of both. Don't worry. I can keep the two apart. Anyway, after *Mary*, Emma will retire from the silver screen . . ."

"Home to Alsace-Lorraine?"

"No. Santa Monica. I want to go on producing movies."

"With William Desmond Taylor?"

The director and Frederika came back to the table. Frederika was delighted. "Gloria Swanson is over there, with what looks like a genuine Latin lover type."

"They all come here," said Caroline, her eyes on Taylor as he took an envelope from his pocket and poured its contents into a glass of water.

"Cocaine?" Blaise was blithe.

Caroline glared at him. Taylor laughed. "No. For my ulcer. Occupational hazard. Once the shooting's over, I want to get as far away from here as possible."

"Summer in Europe," said Caroline.

"Take him to Saint-Cloud." Frederika was cozy.

"I must stay here." Caroline drank real tea from a real teacup.

"Eddy – that's Edward Knoblock – he's lent me his London townhouse, and I'm leaving him my place here in town. We met once before." Taylor turned to Blaise. "Years ago. You were very young. So was I, of course. The English Antique Shop, 246 Fifth Avenue. Remember? I was the manager. Caroline came in, too. But not with you."

"I thought you were an actor."

"I was. But actors have to live. You were with a French-woman . . ."

"Anne de Bieville," murmured Caroline.

"You do have a memory," said Blaise, who had none, at least of Taylor. He also found it disturbing that Taylor should have remembered him after all these years. But then if one had led other lives, it was probably best to confess them before one was found out. Taylor seemed authentic, despite a large diamond ring not usually found on a gentleman's hand. But then this was Hollywood, as Taylor again demonstrated when he produced, at Frederika's request, a platinum cigarette-case containing black cigarettes with gold tips.

The orchestra was now playing "Blue Moon," a new song that Blaise liked to sing when absolutely alone. He was beginning to see how one could succumb to the Tahitian charm of Southern California. The only mystery was how to get work done in so languorous a setting; yet the Hollywood people were never at rest if they could help it. A star could make a dozen feature-length movies in a year and still have time for a divorce and a remarriage. Of course, everyone was very young, except Caroline and Taylor.

While Taylor pointed out the stars to Frederika, Blaise came to the point. "Would you sell me your share– in the paper?"

Caroline looked at him for a long moment, looking, perhaps, for the silver lining. "Why – now?"

"Why – any time? You've lost all interest in it, and Washington, and politics . . ."

"Have I?" The famous – even to her half-brother – eyes opened very wide. They were luminous, and rather bloodshot. "Did I go to sleep out here for a hundred years and now it's time to wake up, and no one's left?"

"Well, *I'm* here. It may have seemed like a hundred years to you, but . . ."

"No. It's gone very fast." Caroline was suddenly serious. "Do I want to sell? I don't know. Do I want to stay here? That depends."

"On the next hundred years?"

Caroline nodded. "Marriage has been discussed," she said under the music.

"Then you will have to stay here. I can't see him . . . uh, happy in Washington."

"*Only* discussed." Caroline was vague. "I don't know. Let's see what happens to *Mary*. Those Elizabethan ruffs are a godsend for aging necks."

A dark Latin lover stopped at their table: it was the Spanish-born star Tony Moreno. There was much flashing of eyes and teeth during the introductions; then Moreno said to Taylor, "Can I see you a moment?" Taylor excused himself, and the two men left the nightclub.

"How handsome," said Frederika, drawing out her syllables, "everyone is."

"That's because we don't allow senators in public places." Caroline was now looking toward the lobby, where, past two uniformed security men, Moreno and Taylor were talking intently. Blaise was beginning to get the range; and he was more intrigued than not by all the possibilities for disaster that Caroline was so compulsively arranging for herself. Suddenly, the two men in the lobby were no longer visible.

At that moment, a tall, elegant, overpainted woman paused at their table, with an escort half her age. "Dear Emma," she said. The accent was deep Southern.

"Charlotte Shelby." Caroline introduced the lady to Blaise and Frederika. The escort was ignored. Blaise rather liked the way that manners had been pared down to their essentials.

"You must come, Mr. and Mrs. Sanford, to pay us a call at the Casa de Margarita, our private mansion on New Hampshire Avenue, that's when we're not really back home on Mummy's plantation in Shreveport, Louisiana."

"I should love to, of course." Frederika exuded her own District of Columbia Southern charm.

"Tell William hello and that little Mary is better." Like Chaplin's yacht in the Vienna Woods, Mrs. Shelby sailed on, escort in tow.

"What was *that?*" asked Frederika.

"An ex-actress named Charlotte Shelby," Caroline began.

"Best known as the mother of Mary Miles Minter," Blaise concluded, complacently.

"How do you know that?" Caroline was startled.

"I always read *Photoplay* magazine. You know, at the barber's . . ."

"You do get around," said Caroline neutrally. Then Taylor returned without Moreno. Caroline whispered something to him, and he waved to Charlotte Shelby across the dance floor and she, graciously, inclined her head. Blaise noticed that despite heavy makeup, the lady's lips were thin and the mouth, compressed into a smile, was grim. Was she jealous of Caroline? Or relieved that Taylor was no longer enamored of the fabled child?

". . . letters," said Taylor. Then he led Caroline onto the dance floor.

"Well," said Frederika.

"Well," said Blaise.

"Do you think Mr. Taylor was being given drugs by the Latin lover?"

"Frederika! You have gone Hollywood, as they like to say out here." But Blaise suspected that that might have been a part of a more complex transaction. He was also beginning to wonder whether or not Caroline might herself have got involved in drugs. Certainly, she was not at all the self that he had once known, but then, admittedly, they had never known each other well. Half-consanguinity was, perhaps, in itself, the equal to none. "Letters," Taylor had said. Whose letters? Blaise wondered.

"She'll come home." Frederika sounded sad. "This can't last for her – for anybody. But I can see the appeal. Imagine a place where no one cares who the new attorney general is or whether Mr. Harding is his puppet."

"I think the attorney general might be the one politician that they'd all be interested in."

Among the papier-mâché palm trees, there were guards – criminals, too. Even the Latin lover, Moreno, looked as if he might slit one's throat simply for pleasure. The false jungle was a very real jungle, and Caroline could have it all, as far as Blaise was concerned. A life-size monkey doll at the base of a palm tree opposite suddenly began to blink glaring red electrical eyes.

3

On the Argyle Lot, now deserted at day's end, bits and pieces of Edinburgh Castle had been re-created, and Caroline and Taylor strolled amidst their handiwork. "Well, now at least we know," said Caroline, "what Mr. Griffith must have felt when he built Babylon."

"Yes," said Taylor, frowning, "and I know what his banker must have felt, too." Although Traxler Productions footed the bill, it was Taylor who worried most about cost. So far, the production was nearly a hundred thousand dollars over its estimated budget and shooting had yet to begin.

Tim had been sardonic. "You could've rented all of Edinburgh for what you're paying." Then he had vanished into the Northwest to make the sort of film that would over-excite Caroline's daughter and son-in-law. Thanks in part to their efforts, the film, with inter-cut footage of Woodrow Wilson, had been banned in most cities. Happily, as the new attorney general, Harry M. Daugherty, was not running for president, Tim might be allowed to continue at large for a while longer. To date, there had been only one scene about Taylor, which Caroline had Emma Traxlered with a nobility worthy of an Elinor Glyn heroine. Tim had most hurt her by being not jealous but mystified by her choice.

"I ride through the gate." Caroline imagined herself on horse-back, sidesaddle, a plume in her hat, the adoring Bothwell at her side. Attempts to get Barthelmess for Bothwell had failed, and an older actor was hired in order to make Caroline look young and helpless. As for Mary's rival, Queen Elizabeth, they had nearly secured Sarah Bernhardt, whose stage version of *Queen Elizabeth* had filled French theaters since the dawn of time. But at the last moment the Divine Sarah had decided not to put at risk her legend a second time on dangerous truth-telling film. They had then hired a distinguished actress of seventy, who was guaranteed to make Caroline look kittenish. La Glyn had, quite seriously, offered her services in the interests of Authenticity, as she was also descended from the Tudor queen, but Caroline had assured her that she was far too handsome to be a foil for plain little Emma Traxler; rather rudely, La Glyn had agreed. "If you put it like that, Madame Traxler, you are absolutely right." To everyone's surprise, Elinor Glyn was now not only writing but producing her own films. She had become a Hollywood success, and was praised by the *Kine Weekly*.

"We'll do all the exteriors first," said Taylor. He took her arm; and she was pleased, as always, when he took the physical initiative. Thus far, nothing had happened between them, and for the first time in Caroline's life, she had developed a sudden blind panic at the thought of age. Suppose there would be, at last, someone whom she wanted – as now – who did not want her? One who pre-ferred young girls like Minter and Normand? What could she do? The demoralizing answer was nothing.

Caroline leaned very lightly against Taylor as they walked along the battlement from which Mary would stare in vain for her lover who, unbeknownst to her, was dead. Caroline felt spontaneous tears of self-pity rush to her eyes. Mary was a role that she was going to have to work very hard *not* to act.

Together they paused on the battlement and looked across the New York street to the high fence that surrounded the lot. All work had stopped for the day, but on certain sets technicians were making last-minute – overtime! – alterations. "Do you really think Mary should meet Elizabeth in the park rather than at the prison?" This was an on-going disagreement.

"We have to get outdoors by then. We've got six interiors in a row. The story's getting too claustrophobic."

"But I like that. It's the way Mary would feel. I mean, she *is* a prisoner." Taylor's profile was nearly perfect. He had had his choice of film parts for years, but after his success in *Captain Alvarez* he had chosen to direct.

"Edward says it's always worked in the park."

Caroline did not much care for the plump New York Englishman Edward Knoblock, who stayed on and on in Taylor's small bungalow, very much underfoot from Caroline's point of view. "That is because Edward has stolen the plot from Schiller, and given him no credit."

"Now, now." Taylor was soothing. "Were it not for theft – tasteful theft, that is – we'd all be out of business here. Why didn't your brother stay longer?"

"He thinks the government will stop if he's not there to guide them. I used to be like that."

"Don't you miss it?"

Reflexively, Caroline counted to three to herself, the way that she had learned to do to insure the effectiveness of a close shot, then she spoke. "Yes, sometimes. This is more fun, of course. But one day I won't be able to do it."

"One day none of us will be able to do anything. Why anticipate?"

At that moment, they were joined by Charles Eyton, the chief of production for Famous Players-Lasky.

"Putting out the lights?" Taylor smiled.

"Don't joke! That's what I have to do. The waste that goes on around here!" Eyton was a very thorough practical man, much involved with everything and everyone at the studio, including outside production companies like Traxler. "Can't wait to get started, I'll bet," he said, frowning at the gate to Edinburgh Castle.

Taylor anticipated him. "We'll sell you the set, if you don't use it until a year after our run."

Eyton nodded, seriously. "I've got an Ivanhoe coming up. Same kind of castle, I guess. I mean, if you've seen one you've seen them all." He turned to Taylor. "It's all squared away. But tell her to grow up."

"That's the one thing only nature can do, Charlie. She isn't grown up."

Taylor drove Caroline to his place on Alvarado Street. The bungalow was part of a building complex that had evolved, as far as Caroline knew, indigenously to Hollywood. A half-dozen bungalows were built on three sides of a courtyard containing palms and a fountain. On the fourth side was sidewalk and street. The owner of the complex occupied the first bungalow and acted as a concierge and armed guard. A well-known actor and his wife, friends of Taylor's, lived across from him. Caroline quite liked the small-town life of the arrangement despite the publicness of all the comings and goings beneath the palms. But then, for privacy, one could enter Taylor's bungalow from Maryland Avenue at the back. Caroline had come that way several times, prepared for love; instead she had got a candle-lit dinner, served by a villainous-looking servant called Eddie Sands; then they played backgammon.

When Caroline had reciprocated, Héloise serving a candle-lit dinner with all the joy of Saint Teresa bathing a leper colony, the evening had ended, again, in backgammon. Caroline had come to hate Mary Miles Minter, who had not yet, in the actuarial sense, grown up.

"That's the whole problem, really." Taylor mixed Caroline a martini. Caroline drank deep. If she was to be frustrated, she might as well be numbed. "She gets these wild crushes on people . . ."

"On you?"

"Among others. Then she writes incriminating letters and poor Charlie Eyton has to buy them up, to keep them from blackmailers and worse."

"Charlotte?"

Taylor nodded. "The last batch of letters were to a director, the father of her child . . ."

"But Charlotte knew all about that at the time." By now, Caroline felt that she knew the passionate Charlotte intimately. Taylor had confessed to a flirtation with mother as well as daughter. So when it had become clear that Taylor was to be the second director – and great love – in Minter's life, Charlotte had behaved like a bayou Medea. On several occasions, Minter would be locked in her room; then Charlotte's mother would help Minter to escape and she would show up at 404 Alvarado and Taylor would then . . . what? Caroline wondered. He had denied having an affair with the child. But then he had also denied his long affair with Mabel Normand. To hear him tell it, he was a sort of healer – like Rasputin, Caroline had sweetly remarked. But so much healing of others had given him an ulcer.

"I can't wait to go to Europe. Anything to get out of here," he said, looking about the very pleasant living room. Knoblock was out to dinner, and they would dine alone and, of course, early. Fortunately, Eddie was a good cook, which made up for very little.

"Perhaps I'll open up Saint-Cloud, or do you hate France?"

"No. No." He smiled at her through a haze of aromatic smoke from a gold-tipped cigarette. "I'd love that, and if you were there. . . ."

Caroline waited, eagerly, for the declaration.

But Taylor only sighed. "The problem is, with both of them, their careers are over, and they don't know it."

"Poor things." Caroline hated "both of them" with a purity that she had not suspected herself capable of. One was a world star at nineteen and a failure; the other a world star of twenty-six, and a dope-addicted crone.

"Of course, Mary doesn't know or care. She hates the movies, hates her life . . ."

"Hates her mother?"

Taylor shrugged. "She says she does. But if she really did, she could always move out."

"A child? A minor – a Mary Miles Minter Minor?" Caroline thought what a pleasure it would be to pull out, one by one, those carefully arranged golden ringlets, grown especially to replace on screen Mary Pickford's, which, when finally cut off, brought an entire nation to despair.

"She has her grandmother." Taylor was thoughtful. "But there's still that contract she signed, giving Charlotte thirty percent . . .'

"Since," said Caroline, bored beyond the call of any duty heretofore known to her, "tiny Minor Mary was a mere gosling at the time of the contract, it is not valid under the laws of this state. Tell her to go to court."

"She's still under-age. You know, she tried to kill herself, with her mother's gun."

Caroline's attention if not sympathy was at last engaged. "Why – a gun?"

"Because Mary thought she was in love with someone that Charlotte wouldn't let her see."

"I divined that. Why," asked Caroline, "does Charlotte have a gun?"

"Southern ladies are used to protecting themselves and their honor, from violation." Taylor was light.

Caroline was even lighter. "In the case of Charlotte Shelby, I suggest a softly murmured 'no' would do the trick. Or, perhaps," she elaborated happily, "an enthusiastic 'yes' might cause even the most devoted rapist to flee."

"We must find you a comedy," said Taylor.

"I *have* found it," said Caroline. This was later proved after dinner. Taylor put one hand on her shoulder, as if he knew exactly how ready, indeed eager, she was. "Yes, William," she whispered. "Yes?"

The fingers burned through the silk of her blouse. "A penny a point," he whispered and led her to the backgammon table.

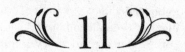

11

1

"My God, how the money rolls in!" sang Jess, tonelessly. Try as he might he could never learn the rest of the song or, indeed, anything other than the one line of chorus that perfectly summed up his situation. In the small parlor of 1509 H Street, Ned McLean was sound asleep on the sofa. Long before midnight when the poker game had broken up, Ned had passed out; and Daugherty had telephoned Evalyn to say that Ned was being well looked after. Now Daugherty was asleep upstairs while a colored cleaning woman removed bottles and overflowing ashtrays from the stale-smelling parlor.

Jess sat at a rolltop desk, doing sums. He was, he knew, handsomely turned out in a chocolate-brown suit with a lavender vest. Had it not been for a nagging ache in the lower right quadrant of his paunch, he was in the pink of condition, both chronic diabetes and asthma at bay. Then he made the first of several telephone calls to his – their – broker Samuel Ungerleider, formerly of Columbus, Ohio. "Whaddaya know?" Jess announced. But Ungerleider knew no more than the previous day's stock market figures. Sam handled investment accounts for the Hardings, Daugherty, Jess and a number of other Ohioans. As Jess was involved in a complex series of speculations, he was always in need of quick cash to cover his margin calls with Sam, who was as honest as Jess was punctilious about coming up with the cash on time. "You'll need eleven, twelve thousand by noon," said Sam.

"You've got it. How's Mr. Daugherty doing?"

"Fine. He don't play dice like you do, Jess."

"And the President?"

"A regular old widow woman . . ."

"That's the Duchess. She won't let him gamble on nothing."

"Lot of money to be made . . ."

"You're telling me. Let's keep it rolling in."

The first caller of the day arrived at seven-thirty. "Whaddaya know?" Jess sprayed the air between them but the man, a lugubrious Virginia bootlegger, seemed not to notice.

"Very kind of you I'm sure, Mr. Smith, to see me so early."

"Any friend of . . . of what's-his-name's a friend of mine." Jess opened and reached into one of the desk's pigeon-holes. From a drawer to which he alone had the key, he withdrew a Treasury Department form. "Now then, I am making you the Virginia-District of Columbia agent for the General Drug Company, with headquarters in Chicago, and in that capacity you would like to withdraw from the Federal custody, for medicinal purposes – how much?"

"One thousand cases of Scotch whisky. Five hundred of the best gin. Seven –"

"Whoa! Whoa! Hold your horses. I can only write so fast."

"Please to forgive me, Mr. Smith. But the thought of having the best to sell to my customers means a whole lot to me . . ."

"Them, too," said Jess. "It's a wonder half the state of Virginia isn't dead from all that illegal hooch they been drinking. There ought to be a law . . ."

The Virginian said, sadly, "Oh, there's a law all right, but no one cares about law these days."

Jess whistled a line or two of "April Showers" as he forged the name of an imaginary Treasury official to the form. "All right, sir, there you go. Present this at any one of the government's bonded warehouses, and they'll hand over the merchandise upon receipt of this bona fide Treasury Department order."

"I'm real grateful, Mr. Smith."

"Alexandria's the easiest warehouse. If there's any trouble, you call me at my office in the Justice Department. That'll be two thousand five hundred dollars, please. In cash like always."

The Virginian counted out the money; and was on his way. The next two callers were in need of inside guidance to political office or preferment. Each paid two thousand dollars for interim instructions. Then as the Attorney General of the United States came down the stairs, the last caller was shown the door. Jess never told Daugherty about any of his private business, and Daugherty never asked.

Daugherty gazed upon Ned McLean and shook his head sadly. "That boy had better get a good hold of himself or they're going to put him away. We should've sent him home last night."

"Well, this is his house, too, isn't it?" Jess was most protective of his friend Ned, who moaned in his sleep. "You want breakfast?"

"No. I'll get something at the Department."

"This a poker night?"

Daugherty grunted. "Ask the Duchess when you see her. I got me a busy day." Daugherty opened the front door. Outside in the street, the Attorney General's car was waiting. The chauffeur saluted Daugherty, and called him "General," the usual title for the nation's chief enforcer of the law. Daugherty quite liked the title; job, too. He got into the car and was driven off to the nearby Department of Justice.

The previous day, Jess had received a message from the White House that the First Lady of the Land wanted him to help her select materials; and so, having given instructions to the grim-faced colored woman on what to do when the owner of the house awakened, Jess stepped out into the bright spring morning and gazed near-sightedly upon the dogwood abloom in the front yard opposite and then, in a mood close to perfect contentment, he walked the short distance to the White House.

The contrast between the mansion now and as it was during the Wilsons' last days was vivid. A few weeks ago, the main gates were padlocked, the public kept away, and only the west wing transacted any business. Now the gates were open; and tourists filed in and out of the state apartments. ("It's *their* White House," the Duchess had proclaimed, as *she* took over.) The guards at the north gate waved Jess through even though he had his Federal Bureau of Investigation badge in hand, a gift from the obsequious assistant director, J. Edgar Hoover, a young man fearful of replacement by one of Daugherty's creatures. But Daugherty had gone by the book; obeyed all laws and most customs.

In many ways, the Harding Administration was the most capable and distinguished of the century, at least according to those editorial writers who did not care for Harding himself. True, one of the country's richest men, Andrew Mellon, was secretary of the Treasury, but his very wealth made it a certainty that he would not have to sell off contraband whisky to cover his broker's margin calls. Also, everyone knew that Mellon would create an atmosphere in which the country's best elements could do well. Although Harding had wanted to raise the income tax on the rich, Mellon had gently dissuaded him, and Wall Street and its newspapers had cheered Mr. Mellon. Also admired was the secretary of state, Charles Evans Hughes, who had run against Wilson in 1916. Equally reassuring was the presence at the Commerce Department of the country's most popular public figure, Herbert Hoover, famed for his competence and honesty while Will Hays, as postmaster general, pursued his high destiny. The secretary of the interior, Senator Fall, had been unanimously hailed by the Senate. Only Daugherty had inspired the cry of cronyism; but then every president was allowed to have at least one political manager on the payroll.

Jess entered the main door. An usher greeted him with the message that Mrs. Harding was in the upstairs family parlor. As Jess crossed to the elevator he was aware that the long line of tourists moving from Red to Blue to Green to East Rooms were staring at *him*, and wondering who this powerful man was, wearing a new Chesterfield coat and thick-rimmed owl-like – for wisdom – glasses. There was a sigh of ecstasy when the private elevator arrived and he stepped in.

In the oval parlor the Duchess had draped materials over every piece of furniture. In attendance was a frightened clerk from Woodward and Lothrop's Department Store.

"Jess Smith, you come in here and get to work. Is this real velvet or is it velveteen?" The clerk dared not speak. Jess fingered the material. There was very little that he did not know about fabrics.

"It's velvet, all right."

"Just wanted to make sure. I'm sure Donald Woodward would never try to cheat us but sometimes mistakes," she glared at the clerk, "get made."

Jess helped her pick out several bolts of material that he was certain would look good on her. Now that Florence Kling Harding was First Lady of the Land, she intended to dress up to her new role. The result was not entirely pleasing in Jess's eyes. For one thing, she had taken to wearing clown spots of rouge on her gray cheeks while her hair was, regularly, mercilessly, marcelled. As diplomatically as Jess could, he steered her away from gold and silver threads for daytime wear and pale pastel chiffons for evening wear. "More suitable, maybe, for the boudoir," said Jess, assuming, unconsciously, his Smith's Emporium wheedling voice. Then, orders given, the clerk departed.

"Sit down, Jess. Warren wants to play poker tonight at H Street. So tell the usuals. I'm not going. That means you make sure he's home before twelve."

Jess said that he would do his best, as always.

"Also, don't let him chew. It's bad for him. Cigars are all right *if* there's no camera around but keep an eagle-eye on him if he chews."

"How do I stop him?"

"You tell him you'll tell me *and* Doc Sawyer. That should do it."

"I'll try, Duchess." But Jess expected that this mission would fail. So addicted was Harding to chewing tobacco that Jess had seen him, on several occasions, unravel a cigarette and put the tobacco in his mouth. "How's the household going?"

The thin mouth opened like a letter-box. "I've got the kitchen under control at last. I tell you, the Wilsons just let everything fall apart. So when Mrs. Wilson said to me – first thing – how good the housekeeper was, and after I saw the house, the first thing I wanted to do was get rid of her. But she's turning out all right. The villain was Mrs. Wilson. She just didn't care about anything except that sick husband of hers. They were extremely selfish people."

The Duchess was now at the birdcage which contained the much-loved, by the Duchess only, canary. "Pete, sing for Mummy.

Pete!" the Duchess commanded; then she, not the sullen Pete, trilled. "I declare that bird gets more temperamental every day. Sulk. Sulk. Sulk. Why didn't you take that job Warren offered you?"

"Oh, you know I like being out on the floor with the customers, like we say in dry goods."

"You're just about the only person from Ohio I can think of who said no to a job." Jess tried to look modest and above the battle. "Of course you're pretty rich," she added. "Pete sings just like a nightingale when he isn't in one of his moods."

Actually, Jess had been delighted when he had been offered the post of commissioner of Indian affairs; and he had been distressed when the western senators had informally told the President that he wouldn't do. W.G. had then asked him if he'd like to be treasurer of the United States, a ceremonial job which involved little more than allowing his signature to be printed on every dollar bill. But as Jess had other plans for dollar bills, he had thanked the President warmly and said he preferred to be of use to the Administration in less formal ways.

Laddie Boy, the President's collie, stormed into the room; leapt upon Jess and barked at the Duchess, who said, "Shut up. Warren's on his way. Here he is."

But it was not the President but Charlie Forbes. "Hiya, Duchess! Hiya, Jess!" Forbes was the President's jester, a round-faced man with owl-like glasses and, despite red hair, a passing resemblance to Jess. "I'm here for lunch. The President's promised wienerwurstels and sauerkraut, so I left my veterans to their affairs and hurried over."

"Charlie." The Duchess disliked any and all sexual allusions. But Charlie was now playing with Laddie Boy, and Jess envied him his easy charm. Where Jess was only called upon to run errands, Charlie Forbes was asked over to cheer everyone up. A builder from Spokane, Washington, Colonel Forbes was a genuine war hero, who had been awarded the Congressional Medal of Honor. Everyone had agreed he was a natural to be director of the Veterans Bureau. A Wilson Democrat, Charlie had been so charmed by Senator and Mrs. Harding, and they by him, in the course of a senatorial junket to the Northwest that he had shifted parties and organized the region for Harding. Finally, Charlie was the only one of W.G.'s playmates that the Duchess doted on. "I just hope Warren gets the lunch he ordered. The cook makes such a fuss every time he asks for sauerkraut. *And* toothpicks. Lord, the problems I'm having with Warren. He tells the butler he wants toothpicks *on the table,* which has never happened before in the White House . . ."

"First president to have his own teeth," said Charlie. "They ought to be proud."

"Then the butler comes to me and I say no, and then Warren goes to the housekeeper and raises his voice . . ."

Laddie Boy bounded out of the room.

"That means Warren's shaking hands in the East Room. Half an hour every morning, no matter what. He *likes* it. Imagine!" The Duchess sighed.

Charlie sighed, "I've got a buyer for Wyoming Avenue."

"You know the price?"

"He'll meet it. Don't worry. He's my legal adviser at the Bureau. Charles Cramer. First-rate. From California. Big law firm."

"I'll hate giving up that house . . ."

"Busy days." Charlie was so full of energy that he made Jess tired just watching him dance about a room. "We're building, building, building. Hospitals everywhere. . . . Oh, Duchess! We're taking Carolyn on, in Personnel."

"Does Warren know?" The Duchess frowned. "She's his sister after all."

"He's happy we could fit her in."

The President and Laddie Boy entered the room together. "Good morning, gentlemen. Duchess. Pete."

"He won't sing," observed the Duchess.

"Jess, tell Harry we'll meet at H Street after supper. So round up the boys."

"Yes, Mr. President." George Christian appeared in the doorway. "Can you see Senator Borah and Senator Day, after lunch?"

"Well, can I? You're the fellow who knows."

"Yes, sir. I can fit them in. Senator Borah says it's important."

"Everything to do with Mr. Borah's important," said the Duchess. "He's a scandal the way he and Alice Longworth are carrying on, not that Nick cares, but poor Mrs. Borah's a martyr, I say . . ."

Harding nodded to Christian, who disappeared; as did Jess. Although he liked to say he hated offices, he very much enjoyed the one that Daugherty had given him on the sixth floor of the Department of Justice. He was paid no salary but he could write letters on Justice Department stationery and, best of all, he had access to the files. In a city where who knew what was all that mattered, he was becoming very knowledgeable indeed. Finally, as right hand to the President's right hand (Daugherty had a private line to the President's office), every door opened for him as he went about *his* business, which was to keep the money rolling in.

2

The family dining room smelled of wieners and sauerkraut, one of Burden's favorite meals. The President received them at the head of the cleared table. He was chewing on a toothpick and he seemed to Burden to have grown, literally, in office. It was not so much that he was stouter – like a glacier, the high stomach had moved another inch up his rib cage – as the aura of largeness about him, the large bronze face, the thick white hair, the black eyebrows, the sense of perfect equilibrium. Burden wondered if, by design, they had all been led to underestimate Harding – by *his* design.

Certainly Harding's first message to Congress had made it very clear that not only was he the president but he was not about to yield any of his powers to the legislative branch, particularly to that Senate which was supposed to have created him. Twice, he had publicly made fun of the notion that he had been installed by senatorial bosses, and Burden had studied the faces of Lodge and Brandegee and Smoot, and found in them a degree of sour corroboration. Lately, the cloakroom Republicans had taken to complaining how "the highbrows" of the Cabinet, Hughes and Hoover, were exercising far too much influence over the President. Now Borah, with help from his Democratic friend James Burden Day, was about to do some influencing of his own.

Harding motioned for the two men to sit on either side of him. Coffee was brought. The dog chewed a bone at Harding's feet. "I figured this was the quietest place, on short notice." Harding waited for the butler with the coffee to go. When the door shut behind him, Harding whispered, "Boys, I tell you this place is like something at the time of those Louises of France, or maybe the Borgias. Everybody's listening to you all the time. Half the time we talk in code so what we say won't end up in Hearst's papers." Harding turned to Burden. "Heard you had kind of a tough race."

"Thanks to you, I nearly lost." Burden's majority had been very small indeed, while two of the state's congressional seats that had never been anything but Democratic had gone Republican. Kitty had been indomitable, and Burden had not been himself, energy much lowered since the flu. Would he ever be well again? he wondered. "Jake Hamon also spent a lot of money in our state, which didn't help."

"Poor Jake." Harding shook his head. "Well, if he had to get killed, I suppose it was more becoming that it was his mistress and not his wife that did the deed."

Borah allowed five minutes for presidential small talk. In some mysterious way, at least mysterious to Burden, the lone wolf of the Senate had made himself its greatest power. In fact, when Lodge and his senatorial coven had tried to re-create the League of Nations without Wilson, Burden had overheard Borah warning Lodge that if he tried to support *any* kind of League, Borah would break him. Lodge had, most icily, said that it was singularly insolent for a young man like Borah to speak in such a fashion to his elder (and, by implication, better), to which Borah had said that there was worse to come if Lodge and his friends tried to betray the electorate. When Lodge had then threatened to resign as majority leader, Borah had thundered, "Resign? Never! We won't let you. We'll throw you out, as an example." Clearly, all the drama these days was on the Republican side. The Democrats were demure; and dour in their electoral defeat.

"Mr. President," Borah began; and Burden felt a chill – thus the great windy tribune addressed the presiding officer of the Senate. Was he going to speak for four hours? Suddenly, Harding was, once again, just a spear-carrier in the Senate, staring, hypnotized, at the greatest of chieftains. "We have had our disagreements in the past. I did not support you until last September when you assured me that *you* would never support our entry into *any* League of Nations." Borah's eyes were fixed on Harding, who blinked, and cupped his right cheek in his right hand and chewed on the stub of an unlit cigar.

Borah took silence for consent. "My fear of foreign entanglements is well-known. But I am hardly an ostrich. I know what will happen should the nations start up an arms-race in a world at peace. Should there be a competitive build-up of fleets, I am here to tell you that we will be at war with Japan within the next quarter-century, and, frankly, I would regard such a war as nothing less than a crime against humanity, started by us in our neglect." Borah drank a glass of water.

Harding took advantage of this pause. He sat up straight. "Senator, it is perfectly clear to me and to Secretary Hughes that the troubles with Japan have already begun, specifically in the matter of who will control the island of Yap now that Germany is gone from the Pacific and, generally, in the matter of who will control our common ocean, the Pacific."

Burden was startled by the usually vague President's sudden mastery of the relevant detail. He looked at Borah out of the corner of his eye and saw that the wide mouth was now slightly ajar – with surprise? Usually when Borah was in the room only Borah spoke. "Now then," the President put down the cigar stub, "it is not our wish around here to get the folks upset all over again over the Yellow Peril – like 1913 when we almost had a war with Japan. On the other hand, I take your point, Senator, about the necessity of coming to terms with them *outside* the League of Nations, which alarms you more than it does me, but then that's the way we are, you and I. For me, the League is a perfectly nice idea which probably wouldn't work even if we were to join . . ."

"Mr. President, should we join the League, our liberties would be surrendered . . ." The Lion of Idaho had begun to roar. But the President raised his hand, and smiled.

"I hadn't quite finished, Senator. Certainly I know your eloquent views on the subject." Harding looked at Burden as if for confirmation. Burden responded with a nod. The President continued. "I am going to prepare a disarmament campaign pretty much along the lines of your December-fourteenth resolution which authorized – or was it directed? – me," Harding's smile was mischievous, "to ask the British and the Japanese governments to join us in cutting back our naval programs by fifty percent or whatever. Mr. Hughes and I have been working on this ever since we got here, though neither of us has had much to say on the subject in public. I've discovered one thing about this job." Harding stretched his arms; then he cradled the back of his neck in his hands. "Someone – in this case you – can come up with a good idea that the President likes, but that's not always enough, because a lot of the time even though he – me – agrees with you on a policy, I have to say no, and sit back, looking sad and forlorn, until you force me to do the right thing."

"In this case, you can count on my forcing you, Mr. President." Borah was somewhat taken aback by Harding's unexpected grasp of the essentials of power. Burden had often noted that for want of good timing, many an excellent policy had failed of enactment. "What's nice here," said the President, "is that disarmament is as popular with the pro-Leaguers like Bryan as it is with you anti-Leaguers. Only Mr. Hearst and Burden's Naval Sub-Committee dislike it, which proves we're on the right track."

Burden smiled. "*I* like it, even if the rest of the sub-committee wants more and more and bigger and better battleships."

"All those contracts!" Harding shook his head in mock wonder. "*All* that paperwork! Just makes your head ache, don't it? Now, gentlemen, I want you on both sides of the Senate to keep the pressure on me. I will look grave and concerned and keep on saying you must not force the hand of the executive, and I'll wonder out loud how on earth you think you could ever bring yourselves to trust the Japanese and the British to live up to their promise to disarm when you don't trust them enough to join them in a League."

Burden heard Borah inhale sharply as this needle found its mark. But the President was in full control of the situation. "So let's keep in close touch during the next few weeks." Harding rose, as did the two senators. Laddie Boy raised his leg against a chair. Harding gave him a shove and said sadly, "I wish he wouldn't do that." Then he turned to Borah. "Let me wind up my fishing expedition with the Japanese. The British are already on board, so they say. We may also have to include the French and the Italians to make them feel good. Then when we're ready, I'll give you a signal to go and put the gun to my head with a Senate resolution, and then, gracefully, I'll give way, and we'll send out invitations for a conference here in Washington, probably some time in July. You see," the President had led them to the door, "I want this country to be known as a defender of the peace, everywhere."

"We're as one on that." Borah shook the President's hand.

"So was Wilson," Burden observed, "but he would've made a brilliant speech prematurely. Then he would've denounced those who disagreed with him and . . . well, I suppose he would've declared martial law, if he could."

"I am a softer president." Harding smiled. "As there's no chance of my ever being known as a great or brilliant president, like Wilson, I can only hope to be one of the better-loved, if any politician can ever be the beneficiary of such an emotion."

"Such a thing," said Borah, plainly impressed, "is very possible."

Harding patted each on the back and led them into the main hall. "Anyway, what I really have going for me is that since nobody has the slightest expectation of me, whatever I do that's any good at all will produce astonishment." Then Harding plunged into a crowd of tourists, shaking hands and visibly spreading euphoria.

As Burden and Borah waited for their car at the north portico, Burden said, "Offhand, I'd say that the Senate is not guiding the President, as previously advertised. Quite the contrary, in fact."

Borah grunted. "It's Hughes and Hoover that do the guiding."

"I'm not so sure."

"What difference does it make?" Borah got into the car first, though Burden was his senior. Burden got in after him. The car smelled of hyacinth, which the driver had picked somewhere – where? – the hyacinth in Rock Creek had come and gone. "As long as we're going in the same direction, everything's all right. It's later, when we differ . . ." Borah's jaw set. He was made for opposition. He was eloquent, honest, intelligent; and he bored Burden to death.

3

Like an imperious lizard, Queen Elizabeth darted this way and that between the cardboard trees, which, despite superb – dim! – lighting, looked exactly like cardboard trees with paper leaves. Queen Elizabeth was very, very old and Mary Queen of Scots was simply old. Caroline sank lower in her chair, and watched herself unpack, one by one, her not very large bag of tricks. How few they were when all was said and done, and all appeared now to be said, done.

In the flickering light from the projection booth, she could see that Charles Eyton had not slumped in his seat; he sat very straight, smoking a cigarette whose smoke made cloud-like patterns in the ray of light that carried within its impulses the images of Traxler Productions' *Mary Queen of Scots,* starring Emma Traxler, a "troubled" production, as Miss Kingsley had called it in the Los Angeles *Times,* one whose budget had gone from one to close to two million dollars "with no young love interest for the flapper set," in the words of the *Kine Weekly.* Since Emma was the mature love interest, Taylor had, much to her relief, cut a subplot involving two young lovers. Now she longed to see dewy lips and unlined necks on the screen, anything other than her admittedly attractive ruff and somewhat less attractive tired eyes. Bothwell was the right age for her, which meant that they were both the wrong age for the movie audience as opposed to the theater, where, viewed at a distance, they would have charmed and convinced.

Caroline shut her eyes during the close shot where she turns on Queen Elizabeth in the cardboard forest. Despite careful lighting, the luminous eyes, beloved by adolescent boys and sapphic women of all ages, shone through a delicate network of very small lines never before visible in her mirror or, presumably, to the most expensive make-up man in the business. Now, like the canals of Mars, they registered thirty times life size on the screen. Caroline was beginning to feel ill. She grasped William's hand, and found it sweaty. He returned the squeeze briefly; then detached his hand and lit a cigarette. There were a number of coughs from the rest of the audience, professionals who would soon be trying to market the long-awaited *Mary*.

A battle scene came as a relief. Then back to Mary's prison, and a great deal of marching up and down, and arms flung this way and that like a Dutch windmill in a gale. At last the ending: a jeering crowd of extras who looked as they always did in every other photoplay. It was said that movie addicts all over the country had memorized the faces of hundreds of extras and whenever a favorite appeared, he was cheered as he fought in the American or French Revolution or languidly gambled at the casino in Monte Carlo or pushed a cart in the slums of Old New York.

Finally: The great doors of the castle open and Mary appears alone, in black, clutching cross, Bible, rosary. She is regal in her bearing yet, somehow, vulnerable, as almost anyone would be whose head is about to be chopped off. Who did she remind Caroline of? Mary was at the foot of the steps to the scaffold when Caroline recalled – Miss Glover, the mathematics teacher at Mlle. Souvestre's, a woman with a never-ending cold, teary eyes and a dripping nose.

Caroline shuddered as she watched Miss Glover, clutching a much-used handkerchief, slowly ascend the steps to where the hooded headsman, ax in hand, awaits her. Wisely, Caroline had decided to keep her ruff on until the very last minute. William had suggested that she keep it on even while her head was being chopped off as no one would know the difference and, besides, an ax that could go clear through a neck could certainly take care of a mere ruff, but Caroline felt that history required a degree of respect.

Cut-away shots to the extras covered the removal of the ruff. Where before they were jeering, now they are suffused with both awe and pity, particularly a burly Highlander, who sports on one hairy wrist an expensive Longine wristwatch. They would have to re-cut, thought Caroline. Tim would have seen that wristwatch in time. Yet for this sort of thing William Desmond Taylor was the better director. But then again *what,* she wondered, panic beginning, *was* this sort of thing?

Mary Queen of Scots looks around her – one last luminous gaze upon a world that she is now about to leave forever. Then, ignoring Knoblock's interpolation of Anne Boleyn's "Such a little neck" ("Who on earth will know?" he had asked, "who said it?"), Mary – no, Miss Glover again – clutches Bible and cross to her bosom. A title card assures the audience that she is en route to a better world where trigonometry is the study of triangles. Then Miss Glover – eternally in thrall to Trinity as the ultimate triangle – approaches the block, kneels, places head on block.

Pity and awe seize the extras just as it will the audience, depending on who is playing the Wurlitzer organ at New York's Strand theater or, if they are lucky enough to be booked into the Capitol, an entire symphony orchestra guaranteed to drag powerful emotions from any audience during those last moments as Miss Glover loses her head and the camera moves from the ax-man's knees to his hooded head to the tower of the castle behind to the stormy sky above where the sun emerges from behind a cloud bank to make a thousand prisms of the camera lens as Mary Queen of Scots' troubled soul is received by angels – gloria, gloria, gloria!

Caroline wanted to kill if not herself Emma Traxler, whose blind vanity had got her into this humiliating mess.

As the lights came on in the projection room, Charles Eyton rose and shook his head rapturously. "Never seen anything like it. Congratulations, both of you."

"It needs a bit of fine-tuning," said William smoothly. "We'll preview at Pasadena and see . . . you know, how it holds."

Charles nodded and daubed at his eyes. "Take it to Bakersfield, too."

So it was as bad as Caroline suspected. Bakersfield meant a working-class, meat-and-potatoes audience who would have hated *Mary* even more had it been good. The Bakersfield audience was also known to talk to the screen, advising the characters on their next plot-moves. Eyton was gone and Caroline accepted the congratulations of her fellow dream-makers. No eyes made contact with hers. She would go back to Washington.

Caroline dropped William off at his house. Although she wanted to talk to Tim, who was shooting a film in Culver City, William asked her to come in, rather more urgently than usual. Fortunately, Eddie was not visible. "Shall I make tea?" he asked.

Caroline said no, she would make herself a drink, which she did, from a console crowded with crystal decanters and silver-framed photographs of great stars, reverently arranged like Roman household deities. As in every other Hollywood house, Mary Pickford was principal goddess. Presumably when she got old and resembled Miss Glover, her picture would be removed from a thousand consoles and the tops of ten thousand pianos, and Gloria Swanson – or someone – would take her place. "Who is this?" For the first time Caroline noticed a picture of a striking if not beautiful woman with a large hat and huge dark eyes.

"Charlotte Shelby. You've met her. Little Mary Minter's mother."

"Little Mary Minter," murmured Caroline, staring at a large photograph of the golden-ringletted child with the large eyes and boiled-potato nose.

Then star faced director. "Bakersfield," said Caroline in a voice that she had never heard herself use before: Lady Macbeth was now within her range. She could do it on stage. The dialogue that she could never learn would be glued to the backs of chairs and columns, and she would thunder the part as she strode, covered with blood, about Glamis Castle or wherever it was in Scotland. No, not Scotland again. She had left all that was celluloid if not mortal of Emma Traxler on the Argyle – Scotland again! – Lot.

"I think, even in Bakersfield, they will be happy." William was comforting. "You're too close to it. That's all. I think the story works remarkably well."

"*It* does, William. I don't." Caroline sat down at his desk, as if it were her own. "The calendar has caught up with me."

"Don't be absurd." He said all that she wanted to hear.

"Do we open at the Capitol?"

William shrugged. "Why not? You're popular in that house. It's what they call classy, and so are you. I'm leaving the first of June." William pressed his diaphragm. He had had for more than a year intermittent pains, as yet undiagnosed.

"Where to?" Caroline did not know whether or not she was being invited to go with him.

"London. I told you. Knoblock's lent me his townhouse in London. I'm leaving him this. A swap. I'll be back in the fall. I need a complete rest." He looked harassed. Although everyone thought that William Desmond Taylor took drugs, there was no sign of it in his behavior, unlike that of Mabel Normand or Wallace Reid, whom the studio supplied with morphine on the set so that he could cope with the day's shooting. Hollywood was growing more and more addicted and the salesmen of drugs –" dealers of cards," as they were sportily known – were everywhere, disguised as Russian princes at dinner parties or as peanut-vendors selling brown paper bags containing cards of cocaine. Caroline often had the sense that she was living in an encoded society to which she alone lacked the key.

"What about *Green Temptation*?" This was to be the next Taylor photo-play, with no part for Caroline.

"Postponed." He looked at her, somewhat anxiously. "Why don't you come, too?"

William had led Caroline so many times down the cactus-strewn path of unrequited desire that she was reluctant to expose herself again to a desert that contained neither honey nor locusts – or was it a mess of herbs? "I'm not sure that I can. The paper . . ." She always mentioned her other life when the current one proved unsatisfactory.

"Of course," he said, too quickly. "I quite understand. I simply thought you might enjoy London and the theater and your European fame . . ."

"In tatters, by now." As Caroline made light of herself and Europe and the movies, she played nervously with a letter on the desk. Over and over again she read to herself the line – black ink on blue notepaper: "I will shoot you and that is a promise." Yet so busy was she with her own performance that she did not take in the words. They were simply so many meaningless scrawls and loops, part of a different plot from the one that she was involved in, another keyless code. It was not until she had half-promised *not* to go, so much more tactical than a half-promise to go, that Caroline realized what she had been reading. But by then she was in bed with Tim for the first time in months. He had come home early from the studio. Héloise had let him in and he had fallen asleep in her bed. Caroline had seized her opportunity.

"What does he see in me?" she asked yet again: some of Tim's answers to this old question pleased her more than others.

"Money." Tim was brisk. He lay beside her, lean and hairy and self-absorbed.

"Why mine? There are so many other people here with more than I've got. He wants me to go to Europe with him. Why?"

"So that you'll introduce him to your grand friends."

"I don't have any. Anyway, he's got more. He already knows all the sort of people that – would know him," she added with precise cruelty.

"He still hasn't gone to bed with you?"

Caroline shook her head. "I assume that I'm too old. He who worships at the shrine of the Three M's will not light so much as a candle to my aged effigy."

"How you mock my religion!"

"Mine, too," said Caroline. She saw herself in a nun's habit, a vow of silence, doing good works in a leper colony. Then she remembered Lubitsch's comment that every actress over forty wanted to play a nun to hide her neck.

"Has it occurred to you that he's one of the boys?" Tim was always quick to separate everyone into one of two strict sexual categories, which, Caroline knew, was not possible in the real world, at least not amongst Parisian ladies whose life work was to keep in perfect equilibrium husband, lover and beloved woman friend.

"Perhaps he is. Some of the time. But do boys write you letters in a woman's handwriting on scented note-paper, threatening to kill you?"

Tim sat up in bed. "Not my kind of boy."

"I shouldn't think *any*one's kind of boy. No, the letter was from a woman. You can always tell. I don't know how. The color of the paper, the exclamation marks. . . . Anyway, it was lying on his desk, and I was sitting at his desk. I didn't mean to read it but of course I did, right in front of him, too, not paying the slightest attention to what it said."

"Did it say 'kill'?"

"'Shoot,' actually."

"Only a man would write 'shoot.'"

"Well, this woman wrote 'shoot.'"

Tim frowned. "Taylor's supposed to be pretty deep into the drug world. A fellow dealer, maybe?"

"I don't know. All I know is – I want to be with him." Precisely why Caroline would want to be at all hours of day and night in the company of a man with whom she had not had an affair was a mystery not only to the patient Tim but to herself. She had now lived quite a long time in the world and she had always managed through luck – bad or good? – or instinct to base her life securely upon herself and not upon others. From Burden to Tim, she had been able to conduct as pleasurable a relationship as she could with men while not allowing any of them into her life beyond, as it were, the bed. Now, bedless, again, *as it were* – how they had mocked Henry James's elaborate elderly style! – and how useful it was when it came to gathering up contradictory emotions in order to sort them out. Bedless, she was jealous in a way that she had never known before. She had, subtly she hoped, quizzed everyone about Taylor. She had flattered the Three dismal M's at parties, and she had responded warmly but wearily to Mabel Normand's charms, which were, like those of so many of the natural stars, calculated to ensnare both sexes. But at the center of all this desire was William Desmond Taylor, a perfect enigma. He was liked by "real" men, even Chaplin was a friend, to the extent that that odd world-spirit could be said even to notice anyone in any guise save audience. The professionals

411

regarded Taylor with admiration; and women were drawn to him. Yet she was quite unable to touch him, much less know him. Good manners – his – kept her from flinging herself upon him. Taylor was a master of distance, who always kept her just out of reach. Ordinarily, if frustrated, Caroline had known enough to move on. But this time she *stayed* on. He talked to her, constantly, of Mary and Mabel, and she listened, with sympathy, as if she were their mother.

"I don't think Mr. Eyton likes Mary Miles . . . I mean, *Mary Queen of Scots.*" Caroline put on her dressing gown.

"Do *you* like it?" Tim lay on the bed, wearing only a single garter which he had forgotten to take off.

"I look very old."

"Probably not as old as you think you do. Remember, you look at yourself a lot closer than the audience will. You over-react."

"I over-act."

"I would've stopped that."

"William tried." She was defensive of her passion. "I suppose I suspected I looked wrong, like Miss Glover, a teacher I had in school. Perhaps," she looked into her dressing-table mirror, "I should bob my hair."

"Then you wouldn't look like Emma Traxler."

"That's the point."

"Forget it. Go to Europe with him. Get away from here for a while. Don't read the reviews. See your friend Mrs. Wharton and try to buy her new book, the one you like and I can't read. All those rich people . . . you'll need long hair for that."

Tim cheered her up both physically and morally. It was curious that as she got older the act of love seemed more and more necessary to her than when she was young, yet morale tended to weaken with each new year, winged years, she thought of them, gliding by ever faster, like bats at sundown.

Caroline reciprocated, and they had an early dinner at the Sunset Inn on Ocean Avenue, where she tried to talk him out of a movie about a lynching in the South. "You're getting typed, as they call it," she said, watching an early near-full moon start its showy progress across the gray Pacific sky. Beneath them, the tide swept slowly in and out, swirling about the restaurant's fragile wooden piles set like stilts upon the sand. Across the dining room, eating heavily and drinking deeply, were a half-dozen comic actors, and their girl friends, known as starlets.

"There should be at least one . . . typed director." But Tim did not look too pleased with his distinction. It was said that he had quarrelled with Ince. As there were not many other studios where he would have so free a hand, and as he had refused to allow Traxler Productions to be "typed," too, that left only Europe, which was not his sort of thing. "The poison-pen letters have stopped," he observed.

"My poor child," Caroline sighed.

"Emma now sends me poison-pen pamphlets. How did she get the way she is?"

"As she has no father, I suppose I'm at fault. But I don't know how."

"Washington?"

"Perhaps. It's hard for us – well, me – to believe that all those speeches our friends make in the Senate and we never listen to, *they* listen to . . ."

"The public?"

Caroline nodded. "The senators who give them, too. They keep making so much of Bolshevism that, I suppose, they believe it all. Like the Huns."

"Just like the Huns." Tim looked up, and his eyes grew round. "Here she comes."

Caroline turned, as Elinor Glyn made her entrance, with three young men, of whom one was a rising star whose name Caroline could never remember.

Miss Glyn's eagle-like eye took in the entire restaurant. When she saw Caroline, she left her own party, swept past the table of comics who paused in their routines to gaze with awe upon a legend. "Dear Miss Traxler!" Caroline and Tim both rose. "Do sit. Please. We're celebrating. I have just received what is called a 'go-ahead' for my second picture . . ."

"Sit down," said Emma Traxler, all business, irony expunged at the thought of trade.

"I shall be making it near *you*, Mr. Farrell, in Culver City, with the charming Mr. Goldwyn, who has just told the press that my name is *anonymous* with sex appeal. A bit of a revulsh, I suppose, but beggars cannot be choosers."

Caroline asked briskly for all details. "I produce," said Glyn. "Mr. Sam Wood directs for me yet again. He is aptly named but no matter. I shall have even greater freedom than I had with Lasky. There is a Mr. Gibbons in the art department who has actually seen a great house from the inside and is nearly a gentleman himself. No more dried palms and elephant feet in the drawing rooms of Mayfair . . ."

"So unlike Sandringham and Osborne," said Caroline, playing the royal card.

"You have stayed in *those* houses?"

"In the old days of Queen Victoria." Caroline had once spent a weekend at Sandringham when the Prince of Wales, not the Queen, was in residence. There were, she recalled, a number of elephant feet containing canes and umbrellas. "But who plays the lead? Gloria Swanson again?"

"That is undecided. But I've got *him! It*, personified. Rudolph Valentino. He's joining us tonight with his two ladies. So charming. Do you speak Italian?"

"Oh, yes!" Caroline or, rather, Emma lied. In the last year, Valentino had become a world star with *The Sheik* and *The Four Horsemen of the Apocalypse.*

"Rodolfo is essentially unspoiled, untouched by the Californian Curse, as I call it. The Evil Fairy that spoils everything, finally, for everyone who comes here in pursuit of fool's gold . . ."

"But the gold's actually pretty real," said Tim, somewhat recovered from his first alarm at the sight of Elinor Glyn.

"But then so are the fools." Caroline smiled radiantly, aware too that, as she did, her face had become a spider's web of lines and so, thanks to this suicidal – tic? – she should not be appearing opposite Rodolfo in *Beyond the Rocks.*

"A tale of innocence meeting sophistication. Of young fresh trusting Theodora . . ."

If not the part of Theodora, then perhaps she could play her mother, thought Caroline wildly, allowing her smile to fade as quickly as was plausible.

"With Rodolfo as the world-weary Lord Bracondale . . ."

Glyn gave her a suspicious look. "The Lambtons are a lot darker than adorable Rodolfo."

"Moors, they say – the Lambtons, that is. Wasn't Shakespeare's dark lady related to them?"

"That was before my time." Wig held high, Elinor Glyn joined her table. No mention had been made of *Mary Queen of Scots*.

"Well, that decides it," said Caroline. "The Californian Curse is upon me. I must flee."

"Where to?"

"Washington? Where else?"

"I thought you were finished with newspapers."

Caroline wondered if, perhaps, she was finished with everything; life, too.

"I could always retreat to France and become an old lady."

Tim shook his head. "You would kill yourself first. Why don't you take all this more seriously?"

"All what?"

"Movies. Why do you think I keep trying to make movies about real life?"

"Because you don't know any better. This is not real life. This is . . . amusement."

Tim shook his head. "No, there's more to it than that. You remember your first picture."

"I was incredibly noble. And I looked marvelous."

Tim sighed. "Actresses. But don't you know what you – what we did? The government wanted every American to hate every German, and we – you and I – pulled it off."

"With some help from a thousand other movies, and the press, and George Creel, and the Germans . . ."

"That's not the point. At a certain moment we made a . . . connection with the public, with the . . . the *Zeitgeist*. We were able to make everyone feel what we wanted them to."

Caroline stared at Elinor Glyn, who was staring at her watch: Rodolfo was late. "You sound like Chaplin when he talks about movies as a Force for Good."

"He's right. Though I don't know what he thinks is good. As it is, we are now supplying the world with all sorts of dreams and ideas. Well, why don't we shape those dreams, deliberately?"

Caroline heard Tim at last, through the great velvety cloud of self-pity in which she had been encased. "You are ambitious," she heard herself saying as she began to emerge from the cloud. "But I see what you mean. There is no country here . . . no real country anywhere, I suppose, except in dreams. But what do you want them to dream?"

Tim shrugged. "Eugene V. Debs?"

Caroline shook her head. "That's just propaganda, and most people know how to ignore special pleading. A dream is something subtle – universal, unnoticeable at the time but then unforgettable. The way Richard Barthelmess walks in *Broken Blossoms*. But I don't see how you – we – anyone – can calculate what will work."

"Then don't calculate. Simply do it. Show things the way they are but carefully angled, the way the camera is, to make the audience see what you want them to see . . ."

"Which is what?"

Tim laughed, and looked very young indeed. "If we knew the answer to that we would know everything and so die happy. Just do it."

Caroline was beginning to get the range. "Up till now," she began to improvise, "we've let the government tell us what to do and pretty much how to do it. So why not," Caroline set her foot with great deliberation upon the road to Damascus, "reverse the procedure and make the government do – and be – what we want them to do and be?"

Tim was delighted. "Years of writing stupid capitalist editorials have trained you well."

"I'm not so sure about the stupid part." Caroline was serene. "But where Hearst invented the news about people, we can . . ." Involuntarily, she shuddered and did not know why.

"We can what?"

"I was going to say we can invent the people. Can we?"

"Why not? They're waiting to be invented, to be told who and what they are."

Caroline suddenly realized that she – and everyone else – had been approaching this new game from the wrong direction. Movies were not there simply to reflect life or tell stories but to exist in their own autonomous way and to look, as it were, back at those who made them and watched them. They had used the movies successfully to demonize national enemies. Now why not use them to alter the viewer's perception of himself and the world? Thus, she would be able to outdo Hearst at last. Self-pity was now replaced by megalomania of the most agreeable sort. She even fell in love with Tim, yet again. What work they could do together now that they knew what the work was! Then, as if blessings could not cease to flow, it was quite clear to her and to Elinor Glyn that Rudolph Valentino had stood her up, while the comedians at the next table made more and more noise until one of them, a very fat man who had been a plumber before stardom, made a trip to the toilet, imitating, as he walked, Elinor Glyn, to all the room's delight save the inventrix of passion, who scowled. Caroline laughed a care-free laugh. Under the table, Tim, unexpectedly, held her hand.

1

Burden nodded, and shivered. Plainly, he was never going to go back to what he had been before the flu. He would simply go forward to the end. Glumly, he stared at the flag-draped pine-wood box that contained the remains of "the unknown soldier," a current fetish all round the world as the world's leaders interred the odd set of unidentified bones, thus honoring, as they liked to put it, the anonymous multitudes that they had sacrificed for nothing at all. The coffin had been placed on a bier hidden by floral wreaths. Burden wondered who – or what – was inside the box.

On the stage at the center of the amphitheater, the world's leaders or their military representatives were solemnly arranging themselves. They had been summoned to Washington for the Arms Limitation Conference. Harding had appropriated Borah's original notion; then he had subtly maneuvered the entire American political establishment into accepting some sort of disarmament. Whether or not Harding and Hughes had brought round the foreign leaders would be apparent the next day when the conference began its work. Meanwhile, this celebration of the unknown soldier was carefully calculated to influence the public everywhere: never again would there be such a slaughter.

Of the foreign dignitaries, the highest-ranking was Aristide Briand, the French prime minister, all in black, a contrast to the bemedalled military men that crowded the platform. Even the former British prime minister, Arthur Balfour, had found a gaudy uniform to wear. How the English enjoyed dressing up! thought Burden sourly. But then his mood was generally bad these days. Life was moving too fast for him or he too slow for it. He gazed without interest at Marshal Foch and Admiral Beatty, at Chinese and Japanese war-lords, their gold and silver braid glistening in the cold morning sun. Earlier, they had all paraded past the White House, and then, having hopelessly tied up traffic, the foreign contingent had somehow got across the Potomac to the cemetery, losing, according to Borah, the President in the process. "His car was last seen," said the Lion of Idaho, with quiet satisfaction, "driving off the road and into the cemetery, a shortcut, you might say, to immortality."

Borah now sat next to Kitty, Mrs. Borah beside Burden. "Did you see poor Mr. Wilson?" Mrs. Borah had the look of an alert sheep.

Burden nodded; and Kitty answered. The uses of a wife in politics were manifold. "He looked so shattered, sitting there in his car, with Edith, who looked so well. She's taken off pounds, I'd say."

"Do you ever go see them?" asked Borah. ᐧ

"No." Burden did not feel as guilty as he should. He had been the former President's political ally, not friend. "I don't think they particularly want visitors. He has his court."

"I wouldn't go out in public if I was in such bad shape." Borah was stern. Certainly the image of the frail half-paralyzed Wilson was an arresting one as he drove past the west end of the White House in the endless train of the unknown soldier. When Harding saw his predecessor pass before him in review, like a ghost of war, he had bowed low, and Wilson had raised a long white hand in response, past to present. Who was future?

Borah was muttering discontentedly. "I don't like the look of all this."

"We merely honor the dead." Burden was pious.

"No, not that. This conference. It's not what I asked for. It's not what I wanted, not at all. Disarm, yes. All of us. But this is going to turn itself into another League of Nations. If it does, I stand opposed. I warned Harding."

Plainly Borah was distressed that the President would get the credit for what he took to be uniquely his own idea.

Whatever adventures the Hardings might have had getting through the traffic, they were now on the stage of the amphitheater. The President was as nobly handsome as ever, in a Chesterfield, and carrying a hat while Mrs. Harding was suitably veiled in black.

The Marine band played the national anthem. A chaplain exhorted God in a most ecumenical way. Then, at exactly noon, a single bugler played taps, and the tears came to Burden's eyes. What was better than to die in youth for one's own kind and country? What was worse than to live on into middle age, a peripheral man of state? The soprano, Rosa Ponselle, sang "I Know That My Redeemer Liveth," and Burden's sadness remained elevated and pure. Then the band played "America," a resolutely tinny anthem calculated to stifle all elevated feeling in Burden or anyone else. He dried his eyes as the Secretary of War came out onto the stage, where a microphone on a metal stick was transmitting by telephone the proceedings to Madison Square Garden in New York and to San Francisco's Auditorium as well as to local crowds in Washington itself. This would be the largest audience in history for any public occasion, thanks to the perfecting of radio.

"Ladies and gentlemen, the President of the United States."

Everyone rose, as Harding, without his coat, stepped forward to the microphone. He made a deprecating gesture to the audience; they were to be seated. He had, as the press liked to say of presidents in their second year, "grown" in office. The somewhat coarse senator – "a character out of a low-life Dreiser novel," Lodge had called him – was now the silver-haired embodiment of all that was good and sane and normal in his country.

Harding struck – as who did not on such occasions? – the Lincoln note. "Standing today on hallowed ground, conscious that all America has halted to share in the tribute of the heart, and mind, and soul to this fellow American, and knowing that the world is noting this expression of the republic's mindfulness, it is fitting to say that his sacrifice, and that of the millions dead, shall not be in vain." The resonant voice almost convinced. But Burden knew, as they all knew, British admirals of the fleet and marshals of France, that life was all that the poor set of bones in the box had had – and lost so that boundaries might be redrawn by shady men

420

of state and profits made by the busy.

"There must be, there shall be the commanding voice of a conscious civilization against armed warfare . . ." Burden wondered how many times after similar wars Capitoline geese had honked the same fervent message in the wake of some awful blood-letting. But all that it took was a generation to forget war's horrors in order to hunger, yet again, for war's thrills and profits. How stupid the human race was, thought Burden, staring at a bemedalled Japanese prince, who was known to be plotting war in the Pacific. Little did the Japanese suspect that now that the gentle polyglot republic of North America had got the taste of blood in its mouth there would be no stopping it. War was money earned. War was the ultimate expression of that racial pride with which the white Caucasian tribe had been so overly endowed. It would have been much more suitable for Harding to do a war-dance, with tomahawk and feathered war-bonnet, borrowed from the Indian chief who stood, most incongruously, at the edge of the bemedalled war-lords. To the beat of tom-toms, they would all shout "Blood!" and the wars would continue, each more destructive than the last until no one on earth was left alive.

"As we return this poor clay to its native soil, garlanded by love and covered with the decorations that only nations can bestow, I can sense the prayers of our people, of all peoples, that this Armistice Day shall mark the beginning of a new and lasting era of peace on earth, good will among men. Let me join in that prayer." The President then said the Lord's Prayer and all those around Burden said it along with him. Senatorial and ambassadorial faces were streaked with tears. Burden was exalted now by his own disdain for so much generalized hypocrisy. Taps and a single set of bones could trigger in him a sense of his own mortality, and of his likeness to all others. But monkish prayers chilled him and a quartet from the Metropolitan Opera singing "The Supreme Sacrifice" reminded him of how cold he was as the President pinned the Congressional Medal of Honor onto the flag that draped the box. He was followed by the other war-lords. While each was adding a medal to the constellation, Burden turned to Borah. "When shall we have our next war?"

Borah looked startled; then he almost smiled. "Twenty years, if we don't disarm now."

"If we do?"

Borah grunted, and Burden said, "In twenty years, if we do disarm. Let's hope we're as lucky next time as we were this time."

Now the pall-bearers appeared. They lifted up the coffin. Led by the Hardings, a procession descended to a marble crypt just beneath the amphitheater. "I don't suppose we'll ever find our car," said Kitty. She was quite unmoved. Somehow, women were never much affected by the grief of warriors or, to be precise, the grief of the tribal elders, dreaming of future wars through a haze of present tears.

2

The Duchess was in a state. "The third letter this week, and what does the Secret Service do? Nothing." Then she rounded on Daugherty. "And that Bureau of Investigation of yours, what do they do?"

"Stolen cars and Bolsheviks are their speciality," Daugherty began, but the Duchess was in full torrent. "The President's life is threatened daily." She held up the letter. "Christmas Day will be his last day on earth, this one says, and you still can't find who sends them, who writes them."

Jess felt sorry for Daugherty, who was now staring glumly out the window at the snow falling on the south lawn. A moment before, the Washington Monument had disappeared in a swirl of snow. The world outside was contracting, while the oval sitting room was too warm for Jess, but then he could not endure too much heat. Along with his other disabilities, he was now officially a diabetic, according to a lugubrious doctor, who told him that he could eat nothing, drink nothing, do nothing. The last joy of his life was to serve Daugherty as "bumper," to use a good Ohio word, to worship the Hardings and to make sure that the money kept rolling in. Life was unfair, he decided. He should have been on top of the world. Now its weight was on top of him. Lately, Lucie Daugherty's health had grown worse and Jess was obliged to look after her in the night so that Daugherty could get some sleep. All three now lived in the Wardman Park Hotel and the door between Daugherty's room and Jess's was always open at night so that Jess could call for help in case he had a bad dream or the insomniac Daugherty could summon Jess for a talk during the late dark watches. There was more fun to be had in Washington Court House, and Jess tried to spend at least a week every month back home, gossiping with Roxy about his grand life which wasn't all that grand, what with diabetes and Lucie Daugherty failing.

Laddie Boy announced the President's approach. "Don't tell Warren!" The Duchess stuck the letters inside her blouse, and bared her teeth in a terrifying smile of welcome.

Harding looked weary despite his recent triumphs. He had astonished the world on November 12 when he had proposed to the Disarmament Conference that the United States was willing to scrap thirty capital ships. The Secretary of State, Charles Evans Hughes, had read off the particulars of Harding's secret plan, to the consternation of the war-lords present. Great Britain, Japan, France and Italy were invited to rid themselves of close to two million tons of war-ships.

Harding had figured that if any word of his plan were to leak to the press, military expansionists everywhere would have time to rally public opinion against disarmament. Hence the thunderbolt, hurled by Hughes in the presence of the benign presidential author. It was Harding's theory that once world opinion was appealed to, there would be no way for the various governments to back down.

Harding's gamble paid off. The world was enthralled, and in the course of a single morning Harding became the central figure on the world's stage, and the most beloved.

But W.G. was the historical Harding only part-time. Most of the time, he was a harassed politician married to the Duchess. Now, in the oval sitting room, he sat down heavily in a chair beside the fire and cupped his right cheek in his right hand. "I'm going to propose to Congress that a single term for the president is quite enough. I can't take much more of this place. Nobody can nowadays. If I can get Congress to limit the presidency to one term, will it apply to me?" W.G. looked at the Attorney General.

"No," said Daugherty. "Besides, Congress can't change the Constitution. They can pass a bill asking for a change, but then it's up to the states to ratify, and that takes years. If you don't like the job, don't run again."

"Warren, have you been eating sauerkraut again?" the Duchess was stern. "It gives him gas so then he thinks he's having a heart attack and that gets him all moody."

"In March 1929, after two terms of this hell, I'll be sixty-five, which is pretty old, and then what?"

"It's sauerkraut." The Duchess rubbed the back of W.G.'s neck. "You're all knotted up."

"If you're going to feel like this when you're the most popular man in the world," said Daugherty, "what are you going to feel like when something goes wrong?"

W.G. groaned, more contentedly than not, as the Duchess's powerful fingers worked over the taut muscles of his neck. "I'm serious about this. I mean the principle, not me. One six-year term would make it possible for us to have some really good presidents for a change . . ."

"Warren! You're morbid."

W.G. sighed and shut his eyes. "Because I have to think all the time about being re-elected, just like everybody else who's lived in this house, I spend most of my time doing favors for this one and that one, so he'll help me out. Well, that is no way to run a government, bribing people. It's a wonder any of our appointments are ever any good, considering why we go and make them!"

"Except for me," said Daugherty, "you've got the most admired Cabinet this century."

"Well, you make up for a lot," said the Duchess with one of her unexpected flashes of black humor. "Now, Warren, about Christmas . . ."

But as the First Lady was about to bring up the subject of the assassination threats, Harding sat up straight and announced: "Harry, I'm pardoning Debs. In time for Christmas."

"Warren!" The Duchess looked more than ever grim. She hated equally communism, labor agitators and Alice Roosevelt Longworth. "We've been through all this."

Indeed they had, and Jess had been part of W.G.'s secret plot to release Debs and all the other political prisoners that Wilson had locked up. Shortly before the inauguration, W.G. had told Daugherty that he should have a talk with Debs and if he seemed to pose no particular threat to the United States, he would be pardoned. Currently, Debs was serving a ten-year sentence in an Atlanta prison. Daugherty had managed the whole thing in his customary unorthodox way. Debs had been put on a train to Washington, without guards. Jess had met him at Union Station, and found him an amiable quick-witted old man. Together they had gone to the Justice Department, where Daugherty had a long talk with the country's leading Socialist, and found no harm in him other than a perverse and potentially dangerous affection for the people at large. W.G. had planned to release Debs on the Fourth of July, 1921, but the New York *Times* had got wind of all this and announced, severely, that Debs "is where he belongs. He should stay there." W.G. had made a number of private unpublishable remarks to the effect that the pro-German sympathies of the *Times* had done far more damage to the Allied cause than the Socialist Party; then he had backed down for the time being. Now the peace treaty with Germany had been signed and the war was officially over.

"We're back to normal," said W.G., as he started a staring contest with Laddie, who, invariably, broke down, with wild cries and a race around the room in order to avoid his master's eyes. "So now it's most becoming that we make peace with all our own folks."

"They will overthrow the government, Warren. You mark my words."

"I don't think Mr. Debs wants to do that." Daugherty was soothing.

"The only thing he wanted when I took him down to the depot, to take him back to jail, was a pound of quill toothpicks." Jess made his contribution to history.

Daugherty shook his head no, which often meant yes. "I'll draw up a commutation, if that's what you want."

"That's what I want, Harry." Laddie Boy gave a howl of ecstatic fear, and raced from the room.

"But they should all sign pledges, saying they'll lead an upright life and obey the laws . . ."

"No." W.G. stood up and, idly, picked dog hairs off his coat. "That sort of a pledge is demeaning. It sounds like he's bargaining with us to go free, and he isn't. I am."

"Why?" asked the Duchess.

"Because this is what I was elected to do. Restore the country. The war's over . . ."

"Mr. Wilson's war." Thus, the Duchess brought herself round. Then one of the Secret Service men appeared at the door; apologetically, he signalled Jess to come with him. The others, preoccupied with pardons, did not notice his departure.

Nan Britton was in the President's office, seated demurely on a sofa beside the open-grate burning fire. Jess wondered what the going price was for the murder of a presidential mistress. Surely, the Italian Black Hand could be persuaded to encase her in cement and file her away in some commodious river. "Oh, Jess! I couldn't stay away after that lovely ceremony in Arlington which we could hear just as clear as could be all the way up in Madison Square Garden."

"Whaddaya know?" Jess was cordial. But he felt slightly nauseated all the time now, and he had pains in his right side which the doctor said were nothing; but his urine smelled of apples and that was a sign of diabetes. He took pills; tried to diet; drank quantities of water.

"Well, Elizabeth Ann is just thriving, with my sister. I'm still going to the Columbia School of Journalism and they all say that I have great talent as a writer, particularly about the emotions."

Was this blackmail? Jess wondered. So far she had not been particularly demanding. W.G. had always helped her out financially, and she had made several visits to the White House, like this, in secret. One of the agents, Jim Sloan, was in constant touch with her, and whenever she wanted to see W.G. she would alert Sloan. The previous summer, W.G. had sent for Nan, or so she had told Jess. They had met in the office on a Sunday like today. But there was no place for them to make love. The guards that marched regularly past the windows of the oval office had an unobstructed view of what went on inside. Finally, W.G. had found a nearby closet and there the star-crossed – Duchess-crossed was more like it – lovers became as one amongst the frock coats and umbrellas, a place only marginally less frightening to Jess than his own sinister downstairs closet in Washington Court House.

"But I've been thinking very seriously about the future." Nan gazed into Jess's eyes. What, he wondered, did W.G. see in her? She was just pretty; nothing more. On the other hand, there was no doubt that she was in love with a man more than old enough to be her father, and she had been in love with him long before the presidency; in fact, most of her life. Jess wondered what it would be like to be so loved.

"I've made one or two visits to the photo-play studios, the ones in New York, and they think that I show considerable potential, that was what they said, for acting because – this was Mr. Hirshan who works for Cosmopolitan Pictures – I have these suppressed emotions that you can *always* see on the screen, like Pola Negri."

"Nan," Jess was careful not to sound too alarmed, "Cosmopolitan is owned by Mr. Hearst, whose newspapers would do anything to find out about you and the President."

"Don't be silly, Jess. How could they ever find out? *We* aren't going to tell them. So who can? Anyway, it looks awfully easy, acting, if you have these emotions for the camera to show, like a radiogram, in a way. Well, I have suppressed emotions all right." Softly, Nan began to cry. Jess noted that she was careful not to make her eyes red or smear her make-up.

"There. There." Jess was avuncular. Then, when she had paused in the course of her audition, he asked, "Why did that new agent come to me just now?"

"Because Jim had to go home at the last minute. So he got his friend to bring me in here. I pretended I was here to see you about Ohio business. Jim's leaving the Secret Service you know."

"I know." It was Jess who had got Sloan a job as Washington manager of Samuel Ungerleider. They were all family, Jess had reported to Daugherty, who had grunted. Certainly, it would never do to have Jim Sloan at large in the world with all that he knew about the President's private life.

"Anyway, from now on I'm to write in care of Arthur Brooks, the colored valet, so Jim tells me, which I don't in the least mind. Anyway," now recovered and eyes shining, "will you go tell him I'm here?"

As Jess got to his feet, Nan crossed to the President's desk, where she picked up a miniature of W.G.'s mother. "He was so devoted to her, everyone says. Doesn't she look precious here? Like Elizabeth Ann, her granddaughter."

Jess returned to the upstairs sitting room. Others had joined the President. General Sawyer, small and shrewd, was laying down the law to the Duchess, who listened to him with perfect docility, for he alone understood her last kidney and its vagaries. Charlie Forbes was delighting the President and Daugherty with excited stories while the Secretary of the Interior sat beside the fire, drinking tea with a disgusted expression. After much debate, the President had decided that in the private apartments – specifically the bedrooms of the White House – the law prohibiting alcohol could be broken but in those parts of the White House that plainly belonged to the nation, the law must be upheld. It was not much of a compromise, but then Prohibition was not much of a law. Nevertheless, W.G. took very seriously the dignity of his place and he would not do anything unseemly if he could help it. Now, of course, he could not help it. Presently, he would be joining Nan in the anteroom closet.

Jess simply stared at the President until W.G. became aware of him. Easily, smilingly, W.G. left the group that was laughing with Charlie Forbes, and came toward Jess, who whispered, "She's in your office."

Harding's smile did not fade; but the eyes were suddenly alert. He glanced at the Duchess and General Sawyer; neither was aware of anything on earth save her kidney. Then the President and Laddie Boy left the room. Only Daugherty had noticed. The blue eye stared at Jess, who nodded. The brown eye blinked, as Daugherty nodded, meaning, no.

Jess sat down beside the Secretary of the Interior, who said,

"Jess, you want to know what I know? Well, what I know is I can't wait to get the hell out of here, and go home to New Mexico." Fall coughed at length into a bandanna-like handkerchief. "Bronchitis." He held up a gnarled hand. "Arthritis. Now pleurisy, they say."

"Ask Doc Sawyer."

"I'd rather go to a veterinarian." Fall eyed the small doctor with disfavor. "I've also got a hole in my lung from this stag which don't help matters. I keep asking the President to let me go but he says it wouldn't be seemly so soon into his Administration. Now I've been stuck with the naval oil reserves because Denby doesn't want to be bothered with them, which means every crook in the country is trying to get his hands on all that government oil." Fall was full of complaints, and Jess was eager to hear each and every one because he had – as who had not? – friends who were keenly interested in acquiring those oil lands held by the government. The Navy believed implicitly that since a war with Japan was bound to come sooner or later, American battleships must have instant access to their own fuel supply. So oil-reserve lands in California and Wyoming had been set aside by President Wilson. Now peace had broken out; and the fleets of the world, instead of growing, were, thanks to Harding, shrinking, and the dim Secretary of the Navy, Denby, had turned the whole business over to the Department of the Interior, a mixed blessing to hear Fall tell it. "Now I've had all the bother since May. Denby's out of it. I'm in it. Favors. *Special* favors," Fall muttered into his huge moustaches. He shook his head bleakly.

"Well, the government can turn a nice profit auctioning off those reserves. That's something." Jess's pulse began to beat faster; this time not diabetes but money had triggered his nervous system.

"If I can." Fall was cryptic. "We had open bidding last summer for Elk Hills, California. Wasn't much in it for us. But a lot of oil . . . lot of profit for the winner."

"Edward Doheny."

Fall glanced at Jess with mild surprise that anyone should have bothered to follow so insignificant a matter. "That's the one." He was noncommittal. "The big problem isn't oil. It's those

Goddamned conservationists, like young Roosevelt." Fall denounced the Under-Secretary of the Navy, who was, like his cousin Franklin and his father Theodore, occupying the family post at the Navy Department.

Jess was surprised at Fall's vehemence, considering the fact that Fall was a Roosevelt Republican, an original Rough Rider, a true progressive, whatever that was.

Then dinner was announced, an informal affair for W.G.'s particular friends in the Administration. Since Jess was not asked as often to these meals as he would have liked, he did not in the least mind being put next to the general counsel of the Veterans Bureau, Charles F. Cramer, a colorless Californian whose main distinction was that he had bought the Hardings' house in Wyoming Avenue. He also thought the world of his boss, Charlie Forbes, a man equally mistrusted by Daugherty and Doc Sawyer, to Jess's surprise, since Daugherty was never censorious and the Doc's only interest in Forbes would have been on the medical side, involving all those hospitals which were supposed to be not only first-rate but highly profitable. Jess suspected, on Daugherty's side, a degree of jealousy. Charlie always made W.G. laugh. Daugherty usually made him frown.

At the moment W.G., somewhat too red in the face, was laughing at one of Charlie's jokes. Presumably, the tryst with Nan had been satisfactory, if brief.

Cramer turned to Jess. "Where are you living now?" Everyone seemed to know that Ned McLean's H Street house had been abandoned the previous month when Daugherty and Lucie and Jess had all three moved into Wardman Park.

"Well, I'm camping out with General Daugherty." Jess took pleasure in his friend's title.

"Thought you were at K Street now." Cramer was not as dim as he appeared. "In the green house."

Jess shook his head. "That's my old friend Howard Mannington. He's set up shop there, doing business, he says. I see him from time to time." That was enough information, Jess decided. The operation at 1625 K Street was a smooth affair. Jess and two old friends were agents for the ever-thirsty General Drug Company.

They also transacted all sorts of business with desperate men who wanted immunity from prosecution or, simply, information from the files of the Justice Department, to which Jess, in his sixth-floor office, had the key. But no matter how much business was done in the little green house on K Street or from Jess's office at the Justice Department, Daugherty, by design, was kept largely uninformed while the President never suspected anything amiss other than a somewhat blatant trafficking with bootleggers on poker nights. "My God, how the money rolls in!" Jess hummed.

3

Blaise looked out the window of Laurel House and, like pre-Edenic God, was pleased at his creation. The house itself was comfortable but not too grand for the Virginia countryside. The mock-Georgian style tended to symmetry, as did Blaise, who had, instinctively, like God when he made Adam, done things in twos – one marble obelisk on the left of the lawn balanced exactly the one on the right. The pool house, now visible through the winter trees, was equally balanced: a pavilion to the left was hers, one to the right was his. Only the original trees were allowed to escape Blaise's binary passion. They loomed like black slashes and scratches drawn against the dirty gray winter sky.

Beyond the trees, far below the level of lawn and house, the swift Potomac River broke upon the confusion of rocks that edged the steep river bank, a sign of nature's lack of art much less symmetry. Here and there, between the rocks, the water had frozen into solid white sheets, and at night, in bed, Blaise liked to listen to the scrape and crunch not to mention the odd shuddering groans of the ice as it shifted in response to the water sweeping down from Great Falls.

Frederika was so delighted to be living in the country that every chance she got, she would cross the river at Chain Bridge to visit friends in Washington, secure in the knowledge that an earthly paradise awaited her on the Virginia side, all ordered garden and wild forests crossed by earthworks from the Civil War, for Laurel House was set on the road to Manassas where, twice, the Union Army had lost to the Confederates at Bull Run. Up near the greenhouses – built originally in an L shape until Blaise rebuilt the base of the L so that it resembled an evenly balanced T – there was a slave cabin complete with original slave. Although long since freed, he had never fled from the cabin of his birth: he went with the property – thus enslaving the owners to him as he had once been to them. Blaise kept the old man on as a not-so-handyman and a source of folk-lore both Confederate and African; the two, Blaise decided, were much the same. The old man had a set-piece that he enjoyed reciting to anyone who'd listen: how all the fine folk had come out from Washington to watch the Union Army defeat the rebels, and how they had passed by his cabin on the road – he had been seven or eight years old then, and he had cheered them on. "But they looked mighty different that night, runnin' for home." He was a loyal son of Virginia; and except for Lincoln hated all Yankees.

Frederika came into his room. "Do shut the window. It's freezing." She wore a summery sort of dress, not suitable for a winter lunch, but then lunch was Christmas dinner at the McLean palace in H Street and any costume was all right in that house of fantasy. Enid and Peter followed their mother into Blaise's room, and Peter climbed his father's leg while Enid complained that it was not fair to leave them on Christmas, despite that morning's orgy of present opening in the pine-scented drawing room where a Christmas tree had been set up, its base surrounded by a thick white snow-like material that contained something very like ground glass which still caused Blaise, who had been Santa Claus, to squirm with discomfort as it clung to his skin.

"We'll be home early, my pets." Frederika was admirably patient and serene with even the crankiest child. "We'll have supper together. Miss Claypoole will take you out in the sleigh, if there's enough snow."

"There's more than enough up at the stables," said Enid, a dark rather glamorous-looking child. Peter nodded and chewed on a red-and-white-striped candy cane taken from the tree and not meant to be eaten. Peter was always hungry. Frederika worried. Blaise did not. Let children enjoy themselves. Later there would be little enough to enjoy, he maintained, as only a man whose life had been entirely easy and largely happy could.

In procession they descended the carved staircase to the main hall, decorated with holly and mistle-toe. Christmas Eve had been their celebration for friends and familiars. Despite Peter's last-minute attempt to get his father to read him Captain Marryat, of all writers, Blaise and Frederika were able to depart without tears.

Snow covered the ground in drifts. The narrow road to Chain Bridge was dangerously icy, and not much helped by the county's addition of rock-salt to its surface. Frederika sat, very alert, as the chauffeur managed the curves like an expert skier. Blaise, who had no fear of accidents – or death? – sat far back in his seat and enjoyed the warmth of the vicuña coverlet.

At Chain Bridge, Frederika relaxed despite the cautionary sight of a Model A Ford that had skidded into the railing. Beneath them the river was filled with shards of ice. The sky over the city was yellow like a cheap diamond. "Evalyn says we're to tell no one but this is the day the President is going to be killed."

"At the McLeans'?"

"If he gets there in one piece. It's very exciting," said Frederika mildly.

"Who would want to kill Warren Harding?"

"The Vice President, I suppose. They say he never speaks but every time I sit next to him at dinner he never stops talking."

"You have that effect on everyone."

"Not you."

"That is a condition of marriage. Long meaningless silences."

They were halfway across the near-deserted city when Frederika observed, "You don't think they'll try, do you?"

"Who'll try what?" Blaise was already in his own world, which, nowadays, involved Paris and a friend's wife and a private room at Prudhomme where, for two centuries, initials had been inscribed on the ancient window pane with diamonds – white and blue but never yellow diamonds.

"The murderers, whoever they are. The Secret Service takes it all very seriously. That's why they were happy to get the President out of the White House and into the I Street house, where, they say, it's easier to guard him, which I doubt."

"I'm sure Evalyn and Ned wrote the letters, just to get the Hardings for Christmas Day."

Frederika shook her head, unconvinced. "They see them all the time. Perhaps anarchists will blow up the house like Mr. Palmer's."

Blaise was greeted warmly by his rival publisher. Ned was on a new regime which he called "English drinking." This involved a first drink at about eleven in the morning and then, at regular intervals throughout the day, he would continue drinking. The result was, so far, satisfactory. Although he was never drunk he was also never sober, very much in the English manner, as Millicent Inverness observed to Blaise, herself a committed Anglophile in these matters.

Evalyn, hung with ill-omened diamonds, did her best to compete with what must have been Washington's largest Christmas tree, whose glittering star just grazed the ceiling of the drawing room, which itself was three times higher than any other drawing room in the city. Splendor was the McLean style, and the Hardings seemed as at home as they were out of place in this palace.

Blaise sat beside the President before the fire while the half-dozen ladies gathered around Evalyn. "Well, Blaise," said Harding, nursing a pale whisky and water. "I can't think of a better place to be killed in."

"Or such an auspicious day."

"Better than April Fool's." Harding chuckled. Blaise had never been able to gauge the President's intelligence. Harding did not read books, and the arts chilled him except for the girlie shows at the Gayety Burlesque theater where he liked to slip, unobserved, into a box, to the delight of the excited manager. But a cultivation of the arts was hardly a sign of practical intelligence. The fact that Harding's career had been one of astonishing success could not be ascribed solely to brute luck or animal charm. Without luck and charm, Harding would probably not have had a political career. But he had had the luck and the charm and something else as well, hard to define because he was so insistently modest. "Mr. Hughes took them by storm," he said with satisfaction, as if only the Secretary of State had been responsible for the terms of the Disarmament Conference. "I thought Admiral Beatty would have a stroke when Mr. Hughes looked right at him, and told him how many ships England would have to scrap."

Harry Daugherty joined them. "May I?" he asked of the sovereign, who nodded. Daugherty sat next to Blaise. "We're surrounded by the press, Mr. President."

"In the event that I join McKinley and Garfield and Lincoln up there in the sky, I want Ned and Blaise to be witnesses of my last hours on earth, omitting no gruesome detail except one." He held high his drink. "The people must never know that I died violating the Eighteenth Amendment. That would be unseemly."

Then Harding, the publisher and editor of the Marion *Star*, took over from the President, and Blaise found him both knowledgeable and interesting in their common trade. As they chatted, Blaise was very much aware of the Secret Service men in the hall and in the next room. Their attention was evenly divided between watching the President and observing all conceivable entrances and exits. The secretary of war, John W. Weeks, was allowed to enter, followed by the black-eyed part-Indian Senator Curtis of Kansas. They were a part of what Harding called his poker cabinet. Blaise found the President to be a curious mixture of an almost Buddhistic stillness interrupted, at regular intervals, by a small boy's restlessness. He must play golf. He must play card games, particularly poker. He must travel as much as his office allowed. Constant motion was a necessary distraction. Yet he could, just as easily, remain as still as a statue, self-contained, smiling, content. All in all, he was a mystery to Blaise, but no less enjoyable for that.

As it was Christmas Day, there was no shop-talk, other than a sour remark from Curtis to the effect that Borah was, yet again, disaffected. "He's mad that you're getting all the credit for *his* Disarmament Conference."

"What can I do?" Harding looked genuinely pained.

"Nothing," said Daugherty. "There's no pleasing that son-of-a-bitch."

"Anyway, we have the votes." Curtis blinked his black eyes at

Blaise, a disconcerting effect. "Whatever treaty you come up with the Senate will give you."

"Thanks," Daugherty turned to Harding, "to your making Lodge a delegate. That was inspired, Mr. President."

"I'll say it was." Harding chuckled. "Fact, it was literally inspired by President Wilson's *not* letting him sit in on the League of Nations. You know," Harding gazed at the Secret Service agent in the hall, "when Wilson and I were driving from the White House to the Capitol, I was trying to make conversation, never an easy thing to do with him when he was well and really hard when he was so sick. Anyway, I don't know how I got onto the subject of elephants, but there we were driving down Pennsylvania Avenue and I'm telling him how these elephants fall in love with their keepers and how jealous they can get, and how, in the case of this one elephant, when her keeper died, she died, too, of grief. Then I looked over and Wilson was crying, and I thought what a strange end to a presidency this was. Strange beginning, too, I suppose, for me."

Christmas dinner was served with the usual McLean lavishness. Ned seemed somewhat bemused by his new regimen but otherwise did not embarrass Evalyn, who quizzed Blaise in great detail about Caroline. "I loved her *Mary Queen of Scots* and I don't see why everyone was so mean about her."

Blaise murmured something about envy; actually, he himself was envious of Caroline's conquest of the movies, and he wondered why. It was not as if he had ever had the slightest ambition along those lines. Yet the fact that, once again, she had moved beyond him was a source of nagging irritation. Fortunately, her recent failure had been most heartening. Without going to any particular effort, he had somehow managed to read every one of her American reviews. She was, at last, too old, was the verdict. He, of course, was older than she but he did not market his face on the screen as she had done.

"Where is she now?"

"I don't know. I think she's in Paris. She opened up Saint-Cloud in the summer but that's no place to be alone in for Christmas. I suppose she's with friends."

"Isn't there a director . . . ? Evalyn was eager to gossip.

"Two directors," said Blaise, now compulsively disloyal. "But I don't think she's with either of them. She may be making a picture in Paris, where old age is rather a plus," he added, wondering if he was leering uncontrollably at Evalyn, who now wanted to discuss Mary Pickford. But then everyone wanted to discuss Mary Pickford.

"If you don't want to play poker with the President, I'm showing Mary's new movie, *Little Lord Fauntleroy*."

"I'll watch," said Blaise, who disliked poker even more than America's sweetheart.

"I got to know her whole family." Evalyn was more involved with Hollywood than Blaise had suspected. But then almost everyone nowadays had two lives, his own and his life at the movies. Although Blaise did his conscious best to ignore Caroline's triumphant new world, he found himself unable not to read any gossip about the stars and he sometimes showed movies at Laurel House when he and Frederika were alone, the ultimate vice.

"Anyway, they are all drunks, the whole lot of them, including Mary and her brother Jack and this wonderful old Irish biddy of a mother who, just before Prohibition came in, went out and bought a whole liquor store and moved all the bottles into her cellar and locked the door to keep Jack out."

"They are most royal these days, the Fairbankses," said Blaise, succumbing yet again to Hollywood. Caroline had taken him to dinner at Pickfair, where social climbing was very much in the air. Titles were resonated at the table; and royalty was referred to by pet names. But then the king and queen of Hollywood would naturally be interested in their own kind. Warned of Miss Pickford's liking for the bottle Blaise had watched her keenly. But she was as demure as her screen self, a rather matronly little girl was the effect that she made in real life, while Fairbanks, now that he had come into his own as a swashbuckling athletic star, tended to gallop about the room, lecturing on strength both physical and moral. Apropos divorce, a sore subject, he announced, "Caesar and Napoleon were both divorced men, and no one can say that *they* were weak!" Thus he classed himself.

Fairbanks's mother-in-law was more engaging, particularly when she confided to Blaise that "Mary gives her most as an actress when she's got a good director on top of her."

After dinner, the sated guests sat about the Christmas tree, waiting for the President to be assassinated. In low voices, the men spoke of the Fatty Arbuckle – Hollywood again – scandal. Harding was particularly fascinated by the details, which the Secretary of War had mastered.

During the course of a wild party in San Francisco, the hugely fat comedian Arbuckle, a one-time plumber as the press never forgot to mention, hurled himself onto a young woman, much experienced at parties, and, inadvertently, he burst her bladder – or so the story went. Daily, the press, including Ned McLean and Blaise, printed horrendous stories about the new Babylon while Hearst daily exhorted the Almighty, if not the police, to destroy this city of the plain and turn all its inhabitants, save Marion Davies, to salt. The hapless Arbuckle had finally brought down the concerted wrath of Puritan America on the sinful movie stars who, after celebrating every sort of immorality on-screen then, off-screen, busily burst the bladders of virgin girls and worse. The patriarchal spirit that deprived all Americans of alcohol was now abroad again in the land, and Blaise was ashamed to be a part of it. But he had little choice in the matter: one newspaper followed another until a story had finally run its course. This one seemed nowhere near its terminus. Aside from Arbuckle and his trial, there were more and more stories about drug addiction among the stars and everyone now agreed that *something must be done.*

Harding echoed the popular cry, without much enthusiasm. "The movie people want the government to come in and police them. But how can we? That isn't our function. Police yourselves, I told Mr. Zukor."

Senator Curtis observed that the Postmaster General had been approached about becoming a czar of the movie business, to pass on everyone's morality. Curtis chuckled, "Can't you see Will Hays, with all them starlets sitting on his lap?"

"I'm sure," said the President, surreptitiously lighting his first cigar – the Duchess was facing in the opposite direction – "that Will has great control and he'll do nothing improper, if he takes the job."

This was news. "Has he been offered the job?" asked Blaise.

Harding nodded. "But don't tell anybody just yet. He hasn't made up his mind. And of course I don't want him leaving the Cabinet, particularly now."

Blaise knew that Fall also wanted to resign, and two resignations at the same time would not be – seemly, to employ one of the President's favorite words.

Daugherty wondered if any movie had ever encouraged anyone to a life of crime or vice. By and large, the men agreed that it was unlikely, unless the sinner was already so disposed. But Curtis came up with an interesting variation. "There's no doubt in my mind that movies and plays and books give people plot ideas, including criminals. The badger game, for instance."

To a man, the politicians beside the Christmas tree shuddered. Harding nodded somberly and said, "There's no doubt that when Senator Gore wouldn't help out those oil men one of them thought of that play, the *Purple* something."

"*Deep Purple,*" said Daugherty.

"What was that all about?" Blaise had only a vague memory of the blind Senator's trial.

"A few years back, there was this real popular play," said Curtis. "Everybody saw it. How a bunch of gangsters set up an innocent man with a woman. Well, one day this woman, a constituent, calls up Senator Gore about getting an appointment to West Point for her son, and she says can he come by her hotel, as she's lame, and so he does, with his secretary, and they all meet in the lobby, and of course Gore's blind and can't see her or what she's up to when she says, let's go up to the mezzanine. But instead of going there, she takes him to her room, tears her dress, starts to scream 'Rape!' and a couple of crooks hired by the oil men come rushing in and say, 'We got you.'"

"Could happen to almost any senator," said Harding sadly.

"It could certainly happen to any senator who happens to be blind." Weeks was precise.

Daugherty was even more precise. "Particularly if the folks out to get you had seen *Deep Purple.*"

When Gore had refused to be blackmailed, charges were brought against him for attempted rape. He had then insisted on standing trial in Oklahoma City. The whole affair had been exceedingly melodramatic, Blaise now recalled, even to the last-minute appearance of a widow from Boston who had observed what had happened from her hotel-room window. Gore was exonerated. "Proving," said Harding, "that no trouble with a woman ever lost a man a vote."

"Unless her bladder bursts," said Curtis.

The Duchess and Evalyn joined the gentlemen. Evalyn said, "I've talked to the Secret Service and they say that the safest place in the house is the sitting room to my bedroom. Ned's up there now, with the cards."

"Be careful, Warren!" The Duchess was genuinely frightened.

"Why, dearie, when am I not?"

Blaise remained with the ladies to see *Little Lord Fauntleroy*. Millicent, Countess Inverness, drifted off to sleep, and snored while the Duchess fidgeted, and Evalyn took her hand from time to time. Blaise day-dreamed; only Frederika was intent upon the adventures of a stocky thirty-year-old matron as she impersonated, in the most sinister way, a pubescent boy.

At first, Blaise thought that a bomb had gone off somewhere upstairs. They all leapt to their feet except Mrs. Harding, who slipped off her chair and now lay like some stranded sea-creature on the parquet floor. "Florence. Here!" Evalyn pulling Mrs. Harding to her feet.

"I know. I know what's happened. It was foretold in the stars. Take me to him. Now. It's all come true. All of it. Just like she said. Oh, God!"

Mrs. Harding was now in the hallway where a Secret Service man smilingly reassured her. "The wind slammed a door shut. That's all."

From far above them, Harding's mellifluous voice could be heard. "Don't worry, Duchess. They missed me."

Mrs. Harding turned fiercely back into the drawing room. "I don't see the joke."

"Unbecoming," said Blaise, delighting in the President's other favorite word. Then he turned to Frederika. "I think he's safe."

They said good night to the Duchess, who was now in full tirade. Like so many forceful women of a certain age, her conscious mind had been gradually replaced by her unconscious. She now tended to say whatever she was thinking, even when she was not, properly speaking, thinking at all. "I know what's going on, you see." She stared vacantly at Blaise. "I always do. That doesn't mean that there's anything I can do. But I try, God knows how I try. What makes it worse is how they're all in on it. Even Laddie Boy who sits in front of the door." Evalyn led Mrs. Harding back to the Christmas tree.

"What was *that* about?" Frederika was intrigued.

"Hysteria," said Blaise. "Poor Harding. I think she's crazy."

"Poor Duchess, to be so misused."

"How?"

"There are mistresses," said Frederika, pulling the coverlet over her knees as the great car glided toward Georgetown.

"I wonder why she cares? She's got him, after all."

"I think," said Frederika, uncharacteristically focussed on a problem not her own, "that he dislikes her and she doesn't know what to do about it."

"Except make scenes."

"*Chagrin d'amour.* I don't suppose it helps having just the one."

"The one what?"

"Kidney," said Frederika with unanalyzable joy.

13

1

Miss Kingsley always put Caroline in a good mood. For one thing, she was a genuine fan of Emma Traxler. For another, she was encyclopedic. There was nothing that she did not know when it came to who was making what movie and why. Caroline always served her tea, and Miss Kingsley always made an art form of taking off her gloves, while discussing the subtleties of Indian as opposed to China tea.

Traxler Productions was having a good season. The release of two westerns had already made up the money lost on *Mary*.

"But when do *you* plan to go before the cameras next?" Miss Kingsley's kindly eye was fixed on Caroline's left ear where the surgeon's knife had cut; then the skin was drawn back and resewn, following the natural line where the ear connected with the head. Hair swept back and in a full light, the scar was still a horrible livid shiny wound to Caroline's own sharp eye. But the Paris surgeon had assured her that it would lose all color soon and no one would ever notice the line.

After much trepidation, Caroline had gone into a clinic outside Paris, and the deed had been done at the beginning of winter. Now she felt that it was safe to show off her restored – if not exactly new – face. She had been lucky. Aside from all the horror stories of operations gone wrong, many an operation had been so successful that the seeker after eternal beauty was startled to see that she – or he – was indeed made beautiful by the unexpected possession of someone else's face. Caroline looked like Emma at her

442

best, who was exactly like, though unlike, the original Caroline long since erased by time and Emma's glory and – now – surgery.

"I have no plans," said Caroline, who had a great many plans. "It was so pleasant being home again in . . ."

"Alsace-Lorraine. I know." Miss Kingsley was very good at keeping straight all the lies that the stars had told her. When Mabel Normand had said something to Miss Kingsley about her childhood in Staten Island, Miss Kingsley had gently reminded her that she had been born and raised on Beacon Hill in Boston. Mabel promised not to make such a slip again.

"Dear old Alsace-Lorraine," sighed Caroline. "Yes. I took the waters there, and lost a great deal of weight."

"I can see. You look amazingly rested and slender." This was Miss Kingsley's code phrase for "plastic surgery." "Ready to go before the cameras again." Code: the star is now ready to face with a brand-new face a new career, having lost the old one to unkindly Father Time.

"Perhaps. I'm talking to William Desmond Taylor about a new project, a life of George Sand, actually."

"Will you wear trousers?" Miss Kingsley frowned at her notebook.

"I think one must, at times. But she was mostly in gowns."

"I deplore, frankly, women in men's clothes. **Mr. Hearst** has an unhealthy passion for this . . . this perversion. **There** is no other word, I fear." Miss Kingsley turned pale pink. "I've discussed it with poor Marion, who says it's what, as she puts it in that cute way of hers, 'Pops wants.'"

"She has not got quite the right bottom for trousers." Caroline was judiciously clinical.

"I trust *you* will wear a long frock coat . . ."

"A Prince Albert, yes. And I shall only pretend to smoke a cigar."

"What you stars must do for your art!" Miss Kingsley shook her head more in pity than awe. "Do you still plan to buy or build your own studio?"

Caroline nodded. Tim had reawakened her ambition. Although she enjoyed acting the part of a movie star in real life, she did not much like becoming an old woman on the screen. The sudden entirely unexpected realliance with Tim had changed her course.

With Tim's help, what Hearst had done with newspapers she would do with the movies. Others had had the same wish but they had been bemused by the notion of art. Griffith had tried to render the Civil War on the screen in "lightning flashes," as President Wilson had poetically put it, but he had got lost in the politics of that huge event. Later, when he made *Intolerance*, he had succumbed to spectacle without mind. Yet Caroline knew what he was doing or trying to do. Like Griffith, Tim believed that the imagination of the public could be laid siege to, and won. But Tim chose, perversely, to appeal to everyone's sense of justice, while Griffith wearied them with grandiose visions of various deadly sins. Caroline knew that the answer was somewhere between the two, in what would look to be nothing more ambitious than a celebration of the ordinary in American life and then – thanks to the luxury of film editing – dreams could be stealthily planted in the viewer's mind. Instinctively, Chaplin had done this from the beginning, and Caroline was confident that once he knew what he was doing, he would lose his art. Self-consciousness was the principal enemy of this strange narrative form. Gradually, she and Tim had worked it all out in a way that neither on his own could have done. They were now both hard at work on a dozen photo-plays, each calculated to appeal to as many people as possible, yet with a certain intrinsic design that, if successful, would subtly alter the way everyone observed the world. Where once Huns and Reds were demonized, human qualities would be apotheosized. The fact that they could so easily fail made the attempt all the more exciting.

"We've thought of buying Inceville at Santa Monica. Or maybe something in the Valley but only," Caroline added quickly, "if you approve."

"My heart shall never go out to the Valley, but if you are there I will come out. That is a solemn promise."

"I shall miss Paramount." Famous Players-Lasky was now more and more known as Paramount Pictures, by order, presumably, of Adolph Zukor, who had also painted the studio green, his favorite color according to Charles Eyton. Yet Zukor was never to be seen in the studio. Instead he reigned over his empire from New York and left movie-making to his employees, a mistake Caroline would not make when she began her new career. Essentially, the movie magnates were not concerned with what was on the screen as long as it was profitable. Those who did care, like Griffith, tended to be self-indulgent and unprofitable. But the magnates must be propitiated. They – or specifically Zukor – owned the movie theaters, and Caroline had done her best to charm the great man who lived in Rockland County, New York, surrounded by relatives. But then all of the movie magnates were family men on the grandest, most tribal scale. They married off their children in the same calculated way as royal families did, and with, often, the same dire results. No wonder they all wanted to make *Mayerling*. Currently, Samuel Goldfish now Goldwyn, brother-in-law of Lasky but mortal enemy of Zukor, wanted Caroline to play the Empress Elizabeth, whose doomed son Rudolph – Barthelmess had said yes to the role – would kill himself at the hunting lodge of Mayerling. Hearst was now threatening to make his *Mayerling* with Marion Davies as the tragic Maria Vetsera.

"Naturally, you have your two favourite directors both on the lot." Grace Kingsley twinkled. "Mr. Farrell's out in the Valley, I'm told, doing a western. I'm due to see him tomorrow."

"Give him," said Caroline, "my love."

Thus far, their realliance as lovers and business partners was in secret. Tim had personal as well as movie commitments to be honored, while Caroline had William Desmond Taylor to – what? She had found it significant that when she had reappeared at the studio, Tim had whistled when he saw her new face. "Is it a success?" she had asked, and he had nodded, while her other "favorite" director had not noticed her surgical master-work. But then Taylor was busy in both his private and his professional life. "*He's* in Projection Room C, e'en as we speak. He's editing *The Green Temptation*, which sounds to me like a winner."

"I certainly hope so." Caroline smiled with great care. There was still some tightness about her mouth, certain to disappear, she had been assured, once the new face had settled in.

"He tells me he can't wait to start on his next new Traxler photoplay. But he wouldn't say what it was."

"We are hoping to do *Mayerling*." Boldly Caroline lied. After all, everyone else had, at one time or another, announced that they were doing the story or, indeed, had done a version. The visit was now worthwhile, and Miss Kingsley had her "scoop." She scribbled happily as Caroline named an ideal – and impossible – cast. No, they would not use Knoblock for the script. He had gone back to England. "Bernard Shaw would be ideal." Caroline was now swept away by fantasy. There was a kind of perfect joy in lying for no specific purpose. "Of course he would have to adjust to our art-form, so unlike the theater. But I'm sure he could pull it off. Otherwise there's always Maurice Maeterlinck." On Maeterlinck's much-heralded visit to Hollywood, he had submitted a script whose protagonist was a bee. Then he had gone back to Belgium.

"Quality. That is what a Traxler movie is all about," Miss Kingsley intoned.

"One tries," whispered Caroline, "one tries," she repeated, quite liking the sound of her own voice.

Then, although each was a lady and Miss Kingsley virginal, they were obliged to discuss that morning's newspaper account of the on-going Arbuckle case. The accidental rupture of Virginia Rappe's bladder had taken place September 7, 1921. It was now February 1, 1922 and the press still continued, each day, to invent new revelations or rake over old ones. Secretly, almost everyone in Hollywood had sided with Arbuckle but the rest of the country, spurred on by Hearst's press, wanted an auto-da-fé with the plump comedian as centerpiece, a flaming torch to morality.

More than ever was Caroline convinced that she and Tim were on the right track. Where it was Hearst's tactic to bestialize the public, they would civilize them, she thought grandly if somewhat uneasily. Certainly she would have to rein in Tim's political enthusiasm. They had agreed that in the ordinary American town that they were going to invent, the voice of reason would eventually win over the people, who would come to realize to what extent they are manipulated. The town must seem very real while at its center there would be a family for the whole nation to love. Above all, there would be no overt preaching: if they had done their work properly, their ends would be achieved subliminally. Both agreed that the noble Emma Traxler, a creature of perfect romance, would never set foot in their town.

"I have just had word from Washington," said Miss Kingsley,

putting on her gloves. "The Postmaster General will not be coming to Hollywood."

"I suppose he still thinks he'll be president one day, and that Hollywood . . ."

". . . is or will be – I promise you – a *highly* suitable background for *any* important venture." Miss Kingsley was a fervent booster of their beleaguered dreamland.

"One day, I suppose so. Of course, he'd have great power here. I wonder if he understands that." Caroline also wondered why she, herself, had not given the subject more thought. There would be ridiculous censorship, of course, but there would also be encouragement for the sort of thing that the virtuous conspirators had in mind. Hays – or some other high federal officer – could act as a bridge between politics and the movies. If Caroline and Tim, somehow, could capture the bridge, the impulses that now came to Hollywood from Washington would be reversed and Mr. Hays, or whoever, would be *their* transmitter from West to East, from the governed to the governors.

At the door to the commissary Caroline and Miss Kingsley parted. Then Caroline entered the dining room, aware that she was still a source of interest. She heard her name through the rattling of dishes and the roar of several hundred conversations. The room smelled of beef stew, and mothballs from Western Costume's costumes.

William waved for her to join him. He was seated with his writer, Julia Crawford Ivers, and his editor, Edy Lawrence. In the past, Caroline had noted with some bewilderment that all of William's intimates were women and yet, as far as she could tell, he was not interested in them sexually. She had come, gradually, to Tim's conclusion. Yet, once, there had been a wife, and, now, there was still very much a daughter, whom he was sending through an expensive New York school. Had he undergone some sea change in middle life, and shifted from nymph to faun? Or was he simply yet another victim of the Californian Curse? – or, more precisely had she been, during the time of her passion, now entirely ended, thanks to backgammon and the return of Tim.

Caroline told them that Will Hays would not be coming to Hollywood.

"Then we'll get Herbert Hoover," said Julia Ivers. "They say it must be a member of the Cabinet."

"Or Supreme Court." Like everyone in Hollywood, Edy Lawrence was not enthusiastic about a supervisor from Washington.

"The worst thing, of course, will be the censorship." Taylor's handsome face was paler than usual. He smoked one black cigarette after another from a gold case which Caroline thought had been stolen the previous July when the man-servant, Eddie Sands, had decamped with most of the contents of the bungalow, as well as Taylor's car. Knoblock had been at the studio when Eddie had disappeared, after first telling Knoblock that he intended to get married in Catalina. But Eddie had gone elsewhere, as checks with Taylor's forged signature began to crop up in different parts of the state. Taylor notified the police; hired a Negro servant, Henry Peavey; bought a new car and engaged a new chauffeur. The whole business had caused him a good deal of distress.

"Where did you find this?" Caroline touched the cigarette-case.

Taylor frowned. "A pawn shop. Where else? The police put me onto it. He seems to prefer the pawn shop to the fence."

"I like Hoover." Julia Ivers was a comfortable sort of woman, who could eat as much macaroni and cheese as she liked while Caroline picked at a sliver of white fish.

"He's honest," said Taylor with no great conviction.

"What about censorship?" Caroline's interest in Taylor's domestic problems had long since been satisfied.

"Isn't it inevitable? The Motion Picture Producers and Distributors want someone to clean up, whatever that means, the movie business, and make the world forget poor Fatty Arbuckle."

"To be paid one hundred fifty thousand dollars a year." Mrs. Ivers sounded mournful.

Then they discussed the usual subject – movies. Who was making what and where and for how much. At the end of lunch, Taylor turned to Caroline. "I think I've got a project for us. Charlie Eyton and I had a talk just before lunch."

"Not *The Rocks of Valpré*. I'm too old."

Mrs. Ivers shook her head. "The story's too dull, anyway. Not enough action."

"But there's a wonderful part for Mary." Taylor sighed. "Anyway, I'm outvoted. No, something else. Can I take you home? At five? We'll talk in the car."

Caroline returned to her office to find Tim, dressed like a cattle wrangler, talking on two telephones, while the secretary smiled an unfocussed happy smile. Absently, Caroline tapped his head; then she went into her office, where scripts were piled beneath icons of Emma Traxler, suffering and aging from one station of life's way to the next. Well, there could be a rebirth soon. She looked young again; but did she still resemble Emma? That was the question whose answer, if negative, would come too late on film. Fortunately, Emma's days were now numbered. There would be one more glamorous film, then Emma would remove forever her spectacular earrings, and pass into history.

Tim joined her. "I finished up early. Westerns don't get any easier. There's no new way to film a horse. There never will be a new way."

"Why don't we try *people* in westerns? The way we will in our town."

"The form's too stylized. We just use characters, and they're about all used up. I hear Taylor's got something for you."

"Word gets around. He'll tell me after five. Do you think I look like – you know, Emma?"

Tim came very close to her and squinted down into her face. She was, at this moment, simply an object to be photographed and the director was studying the contours of the round stone-like head to see what needed light, what needed shadow. "Yes. You'll give a good impression of her."

"Only that?"

"There's always some change. Don't worry. You know, Taylor's having trouble getting a picture for Minter."

"Trouble? Here? Impossible. She's a Paramount star."

"They want to can her. Buy her out."

"Why? She's no worse than any of the others." Caroline had always had difficulty telling one pretty golden-haired dwarf from another. They came in shoals, according to fashion, and vanished as quickly when the style changed. Only Mabel Normand was distinctive and unlike anyone else; and, of course, she was now becoming unemployable. Apparently, cocaine deranged performances. At twenty-nine Wallace Reid was at the end of his career and probably life, thanks to morphine. Thanks to the Arbuckle scandal, the press was excitedly hinting at their names; soon hints would become accusations, and careers would end. Caroline was now convinced that a czar of the movies was needed. In the past, whenever those in power decided to take over the railroads or the coal mines, the press would obediently cease its lurid fictions and false alarms. Plainly, Hollywood needed a rest; and Caroline and Tim an ally.

Meanwhile, Mary Miles Minter and her mother were more trouble than they were worth. Also, in the cold light of commerce, the idea of replacing Mary Pickford had been a bad one. There was only one Pickford and no substitute was needed. Although Minter, now nineteen or twenty, was good for another decade or two as a pubescent star, the public had lost interest in little girls with golden ringlets and fun-loving ways. "I suppose they'll buy her out one of these days."

"Poor William," was all that Caroline would think to say.

"She's told everyone she's going to marry him." Tim looked at Caroline to see what her reaction would be but Caroline was careful not to react. Although she no longer felt anything for Taylor, she was still his friend and wished him well.

"I don't think he really wants a second daughter." Caroline looked at a poster of Emma Traxler drinking a cocktail with a hectic jazzy smile. An air-brush had entirely erased all but the salient features.

"Particularly one equipped with such a mother."

"But Mary Miles would be marrying him to get rid of her mother."

"I don't think that's possible. Mrs. Shelby collects a third of everything her adorable child makes for as long as the child shall live – or at least until the ringlets fall out."

"Poor William," said Tim; he stood up. "I've got to go see Ince, about buying Santa Monica."

"Where we shall build our permanent absolutely real imaginary town. Which story do we do first?"

Tim grinned. "What about who killed President McKinley?"

"Who did?"

"Theodore Roosevelt and Standard Oil. You see, they hired this crazed anarchist and gave him a gun, but no one knows they've done it except his kindly old mother, who lives in our town."

"You will," said Caroline, "end in jail."

Taylor's car and driver were parked before the main studio gate on Vine Street, where the fans kept constant vigil. The fact that they all recognized the new Emma was most heartening, and Caroline signed autographs while making her way, resolutely, to the car, Taylor beside her.

"Do you mind if I do some errands on the way?"

Caroline did not mind.

"Robinson's Department Store, Fellows." Taylor turned to Caroline.

"I've got to find a present for Mabel. She's pretty low right now."

"I thought she was working for Sennett."

"That's why she's low. She's in trouble."

"Drugs."

"She's tried very hard. I've helped her as much as you can ever help anybody . . . help themselves."

Caroline remained in the car while Taylor went into Robinson's. "Could I have your autograph, Miss Traxler?" The chauffeur was young and fresh-faced. Emma's dazzling smile no longer made Caroline uneasy. She wrote Emma's name in a Woolworth's notebook. There were a dozen other signatures in the book but she did not dare riffle the pages, as she returned book and pen. "It's sure a great honor getting to drive you, and all the other big stars."

Caroline simpered briefly. "Is there any news about Eddie . . . Eddie Sands?"

The boy frowned. "Well, he's been signing Mr. Taylor's name to checks up in Fresno and Sacramento. Then there was this pawn shop where he hocked some things, using a name Mr. Taylor recognized. But that's all."

Taylor was back in the car. "Nothing I wanted. Let's go by the bank," he said to Fellows. "My God," he said to Caroline, money on his mind, "this income tax business is a nuisance."

"And expensive."

Taylor nodded. "I wish you'd work on your friends in Washington to let up on us." They were driving along a dusty lane lined with eucalyptus trees which would, presently, cross Sunset

Boulevard. The day was bright, blue and cold. "I told you Eddie's been forging my name to checks . . ."

"Another nuisance."

Taylor laughed suddenly. "The real nuisance is that he's such a good forger I can't tell his writing from my own. Marjorie Berger's coming over to the house this evening with all the receipted checks."

"Anyway, you're lucky he's gone."

Taylor gave her a quick curious look. Then he said, somewhat ambiguously, "Am I?" After the bank and a stop at Fowler's Bookstore, they went on to Alvarado Street, where Caroline was shown into the familiar drawing room by the new Negro servant, an agreeable somewhat nervous man, plainly devoted to Taylor. "Miss Berger called to say she'll be here at six-thirty, sir. Then another lady called, but didn't leave her name."

"Thank you, Henry." Taylor went over to his desk and picked up a script. *"Monte Carlo,"* he said. "There's a wonderful part for you. The star's part," he added quickly. "You're a White Russian grand duchess, working as a maid for this rich American lady – very vulgar. You go to Monte Carlo with her, and there's your fiancé from St. Petersburg, who's supposed to have died in the Revolution."

"I know the story," said Caroline, sweetly, she hoped. "What do I wear?" He told her. She was thrilled.

"I think I can really get Valentino for this one."

"I'll do it." Caroline looked about the room where she had played so many games of backgammon. Now she felt nothing, nothing at all. Taylor suggested that she take his car home while he walked to his dancing class in Orange Street. "I'm learning the tango," he said, and kissed her cheek.

Caroline was awakened by the telephone, which had merged, most unpleasantly, with a dream involving a train's departure without her. As she ran beside the train pulling out of the station, the conductor, Eddie Sands, grinned at her, and rang a bell and said in what sounded to be German – Alsatian? – "All aboard." Yet her luggage was on the train, including a Poussin painting and a childhood doll with one arm. "I must get aboard," said Caroline, into the receiver.

"What?" It was a man's voice, a familiar voice.

Caroline was now awake. She looked at the luminous dial on her bedside clock: nine-thirty. She had slept late. "I'm sorry," she said. "Who is this?"

"Charlie Eyton." The voice sounded tense, and unlike its owner's usual soothing head-of-studio drone. "Have the police called you?"

"What about?" Caroline sat up in bed, completely alert.

"Taylor's been murdered. I think you better get down here, to my office. They'll want to question you. The police. The press, too. But don't talk to them. Everybody who saw Bill yesterday's being questioned. Luckily, I've got all the letters . . ."

"What letters?" she asked stupidly.

"Yours to him. Don't worry. I've got the whole lot. I've already been to Alvarado Street. Anyway, we've got to work on a statement for you to make . . ."

"Why was he murdered? I mean, *how* was he murdered?" Caroline was having great trouble absorbing so grotesque a fact.

"He was shot in the back a couple of hours after you left him."

"That would be *after* his tango class in the Orange Street dance studio." Caroline was shrewd and precise in her shock.

"Sure. Sure." Eyton hung up.

Caroline warned Héloise not to speak to anybody in her absence. "There's been an accident," she said. "Poor Mr. Taylor's dead."

"I knew it!" When it came to disaster, Héloise was never taken by surprise.

"Of course you did." Caroline left the apartment and got into her car. The Japanese gardener greeted her politely. The day was cold and perfect. Sunset Boulevard was almost deserted. So many times she had driven like this through empty streets to studios near and far as well as to locations where it was often necessary to start out before the sun rose. If she ever looked back over this extraordinary period in her life, she would recall, first, the sun coming up over the studio ranch in the San Fernando Valley and then the torturing blaze of klieg lights in her eyes. "Interlock." The rest was confusion.

Charles Eyton was at his desk, speaking on the telephone. He waved Caroline to a chair. "Yes, it was murder. At first they said

453

natural causes but then the coroner rolled him over and saw that he'd been shot in the back. When? Around seven, seven-thirty last night. Yes, all hell is going to break loose." He hung up. "I'm sorry to rout you out, but we've got to co-ordinate our stories."

"We?"

"Yes. *We.* The studio. The movie business. This could be worse than Fatty Arbuckle."

"Oh," was all that Caroline could manage. Then she thought how delighted Blaise would be that her acting career, what was left of it, would end in such a spectacular *Götterdämmerung*. Would scandal also affect what she had come to think of as the real imaginary American town?

"The colored man found him at seven-thirty this morning on the floor. In the living room. He called the police. He called me, thank God. I sent our people over to take away anything that would look bad for the studio. Bootleg whisky, love letters. Articles of feminine apparel."

"I shouldn't have thought that there would be many of those."

Eyton gave her a hard look; but said nothing. "We got the bottles out. I personally got the letters. While the police were busy questioning the neighbors, I went upstairs." He indicated three stacks on his desk. "Letters from you and Mabel Normand and Claire Windsor and Mary Miles Minter . . ."

"Nothing incriminating – in my letters, anyway."

"No. But that won't stop the press from running full-page pictures of you as a foreign temptress, capable of an act of passion."

"No, it won't," said Caroline bleakly. "After all, I am the press, too."

Eyton was suddenly all apparent candor. "You can help us. A lot. First . . ."

"First, what happened?"

"Who knows? Taylor came home with you. Went out again for a walk – to your tango class, I suppose. They'll check it out. Then he came back to the house, where his accountant, Marjorie Berger, was waiting for him. That was six-fifteen. An hour later Mabel Normand arrived. Her chauffeur waited for her in Alvarado Street, in full view of everyone in the court. Then the colored man, who let her in, went home. At around seven-thirty, Taylor walked Mabel to her car. She had a paper bag of peanuts in her hand." Eyton paused to see if Caroline grasped the significance of the peanuts, but Caroline chose to acknowledge nothing. "Then Mabel was driven away, and Taylor went inside the bungalow and a few minutes later the neighbors heard what sounded like a shot, which was a shot, the shot that killed him, but since it could have been an automobile's exhaust or a firecracker, nobody thought anything about it."

"Do the police know about Mabel?"

Eyton nodded.

"This will not exactly help her career."

"If we all work together, we can all stay clear of this thing. As you know, we can pretty much control the press from the studio, if we're all agreed on just what we want to feed them."

"Can you control the police?"

There was a pause. Then Eyton shrugged. "We always have. It's expensive. You have to pay off everybody, which means the district attorney, too, and he comes high."

Caroline was beginning to grasp the nature of the problem. "What is it that we must all agree to?"

"Do you have any idea who killed William?" The tone was so casual that Caroline found herself smiling politely.

"I didn't, of course."

"Of course." Eyton was now smiling at Caroline, as if a preview at Bakersfield had gone unexpectedly well. Back of Eyton's chair, a portrait of Adolph Zukor glowered at them. Above the picture, like heraldic devices, two polo mallets were crossed, a gift from Cecil B. DeMille.

"Mabel didn't either. So if it's to be a star, that leaves only Mary Miles Minter, doesn't it?" Caroline's journalistic sense was aroused. Consumed by a passion far too large for her tiny frame and frustrated yet again in her lust, the golden-ringletted dwarf swept to the floor the backgammon set whilst firing her pistol into William Desmond Taylor, aged Joseph to her nubile Madame Potiphar.

"But why do you think it has to be a star?" Eyton's question was more of a statement.

"Because the press will insist that it's one of us, which is why you've asked me here. Isn't it?"

Eyton sighed. "I guess I can handle just about any actor in the business, but to deal with one who's also a publisher . . ." The voice trailed off.

"There was a letter last summer, to William, which I read by accident. Someone wrote that he – or she, I never saw the signature – would shoot him. Did you find that letter?"

Eyton shook his head. "No. But I found one from Eddie Sands. A recent letter. A blackmail letter. Now it's my view that last night Eddie paid Bill a call, and asked maybe for money and there was this quarrel, and then Eddie . . ." Eyton suddenly pointed a forefinger at Caroline, who winced. "Naturally it's a bit early for the police to make an announcement, but I have a hunch they're just about convinced he did it – as is the district attorney, Mr. Woolwine. So that means the heat is off us and there will be a nation-wide manhunt."

"Will they find Eddie?"

"I don't know." Eyton touched the stack of letters. "I hope not. It would be better if he had an accident first. That is, before he was arrested."

Caroline and Eyton looked at one another. She had never suspected that this very amiable highly ordinary man could be so swift in his responses, and so ruthless. "What," asked Caroline at last, "does Eddie know?"

Eyton held up one of the letters. "I have no way of knowing what he knows but I do know what he was threatening. If Taylor didn't drop the charges against him, he says here that he will expose him."

"Men?"

"Boys." Eyton unexpectedly smiled. "If the press gets on to this, Hollywood has had it. Thanks to Arbuckle, we're being boycotted all through the Bible Belt. One more scandal, and . . ."

"Boycott." In context, Caroline found the word darkly witty. "Let us say we – you – can control the press. How do you control the police investigation?"

"By paying them to go after Eddie."

"Suppose they find him, and he tells – *his* story?"

"We'll have to pay them *not* to find him – alive, anyway."

"An accident?"

Eyton nodded. "Meanwhile, we're turning Bill into a lady-killer, a real Don Juan. In a couple of weeks I'll confess to having got off with some letters from some of his glamorous lady friends on the ground that I did not want innocent people involved in this sad and tragic affair. So I will turn every single one of the letters over to the police except for the ones I keep."

"Are the others as dull as mine?"

"Mary Miles Minter's aren't dull at all. Fact, they're a lot better than any of the movies she's been doing lately. She writes how she expects Bill to marry her so that she can get away from her mother who locks her up when she suspects she's on the prowl but things are coming to a head now, because the last time Mrs. Shelby locked her up Mary took a gun and tried to kill herself."

Caroline saw the letter on William's desk; saw the large bold handwriting; saw the word "shoot." "That means she has a gun. That means we know who killed him, don't we?"

"Do we?" Eyton was mild. "Well, I suppose we do when you come right down to it. It was Eddie who'd been blackmailing his old employer about his . . . lady friends, as we'll call them. Actually we didn't take away the feminine apparel that we found in the house. We even left a pink dressing gown with three M's embroidered on it. So he'll be depicted as another Casanova, which is all right by the studio, and though a number of famous ladies will be mentioned as possible victims or would-be victims of his normal passions, only Mary and Mabel may come out of this just a little bit tarnished, and poor Mabel wouldn't't've been involved at all if she hadn't decided to come by and say hello just before Eddie shot him."

"Drugs?"

"We found nothing. The police found nothing." If Eyton was lying he was most convincing. "Hollywood is once again pure and blameless – in that department, anyway." Eyton smiled. "But those peanuts in that brown paper bag." He shook his head.

Caroline rose. "When the police question me . . ."

"Tell the truth. What else? But you might, if you want to, mention Eddie as a possible killer. It would be a big help if you did." Eyton was on his feet, always polite. "You know the colored man, Henry Peavey, was due in court today and Bill was going to testify to his good character."

"In court for what?"

"Soliciting boys. In Westlake Park."

"For himself?"

"For his employer, he tells me. The police have found a bunch of keys that don't fit any of the locks at 404 Alvarado Street. Apparently, there is another apartment somewhere else . . ."

"A *garconniére*."

"I'm afraid I don't know any French." Eyton showed Caroline to the door. "Just a bit of Tijuana Spanish."

2

By the middle of March, Emma Traxler was again before the cameras, directed by her all-time favorite megaphoner, Timothy X. Farrell, as Grace Kingsley put it in a long story for the Los Angeles *Times*. Apparently, Emma had intended to give up the bright lights of Hollywood for her native Alsace-Lorraine, where her moated family castle was ever at her disposal. But letters from fans all round the world had convinced her that she should return to the screen in a photo-play to be directed by William Desmond Taylor. Caroline shuddered every time she saw the name, which was several times a day.

As Eyton had predicted, the scandal was huge but delicately orchestrated. Emma was simply one of a number of glamorous stars that he had pursued. Beyond a single deposition to the Los Angeles Police Department, Caroline had been bothered by no one official. But what the police were releasing to the public and what Eyton was manufacturing were often contradictory. The pink nightgown with the three M's was discussed in every paper; yet the police affected not to have seen it. Had Eyton invented the whole thing to involve Minter more deeply in the plot? As it was, Eyton was feeding Minter's love letters to the *Examiner*. Fortunately, Mary herself had a perfect alibi for the fatal night. She was at home, reading aloud to her mother and sister. Yet, somewhat mysteriously, on the morning after the murder, she had come to the Alvarado house *before* the newspapers had spread the news of

Taylor's death. On the other hand, the telephones of Hollywood had not stopped ringing all that morning and everyone in any way concerned knew of the murder. While the press continued to print salacious stories about Taylor's womanizing, the police spoke only of the thief, Eddie, who had vanished.

Caroline sat in her dressing room just off the sound-stage, where the casino at Monte Carlo had been re-created. She had taken over Taylor's script for Traxler Productions. A former grand duchess she was now a lady's maid, decked out in her employer's splendor for an anonymous night at a masked ball.

Caroline lay on an incline board in order to keep her hair and dress pristine. More than ever, she felt like a doll being manipulated, not unpleasurably, by Tim. There was comedy as well as Traxler heartbreak in her role, and although the new face was not yet entirely hers, it photographed well. Certainly she looked a decade younger than poor Mary Queen of Scots, who had been forced to undergo the Renaissance's only solution to age, a beheading with an ax.

Suddenly the door to the dressing room opened. "Tim," said Caroline, since he was the only one who could come and go without knocking. But it was not Tim. It was Mabel Normand.

"Em, can I see you?" For reasons unknown, Mabel had always called her Em. But then better the bleak Em than the full panoply of the sombre three M's.

"Of course." Caroline turned to her dresser. "Could you wait outside, please?" The dresser departed and Mabel turned on both taps in the wash basin. "They can't record you with the water running."

"Who can't record what?"

"Anybody. The police." Mabel crossed the room, toes turned in, hands turned out; the effect was, as always, enchanting and curiously boyish. Had that been Mabel's appeal to William Desmond Taylor? "Will you do me a favor, Em?" The long upper lip was suddenly that of Huck Finn in a winsome mood.

"If I can." Caroline was cautious. She also felt a fool, Lying on an incline board, unable to move for fear of losing sequins from her gown or disturbing the fantastic arrangement of her hair, a towering beehive buttressed with braids not her own and jewels.

"You're having dinner at Pickfair tonight."

"Are you coming, too?"

"Me? I'm never invited there. Thank God. But tonight it's for all the bigwigs of the Motion Picture Producers and Distributors. Now, listen, Em. There's this blacklist in the town. It's not official – yet. But everybody knows about it. Because of all this Central Casting Agency business."

The new committee had announced that in order to maintain high moral standards within the motion-picture business, all players would be obliged to join an agency that would, somehow, determine if they were morally worthy of being transformed into shadows upon a screen. "I thought it was to keep out the . . . the . . ."

"The hookers. Well, sure. But it also has to do with drugs and politics and anything else they happen to think up. Well, I'm on the blacklist."

"How do you know?"

"Mack, Mack Sennett. He told me. *He* isn't bothered, but that's all the work I can get. No one else is ever going to hire me again until the word comes down from whoever Washington sends out here. So will you talk to whoever that is? About me?"

"Yes." Caroline felt virtuous; she was also aroused by yet another example of American hypocrisy in full cry. "Do you think it's drugs?" She was blunt.

"No. It's William Desmond Taylor. You see, I'm sort of a suspect. In the press, that is." Mabel sat at Caroline's dressing table and, reflexively, began to make herself up as if for a scene. Caroline was fascinated by her swift professionalism. But then Mabel knew more about movies than any woman in the business.

"But you're not a real suspect, are you? I mean, the police . . ."

"Are you kidding?" Mabel chuckled. "The fix is in. The district attorney's been paid off. He'll go on looking for Eddie Sands, until the whole thing just peters out. Eddie's dead, by the way."

Startled, Caroline moved her head, breaking off a section of her hair. Mabel leapt to her feet; picked up the braid and expertly reattached it to the glittering beehive. "They found him in the Connecticut River. A bullet in his head. They said it was suicide."

"Who's they?"

"The police in Darien, Connecticut."

"Why didn't they tell the Los Angeles police?"

"They did. That's how we know. Only Woolwine – the D.A. – says he's not convinced it's really Eddie, and so the manhunt goes on. They'll get tired of it, the press. But I'd like to go back to work before then."

"I'll certainly talk to the . . . bigwigs tonight."

"They're all afraid of you." Mabel was precise and blunt. "Everyone in politics is afraid of people who own newspapers. The way we are, too. The way I am, anyway. I miss Bill."

"I'm not sure that I do." Caroline was not certain just what she thought of the whole extraordinary business. In a sense she was still literally shocked by what had happened. Certainly it seemed odd that she would never again see him at lunch in the commissary or over the backgammon board in Alvarado Street. "Who," Caroline was suddenly inspired to ask, "killed him?"

"Don't you know?" The boy's face was suddenly mischievous and the eyes were bright.

"How could I?"

"I thought you'd figured it out. I did even before Mary told me."

"Surely she didn't kill him."

"Well," Mabel was enjoying herself, "let's say she was a logical suspect. The police found three long golden hairs on Bill's jacket. Neither you nor I have – at the moment, anyway – long golden hair."

"Wasn't she at home, reading aloud to her mother and sister?" Caroline knew the catechism of that famous evening in all its intricate detail.

"No. She was upstairs when I came to call."

Caroline stared, as best she could out of the corner of her eye, at Mabel, who was now trying on a pair of Emma Traxler's long lashes. "How do you know?"

"She told me."

"Why? You'd be the last person I'd tell, in that situation."

Mabel sighed. "They don't look right on me, do they?" She blinked her eyes at her reflection in the mirror.

461

"No," said Caroline. "They are for an aging grand duchess at the Casino in Monte Carlo, not 'our Mabel.'"

"The next day, little Mary rang me: could we meet? We did. I can't stand her and she can't stand me and no one can stand that mother of hers, the Louisiana belle."

"Why did Mary want to see you?"

Mabel took off the lashes, and turned to face Caroline directly. "She wanted to know if Bill had said anything about her being in the house when he hustled me out the door and walked me to my car and gave me this book by Freud, which he said was better than my usual reading, the *Police Gazette.* I told Mary, yes. He told me." The grin was impish. "Of course he hadn't. But she fell for it. Then she told me what happened. After I drove off, Charlotte came into the house. She'd been hiding outside the bungalow, spying on her little girl. You can imagine how surprised she was to see me on the premises. Then, when I was off the premises, Charlotte went inside the house and shot Bill dead, as she'd been threatening to do if he married her meal ticket, which little Mary had told her he planned to do and which, poor bastard, he had no intention of doing. Anyway, she shot him right in front of her daughter, which makes little Mary – technically – an accomplice."

"Do the police know this?"

Mabel nodded. "The three blond hairs cinched it for them, which is why with all the stories about all of us, the only real evidence has never been given the press and never will be. Charlotte's personally paying off the D.A. Mary says Woolwine insists on taking the money in cash."

"What must it be like to have a mother . . . a *living* mother . . . who is a murderess." Caroline's own mother had contrived the death of the first Mrs. Sanford, and Caroline had never been able to rid herself of a sense of inherited sin.

"Well, it gives them a lot to talk about, I suppose."

There was a knock at the door. "On the set, please, Miss Traxler." Then the make-up man and wardrobe mistress were in the room, transforming Caroline first into Emma and then into the Grand Duchess Olga in disguise.

"You look really wonderful." Mabel sounded sincere. "I wish I could dress like that." Mabel turned off the wash-basin taps.

"I wish I could act like you." Caroline was absolutely sincere.

"Act? I've never *acted* a day in my life that I know of. Help me, Em." Mabel threw Caroline a kiss and departed.

Caroline then walked onto the set and received a round of applause, led by Tim. The string orchestra played Offenbach. "Give me any mask," said the Grand Duchess to her maid. "Tonight I am someone else. I wonder who?"

At six o'clock that evening, Caroline knew exactly who she was – Mrs. Sanford of the Washington *Tribune*. She rang the paper and got Mr. Trimble, who stayed late, unlike Blaise, who left early.

"Mrs. Sanford – Caroline," the voice was that of an old man now, "or maybe I should say Emma . . ."

"Emma Traxler goes into retirement next year and Mrs. Sanford becomes a full-time movie producer . . ."

"Come back to the paper . . ."

"This is better than a paper, once I'm out of the papers . . ."

"We're playing it down, as much as we can. That place sure sounds like a real mess."

"Exactly." Caroline was brisk. "That's why I want you to write an editorial, one of your fierce Cotton Mather numbers, insisting that Will Hays, for the good of the nation – of the world – become our czar. He's said no already, but I think he can be convinced if we say that the person who cleans up Hollywood could very well be elected president by a grateful nation. You know the line."

Mr. Trimble spent some time coughing on the other end. Then he said, "I know Hays pretty well. If he thought we – you and Blaise and the *Trib* – would support him for president, he'd probably go along . . ."

"Tell him we will. Tell him Hearst will, too. That I can guarantee him Hearst's support . . ."

"Can you?"

"Who knows? But I can get Hearst to write an editorial just like ours asking for Hays to take the job."

"I guess you know, there's a lot of trouble brewing here for the Administration, so now's maybe a good time to get out of the

Cabinet. Tell me, what's this Mary Miles Minter like?"

"She is a dwarf, aged sixty." For a moment they gossipped.

Then Caroline said, "After the editorial runs, why don't you go see Mr. Hays, and tell him how much this means to us, and so on."

Mr. Trimble knew what was expected of him; and they bade each other good-by.

Tim came into the bedroom, already in his dinner clothes. Pickfair was early but formal. "I think we'll get Mr. Hays," said Caroline.

"What's he like?"

"A dwarf, aged sixty. No, sorry. What's he *like*? A very ambitious mouse. If we help him politically, he'll help us . . . populate our imaginary town. I think he'll be easy."

Tim nodded; and smiled. Caroline had come back to life, as Caroline. It was not yet time to stop.

3

Jess slowly, painfully lowered himself into his usual chair in the lobby of the Wardman Park Hotel. The truss that kept the wound in his unhealed belly together was tight, and smelled disagreeably of witch hazel. It took him an hour to dress nowadays. When he had plaintively asked the surgeon if his appendix scar would ever heal, he had been told that for a diabetic the healing process was always a slow one. The only good news in what had been a relentlessly bad year was the appearance of insulin, a new medicine that was saving the lives of diabetics everywhere. For the first time in years Jess could eat and drink normally.

Jess held a copy of the Washington *Tribune* in one hand. In the unlikely event that he saw someone he didn't want to talk to, the paper would cover his face, as he carefully studied the stock market. Otherwise, he simply stared at the people coming and going. Members of Congress and high government officials lived in the hotel, and it was possible to transact quite a lot of unexpected business in the shadowy lobby with its thick carpeting and heavy old-fashioned arm chairs, and the spittoons thoughtfully set nearby.

An Ohio congressman stopped by to say hello. "It was a close thing, Jess, boy, a close thing."

"Sit down." Jess was eager for news of the recent election, in which the Republican Party had lost eighty-eight seats in the House of Representatives and seven seats in the Senate. The party still controlled both houses of Congress but everyone agreed that the people were in a restive mood and Harding's re-election in 1924 was by no means a sure thing.

"We lost Frank Mondell, best floor leader the House ever had. And Lodge barely squeaked in." The congressman shook his head sadly. "It's the radicals, Jess. And the progressives, the madmen like La Follette and Norris. They're out there busy inciting the folks to revolution, just like Russia."

Jess agreed that if the election had demonstrated anything it was that the radical element was on the rise and that the quiet sensible conservatism of Harding was being rejected. But the set-back had had an energizing effect on the White House. W.G. had promptly summoned Congress into a special session two weeks before December 4, when the regular winter session began. W.G. was about to crack the whip at last.

"I just hope he can ride herd on these wild men." The congressman ran his fingers through an enviably full head of gray hair. "Seen much of Charlie Forbes lately?"

Jess's heart began to beat a little faster as it always did when the subject was business. "Every now and then. He's been travelling a lot this year. Charlie Cramer's been running the bureau for him. Yeah, I see a bit of him. Nice guy. You know?"

The congressman nodded. "They say Charlie – Forbes, that is – is going to take Fall's place at Interior when Fall steps down."

"Yes," said Jess, and nothing more because he knew nothing of the matter and someone in his situation, as the right arm to the President's right arm, was supposed to know everything.

"So then Forbes goes to Interior?"

"Well," Jess did his best to look sly, "yes, to Fall's going home. He's in bad shape physically and his two sons died, you know?"

"Well, I think Charlie Forbes would be a real live wire in this job. Yes, sir." Suddenly the congressman chuckled. "Friend of mine sold the Veterans Bureau seventy thousand gallons of this four-cents-a-gallon floor wax which they then bought for close to a dollar a gallon."

"That's a lot of floor wax." Through his vest, Jess tugged at the right end of his truss, which had begun to curl in on itself.

"Enough floor wax for those hospitals for a hundred years." Jess made amiable sounds; and the congressman went on his way.

Jess had managed to do some business with Forbes, but not much, because Daugherty deeply disliked him. There was always a certain amount of money floating around in an agency like the Veterans Bureau, and Forbes was getting a reputation for care-lessness when it came to giving out contracts for new hospitals. Daugherty was positive that Forbes was an out-and-out crook while the President was satisfied that he was, at worst, too much in a hurry to make a name for himself in the bureaucracy so that he could move up the ladder to the Cabinet itself. Jess made it a point never to volunteer information to Daugherty on the subject of business. By and large, the Attorney General was not one to arouse someone else's sleeping dog. As it was, he had quite enough to worry about. Despite W.G.'s complaints about the presidency, he was eager to be renominated and re-elected, and it was up to Daugherty to make sure that nothing went wrong. Meanwhile, Lucie Daugherty was in Johns Hopkins Hospital and their alco-holic son, Draper, was about to be institutionalized, while Daugherty himself was obliged to fight off fourteen charges of impeachment, the work of a fanatic congressman who found the Attorney General too lax in prosecuting the trusts. Since everyone knew that organized labor was behind the impeachment pro-ceedings, the Congress threw the whole thing out. But Daugherty was physically exhausted, and Jess was not going to add to his bur-den if he could help it; quite the contrary.

During the next hour, Jess did a fair amount of business of the sort that he filed away in his mind as "guidance": whom to see about what. Then he pulled himself carefully to his feet in order not to disturb the open scar beneath the truss, which might, even now, with luck, be healing. The Wardman Park doorman helped him into a cab, as if he were made of glass. "The White House,"

Jess announced to the driver, a phrase he never tired of using.

The Duchess was in her wheelchair; at her side was tiny Doc Sawyer, in his uniform as surgeon general of the Army. Both looked somewhat forlorn in the large oval sitting room with its bright fire. "Well, Jess, you stay away when a body's sick." The high nasal voice was as strong as ever. "Don't think I don't know."

"Now, Duchess, you know I was here every day in August, wasn't I, Doc?"

"Well, I was in a coma, so *that* didn't do me much good, did it? Evalyn's just been here. She brought me this." The Duchess held up a lace bed-cap, cut in the shape of a crown. "Doc says I'll be up for Christmas, but I don't see how. I'm so weak, I'm like a dishrag, and I'm getting dropsical, too." With sombre joy, the Duchess chanted her list of symptoms. But, as Daugherty had said, she'd earned the right to bore everyone with her illnesses because she had nearly died in August when the remaining kidney had become infected. Although Doc Sawyer was only a homeopathic practitioner, he had somehow, yet again, saved her life. Either he was a better doctor than anyone suspected or Florence Kling Harding was an unkillable old bird.

Once illnesses had been exchanged – the Duchess was morbidly interested in Jess's unhealed scar – she gave him a half-dozen sheets of White House note-paper, covered with her best handwriting. "Christmas presents. You're the only one who knows how to buy things on the cheap that don't look cheap. We've got to economize, you know. The stock market . . ." She sighed. Jess knew exactly what W.G. had lost. "We may have to sell the *Star*."

"Would he really do that?" Harding without the Marion *Star* simply wasn't Harding. But then if he was to be president for another six years he'd be too old to ever run it again.

"We've had a good offer. Anyway, see what you can do about those presents." The President's valet, Brooks, appeared at the door. "All right. I'm ready. I'm exhausted. Oh, Jess, I had a call from Madame Marcia. Guess what she said?"

Jess shook his head dumbly. "Beats me, Duchess."

"Well, she knew all about the flu, but she could've read that in the papers, couldn't she? Anyway, what she wanted to see me about was the opposition of the moon to the sun and Saturn, which is very serious. Because it means that Warren can't depend on his friends. She said he should be suspicious of the ones he should trust and trust those he's usually suspicious of."

"That's a pretty wide field, Duchess."

"Uh huh," she said, noncommittally, as Brooks started to push her chair.

"Want me to go with you?" asked Doc.

The Duchess shook her head, as Brooks pushed her wheelchair into the hallway. "I can manage," she said, putting on her lace crown.

Jess moved to the edge of his chair, preparatory for departure.

Suddenly Doc sat down in the chair opposite him. "I want to talk to you, Jess." The little man's voice was cold and his gaze unnerving.

"Sure thing. Whaddaya know?" asked Jess reflexively.

"I know Charlie Forbes is a crook. What do you know?"

Something was going very wrong indeed if twice in the same day two such different people as an Ohio congressman and Doc were on to the Court Jester, as the press called Charlie.

"Well, Doc, I don't know I *know* that. There was all that fuss about Perryville, Maryland, last month, but that's all over. Isn't it?"

"No." Doc stared fixedly at Jess. "I'm surgeon general of the Army. I've got a job to do for all the Army, including veterans. Charlie's been selling off everything that isn't nailed down for pennies to the government and dollars to himself."

Jess was now feeling distinctly unwell. The wound in his right side was burning: he suddenly visualized a heifer being branded. "I thought the President stopped the sales and then Charlie explained everything and now everything's all right, and that the only stuff they've been selling was old and useless."

"*You* do business with Charlie?"

That was the question. Jess's face became hot; mouth dry. He longed for water, a gallon of cool water. "Doc, you know Daugherty don't get on with Charlie, and so I don't either. Oh, he comes to K Street for poker and booze, like you do, but that's all."

"I'm there for the poker and the booze. That's true. But some of the other fellows aren't, are they?"

468

"I don't know what you're talking about." Jess's fear was turning to anger.

"I suppose not. Sooner or later, I'm going to have to blow the whistle on Charlie Forbes."

"Go ahead." Jess knew that Doc would do nothing without the President's approval.

"I just want to make sure there's only Forbes involved." Doc stared again at Jess, who looked away. All he could think of now was water.

"If Charlie's really up to something, he can't be doing it all by himself. Can he?"

"Well," said Doc, "I meant aside from him and his friends, like Charlie Cramer. I just hope nobody else from the K Street house is involved, like Mannington."

"They're not." Jess was fairly certain that what he said was true.

"Good."

"You know if you're really going to . . . blow the whistle like you say, go to the General."

"Daugherty?"

Jess nodded. "He'll be happy to put Charlie Forbes in jail. It's just the President who'll be upset, particularly now he's going to run for re-election."

"He won't run." Doc was suddenly bleak.

"He is running."

"He thinks he is. But he isn't going to be here in two years."

As the truss suddenly doubled in on itself, Jess felt as if a hot knife had stabbed him. "I don't get it."

"His heart's going fast."

"How do you know? You're not his doctor."

"That's why I can say it. He's just running down, like an old clock. I see it in his face, his eyes, the way he can't breathe when he lies down unless Brooks props him up with pillows."

"Can't you do anything?"

Doc Sawyer shook his head. "Some things there's nothing you can do about but just stand by and watch, and wait."

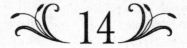

1

James Burden Day put his feet on the brass fender, and stared at the burning coals in the grate. February was a melancholy month at best, made only bearable for a senator by the knowledge that Congress would adjourn in a few weeks, and the round of committee meetings would end, except, of course, when they did not. Currently, those who were not ill with flu were simply sick of winter and politics while the country itself had never before seemed so out-of-focus. For the moment bad economic times were over. But Harding's normalcy was still a dream. Everywhere, working men were on strike or threatening to strike, and in the Senate cloakroom there were long idle conversations about the advantages and disadvantages of revolution, dictatorship, sheer chaos. Meanwhile, the President was recovering from influenza, and Burden had been sent for.

"What," asked Cabot Lodge, in the chair beside him, "is the subject of your meeting? If I do not pry, of course." Lately, the ghostly old man had taken to dropping in on Burden. He was, simply, lonely in the cold windy Senate Office Building. Although Lodge was Senate majority leader he tended now to delegate his powers to others. Between the death of his beloved wife and probably even more beloved poet son, Bay, Lodge had no one left to love; worse for someone of his temperament, he had no one to hate. The President was not only a fellow Republican but absolutely unhateful. For some reason, Lodge had always been well disposed toward Burden, even though Burden was now, in effect if not in title, the Democratic minority leader. Caroline was a link, of course; and there was always the court of Henry Adams, now as dispersed as that of King Arthur.

"The subject will be *you.*" Burden smiled at Lodge, who allowed his white beard to twitch in response.

"The International Court."

Burden nodded. "Harding wants us to join . . ."

"*Hughes* wants us to join, and Harding does what he tells him to. Hughes is a lawyer. I hate lawyers. No lawyer can resist a court of any kind. Have you noticed?"

"Depends on the venue."

"Exactly. Well, this is tied in with the League of Nations, and so we can never . . ."

"Never! Never!"

"Never," whispered Lodge with some satisfaction. "Join!" The pale marble face was ever so slightly flushed. Anything to do with the League of Nations put him in a good mood. "The Foreign Relations Committee is split. Eight to eight on the issue. As chairman, I'll naturally want more time to consider the matter. Anyway, we're adjourning soon, and there's no real hurry. They say Hughes is in bed with the flu."

Miss Harcourt entered with Burden's notes on the International Court. "Mrs. Sanford rang. She said it wasn't important. But if you get a chance . . ."

"Is she at Laurel House?"

"I'm sorry, Senator. I should've identified her more precisely. It is Mrs. John Apgar Sanford. She's back in Georgetown." Whatever Miss Harcourt may have suspected she betrayed nothing, ever.

"Caroline has come home to us." Lodge smiled at the prospect.

"So it would seem. I must get Kitty to call her."

"What a curious thing to have become, a photo-play star." Lodge shook his head in wonder. "She never seemed the type who wanted to . . . to dress up. But then she was raised in France. That explains so much." Lodge was bleak. The glittering lost son, Bay Lodge, had lived abroad, in France. "I miss not having Henry to travel with, as vile as he could be, and that was very vile indeed."

"We are so . . . so . . ." Burden was not sure which word would suit his own bad mood. He made a choice. "Mediocre nowadays. Except for you, of course . . ."

"And you, Burden. You'll be president one of these days, for what that's worth."

Burden nodded. "And what that's worth is not so much, I'd say. *We* don't seem to matter in this modern world." Burden realized that he was speaking like a very old man to a really old man who was at the end; but Burden was not old, not at the end. He had never doubted that he would be president in time. But time had become chilly and remote and less and less familiar, and his own place in it of little consequence.

"Politicians only matter when there's war. The observation is not original. But no less true for that. War created Lincoln. Roosevelt. Wilson." Lodge frowned at the thought of his ancient enemy, now living like an exiled, wounded king in S Street. He changed the subject. "Harding thinks you Democrats will give him the International Court."

"I suppose so." Burden was guarded. They were now rival political gamesmen. "You'll be giving him your committee report any day now, won't you?"

"Why such unseemly haste?"

"Because the Sixty-seventh Congress ends Sunday, March thirteenth."

"But by the time Hughes replies, it will be another Congress, another epoch. Tell Harding we're with him, of course. We want a court. It's just that we don't want *this* court with all its ties to the League."

Burden nodded. It was going to be the League of Nations fight yet again. To everyone's surprise, Harding was threatening to take the issue to the country. Imperceptibly, the amiable soft-headed senator had turned into a hard-minded president, most jealous of his own powers as the executive.

Together Burden and Lodge made their way down the high-ceilinged hall of the Senate Office Building. As it was February and dark, cheerless lights had been switched on, emphasizing the gloom. At Lodge's office they paused. "What do you hear about Fall?" asked the old man.

"Nothing. He's gone back to New Mexico, hasn't he?"

"He's been leasing the naval oil reserves to just about everybody."

"That was his job."

"Yes. Of course." Lodge stepped into his own office.

Still weak from the flu, the President was not in the west wing of the White House. He could be found, Burden was told, in the upstairs sitting room. An usher offered to escort him to the main residence, but Burden said that he knew the way well. En route, he recognized several Secret Service men and was greeted by the President's secretary, George Christian, who was coming from the living quarters. "The President's upstairs," he said.

As Burden stepped into the main hall of the White House, he was struck by the emptiness. It reminded him of the last Wilson year. But then sightseers seldom appeared on cold February days, while the usual business of the executive was transacted in the west wing.

As Burden walked over to the elevator, he heard a loud furious voice from the Red Room. Simultaneously, two ladies were being received at the main entrance by the chief usher. Burden was alarmed: they must not hear whatever was going on.

Quickly, Burden crossed to the Red Room, where he found the President of the United States shaking the Director of the Veterans Bureau by the neck. "You God-damned double-crossing bastard!" With one last shove, the scarlet-faced Harding flung Forbes against the red-damasked wall. Forbes's glasses fell to the floor. His ginger hair was all on end.

"Mr. President," said Burden. Harding glared blindly at him for a moment, completely disoriented. Then he recovered himself; became his seemly, becoming presidential self. "Senator Day. Yes. We have an appointment. Let's go into the next room." Neither acknowledged the presence of the ashen Charlie Forbes.

In the oval Blue Room, Harding sat, back to the window. He was breathing with great difficulty.

"I gather," said Burden formally, "you want to know how the vote will go on the Court bill."

"Yes. Yes." Harding took a deep shaky breath. "Peculiar situation when a Republican president has to rely on the Democrats to get his program through the Senate." He attempted a smile; and failed. "In this job it's not your enemies you have to worry about; it's your friends." The reference to Forbes was clear.

As Burden formally analyzed the Senate's mood, he wondered just what had gone wrong. Everyone knew that the Court Jester spent money lavishly. Everyone assumed that he no doubt received presents from contractors, a venerable custom for government officials with contracts to let. But the thought that there might be serious corruption had not occurred to Burden even though two fellow senators, Wadsworth and Reed, were certain that something was wrong. Burden had put their suspicions down to partisan zeal.

"I'm going to take a swing around the circle in May or June, ending up in Alaska. I know it's going to look like I'm campaigning for re-election but I'm not, really. I just want to set the record straight on my troubles with the Senate."

Burden was reminded of Wilson. How extraordinary these presidents were in their own eyes! Even the modest Harding had succumbed to the crown's hypnotic glitter, and had come to believe that if he merely showed himself to the people, his enemies would be routed. "Well, it's always good to get away from Washington."

"I'll say." Harding offered Burden a cigar, which he refused. Then Harding tried to light one for himself but his hands trembled, and he could not. Burden lit the cigar for him. "The flu never really goes away, does it?" Harding puffed a cloud of smoke as if he wanted to vanish.

"It goes, all right. But it takes its time. In my case a year before I felt myself again."

"Yes." The smoke cleared. Harding's olive-skinned face was now sallow. High blood pressure, Burden decided; due to overweight. As if Harding had read his thoughts, he said, "I'm starting on a strict diet this year. No more whisky, fewer cigars, more exercise, though I don't have the get-up-and-go I used to have."

"That will come back." It was odd to think that he, James Burden Day, was very apt to be the Democratic nominee for president in

1924 running against this amiable man. If the times were prosperous, Harding would win. If not, Burden would be installed in this altogether too familiar place.

"I'm calling my trip a voyage of understanding," Harding began; and ended. Then he said, "I'd appreciate it if you said nothing about what happened in there."

"If you ask me not to, I won't. But I think you should probably tell me what it's all about because if it's public business I'll find out anyway."

Harding rested his right cheek in his right hand. He shut his eyes. "It's the Perryville, Maryland, business. Charlie told me everything was all right and I believed him. But the Attorney General didn't. He's just wound up an investigation. Charlie is going to resign."

"That means the Senate will investigate."

"I suppose we'll have to. I mean," Harding's attempt at a smile was ghastly, *"you'll* have to. Sometimes I keep thinking I'm still on the Hill and not down here – at the bottom of this damned well. What a time for this to happen!" Harding shook his head. "Daugherty's close to a break-down with all his troubles, and I'm a bit down myself . . ."

"Well, there's one good thing. Congress adjourns in a few weeks. There can't be much of an investigation till October, November."

"I thought I knew Charlie Forbes as well as I've ever known anybody, and then . . ." But Harding was not about to tell Burden what Forbes had done, nor would Burden ask. Executive and legislative not to mention Republican and Democrat, must keep their distance at such a time. Burden doubted if Forbes could have got away with very much in so conspicuous a job. Bribes were an everyday affair in government, and there were agreed-upon limits to what an officeholder might demand. During the war, Burden had been offered numerous bribes by naval contractors and he had refused them all on the ground that not only was it a wrong thing to do but, if found out, the career was at an end. On the other hand, he was not censorious. What others chose to do was their business not his. By and large, the great political players stayed reasonably clean. Harding was honest as far as Burden knew, which was quite a lot: the Senate was a relatively small club and who got money from whom was generally if not precisely known. Before 1917, Borah, the incorruptible, was thought to have taken money from one George Sylvester Viereck, who had been in charge of disbursements in the Kaiser's name. A charming and cultivated figure, Viereck had tried to charm and cultivate Burden, who had not responded.

But the lines were vague at best, and when it came to campaign contributions there was moral chaos. In 1904, Theodore Roosevelt had gone begging to every rich magnate in the land. "We bought him," Frick was supposed to have said later, "but he didn't stay bought." Actually, Roosevelt had been sufficiently honorable to give value for money paid. That was the rule of the game, and one broke it at one's peril. Ohio politicians tended either to the small-time, like Jess Smith, helping out bootleggers, or they were, like Mark Hanna, huge national operators, selling their presidents, like oil stock. Of the lot, Harding was, perhaps, the most honest, while the much-maligned Daugherty appeared to be above temptation except when it came to raising money for Harding; then he rivalled Hanna.

"Well, we've still got Charlie Cramer at the bureau." Harding stubbed out his cigar. "He'll straighten everything out once Forbes is gone. Burden, I'd be most grateful if you said nothing about Forbes's resigning until he actually has, in the next week or so."

"I won't."

"Good." Harding smiled; a normal color had returned to his face. "They tell me I may be up against you in '24."

Burden laughed. "I hear that every four years but they always find someone else."

"Personally – selfishly – I hope they do again. You'd be hard to beat."

Burden gave the President a folder containing his reflections on the International Court; and departed.

Burden let himself in the side door of the Sanford Massachusetts Avenue house, now up for sale. Whenever Blaise or Frederika wanted to stay over in town, they would use the upper part of the house; the rest was empty, dark, cold.

Frederika wore a negligee. "Come in. Shut the door. The house is freezing." She shivered even though her sitting room was as warm as a greenhouse with a great fire and masses of flowers everywhere. She liked it to be known that she gardened seriously. Actually, she did not know one flower from another and preferred goldenrod to chrysanthemums. The conservatories at Laurel House were well tended by professional gardeners, and Frederika never went near them.

Burden sat beside the fire while Frederika made a cocktail containing gin. Since Prohibition, each felt obliged to drink more than ever before. Luckily, neither was addicted, unlike half the Senate – and their wives. "Harding's gone on the wagon."

"Poor man."

"He owes it to the Constitution . . ."

"His?"

"Ours. Both, I suppose."

"Have you seen Caroline?"

Burden shook his head. New mistress quite liked old mistress, who made no fuss of any kind. Then, suddenly, on cue, the door to the sitting room was flung open and there stood Caroline herself, with Blaise behind her.

Burden's first alarm turned, unexpectedly, to mirth. There they were, the four of them, like some intricate equation that, with time, kept bringing forth new answers or, more precisely, data, since there were no answers in life.

"You have caught us at last," Frederika observed dispassionately. She embraced Caroline; and patted Blaise's cheek. Burden had always assumed that Blaise knew everything; now he wondered if, perhaps, Blaise had *not* known because – sad thought! – he did not care one way or the other.

"This is cozy," said Blaise neutrally and sat beside the fire. "I had no idea you were giving a party," he said to Frederika.

"I wasn't. Until you two made it one. Burden has been telling me all about Mr. Forbes and the Veterans Bureau . . ."

"I am home," said Caroline, smiling fondly at Burden. "Where I live, you would be talking about how much *Robin Hood* really grossed last week at the Capitol . . . the one on Broadway, not ours."

"What," asked Frederika, "is Douglas Fairbanks really like?"

"Very athletic."

"I can see that on the screen. But – in person."

"There is no person in person," said Caroline, who looked like someone Burden had never known except on the screen. She had managed to simplify her face so that now it was nothing but a number of perfect features in strict harmony with each other. Kitty was certain that surgery had been resorted to, but Burden thought not. The camera had burned away all imperfections, and fame had done the rest.

"How long will you stay?" Burden was casual.

"As long as I have to. I must wait for the scandal to die down."

"How I envy you!" Frederika was perfectly sincere in this. "I wish I could have my picture in the tabloids. Frederika Sanford . . ."

"Traxler is our movie name," said Blaise, gazing thoughtfully at Burden, whose cheeks were suddenly warm.

"All right. Frederika Traxler, *femme fatale,* the pearl of Transylvania . . ."

"Alsace-Lorraine, dear." Caroline's smile was dazzling.

"Whatever. Were you really the last person to see that director?"

"The last but two. At least." Caroline's smile began to fade exactly as it did on film.

"Who killed him?" Blaise turned to Caroline.

"Eddie Sands, they say. The servant. Anyway, this is not the sort of case that anyone wants to solve. We put it all down to the Californian Curse."

"Mary Miles Minter's pink dressing gown in his closet!" Frederika shuddered with pleasure. "Mabel Normand in the middle of the night . . ."

"Shortly before eight in the evening." Caroline was precise.

"I thought him charming, that evening at the Coconut Grove. But I had no idea he was such a . . . a voluptuary?"

"Was he?" asked Blaise.

"I saw no sign of it." Caroline stopped smiling and, nonsmiling, began to resemble a younger version of her own self. "He was more . . . fatherly with the movie ladies. He was always the best of friends. Anyway, my new friend Will Hays is cleaning up Hollywood, and I'm helping him."

Burden wondered how he could explain, first, his immediate departure from the Sanford family bosom and, second, his presence in Frederika's room. "We're having," he began, "more scandals here than Hollywood . . ."

"But our cast is so unattractive." Frederika began to recomb her hair. Caroline watched her with a professional eye. Blaise rang for Frederika's maid, the only servant in the house.

"Mr. Harding is very handsome." Caroline looked at herself in Frederika's mirror and saw Burden. He raised an eyebrow – in greeting?

"I don't think he's involved, poor bastard." Blaise turned to Burden. "What do you think?"

"Harding's honest. But he's managed to surround himself with all these poker-playing small-time chiselers. Like Charlie Forbes." After Forbes's encounter with the President, he had fled to Europe, from where, on February 15, he had resigned. As Burden had predicted, shortly before adjournment, the Senate ordered an investigation of the Veterans Bureau. Then Congress went home, and the Hardings and the McLeans went to Florida together.

"Forbes isn't such a small-time chiseler. You've heard about Cramer, haven't you?"

Currently, the Veterans Bureau was being administered by its general counsel, Charles F. Cramer. "Is he involved, too?" asked Burden.

Blaise nodded. "Very much so, I'd say. Or was. Last night he shot himself in the head. In Harding's old house."

"Cramer's dead?" Burden was astonished. Never before in his experience had politics veered off into overt crime, covert death.

"Yes. They say he left two letters but they've disappeared."

"She was charming," said Frederika. "Mrs. Cramer. What was her name?"

No one answered. Then Burden said what each was thinking.

"Cramer was supposed *not* to have been involved in Forbes's deals."

"He must have known," Blaise was emphatic. "And if he knew, he should have gone public. He is – was – a lawyer, after all. Anyway, according to my reporter who was in the house, there was a clipping about the Senate investigation on his desk."

"He would have had to testify . . ." Burden stopped, suddenly aware of the possibility of a scandal so vast that it could bring down the Administration.

Caroline completed his thought. "But if someone did not want him to testify, they would shoot him and make it look like a suicide."

"Or a movie," said Frederika. "Nonie, I think, is her name."

"I have been living in a movie murder case." Caroline was hard. "It is not pleasant, let me tell you."

"Where's Daugherty?" Burden turned to Blaise.

"Somewhere in Florida. Sick."

The maid arrived with whisky for the master of the house. Burden used her arrival as pretext for departure; and bade his three lovers a fond farewell.

2

Usually May was Jess's favorite time at Deer Creek, but nothing pleased him now because nothing that he could do would ever please Daugherty again. For the most part, the two men sat in their rocking chairs, staring straight ahead at the woods in full leaf. In silence they had eaten the hamburgers that Jess had cooked. Now Daugherty was yawning; ready for his afternoon nap. It had taken him three months to recover from the flu. After Florida, he had gone alone to North Carolina; then back to Washington Court House and the shack at Deer Creek which they had both used for years as a getaway from the world. But the world could not be got away from if you were attorney general.

"Maybe," said Daugherty suddenly, "you should stay on here."

"Here? In the shack?"

"No. Washington Court House. That other Washington's nothing but trouble for you now. Me, too." Daugherty rocked more quickly in his chair.

Jess waited to be told what kind of trouble, but Daugherty was silent. "Well, there was the Charlie Forbes and Cramer business. But that's all over. I mean, what else is there?"

Daugherty grunted; and slowed down his rocking. "There's Fall."

For a year the conservationists had been attacking Fall for his indifference to nature, a likeable trait in Jess's eyes. Then La Follette had got into the act, and asked for a Senate investigation of all the oil leases given out by the Department of the Interior. Senator Walsh of Montana was assigned the task of finding out why the Navy lands had been turned over to Interior and on what principle Fall had then leased the lands to private exploiters. Nothing of interest had come to light. The Secretary of the Navy did not want to be burdened with such vast oil reserves, pending some distant war with Japan. The Secretary of the Interior had then asked to take them over and the President had agreed. All this was done openly. Edward Doheny had taken a lease on Naval Reserve Number One at Elk Hills, California, and Harry Sinclair had taken a lease on Naval Reserve Number Three at Teapot Dome, Wyoming. All of this was straightforward, or so it seemed. Yet the Senate investigation of Fall was due to continue when Congress convened in October, simultaneous with the investigation of the Veterans Bureau.

"What's Fall done?"

"Who knows? It's what Walsh thinks he's done that matters to us."

"Like take a . . . a commission from Doheny?"

"A bribe. Sure. And one from Sinclair, too. He's travelling with Sinclair right now, the damned fool. I asked him not to, but he thinks he's God on earth, and so he and Harry Sinclair are prospecting for oil together in Russia."

"Partners."

"And for just how long have you two gentlemen been partners?"

Daugherty assumed a loud inquisitorial voice. "Oh, it's going to be hell. For the President. Thank God he's leaving town. He needs a rest. So do I." Daugherty stood up and stretched. "I'm going to take my nap."

"O.K., General. I'll hold the fort." Daugherty went inside, and Jess rocked back and forth, soothed by the motion. The truss bothered him less now that the scar was beginning to heal, but lately he had been having odd dizzy spells and moments of confusion when he was awake and terrible dreams when he was not. The doctor had unhelpfully assured him that this was perfectly normal for a diabetic, who had nothing to fear as long as he remembered to take his insulin shots.

Despite three months of convalescence, Daugherty was still not himself. He was irritable with Jess, something he had never been before. For Jess, Daugherty had always been the ideal older brother, wise and humorous and kind. In twenty years, they had never exchanged a harsh word. Jess would have committed murder for Daugherty; he would even have gone into the downstairs coat closet without a light, if Daugherty asked him to. Since the thought of that closet made his pulse race, he made himself think of something pleasant, like the trip to Alaska. Most of the Cabinet would be on the train with the President, and they would make leisurely stops across the country so that W.G. could bloviate and get his strength back, renewed by the crowds who loved him even if the Senate did not. Jess would join the President in his bridge games.

"Jess!" With a start, Jess opened his eyes. He had fallen asleep in the rocker. Standing over him was one of the courthouse gang from Columbus. An early supporter of Harding, he only came around when he wanted something.

"Whaddaya know?" said Jess.

"I know I got to talk to the General. He's here, isn't he?"

Jess nodded. "But he's taking a nap like always after lunch. Come back later."

The man shook his head. "I can't. I got business over to Marion. I just want a couple words with him. That's all."

Finally, reluctantly, Jess agreed. He went inside the shack and climbed the dry-rotted stairs to Daugherty's bedroom. He listened to the snoring a moment; then he called out, "General. There's a friend come to see you."

With an oath, Daugherty was on his feet. "Damn it!" he repeated, as he came out of the room and went downstairs. Jess, alarmed, stayed in his own room until the interview ended some five minutes later when there was a sound of a car moving off, followed by Daugherty's heavy stride on the stairs, and then a tirade of the sort that Jess had never heard before from Daugherty or, indeed, from anyone.

The subject *seemed* to be the sacredness of the afternoon nap, but all sorts of other things were said until Jess decided that he was probably still asleep in the rocker and this was a typical diabetic nightmare. Presently, he would wake up. But he didn't. Daugherty was now dressed and packed and he had called for his car and driver to take him to Washington Court House. "You can get back to town on your own," he said, and slammed the front door behind him.

Jess went to the telephone, and rang Roxy. But she wasn't home. He made two more calls: no one was answering. Then Daugherty opened the front door and said, "Come on, I'll take you into town."

They did not speak for most of the short drive. Daugherty stared out his window, and Jess out his. The driver was sealed off in the front, for privacy's sake.

When they got to the main street, Daugherty told the driver to stop near Jess's store. Daugherty avoided Jess's gaze when he said, "I meant it about your staying on here, staying away from Washington. It's getting too hot."

"I haven't done anything." Jess was almost too wounded to defend himself. He had done nothing, except the sort of odds and ends that practically everyone else did in his situation. "I never had anything to do with Charlie or Fall."

"There's K Street, there's Mannington." Daugherty still did not look at him. "The President wants you out of Washington."

"W.G.?" Jess was stunned.

"I've also got to tell you you're not going to Alaska with him. He told me to take your name off the list."

483

Other things were said. But Jess was confused. He hated firearms. Daugherty was like a madman. The car stopped.

Blindly, Jess got out of the car. Several cronies greeted him. He shook a half-dozen hands. Then, as the car bore the Attorney General away, Jess went into Carpenter's hardware store and bought a pistol and a round of ammunition. The proprietor was amazed. "Why, Jess. I never knew you to touch one of these before."

"It's for the Attorney General. Nowadays you got to protect yourself." Jess did not mind the cold hard feel of the gun as much as he had thought he would. What else had Daugherty said to him? Or had he dreamed it all? What he *thought* Daugherty had said in the car, he couldn't have said. It was just a nightmare.

Roxy wanted to go to a dinner dance at the Scioto Country Club, and Jess indulged her. Now that everything was decided, he felt at ease with the world if not his own body, which was not responding as well as it should to insulin. He was more and more subject to fits which left him shaken and disoriented. But all would soon be well. Daugherty had telephoned him that afternoon at the emporium. They would go back to Washington together and Daugherty would then move into the White House while Jess would go back to Wardman Park to wind up his affairs. It was like old days, almost.

The orchestra was a good one, and the latest favorite, "Tea for Two," tempted Jess to dance, but Roxy said, "No. It's too much strain on you. Besides, I hate feeling that truss up against me."

"Not for much longer," said Jess. All around them there were signs of prosperity. Something was happening in the country. Everybody's business was good. There was a powerful smell of roast beef and Havana cigars in the large dining room with the dance floor and orchestra at the far end. Jess knew everyone in the room and everyone knew and liked Jess. But as tonight he wanted to enjoy Roxy, he kept to a minimum his "whaddaya knows?"

"You're all right now, aren't you?" Roxy had been worried the day before when he was suffering from a kind of waking dream in which the words of Daugherty at Deer Creek were mingled with nightmare visions of crabs and galoshes and pistols, and the dark. He knew that he had talked wildly to Roxy. But now he was in perfect control of himself. Events would take their course according to *his* plan and no other.

"What did you mean when you said, 'They passed it to me'?"

"I was just having one of those spells I get every now and then." From a coffeepot, Jess poured himself a gin martini. "You'll miss me when I'm gone?"

"I always do. Some of the time, anyway. I'm pretty busy. You know."

"I'm giving you my Cole sedan."

The orchestra played "Yes, We Have No Bananas," a title that irritated Jess no end. Why "yes" if there are none?

The train ride back to Washington was also just like old times, almost. Daugherty was agreeable, very much like his usual self. It was agreed that Jess do away with all his records in case the various investigations were to spread beyond the Veterans Bureau and the naval oil reserves. Daugherty did not think that the Senate would find out anything other than the well-known fact that Forbes was a thief, acting on his own, while Fall, a favorite of the Senate, was no more than an obliging friend to the oil magnates.

"We've been tapping Senator Walsh's telephones." Daugherty fixed his blue eye humorously on Jess; through the window the flat Ohio landscape was giving way to mountainous West Virginia. "He's headed nowhere, I'd say. Fall's too shrewd an old bird." The blue eye suddenly winked, for no reason. "But Charlie Forbes will go to jail for thirty years if I have any say."

"What about Charlie Cramer?" Jess had not believed the suicide story. You only killed yourself if you were really sick with something, like diabetes before the days of insulin.

"What about him?"

"Was he in on it, with Forbes?"

"Why else would he go shoot himself?" The brown eye had joined the left eye in staring at Jess.

"Well, somebody could've shot him to shut him up, couldn't they?"

"Burns would've known." Daugherty had a lot more faith in his director of the Federal Bureau of Investigation than Jess or anyone else had. William J. Burns was an old friend of Daugherty's from

Columbus, where he had established the Burns National Detective Agency. So close was Burns to Daugherty that Burns had eventually moved into Wardman Park, taking an apartment directly under the one that Daugherty shared with Jess. As a result, Jess had always been jealous of the intimacy between the two and he suspected that there were secrets Daugherty shared with Burns that he did not with Jess.

Jess had never played golf well; today he was at his worst. But the others were tolerant as they made their way around the golf course at Friendship, under a dark sky. Although the McLeans were in Virginia, at their Leesburg place, friends were encouraged to use the course any time.

Among the players was Warren F. Martin, Daugherty's special assistant at the Justice Department, a man Jess had never got to know particularly well, and the President's personal doctor, Lieutenant Commander Boone, an amiable fellow who, finally, aware that Jess was sweating too much even for a damp airless day, said, "Let's go in. Jess here's having a menopausal response."

But Jess said no. He'd play to the ninth hole. Then they all went back to the clubhouse. Jess stayed a moment but refused a drink from the waiter. "Looking forward to the trip next month?" Boone was an amiable man and, reputedly, a good doctor.

"I'm not going." Jess looked at Martin, who looked somewhat guiltily away. Martin knew of his disgrace. Daugherty had told him. How many others knew?

"Shame. Sounds like it's going to be fun. Is the General coming?"

"No," said Martin. "He's staying put. He's been away from his desk almost three months." So Martin answered a question addressed to Jess Smith, Daugherty's bumper and best friend. The curtain was coming down fast.

Jess drove his Cole sedan from Friendship to the Justice Department, where he was greeted as if nothing had happened. At least Daugherty hadn't told the guards. Jess cleared out the files in his sixth-floor office; then he drove to the White House, where, again as if nothing had happened, the guards waved him through the gate to the executive offices. In the reception hall, he told the usher in charge that he had an appointment with the President, which was not exactly true. But he was not kept waiting long. As he walked down the corridor, past the coat closet, he shuddered, as he did at the thought of any closet, so like a coffin, except that in this particular closet W.G. and Nan had made love standing up? Or was there room enough for the two of them to lie on the floor?

The President was standing at his desk, looking out the window at the south lawn, a radiant green in the late-afternoon light. Then he turned and Jess was struck by how putty-gray his face was, by how fat he'd become. But the smile was as beguiling as ever, and the hand-clasp firm. "Well, Mr. President, I'm doing like I was told. I'm clearing out of town."

"Sit down, Jess." Harding remained standing, an unlit cigar in his right hand. "I'm really sorry it had to end like this. You've been a good friend to the Duchess and me, but we're in for a lot of trouble come October when Congress gets back. I've been too trusting, the Duchess says. But I don't think I am. I figure that people who're doing well doing the right thing won't be dumb enough to get themselves in trouble by doing the wrong thing."

"Yes, sir." Jess felt as if he was a disembodied pair of eyes resting high up in the chandelier, watching the two of them in the distance. "I don't think any of us in the K Street house . . ."

"Jess, Jess." The President motioned for him to stop; then he sat behind the desk and cradled his head in his hand. "I know all about K Street. Or I know as much as I want to know, and I wish to God I didn't know what I do. I don't blame you. I guess it's my fault thinking you'd know the difference between the capital here and Washington Court House, and what's seemly here and what isn't."

"Well, I did my best. For everybody, or tried to." Jess hoped that he would not start to cry.

"I know. I know. If it weren't for . . . the Veterans Bureau mess . . ." The President did not go on; he also could not say the name Charlie Forbes.

"What shall I do with the Ungerleider accounts?"

The President shrugged. "You can publish mine in the *Post* for all I care. It just shows that I've been as unlucky in the stock market as everything else. I'm selling the *Star*."

"I'm sorry, W.G." Somehow the thought of the Marion *Star* and Harding transported, if only briefly, the two figures at the far end of the oval office back to a happier better time when W.G. was a newspaper editor and Jess the proprietor of a dry-goods emporium in the next town. They had come such a long way, to this evil house and uncommon end.

"I had to. We need the money." The President stood up. Jess rejoined his ailing body at the desk and shook Harding's hand for the last time.

It was evening when Jess parked his Cole sedan in the garage beneath Wardman Park. Then he took the elevator to his floor. As he unlocked the door to the living room of the suite, he was aware that something was not right. Then he saw Martin, in his shirt sleeves, seated at the desk, talking on the telephone.... "I won't know till he gets here." Then Martin must have heard the heavy sound of Jess's breathing. He said into the receiver, "I'll call you back." Martin smiled at Jess; he always smiled. He was a dozen years younger than Jess.

"The General was worried about you. So he asked me to sleep over, knowing how you don't like being alone at night."

"Fine," said Jess. There were two bedrooms in the suite with a living room between. Martin's suitcase was on Daugherty's bed.

Jess went into his own bedroom, and shut the door. Then he opened his briefcase and withdrew all the bank statements, receipts, letters. He had also collected everything that pertained to the President and Daugherty. Beside his desk, there was a large solid metal wastebasket. Methodically, one by one, he put the papers into the basket, and set them afire. A cool breeze blew the smoke out the open window. In the distance thunder sounded. Why, of all people, Martin?

Suddenly, Jess was inspired. He telephoned the McLeans in Leesburg. Evalyn came on the line. "It's Jess," he announced.

"Back from Ohio?"

"For a while. Listen. I wonder if I could come down there and spend maybe a couple, three days."

"Of course you can. There's plenty of room, Lord knows. Are you all right?"

"I'm a little upset. I guess you know, business, and things."

"I know," said Evalyn, who probably did know a great deal.

"I'll start soon as I can." Jess hung up. Thunder sounded even louder, rain started to fall in sheets.

Jess dozed off. The last of the papers was now ash. He woke up with rain in his face. He looked at his watch. It was after ten. He shut the window. Then he telephoned Evalyn again; told her it was raining too hard to drive. She told him to come in the morning. He would be there at seven, he said. On the dot. It would be light out then. He didn't like to drive in the dark or, indeed, do anything without a light on somewhere.

Jess dozed off again. He dreamed of monsters, closets, horrors that he could sense but could not see. He dreamed that he heard a key turning in a lock and a door being opened. Then came an explosive thunder-clap, lightning, darkness.

3

Warren T. Martin and Lieutenant Commander Joel T. Boone leapt to their feet as Brooks announced, "Gentlemen, the President."

Harding entered the oval sitting room. He was in pyjamas and dressing gown, and only half his face had been shaved. With a towel he wiped shaving cream from the unshaven side. "What happened?" He motioned for them to sit.

"Well, sir," Martin began, nervously pulling at the fingers of his right hand with his left, "at about six-thirty this morning, I heard what sounded like somebody had slammed a door, or maybe thunder because there was this bad storm most of last night. I tried to go back to sleep but I couldn't. Then I got up to see how Jess was. The door to his bedroom was open and I looked in and there he was, lying on the floor, his head in this wastebasket full of ashes, with this pistol in his hand. He had shot himself in the head, on the left side."

Harding held the right side of his own head, as if to shield it from a second bullet. "Did he leave a letter, or anything?"

"No, sir. He'd burned up a lot of papers in the wastebasket, before he . . ." Martin's mouth was dry. He swallowed hard. "Then I called Mr. Burns, who lives in the apartment on the floor just below, and he called you, sir, and you sent Commander Boone here, as a medical man, and he saw the body."

Harding looked at Boone. "You must speak to the press. Tell them . . . he shot himself because . . ." Harding rubbed his eyes.

"Because, sir, he was in a diabetic depression, and had suffered from such depression ever since last year when his appendix was removed and the scar would not heal. As there was no reason for a post-mortem, I surrendered the body to Mr. Burns of the F.B.I."

"He's sending the remains back to Washington Court House for interment," said Martin.

Harding rose. "Commander, go down to the press office and make your statement. Thank you, both." Harding shook hands with each man, and saw them to the door.

Harding then sat at the window, and looked out at the Washington Monument, like a white needle in the bright morning sun. From the hallway, he heard a door slam shut. Then he heard Daugherty's voice. "What's wrong with this phone in my room? I can't get Mr. Smith on my extension."

Whatever the usher answered was not audible to the President. But from Daugherty's face, it was clear that he had been told: he stood in the middle of the oval sitting room, unable to speak.

"Jess did it," said Harding. "But first he burned a lot of papers. There was nothing left in his room. No message, nothing."

"He shot himself, with that gun he bought last week in Washington Court House."

"With a pistol, they said. Martin found him. He phoned me. I sent over Dr. Boone. Then Burns took over. The body's on its way home now."

"Where did he shoot himself?"

Harding placed his left hand against the left side of his head. "Here," he said.

490

"But Jess was right-handed," said the Duchess. She stood in the doorway, wearing an elaborate silk dressing gown.

"Perhaps I heard wrong," said the President. He shook his head. "First Cramer. Now Jess. There is a curse on us, I swear."

"And tonight of all nights we have the Sanfords for supper. I'll call them off."

"No, no. That wouldn't be seemly."

"Or wise." Daugherty gave a great long moan all on a single exhalation of breath.

Blaise and Frederika had been surprised to be asked to a White House family dinner party, and even more surprised that after the front-page story of Jesse Smith's suicide, the dinner had not been cancelled.

The President was all grave politeness, but nothing more. He seemed distracted. The Attorney General spoke hardly at all. The First Lady of the Land did her best to make small talk. Since one publisher made her think of another publisher, she discussed Ned McLean at some length. "I think he's done well by the *Post*. I know people don't think he's serious. But over-all linage of advertising is three percent better than last quarter." Blaise recalled that Mrs. Harding herself had run a newspaper for years. They spoke of advertising rates, while Frederika tried to amuse the President.

"Has a president ever been to Alaska before?"

. Harding stared at her blankly; then he appeared to play back her question in his head. "No. I'm the first. I can't wait to get out of here, let me tell you."

"I just saw your itinerary, Mr. President. You're very ambitious. All those stops along the way, in all that heat."

Mrs. Harding looked up at this. "Doc Sawyer doesn't want you to go at all. Says it's too much. I agree."

"It's my job." Blaise noted how sallow the President's face was; also, jowls had begun to appear; when he looked down, heavy jowls flowed over his stiff collar. Blaise wondered if there was any truth to the story of Harding's Negro blood; he also wondered why Jess Smith had killed himself. The *Tribune* reporter had been most suspicious of the fact that no one had seen the body except a

White House doctor and the director of the Federal Bureau of Investigation. Also, it was remarkably convenient that Jess should kill himself in Daugherty's hotel suite with an agent from the Justice Department in the next room and Mr. Burns of the F.B.I. on the floor beneath. Then, instead of an examination by a police coroner as the law required, a White House naval physician had been called in. But why, asked Blaise, would Daugherty want his closest friend killed? Why, asked the reporter, were so many papers burned and then the one person who knew their contents killed?

Mrs. Harding proposed that they watch a film in the second-floor corridor, and everyone was much relieved that there would no longer be any need to make conversation.

As Frederika and Blaise followed the President and Mrs. Harding down the corridor, past the projectionist to where five arm chairs had been arranged, Frederika whispered to Blaise, "It's like an evening with the Macbeths."

"Do shut up," said Blaise.

The film was *Monte Carlo,* starring Emma Traxler. "We hope you haven't seen it," said Mrs. Harding.

"No," said Frederika, "we haven't. Caroline always asks us not to."

As Emma Traxler made her entrance in a ball gown at the Winter Palace, Mrs. Harding observed, "I guess that sister of yours is the best-looking newspaper publisher in Washington." For the first time that evening everyone laughed except Daugherty, who gave a long-drawn-out "Oh."

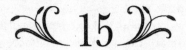

15

1

Burden and his blind neighbor, former Senator Thomas Gore, gazed upon the moonlit woods where Gore was building a house. Defeated in 1920 after three terms in the Senate, Gore was practicing law in Washington and for the first time making money. "The house will be just out of view, three hundred yards to the northwest of that hill." The blind man pointed accurately with his cane. Burden had always been delighted by the way that Gore would hold a manuscript in his hand when he spoke and, from time to time, would pretend to look at it, as if to check a statistic or the exact wording of a Latin quotation. Although two separate accidents had blinded him by the time he was ten, there was a legend that he had been elected Oklahoma's first senator by pretending not to be blind. Hence, the pretense of reading, of seeing.

During dinner the wives had talked, now the wives were talking in the living room and the men were enjoying the warm August night. Fireflies blinked in the dark woods. The moon was behind clouds. Burden shut his eyes to see what it was like not to see. Unbearable, he decided. They spoke of the investigation of Fall. "He's an old friend," said Gore. "I won't speculate on what he did or didn't do. But Sinclair and Doheny are hard to discourage once they've got you in their sights."

"Well, *you* turned them in." Some years earlier, Gore had created a sensation in the Senate by revealing that he had been offered a bribe by an oil company. No one had ever done that before and, privately, Gore's eccentricity was deplored in the cloakroom. "I'd *starve* if it wasn't for my friends!" a Southern states-man had declaimed.

"I wonder now if I would've done what I did if I'd been as broke as Fall is. You never can tell what you might do in a different situation."

"I don't think you or I would take a bribe, ever." Burden was firm.

"But then there are the contributions." Gore sighed. "That's where things can get right shadowy. You know, back in 1907, my first campaign, I had no money at all. Literally. Fact, I was in debt because instead of practicing law I'd been politicking, to get Oklahoma into the Union, and so on. Anyway, after I was nominated I was standing in front of the barber shop in Lawton, thinking what a fix I was in, when a stranger came up and said, 'Here, take this,' and gave me an envelope. Then he was gone. Well, inside that envelope was a thousand dollars." Gore laughed. "I love telling that story because I've never met anybody who believes it. But that's the way it happened."

"You plan to come back, don't you?"

Gore looked at him. In the moonlight his single glass eye shone, while the blind one was dull and reflected no light. "When I went down in the Harding sweep, I thought it was the end of the world. Then I pulled myself together and said to myself, Here you are, fifty years old, and you've been a senator since you were thirty-seven and never had a chance to make a penny. So take time off. Build a house in Rock Creek Park. Then go back. I wrote a note and hid it in the Senate chamber, saying I'd be back one day. Funny," he held his cane in front of him like a dowsing rod, "right after I hid that scrap of paper, I went into the cloakroom to collect my gear – this was the last day of the session – and suddenly I felt two arms around me and I was being given a bear-hug and I said, 'Who is it?' and this voice said, 'Just an old duffer, going off to be hung,' and it was Harding."

Burden recalled how radiant Harding had looked on his last day as a senator, gently teasing those senators who had taken all the credit for his election. Now he was sick in a hotel room in San Francisco. Officially he was supposed to have contracted ptomaine poisoning. But ptomaine poisoning was quick to pass, and the

President had been ill for five days, and the balance of his tour was cancelled. There was talk of heart trouble. "He had so much luck for so long," Burden said. "Now the people are getting ready to turn on him."

"Sooner or later, they turn on everybody." Gore sighed. "I tell you, if there was any race other than the human race, I'd go join it."

Burden had forgotten how much he'd missed Gore's black wit. When forced to take a stand on Prohibition, a dangerous thing to do for a Bible Belt politician, Gore had said that he thought the Eighteenth Amendment was a very fine thing. "Because now the Drys have their law and the Wets have their whisky, and everybody's happy."

Kitty came out onto the porch. "The White House is calling. Mr. Christian's office."

"So late?" Burden went into the hall; he picked up the receiver. "This is Senator Day."

An unidentified voice said, "I'm sorry to bother you so late but Mr. Christian thinks you should know that the President is dead."

"Dead? What?" Burden sat down on top of the refectory table, something not allowed in Kitty's by-laws.

"Apoplexy, they say. Mr. Christian wanted you to know before the papers report it." Burden thanked the unknown man. Then he rang Lodge. Had he heard the news? Lodge had not. When Burden told him, Lodge exclaimed, "Oh, my God! This is terrible. *Unthinkable.*" He seemed truly shattered.

"Well, yes, it's pretty awful, at his age and everything. But I didn't know you two were so close."

"We weren't." Lodge's voice had regained its usual cold balance. "I'm upset because Calvin Coolidge is now the president. *Calvin Coolidge.* What a humiliation for the country, that dreadful little creature in his dreadful little two-family house."

In the living room, the Gores and Kitty responded more sympathetically. Kitty was not surprised. "You could tell he was getting sicker and sicker this last year. He was always a bad color, and so swollen-looking. I'm sure it was an old-fashioned stroke."

Gore thought that Harding was probably well out of it. "He was much too nice a man for the presidency."

495

Burden sat on a sofa, and drank Coca-Cola. "You know, he wasn't going to run again with Coolidge."

"Who did he want?" asked Mrs. Gore.

"Charlie Dawes. So Dawes told me. He couldn't stand Coolidge. Nobody can. In the Cabinet he just sits and stares."

"Now he has it all," said Gore. "You'll be running against him, I expect."

"If nominated . . ." Burden felt the familiar tide of ambition begin its rise. Who else was there? Cox would not be acceptable after his disastrous defeat in 1920. Franklin Roosevelt was a cripple from polio and would never walk – much less run for office – again. The governor of New York, Al Smith, was a Roman Catholic. Hearst was dead politically to all but himself. McAdoo had no following. James Burden Day against Calvin Coolidge seemed now to be inevitable, with the inevitable result. Burden shuddered with delight and fear; and thought of his father.

2

Caroline stood on the terrace of Laurel House and looked down at the river. "It is All Souls' Eve," she observed to no one but herself. Blaise and Frederika had decided to entertain everyone in Washington, and, somehow, they had picked the evening of November 1, when the souls of the dead were abroad or asleep or somewhere, waiting to be – what? – propitiated: she could not remember exactly what. Mlle. Souvestre had driven all religion out of her soul, including the attractive pagan.

The night was ominously warm, and a last summer storm was approaching the house. Time of equinox, she thought, time of change. But then *was* this the equinox? The science teacher had not been as successful in filling the niches in her mind which Mademoiselle had so ruthlessly emptied of their idols.

Tim had come out on the terrace. He wore evening dress; and looked older than he was. "Do they do nothing here but talk politics?"

"The gentry talk horses – and blood lines. Theirs and the horses. My father talked about music," she added, wondering how that curious man had suddenly slipped back into her memory. "All Souls'," she said, in explanation to herself. "My father's spirit is abroad tonight. But I'd rather see my mother's."

"Your namesake."

"Partly. Emma de Traxler Schuyler d'Agrigente Sanford. It is too long for a marquee."

"What about for a life?"

"I don't think she thought so. But I don't know. I don't remember her."

From the lower terrace, a couple emerged from the darkness. Plainly, they had been at the pool house. "Young lovers," said Caroline tolerantly, holding up the lorgnette that was both a decoration and necessary to see with.

"Not so young," said Tim, whose far-sightedness complemented her myopia.

"Caroline," said Alice Longworth, with a bright smile. "What a lovely party. What a lovely place. What a lovely film star you are. Act for us."

"I *am* acting for you. I am smiling tolerantly, and recalling the fevers of my long-past youth. I am Marschallin at last."

Senator Borah found none of this amusing. He shook hands solemnly with Caroline and Tim. "We were looking over the place," he said. "I hadn't realized it was so big."

"The pool house is a great success," said Caroline. "It is All Souls' Night." She turned to Alice, handsome in blue and as happy as that restless creature could be.

"So it is. I think I've met them all by now. After all, everyone who's interesting is dead. We better go join them – in hell, I suppose."

"You do. I'm going inside." The Lion of Idaho opened the French door and stepped into the crowded drawing room.

"Do you find maternity rewarding?" asked Alice.

"My daughter's here tonight," was Caroline's non-answer.

"I remember when you had her, years and years ago. Have I missed anything?"

"A great deal of trouble."

"I'm almost forty." In the half-light from the drawing room, Alice looked pale, like a phantom, a restless soul.

497

"Well, it does wonders for your skin. But then you have perfect skin. So you need not . . . replicate."

"What a disgusting word," said Alice, and went inside.

"She's worried," Caroline observed.

"About getting pregnant? From Senator Walsh?"

"Borah. No. Oil. Her brothers Ted and Archie Roosevelt are involved with Mr. Sinclair. If he gets involved in the Teapot Dome hearings . . . Why do I talk about these things when I'm out of it?"

Tim's face was half in shadow and so he half smiled at her. Through the French windows the guests could be seen, moving about in what looked to be some hieratic dance. "I think you're more in it now than you ever were before. That's if we pull it off."

Caroline had not made the connection, but, of course, he was right. "Because now we'll be acting in the first place instead of reacting, the way the press usually has to do. Here comes our transmitter."

Will Hays stepped out onto the terrace. The light back of him made his huge ears glow pink as they stood out from his neat rodentine head. "My two favorite producers," he said, with a show of proprietary warmth.

"And our preferred candidate for president." Caroline laid it on with her ancient skill, more Sanford than Traxler.

Hays held up a curved rodentine paw. "Now, now, that's quite a ways down the road if it's there at all." The ears shone like rubies. "Say, I like that first photo-play of yours a whole lot, what I read, anyway, not that I know much about these things. But it's got a lot of heart, sort of Booth Tarkington stuff, which I really like, you know, small town, family life, kid growing up, the whole thing's very truthful . . ."

"Only," said Caroline, who could detect a demur in even the most enthusiastic panegyric.

"Only . . . well, I was thinking about what you said about how everything that goes on in this town of yours will be like what's going on in the country, only you'll sort of point up maybe what's wrong or not quite right. So I was thinking about this really serious problem we've got now with drugs and how you just might show how dope can kill young people . . ."

"Mr. Hays," it was Tim to the rescue, "the whole point to our sort of picture is not to melodramatize things. Drugs are a big problem in and around Hollywood Boulevard, but nobody would know where to find them in our town, and I don't think we should go and give the audience ideas."

Hays was still for a minute; then he nodded, "You've got a point there . . ."

"Besides," said Caroline, "the boy's experience with cigarettes, where he gets sick, is exactly the same thing as drug-taking only it's more typical."

Hays dropped the subject. "I also liked your old newspaper editor. Why, I've known that sort of man all my life. Somebody who's always trying to do good but it's always uphill work."

Both Caroline and Tim laughed. The old newspaper editor, who managed, always, to be so smugly in the wrong on every subject, had been carefully based on a year's observation of Will Hays in action. Through the window closest, Caroline could see her daughter Emma, haranguing a terrified-looking senator.

"When do you folks release your first picture, the one I read?"

"January 1924," said Tim. "The first Sanford-Farrell Studio movie will open at the Strand in New York, New Year's Day. We're calling it *Hometown*."

"No more Traxler Productions?" Hays, like McAdoo before him, had taken mightily to the corporate end of movie-making.

"Emma Traxler died earlier this year," said Caroline, with quiet joy. "At Monte Carlo. She drank one glass of champagne too many and waltzed one time too often. She simply fell asleep and breathed her last, eyes shut."

"We'll sure miss her," said Hays, sincerely, as if of someone real. But then Emma Traxler had been very real to a great many people, including Caroline on certain mad days. "That's quite a big studio you're building yourselves out at Santa Monica."

Frederika was standing now in the doorway. "Everyone wants to talk to you, Mr. Hays, about Fatty Arbuckle. You must come in, and tell all."

"I hope they'll want to hear something more wholesome than

499

that." Hays went inside. Frederika smiled at her sister-in-law. "Is it true that you two are getting married?"

"No," said Caroline. "It would give my daughter and Mr. Hays too much pleasure."

"Good. Then you need never divorce." Frederika returned to her party.

Caroline shivered. "All souls are chilly on their night out. Now I shall go get us some money for the studio." Before Tim could ask how, Caroline had gone inside.

Millicent Inverness, now Mrs. Daniel Truscott Carhart, greeted Caroline warmly. "I have given up drink," she said. "It is part of my new life."

"You look years younger," Caroline lied easily. Always punctilious, Millicent had waited until the Earl was safely dead before she remarried. Mr. Carhart was a dim New Englander connected in some way with the Smithsonian Institution, itself one of Washington's on-going mysteries that Caroline had never penetrated nor, indeed, tried to.

"I saw your daughter a moment ago. She appears to be divorced from that nice young man. I have some difficulty understanding her. She speaks so rapidly."

Emma had indeed been divorced. Now she was working with the Federal Bureau of Investigation, exposing those Communists who had managed to infiltrate the government. Mother and daughter met as seldom as possible. Emma refused to speak to Tim, on moral as well as political grounds. Emma had also found God and was a regular at mass, where Héloise encountered her, and got what news there was.

"She is trying to atone for her butterfly mother," said Caroline. "She is serious. I am frivolous."

"Oh, no, you're not, honey," said Millicent Carhart, settling into her new Americanism and very much the niece of a folksy – but which one? – president.

Blaise was seated in the wood-panelled study where hung the portrait of Aaron Burr, Caroline's ancestor not Blaise's; yet he was a significant icon to each. Blaise was talking to the aged Trimble, who seldom went out anymore.

"Here we three are," said Caroline. "The *Tribune* made flesh."

"I'm shucking mine off pretty damn soon," said Trimble glumly. "I hadn't realized that age was such a God-damned mess."

Caroline sat with her co-publishers. "Am I interrupting?"

Blaise shook his head. The handsome pony body had vanished beneath new flesh; he was definitely stout and the once-pale face was ruddy. He looked a clubman. She wondered about his private life. There must be someone; otherwise, he would not have accepted so easily Frederika's affair with Burden.

"It seems," said Blaise, "that last summer when our late President was in Kansas City, Mrs. Fall visited him secretly at the Muehlbach Hotel. No one knows what she told him but he was never the same again. Then, when he was in Alaska, he got a coded message from the White House, and this made him very agitated, according to Herbert Hoover, who was there. So he must have known a lot of what we're learning."

"Just known?" asked Caroline. "Or was he in on it?"

"The problem is how do you get all this to the public." Despite his age, Trimble never ceased to be an inquisitive editor. "Harding died one of the most popular presidents in history."

"The Senate hearings will change all that," said Blaise. "Forbes will go to jail. Fall, too. Maybe Daugherty, if half of what they say about him is true."

"Did he murder Jess Smith?" For Caroline, the Smith affair was the most intriguing of all.

"Daugherty was asleep in the White House when Smith was shot," said Trimble. "Of course, his deputy was with Smith in the apartment. Then Mr. Burns of the F.B.I. came upstairs and took the gun that killed him, and mislaid it, he says."

Frederika was at the door, splendid in white and gold. "Come out, you three. You do enough plotting at the office. The President's here." In the hallway, the small orchestra was playing "Hail to the Chief."

"Oh, God," said Blaise. The three stood up. "I'd rather spend an hour at the dentist than five minutes trying to talk to that man."

When Millicent Carhart had been placed next to the new President at dinner, she had said, "I've just made a ten-dollar bet that I can get you to say more than three words to me." The President had then turned his wizened-apple head toward her and, in his highly imitable Yankee voice, said, "You lose."

At the door to the library, Caroline pulled Blaise back. Trimble went on ahead into the hallway, where a crowd was gathering about the Coolidges.

"Do you still want to buy my share of the *Tribune?*"

Blaise gave her a long, curious look; then he nodded.

"Good. I'll tell my lawyer to talk to your lawyer. It will be like the old days."

"Why?"

"Why not? I've come to the end of this. That's all. Besides, I need the money for the Sanford-Farrell Studio."

"Are you really settling in out there?"

Caroline nodded. "After all, that's the only world there is now, what we invent."

"Invent or reflect?"

"What we invent others reflect, if we're ingenious enough, of course. Hearst showed us how to invent news, which we do, some of the time, for the best of reasons. But nothing we do ever goes very deep. We don't get into people's dreams, the way the movies do – or can do."

"The way you and Tim mean to do. Well, it must be very nice to be so . . . creative."

"Are you envious?"

"Yes."

"I *am* pleased."

Then Blaise went into the hallway to greet the President, who was, like some white knight – in the press, at least – purifying the nation's political life just as Will Hays was doing the same for Hollywood, only Coolidge had no secret advisers and Hays, unknown to him, did.

Comfortably, Caroline, now entirely herself, one person at last, stared into the fire and thought of all the souls that she had known and if they were indeed abroad tonight, they would be all fire and air, light and shadow so fixed upon her memory that she might, if she chose, transfer them to strips of film that the whole world could then forever imagine until reel's end.